BRAVE NEW WORLDS

Other Books edited by John Joseph Adams

Wastelands
Seeds of Change
The Living Dead
By Blood We Live
Federations
The Improbable Adventures of Sherlock Holmes
The Living Dead 2
The Way of the Wizard

Forthcoming Anthologies

The Mad Scientist's Guide to World Domination
The Book of Cthulhu

BRAVE NEW WORLDS

EDITED BY JOHN JOSEPH ADAMS

NIGHT SHADE BOOKS
SAN FRANCISCO

First Edition

ISBN 978-1-59780-221-5

Printed in Canada

Night Shade Books
Please visit us on the web at
http://www.nightshadebooks.com

For Christie

CONTENTS

INTRODUCTION

by John Joseph Adams

Nineteen Eighty-Four, Fahrenheit 451, and, of course, the book this anthology is named for—*Brave New World*—are the cornerstones of dystopian literature in novel form, but there has never, to my knowledge, been an anthology collecting all the best, classic works of dystopian short fiction in one volume. This book aims to do exactly that, spanning from 1948 to the present day, from what is perhaps *the* classic dystopian short story—"The Lottery" by Shirley Jackson—to stories just published in the last two years but which will surely stand the test of time.

The roots of the word dystopia—dys- and -topia—are from the Ancient Greek for "bad" and "place," and so we use the term to describe an unfavorable society in which to live. "Dystopia" is not a synonym for "post-apocalyptic"; it also is not a synonym for a bleak, or darkly imagined future. In a dystopian story, society itself is typically the antagonist; it is society that is actively working against the protagonist's aims and desires. This oppression frequently is enacted by a totalitarian or authoritarian government, resulting in the loss of civil liberties and untenable living conditions, caused by any number of circumstances, such as world overpopulation, laws controlling a person's sexual or reproductive freedom, and living under constant surveillance.

Whether or not a society is perceived as a dystopia is usually determined by one's point of view; what one person may consider to be a horrible dystopia, another may find completely acceptable or even nigh-utopian. For instance, if you don't care about procreating, then living in a world in which the birth rate is strictly regulated wouldn't seem very dystopic to you; to someone who values that very much, however, having society tell you how, when (or how often) you can procreate would seem like something out of a nightmare. Or a person who doesn't enjoy reading or intellectual thinking might not care if books are banned… or even hunted down and destroyed, as in *Fahrenheit 451*, whereas you, dear reader, would probably care very much.

Many societies in fiction are depicted as utopias when in fact they are dystopias; like angels and demons, the two are sides of the same coin. This seemingly paradoxical situation can arise because, in a dystopia, the society often gives up

A in exchange for B, but the benefit of B blinds the society to the loss of A; it is often not until many years later that the loss of A is truly felt, and the citizens come to realize that the world they once thought acceptable (or even ideal) is not the world they thought it was. That's part of what is so compelling—and insidious—about dystopian fiction: the idea that you could be living in a dystopia and not even know it.

Dystopias are often seen as "cautionary tales," but the best dystopias are not didactic screeds, and the best dystopias do not draw their power from whatever political/societal point they might be making; the best dystopias speak to the deeper meanings of what it is to be one small part of a teeming civilization... and of what it is to be human.

And so here are thirty-three such stories, representing the best of what dystopian fiction has to offer. So read them, and be glad that doing so won't bring firemen to your door to burn all your books—and your house with them.

THE LOTTERY

by Shirley Jackson

Shirley Jackson, best known for penning this classic story, was the author of several novels, such as *We Have Always Lived in the Castle* and *The Haunting of Hill House,* the latter of which has been adapted to film twice (both times as *The Haunting*). She is also the author of dozens of short stories, which appeared in magazines including *The New Yorker, Collier's, Good Housekeeping, Harper's, Mademoiselle, The New Republic,* and *The Magazine of Fantasy & Science Fiction.*

Frequently anthologized and taught in classrooms around the world, "The Lottery" is a masterwork of dystopian fiction, and is a story whose influence can be felt in several of the other stories in this anthology.

Literature of the early twentieth-century is rich with characters struggling to understand the dwindling importance of rural life. Whether the small towns and agrarian communities were rejected by the characters or if their loss left them pining, there could be no doubt that rural communities were drying up. From Sherwood Anderson to John Steinbeck to the stage of Thornton Wilder, writer after writer tried to capture the end of era.

Science fiction and fantasy writers tackled the topic, too. Many of Ray Bradbury's greatest pieces are saturated with nostalgia for lost times in little country towns. In our first story, we offer you one of those small towns, a place not so different from Bradbury's beloved Green Town, Illinois. Like Green Town, it's full of ordinary people working hard to get by, who are drawn together by an annual ritual.

The morning of June 27th was clear and sunny, with the fresh warmth of a full-summer day; the flowers were blossoming profusely and the grass was richly green. The people of the village began to gather in the square, between the post office and the bank, around ten o'clock; in some towns there were so many people that the lottery took two days and had to be started on June 26th, but in this village, where there were only about three hundred people, the whole lottery took less than two hours, so it could begin at ten o'clock in the morning and still be through in time to allow the villagers to get home for noon dinner.

The children assembled first, of course. School was recently over for the summer, and the feeling of liberty sat uneasily on most of them; they tended to gather together quietly for a while before they broke into boisterous play, and their talk was still of the classroom and the teacher, of books and reprimands. Bobby Martin had already stuffed his pockets full of stones, and the other boys soon followed his example, selecting the smoothest and roundest stones; Bobby and Harry Jones and Dickie Delacroix—the villagers pronounced this name "Delacroy"—eventually made a great pile of stones in one corner of the square and guarded it against the raids of the other boys. The girls stood aside, talking among themselves, looking over their shoulders at the boys, and the very small children rolled in the dust or clung to the hands of their older brothers or sisters.

Soon the men began to gather, surveying their own children, speaking of planting and rain, tractors and taxes. They stood together, away from the pile of stones in the corner, and their jokes were quiet and they smiled rather than laughed. The women, wearing faded house dresses and sweaters, came shortly after their menfolk. They greeted one another and exchanged bits of gossip as they went to join their husbands. Soon the women, standing by their husbands, began to call to their children, and the children came reluctantly, having to be called four or five times. Bobby Martin ducked under his mother's grasping hand and ran, laughing, back to the pile of stones. His father spoke up sharply, and Bobby came quickly and took his place between his father and his oldest brother.

The lottery was conducted—as were the square dances, the teenage club, the Halloween program—by Mr. Summers, who had time and energy to devote to civic activities. He was a round-faced, jovial man and he ran the coal business, and people were sorry for him, because he had no children and his wife was a scold. When he arrived in the square, carrying the black wooden box, there was a murmur of conversation among the villagers, and he waved and called, "Little late today, folks." The postmaster, Mr. Graves, followed him, carrying a three-legged stool, and the stool was put in the center of the square and Mr. Summers set the black box down on it. The villagers kept their distance, leaving a space between themselves and the stool, and when Mr. Summers said, "Some of you fellows want to give me a hand?" there was a hesitation before two men, Mr. Martin and his oldest son, Baxter, came forward to hold the box steady on the stool while Mr. Summers stirred up the papers inside it.

The original paraphernalia for the lottery had been lost long ago, and the black box now resting on the stool had been put into use even before Old Man Warner, the oldest man in town, was born.

Mr. Summers spoke frequently to the villagers about making a new box, but no one liked to upset even as much tradition as was represented by the black box. There was a story that the present box had been made with some pieces of the box that had preceded it, the one that had been constructed when the first people settled down to make a village here. Every year, after the lottery, Mr. Summers began talking again about a new box, but every year the subject was allowed to fade off without anything's being done. The black box grew shabbier each year; by now it was no longer completely black but splintered badly along one side to show the original wood color, and in some places faded or stained.

Mr. Martin and his oldest son, Baxter, held the black box securely on the stool until Mr. Summers had stirred the papers thoroughly with his hand. Because so much of the ritual had been forgotten or discarded, Mr. Summers had been successful in having slips of paper substituted for the chips of wood that had been used for generations. Chips of wood, Mr. Summers had argued, had been all very well when the village was tiny, but now that the population was more than three hundred and likely to keep on growing, it was necessary to use something that would fit more easily into the black box. The night before the lottery, Mr. Summers and Mr. Graves made up the slips of paper and put them in the box, and it was then taken to the safe of Mr. Summers's coal company and locked up until Mr. Summers was ready to take it to the square next morning. The rest of the year, the box was put away, sometimes one place, sometimes another; it had spent one year in Mr. Graves's barn and another year underfoot in the post office, and sometimes it was set on a shelf in the Martin grocery and left there.

There was a great deal of fussing to be done before Mr. Summers declared the lottery open. There were the lists to make up—of heads of families, heads of households in each family, members of each household in each family. There was the proper swearing-in of Mr. Summers by the postmaster, as the official of the lottery; at one time, some people remembered, there had been a recital of some sort, performed by the official of the lottery, a perfunctory, tuneless chant that had been rattled off duly each year; some people believed that the official of the lottery used to stand just so when he said or sang it, others believed that he was supposed to walk among the people, but years and years ago this part of the ritual had been allowed to lapse. There had been, also, a ritual salute, which the official of the lottery had had to use in addressing each person who came up to draw from the box, but this also had changed with time, until now it was felt necessary only for the official to speak to each person approaching. Mr. Summers was very good at all this; in his clean white shirt and blue jeans, with one hand resting carelessly on the black box, he seemed very proper and important as he talked interminably to Mr. Graves and the Martins.

Just as Mr. Summers finally left off talking and turned to the assembled villagers, Mrs. Hutchinson came hurriedly along the path to the square, her sweater thrown over her shoulders, and slid into place in the back of the crowd. "Clean forgot what day it was," she said to Mrs. Delacroix, who stood next to her, and they both laughed softly. "Thought my old man was out back stacking wood," Mrs. Hutchinson went on, "and then I looked out the window and the kids was gone, and then I remembered it was the twenty-seventh and came a-running." She dried her hands on her apron, and Mrs. Delacroix said, "You're in time, though. They're still talking away up there."

Mrs. Hutchinson craned her neck to see through the crowd and found her husband and children standing near the front. She tapped Mrs. Delacroix on the arm as a farewell and began to make her way through the crowd. The people separated good-humoredly to let her through; two or three people said, in voices just loud enough to be heard across the crowd, "Here comes your Missus, Hutchinson," and "Bill, she made it after all." Mrs. Hutchinson reached her husband, and Mr. Summers, who had been waiting, said cheerfully, "Thought we were going to have to get on without you, Tessie." Mrs. Hutchinson said, grinning, 'Wouldn't have me leave m'dishes in the sink, now, would you, Joe?" and soft laughter ran through the crowd as the people stirred back into position after Mrs. Hutchinson's arrival.

"Well, now," Mr. Summers said soberly, "guess we better get started, get this over with, so's we can go back to work. Anybody ain't here?"

"Dunbar," several people said. "Dunbar, Dunbar."

Mr. Summers consulted his list. "Clyde Dunbar," he said. "That's right. He's broke his leg, hasn't he? Who's drawing for him?"

"Me, I guess," a woman said, and Mr. Summers turned to look at her. "Wife draws for her husband," Mr. Summers said. "Don't you have a grown boy to do it for you, Janey?" Although Mr. Summers and everyone else in the village knew the answer perfectly well, it was the business of the official of the lottery to ask such questions formally. Mr. Summers waited with an expression of polite interest while Mrs. Dunbar answered.

"Horace's not but sixteen yet," Mrs. Dunbar said regretfully. "Guess I gotta fill in for the old man this year."

"Right," Mr. Summers said. He made a note on the list he was holding. Then he asked, "Watson boy drawing this year?"

A tall boy in the crowd raised his hand. "Here," he said. "I'm drawing for m'mother and me." He blinked his eyes nervously and ducked his head as several voices in the crowd said things like "Good fellow, Jack," and "Glad to see your mother's got a man to do it."

"Well," Mr. Summers said, "guess that's everyone. Old Man Warner make it?"

"Here," a voice said, and Mr. Summers nodded.

A sudden hush fell on the crowd as Mr. Summers cleared his throat and looked at the list. "All ready?" he called. "Now, I'll read the names—heads of families first—and the men come up and take a paper out of the box. Keep the paper folded in your hand without looking at it until everyone has had a turn. Everything clear?"

The people had done it so many times that they only half listened to the directions; most of them were quiet, wetting their lips, not looking around. Then Mr. Summers raised one hand high and said, "Adams." A man disengaged himself from the crowd and came forward. "Hi, Steve," Mr. Summers said, and Mr. Adams said, "Hi, Joe." They grinned at one another humorlessly and nervously. Then Mr. Adams reached into the black box and took out a folded paper. He held it firmly by one corner as he turned and went hastily back to his place in the crowd, where he stood a little apart from his family, not looking down at his hand.

"Allen," Mr. Summers said. "Anderson.... Bentham."

"Seems like there's no time at all between lotteries any more," Mrs. Delacroix said to Mrs. Graves in the back row. "Seems like we got through with the last one only last week."

"Time sure goes fast," Mrs. Graves said.

"Clark.... Delacroix."

"There goes my old man," Mrs. Delacroix said. She held her breath while her husband went forward.

"Dunbar," Mr. Summers said, and Mrs. Dunbar went steadily to the box while one of the women said, "Go on, Janey," and another said, "There she goes."

"We're next," Mrs. Graves said. She watched while Mr. Graves came around from the side of the box, greeted Mr. Summers gravely, and selected a slip of paper from the box. By now, all through the crowd there were men holding the small folded papers in their large hands, turning them over and over nervously. Mrs. Dunbar and her two sons stood together, Mrs. Dunbar holding the slip of paper.

"Harburt.... Hutchinson."

"Get up there, Bill," Mrs. Hutchinson said, and the people near her laughed.

"Jones."

"They do say," Mr. Adams said to Old Man Warner, who stood next to him, "that over in the north village they're talking of giving up the lottery."

Old Man Warner snorted. "Pack of crazy fools," he said. "Listening to the young folks, nothing's good enough for them. Next thing you know, they'll be wanting to go back to living in caves, nobody work any more, live that way for a while. Used to be a saying about 'Lottery in June, corn be heavy soon.' First thing you know, we'd all be eating stewed chickweed and acorns. There's always been a lottery," he added petulantly. "Bad enough to see young Joe Summers up there joking with everybody."

"Some places have already quit lotteries," Mrs. Adams said. "Nothing but trouble in that," Old Man Warner said stoutly. "Pack of young fools."

"Martin." And Bobby Martin watched his father go forward. "Over-dyke.... Percy."

"I wish they'd hurry," Mrs. Dunbar said to her older son. "I wish they'd hurry."

"They're almost through," her son said.

"You get ready to run tell Dad," Mrs. Dunbar said.

Mr. Summers called his own name and then stepped forward precisely and selected a slip from the box. Then he called, "Warner."

"Seventy-seventh year I been in the lottery," Old Man Warner said as he went through the crowd. "Seventy-seventh time."

"Watson." The tall boy came awkwardly through the crowd. Someone said, "Don't be nervous, Jack," and Mr. Summers said, "Take your time, son."

"Zanini."

After that, there was a long pause, a breathless pause, until Mr. Summers, holding his slip of paper in the air, said, "All right, fellows." For a minute, no one moved, and then all the slips of paper were opened. Suddenly, all the women began to speak at once, saying, "Who is it?," "Who's got it?," "Is it the Dunbars?," "Is it the Watsons?" Then the voices began to say, "It's Hutchinson. It's Bill," "Bill Hutchinson's got it."

"Go tell your father," Mrs. Dunbar said to her older son.

People began to look around to see the Hutchinsons. Bill Hutchinson was standing quiet, staring down at the paper in his hand. Suddenly, Tessie Hutchinson shouted to Mr. Summers, "You didn't give him time enough to take any paper he wanted. I saw you. It wasn't fair!"

"Be a good sport, Tessie," Mrs. Delacroix called, and Mrs. Graves said, "All of us took the same chance."

"Shut up, Tessie," Bill Hutchinson said.

"Well, everyone," Mr. Summers said, "that was done pretty fast, and now we've got to be hurrying a little more to get done in time." He consulted his next list. "Bill," he said, "you draw for the Hutchinson family. You got any other households in the Hutchinsons?"

"There's Don and Eva," Mrs. Hutchinson yelled. "Make them take their chance!"

"Daughters draw with their husbands' families, Tessie," Mr. Summers said gently. "You know that as well as anyone else."

"It wasn't fair," Tessie said.

"I guess not, Joe," Bill Hutchinson said regretfully. "My daughter draws with her husband's family, that's only fair. And I've got no other family except the kids."

"Then, as far as drawing for families is concerned, it's you," Mr. Summers said in explanation, "and as far as drawing for households is concerned, that's you, too. Right?"

"Right," Bill Hutchinson said.

"How many kids, Bill?" Mr. Summers asked formally.

"Three," Bill Hutchinson said. "There's Bill, Jr., and Nancy, and little Dave. And Tessie and me."

"All right, then," Mr. Summers said. "Harry, you got their tickets back?"

Mr. Graves nodded and held up the slips of paper. "Put them in the box, then," Mr. Summers directed. "Take Bill's and put it in."

"I think we ought to start over," Mrs. Hutchinson said, as quietly as she could. "I tell you it wasn't fair. You didn't give him time enough to choose. Everybody saw that."

Mr. Graves had selected the five slips and put them in the box, and he dropped all the papers but those onto the ground, where the breeze caught them and lifted them off.

"Listen, everybody," Mrs. Hutchinson was saying to the people around her.

"Ready, Bill?" Mr. Summers asked, and Bill Hutchinson, with one quick glance around at his wife and children, nodded.

"Remember," Mr. Summers said, "take the slips and keep them folded until each person has taken one. Harry, you help little Dave." Mr. Graves took the hand of the little boy, who came willingly with him up to the box. "Take a paper out of the box, Davy," Mr. Summers said. Davy put his hand into the box and laughed. "Take just one paper," Mr. Summers said. "Harry, you hold it for him." Mr. Graves took the child's hand and removed the folded paper from the tight fist and held it while little Dave stood next to him and looked up at him wonderingly.

"Nancy next," Mr. Summers said. Nancy was twelve, and her school friends breathed heavily as she went forward, switching her skirt, and took a slip daintily from the box. "Bill, Jr.," Mr. Summers said, and Billy, his face red and his feet overlarge, nearly knocked the box over as he got a paper out. "Tessie," Mr. Summers said. She hesitated for a minute, looking around defiantly, and then set her lips and went up to the box. She snatched a paper out and held it behind her.

"Bill," Mr. Summers said, and Bill Hutchinson reached into the box and felt around, bringing his hand out at last with the slip of paper in it.

The crowd was quiet. A girl whispered, "I hope it's not Nancy," and the sound of the whisper reached the edges of the crowd.

"It's not the way it used to be," Old Man Warner said clearly. "People ain't the way they used to be."

"All right," Mr. Summers said. "Open the papers. Harry, you open little Dave's."

Mr. Graves opened the slip of paper and there was a general sigh through the crowd as he held it up and everyone could see that it was blank. Nancy and Bill, Jr., opened theirs at the same time, and both beamed and laughed, turning around to the crowd and holding their slips of paper above their heads.

"Tessie," Mr. Summers said. There was a pause, and then Mr. Summers looked at Bill Hutchinson, and Bill unfolded his paper and showed it. It was blank.

"It's Tessie," Mr. Summers said, and his voice was hushed. "Show us her paper, Bill."

Bill Hutchinson went over to his wife and forced the slip of paper out of her hand. It had a black spot on it, the black spot Mr. Summers had made the night before with the heavy pencil in the coal-company office. Bill Hutchinson held it up, and there was a stir in the crowd.

"All right, folks," Mr. Summers said. "Let's finish quickly."

Although the villagers had forgotten the ritual and lost the original black box, they still remembered to use stones. The pile of stones the boys had made earlier was ready; there were stones on the ground with the blowing scraps of paper that had come out of the box. Mrs. Delacroix selected a stone so large she had to pick it up with both hands and turned to Mrs. Dunbar. "Come on," she said. "Hurry up."

Mrs. Dunbar had small stones in both hands, and she said, gasping for breath, "I can't run at all. You'll have to go ahead and I'll catch up with you."

The children had stones already, and someone gave little Davy Hutchinson a few pebbles.

Tessie Hutchinson was in the center of a cleared space by now, and she held her hands out desperately as the villagers moved in on her. "It isn't fair," she said. A stone hit her on the side of the head.

Old Man Warner was saying, "Come on, come on, everyone." Steve Adams was in the front of the crowd of villagers, with Mrs. Graves beside him.

"It isn't fair, it isn't right," Mrs. Hutchinson screamed, and then they were upon her.

RED CARD

by S. L. Gilbow

S. L. Gilbow is a relatively new writer, with five stories published to date, four in *The Magazine of Fantasy & Science Fiction* and one in my anthology *Federations*. Gilbow served twenty-six years in the Air Force, and has been on dozens of deployments, and has flown more than 2000 hours as a B-52 navigator. He currently makes his living by teaching English at a public high school in Norfolk, Virginia.

Everyone knows that James Bond has a "license to kill." As an international spy, he must sometimes fight for his life. But he's a trained government employee, specially selected for Her Majesty's Service. But could you trust just *anyone* with a license to kill?

What about your neighbor?

Or your boss?

In fact, what if the government gave everybody one free pass to shoot one person, *any person*, for whatever reason?

That's the premise of our next story. S. L. Gilbow says that the idea for "Red Card" actually came from a conversation he had with his daughter, Mandy. "One day after a driver cut me off in heavy traffic, I... turned to my daughter and said, 'Everyone should be allowed to shoot one person without going to prison.' My daughter thought for a second then turned to me and said, 'Dad, if that were true you would have been dead a long time ago.'"

Mr. Gilbow might have lived to write this story. But in the world he's imagined, not everyone is so lucky.

L ate one April evening, Linda Jackson pulled a revolver from her purse and shot her husband through a large mustard stain in the center of his T-shirt. The official after incident survey concluded that almost all of Merry Valley approved of the shooting. Sixty-four percent of the townspeople even rated her target selection as "excellent." A few, however, criticized her, pointing out that shooting your husband is "a little too obvious" and "not very creative."

Dick Andrews, who had farmed the fertile soil around Merry Valley for over thirty years, believed that Larry Jackson, more than anyone else in town, needed to be killed. "I never liked him much," he wrote in the additional comments section of the incident survey. "He never seemed to have a good word to say about anybody."

"Excellent use of a bullet," scrawled Jimmy Blanchard. Born and raised in Merry Valley, he had known Larry for years and had even graduated from high school with him. "Most overbearing person I've ever met. He deserved what he got. I'm just not sure why it took so long."

Of course, a few people made waves. Jenny Collins seemed appalled. "I can hardly believe it," she wrote. "We used to be much more discerning about who we killed, and we certainly didn't go around flaunting it the way Linda does." Jenny was the old-fashioned kind.

Linda would never have called her actions "flaunting it." Of course she knew what to do after shooting Larry. She had read *The Enforcement Handbook* from cover to cover six times, poring over it to see if she had missed anything, scrutinizing every nuance. She had even committed some of the more important passages to memory: *Call the police immediately after executing an enforcement—Always keep your red card in a safe, dry place—Never reveal to anyone that you have a red card—Be proud; you're performing an important civic duty.*

But flaunting it? No, Linda blended in better than anyone in town, rarely talked and never called attention to herself. She spent most of her days at the Merry Valley Public Library, tucked between rows of antique shelves, alone, organizing a modest collection of old books. In the evening she fixed dinner. After Larry had eaten, cleaned up and left the house for "some time alone," Linda would lie in bed reading Jane Austen. No, Linda never flaunted anything—never had much to flaunt.

After she shot her husband, Linda returned the revolver to her purse and collapsed onto her oversized couch. She then picked up the telephone, set it in her lap, and tugged at her long, pale bangs—a nervous habit that drove Larry crazy. She had once considered cutting them to make him happy, but Sarah Hall from across the street had commented on how nice they looked. "They really bring out your eyes," Sarah had said. "They make you look as pretty as a princess."

Linda would never have called herself pretty, but she always looked as nice as she could. Her makeup—tasteful and modest—came straight off of page twenty-seven of the current issue of *Truly Beautiful*. She applied her eyeliner, mascara, lipstick and blush precisely according to the instructions, copying every detail of the model's face, framing each eye with two delicate, taupe lines. But she realized she could do no better than pass as the model's homely cousin.

Linda let go of her bangs, lifted the receiver and dialed a number from a yellow sticker plastered across the phone; the sticker doubled as an ad for Bob's Pizza

Heaven, so she dialed carefully.

"Merry Valley Police Department."

"I'd like to report an enforcement," said Linda.

"Linda?"

"Yes," she replied, trying to recognize the voice.

"This is Officer Hamilton."

"Oh, thank goodness," she said, unable to hide her relief. She admired Officer Hamilton. Once, while making his usual patrol through Merry Valley, he had pulled over to help her carry two bags of groceries, heavy with the dead weight of frozen meat and canned vegetables. He was probably just fighting boredom, but she still appreciated the help. You rarely found that kind of service anymore.

`Linda paused, wondered what tone to strike, and settled on matter-of-fact. "I've just shot someone. *The Enforcement Handbook* says I'm supposed to call you."

"That's right," said Officer Hamilton. "Chapter three, I think. Who did you shoot?"

"My husband."

"Is he dead?" he asked.

Linda studied Larry, sensitive to any movement, the slightest twitch. "He's not moving." she said. "He hasn't moved since I shot him."

"How many times did you shoot him?"

"Once," she said.

"I'd recommend you shoot him one more time just to be sure," said Officer Hamilton.

"No," said Linda, "I'm sure he's dead enough." *The Enforcement Handbook* recommended at least two shots, but the thought of shooting Larry again bothered Linda. The first shot hadn't been easy, in spite of what the handbook said.

"Fine then, but you'll need to come down to the station to fill out the paperwork."

"Of course," she said. "Do I need to call someone to pick him up?" The handbook hadn't mentioned how to remove the body.

"We'll take care of that," said Officer Hamilton. "Just come down to the station and don't forget to bring your red card. You do have a red card, don't you?"

"I do," she said.

"Wonderful," said Officer Hamilton.

"And I'll bring the revolver," she said, paraphrasing a portion from chapter two of the handbook.

"And any spare ammunition you didn't use," said Officer Hamilton. "We can reissue it with the card."

Linda hung up, set the phone on the floor, and rose from the couch. She looked at Larry, and the longer she looked at him the more she expected him to move; it seemed so unnatural for him to be so still, so silent—he had always been in motion. Early in their courtship she pictured him as a hummingbird—a large, gawky hummingbird—but lately she saw him as something else—perhaps a mongoose.

"Larry," she said without taking her eyes off him. She wondered if she should follow Officer Hamilton's advice and shoot him again. But there was no movement, no sound. She thought he looked like he was asleep, but then she remembered the constant rolling and snoring that marked his nights. No second shot would be needed.

Linda felt an urge to wash. She stepped around Larry's body, crossed the living room and passed through the spare bedroom into the bathroom. Linda filled the sink with warm water, adding a delightful mixture of strawberry and watermelon soap. The crimson color had never bothered her before, but now she braced herself as she plunged her hands into the water. She scrubbed her hands for more than minute; it seemed like the right thing to do.

After she dried her hands on a monogrammed towel, Linda went to her bedroom. Larry and Linda referred to it as the "spare bedroom," but it was the one room Linda had all to herself, her refuge from Larry when he got wild—even wilder than usual. The room became her sanctuary, and Larry rarely entered it. Not that Linda forbid him to do so. It's just that Linda had filled it with things that made him uncomfortable. A large four-poster bed dominated the center of the room. On top of the bed were a handmade quilt, a pile of embroidered throw pillows, and a stuffed animal Larry had given to Linda years ago. Linda called the animal "Sally Cat" but lately had considered the possibility that it might be a ferret. Beside the bed stood an antique vanity bordered by two windows, each framed with lace curtains adorned with a delicate tea rose pattern. The room radiated Linda; there was nothing about Larry in it.

Linda scanned her closet and filtered through a row of clothes she had worn only once—a wedding dress, a pink prom dress, and an evening gown. She finally settled on a gathered lavender dress. She had once worn it to The Merry Valley Bistro, the one restaurant in town Linda looked forward to. Larry criticized her for being overdressed, and she hadn't worn the dress since. But tonight it seemed right—the lavender dress and a matching pair of high heeled shoes. Linda wasn't sure who might be at the police station, but crowds had a way of forming in Merry Valley, and she wanted to be presentable. "Besides," she thought, "there's no chance of Larry objecting."

When she finished dressing, Linda gathered the red card, the government revolver, and the last two rounds of ammunition, and dropped them into her purse. She checked her makeup in the vanity mirror and then, deciding she was in no mood to drive, called a taxi.

She opened the front door, paused, and surveyed the living room one last time. "Damn it, Larry," she said. "I gave you fair warning."

Linda stepped into the dark night of a new moon. Her outdoor light had burned out weeks ago, but the porch light on Sarah Hall's house across the street blazed like a beacon, allowing Linda to navigate her steps safely. Sarah, swaying in time to a big band tune coming from her living room, deadheaded flowers that grew in large pots that framed her house. She was a large, nocturnal woman with a strong jaw and an unmistakable silhouette.

As Linda neared the street, Sarah was attracted by the unexpected movement and gave a friendly wave. Linda wished she hadn't been noticed, but if she had to deal with anyone tonight, besides the police—which at this point seemed inevitable—it might as well be Sarah. Linda liked Sarah and believed Sarah liked her too. She liked the way she complimented her bangs; she liked the cheesecakes she occasionally brought over; she liked her sisterly advice. Often Linda would call Sarah when Larry acted up. "You should get help," Sarah would say. Linda would agree and then tell her how she was starting to get things under control, how she and Larry were going to work things out with just a little more time, but Linda knew that the time needed to work things out with Larry was most aptly measured in geological terms.

Linda stopped between two small pear trees to wait for the taxi. She stooped under one and felt the soil—she would need to water it tomorrow. Larry had purchased the trees on the way back from their honeymoon five years ago. The trees were the only fond memory she had of that week.

Larry had surprised her with a Caribbean cruise, although Linda thought they had decided to go to New York. They spent two days in the Bahamas, but Linda refused to count it as one of the places she had actually visited since she never left the ship.

"You ever been on a cruise before?" Larry asked as they entered their suite.

The question surprised Linda. Surely they had discussed cruises in the five months they had known each other. She thought for a moment, but no such conversation came to mind. "No," she said, "this will be my first time."

"You're going to love it here," he said.

But she didn't. Within two hours she was heaving into the toilet.

"You should give it more of a chance," Larry said.

"I'll try," she said.

"It's all in your attitude."

"I think I'm feeling a little better," she whispered, trying to prove him right. Then she grabbed the rim of the toilet and vomited again.

Larry spent the rest of their honeymoon pacing the ship's deck. Occasionally, between doses of Dramamine, Linda would look out the cabin window. She had never seen so much water. Larry refused to join her, refused to eat with her, refused to talk to her. He had decided to boycott any activity that included Linda.

Linda stood under the pear tree until the taxi arrived. As it pulled over, Sarah dropped her pruning sheers and dashed across the street.

"Sarah, I would to love talk but I need to go."

"I would say so." Sarah opened the taxi door and slid into the back seat; she waved for Linda to join her. Linda crawled in.

"Just tell me, dear," said Sarah, "why did you shoot him?"

"Where to?" asked the driver.

"The police station," said Linda.

The taxi sped into the night.

Linda stared out the window as the simple homes of Merry Valley slipped by. She felt Sarah's strong hands grab her arm and pull her close. "Now don't you worry," said Sarah. "You're not worried, are you?"

"A little," admitted Linda.

"There's nothing to it. Really. I had a cousin once who used a red card, and he said it was the easiest thing he ever did."

"Who'd he use it on?" asked Linda.

"I don't remember. It's been years. At least five and it wasn't around here."

"He said it was easy?"

"I think he shot a speeder. He always hated careless drivers."

Linda buried her face into the fat flesh of Sarah's right arm. She wanted to cry. The handbook had mentioned this—*Shooter's Regret. It will pass*, the handbook stated, *just trust your decision, trust your instincts.*

"When I was young, I used to drive around with my cousin," said Sarah. "He would yell at people all the time. Yell at them for going too slow, for going too fast, for cutting him off. I wasn't surprised when I heard he had used a red card."

"It wasn't easy," said Linda.

"Think he got an award for it. Used the card the same week he got it. A lot of people like to see the cards circulate. Lets more people take part in the system."

"How'd you know I used a red card?"

"Why, dear, I heard it on the radio. They broke into 'Phil's Follies.' There's nothing as exciting as one of the cards being used."

"I guess," said Linda. She didn't mind excitement; she just didn't want the excitement to revolve around her.

By the time Linda and Sarah arrived at the police station, a small crowd had already gathered. Sarah wrapped an arm around Linda and pulled her close. "OK, dear, you ready for this?"

Linda nodded.

"You stay by me," she snapped with authority. Linda pulled in close for protection.

Linda recognized several faces in the crowd—Jerry Miles, Freddy Nevers, and Ann Davidson. She knew them well enough to carry on casual conversation at The Happy Druggist—Jerry's store—or Mel's Fill 'em Up where Freddy and Ann worked. There were also half a dozen people not quite as familiar to her, but she had seen them all around town at one time or another.

Freddy Nevers called her name, and Jerry Miles even shouted a little encouragement: "Way to go!"

Deputy Williams met Linda and Sarah at the entrance to the police station and escorted them to the reception counter. At one point, Jerry, excited at having his monotonous evening livened up a little, dashed toward Linda to congratulate her, but Deputy Williams reached out and shoved him back. Linda gave the deputy an appreciative glance. "Where were you when I needed you?" she thought.

Barry Giles, lead reporter for Channel Seven, moved as close to Linda as he could, microphone in hand, ready to broadcast the details to all of Merry Valley. "How did it happen, Mrs. Jackson?" he called out.

Linda started to answer, but the deputy interrupted in a low forceful voice he saved for his most serious duties. "There'll be time for that later."

Officer Hamilton was waiting for Linda behind a mahogany reception desk. Linda pulled a revolver out of her purse and laid it gently in front of him. After Officer Hamilton confirmed the revolver to be official government property, the crowd, giving Linda some space out of politeness while inching forward out of curiosity, waited for the inevitable. Linda reached into her purse and pulled out the red card. The card didn't seem special. It was small, only half the size of a postcard, with rounded corners and a smooth edge. The one mark on it was an ordinary bar code.

"Son of a gun," said Barry.

"Killed by a librarian with a red card," said Jerry. "That's got to be embarrassing."

"I knew she had it," said a voice Linda didn't recognize.

"Like hell you did," came a muffled response.

Officer Hamilton slid the card under an electronic reader and, with a nod, confirmed its authenticity.

"How long you been holding it?" asked someone from the crowd.

Officer Hamilton checked the reading. "Four years," he said, impressed at Linda's self-restraint. The crowd nodded its approval.

"My goodness," said Barry. "Most of the other tickets have been circulating a lot faster than that."

"Sure have," said Officer Hamilton.

"How long have they been out?" Barry asked.

"A couple have been out for almost a year and one for about nine months. I'm not sure about the other two. I'd have to look it up."

"Looks like another one's going back into circulation," someone said. The crowd hummed with excitement.

Officer Hamilton led Linda away from the crowd. Linda glanced back at Sarah who signaled that she would be in the waiting room, an unimpressive area set off by grey partitions. It contained little more than four chairs, a television dangling from the ceiling, and two ash trays. "Thanks," mouthed Linda.

They ended up in a small, secluded room in the back of the station. Linda took her place in a wooden chair behind an aging table. On a corner shelf stood a drip coffeepot containing the last few drops after a long day.

Officer Hamilton held up a Styrofoam cup. "Coffee? Looks like there's enough for one more cup."

"No thanks," said Linda. She could have actually used a cup of coffee, but not from that pot.

Officer Hamilton sat in the chair across from Linda. "Well," he said, "The enforcement isn't over…"

"Until the paperwork's done," finished Linda, quoting the handbook. "This is the hard part, isn't it?"

"There's no hard part," he said. "It's all easy." He smiled, placed an official looking form on the table and put on a pair of bifocals. He read the form quickly to himself, vocalizing a few key phrases, orienting himself on how to proceed.

"Are you ready?" he finally asked. Linda nodded.

"What is your name?"

Linda gave him a "you've got to be kidding me" look.

"These are standard questions, Linda. Just humor me."

"Linda Jackson."

"Gender?"

Linda didn't even answer. "Female," said Officer Hamilton in response to his own question. "Marital Status?"

"Widowed," said Linda.

"Oh yes," he said. "That's kind of why we're here, isn't it."

"It is."

"Where did you execute the enforcement?"

"In my living room."

"Why did you execute the enforcement?"

"Is that important?" asked Linda.

"We track these things for statistical purposes."

"I think the real question should be why didn't I do it sooner."

"Why didn't you? You've had the red card for almost four years."

"I don't know. At first I didn't want to use it because then I wouldn't have one. But later it just became a challenge."

"A challenge?"

"Sometimes he would egg me on, dare me to use it."

"He knew you had a red card?"

Linda wasn't sure how to answer this. She knew she wasn't supposed to tell Larry about the red card.

"Just answer honestly," said Officer Hamilton. "You have nothing to worry about. You performed an enforcement while in possession of a valid red card. That's it. It's that simple. These questions are just to help us improve the program."

"He knew," said Linda. "He's known for years. It was a mistake to tell him because then he would test me. It was like Russian roulette."

Officer Hamilton made a quick note.

"Is that alright? Am I in trouble?"

"Well some people view it as having an unfair advantage over other citizens.

But in this case it doesn't seem to have made a difference."

"But it should have made a difference." Linda looked at Officer Hamilton and wondered if she was getting through to him. She wanted to tell him how things were supposed to be different, how they were supposed to get better, slowly, incrementally, but better. Her plans were never to kill Larry but to keep him alive, to keep him alive forever. "It should have made a big difference," she said. "He knew I had a card."

"Had he been drinking?"

"He'd been out messing around. He always seemed to be going someplace."

"Why did you shoot him?" asked Officer Hamilton, trying the question one more time.

"I really don't know," said Linda. "I think I just snapped."

"Linda," he said. His eyes narrowed. "People with red cards are allowed to snap. It's their duty to snap."

Officer Hamilton pressed on with questions for almost half an hour. How did you feel? Where did you keep your card? Did the handbook prepare you for your role as an enforcer? Linda answered as best she could, but she was ready for it all to end.

Finally, Officer Hamilton put down his pencil. "That's it," he said.

"Really?"

"That wasn't so bad was it?"

"Not too bad. Anything else?"

"Just a word of advice," said Officer Hamilton. "If you ever get another red card, don't tell anyone. I don't even know who has them. The program is random and anonymous. That's what makes it work. If you start taking those factors out, the program loses its effectiveness."

"Of course," she said, a little embarrassed at having made such a careless mistake.

Officer Hamilton released Linda and led her to the hallway out. "Do you need a ride?" he asked.

"I'll go back with Sarah," she said. "I could use a restroom though."

In the restroom, Linda checked herself in the mirror. Her lipstick had faded from the right side of her upper lip, and black mascara crept up towards her eyebrow. Her blush had cracked except for the glow on her nose. The night had been hard on her face; she looked old and tired. She freshened her lipstick, brushed her hair, and killed the shine on her nose. It seemed futile. She would need to check *Truly Beautiful* for a look that could hold up better.

Linda left the restroom and walked down the long hall to join Sarah in the waiting area. She paused at the end of the hall, dwarfed by the grey partitions that separated the waiting area from the rest of the police station. She could hear voices, several of them, mingling, Sarah's dominant among them.

Linda looked above the partition and saw a small television, muted and pathetic, hanging from the ceiling. The television's color had shifted long ago, and a bald, blue man in a sweater dispensed advice. She thought she might have seen him before. He seemed vaguely familiar. Was his name Richard? She wasn't sure, but he seemed like a Richard to her. Maybe it wasn't advice; he could be warning her about something, some disaster, some great flood.

"Well I know what I'll do if I get the card next," she heard Jerry Miles say.

"Shoot yourself?" asked Freddy Nevers.

"Never mind, I just changed my plan," cackled Jerry.

"Well, if either of you get a card, let me know," said Sarah. "You tend to live a lot longer if you know who has the cards."

Richard now held a green spray bottle. He was selling something. Of course. Why advise or warn when you can sell. Linda decided to wait until the conversation settled down a little more before joining Sarah. Conversations tended to die once Linda entered into them.

"I never know who has the cards," said Jerry.

"I try to make it my business," said Sarah. "I try to make everything my business." She spit out the words as if they were rehearsed.

Richard, energetic and passionate now, waved the bottle about in his left hand. He held up a shirt and sprayed it. Linda moved closer to the television, but she couldn't tell if the spray had any effect. Richard sprayed the bottle on the floor and then on himself. He was obviously proud of its versatility. He looked straight at Linda and urged her to buy his product. She needed it. She needed to have what he was selling.

"What about Linda?" asked Jerry.

"I've known Linda for years," said Sarah. "Her husband too."

"I knew her," said Freddy.

"But not like I knew her, dear."

Linda hated to interrupt; Sarah seemed to be enjoying herself. She wondered what it would be like to enjoy yourself. Linda continued to watch the commercial, one of those long ones, one of those that could go on for five minutes. Richard had toned down the sell and appeared to be whispering, enunciating every word. He had two bottles now, one cradled under each arm, and he was talking to Linda, directly to Linda, only to Linda.

"Well, she shops at my store," said Jerry. "Buys a lot of makeup. Careful shopper. Always did like her."

"Sweetheart, you have to like someone who has a red card," said Sarah. "Kind of dangerous not to."

"How would I have known she had a red card?" asked Jerry.

"I knew," said Sarah.

"You knew she had a red card?"

"Of course she had the card."

"I suspected, but I was never sure," said a voice Linda didn't recognize. He seemed to be acting more important than he actually was.

"I've known it for years. I'm surprised you all didn't know." Sarah paused for effect. "Oh, I forgot, you all weren't sleeping with her husband?" The crowd laughed. "Well, I guess I won't have to like her anymore," said Sarah.

Richard made his final plea. Under him flashed a phone number, barely legible, followed by the words, "Miracle Madness, for when clean isn't clean enough." Linda listened for the conversation to continue, but it had stalled. Even Sarah was silent.

Linda pulled back into the hall, found a phone near the ladies' restroom, and called the toll free number.

"I want to place an order," said Linda.

"Which product?"

"Miracle Madness."

"Oh, you are going to love it. And with that you get Miracle Madness Plus."

After Linda had provided her billing information, she joined Sarah and the others in the waiting room. "Sarah," she said as she rounded the partition, "I'm all done now."

"Wonderful," said Sarah. "You've had a hard day and it's time to get you home."

When the taxi dropped them off at Linda's place well after midnight, Sarah was in full motion, feeding off the energy of the evening. Linda had been quiet during the drive home, but she didn't need to speak since Sarah had rambled on without stopping. Sarah had pretty well resolved most of Linda's problems. She had told her how to improve her career—*after all you can't stay a librarian your entire life.* She had told her how to improve her looks—*those bangs just have to go; they do absolutely nothing for you.* She had told her how to improve her general disposition—*you have got to stop moping about.*

Finally Linda asked, "What do I do now?"

"What do you mean?"

"The handbook never talked about this part. I don't know what to do next."

"Well," said Sarah, "tomorrow we need to plan Mr. Jackson's funeral. I guess that would be next."

"Of course," said Linda.

"Then we bury him, and then you get on with your life."

"We need to plan a funeral," said Linda.

"Now don't be afraid to call if you need anything," said Sarah as they entered the house. "Really. Anything at all."

"Anything?"

"Absolutely. Whatever you need."

"Can I stay with you?" asked Linda.

"Stay with me?"

Linda nodded.

"At my house?"

"For a while. At least a day or two. Longer if I could."

"You really need to get back on your feet," said Sarah. "*This* is your home and it doesn't do any good to run from it. *This* is your place."

"My place," said Linda. She stood over the spot where Larry had lain. Now that he was gone, the room seemed much more open, almost cavernous.

Sarah joined her. "Is this it?" she asked.

"He fell right here next to the coffee table," replied Linda.

"They really are quite efficient. The enforcement program is run so well."

"It is," agreed Linda, noticing that even the blood had been cleaned up. All that remained was a small stain, barely noticeable, no worse than the tea spill on the other side of the room. But Linda would get all the stains out, the blood, the tea, everything. After all, Miracle Madness was on its way.

"I can stay for a bit," said Sarah, turning on the television. She folded onto the couch, pried her shoes off, and clicked through channels looking for the television version of "Phil's Follies."

"Stay for as long you can," said Linda. "I'll be with you in a moment. After I change." The lavender dress was beginning to weigh on her.

In her bedroom, Linda slipped off her high heels and set them in her closet. She then pulled off her dress and hung it neatly on a padded hanger. She lay down on her bed, closed her eyes, and folded her hands over her face. She exhaled, bathing her eyes and nose in the warmth of her own breath. She opened her mouth and made a guttural sound that echoed off her cupped hands.

She rolled onto her stomach, grabbed her stuffed cat, Sally, and pulled her close. She wanted to be a cat. No, a ferret, she would rather be a ferret. Linda slid off the bed and crouched on her hands and knees, almost feral. She could sleep here. She could sleep on the carpet once it was clean. That would be soon; Miracle Madness was coming.

"When clean isn't clean enough," she moaned.

Linda reached under the bed and felt around blindly. She pulled out a shoe box adorned with a lavender bow—a beautiful bow she had tied nine months earlier. She loved tying bows and she was proud of this one, bold and perfectly proportioned. Lavender—she loved lavender. Linda untied the bow and carefully slid the ribbon off the box. She opened the box, pulled out a red card and a small revolver, and finally cried for the first time that night.

TEN WITH A FLAG

by Joseph Paul Haines

Joseph Paul Haines is the author of several stories, which have appeared in magazines such as *Interzone, Aeon Magazine,* and *Abyss & Apex.* He is also the editor, with Samantha Henderson, of the anthology *From the Trenches,* and his short story collection, *Ten With a Flag and Other Playthings,* came out in November. This story first appeared in *Interzone* and was adapted to audio on the *Transmissions From Beyond* podcast.

Newly pregnant women face a great deal of difficult decisions, and modern medical procedures have only made those decisions more complex. Once, women expected to struggle through forty uncomfortable weeks, drive to the hospital, and go through the rigors of labor with their babies' entire future being a mystery. Boy or girl, no one knew. Healthy or ailing, no one could guess.

But today, a woman is confronted with medical technology almost from her first obstetric appointment. Should she have an ultrasound? What kinds of blood tests should she take? Should she ask for maternal serum screening? Is amniocentesis in order?

These are the questions facing today's pregnant woman. What about the mothers of the future? What kind of tests will be offered to them? What kind of choices will they need to make?

Our next story takes us into that future. Here is a world where it is possible to know too much about your baby's potential—or at least, a place where the *government* knows too much.

J ohnnie didn't talk while he was driving. Normally it would drive me a little crazy, sitting there in traffic and not saying a word, but this time it didn't bother me. There was too much on my mind. Truth was, I hoped he wouldn't talk so that I could have some time to think. But when he pulled onto the freeway, I knew I wasn't going to get that lucky.

It only took him a couple of seconds to connect to the traffic web. Johnnie didn't like being out of control, it was one of the things I'd found endearing in him; quaint even. This time though, he didn't even double check the connection. The steering wheel folded and collapsed into the dash, and he turned to face me. "What does that mean, exactly?" he asked. "Did the doctor say anything else?"

I shook my head. "He said he'd have to check, but he'd never heard of the combination coming up before."

"He'd have to check?"

"Yeah."

"Did he say anything else?"

"I told you, he said he'd have to check." I didn't know what to say. It was still sinking in.

Johnnie leaned back in his seat and stared out his window. I could tell he was getting ready to turn around and go back. We'd only been married three years, but I could read some of his expressions like a book. "How's that even possible?" he asked. "I mean, is the baby okay?"

"The baby is fine."

"Now I wish we didn't know."

I turned away from him. "You agreed we should get the test done."

"I know, but...*damn*."

"Don't you think it's better knowing?"

"How do you get a ten and a flag?" he asked.

"He said he'd have to check," I repeated.

"But the baby's fine?"

"Yes."

"Are you sure he said ten?"

I nodded. "Ten."

Johnnie crossed his arms and chewed on his bottom lip. I think he mumbled something, but at that point I didn't want to hear it.

We didn't talk for a while after that. I was contented to sit and watch the other transports as we cut in and out of traffic. It was like watching a school of fish swimming together, weaving at the same time. We rushed along at speeds of over two hundred kilometers with no more than a meter separating our vehicles, our safety in the control of the central traffic computer. Sometimes it was easier to let something bigger than yourself take control. It had a plan, and although you couldn't always see it, you knew you'd never wreck.

It wasn't until we sped past our off-ramp that I began to get concerned.

"Where we going?" I asked.

Johnnie didn't answer. He punched up the navigation screen and sighed. "What the hell?"

"What?"

"We've been redirected. We have an appointment with Human Services. Now."

"Now?"

"Yeah, they've even rescheduled my work-shift for this afternoon and notified the office."

"Do you think it's about the test results?" I had expected some reaction from Human Services, just not this quick. I folded my hands in my lap to keep from tapping my fingers. Johnnie didn't like to see me get nervous.

"It doesn't say."

"Great." There was nothing else to do but sit back and enjoy the ride. We were just passengers.

Central had control.

"I understand you must be apprehensive," the agent said. He was a small man, this Mr. White, and the huge, empty desk he sat behind made him look even smaller. "Results like these can cause a great deal of confusion."

Johnnie started to say something. I squeezed his hand before he could. The last thing we needed was to anger a government official, particularly one as high up as Mr. White seemed to be. It was best to remain compliant until he finished.

"The important thing to remember is that your baby rated a ten. Your child will be an asset to the Nation. Only one in fifty thousand couples who go through the procedure come up with these results. It's a credit to the two of you as citizens.

"As such, the state has raised both your rating to eight, effective immediately. Congratulations."

Johnnie and I stared at each other. Eights? That was two levels higher than our current rating. Eight meant ten hours of work as opposed to forty. Eight meant no more scraping by between allowance periods. Eight meant a much bigger apartment. Eight meant no more late nights while Johnnie stayed at work to improve his production numbers.

Eight meant no more looking over our shoulders.

"Thank you, Mr. White." But of course, Johnnie couldn't keep his mouth shut. "I've just one question, though. The flag? How can there be a flag with a rating of ten?"

Mr. White pursed his lips. It was quite an odd gesture, almost feminine and I had to keep myself from giggling.

Eight didn't mean you could just randomly disrespect government officials.

"Well," he said, "there is that question. To be perfectly honest, I've never seen it come up before. But in your case, I don't think it's something to worry about. Your child rated a ten and you are now eights. I don't see how there could be a problem. The government won't, of course, stand in the way if you decide to invoke your option."

"What if we do?" Johnnie asked. I squeezed his hand tighter but he just pulled his away from my grasp and continued, "What would happen to us?"

Mr. White smiled. There was little humor in it. "Happen, sir?"

"If we use the option to terminate the pregnancy, what would happen to us?"

"Why would you do that, sir? Your child is a ten. He or she will be a great credit to the nation and improve life for all of the citizenry. What citizen would even consider that?"

Johnnie shook his head. "Well, the flag. I'm worried about it."

"Worried about it?" Mr. White picked up his pen and scribbled something on his tablet.

"Yes," Johnnie answered.

"Your child is a ten, sir," Mr. White repeated. "That should be enough to make you forget about the flag."

"Well, it doesn't. It certainly didn't keep Central from issuing the flag. Why would they have issued a flag unless there was some concern?"

Mr. White tapped his pen on his desk a few times, and leaned forward. "How much do you know about the CDP test?"

"Central looks into the future and determines the baby's community viability," Johnnie said. "That's really all there is to it, right?"

Mr. White chuckled. "Well, that's not really accurate. Central can't look into the future. That's impossible," he said, chuckling. "What it does do is predict the future based off of the child's cellular past, the parent's cellular past and other environmental factors. You see, once you can witness the cellular history of an individual, you can predict future activity through sheer computational power. Central has an over ninety-nine percent success rate with this test. We don't question the results."

I knew Johnnie wasn't going to take the hint so I cut him off before he could do more damage. "It's just so confusing, Mr. White," I said, smiling as wide as I could. "Aren't flags usually reserved for children with... well, problems?"

"Actually," he said, "the flag is just an indication that the parents will have to make a sacrifice. Sometimes it means that the child will be handicapped, and the parents will have to work additional hours to make up for the extra burden on the State. All we know is that when a flag comes up, the sacrifice necessary from the parents is sufficient to warrant giving them the option to terminate the pregnancy. It's how we protect your freedoms as individuals.

"The State values that highly." He smiled.

"But our child is a ten," I said. "Tens can't be a burden on the State by definition. They are the ones that make the State better."

"That's true. Which is why I'm not overly concerned with the flag. And neither should you. Your child will be an asset to the State. You'll have to make a sacrifice, but what parent doesn't?"

I knew I had to phrase my next question carefully. "And there's no indication as to what form that sacrifice might take?"

"You know I can't answer that," Mr. White said. "And you know you shouldn't even be asking. Knowledge of the results can affect their outcome."

"I see. Well, thank you—"

"You didn't answer my question," Johnnie said. "What happens if we take the flag option?"

Mr. White fidgeted in his chair. "Well, your promotion will be cancelled, for one thing." He grabbed a folder from the stack of papers and flipped it open. "You're a six now, correct?"

Johnnie nodded.

"Hmm," Mr. White said, flipping through pages. "Did you know that your boss had put in for a rate reduction?"

"Excuse me?" Johnnie leaned forward in his seat. I could see his cheeks turning red. "I work harder than—"

"Says here," Mr. White interjected, "that your boss seems to think that although you spend fifty hours a week on the job, your production levels only account for thirty hours worth of work. He recommended you be downgraded to a five so that you can actually accomplish forty hours worth of work in sixty hours time."

"That's not right. I work harder than—"

"But you don't have to worry about that anymore," Mr. White said, smiling wider. "You've been promoted to an eight."

Johnnie's mouth hung open. It was time to get out of there. "Thank you, Mr. White. We both appreciate your time."

Johnnie was still dazed by the time we got back to the transport. It didn't help matters any that it wasn't the same one we had left in the parking garage. It was bigger. Longer. It was a transport belonging to a couple of eights. There was no driver's seat.

Central had control.

"A demotion?" Johnnie said. "I can't believe that—"

"No," I said, nodding toward the speaker panel on the dashboard. "A promotion. What great luck." Doubt gnawed at my insides, but this wasn't the place to discuss it.

We sat quietly while Central directed the car onto the freeway. Once again, we passed our off-ramp without slowing.

"Central," Johnnie said. "List destination."

The soft voice of Central command filled the cabin, "Your new residence, sir."

"New residence, of course."

"You have eighteen voice messages, sir, all offering congratulations on your promotion and the impending boon to the Nation that your son's birth will deliver. Would you like to hear them?"

So it was a boy.

Neither of us felt much like celebrating. "Not now, Central," I said. "Just take us home."

We'd managed to go a full week without appearing in public. The raise meant Johnnie could work from home, so we didn't have to go out if we didn't want but we both knew we'd stayed hidden as long as we could. I'd convinced Johnnie to show our faces at the opera—I'd never been to the opera; it was one of the perks of the promotion and I was looking forward to the evening—but even that had been a struggle. Since we'd come home from Human Services, he'd spent all his free time in front of the computer. He wouldn't even discuss the test results with me.

My wardrobe had picked out a deep-blue chiffon evening gown for me. I dressed in front of the full length mirror and once I was ready, the lights dimmed while the environmental controls chose the scent of roses to fill the room. It was the first time in weeks I'd felt relaxed. A night out would do us good. I only hoped Johnnie would be in a similar mood.

Instead, I found Johnnie still sitting in front of the computer. He hadn't yet started to get ready. "We'll be late," I said.

He glanced my direction and did a double-take. "You look beautiful."

I crossed one ankle over the other, dipped my chin and looked up at him. "Then get up, get dressed and take me on a date."

He sighed, took a deep breath and said, "I *do* so very love you, you know."

"Then get dressed."

He pushed himself away from the desk and walked toward his dressing room.

"And don't even try," I called after him, "to pick something out yourself. Just wear what your wardrobe chooses. You'd never match this color if you had all night."

"I'm not completely useless."

"Oh honey, I know that," I said, smiling as sweetly as possible. "You're only useless when trying to dress yourself. Now hurry up!"

We made it out the door on time.

Our new transport was no where to be seen. An older model pulled up in front of our building.

"I requested a downgrade for the evening," Johnnie said. "I felt like driving."

I shook my head. "As long as you get us there on time."

He held my door open and closed it behind me. I waited until we left the parking lot and slid my hand onto his leg. It was good to be out again. Even though the new apartment had plenty of room, it just felt great to get out from behind the walls, to get back into the world again.

Once we'd turned onto the surface streets, Johnnie engaged the auto-drive and leaned back in his seat. "I thought you said you wanted to drive?"

"I lied. I just wanted to talk to you without a speaker."

My good mood evaporated. "Do we have to do this now?"

"Did you know," he asked without acknowledging my question, "that in the four cases where a mother has died in childbirth over the last ten years, the flag option had been available in every case?"

My stomach turned. "So? That doesn't mean—"

"No, no, it doesn't mean—"

"So why are you bringing this up?" I asked. "Don't you think I'm frightened enough already?"

Johnnie leaned closer to me. "But it doesn't mean it isn't possible, either. We've got to consider it."

"It could also mean that our son will have a learning disability, and we'll have to work particularly hard to get him through it." My cheeks were burning. I understood his concern, but I couldn't believe he was going to ruin our first night out together in ages.

He crossed his arms. "And it could mean you're in danger. How are we supposed to know? Who's to say the child actually needs us to be a ten?"

"We can't know. Knowledge of future events can change the outcome. He's a ten. That's all that's important."

"Bullshit."

My jaw dropped.

"That's not *all* that's important by a long-shot."

"Of course it is." Instinct made me look around to see that no one was in the car with us. "You don't interfere with something like that. It's almost treasonous."

"Of course it isn't treasonous. The State wouldn't have given us the flag otherwise. It's our right."

My eyes filled with tears. "But he's going to be a ten. He's going to be a perfect little boy."

"Yes, he will," Johnnie replied, taking my hand in his. He brushed a tear from my cheek and added, "But perfect for who?"

I knew we weren't going to the opera even before we sped past the turn-off to the Cultural District, but it didn't get any easier once we were sitting inside Dr. Jones' office, waiting for him to finish his examination. "Well," he said, looking down at me from over the edge of his bifocals, "there's no genetic contra indicators, no signs of pre-toxemia, no anemia, nothing that would give me even a moment's hesitation about your health or that of your child." He seemed tired and his thin, grey hair puffed up more on one side of his head than the other.

Johnnie ran his fingers through his hair. "I just don't get it."

"Maybe it's not for us to get," I offered. "But there's nothing wrong with me. I'm not in any danger so we can stop worrying—"

"That doesn't mean that something couldn't show up later though, right?"

"Johnnie, I—"

"Nothing is certain, sir," Dr. Jones replied.

"Johnnie!" I grabbed his wrist and clamped down. He whipped his head around to look at me, and that's when I finally saw it: He was terrified. Sweat beaded his upper lip and he couldn't keep his eyes on any one thing.

"But it's still your choice," Dr. Jones said. "No one is going to stop you from choosing to exercise your option. The flag is there for a purpose."

I stared Johnnie in the eye, hoping he'd notice the slight side-to-side shake

I was giving him.

"I think we should use the flag," he said.

My skin froze. "No," I whispered.

"There will be other babies," he said. "Ones without a flag. We don't need the raises. I can't stand the thought of losing you. Tell her she can have other babies, Doctor."

"Of course you can have other babies," Dr. Jones said, "but let's not overlook—"

"Why should we have to make a sacrifice?" Johnnie asked, kneeling down in front of me. "We've been given the option. There wouldn't be a flag if there wasn't a problem. You know that."

I tried to speak, but nothing came out of my mouth. He was right. There was something wrong; some kind of difficulty we'd have to face if we had this baby. Difficulties we most likely wouldn't have to face with another baby. But this one was a ten! He could be a great composer or an artist. He could discover medicine that cured the last remaining diseases. He could do anything! I *knew* that, felt it with every beat of my heart.

The State knew that too.

But what was the cost?

I looked at Johnnie and felt very cold.

"I can't make this decision," I said. I pulled him in close and rested my cheek against his and whispered in his ear. "You make it. Make it for both of us."

He kissed my temple, then my cheek, then my ear. His warm breath caught in his throat. He pulled away, turned to Dr. Jones and said, "We'll take the option."

What little air remained in my chest rushed out of me. The room spun.

"Very well," Dr. Jones said. He removed a gown from a drawer beneath the examination table and handed it me. "I'll give you a moment to get ready," he said, and left the room.

We didn't talk. I changed into the dressing gown and sat back up on the table. The longer we sat, waiting, the smaller the room seemed to get. I wanted Johnnie to say something; anything, but he just sat there, trying his best to smile when I looked at him.

After a few minutes, Dr. Jones re-joined us. He wasn't alone.

Mr. White from Human Services stood in the doorway, flanked by a half dozen Constables. "That will be all, Doctor."

Johnnie stepped in front of me. "What are you doing? This is our decision."

"And you made it," Mr. White said. He appeared even smaller out from behind his desk.

Johnnie shook his head and held his arms to the side, trying in vain to shield me from the Constables. "You said you wouldn't interfere."

Mr. White smiled. "We didn't. We allowed you to make your decision of your own free will." He stepped inside the door and removed a stun-gun from behind his back. "No one ever said we'd let you go through with it, though. The flag is an option, not a right. Arrest him."

The Constables fell on him them. Johnnie tried to resist, but one kick in the stomach was all it took to end that. Within ten seconds they had him out of the room, leaving only myself and Mr. White. "Go ahead and get changed," he said. "I'll wait for you outside."

I dressed slowly. It was as if every memory I had of Johnnie came back to me right then. The dates, our wedding, the fights, the make-ups; all of it. I'd just stood there and let them take him. I wanted to cry, but held it back. Whatever happened to us, I'd be strong. I pulled my shoulders back and opened the door.

Mr. White was waiting for me. He was still alone. "We understand this wasn't your choice. That's correct, isn't it?"

My flesh raised with a sudden chill. "That's right."

"Good," he said, lips drawn tight and thin with his smile.

"What's going to happen to Johnnie?"

Mr. White offered me his hand and helped me step down from the examination table. "He'll be reduced to a one or two, of course. Put to manual labor. If he keeps himself clean, he could even work back up to a four or five."

I knew Johnnie wouldn't want me to live that way.

"Of course your marriage is annulled. You're free to choose whomever you'd like to replace him from the other eights or nines."

"Replace him?"

Mr. White grimaced. "I'm sorry, I'm afraid I'm not terribly good with certain social graces. Please forgive me. Of course you'll want to take some time to yourself. But when you're ready, choose who you will."

By the time we walked outside, the Constables had Johnnie packed into a separate transport and were pulling out into traffic. I watched them drive away, wondering if I'd ever see him again. Either way, I knew he'd want me to take care of our baby. "Mr. White?" I asked, my senses beginning to return. "Can you tell me anything about the flag? It seems like I deserve to know something."

"What flag, dear?"

"The flag on my baby, of course."

"There is no flag on your baby. You made your sacrifice, just as Central predicted you would."

"You mean…"

Mr. White chuckled. "Of course we knew what your husband would do. Central is over ninety-nine percent accurate, remember. We don't question its results." My transport pulled up to the curb and Mr. White helped me inside. "Central," he said, "take the lady home. She's had a hard night."

"Mr. White?" I asked. "One last thing?"

He folded his hands in front of him. "Yes?"

"My baby? Can you give me any hint about what makes him so important?"

Mr. White glanced over his shoulder, then leaned into the car. "I can't be specific, you know that, right?"

"Of course."

"Let's just say that I wouldn't be surprised to see him in Human Services."

That I *hadn't* expected. "Human Services?"

"Well, look at it this way, dear. He's already uncovered one traitor to the State, and he hasn't even been born yet." He then leaned back, with that tight, thin smile still stretched across his face, and slammed shut the door.

The transport sped away, whisking me home.

There was no driver.

Central was in control.

THE ONES WHO WALK AWAY FROM OMELAS

by Ursula K. Le Guin

Ursula K. Le Guin is the author of innumerable SF and fantasy classics, including *The Left Hand of Darkness, The Lathe of Heaven, The Dispossessed,* and *A Wizard of Earthsea* (and the others in the Earthsea Cycle). She has been named a Grand Master by the Science Fiction Writers of America, and is the winner of five Hugos, six Nebulas, two World Fantasy Awards, and twenty Locus Awards. She's also a winner of the Newbery Medal, The National Book Award, the PEN/Malamud Award, and was named a Living Legend by the Library of Congress.

Our next piece first appeared in 1973 in *New Dimensions 3,* an anthology edited by the legendary Robert Silverberg. Unusual for its story structure, which includes no protagonist, its exceptional narrative voice, and purposeful reader engagement have made it a landmark American short story. Reprinted many times, "The Ones Who Walk Away from Omelas" brilliantly captures life in a perfect society, a total utopia…until you do a little digging.

Omelas—which, if you're curious, is derived from Salem spelled backwards (Le Guin is a longtime Oregonian and has a self-proclaimed quirk of reading road signs backward)—is a city of joy and beauty, and the tale is careful to unfold each of its splendors. There has never been such a resoundingly happy place to live. There is no crime, no war, and even the drugs are harmless.

But how is it possible for any place to achieve this level of easy delight? And at what price does it come?

Or more importantly: if you lived in Omelas, would you be willing to pay it?

With a clamor of bells that set the swallows soaring, the Festival of Summer came to the city Omelas, bright-towered by the sea. The rigging of the boats in harbor sparkled with flags. In the streets between houses with red roofs and painted walls, between old moss-grown gardens and under avenues of trees, past great parks and public buildings, processions moved. Some were decorous: old people in long stiff robes of mauve and grey, grave master workmen, quiet, merry women carrying their babies and chatting as they walked. In other streets the music beat faster, a shimmering of gong and tambourine, and the people went dancing, the procession was a dance. Children dodged in and out, their high calls rising like the swallows' crossing flights over the music and the singing. All the processions wound towards the north side of the city, where on the great water-meadow called the Green Fields boys and girls, naked in the bright air, with mud-stained feet and ankles and long, lithe arms, exercised their restive horses before the race. The horses wore no gear at all but a halter without bit. Their manes were braided with streamers of silver, gold, and green. They flared their nostrils and pranced and boasted to one another; they were vastly excited, the horse being the only animal who has adopted our ceremonies as his own. Far off to the north and west the mountains stood up half encircling Omelas on her bay. The air of morning was so clear that the snow still crowning the Eighteen Peaks burned with white-gold fire across the miles of sunlit air, under the dark blue of the sky. There was just enough wind to make the banners that marked the racecourse snap and flutter now and then. In the silence of the broad green meadows one could hear the music winding through the city streets, farther and nearer and ever approaching, a cheerful faint sweetness of the air that from time to time trembled and gathered together and broke out into the great joyous clanging of the bells.

Joyous! How is one to tell about joy? How describe the citizens of Omelas?

They were not simple folk, you see, though they were happy. But we do not say the words of cheer much any more. All smiles have become archaic. Given a description such as this one tends to make certain assumptions. Given a description such as this one tends to look next for the King, mounted on a splendid stallion and surrounded by his noble knights, or perhaps in a golden litter borne by great-muscled slaves. But there was no king. They did not use swords, or keep slaves. They were not barbarians. I do not know the rules and laws of their society, but I suspect that they were singularly few. As they did without monarchy and slavery, so they also got on without the stock exchange, the advertisement, the secret police, and the bomb. Yet I repeat that these were not simple folk, not dulcet shepherds, noble savages, bland utopians. They were not less complex than us. The trouble is that we have a bad habit, encouraged by pedants and sophisticates, of considering happiness as something rather stupid. Only pain is intellectual, only evil interesting. This is the treason of the artist: a refusal to admit the banality of evil and the terrible boredom of pain. If you can't lick 'em, join 'em. If it hurts, repeat it. But to praise despair is to condemn delight, to embrace violence is to lose hold of everything else. We have almost lost hold; we can no longer describe a happy man, nor make any celebration of joy. How can I tell you about the people of Omelas? They were not naive and happy children—though their children were, in fact, happy. They were mature, intelligent, passionate adults whose lives were not wretched. O miracle! but I wish I could describe it better. I wish I could convince you. Omelas sounds in my words like a city in a fairy tale, long ago and far away, once upon a time. Perhaps it would be best if you imagined it as your own fancy bids, assuming it will rise to the occasion, for certainly I cannot suit you all. For instance, how about technology? I think that there would be no cars or helicopters in and above the streets; this follows from the fact that the people of Omelas are happy people. Happiness is based on a just discrimination of what is necessary, what is neither necessary nor destructive, and what is destructive. In the middle category, however—that of the unnecessary but undestructive, that of comfort, luxury, exuberance, etc.—they could perfectly well have central heating, subway trains, washing machines, and all kinds of marvelous devices not yet invented here, floating light-sources, fuelless power, a cure for the common cold. Or they could have none of that: it doesn't matter. As you like it. I incline to think that people from towns up and down the coast have been coming in to Omelas during the last days before the Festival on very fast little trains and double-decked trams, and that the train station of Omelas is actually the handsomest building in town, though plainer than the magnificent Farmers' Market. But even granted trains, I fear that Omelas so far strikes some of you as goody-goody. Smiles, bells, parades, horses, bleh. If so, please add an orgy. If an orgy would help, don't hesitate. Let us not, however, have temples from which issue beautiful nude priests and priestesses already half in ecstasy and ready to copulate with any man or woman, lover or stranger, who desires union with the deep godhead of the blood, although that was my first idea. But really it would be better not to have any temples in Omelas—at least, not manned temples. Religion yes, clergy no. Surely the beautiful nudes can just wander about, offering themselves like divine soufflés to the hunger of the needy and the rapture of the flesh. Let them join the processions. Let tambourines be struck above the copulations, and the glory of desire be proclaimed upon the gongs, and (a not unimportant point) let the offspring of these delightful rituals be beloved and looked after by all. One thing I know there is none of in Omelas is guilt. But what else should there be? I thought at first there were no drugs, but that is puritanical. For those who like it, the faint insistent sweetness of drooz may perfume the ways of the city, drooz which first brings a great lightness and brilliance to the mind and limbs, and then after some hours a dreamy languor, and wonderful visions at last of the very arcana and inmost secrets of the Universe, as well as exciting the pleasure of sex beyond all belief; and it is not habit-forming. For more modest tastes I think there ought to be beer. What else, what else belongs in the joyous city? The sense of victory, surely, the celebration of courage. But as we did without clergy, let us do without soldiers. The joy built upon successful slaughter is not the right kind of joy; it will not do; it is fearful and it is trivial. A boundless and generous contentment, a magnanimous triumph felt not against some outer enemy but in communion with the finest and fairest in the souls of all men everywhere and the splendor of the world's summer: this is what swells the hearts of the people of Omelas, and the victory they celebrate is that of life. I really don't think many of them need to take drooz.

Most of the processions have reached the Green Fields by now. A marvelous smell of cooking goes forth from the red and blue tents of the provisioners. The faces of small children are amiably sticky; in the benign grey beard of a man a couple of crumbs of rich pastry are entangled. The youths and girls have mounted their horses and are beginning to group around the starting line of the course. An old woman, small, fat, and laughing, is passing out flowers from a basket, and tall young men wear her flowers in their shining hair. A child of nine or ten sits at the edge of the crowd, alone, playing on a wooden flute. People pause to listen, and they smile, but they do not speak to him, for he never ceases playing and never sees them, his dark eyes wholly rapt in the sweet, thin magic of the tune.

He finishes, and slowly lowers his hands holding the wooden flute.

As if that little private silence were the signal, all at once a trumpet sounds from the pavilion near the starting line: imperious, melancholy, piercing. The horses rear on their slender legs, and some of them neigh in answer. Sober-faced, the young riders stroke the horses' necks and soothe them, whispering, "Quiet, quiet, there my beauty, my hope...." They begin to form in rank along the starting line. The crowds along the racecourse are like a field of grass and flowers in the wind. The Festival of Summer has begun.

Do you believe? Do you accept the festival, the city, the joy? No? Then let me describe one more thing.

In a basement under one of the beautiful public buildings of Omelas, or perhaps in the cellar of one of its spacious private homes, there is a room. It has one locked door, and no window. A little light seeps in dustily between cracks in the boards, secondhand from a cobwebbed window somewhere across the cellar. In one corner of the little room a couple of mops, with stiff, clotted, foul-smelling heads, stand near a rusty bucket. The floor is dirt, a little damp to the touch, as cellar dirt usually is. The room is about three paces long and two wide: a mere broom closet or disused tool room. In the room a child is sitting. It could be a boy or a girl. It looks about six, but actually is nearly ten. It is feeble-minded. Perhaps it was born defective, or perhaps it has become imbecile through fear, malnutrition, and neglect. It picks its nose and occasionally fumbles vaguely with its toes or genitals, as it sits hunched in the corner farthest from the bucket and the two mops. It is afraid of the mops. It finds them horrible. It shuts its eyes, but it knows the mops are still standing there; and the door is locked; and nobody will come. The door is always locked; and nobody ever comes, except that sometimes—the child has no understanding of time or interval—sometimes the door rattles terribly and opens, and a person, or several people, are there. One of them may come in and kick the child to make it stand up. The others never come close, but peer in at it with frightened, disgusted eyes. The food bowl and the water jug are hastily filled, the door is locked, the eyes disappear. The people at the door never say anything, but the child, who has not always lived in the tool room, and can remember sunlight and its mother's voice, sometimes speaks.

"I will be good," it says. "Please let me out. I will be good!" They never answer. The child used to scream for help at night, and cry a good deal, but now it only makes a kind of whining, "eh-haa, eh-haa," and it speaks less and less often. It is so thin there are no calves to its legs; its belly protrudes; it lives on a half-bowl of corn meal and grease a day. It is naked. Its buttocks and thighs are a mass of festered sores, as it sits in its own excrement continually.

They all know it is there, all the people of Omelas. Some of them have come to see it, others are content merely to know it is there. They all know that it has to be there. Some of them understand why, and some do not, but they all understand that their happiness, the beauty of their city, the tenderness of their friendships, the health of their children, the wisdom of their scholars, the skill of their makers, even the abundance of their harvest and the kindly weathers of their skies, depend wholly on this child's abominable misery.

This is usually explained to children when they are between eight and twelve, whenever they seem capable of understanding; and most of those who come to see the child are young people, though often enough an adult comes, or comes back, to see the child. No matter how well the matter has been explained to them, these young spectators are always shocked and sickened at the sight. They feel disgust, which they had thought themselves superior to. They feel anger, outrage, impotence, despite all the explanations. They would like to do something for the child. But there is nothing they can do. If the child were brought up into the sunlight out of that vile place, if it were cleaned and fed and comforted, that would be a good thing, indeed; but if it were done, in that day and hour all the prosperity and beauty and delight of Omelas would wither and be destroyed. Those are the terms. To exchange all the goodness and grace of every life in Omelas for that single, small improvement: to throw away the happiness of thousands for the chance of the happiness of one: that would be to let guilt within the walls indeed.

The terms are strict and absolute; there may not even be a kind word spoken to the child.

Often the young people go home in tears, or in a tearless rage, when they have seen the child and faced this terrible paradox. They may brood over it for weeks or years. But as time goes on they begin to realize that even if the child could be released, it would not get much good of its freedom: a little vague pleasure of warmth and food, no doubt, but little more. It is too degraded and imbecile to know any real joy. It has been afraid too long ever to be free of fear. Its habits are too uncouth for it to respond to humane treatment. Indeed, after so long it would probably be wretched without walls about it to protect it, and darkness for its eyes, and its own excrement to sit in. Their tears at the bitter injustice dry when they begin to perceive the terrible justice of reality, and to accept it. Yet it is their tears and anger, the trying of their generosity and the acceptance of their helplessness, which are perhaps the true source of the splendor of their lives. Theirs is no vapid, irresponsible happiness. They know that they, like the child, are not free. They know compassion. It is the existence of the child, and their knowledge of its existence, that makes possible the nobility of their architecture, the poignancy of their music, the profundity of their science. It is because of the child that they are so gentle with children. They know that if the wretched one were not there sniveling in the dark, the other one, the flute-player, could make no joyful music as the young riders line up in their beauty for the race in the sunlight of the first morning of summer.

Now do you believe in them? Are they not more credible? But there is one more thing to tell, and this is quite incredible.

At times one of the adolescent girls or boys who go to see the child does not go home to weep or rage, does not, in fact, go home at all. Sometimes also a man or woman much older falls silent for a day or two, and then leaves home. These people go out into the street, and walk down the street alone. They keep walking, and walk straight out of the city of Omelas, through the beautiful gates. They keep walking across the farmlands of Omelas. Each one goes alone, youth or girl, man or woman. Night falls; the traveler must pass down village streets, between the houses with yellow-lit windows, and on out into the darkness of the fields. Each alone, they go west or north, towards the mountains. They go on. They leave Omelas, they walk ahead into the darkness, and they do not come back. The place they go towards is a place even less imaginable to most of us than the city of happiness. I cannot describe it at all. It is possible that it does not exist. But they seem to know where they are going, the ones who walk away from Omelas.

EVIDENCE OF LOVE IN A CASE OF ABANDONMENT:

ONE DAUGHTER'S PERSONAL ACCOUNT

by M. Rickert

M. Rickert's stories have been appearing regularly in *The Magazine of Fantasy & Science Fiction* for several years, starting in 1999 with her first publication, "The Girl Who Ate Butterflies." Her work has also appeared in SCI FICTION and the anthologies *Wastelands, Poe,* and *Feeling Very Strange.* A new collection of her short fiction, *Holiday,* came out in November. Her first collection, *Map of Dreams,* won the World Fantasy Award and the William L. Crawford Award for best first book-length work of fantasy, and her story, "Journey to the Kingdom" won her another World Fantasy Award and was a finalist for the Nebula Award. This story was a finalist for the Stoker, British SF, and Shirley Jackson awards.

In 1979, Ruhollah Khomeini—Islamic scholar and fundamentalist—became the Supreme Leader of Iran. In this position, Khomeini served as the highest political and religious figure of the nation. Under his leadership, a revolution swept across the country, brushing aside years of Western influences. Women with college educations stepped down from their work as doctors, educators, and business associates, and returned to their traditional place in the home. They put on their veils and scarves and became invisible to everyone except their closest family members.

Rickert says that our next story was meant to take a sort of sideways look at what has already happened to women in countries where their freedom is denied. It's a story set in an America that has made its own conservative revolution. It's a world with harsh rules for women, and a strict delineation of acceptable behavior.

In a such a place, where women have given up their reproductive freedoms, there are only two choices: be a good girl—or die.

"When I, or people like me, are running the country, you'd better flee, because we will find you, we will try you, and we'll execute you. I mean every word of it. I will make it part of my mission to see to it that they are tried and executed."

—Randall Terry, founder of Operation Rescue

It took a long time to deduce that many of the missing women could not be accounted for. Executions were a matter of public record then and it was still fairly easy to keep track of them. They were on every night at seven o'clock, filmed from the various execution centers. It was policy back then to name the criminal as the camera lingered over her face. Yet women went missing who never appeared on execution. Rumors started. Right around then some of the policies changed. The criminals were no longer named, and execution centers sprung up all over the country so it was no longer possible to account for the missing. The rumors persisted though, and generally took one of two courses; Agents were using the criminals for their own nefarious purposes, or women were sneaking away and assembling an army.

When my mother didn't come home, my father kept saying she must have had a meeting he'd forgotten about, after all, she volunteered for Homeland Security's Mothers in Schools program, as well as did work for the church, and the library. That's my mom. She always has to keep busy. When my father started calling hospitals, his freckles all popped out against his white skin the way they get when he's upset, and I realized he was hoping she'd had an accident, I knew. The next morning, when I found him sitting in the rocker, staring out the picture window, their wedding album in his lap, I really knew.

Of course I am not the only abandoned daughter. Even here, there are a few of us. We are not marked in any way a stranger could see, but we are known in our community. Things are better for those whose mothers are executed. They are a separate group from those of us whose mothers are unaccounted for, who may be so evil as to escape reparation for their crimes, so sick as to plan to attack the innocent ones left behind.

I am obsessed with executions, though there are too many to keep track of, hard as I try to flip through the screens and have them all going on at once. I search for her face. There are many faces. Some weeping, some screaming, some with lips trembling, or nostrils flaring but I never see her face. Jenna Offeren says her mother was executed in Albany but she's lying. Jenna Offeren is a weak, annoying person but I can't completely blame her. Even my own father tried it. One morning he comes into my room, sits at the edge of my bed and says, "Lisle, I'm sorry. I saw her last night. Your mother. They got her." I just shook my head. "Don't try to make me feel better," I said, "I know she's still alive."

My mother and I, we have that thing some twins have. That's how close we've always been. Once, when I was still a little kid, I fell from a tree at Sarah

T.'s house and my mom came running into the backyard, her hair a mess, her lipstick smeared, before Mrs. T. had even finished dialing the cell. "I just knew," mom said, "I was washing the windows and all of a sudden I had this pain in my stomach and I knew you needed me. I came right over." My wrist was broke (and to this day hurts when it's going to rain) and I couldn't do my sewing or synchronized swimming for weeks, but I almost didn't mind because, back then I thought me and mom had something special between us, and what happened with my wrist proved it. Now I'm not so sure. Everything changes when your mother goes missing.

I look for her face all the time. Not just on the screens but on the heads of other women, not here, of course, but if we go to Milwaukee, or on the school trip to Chicago, I look at every women's face, searching for hers. I'm not the only one either. I caught Jenna Offeren doing the same thing, though she denied it. (Not mine, of course. Hers.)

Before she left us, Mom was not exactly a happy person, but what normal American girl goes around assuming that her own mother is a murderer? She even helped me with my project in seventh year, cutting out advertisements that used that model, Heidi Eagle, who was executed the year before, and I remember, so clearly, mom saying that Heidi's children would have been beautiful, so how was I to know that my own mother was one of the evil doers?

But then what did I think was going on with all that crying? My mother cried all the time. She cried when she was doing the dishes, she cried when she cleaned the toilets, she even cried in the middle of laughing, like the time I told her about Mr. Saunders demonstrating to us girls what it's like to be pregnant with a basketball. The only time I can ever remember my mom saying anything traceable, anything that could be linked from our perfect life to the one I'm stuck in now, was when she found a list of boys names on my T.S.O. and asked if they were boys I had crushes on. I don't know what she was thinking to say such a thing because there were seven names on that list and I am not a slut, but anyhow, I explained that they were baby names I was considering for when my time came and she got this look on her face like maybe she'd been a hologram all along and was just going to fade away and then she said, "When I was your age, I planned on being an astronaut."

My cheeks turned bright red, of course. I was embarrassed for her to talk like that. She tried to make light of it by looking over the list, letting me know which names she liked (Liam and Jack) and which she didn't (Paul and Luke.) If the time ever comes (and I am beginning to have my doubts that it will) I'm going to choose one of the names she hated. It's not much, but it's all I have. There's only so much you can do to a mother who is missing.

My father says I'm spending too much time watching screens so he has insisted that we do something fun together, "as a family" he said, trying to make it sound cheerful like we aren't the lamest excuse for family you've ever seen, just me and him.

There's plenty of families without mothers, of course. Apparently this was initially a surprise to Homeland Security, it was generally assumed that those women who had abortions during the dark times never had any children, but a lot of women of my mother's generation were swayed by the evil propaganda of their youth, had abortions and careers even, before coming back to the light of righteous behavior. So having an executed mother is not necessarily that bad. There's a whole extra shame in being associated with a mother who is missing however, out there somewhere, in a militia or something. (With the vague possibility that she is not stockpiling weapons and learning about car bombs, but captured by one of the less ethical Agents, but what's the real chance of that? Isn't that just a fantasy kids like Jenna Offeren came up with because they can't cope?) At any rate, to counteract the less palatable rumor, and the one that puts the Agents in the worse light, Homeland Security has recently begun the locks of hair program. Now they send strands of criminal's hair to the family and it's become a real trend for the children to wear it in see-through lockets. None of this makes sense, of course. The whole reason the executions became anonymous in the first place was to put to rest the anarchist notion that some women had escaped their fate, but Homeland Security is not the department of consistency (I think I can say that) and seems to lean more towards a policy of confusion. The locks of hair project has been very successful and has even made some money as families are now paying to have executed women's corpses dug up for their hair. At any rate, you guessed it, Jenna shows up at execution with a lock of hair necklace that she says comes from her mother but I know it's Jenna's own hair, which is blonde and curly while her mom's was brownish gray. "That's 'cause she dyed it," Jenna says. I give up. Nobody dyes their hair brownish gray. Jenna has just gone completely nuts.

It seems like the whole town is at execution and I realize my father's right, I've been missing a lot by watching them on screen all the time. "Besides, it's starting to not look right, never going. It was different when your mother was still with us," he said. So I agreed, though I didn't expect much. I mean no way would they execute my mom right here in her home town. Sure, it happens but it would be highly unlikely, so what's the point? I expected it to be incredibly boring like church, or the meetings of The Young Americans, or Home Ec class but it wasn't anything like any of that. Screens really give you no idea of the excitement of an execution and if you, like me, think that you've seen it all because you've been watching it on screen for years, I recommend you attend your own hometown event. It just might surprise you. Besides, it's important to stay active in your community.

We don't have a stadium, of course, not in a town of a population of eight thousand and dwindling, so executions are held on the football field the first Wednesday of every month. I was surprised by the screens displayed around the field but my father said that was the only way you could get a real good look at the faces, and he was right. It was fascinating to look at the figure in the center of the field, how small she looked, to the face on the screen, freakishly large. Just like on screen at home, the women were all ages from grandmothers to women my mother's age and a few probably younger. The problem is under control now. No one would think of getting an abortion. There's already talk about cutting back the program in a few years and I feel kind of sentimental about it. I've grown up with executions and can't imagine what kids will watch instead. Not that I would wish this on anyone. It's a miserable thing to be in my situation. Maybe no one will even want me now. I ask my dad about this on the way to execution, what happens to girls like me and for a while he pretends he doesn't know what I'm talking about until I spell it out and he can't act all Homeland Security. He shakes his head and sighs. "It's too soon to say, Lisle. Daughters of executed moms, they've done all right, maybe you know, not judges' wives, or Agents', or anyone like that, but they've had a decent time of it for the most part. Daughters of missing moms, well, it's just too soon to tell. Hey, maybe you'll get to be a breeder." He says it like it's a good thing, giving up my babies every nine or ten months.

"I hate mom," I say. He doesn't scold me. After all, what she did, she did to both of us.

It seems like the whole town is here, though I know this can't be right because it's the first time I've come since I was a kid, and that would be statistically improbable if we were the only ones who never came back, but, even though I am certain it's not the whole town, I'd have to say it's pretty close to it. Funny how in all these faces and noise and excitement I can see who's wearing locks of hair lockets as if they are made of shining light, which of course they are not. I could forgive her, I think— and I'm surprised by the tears in my eyes— if she'd just do the right thing and turn herself in. Maybe I'm not being fair. After all, maybe she's trapped somewhere, held prisoner by some Agent and there's nothing she can do about it. I, too, take comfort in this little fantasy from time to time.

Each execution is done individually. She walks across the entire field in a hood. The walk takes a long time 'cause of the shackles. I can think of no reasonable explanation for the hood, beyond suspense. It is very effective. The beginning of the walk is a good time to take a bathroom break or get a snack, that's how long it takes. No one wants to be away from his seat when the criminal gets close to the red circle at the center of the field. The closer she gets to the circle (led by one of the Junior Agents, or, as is the case tonight, by one of the children from the town's various civic programs) the more quiet it gets until eventually the only noise is the sound of chains. I've heard this on screen a million times but then there is neighborhood noise going on, cars, maybe someone talking on a cell, dogs barking, that sort of thing, but when the event is live there's no sound other than maybe a cough or a baby crying. I have to tell you all those people in the same space being quiet, the only sound the chains rattling around the criminal's ankles and wrists, well it's way more powerful than how it seems on screen. She always stands for a few seconds in the center of the circle but she rarely stands still. Once placed in position, hands and feet shackled, she displays her fear by wavering, or the shoulders go up, sometimes she is shaking so bad you can see it even if you're not looking on screen.

The child escort walks away to polite applause and the Executioner comes to position. He unties the hood, pauses for dramatic effect (and it is dramatic!) then plucks the hood off, which almost always causes some of her hair to stand out from her head, as though she's been electrocuted, or taken off a knit cap on a snowy day, and at that moment we turn to the screen to get a closer look. I never get bored of it. The horror on their faces, the dripping nostrils, the spit bubbling from lips, the eyes wet with tears, wide with terror. Occasionally there is a stoic one, but there aren't many of these, and when there is, it's easy enough to look away from the screen and focus on the big picture. What had she been thinking? How could she murder someone so tiny, so innocent and not know she'd have to pay? When I think of what the time from before was like I shudder and thank God for being born in the Holy times. In spite of my mother, I am blessed. I know this, even though I sometimes forget. Right there, in the football field bleachers I fold my hands and bow my head. When I am finished my father is giving me a strange look. "If this is too upsetting we can leave," he says. He constantly makes mistakes like this. Sometimes I just ignore him, but this time I try to explain. "I just realized how lucky I am." I can't think of what else to say, how to make him understand so I simply smile. Right then the stoic woman is shot. When I look I see the gaping maul that was her head, right where that evil thought was first conceived to destroy the innocent life that grew inside her. Now she is neither stoic nor alive. She lies in a heap, twitching for a while, but those are just nerves.

It's getting late. Some people use this time to usher their young children home. When we came, all those years ago, my mom letting me play with her gold chain while I sat in her lap, we were one of the first to leave, though I was not the youngest child in attendance. My mother was always strict that way. "Time for bed," she said cheerfully, first to me, and then by way of explanation, pressing my head tight against her shoulder, trying to make me look tired, pressing so hard that I started crying, which, I now realize, served her purpose.

My father says he has to use the bathroom. There is a pocket of space around me when he leaves. My father is gone a long time. This is unusual for the men's bathroom and I must admit I get a little worried about him, especially as the woman approaches the target circle but right when I am starting to think he's going to be too late, he comes, his head bent low so as not to obstruct the view. He sits beside me at what is the last possible second. He shrugs and looks like he's about to say something. Horrified, I turn away. It would be just like him to talk at a time like this.

The girl (from the Young and Beautiful club) dressed all in white with a flower wreathe on her head (and a locks of hair locket glimmering on her chest) walks away from the woman. The tenor of applause grows louder as the Executioner approaches. We are trying to show how much we've appreciated his work tonight. The Executioners are never named. They travel in some kind of secret rotation so no one can ever figure it out, but over time they get reputations. They wear masks, of course, or they would always be hounded for autographs, but are recognized, when they are working, by the insignia on their uniforms. This one is known as Red Dragon for the elaborate dragon on his chest. The applause can be registered on the criminal who shakes like Jell-o. She shakes so much that it is not unreasonable to wonder if she will be one of the fainters. I hate the fainters. They mess with the dramatic arc, all that build up of the long walk, the rattling chains, the Executioner's arrival, only to have the woman fall in a large heap on the ground. Sometimes it takes forever to revive her, and some effort to get her to stand, at which point the execution is anti-climatic.

The Executioner, perhaps sensing this very scenario, says something to Jell-o woman that none of us can hear but she suddenly goes still. There is scattered applause for Red Dragon's skill. He turns towards the audience, and, though he wears his mask, there is something in his demeanor which hushes the crowd. We are watching a master at work. Next, he steps in front of the woman, reaches with both hands around her neck, creating the effect of a man about to give a kiss. We are all as still as if we are waiting for that kiss. With one gesture, he unties the string, and in the same breath reaches up and pulls off the hood. We gasp.

Mrs. Offeren's face fills the screen. Someone screams. I think it is Jenna. I am torn between looking for her in the crowd, and keeping my attention on her mother, whose head turns at the sound so there is only a view of her giant ear but the Executioner says something sharp and she snaps her head back to attention. The screen betrays that her eyes peer past the Executioner, first narrow than wide, and her lips part at the moment she realizes she is home. Her eyes just keep moving after that, searching the crowd, looking for Jenna, I figure, until suddenly, how can it be suddenly when it happens like this every time, but it is suddenly, her head jerks back with the firecracker sound of the shot, she falls from the screen. She lies on the ground, twitching, the red puddle blossoming around her head. Jenna screams and screams. It is my impression that no one does anything to stop her. Nor does anyone use this break to go to the snack shop, or the bathroom, or home. I don't know when my father's hand has reached across the space between us but at some point I realize it rests, gently, on my thigh, when I look at him, he squeezes, lightly, almost like a woman would, as though there is no strength left inside him. They quickly cut some of Mrs. Offeren's hair before it gets too bloody, and bag it, lift her up, clumsily so that at first her arm and then her head falls towards the ground (the assistants are tired by this time of night) load her into the cart. We listen to the sound of the wheels that need to be oiled and the faint rattle of chains as the cart lumbers across the field. Jenna weeps audibly. The center of the red circle is coated in blood. I pretend it is a Rorschach and decide it looks exactly like a pterodactyl. The cleaning crew comes and hoses it down. That's when people start moving about, talk, rush to the bathroom, take sleeping children home, but it goes mostly silent again when the Offeren family stands up. The seven of them sidle down the bleacher and walk along the side of the field.

I watch the back of Jenna's head, her blonde curls under the lights, almost golden like a halo, though no one, not even the most forgiving person is ever going to mistake Jenna for someone holy. Her mother was a murderer, after all. Yet I realize she'll soon replace that stupid fake locket with a real one while I have nothing. She might even get to marry a Police or a trash collector, even a teacher, while the best I can hope for is a position at one of the orphanages. My dad's idea that I might be a breeder someday seems highly optimistic.

"Let's go," I say.

"Are you sure? Maybe the next one…" But he doesn't even finish the thought. He must see something in my face that tells him I am done with childish fantasies.

She's never coming back. Whatever selfish streak caused her, all those years ago to kill one child is the same selfish streak that allows her to abandon me now.

We walk down the bleachers. Everyone turns away from us, holding their little kids close. My father walks in front of me, with his head down, his hands in his pockets. By the time we get to the car in the parking lot we can hear the polite applause from the football field as another woman enters the circle. He opens his door. I open mine. We drive home in silence. I crane my neck to try to look up at the sky as if I expect to find something there, God maybe, or the living incarnation of the blood pterodactyl but of course I see neither. There is nothing. I close my eyes and think of my mother. Oh, how I miss her.

THE FUNERAL

by Kate Wilhelm

Kate Wilhelm is the winner of three Nebulas, two Hugos, and two Locus awards, and is an inductee to the Science Fiction Hall of Fame. Her short fiction has appeared in *The Magazine of Fantasy & Science Fiction, Omni, Asimov's Science Fiction, Amazing Stories, Orbit,* and has been collected in several volumes, notably in *The Mile-Long Spaceship; Listen, Listen;* and *The Infinity Box.* Her SF novels include *Where Late the Sweet Birds Sang, Juniper Time, Welcome Chaos,* and the Constance and Charlie series (*The Hamlet Trap* et seq.). She has also written several legal thrillers, beginning in 1991 with *Death Qualified.* The latest of these "Barbara Holloway" mysteries, *Cold Case,* was released in 2008.

The story of two boys' quest for freedom, *Adventures of Huckleberry Finn* is one of the greatest American novels. Jim wants to escape slavery. Huck wants to get away from his horrible father. Their adventures rafting down the Mississippi River have become a part of the American identity, stirring up hopes and dreams inside the hearts of generations of dissatisfied children.

Our next story is set in a regimented society that, like the antebellum South, maintains some people are property, without voice and fully disposable. For girls like Clara, their lives are spent in frightened obedience, waiting for their futures to be set for them. Only the dying words of one mad woman offer Clara hope: the hint of a secret cave, a mysterious hideout that no one has ever found.

The Widow Douglas was always trying to "sivilize" Huck Finn—but she could never bend his indomitable spirit. If she could escape from her world, perhaps Clara could teach him a thing or two.

N o one could say exactly how old Madam Westfall was when she finally died. At least one hundred twenty, it was estimated. At the very least. For twenty years Madam Westfall had been a shell containing the very latest products of advances made in gerontology, and now she was dead. What lay on the viewing dais was merely a painted, funereally garbed husk.

"She isn't real," Carla said to herself. "It's a doll, or something. It isn't really

Madam Westfall." She kept her head bowed, and didn't move her lips, but she said the words over and over. She was afraid to look at a dead person. The second time they slaughtered all those who bore arms, unguided, mindless now, but lethal with the arms caches that they used indiscriminately. Carla felt goose bumps along her arms and legs. She wondered if anyone else had been hearing the old Teacher's words.

The line moved slowly, all the girls in their long grey skirts had their heads bowed, their hands clasped. The only sound down the corridor was the sush-sush of slippers on plastic flooring, the occasional rustle of a skirt.

The viewing room had a pale green plastic floor, frosted-green plastic walls, and floor-to-ceiling windows that were now slits of brilliant light from a westering sun. All the furniture had been taken from the room, all the ornamentation. There were no flowers, nothing but the dais, and the bedlike box covered by a transparent shield. And the Teachers. Two at the dais, others between the light strips, at the doors. Their white hands clasped against black garb, heads bowed, hair slicked against each head, straight parts emphasizing bilateral symmetry. The Teachers didn't move, didn't look at the dais, at the girls parading past it.

Carla kept her head bowed, her chin tucked almost inside the V of her collarbone. The serpentine line moved steadily, very slowly. "She isn't real," Carla said to herself, desperately now.

She crossed the line that was the cue to raise her head; it felt too heavy to lift, her neck seemed paralyzed. When she did move, she heard a joint crack, and although her jaws suddenly ached, she couldn't relax.

The second green line. She turned her eyes to the right and looked at the incredibly shrunken, hardly human mummy. She felt her stomach lurch and for a moment she thought she was going to vomit. "She isn't real. It's a doll. She isn't real!" The third line. She bowed her head, pressed her chin hard against her collarbone, making it hurt. She couldn't swallow now, could hardly breathe. The line proceeded to the South Door and through it into the corridor.

She turned left at the South Door and, with her eyes downcast, started the walk back to her genetics class. She looked neither right nor left, but she could hear others moving in the same direction, slippers on plastic, the swish of a skirt, and when she passed by the door to the garden she heard laughter of some Ladies who had come to observe the viewing. She slowed down.

She felt the late sun hot on her skin at the open door and with a sideways glance, not moving her head, she looked quickly into the glaring greenery, but could not see them. Their laughter sounded like music as she went past the opening.

"That one, the one with the blue eyes and straw-colored hair. Stand up, girl."

Carla didn't move, didn't realize she was being addressed until a Teacher pulled her from her seat.

"Don't hurt her! Turn around, girl. Raise your skirts, higher. Look at me, child. Look up, let me see your face…."

"She's too young for choosing," said the Teacher, examining Carla's bracelet.

"Another year, Lady."

"A pity. She'll coarsen in a year's time. The fuzz is so soft right now, the flesh so tender. Oh, well…" She moved away, flicking a red skirt about her thighs, her red-clad legs narrowing to tiny ankles, flashing silver slippers with heels that were like icicles. She smelled… Carla didn't know any words to describe how she smelled. She drank in the fragrance hungrily.

"Look at me, child. Look up, let me see your face… The words sang through her mind over and over. At night, falling asleep, she thought of the face, drawing it up from the deep black, trying to hold it in focus: white skin, pink cheek ridges, silver eyelids, black lashes longer than she had known lashes could be, silver-pink lips, three silver spots—one at the corner of her left eye, another at the corner of her mouth, the third like a dimple in the satiny cheek. Silver hair that was loose, in waves about her face, that rippled with life of its own when she moved. If only she had been allowed to touch the hair, to run her finger over that cheek… The dream that began with the music of the Lady's laughter ended with the nightmare of her other words: "She'll coarsen in a year's time…."

After that Carla had watched the changes take place on and within her body, and she understood what the Lady had meant. Her once smooth legs began to develop hair; it grew under her arms, and, most shameful, it sprouted as a dark, coarse bush under her belly. She wept. She tried to pull the hairs out, but it hurt too much, and made her skin sore and raw. Then she started to bleed, and she lay down and waited to die, and was happy that she would die. Instead, she was ordered to the infirmary and was forced to attend a lecture on feminine hygiene. She watched in stony-faced silence while the Doctor added the new information to her bracelet. The Doctor's face was smooth and pink, her eyebrows pale, her lashes so colorless and stubby that they were almost invisible. On her chin was a brown mole with two long hairs. She wore a straight blue-grey gown that hung from her shoulders to the floor. Her drab hair was pulled back tightly from her face, fastened in a hard bun at the back of her neck. Carla hated her. She hated the Teachers. Most of all she hated herself. She yearned for maturity.

Madam Westfall had written: "Maturity brings grace, beauty, wisdom, happiness. Immaturity means ugliness, unfinished beings with potential only, wholly dependent upon and subservient to the mature citizens."

There was a True-False quiz on the master screen in front of the classroom. Carla took her place quickly and touch-typed her ID number on the small screen of her machine.

She scanned the questions, and saw that they were all simple declarative statements of truth. Her stylus ran down the True column of her answer screen and it was done. She wondered why they were killing time like this, what they were waiting for. Madam Westfall's death had thrown everything off schedule.

Paperlike brown skin, wrinkled and hard, with lines crossing lines, vertical, horizontal, diagonal, leaving little islands of flesh, hardly enough to coat the bones. Cracked voice, incomprehensible: they took away the music from the air… voices from the skies… erased pictures that move… boxes that sing and sob… Crazy talk. And,… only one left that knows. Only one.

Madam Trudeau entered the classroom and Carla understood why the class had been personalized that period. The Teacher had been waiting for Madam Trudeau's appearance. The girls rose hurriedly. Madam Trudeau motioned for them to be seated once more.

"The following girls attended Madam Westfall during the past five years." She read a list. Carla's name was included on her list. On finishing it, she asked, "Is there anyone who attended Madam Westfall whose name I did not read?"

There was a rustle from behind Carla. She kept her gaze fastened on Madam Trudeau. "Name?" the Teacher asked.

"Luella, Madam."

"You attended Madam Westfall? When?"

"Two years ago, Madam. I was a relief for Sonya, who became ill suddenly."

"Very well." Madam Trudeau added Luella's name to her list. "You will all report to my office at eight A.M. tomorrow morning. You will be excused from classes and duties at that time. Dismissed." With a bow she excused herself to the class Teacher and left the room.

Carla's legs twitched and ached. Her swim class was at eight each morning and she had missed it, had been sitting on the straight chair for almost two hours, when finally she was told to go into Madam Trudeau's office. None of the other waiting girls looked up when she rose and followed the attendant from the anteroom. Madam Trudeau was seated at an oversized desk that was completely bare, with a mirrorlike finish. Carla stood before it with her eyes downcast, and she could see Madam Trudeau's face reflected from the surface of the desk. Madam Trudeau was looking at a point over Carla's head, unaware that the girl was examining her features.

"You attended Madam Westfall altogether seven times during the past four years, is that correct?"

"I think it is, Madam."

"You aren't certain?"

"I… I don't remember, Madam."

"I see. Do you recall if Madam Westfall spoke to you during any of those times?"

"Yes, Madam."

"Carla, you are shaking. Are you frightened?"

"No, Madam."

"Look at me, Carla."

Carla's hands tightened, and she could feel her fingernails cutting into her hands. She thought of the pain, and stopped shaking.

Madam Trudeau had pasty white skin, with peaked black eyebrows, sharp black eyes, black hair. Her mouth was wide and full, her nose long and narrow. As she studied the girl before her, it seemed to Carla that something changed in her expression, but she couldn't say what it was, or how it now differed from what it had been a moment earlier. A new intensity perhaps, a new interest.

"Carla, I've been looking over your records. Now that you are fourteen it is time to decide on your future. I shall propose your name for the Teachers' Academy on the completion of your current courses. As my protégée, you will quit the quarters you now occupy and attend me in my chambers...." She narrowed her eyes, "What is the matter with you, girl? Are you ill?"

"No, Madam. I... I had hoped. I mean, I designated my choice last month. I thought..."

Madam Trudeau looked to the side of her desk where a records screen was lighted. She scanned the report, and her lips curled derisively. "A Lady. You would be a Lady!" Carla felt a blush fire her face, and suddenly her palms were wet with sweat. Madam Trudeau laughed, a sharp barking sound. She said, "The girls who attended Madam Westfall in life shall attend her in death. You will be on duty in the Viewing Room for two hours each day, and when the procession starts for the burial services in Scranton, you will be part of the entourage. Meanwhile, each day for an additional two hours immediately following your attendance in the Viewing Room you will meditate on the words of wisdom you have heard from Madam Westfall, and you will write down every word she ever spoke in your presence. For this purpose there will be placed a notebook and a pen in your cubicle, which you will use for no other reason. You will discuss this with no one except me. You, Carla, will prepare to move to my quarters immediately, where a learning cubicle will be awaiting you. Dismissed."

Her voice became sharper as she spoke, and when she finished the words were staccato. Carla bowed and turned to leave.

"Carla, you will find that there are certain rewards in being chosen as a Teacher."

Carla didn't know if she should turn and bow again, or stop where she was, or continue. When she hesitated, the voice came again, shorter, raspish. "Go. Return to your cubicle."

The first time, they slaughtered only the leaders, the rousers,... would be enough to defuse the bomb, leave the rest silent and powerless and malleable....

Carla looked at the floor before her, trying to control the trembling in her legs. Madam Westfall hadn't moved, hadn't spoken. She was dead, gone. The only sound was the sush, sush of slippers. The green plastic floor was a glare that hurt her eyes. The air was heavy and smelled of death. Smelled the Lady, drank in the fragrance, longed to touch her. Pale, silvery-pink lips, soft, shiny, with two high peaks on the upper lip. The Lady stroked her face with fingers that were soft and cool and gentle.

...when their eyes become soft with unspeakable desires and their bodies show signs of womanhood, then let them have their duties chosen for them, some to bear the young for the society, some to become Teachers, some Nurses, Doctors, some to be taken as Lovers by the citizens, some to be...

Carla couldn't control the sudden start that turned her head to look at the mummy. The room seemed to waver, then steadied again. The tremor in her legs became stronger, harder to stop. She pressed her knees together hard, hurting them where bone dug into flesh and skin. Fingers plucking at the coverlet. Plucking bones, brown bones with horny nails.

Water. Girl, give me water. Pretty pretty. You would have been killed, you would have. Pretty. The last time they left no one over ten. No one at all. Ten to twenty-five.

Pretty. Carla said it to herself. *Pretty.* She visualized it as p-r-i-t-y. *Pity with an r. Scanning the dictionary for p-r-i-t-y. Nothing. Pretty. Afraid of shiny, pretty faces. Young, pretty faces.*

The trembling was all through Carla. Two hours. Eternity. She had stood here forever, would die here, unmoving, trembling, aching. A sigh and the sound of a body falling softly to the floor. Soft body crumbling so easily. Carla didn't turn her head. It must be Luella. So frightened of the mummy. She'd had nightmares every night since Madam Westfall's death. What made a body stay upright, when it fell so easily? Take it out, the thing that held it together, and down, down. Just to let go, to know what to take out and allow the body to fall like that into sleep. Teachers moved across her field of vision, two of them in their black gowns. Sush-sush. Returned with Luella, or someone, between them. No sound. Sush-sush.

The new learning cubicle was an exact duplicate of the old one. Cot, learning machine, chair, partitioned-off commode and wash basin. And new, the notebook and pen. Carla never had had a notebook and pen before. There was the stylus that was attached to the learning machine, and the lighted square in which to write, that then vanished into the machine. She turned the blank pages of the notebook, felt the paper between her fingers, tore a tiny corner off one of the back pages, examined it closely, the jagged edge, the texture of the fragment; she tasted it. She studied the pen just as minutely; it had a pointed, smooth end, and it wrote black. She made a line, stopped to admire it, and crossed it with another line. She wrote very slowly, "Carla," started to put down her number, the one on her bracelet, then stopped in confusion. She never had considered it before, but she had no last name, none that she knew. She drew three heavy lines over the two digits she had put down.

At the end of the two hours of meditation she had written her name a number of times, had filled three pages with it, in fact, and had written one of the things that she could remember hearing from the grey lips of Madam Westfall: "Non-citizens are the property of the state."

The next day the citizens started to file past the dais. Carla breathed deeply, trying to sniff the fragrance of the passing Ladies, but they were too distant. She watched their feet, clad in shoes of rainbow colors: pointed toes, stiletto heels; rounded toes, carved heels; satin, sequined slippers.... And just before her duty ended for the day, the Males started to enter the room.

She heard a gasp, Luella again. She didn't faint this time, merely gasped once. Carla saw the feet and legs at the same time and she looked up to see a male citizen. He was very tall and thick, and was dressed in the blue-and-white clothing of a Doctor of Law. He moved into the sunlight and there was a glitter from gold at his wrists and his neck, and the gleam of a smooth polished head. He turned past the dais and his eyes met Carla's. She felt herself go lightheaded and hurriedly she ducked her head and clenched her hands. She thought he was standing still, looking at her, and she could feel her heart thumping hard. Her relief arrived then and she crossed the room as fast as she could without appearing indecorous.

Carla wrote: "Why did he scare me so much? Why have I never seen a Male before? Why does everyone else wear colors while the girls and the Teachers wear black and grey?"

She drew a wavering line figure of a man, and stared at it, and then Xed it out. Then she looked at the sheet of paper with dismay. Now she had four ruined sheets of paper to dispose of.

Had she angered him by staring? Nervously she tapped on the paper and tried to remember what his face had been like. Had he been frowning? She couldn't remember. Why couldn't she think of anything to write for Madam Trudeau? She bit the end of the pen and then wrote slowly, very carefully: "Society may dispose of its property as it chooses, following discussion with at least three members, and following permission which is not to be arbitrarily denied."

Had Madam Westfall ever said that? She didn't know, but she had to write something, and that was the sort of thing that Madam Westfall had quoted at great length. She threw herself down on the cot and stared at the ceiling. For three days she had kept hearing the Madam's dead voice, but now when she needed to hear her again, nothing.

Sitting in the straight chair, alert for any change in the position of the ancient one, watchful, afraid of the old Teacher. Cramped, tired and sleepy. Half listening to mutterings, murmurings of exhaled and inhaled breaths that sounded like words that made no sense.... Mama said hide child, hide don't move and Stevie wanted a razor for his birthday and Mama said you're too young, you're only nine and he said no Mama I'm thirteen don't you remember and Mama said hide child hide don't move at all and they came in hating pretty faces....

Carla sat up and picked up the pen again, then stopped. When she heard the words, they were so clear in her head, but as soon as they ended, they faded away. She wrote: "hating pretty faces... hide child... only nine." She stared at the words and drew a line through them.

Pretty faces. Madam Westfall had called her pretty, pretty.

The chimes for social hour were repeated three times and finally Carla opened the door of her cubicle and took a step into the anteroom, where the other protégées already had gathered. There were five. Carla didn't know any of them, but she had seen all of them from time to time in and around the school grounds.

Madam Trudeau was sitting on a high-backed chair that was covered with black. She blended into it, so that only her hands and her face seemed apart from the chair, dead-white hands and face. Carla bowed to her and stood uncertainly at her own door.

"Come in, Carla. It is social hour. Relax. This is Wanda, Louise, Stephanie, Mary, Dorothy." Each girl inclined her head slightly as her name was mentioned. Carla couldn't tell afterward which name went with which girl. Two of them wore the black-striped overskirt that meant they were in the Teachers' Academy. The other three still wore the grey of the lower school, as did Carla, with black bordering the hems.

"Carla doesn't want to be a Teacher," Madam Trudeau said dryly. "She prefers the paint box of a Lady." She smiled with her mouth only. One of the academy girls laughed. "Carla, you are not the first to envy the paint box and the bright clothes of the Ladies. I have something to show you. Wanda, the film."

The girl who had laughed touched a button on a small table, and on one of the walls a picture was projected. Carla caught her breath. It was a Lady, all gold and white, gold hair, gold eyelids, filmy white gown that ended just above her knees. She turned and smiled, holding out both hands, flashing jeweled fingers, long, gleaming nails that came to points. Then she reached up and took off her hair.

Carla felt that she would faint when the golden hair came off in the Lady's hand, leaving short, straight brown hair. She placed the gold hair on a ball, and then, one by one, stripped off the long gleaming nails, leaving her hands just hands, bony and ugly. The Lady peeled off her eyelashes and brows, and then patted a brown, thick coating of something on her face, and, with its removal, revealed pale skin with wrinkles about her eyes, with hard, deep lines beside her nose down to her mouth that had also changed, had become small and mean. Carla wanted to shut her eyes, turn away, and go back to her cubicle, but she didn't dare move. She could feel Madam Trudeau's stare, and the gaze seemed to burn.

The Lady took off the swirling gown, and under it was a garment Carla never had seen before that covered her from her breasts to her thighs. The stubby fingers worked at fasteners, and finally got the garment off, and there was her stomach, bigger, bulging, with cruel red lines where the garment had pinched and squeezed her. Her breasts drooped almost to her waist. Carla couldn't stop her eyes, couldn't make them not see, couldn't make herself not look at the rest of the repulsive body.

Madam Trudeau stood up and went to her door. "Show Carla the other two films." She looked at Carla then and said, "I order you to watch. I shall quiz you on the contents." She left the room.

The other two films showed the same Lady at work. First with a protégée, then with a male citizen. When they were over Carla stumbled back to her cubicle and vomited repeatedly until she was exhausted. She had nightmares that night.

How many days, she wondered, have I been here now? She no longer trembled, but became detached almost as soon as she took her place between two of the

tall windows. She didn't try to catch a whiff of the fragrance of the Ladies, or try to get a glimpse of the Males. She had chosen one particular spot in the floor on which to concentrate, and she didn't shift her gaze from it.

They were old and full of hate, and they said, let us remake them in our image, and they did.

Madam Trudeau hated her, despised her. Old and full of hate…

"Why were you not chosen to become a Woman to bear young?"

"I am not fit, Madam. I am weak and timid."

"Looks at your hips, thin, like a Male's hips. And your breasts, small and hard." Madam Trudeau turned away in disgust. "Why were you not chosen to become a Professional, a Doctor, or a Technician?"

"I am not intelligent enough, Madam. I require many hours of study to grasp the mathematics."

"So. Weak, frail, not too bright. Why do you weep?"

"I don't know, Madam. I am sorry."

"Go to your cubicle. You disgust me."

Staring at a flaw in the floor, a place where an indentation distorted the light, creating one very small oval shadow, wondering when the ordeal would end, wondering why she couldn't fill the notebook with the many things that Madam Westfall had said, things that she could remember here, and could not remember when she was in her cubicle with pen poised over the notebook.

Sometimes Carla forgot where she was, found herself in the chamber of Madam Westfall, watching the ancient one struggle to stay alive, forcing breaths in and out, refusing to admit death. Watching the incomprehensible dials and tubes and bottles of fluids with lowering levels, watching needles that vanished into flesh, tubes that disappeared under the bedclothes, that seemed to writhe now and again with a secret life, listening to the mumbling voice, the groans and sighs, the meaningless words.

Three times they rose against the children and three times slew them until there were none left none at all because the contagion had spread and all over ten were infected and carried radios….

Radios? A disease? Infected with radios, spreading it among young people?

And Mama said hide child hide and don't move and put this in the cave too and don't touch it.

Carla's relief came and numbly she walked from the Viewing Room. She watched the movement of the black border of her skirt as she walked and it seemed that the blackness crept up her legs, enveloped her middle, climbed her front until it reached her neck, and then it strangled her. She clamped her jaws hard and continued to walk her measured pace.

The girls who had attended Madam Westfall in life were on duty throughout the school ceremonies after the viewing. They were required to stand in a line behind the dais. There were eulogies to the patience and firmness of the first Teacher. Eulogies to her wisdom in setting up the rules of the school. Carla tried

to keep her attention on the speakers, but she was so tired and drowsy that she heard only snatches. Then she was jolted into awareness. Madam Trudeau was talking.

"...a book that will be the guide to all future Teachers, showing them the way through personal tribulations and trials to achieve the serenity that was Madam Westfall's. I am honored by this privilege, in choosing me and my apprentices to accomplish this end...."

Carla thought of the gibberish that she had been putting down in her notebook and she blinked back tears of shame. Madam Trudeau should have told them why she wanted the information. She would have to go back over it and destroy all the nonsense that she had written down.

Late that afternoon the entourage formed that would accompany Madam Westfall to her final ceremony in Scranton, her native city, where her burial would return her to her family.

Madam Trudeau had an interview with Carla before departure. "You will be in charge of the other girls," she said. "I expect you to maintain order. You will report any disturbance, or any infringement of rules, immediately, and if that is not possible, if I am occupied, you will personally impose order in my name."

"Yes, Madam."

"Very well. During the journey the girls will travel together in a compartment of the tube. Talking will be permitted, but no laughter, no childish play. When we arrive at the Scranton home, you will be given rooms with cots. Again you will all comport yourselves with the dignity of the office which you are ordered to fulfill at this time."

Carla felt excitement mount within her as the girls lined up to take their places along the sides of the casket. They went with it to a closed limousine, where they sat knee to knee, unspeaking, hot, to be taken over smooth highways for an hour to the tube. Madam Westfall had refused to fly in life, and was granted the same rights in death, so her body was to be transported from Wilmington to Scranton by the rocket tube. As soon as the girls had accompanied the casket to its car, and were directed to their own compartment, their voices raised in a babble. It was the first time any of them had left the school grounds since entering them at the age of five.

Ruthie was going to work in the infants' wards, and she turned faintly pink and soft-looking when she talked about it. Luella was a music apprentice already, having shown skill on the piano at an early age. Lorette preened herself slightly and announced that she had been chosen as a Lover by a gentleman. She would become a Lady one day. Carla stared at her curiously, wondering at her pleased look, wondering if she had not been shown the films yet. Lorette was blue-eyed, with pale hair, much the same build as Carla. Looking at her, Carla could imagine her in soft dresses, with her mouth painted, her hair covered by the other hair that was cloud-soft and shiny.... She looked at the girl's cheeks flushed with excitement at the thought of her future, and she knew that with or without the paint box, Lorette would be a Lady whose skin would be smooth,

whose mouth would be soft…

"The fuzz is so soft now, the flesh so tender." She remembered the scent, the softness of the Lady's hands, the way her skirt moved about her red-clad thighs.

She bit her lip. But she didn't want to be a Lady. She couldn't ever think of them again without loathing and disgust. She was chosen to be a Teacher.

They said it is the duty of society to prepare its non-citizens for citizenship but it is recognized that there are those who will not meet the requirements and society itself is not to be blamed for those occasional failures that must accrue.

She took out her notebook and wrote the words in it.

"Did you just remember something else she said?" Lisa asked. She was the youngest of the girls, only ten, and had attended Madam Westfall one time. She seemed to be very tired.

Carla looked over what she had written, and then read it aloud. "It's from the school rules book," she said. "Maybe changed a little, but the same meaning. You'll study it in a year or two."

Lisa nodded. "You know what she said to me? She said I should go hide in the cave, and never lose my birth certificate. She said I should never tell anyone where the radio is." She frowned. "Do you know what a cave is? And a radio?"

"You wrote it down, didn't you? In the notebook?"

Lisa ducked her head. "I forgot again. I remembered it once and then forgot again until now." She searched through her cloth travel bag for her notebook and when she didn't find it, she dumped the contents on the floor to search more carefully. The notebook was not there.

"Lisa, when did you have it last?"

"I don't know. A few days ago. I don't remember."

"When Madam Trudeau talked to you the last time, did you have it then?"

"No. I couldn't find it. She said if I didn't have it the next time I was called for an interview, she'd whip me. But I can't find it!" She broke into tears and threw herself down on her small heap of belongings. She beat her fists on them and sobbed. "She's going to whip me and I can't find it. I can't. It's gone."

Carla stared at her. She shook her head. "Lisa, stop that crying. You couldn't have lost it. Where? There's no place to lose it. You didn't take it from your cubicle, did you?"

The girl sobbed louder. "No. No. No. I don't know where it is."

Carla knelt by her and pulled the child up from the floor to a squatting position. "Lisa, what did you put in the notebook? Did you play with it?"

Lisa turned chalky white and her eyes became very large, then she closed them, no longer weeping.

"So you used it for other things? Is that it? What sort of things?"

Lisa shook her head. "I don't know. Just things."

"All of it? The whole notebook?"

"I couldn't help it. I didn't know what to write down. Madam Westfall said too much. I couldn't write it all. She wanted to touch me and I was afraid of her and

I hid under the chair and she kept calling me, 'Child, come here, don't hide, I'm not one of them. Go to the cave and take it with you.' And she kept reaching for me with her hands. I... They were like chicken claws. She would have ripped me apart with them. She hated me. She said she hated me. She said I should have been killed with the others, why wasn't I killed with the others."

Carla, her hands hard on the child's shoulders, turned away from the fear and despair she saw on the girl's face.

Ruthie pushed past her and hugged the child. "Hush, hush, Lisa. Don't cry now. Hush. There, there."

Carla stood up and backed away. "Lisa, what sort of things did you put in the notebook?"

"Just things that I like. Snowflakes and flowers and designs."

"All right. Pick up your belongings and sit down. We must be nearly there. It seems like the tube is stopping."

Again they were shown from a closed compartment to a closed limousine and whisked over countryside that remained invisible to them. There was a drizzly rain falling when they stopped and got out of the car.

The Westfall house was a three-storied, pseudo-Victorian wooden building, with balconies and cupolas, and many chimneys. There was scaffolding about it, and one of the three porches had been torn away and was being replaced as restoration of the house, turning it into a national monument, progressed. The girls accompanied the casket to a gloomy, large room where the air was chilly and damp, and scant lighting cast deep shadows. After the casket had been positioned on the dais which also had accompanied it, the girls followed Madam Trudeau through narrow corridors, up narrow steps, to the third floor where two large rooms had been prepared for them, each containing seven cots.

Madam Trudeau showed them the bathroom that would serve their needs, told them goodnight, and motioned Carla to follow her. They descended the stairs to a second-floor room that had black, massive furniture: a desk, two straight chairs, a bureau with a wavery mirror over it, and a large canopied bed.

Madam Trudeau paced the black floor silently for several minutes without speaking, then she swung around and said, "Carla, I heard every word that silly little girl said this afternoon. She drew pictures in her notebook! This is the third time the word cave has come up in reports of Madam Westfall's mutterings. Did she speak to you of caves?"

Carla's mind was whirling. How had she heard what they had said? Did maturity also bestow magical abilities? She said, "Yes, Madam, she spoke of hiding in a cave."

"Where is the cave, Carla? Where is it?"

"I don't know, Madam. She didn't say."

Madam Trudeau started to pace once more. Her pale face was drawn in lines of concentration that carved deeply into her flesh, two furrows straight up from the inner brows, other lines at the sides of her nose, straight to her chin, her mouth tight and hard. Suddenly she sat down and leaned back in the chair. "Carla, in

feel better after you get out in the sunshine and fresh air."

"Chrysanthemums, dahlias, marigolds. No, the small ones there, with the brown fringes…" Luella pointed out the various flowers to the other girls. Carla walked in the rear, hardly listening, trying to keep her eye on Lisa, who also trailed behind. She was worried about the child. Lisa had not slept well, had eaten no breakfast, and was so pale and wan that she didn't look strong enough to take the short garden walk with them.

Eminent personages came and went in the gloomy old house and huddled together to speak in lowered voices. Carla paid little attention to them. "I can change it after I have some authority," she said to a still inner self who listened and made no reply. "What can I do now? I'm property. I belong to the state, to Madam Trudeau and the school. What good if I disobey and am also whipped? Would that help any? I won't hit her hard." The inner self said nothing, but she thought she could hear a mocking laugh come from the mummy that was being honored.

They had all those empty schools, miles and miles of school halls where no feet walked, desks where no students sat, books that no students scribbled up, and they put the children in them and they could see immediately who couldn't keep up, couldn't learn the new ways, and they got rid of them. Smart. Smart of them. They were smart and had the goods and the money and the hatred. My God, they hated. That's who wins, who hates most. And is more afraid. Every time.

Carla forced her arms not to move, her hands to remain locked before her, forced her head to stay bowed. The voice now went on and on and she couldn't get away from it.

…rained every day, cold freezing rain and Daddy didn't come back and Mama said, hide child, hide in the cave where it's warm, and don't move no matter what happens, don't move. Let me put it on your arm, don't take it off, never take it off show it to them if they find you show them make them look….

Her relief came and Carla left. In the wide hallway that led to the back steps she was stopped by a rough hand on her arm. "Damme, here's a likely one. Come here, girl. Let's have a look at you." She was spun around and the hand grasped her chin and lifted her head. "Did I say it! I could spot her all the way down the hall, now couldn't I? Can't hide what she's got with long skirts and that skinny hairdo, now can you? Didn't I spot her!" He laughed and turned Carla's head to the side and looked at her in profile, then laughed even louder.

She could see only that he was red-faced, with bushy eyebrows and thick grey hair. His hand holding her chin hurt, digging into her jaws at each side of her neck.

"Victor, turn her loose," the cool voice of a female said then. "She's been chosen already. An apprentice Teacher."

He pushed Carla from him, still holding her chin, and he looked down at the skirts with the broad black band at the bottom. He gave her a shove that sent her into the opposite wall. She clutched at it for support.

"Whose pet is she?" he said darkly.

"Trudeau's."

He turned and stamped away, not looking at Carla again. He wore the blue and white of a Doctor of Law. The female was a Lady in pink and black.

"Carla. Go upstairs." Madam Trudeau moved from an open doorway and stood before Carla. She looked up and down the shaking girl. "Now you understand why I apprenticed you before this trip? For your own protection."

They walked to the cemetery on Saturday, a bright, warm day with golden light and the odor of burning leaves. Speeches were made, Madam Westfall's favorite music was played, and the services ended. Carla dreaded returning to the dormitory. She kept a close watch on Lisa, who seemed but a shadow of herself. Three times during the night she had held the girl until her nightmares subsided, and each time she had stroked her fine hair and soft cheeks and murmured to her quieting words, and she knew it was only her own cowardice that prevented her saying that it was she who would administer the whipping. The first shovelful of earth was thrown on top of the casket and everyone turned to leave the place, when suddenly the air was filled with raucous laughter, obscene chants, and wild music. It ended almost as quickly as it started, but the group was frozen until the mountain air became unnaturally still. Not even the birds were making a sound following the maniacal outburst.

Carla had been unable to stop the involuntary look that she cast about her at the woods that circled the cemetery. Who? Who would dare? Only a leaf or two stirred, floating downward on the gentle air effortlessly. Far in the distance a bird began to sing again, as if the evil spirits that had flown past were now gone.

"Madam Trudeau sent this up for you," Luella said nervously, handing Carla the rod. It was plastic, three feet long, thin, flexible. Carla looked at it and turned slowly to Lisa. The girl seemed to be swaying back and forth.

"I am to administer the whipping," Carla said. "You will undress now."

Lisa stared at her in disbelief, and then suddenly she ran across the room and threw herself on Carla, hugging her hard, sobbing. "Thank you, Carla. Thank you so much. I was so afraid, you don't know how afraid. Thank you. How did you make her let you do it? Will you be punished too? I love you so much, Carla." She was incoherent in her relief and she flung off her gown and underwear and turned around.

Her skin was pale and soft, rounded buttocks, dimpled just above the fullness. She had no waist yet, no breasts, no hair on her baby body. Like a baby she had whimpered in the night, clinging tightly to Carla, burying her head in the curve of Carla's breasts.

Carla raised the rod and brought it down, as easily as she could. Anything was too hard. There was a red welt. The girl bowed her head lower, but didn't whimper. She was holding the back of a chair and it jerked when the rod struck.

It would be worse if Madam Trudeau was doing it, Carla thought. She would try to hurt, would draw blood. Why? Why? The rod was hanging limply, and she knew it would be harder on both of them if she didn't finish it quickly. She raised it and again felt the rod bite into flesh, sending the vibration into her arm, through her body.

Again. The girl cried out, and a spot of blood appeared on her back. Carla stared at it in fascination and despair. She couldn't help it. Her arms wielded the rod too hard, and she couldn't help it. She closed her eyes a moment, raised the rod and struck again. Better. But the vibrations that had begun with the first blow increased, and she felt dizzy, and couldn't keep her eyes off the spot of blood that was trailing down the girl's back. Lisa was weeping now, her body was shaking. Carla felt a responsive tremor start within her.

Eight, nine. The excitement that stirred her was unnameable, unknowable, never before felt like this. Suddenly she thought of the Lady who had chosen her once, and scenes of the film she had been forced to watch flashed through her mind.... remake them in our image. She looked about in that moment frozen in time, and she saw the excitement on some of the faces, on others fear, disgust and revulsion. Her gaze stopped on Helga, who had her eyes closed, whose body was moving rhythmically. She raised the rod and brought it down as hard as she could, hitting the chair with a noise that brought everyone out of his own kind of trance. A sharp, cracking noise that was a finish.

"Ten!" she cried and threw the rod across the room.

Lisa turned and through brimming eyes, red, swollen, ugly with crying, said, "Thank you, Carla. It wasn't so bad."

Looking at her, Carla knew hatred. It burned through her, distorted the image of what she saw. Inside her body the excitement found no outlet, and it flushed her face, made her hands numb, and filled her with hatred. She turned and fled.

Before Madam Trudeau's door, she stopped a moment, took a deep breath, and knocked. After several moments the door opened and Madam Trudeau came out. Her eyes were glittering more than ever, and there were two spots of color on her pasty cheeks.

"It is done? Let me look at you." Her fingers were cold and moist when she lifted Carla's chin. "Yes, I see. I see. I am busy now. Come back in half an hour. You will tell me all about it. Half an hour." Carla never had seen a genuine smile on the Teacher's face before, and now when it came, it was more frightening than her frown was. Carla didn't move, but she felt as if every cell in her body had tried to pull back.

She bowed and turned to leave. Madam Trudeau followed her a step and said in a low vibrant voice, "You felt it, didn't you? You know now, don't you?"

"Madam Trudeau, are you coming back?" The door behind her opened, and one of the Doctors of Law appeared there.

"Yes, of course." She turned and went back to the room.

Carla let herself into the small enclosed area between the second and third floors, then stopped. She could hear the voices of girls coming down the stairs, going on duty in the kitchen, or outside for evening exercises. She stopped to wait for them to pass, and she leaned against the wall tiredly. This space was two and a half feet square perhaps. It was very dank and hot. From here she could hear every sound made by the girls on the stairs. Probably that was why the second door had been added, to muffle the noise of those going up and down. The girls had stopped on the steps and were discussing the laughter and obscenities they had heard in the cemetery.

Carla knew that it was her duty to confront them, to order them to their duties, to impose proper silence on them in public places, but she closed her eyes and pressed her hand hard on the wood behind her for support and wished they would finish their childish prattle and go on. The wood behind her started to slide.

She jerked away. A sliding door? She felt it and ran her finger along the smooth paneling to the edge where there was now a six-inch opening as high as she could reach and down to the floor. She pushed the door again and it slid easily, going between the two walls. When the opening was wide enough she stepped through it. The cave! She knew it was the cave that Madam Westfall had talked about incessantly.

The space was no more than two feet wide, and very dark. She felt the inside door and there was a knob on it, low enough for children to reach. The door slid as smoothly from the inside as it had from the outside. She slid it almost closed and the voices were cut off, but she could hear other voices, from the room on the other side of the passage. They were not clear. She felt her way farther, and almost fell over a box. She held her breath as she realized that she was hearing Madam Trudeau's voice:

"...be there. Too many independent reports of the old fool's babbling about it for there not to be something to it. Your men are incompetent."

"Trudeau, shut up. You scare the living hell out of the kids, but you don't scare me. Just shut up and accept the report. We've been over every inch of the hills for miles, and there's no cave. It was over a hundred years ago. Maybe there was one that the kids played in, but it's gone now. Probably collapsed."

"We have to be certain, absolutely certain."

"What's so important about it anyway? Maybe if you would give us more to go on we could make more progress."

"The reports state that when the militia came here, they found only Martha Westfall. They executed her on the spot without questioning her first. Fools! When they searched the house, they discovered that it was stripped. No jewels, no silver, diaries, papers. Nothing. Steve Westfall was dead. Dr. Westfall dead. Martha. No one has ever found the articles that were hidden, and when the child again appeared, she had true amnesia that never yielded to attempts to penetrate it."

"So, a few records, diaries. What are they to you?" There was silence, then he laughed. "The money! He took all his money out of the bank, didn't he?"

"Don't be ridiculous. I want records, that's all. There's a complete ham radio, complete. Dr. Westfall was an electronics engineer as well as a teacher. No one could begin to guess how much equipment he hid before he was killed."

Carla ran her hand over the box, felt behind it. More boxes.

"Yeah yeah. I read the reports, too. All the more reason to keep the search nearby. For a year before the end a close watch was kept on the house. They had to walk to wherever they hid the stuff. And I can just say again that there's no cave around here. It fell in."

"I hope so," Madam Trudeau said.

Someone knocked on the door, and Madam Trudeau called, "Come in."

"Yes, what is it? Speak up, girl."

"It is my duty to report, Madam, that Carla did not administer the full punishment ordered by you."

Carla's fists clenched hard. Helga.

"Explain," Madam Trudeau said sharply.

"She only struck Lisa nine times, Madam. The last time she hit the chair."

"I see. Return to your room."

The man laughed when the girl closed the door once more. "Carla is the golden one, Trudeau? The one who wears a single black band?"

"The one you manhandled earlier, yes."

"Insubordination in the ranks, Trudeau? Tut, tut. And your reports all state that you never have any rebellion. Never."

Very slowly Madam Trudeau said, "I have never had a student who didn't abandon any thoughts of rebellion under my guidance. Carla will be obedient. And one day she will be an excellent Teacher. I know the signs."

Carla stood before the Teacher with her head bowed and her hands clasped together. Madam Trudeau walked around her without touching her, then sat down and said, "You will whip Lisa every day for a week, beginning tomorrow."

Carla didn't reply.

"Don't stand mute before me, Carla. Signify your obedience immediately."

"I... I can't, Madam."

"Carla, any day that you do not whip Lisa, I will. And I will also whip you double her allotment. Do you understand?"

"Yes, Madam."

"You will inform Lisa that she is to be whipped every day, by one or the other of us. Immediately."

"Madam, please..."

"You speak out of turn, Carla!"

"I... Madam, please don't do this. Don't make me do this. She is too weak...."

"She will beg you to do it, won't she, Carla? Beg you with tears flowing to be the one, not me. And you will feel the excitement and the hate and every day you will feel it grow strong. You will want to hurt her, want to see blood spot her bare back. And your hate will grow until you won't be able to look at her without being blinded by your own hatred. You see, I know, Carla. I know all of it."

Carla stared at her in horror. "I won't do it. I won't."

"I will."

They were old and full of hatred for the shiny young faces, the bright hair, the straight backs and strong legs and arms. They said: let us remake them in our image and they did.

Carla repeated Madam Trudeau's words to the girls gathered in the two sleeping rooms on the third floor. Lisa swayed and was supported by Ruthie. Helga smiled.

That evening Ruthie tried to run away and was caught by two of the blue-clad Males. The girls were lined up and watched as Ruthie was stoned. They buried her without a service on the hill where she had been caught.

After dark, lying on the cot open-eyed, tense, Carla heard Lisa's whisper close to her ear. "I don't care if you hit me, Carla. It won't hurt like it does when she hits me."

"Go to bed, Lisa. Go to sleep."

"I can't sleep. I keep seeing Ruthie. I should have gone with her. I wanted to, but she wouldn't let me. She was afraid there would be Males on the hill watching. She said if she didn't get caught, then I should try to follow her at night." The child's voice was flat, as if shock had dulled her sensibilities.

Carla kept seeing Ruthie too. Over and over she repeated to herself: I should have tried it. I'm cleverer than she was. I might have escaped. I should have been the one. She knew it was too late now. They would be watching too closely.

An eternity later she crept from her bed and dressed quietly. Soundlessly she gathered her own belongings, and then collected the notebooks of the other girls, and the pens, and she left the room. There were dim lights on throughout the house as she made her way silently down stairs and through corridors. She left a pen by one of the outside doors, and very cautiously made her way back to the tiny space between the floors. She slid the door open and deposited everything else she carried inside the cave. She tried to get to the kitchen for food, but stopped when she saw one of the Officers of Law. She returned soundlessly to the attic rooms and tiptoed among the beds to Lisa's cot. She placed one hand over the girl's mouth and shook her awake with the other.

Lisa bolted upright, terrified, her body stiffened convulsively. With her mouth against the girl's ear Carla whispered, "Don't make a sound. Come on." She half led, half carried the girl to the doorway, down the stairs, and into the cave and closed the door.

"You can't talk here, either," she whispered. "They can hear." She spread out the extra garments she had collected and they lay down together, her arms tight about the girl's shoulders. "Try to sleep," she whispered. "I don't think they'll find us here. And after they leave, we'll creep out and live in the woods. We'll eat nuts and berries...."

The first day they were jubilant at their success and they giggled and muffled the noise with their skirts. They could hear all the orders being issued by Madam Trudeau: guards in all the halls, on the stairs, at the door to the dorm to keep other girls from trying to escape also. They could hear all the interrogations, of the girls, the guards who had not seen the escapees. They heard the mocking voice

ıg Madam Trudeau's boasts of absolute control.
to steal food for them, and, more important, water.
everywhere. She returned emptyhanded. During
her sleep and Carla had to stay awake to quiet the
sh.
will you?" she begged over and over.
too quiet. She didn't want Carla to move from her
nd in her hot, dry hand and now and then tried to
ıs too weak now. Carla stroked her forehead.
wrote in the notebooks, in the dark, not knowing
s or on blank pages. She wrote her life story, and
say. She wrote her name over and over, and wept
She wrote nonsense words and rhymed them with
ote of the savages who had laughed at the funeral
all die over the winter months. She thought that
ote of the golden light through green-black pine
noss underfoot. She wrote of Lisa lying peacefully
e amidst riches that neither of them could ever
ıe could no longer write, she drifted in and out of
listening to the birds' songs, hearing the raucous
o beautiful.

O HAPPY DAY!

by Geoff Ryman

Geoff Ryman is the author of the novels *The Warrior Who Carried Life, The Unconquered Country, The Child Garden, Was, 253, Lust, Air,* and *The King's Last Song.* His short fiction has appeared in *The Magazine of Fantasy & Science Fiction, Interzone, Tor.com, New Worlds,* and has frequently been reprinted in Gardner Dozois's *Year's Best Science Fiction* series. Most of his short work can be found in the collections *Unconquered Countries* and the recent *Paradise Tales and Other Stories.* He is a winner of the World Fantasy Award, the John W. Campbell Memorial Award, the Arthur C. Clarke Award, the Philip K. Dick Award, the Tiptree Award, and the British Science Fiction Award. He is also the editor of the recent anthology *When It Changed.* Another story of his appears elsewhere in this volume.

What is the role of violence in society? Is there a place for it? Is there a way to make violence socially acceptable? Or should it be eliminated—at any price?

Our next dystopia gives violence a cold looking-over, and after the examination is complete, no one is left innocent. Like Golding's *Lord of the Flies,* where the wrong conditions turn harmless school boys into malevolent brutes, "O Happy Day" watches people we often stereotype as gentle innocents turn beastly. Women prove themselves as capable of mindless cruelty as men. Homosexual men succumb to fisticuffs and in-fighting just as nastily as any straight men. No one is immune to the temptation of violence.

What this story really probes is the borderline that divides violence from *evil,* the line where aggression becomes a true stain of wickedness. And it asks: is there anything we can do to wash away the stain?

They're fooled by history. They think they won't be killed until they get into camps. So when we load them onto a different train, they go willingly. They see an old country railroad station with a big red hill behind it, and they think it's just a stop along the way.

They slip down from the cars and can't keep their feet on the sharp-edged rubble of the track. They're all on testosterone specifics, a really massive dose.

They're passive and confused, and their skin has a yellow taint to it, and their eyes stare out of patches of darkness, and they need a shave. They smell. They look like a trainload of derelicts. It must be easier to kill people who look like that, easier to call them Stiffs, as if they were already dead.

We're probably on specifics, too, but a very mild dose. We have to work, after all.

We load the Stiffs into cars, the Cars with the special features, and the second train goes off, and ten minutes later it comes back, and we unload them, dead, and that is life under what we call the Grils.

We are the Boys. We get up each morning and we shave. We're male, so we shave. Some of us do our make-up then, a bit of lipstick and slap, and an earring maybe. Big Lou always wore an earring and a tight short-sleeved T-shirt that showed off his arms. It was very strange, all those muscles with his pudding basin haircut and hatchet face, all pressed and prim around the lips.

Big Lou thought what was happening was good. I remember him explaining it to me my first day, the day he recruited me. "Men are violent," he said. "All through history, you look at violence, and it's male. That was OK in the jungle, but not now, with the gangs and the bombs and everything else. What is happening here is simple evolutionary necessity. It's the most liberating event in human history. And we're part of it." Then he kissed me. It was a political kiss, wet and cold. Then he introduced me to the work.

After we unload the trains, we strip the corpses. There are still shortages, so we tie up the clothes in bundles and save everything else of value—money, watches, cigarette lighters—and send them back on the train. It would be a terrible job for anyone, but it's worse for a faggot. Most of the bodies are young. You feel tender toward them. You want them to wake up again and move, and you think, surely there must be something better to do with this young brown body than kill it? We work very quickly, like ants on a hill.

I don't think we're mad. I think the work has become normal for us, and so we're normal within it. We have overwhelming reasons for doing it. As long as we do this work, as long as there is this work to do, we stay alive. Most of the Boys volunteered, but not for this. At first, it was just going to be internal deportation, work camps for the revolution. They were just going to be guards. Me, I was put on that train to die, and I don't know why. They dope whole areas, and collect the people they want. Lou saw me on the platform, and pulled me in. Recruited me, he called it. I slept with him, out of gratitude and fear. I still remember sleeping with him.

I was the one who recruited Royce. He saw me first. He walked up to me on the gravel between the trains, nothing out of the ordinary, just a tall black man in rumpled khaki. He was jingling the keys in his pockets, housekeys, as if he was going to need them again. He was shaking, and he kept blinking, and swaying where he stood, and he asked in a sick and panicky voice, "It's cold. It's cold. Isn't there any food?"

The information that he was good-looking got through slowly. The reaction was neutral, like you'd get from looking at a model on a billboard. Then I thought: in ten minutes' time, he's going to be dead.

You always promise yourself "just once." Just once, you'll tell the boss off; just once, you'll phone in sick and go out to the lakes. Just once. So here, I thought, is my just once: I'm going to save one of them.

"Are you gay?" I asked him I did it without moving my lips. The cameras were always on us.

"What?" Incomprehension.

Oh God, I thought, he's going to be difficult, this is dumb. I got scared.

"What did you ask me?"

"Nothing. Go on." I nodded toward the second train.

"Am I gay?" He said it quickly, glancing around him. I just nodded.

The last of the other Stiffs were being loaded on, the old ones, who had to be lifted up. I saw Big Lou look at us and start walking toward us, sauntering, amiable, with a diamanté earring.

"Yes," said Royce. "Why?"

"Make like you know me. My name's Richard."

"Royce," he said, but I couldn't catch it.

Then Lou was standing next to us. "A little tête-à-tête?" he asked.

"Hi Lou," I said. I leaned back on my heels, away from him. "We got ourselves a new recruit."

"Don't need one, Rich," he said, still smiling

"Lou, look. We were lovers. We lived together for two years. We did a lot of work for the movement together. He's OK, really."

Lou was looking at Royce, at Royce's face. Being black was in Royce's favor, ideologically. All the other Boys were white. No one wanted the Station to be accused of racism.

"I don't believe a word of it," said Lou. "But OK."

Lou walked toward one of the cameras. "Hey!" he shouted up to it. The camera was armed. It turned toward him, slowly. "We've got a new recruit."

"What was that?" asked the camera, or rather the voice of the Gril behind it. The sound was flat and mechanical, the tone offhand and bored.

"A new recruit. A new Boy. He's with us, so don't burn him, OK?"

"OK, OK," said the camera. Lou turned back, and patted Royce's bare, goose-pimpled arm. Royce lurched after him, and I grabbed hold of his shirt to stop him I was frightened he was going to get back onto the train. I waited until it was pulling out, creaking and crashing, so that the noise would cover what I said.

"It's terrible here," I told Royce. "But it's better than dying. Watch what you say. The cameras don't always hear, but usually they can. It's all right to look disgusted. They don't mind if you look a bit sick. They like us to do the job with distaste. Just don't ever say you think it's wrong."

"What's wrong?" he asked, and I thought: Oh God, he doesn't know. He doesn't know what's going on here. And I thought: now what do I do with him?

I showed him around the Station. It's a small, old-fashioned building made of yellow and black brick, with no sign on it to tell us where we are. One hundred years ago women in long dresses with children would have waited on its platform for the train to take them shopping in the city. There would have been a ticket-seller behind the counter who knew all the women by their last name, and who kept a girlie calendar pinned on the wall. His booth still has ornate iron bars across it, the word "Tickets" in art nouveau scrolling, still slightly gilded. The waiting room is full of temporary metal beds. The walls are painted a musty pistachio, and the varnish on the wooden floor has gone black. There are games machines in the corner, and behind the ticket counter is an electric cooker. We eat sitting on our beds. There are cold showers, outside by the wall, and there are flower boxes in the windows. James the Tape Head—he's one of the Boys—keeps them full of petunias and geraniums. All around it and the hill behind are concentric rows of wire mesh, thirty feet high and thirty feet deep, to keep the Stiffs controlled, and us in. It isn't a Station, it's a mass graveyard, for them and probably for us.

I tried to get Royce to go to bed, but he wouldn't. He was frightened to be left alone. He followed me out onto the platform where we were unloading the Stiffs, rolling them out. Sometimes the bodies sigh when they hit the concrete.

Royce's eyes went as wide as a rabbit's that's been run over by a car.

"What are you doing? What are you doing?" he yelped, over and over.

"What the fuck does it look like?" I said.

We strip them on the platform, and load them into trolleys. We shake them out of their trousers, and go through the pockets. Getting them out of their shirts is worse; their arms flop, and their heads loll. We're allowed to leave them in their underwear.

"They're doing it. Oh God, oh Jesus, they're killing them! Nobody knows that! Nobody believes that!"

"Help me carry them," I said. I said it for his sake. He shook his head, and stepped back, and stumbled over arms and legs and fell into a tangle of them.

Only the worst, we're told, only the most violent of men. That means the poor bastards who had to pick up a gun, or join a gang, or sign up for the police or the army. In other words, most of the people we kill are either black or Latino. I tried to tell them, I tried to tell the women that would happen.

Royce was suddenly sick. It was partly the drugs wearing off. Charlie and I hoisted him up and dragged him, as limp as a Stiff, into the showers. We got him cleaned up and into bed—my bed, there wasn't any other—and after that he was very quiet. Everybody was interested in him. New dog in the pound. Harry offered him one of his peppermints. Harry came up smiling, but then Harry is always smiling like the Man who Laughed, yellow teeth in a red beard. He'd got the peppermints off a Stiff. Royce didn't know how precious they were. He just shook his head, and lay there staring under the blanket, as one by one we all came back from the platform. Lou was last, thumping in and sighing, like he was satisfied with something. He slumped down on my bed next to Royce's knees, and I thought: uh-oh, Lou likes him too.

"Bad day, huh," Lou said. "Listen, I know, the first day is poison. But you got to ask yourself why it's happening."

"Why is it?" asked Royce, his face and mouth muffled in the crook of his elbow. He sounded like he was going to be sick again.

"Why?" Lou sounded shocked. "Royce, you remember how bad things got. The assassinations, the military build-up, the bombs?"

Only in America: the gangs got hold of tactical nuclear weapons. They punched out their rivals' turf: parts of Detroit, Miami, Houston, Chicago and then the big DC.

"I know," said Royce. "I used to live in Los Angeles."

Los Angeles came later. I sometimes wonder now if Los Angeles wasn't a special case. Ever hear of the Reichstag fire? Lou went respectful and silent, and he sat back, head bowed. "I am really sick at heart to hear that. I am so sorry. It must be like your whole past life has been blown away. What can I say? You probably know what I'm talking about better than anyone else here. It just had to be stopped, didn't it?"

"It did stop," said Royce.

"Yeah, I know, and that was because of the testosterone specifics. The women gave us that. Do you remember how great that felt, Royce? How calm you felt. That's because you'd been released from your masculinity, the specifics set men free from themselves. It was a beautiful thing to do."

Lou rocked back on the bed, and recited the old doggerel slogan. "TSI, in the water supply, a year-round high. I remember the first day I could leave my gun at home, man. I got on the subway, and there was this big Kahuna, all beads and tattoos, and he just smiled at me and passed me a joint. I really thought the specifics were the answer. But they hurt women, not many, but that's enough. So the specifics were withdrawn, and look what happened. Six months later, Los Angeles went up. The violence had to stop. And that's what we're going for here, Royce. Not men per se, but violence: the military, the police, criminals, gangsters, pornographers. Once they go, this whole thing here stops. It's like a surgical operation."

"Could you let me sleep?" Royce asked.

"Yeah sure," said Lou gently, and leaned forward and kissed him "Don't worry, Royce, we take care of our own here. These guys are a really great bunch of people. Welcome home."

The Boys went back to playing computer games in the waiting room. Bleep bleep bleep. One of the guys started yelling because a jack was missing from his deck of cards. James the Tape Head sat on his bed, Mozart hissing at him through his headphones. I looked at Royce, and I thought of him: you are a good person.

That's when I began to have the fantasy. We all have the fantasy, of someone good and kind and strong, who sees who we really are when we're not messed up. Without knowing I was doing it, I began to make Royce my fantasy, my beautiful, kind, good man. The strange thing was that in a way the fantasy was true. So was it a fantasy at all?

The next day—it was the very next day—Royce began his campaign.

I volunteered us both to get the food. The food comes down the tracks very early in a little automatic car. Someone has to unload it and take it into the kitchen. I wanted to get Royce and me away from the Boys to talk. He was unsure of me; he pulled on his socks and looked at me, solemnly, in the eye. Fair enough, I thought, he doesn't know me. Lou loaned him a big duffle coat, and Royce led us both out through the turnstiles and onto the platform.

We didn't have our talk. Like he was stepping out onto a stage, under the cameras, Royce started to play a part. I don't like to say this, but he started to play the part of a black man. It was an act, designed to disarm. He grinned and did a Joe Cool kind of movement. "Hey! How are you?" he said to one particular camera.

The camera stayed still, and silent.

"You can't fool me, I know there's someone there. What's your name?" he asked it. Silence, of course.

"Aw, come on, you can tell me that, can't you? Listen I have got a terrible name. It's Royce. How would you like to be called after a car? Your name can't be as bad as that. What is it? Grizelda? Hortensia? My favorite aunt's called Hortensia. How about Gertrude? Ever read Hamlet? What about… Lurleen?"

There was a hollow sound, like in a transatlantic phone call, when you talk over someone and it cuts out what they're saying for a couple of seconds afterwards. The camera did that. It had turned off its voice. And I thought, I didn't know it could do that; and I thought, why did it do it?

"Look. I have to call you something. My sister is called Alice. You don't mind if I call you Alice? Like in Wonderland?" Royce stepped forward. The camera did not have to bristle; its warm-up light went on.

"You see, Alice. I—uh—have a personal question."

The camera spoke. "What is it?" The voice was sharp and wary. I had the feeling that he had actually found her real name.

"Alice—uh—I don't want to embarrass anyone, but, um, you see, I got this little emergency, and everywhere I look there are cameras, so, um, where can I go?"

A pause from the camera. "I'm sorry," it said. "There are toilet facilities, but I'm afraid we have to keep you under observation."

"Really, I don't do anything that much different from anyone else."

"I'm sure you don't."

"I mean sometimes I try it standing on the seat or in a yoga position."

"Fine, but I'm afraid you'll still have to put up with the cameras."

"Well I hope you're recording it for posterity, 'cause if you get rid of all the men, it'll have real historical interest."

There was a click from the camera again. I stepped out of the line of fire. Royce presented himself at the turnstiles, and they buzzed to let him through. He made his way toward the john singing "That's Entertainment."

All the cameras turned to watch him.

Just before he went into the shed, he pulled out his pecker and waggled it at them. "Wave bye-bye," he said.

He'll get us all killed, I thought. The john was a trench with a plywood shed around it, open all along one side. I went to the wire mesh behind it, to listen.

"Alice?" I heard him ask through the plywood.

"I'm not Alice," said another voice from another camera. She meant in more ways than one, she was not Alice. "Uh—Hortensia? Uh. There's no toilet paper, Hortensia."

"I know."

"Gee, I wish you'd told me first."

"There are some old clothes on the floor. Use some of them and throw them over the side."

Dead men's shirts. I heard a kind of rustle and saw a line of shadow under the boards, waddling forward, crouched.

"I must look like a duck, huh?"

"A roast one in a minute."

Royce was quiet for a while after that. Finally he said, grumbling, "Trust me to pick tweed."

He kept it up, all morning long, talking to the Grils. During breakfast, he talked about home cooking and how to make tostadas and enchiladas. He talked about a summer job he'd had in Los Angeles, working in a diner that specialized in Kosher Mexican Food. Except for Royce, everyone who worked there including the owners was Japanese. That, said Royce, shaking his head, was LA. He and his mother had to move back east, to get away from the gang wars.

As the bodies were being unloaded, Royce talked about his grandmother. He'd lived with her when he was a child, and his father was dying. His grandmother made ice cream in the bathtub. She filled it full of ice and spun tubs of cream in it. Then she put one of the tubs in a basket with an umbrella over it on the front of her bicycle. She cycled through the neighborhood, selling ice cream and singing "Rock of Ages." She kept chickens, which was against the zoning regulations, and threw them at people who annoyed her, especially policemen. Royce had a cat, and it and a chicken fell in love. They would mew and cluck for each other, and sit for contented hours at a time, the chicken's neck snugly and safely inside the cat's mouth.

It was embarrassing, hearing someone talk. Usually we worked in silence. And the talk was confusing; we didn't think about things like summer jobs or household pets anymore. As the bodies were dumped and stripped, Royce's face was hard and shiny with sweat, like polished wood.

That afternoon, we had our talk. Since we'd gotten the food, it was our turn to cook lunch. So I got him away from the Boys.

We took our soup and crackers up to the top of the mound. The mound is dug out of a small hill behind the Station. James makes it in his bulldozer, listening to Mozart. He pulls the trolleys up a long dirt ramp, and empties them, and smooths the sandstone soil over each day's addition of Stiffs. I get the feeling he thinks he works like Mozart. The mound rises up in terraces, each terrace perfectly level, its slope at the same angle as the one below it. The dirt is brick red and there are seven levels. It looks like Babylon.

There are cameras on top, but you can see over the fence. You can see the New England forest. It looks tired and small, maybe even dusty, as if it needed someone to clean the leaves. There's another small hill. You can hear birds. Royce and I climbed up to the top, and I gathered up my nerve and said, "I really like you."

"Uh-huh," he said, balancing his soup, and I knew it wasn't going to work.

Leave it, I thought, don't push, it's hard for him, he doesn't know you.

"You come here a lot," he said. It was a statement.

"I come here to get away."

Royce blew out through his nostrils: a kind of a laugh. "Get away? You know what's under your feet?"

"Yes," I said, looking at the forest. Neither one of us wanted to sit on that red soil, even to eat the soup. I passed him his crackers, from my coat pocket.

"So why did you pick me? Out of all the other Stiffs?"

"I guess I just liked what I saw."

"Why?"

I smiled with embarrassment at being forced to say it; it was as if there were no words for it that were not slightly wrong. "Because I guess you're kind of good-looking and I... just thought I would like you a lot."

"Because I'm black?"

"You are black, yes."

"Are most of your boyfriends black?"

Bull's-eye. That was scary. "I, uh, did go through a phase where I guess I was kind of fixated on black people. But I stopped that, I mean, I realized that what I was actually doing was depersonalizing the people I was with, which wasn't very flattering to them. But that is all over. It really isn't important to me now."

"So you went out and made yourself sleep with white people." He does not, I thought, even remotely like me.

"I found white people I liked. It didn't take much."

"You toe the line all the way down the line, don't you?" he said.

I thought I didn't understand.

"Is that why you're here?" A blank from me. "You toe the line, the right line, so you're here."

"Yes," I said. "In a way. Big Lou saw me on the platform, and knew me from politics. I guess you don't take much interest in politics." I was beginning to feel like hitting back.

"Depends on the politics," he said, briskly.

"Well you're OK, I guess. You made it out."

"Out of where?"

I just looked back at him. "Los Angeles."

He gave a long and very bitter sigh, mixed with a kind of chortle. "Whenever

I am in this... situation, there is the conversation. I always end up having the same conversation. I reckon you're going to tell me I'm not black enough."

"You do kind of shriek I am middle class."

"Uh-huh. You use that word class, so that means it's not racist, right?"

"I mean, you're being loyal to your class, to which most black people do not belong."

"Hey, bro', you can't fool me, we're from the same neighborhood. That sort of thing?" It was imitation ghetto. "You want somebody with beads in his hair and a beret and a semi who hates white people, but likes you because you're so upfront movement? Is that your little dream? A big bad black man?"

I turned away from him completely.

He said, in a very cold still voice. "Do you get off on corpses, too?"

"This was a mistake," I said. "Let's go back."

"I thought you wanted to talk."

"Why are you doing this?"

"Because," he said, "you are someone who takes off dead men's watches, and you look like you could have been a nice person."

"I am," I said, and nearly wept, "a nice person."

"That's what scares the shit out of me."

"You think I want this? You think I don't hate this?" I think that's when I threw down the soup. I grabbed him by the shirt sleeves and held him. I remember being worried about the cameras, so I kept my voice low and rapid, like it was scuttling.

"Look, I was on the train, I was going to die, and Lou said, you can live. You can help here and live. So I did it. And I'm here. And so are you."

"I know," he said, softly.

"So OK, you don't like me, I can live with that, fine, no problem, you're under no obligation, so let's just go back."

"You come up here because of the forest," he said.

"Yes! Brilliant!"

"Even mass murderers need love too, right?"

"Yes! Brilliant!"

"And you want me to love you? When you bear the same relation to me, as Lou does to you?"

"I don't know. I don't care." I was sitting down now, hugging myself. The bowl of soup was on the ground by my foot, tomato sludge creeping out of it. I kicked it. "Sorry I hassled you."

"You didn't hassle me."

"All I want is one little part of my life to have a tiny corner of goodness in it. Just one little place. I probably won't, but I feel like if I don't find it soon, I will bust up into a million pieces. Not love. Not necessarily. Just someone nice to talk to, who I really like. Otherwise I think one day I will climb back into one of those trains." When I said it, I realized it was true. I hadn't known I was that far gone. I thought I had been making a play for sympathy.

Royce was leaning in front of me, looking me in the face. "Listen, I love you."

"Bullshit." What kind of mind-fuck now?

He grabbed my chin, and turned my head back round. "No. True. Not maybe in the way you want, but true. You really do look, right now, like one of those people on the train. Like someone I just unloaded."

I didn't know quite what he was saying, and I wasn't sure I trusted him, but I did know one thing. "I don't want to go back to that bunkhouse, not this afternoon."

"OK. We'll stay up here and talk."

I felt like I was stepping out onto ice. "But can we talk nicely? A little bit less heavy duty?"

"Nicely. Sounds sweet, doesn't mean anything. Like the birds?"

"Yes," I said. "Like the birds."

I reckon that, altogether, we had two weeks. A Lullaby in Birdland. Hum along if you want to. You don't need to know the words.

Every afternoon after the work, Royce and I went up the mound and talked. I think he liked talking to me, I'll go as far as that. I remember one afternoon he showed me photographs from his wallet. He still had a wallet, full of people.

He showed me his mother. She was extremely thin, with dark limp flesh under her eyes. She was trying to smile. Her arms were folded across her stomach. She looked extremely kind, but tired.

There was a photograph of a large red brick house. It had white window sills and a huge white front door, and it sagged in the way that only very old houses do.

"Whose is that?" I asked.

"Ours. Well, my family's. Not my mother's. My uncle lives there now."

"It's got a Confederate flag over it!"

Royce grinned and folded up quietly; his laughter was almost always silent. "Well, my great-grandfather didn't want to lose all his slaves, did he?"

One half of Royce's family were black, one half were white. There were terrible wedding receptions divided in half where no one spoke. "The white people are all so embarrassed, particularly the ones who want to be friendly. There's only one way a black family gets a house like that: Grandfather messed around a whole bunch. He hated his white family, so he left the house to us. My uncle and aunt want to open it up as a Civil War museum and put their picture on the leaflet." Royce folded up again. "I mean, this is in Georgia. Can you imagine all those rednecks showing up and finding a nice black couple owning it, and all this history about black regiments?"

"Who's that?"

"My cousin. She came to live with us for a while."

"She's from the white half."

"Nope. She's black." Royce was enjoying himself. The photograph showed a rather plump, very determined teenage girl with orange hair, slightly wavy, and freckles.

"Oh." I was getting uncomfortable, all this talk of black and white.

"It's really terrible. Everything Cyndi likes, I mean everything, is black, but her father married a white woman, and she ended up like that. She wanted to be black so bad. Every time she met anyone, she'd start explaining how she was black, really. She'd go up to black kids and start explaining, and you could see them thinking 'Who is this white girl and is she out of her mind?' We were both on this program, so we ended up in a white high school and that was worse because no one knew they'd been integrated when she was around. The first day this white girl asked her if she'd seen any of the new black kids. Then her sister went and became a top black fashion model, you know, features in Ebony, and that was it. It got so bad, that whenever Cyndi meant white, she'd say 'the half of me I hate.'"

"What happened to her?"

"I think she gave up and became white. She wanted to be a lawyer. I don't know what happened to her. She got caught in LA."

I flipped over the plastic. There was a photograph of a mother and a small child. "Who's that?"

"My son," said Royce. "That's his mother. Now she thinks she's a witch." An ordinary looking girl stared sullenly out at the camera. She had long frizzy hair and some sort of ethnic dress. "She'll go up to waiters she doesn't like in restaurants and whisper spells at them in their ears."

"How long ago was this?" I felt an ache, as if I'd lost him, as if I had ever had him.

"Oh ten years ago, before I knew anything. I mean, I wouldn't do it now. I'd like any kid of mine to have me around, but his mother and I don't get on. She told my aunt that she'd turned me gay by magic to get revenge."

"Were they in LA too?"

Royce went very still, and nodded yes.

"I'm sorry," I said.

He passed me back the wallet. "Here. That's all of them. Last time we got together."

There was a tiny photograph, full of people. The black half. On the far right was a very tall, gangling fifteen-year-old, looking bristly and unformed, shy and sweet. Three of the four people around him were looking at him, bursting with suppressed smiles. I wish I'd known him then, as well. I wanted to know him all his life.

"I got a crazy, crazy family," he said, shaking his head with affection. "I hope they're all still OK." It was best not to think about what was happening outside. Or inside, here.

It was autumn, and the sun would come slanting through the leaves of the woods. It would make a kind of corona around them, especially if the Boys were burning garbage and there was smoke in the air. The light would come in shafts, like God was hiding behind the leaves. The leaves were dropping one by one.

There was nothing in the Station that was anything to do with Royce. Everything that made him Royce, that made him interesting, is separate. It is the small real things that get obliterated in a holocaust, forgotten. The horrors are distinct and do not connect with the people, but it is the horrors that get remembered in history.

When it got dark, we would go back down, and I hated it because each day it was getting dark earlier and earlier. We'd get back and find that there had been—oh—a macaroni fight over lunch, great handprints of it over the windows and on the beds, that had been left to dry. Once we got back to the waiting room, and there had been a fight, a real one. Lou had given one of the Boys a bloody nose, to stop it. There was blood on the floor. Lou lectured us all about male violence, saying anyone who used violence in the Station would get violence back.

He took away all of Tom's clothes. Tom was beautiful, and very quiet, but sometimes he got mad. Lou kicked him out of the building in punishment. It was going to be a cold night. Long after the Grils had turned out the lights, we could hear Tom whimpering, just outside the door. "Please, Lou. It's cold. Lou, I'm sorry. Lou? I just got carried away. Please?"

I felt Royce jump up and throw the blanket aside. Oh God, I thought, don't get Lou mad at us. Royce padded across the dark room, and I heard the door open, and I heard him say, "OK, come in."

"Sorry, Lou," Royce said. "But we all need to get to sleep." Lou only grunted. "OK," he said, in a voice that was biding its time.

And Royce came back to my bed.

I would hold him, and he would hold me, but only, I think, to stop falling out of the bed. It was so narrow and cold. Royce's body was always taut, like each individual strand of muscle had been pulled back, tightly, from the shoulder. It was as tense through the night as if it were carrying something, and nothing I could do would soothe it. What I am trying to say, and I have to say it, is that Royce was impotent, at least with me, at least in the Station. "As long as I can't do it," he told me once on the mound, "I know I haven't forgotten where I am." Maybe that was just an excuse. The Boys knew about it, of course. They listened in the dark and knew what was and was not happening.

And the day would begin at dawn. The little automatic car, the porridge and the bread, the icy showers, and the wait for the first train. James the Tape Head, Harry with his constant grin, Gary who was tall and ropey, and who kept tugging at his pigtail. He'd been a trader in books, and he talked books and politics and thought he was Lou's lieutenant. Lou wasn't saying. And Bill the Brylcreem, and Charlie with his still, and Tom. The Boys. Hating each other, with no one else to talk to, waiting for the day when the Grils would burn us, or the food in the cart would have an added secret ingredient. When they were done with us.

Royce talked, learning who the cameras were.

There were only four Grils, dividing the day into two shifts. Royce gave them names. There was Alice and Hortensia, and Miss Scarlett who turned out to be from Atlanta. Only one of the Grils took a while to find a name, and she got it the first day one of the cameras laughed.

She'd been called Greta, I think because she had such a low, deep voice. Sometimes Royce called her Sir. Then one morning, Lou was late, and as he came, Royce said. "Uh-oh. Here comes the Rear Admiral."

Lou was very sanctimonious about always taking what he assumed was the female role in sex. The cameras knew that; they watched all the time. The camera laughed. It was a terrible laugh; a thin, high, wailing, helpless shriek.

"Hey, Sir, that's really Butch," said Royce, and the name Butch stuck.

So did Rear Admiral. God bless all who sail in him.

"Hiya, Admiral," gasped the camera, and even some of the Boys laughed too.

Lou looked confused, a stiff and awkward smile on his face. "It's better than being some macho prick," he said.

That night, he took me to one side, by the showers.

"Look," he said. "I think maybe you should get your friend to ease up a bit."

"Oh Lou, come on, it's just jokes."

"You think all of this is a joke!" yelped Lou.

"No."

"Don't think I don't understand what's going on." The light caught in his eyes, pinprick bright.

"What do you think is going on, Lou?"

I saw him appraising me. I saw him give me the benefit of the doubt. "What you've done, Rich, and maybe it isn't your fault, is to import an ideological wild card into this station."

"Oh Lou," I groaned. I groaned for him, for his mind.

"He's not with us. I don't know what these games are that he's playing with the women, but he's putting us all in danger. Yeah, sure, they're laughing now, but sooner or later he'll say the wrong thing, and some of us will get burned. Cooked. And another thing. These little heart to heart talks you have with each other. Very nice. But that's just the sort of thing the Station cannot tolerate. We are a team, we are a family, we've broken with all of that nuclear family shit, and you guys have re-imported it. You're breaking us up, into little compartments. You, Royce, James, even Harry, you're all going off into little corners away from the rest of us. We have got to work together. Now I want to see you guys with the rest of us. No more withdrawing."

"Lou," I said, helpless to reply. "Lou. Fuck off."

His eyes had the light again. "Careful, Rich."

"Lou. We are with you guys twenty-two hours a day. Can you really not do without us for the other two? What is wrong with a little privacy, Lou?"

"There is no privacy here," he said. "The cameras pick up just about every word. Now look. I took on a responsibility. I took on the responsibility of getting all of us through this together, show that there is a place in the revolution for good gay men. I have to know what is going on in the Station. I don't know what you guys are saying to each other up there, I don't know what the cameras are hearing. Now you lied to me, Rich. You didn't know Royce before he came here, did you. We don't know who he is, what he is. Rich, is Royce even gay?"

"Yes! Of course!"

"Then how does he fuck?"

"That's none of your business."

"Everything here is my business. You don't fuck him, he doesn't fuck you, so what goes on?"

I was too horrified to speak.

"Look," said Lou, relenting. "I can understand it. You love the guy. You think I don't feel that pull, too, that pull to save them? We wouldn't be gay if we didn't. So you see him on the platform, and he is very nice, and you think, Dear God, why does he have to die?"

"Yes."

"I feel it! I feel it too!" Lou made a good show of doing so. "It's not the people themselves, but what they are that we have to hold onto. Remember, Rich, this is just a program of containment. What we get here are the worst, Rich, the very worst—the sex criminals, the transsexuals, the media freaks. So what you have to ask yourself, Rich, is this: what was Royce doing on that train?"

"Same thing I was. He got pulled in by mistake."

Lou looked at me with a kind of blank pity. Then he looked down at the ground. "There are no mistakes, Rich. They've got the police files."

"Then what was I doing on the train?"

Lou looked back up at me and sighed. "I think you probably got some of the women very angry with you. There's a lot of infighting, particularly where gay men fit in. I don't like it. It's why I got you out. It may be something similar with Royce."

"On the train because I disagreed with them?" Everything felt weak, my knees, my stomach.

"It's possible, only possible. This is a revolution, Rich. Things are pretty fluid."

"Oh God, Lou, what's happening?"

"You see why we have to be careful? People have been burned in this station, Rich. Not lately, because I've been in charge. And I intend to stay in charge. Look."

Lou took me in his arms. "This must be really terrible for you, I know. All of us were really happy for you, when you and Royce started. But we have to protect ourselves. Now let's just go back in, and ask Royce who and what he is."

"What do you mean?"

"Just ask him. In front of the others. What he was. And not take no for an answer." He was stroking my hair.

"He'll hate me if I do that!" I tried to push him away. He grabbed hold of my hair, and pulled it, smiling, almost as if he were still being sexy and affectionate.

"Then he'll just have to get over that kind of mentality. What has he got to hide if he needs privacy? Come on, Rich. Let's just get it over with." He pulled me back, into the waiting room.

Royce took one look at us together as we came in, and his face went still, as if to say, "Uh-huh. This is coming now, is it?" His eyes looked hard into mine, and said, "Are you going to put up with it?" I was ashamed. I was powerless.

"Rich has a confession to make," said Lou, a friendly hand still on the back of my neck. "Don't you, Rich?"

They all seemed to sit up and close in, an inquisition, and I stood there thinking, Dear God, what do I do? What do I do?

"Rich," Lou reminded me. "We have to go through this. We need to talk this through."

Royce sat there, on our bed, reclining, waiting.

Well, I had lied. "I don't really know who Royce is. We weren't lovers before. We are lovers now."

"But you don't know what he was doing, or who he was, do you, Rich?"

I just shook my head.

"Don't you want to know that, Rich? Don't you want to know who your lover was? Doesn't it seem strange to you that he's never told you?"

"No," I replied. "We all did what we had to do before the revolution. What we did back then is not who we are." See, I wanted to say to Royce, I'm fighting, see I'm fighting.

"But there are different ways of knuckling under, aren't there, Rich? You taught history. You showed people where the old system had gone wrong. You were a good, gay man."

Royce stood up, abruptly, and said, "I was a prison guard."

The room went cold and Lou's eyes gleamed.

"And there are different ways of being a prison guard. It was a detention center for juveniles, young guys who might have had a chance. Not surprisingly, most of them were black. I don't suppose you know what happens to black juvenile prisoners now, do you? I'd like to know."

"Their records are looked at," said Lou. "So. You were a gay prison guard in charge of young men."

"Is that so impossible?"

"So, you were a closet case for a start."

"No. I told my immediate superior."

"Immediate superior. You went along with the hierarchy. Patriarchy, I should say. Did you have a good time with the boys?"

"This camp is a hierarchy, in case you hadn't noticed. And no, I kept my hands off the boys. I was there to help them, not make things worse."

"Helping them to be gay would be worse?" Every word was a trap door that could fall open. The latch was hatred. "Did you ever beat one of the boys up? Did you deal dope on the side?"

Royce was still for a moment, his eyes narrow. Then he spoke.

"About four years ago, me and the kids put on a show. We put on a show for the girls' center. The girls came in a bus, and they'd all put their hair in ringlets, and they walked into the gym with too much make-up on, holding each other's hands, clutching each other's forearms, like this, because they were so nervous. And the kids, the boys, they'd been rehearsing, oh, for weeks. They'd built and painted a set. It was a street, with lights in the windows, and a big yellow moon. There was this one kid, Jonesy. Jonesy kept sticking his head through the curtain before we started. 'Hey everybody! I'm a star!'"

Royce said it again, softly. "Hey everybody, I'm a star. And I had to yell at him, Jonesy, get your ass off that stage. The girls sat on one side of the gym, and the boys on the other, and they smiled and waved and threw things at each other, like gum wrappers. It was all they had."

Royce started to cry. He glared at Lou and let the tears slide down his face. "They didn't have anything else to give each other. The show started and one of the kids did his announcing routine. He'd made a bow tie out of a white paper napkin, and it looked so sharp. And then the music came up and one of the girls just shouted. 'Oh, they're going to dance!' And those girls screamed. They just screamed. The boys did their dance on the stage, no mistaking what those moves meant. The record was 'It's a Shame.'"

His face contorted suddenly, perhaps with anger. "And I had to keep this god-damned aisle between them, the whole time."

"So?" said Lou, unmoved.

"So," said Royce, and gathered himself in. He wiped the moisture from his face. "So I know a lot about prisons. So, some of those kids are dead now. The boys and the girls wanted each other. That must be an ideological quandary for you, Lou. Here's a big bad guard stopping people doing what they want, but what they want to do is het-ero-sex-u-ality." He turned it into a mock dirty word, his eyes round.

"No problem," said Lou. "All women are really lesbians."

Royce stared at him for a moment. Then he began to laugh.

"I wouldn't expect you to understand. But the first experience of physical tenderness that any woman has is with her mother."

"Gee, I'm sure glad my old aunt Hortensia didn't know that. She would be surprised. Hey, Alice. Are you a dyke?"

Lou went pale, and lines of shadow encircled his mouth.

"Yes," said Alice, the camera.

"Well, I'm a faggot, but it doesn't mean everyone else is."

Lou launched himself from the bed, in a fury. He was on his feet, and shouting, flecks of spit propelled from his mouth.

"You do not use demeaning language here!" His voice cracked.

Alice had been working nine hours, and now she was alone, on the night shift. She had been watching, silently, for nine hours. Now, she wanted to talk.

"I had a girlfriend once who was straight," she said. "No matter how hard she tried, women just didn't bring her off. Mind you, that's better than those lust lesbians. They just want your body. Me, I'm totally dedicated to women, but it's a political commitment. It's something I decided. I don't let my body make my decisions for me."

"Yeah, I know what you mean," said Royce. "It's these lust faggots, I can't stand." He cast his eyes about him at the Boys, and they chuckled.

"We do not use the word 'dyke' in this station," said Lou.

Royce looked rather sad and affectionate, and shook his head. "Lou. You are such a prig. Not only are you a prig. You are a dumb prig."

The floor seemed to open up under my feet with admiration. Only Royce could have said that to Lou. I loved him, even though I did not love myself. The Boys chuckled again, because it was funny, and because it was true, and because it was a little bit of a shock.

"Alice," said Lou. "He has just insulted women."

"Funny," said Alice. "I thought he'd just insulted you."

Lou looked like he was in the middle of a nightmare; you could see it in his face. "Alice is being very tolerant, Royce. But from now on, you talk to and about the women with respect. If you want to live here with us, there are a few ground rules."

"Like what?"

"No more jokes."

Royce was leaning against the bar at the foot of our bed, and he was calm, and his ankles were crossed. He closed his eyes, and smiled. "No more jokes?" he asked, amused.

"You mess around with the women, you put us all in danger. You keep putting us in danger, you got to go."

"Lou," said Alice. "Can I remind you of something? You don't decide who goes on the trains. We do."

"I understand that, Alice." He slumped from the shoulders and his breath seeped out of him. He seemed to shrink.

"Lou," said Royce. "I think you and I are on the same side?" It was a question.

"We'd better be," said Lou.

"Then you do know why I talk to the women."

"Yeah," said Lou. "You want to show off. You want to be the center of attention. You don't want to take responsibility for anything."

He didn't understand. Lou was dangerous because he was stupid.

"I've been a prison guard," said Royce, carefully. "I know what it's like. You're trapped, even worse than the prisoners."

"So?" He was going to make Royce say it, in front of a camera. He was going to make him say that he was talking to the Grils so that they would find it hard to kill us when the time came.

"I'm talking to the women, so that they'll get to know us," said Royce, "and see that there is a place for gay men within the revolution. They can't know that unless we talk to them. Can they?"

Bull's-eye again. That was the only formulation Lou was ever likely to accept.

"I mean, can they, Lou? I think we're working with the women on this thing together. There's no need for silence between us, not if we're on the same side. OK, so maybe I do it wrong. I don't want to be the only one who does all the talking. We all should talk to them, Lou, you, me, all of us. And the women should feel that they can talk with us as well."

"Oh yeah, I am so bored keeping schtum," said Alice.

Lou went still, and he drew in a deep breath. "OK," he said. "We can proceed on that basis. We all communicate, with each other and with the cameras. But Royce. That means no more withdrawing. No more going off in a corner. No more little heart to hearts on the mound."

"I didn't know that was a problem, Lou. There will be no more of those."

"OK, then," said Lou, murmurous in defeat. Royce strode toward him, both hands outstretched, and took Lou's hand in both of his.

"This is really good, Lou. I'm really glad we talked."

Lou looked back at him, looking worn and heavy, but he was touched. Big Lou was moved, as well, and he gave a slightly forlorn flicker of a smile.

So Royce became head of the Station.

He gave me a friendly little nod, and moved his things away from our bed. He slept in Tom's; Tom never did. It didn't matter, because I still had my little corner of goodness, even if we didn't talk. Royce was still there, telling jokes. I was happy with that because I knew that I had deserted him before he had deserted me; and I understood that I was to be the visible victory he gave to Lou. None of that mattered. Royce had survived. I didn't cry the first night alone; I stopped myself. I didn't want the Boys to hear.

Things started to change. The cameras stopped looking at us on the john. We could see them turn and look away. Then one morning, they were just hanging, dead.

"Hey, Rich!" Harry called me. It was me and Harry, unloading the food cart, as winter finally came. Harry was hopping up and down in front of the camera. He leapt up and tapped it, and the warm-up light did not even go on.

"They've turned it off, Rich! The camera's off. It's dead!"

He grabbed my arms, and spun me around, and started doing a little dance, and I started to hoot with laughter along with him. It was like someone had handed you back part of your pride. It was like we were human enough to be accorded that again.

"Hey Royce, the camera in the john's off!" shouted Harry, as we burst through the canteen doors with the trolley.

"Maybe they're just broken," said Gary, who was still loyal to Lou.

"Naw, man, they'd be telling us to fix it by now. They've turned it off!"

"That so, Alice?" Royce asked the camera in the canteen.

"Oh. Yeah," said Alice. Odd how a mechanical voice could sound so much more personal than a real one, closer somehow, as if in the middle of your ear.

"Thanks, Alice."

"'S OK," said Alice, embarrassed. "We explained it to the Wigs. We told them it was like pornography, you know, demeaning to us. They bought it. Believe me, you guys are not a lovely sight first thing in the morning."

I could see Royce go all alert at that word "Wig," like an animal raising its ears. He didn't mention the Wigs again until later that afternoon.

"Alice, is our talking ever a problem for you?"

"How d'you mean?"

"Well, if one of the Wigs walked in…"

Alice kind of laughed. "Huh. They don't get down this far. What do you know about them, anyhow?"

"Nothing. Who are they?"

"Mind your own business. The people who run things."

"Well if someone does show up and you want us to shut up, just sneeze, and we'll stop talking."

"Sneeze?"

"Well, you could always come right out and say cool it guys, there's someone here."

"Hey Scarlett," said Alice. "Can you sneeze?"

"Ach-ooo," said Miss Scarlett, delicately.

"Just testing, guys," said Alice.

Big Lou hung around, trying to smile, trying to look like somehow all this was going on under his auspices. Nobody was paying attention.

The next day, the train didn't show.

It was very cold, and we stood on the platform, thumping our feet, as the day grew more sparkling, and the shadows shorter.

"Hey, Butch, what's up?" Royce asked.

"I'll check, OK?" said the camera. There was a long silence.

"The train's broken down. It's in a siding. It'll be a while yet. You might as well go back in, have the day off."

That's how it would begin, of course. No train today, fellas, sorry. No need for you, fellas, not today, not ever, and with what you know, can you blame us? What are ten more bodies to us?

Trains did break down, of course. It had happened before. We'd had a holiday then, too, and the long drunken afternoon became a long drunken day.

"Well let's have some fun for a change," said Lou. "Charlie, you got any stuff ready? Let's have a blow-out, man."

"Lou," said Royce, "I was kind of thinking we could get to work on the hot water tank."

"Hot water tank?" said Lou. "Are we going to need it, Royce?" There was a horrified silence. "So much for talking. Go on, Charlie, get your booze."

Then Lou came for me. "How about a little sex and romance, Rich?" Hand on neck again.

"No thanks, Lou."

"You won't get it from him, you know."

"That's my problem. Lou, lay off."

"At least I can do it." Grin.

"Surprise, surprise," I said. His face and body were right up against mine, and I turned away. "You can't get at him through me, you know, Lou. You just can't do it."

Lou relented. He pulled back, but he was still smiling. "You're right," he said. "For that, he'd have to like you. Sucker." He flicked the tip of my nose with his fingers, and walked away.

I went and sat down beside Royce. I needed him to make everything seem normal and ordinary. He was leaning on his elbows, plucking at the grass. "Hi," I said. It was the first time we'd spoken since the inquisition.

"Hi," he said, affectionate and distant.

"Royce, what do you think's going to happen?"

"The train will come in tomorrow," he said.

"I hate it when it comes in," I said, my breath rattling out of me in a kind of chuckle, "and I hate it when it doesn't. I just hate it. Royce, do you think we could go to work on the tank?"

He considered the implications. "OK," he said. "Charlie? Want to come work with us on the tank?"

Charlie was plump with a gray beard, and had a degree in engineering, a coffee tin and a copper coil. He was a sort of Santa Claus of the booze. "Not today," he said, cheerily. "I made all of this, I might as well get to drink some of it myself." It was clear and greasy-looking and came in white plastic screw-top bottles.

Charlie had sacrificed one of the showers to plumb in a hot water tank. We'd hammered the tank together out of an old train door. It was more like a basin, really, balanced in the loft of the Station. There were cameras there, too.

Royce sat looking helplessly at an electric hot plate purloined from the kitchen stove. We'd pushed wiring through from the floor below. "Charlie should be here," he said.

"I really love you, Royce."

He went very still for a moment. "I know," he said. "Rich, don't be scared. You're afraid all the time."

"I know," I said, and felt my hand tremble as I ran it across my forehead.

"You gotta stop it. One day, you'll die of fear."

"It's this place," I said, and broke down, and sat in a heap. "I want to get out!"

He held me, gently. "Someday we'll get out," he said, and the hopelessness of it made me worse. "Someday it'll be all right."

"No, it won't."

"Hi, guys," said Alice. "They're really acting like pigs down there."

"They're scared," said Royce. "We're all scared, Alice. Is that train going to come in tomorrow?"

"Yup," she said brightly.

"Good. You know anything about electricity?"

"Plenty. I used to work for Bell Telephone."

Royce disengaged himself from me. "OK. Do I put the plate inside the tank or underneath it?"

"Inside? Good Lord no!"

So Royce went back to work again, and said to me, "You better go back down, Rich."

"The agreement?" I asked, and he nodded yes. The agreement between him and Lou.

When I got down, the Boys looked like discarded rags. There was piss everywhere, and blood on Lou's penis.

I went up to the top of the mound. All the leaves were gone now. For about the first time in my life, I prayed. Dear God, get me out of here. Dear God, please, please, make it end. But there wasn't any answer. There never is. There was just an avalanche inside my head.

I could shut it out for a while. I could forget that every day I saw piles of corpses bulldozed and mangled, and that I had to chase the birds away from them, and that I peeled off their clothes and looked with inevitable curiosity at the little pouch of genitals in their brightly colored underwear. And the leaking and the sudden hemorrhaging and the supple warmth of the dead, with their marble eyes full of seeming questions. How many had we killed? Was anybody keeping count? Did anyone know their names? Even their names had been taken from them, along with their wallets and watches.

Harry had found his policeman father among them, and had never stopped smiling afterwards, saying "Hi!" like a cartoon chipmunk without a tail.

I listened to the roaring in my head as long as I could and then I went back down to the Boys. "Is there any booze left, Charlie?" I asked, and he passed me up a full plastic bottle, and I drank myself into a stupor.

It got dark and cold, and I woke up alone, and I pulled myself up, and walked back into the waiting room, and it was poison inside. It was as poison as the stuff going sour in our stomachs and brains and breath. We sat in twitchy silence, listening to the wind and our own farts. Nobody could be bothered to cook. Royce was not there, and my stomach twisted around itself like a bag full of snakes. Where was he? What would happen when he got back?

"You look sick," said Lou in disgust. "Go outside if you have to throw up."

"I'm fine, Lou," I said, but I could feel a thin slime of sweat on my forehead.

"You make me sick just looking at you," he said.

"Funny. I was just thinking the same about you." Our eyes locked, and there was no disguising it. We hated each other.

It was then that Royce came back in, rubbing his head with a towel. "Well, there are now hot showers," he announced. "Well, tepid showers. You guys can go clean up."

The Boys looked up to him, smiling. The grins were bleary, but they were glad to see him.

"Phew-wee!" he said, and waved his hand in front of his face. "That's some stuff you come up with, Charlie, what do you make it out of, burnt tires?"

Charlie beamed. "Orange peel and grass," he said proudly. I thought it was going to be all right.

Then Lou stood up out of his bed, and flopped naked toward Royce. "You missed all the fun," he said.

"Yeah, I know, I can smell it."

"Now who's being a prig?" said Lou. "Come on, man, I got something nice to show you." He grabbed hold of Royce's forearm, and pulled him toward his own bed. Tom was in it, lying face down, like a ruin, and Lou pulled back the blanket. "Go on, man."

Tom was bleeding. Royce's face and voice went very hard, and he pulled the blanket back up. "He's got an anal fissure, Lou. He needs to be left alone. It could get badly infected."

Lou barked, like a dog, a kind of laugh. "He's going to die anyway!"

Royce moved away from his bed. With Tom in it, he had no place to sit down. Lou followed him. "Come on, Royce. Come on. No more pussyfooting." He tried to put his hand down the front of Royce's shirt. Royce shrugged it away, with sudden annoyance. "Not tonight."

"Not ever?" asked Lou, amused.

"Come on, Royce, give it up man," said Harry. He grabbed Royce playfully, about the waist. "You can't hold out on us forever." He started fumbling with the belt buckle. "Hell, I haven't eaten all day."

"Oh yes you have," said Lou, and chuckled.

"Harry, please let go," said Royce, wearily.

The belt was undone, and Lou started pulling out his shirt. "Let go," warned Royce. "I said let go," and he moved very suddenly. His elbow hit Harry in the mouth, and he yelped.

"Hey, you fucker!"

"You turkey," said Lou.

And all the poison rose up like a wave. Oh, this was going to be fun, pulling off all of Royce's clothes. Gary, and Charlie, they all came, smiling. There was a sound of cloth tearing and suddenly Royce was fighting, fighting very hard, and suddenly the Boys were fighting too, grimly. They pulled him down, and he tried to hit them, and they held his arms, and they launched themselves on him like it was a game of tackle football. I thought, there is a word for this. The word is rape.

"Alice!" I shouted up to the camera. "Alice, stop them! Alice? Burn one of them, stop it!"

Then something slammed into the back of my head, and I fell, the floor scraping the skin of my wrists and slapping me across the cheeks. Then I was pulled over, and Lou was on top of me, forearm across my throat.

"Booby booby booby booby," he said, all blubbery lips, and then he kissed me. Well, he bit my upper lip. He bit it to hold me there; he nearly bit through it with his canine teeth, and my mouth was full of the taste of something metallic: blood.

The sounds the Boys made were conversational, with the odd laugh. Royce squealed like a pig. It always hurts beyond everything the first time. It finally came to me that Royce wasn't gay, at least not in any sense that we would understand. I looked up at the camera, at its blank, glossy eye, and I could feel it thinking: these are men; this is what men do; we are right. We are right to do this to them. For just that moment, I almost agreed.

Lou got up, and Charlie nestled in next to me, fat and naked, white hairs on his chest and ass, and he was still beaming like a baby, and I thought: don't you know what you've done? I tried to sit up, and he went no, no, no and waggled a finger at me. It was Lou's turn to go through him. "Rear Admiral, am I?" asked Lou.

When he was through, Charlie helped me to my feet. "You might as well have a piece," he said, with a friendly chuckle. Lou laughed very loudly, pulling on his T-shirt. The others were shuffling back to their beds in a kind of embarrassment. Royce lay on the floor.

I knelt next to him. My blood splashed onto the floor. "Can you get up, Royce?" I asked him. He didn't answer. "Royce, let's go outside, get you cleaned up." He didn't move. "Royce, are you hurt? Are you hurt badly?" Then I called them all bastards.

"It was just fun, man," said Harry.

"Fun!"

"It started out that way. He shouldn't have hit people."

"He didn't want to do it. Royce, please. Do you want anything? Is anything especially painful?"

"Just his ass," said Lou, and laughed.

"He'll be OK," said Charlie, a shadow of confusion on his face.

"Like fuck he will. That was some way to say thanks for all he's done. Well? Are any of you going to give me a hand?"

Harry did. He helped me to get Royce up. Royce hung between us like a sack.

"It's that fucking poison you make, man," said Harry to Charlie.

"Don't blame me. You were the first, remember."

"I was just playing."

They began to realize what they'd done. He was all angles, like a doll that didn't work anymore.

"What the fuck did you do?" I shouted at them. He didn't seem to be bruised anywhere. "Jesus Christ!" I began to cry because I thought he was dead. "You fucking killed him!"

"Uh-uh, no," said Gary. "We didn't."

"Pisshead!"

Charlie came to help too, and we got him outside, and into the showers, and he slumped down in the dark. I couldn't find a rag, so we just let the lukewarm water trickle down over him. All we did was get him wet on an evening in November.

"It's cold out here, we got to get him back in," said Harry.

Royce rolled himself up onto his knees, and looked at me. "You were there."

"I wasn't part of it. I tried to stop it."

"You were there. You didn't help."

"I couldn't!"

He grunted and stood up. We tried to help him, but he knocked our hands away. He sagged a bit at the knees, but kept on walking, unsteadily. He walked back into the waiting room. Silently, people were tidying up, straightening beds. Royce scooped up his clothes with almost his usual deftness. He went back to his bed, and dropped down onto it, next to Tom, and began to inspect his shirt and trousers for damage.

"The least you could have done!" I said. I don't know what I meant.

Lou was leaning back on his bed. He looked pleased, elbows sticking out from the side of his head. "Look at it this way," he said. "It might do him some good. He shouldn't be so worried about his little problem. He just needs to relax a bit more, try it on for size. The worst thing you can do with a problem like that is hide from it."

If I'd had an axe, I would have killed him. He knew that. He smiled.

Then the lights went out, without warning as always, but two hours early.

There was snow on the ground in the morning, a light dusting of it on the roof and on the ground. There was no patter. Royce did not talk to the cameras. He came out, wearing his jacket; there was a tear in his shirt, under the armpit. He ate his breakfast without looking at anyone, his face closed and still. Hardly anyone spoke. Big Lou walked around with a little half-grin. He was so pleased, he was stretched tight with it. He'd won; he was Boss again. No one used the showers.

Then we went out, and waited for the train.

We could see its brilliant headlight shining like a star on the track.

We could see the layers of wire-mesh gates pulling back for it, like curtains, and close behind it. We began to hear a noise coming from it.

It was a regular, steady drumming against metal, a bit like the sound of marching feet, a sound in unison.

"Yup," said Charlie. "The drugs have worn off."

"It's going to be a bastard," said Gary.

Lou walked calmly toward the cameras. "Alice? What do we do?" No answer. "We can't unload them, Alice. Do we just leave them on the train, or what?" Silence. "Alice. We need to know what you want done."

"Don't call me Alice," said the camera.

"Could you let us back in, then?" asked Lou.

No answer.

The train came grinding into the platform, clattering and banging and smelling of piss. We all stood back from it, well back. Away from us, at the far end of the platform, James stood looking at the silver sky and the snow in the woods, his back to us, his headphones on. We could hear the thin whisper of Mozart from where we stood. Still looking at the woods, James sauntered toward the nearest carriage.

"James!" wailed Charlie. "Don't open the door!"

"Jim! Jimmy! Stop!"

"James! Don't!"

He waved. All he heard was Mozart, and a banging from the train not much louder than usual. With a practiced, muscular motion, he snapped up the bolt, and pulled it back, and began to swing open the door.

It burst free from his grasp, and was slammed back, and a torrent of people poured down out of the carriage, onto him. His headphones were only the first thing to be torn from him. The Stiffs were all green and mottled, like leaves. Oh Christ, oh Jesus. Uniforms. Army.

We turned and ran for the turnstile. "Alice! God-damn it, let us in!" raged Lou. The turnstile buzzed, angrily, and we scrambled through it, caught up in its turning arms, crammed ourselves into its embrace four at a time, and we could hear feet running behind us. I squeezed through with Gary, and heard Charlie behind us cry out. Hands held him, clawed at his forehead. Gary and I pulled him out, and Lou leapt in after us, and pulled the emergency gate shut.

They prowled just the other side of a wire mesh fence, thick necked, as mad as bulls, with asses as broad as our shoulders. "We'll get you fuckers," one of them promised me, looking dead into my eyes. They trotted from door to door of the train, springing them. They began to rock the turnstile back and forth. "Not electric!" one of them called. They began to pull at the wire mesh. We had no weapons.

"Hey! Hey, help!" we shouted. "Alice, Scarlett. Help!"

No answer. As if in contempt, the warm-up lights went on. "We're using gas," said Alice, her voice hard. "Get your masks."

The masks were in the waiting room. We turned and ran, but the cameras didn't give us time. Suddenly there was a gush of something like steam, in the icy morning, out from under the platform. I must have caught a whiff of it. It was like a blow on the head, and my feet crossed in front of each other instead of running I managed to hold my breath, and Royce's face was suddenly in front of me, as still as a stone, and he pushed a mask at me, and pulled on his own, walking toward the gate. I fumbled with mine. Harry, or someone, all inhuman in green, helped me. I saw Royce walking like an angel into white, a blistering white that caught the winter sunlight in a blaze. He walked right up to the fence, and stood in the middle of the poison, and watched.

The gas billowed, and the people billowed too, in waves. They climbed up over each other, in shifting pyramids, to get away, piling up against the fence. Those on top balanced, waving their arms like surfers, and there were sudden flashes of red light through the mist, and bars of rumpled flesh appeared across their eyes. One of them had fine light hair that burst into flame about his head. He wore a crown of fire.

The faces of those on the bottom of the heap were pressed against the fence into diamond shapes, and they twitched and jittered. The whole wave began to twitch and jitter, and shake, against the fence.

It must have been the gas in my head. I was suddenly convinced that it was nerve gas, and that meant that the nerves of the dead people were still working, even though they were dead. Even though they were dead, they would shake and judder against the fence until it fell, and then they would walk toward us, and take us into their arms, and talk to us in whispers, and pull off the masks.

I spun around, and looked at the mound, because I thought the dead inside it would wake. It did seem to swim and move, and I thought that Babylon would crack, and what had been hidden would come marching out. The dead were angry, because they had been forgotten.

Then the mist began to clear, blown. I thought of dandelion seeds that I had blown like magic across the fields when I was a child.

"Hockey games," I said. I thought there had been a game of hockey. The bodies were piled up, in uniforms. They were still. We waited. Harry practiced throwing stones.

"What a mess," said Gary.

There were still wafts of gas around the bottom of the platform. We didn't know how long we would have to wait before it was safe.

Suddenly Lou stepped forward. "Come on, let's start," he said, his voice muffled by the mask. He pulled back the emergency gate. "We've got masks," he said.

None of us moved. We just didn't have the heart.

"We can't leave them there!" Lou shouted. Still none of us moved.

Then Royce sat down on the grass, and pulled off his mask, and took two deep breaths. He looked at the faces in front of him, a few feet away, purple against the mesh.

"Alice," he said. "Why are we doing this?"

No answer.

"It's horrible. It's the worst thing in the world. Horrible for us, horrible for you. That's why what happened last night happened, Alice. Because this is so terrible. You cage people up, you make them do things like this, and something goes, something inside. Something will give with you, too, Alice. You can't keep this up either. Do you have dreams, Alice? Do you have dreams at night about this? While the Wigs are at their parties, making big decisions and debating ideology? I don't believe anyone could look at this and not feel sick."

"You need to hear any more?" Lou asked the cameras, with a swagger.

"I mean. How did it happen?" Royce was crying. "How did we get so far apart? There were problems, sure, but there was love, too. Men and women loved each other. People love each other, so why do we end up doing things like this? Can you give me a reason, Alice?"

"You do realize what he's saying, don't you?" asked Lou. He pulled off his mask, and folded his arms. "Just listen to what is coming out of his closet."

"I am not going to move those bodies, Alice," said Royce. "I can't. I literally cannot move another body. I don't think any of us can. You can kill us all if you want to. But then, you'd have to come and do it yourselves, wouldn't you?"

Lou waited. We all waited. Nothing happened.

"They'll—uh—start to stink if we don't move them," said Gary, and coughed, and looked to Lou.

"If we don't move them," said Harry, and for once he wasn't smiling, "another train can't come in."

"Alice?" said Lou. "Alice?" Louder, outraged. "You hear what is happening here?"

There was a click, and a rumbling sound, a sort of shunting. A gate at the far end of the platform rolled back. Then another, and another, all of them opening at once.

"Go on," said Alice.

We all just stood there. We weren't sure what it meant, we didn't even know that all those gates could open at once.

"Go on. Get out. Hurry. Before one of the Wigs comes."

"You mean it?" Harry asked. We were frightened. We were frightened to leave.

"We'll say you got killed in the riot, that you were gassed or something. They'll never know the difference. Now move!"

"Alice, god-damn it, what are you doing, are you crazy?" Lou was wild.

"No. She ain't crazy. You are." That was Royce. He stood up. "Well you heard her, haul some ass. Charlie, Harry, you go and get all the food there is left in the canteen. The rest of you, go get all the blankets and clothes, big coats that haven't been shipped back. And Harry, fill some jugs with water."

Lou didn't say anything. He pulled out a kitchen knife and he ran toward Royce. Royce just stood there. I don't think he would have done anything. I think he was tired, tired of the whole thing. I mean he was tired of death. Lou came for him.

The Grils burned him. They burned Lou. He fell in a heap at Royce's feet, his long, strong arms all twisted. "Aw hell," said Royce, sad and angry. "Aw hell."

And a voice came cutting into my head, clear and blaring. I was crazy. The voice said, "This is radio station KERB broadcasting live from the First Baptist Church of Christ the Redeemer with the Reverend Thomas Wallace Robertson and the Inglewood Youth Choir, singing O Happy Day."

And I heard it. I heard the music. I just walked out onto the platform, reeling with the sound, the mass of voices inside my head, and I didn't need any blankets. O Happy Day! When Jesus wash! And Los Angeles might be gone, and Detroit and Miami, a lot of things might be gone, but that Sunday night music was still kicking shit, and if there wasn't a God, there was always other people, and they surprised you. Maybe I'd been fooled by history too. I said goodbye to the cameras as I passed them. Goodbye Alice. Goodbye Hortensia. See ya, Scarlet. Butch, I'm sorry about the name.

They were making funny noises. The cameras were weeping.

I walked on toward the open gate.

For America

PERVERT

by Charles Coleman Finlay

Charles Coleman Finlay is the author of the novels *The Prodigal Troll, The Patriot Witch, A Spell for the Revolution,* and *The Demon Redcoat.* Finlay's short fiction—most of which appears in his collection, *Wild Things*—has been published in several magazines, such as *The Magazine of Fantasy & Science Fiction, Strange Horizons,* and *Black Gate,* and in anthologies, including *The Best of All Flesh* and my own *By Blood We Live, The Way of the Wizard,* and *The Living Dead 2.* He has twice been a finalist for the Hugo and Nebula awards, and has also been nominated for the Campbell Award for Best New Writer, the Sidewise Award, and the Theodore Sturgeon Award.

Sexuality is more than just bodily urges; it's more than who you ask on a date. Sexuality permeates almost every aspect of the lives we lead, and our cultural experiences will influence our sexual choices. We dream of love at first sight, but find that society not only influences who we will see, but the kind of love we are allowed to fall into.

This next tale is the story of a man torn between the passion within him and the strictures of a society very different from our own. In his world, religion and biology have colluded to make people with his sexual urges not only uncommon, but unacceptable. Duty and temptation catch him in a Gordian knot even the most hardened dominatrix would find too binding.

This story was a finalist in the 2005 Gaylactic Spectrum Awards for its thoughtful discussion of sexuality and how society regulates our sex lives. Here is all the passion of sex, the melancholy of unexpressed love—and the bitterness of a life lived in perversion.

T here are two kinds of people in the world, homosexuals and hydrosexuals. And then there are perverts like me.

So far as I know, there is not a word, not even a bit of slang, to describe my particular depravity. But then I have never spoken of it to anyone, nor written of it before now, and we do not invent words for the things we dare not speak or write.

Everyone knows I am different, though. They can tell.

Jamin and Zel stroll through the corridor of the apartment building where we all live. I can tell it's them coming because I leave my door cracked open to show everyone I have nothing to hide. Zel's distant voice caroms off the walls, fluctuating in pitch with the peaks and rhythms of the stories he tells; Jamin's subdued, distinctive laugh barks out at regular intervals. For thirty or forty seconds before they arrive, I hear their approach, and dread it. They are my best friends.

I sit in the exact center of the cerulean blue sofa, arms resting on its bell-shaped back, palms damp against the silky fabric. The voice of Noh Sis, last year's most popular singer, warbles from the stereo speakers, making a dirge of joy amid the interweaving of sitar and clarinets. Closing my eyes, I count the notes and half-notes by measure, now the sorrowful tone in the end-rhyme of *love*, Zel's exclamation, a series of mournful sitar chords, Jamin's laugh.

And the tap at the door.

I lift my head as if surprised to see them, smile as if happy. "Hey!"

Zel throws wide his arms in an extravagant gesture of greeting, and says with dead seriousness, "Arise! Arise like the evening star and brighten the way into night for us!"

Jamin grins, nods at me. "Hello."

They are both tall, and handsome, and completely at ease in themselves. Jamin is balding, so he shaves his head; he has quiet, wolfish features, and always wears plain, businesslike clothes, immaculately tailored and pressed. Zel is the shaggy, adorable puppy, all awkward limbs and endless energy.

I wipe my hands on my thighs, arise, and embrace them in turn with only a dry quick kiss on the cheek. "Where are you going?"

"*We,*" Zel exclaims, "we, for surely you are joining us—we won't have a speck of fun without you!"

Jamin grins—he always grins—and says, "*Heart Nouveau.*"

Heart Nouveau is our club. We've been hanging out there since it opened, just around the time that we were finishing school. All our friends go there. It's the kind of place so packed and dark you can't see any decor beyond the dance floor.

"Not tonight," I answer. "Work exhausted me today."

My work itself is not hard, but while I'm working my soul dances like a dervish until I think I will collapse.

Zel immediately begins pleading, making dance gyrations, beckoning me to join, but Jamin, with his hands folded at his waist in front of him, says quietly, "Thinking about marrying this weekend, are you?"

"Ah—"

Zel's eyes widen at this revelation and he ceases the call to fun. The two of them are a happy couple. They know that I am different from them and do their best to fit me into their view of the world, and the way it works.

"—been thinking about it," I admit.

"Pshaw! Don't think about it, just do it!" says Zel as Jamin backs out the doorway, whispering to me, "I'll call you tomorrow."

Their voices resume their previous pattern as they continue their journey down the corridor toward the stairs. Pushing the door closed, I let my face lean against it, eyes shut for a moment, while I twist the lock. Then I go and fall onto the sofa, lifting my head only long enough to replay the previous song at a higher volume. The chorus opens the song: "I want to set myself on fire and plunge into the oceans of your love."

My face presses against the water blue color of the pillows, trying to drown in them. "That's it—I'm only nervous about marrying this weekend," I lie aloud to myself.

It's natural to be nervous about it the first time. I'll just do it, like Zel says, and then everything will be better.

You would think, as much as I practice lying to myself, I'd be better at it by now.

In the morning, I swath myself in my work robes—cheery layers of nectarine and lemon fabric, sherbet smooth. Covering my head and face, I walk down to the street and catch the bus into the city. The road bridges a green river of trees and grass that divides one quarter of the city from another. Through the bus's window I watch the women emerging from their apartment blocks and little homes.

When the bus reaches the corner, they climb onboard, taking seats on their side and evening out the ride so it doesn't feel so much like we'll tip over. We rattle along past road construction, the men working behind screens so their presence out of robes won't disturb weaker minds. The sun already pelts down mercilessly and they will have to leave off working soon.

We arrive at the Children's Center, a long concrete brick of a building with windows shielded from the sun by an open grid of deep squares made of the same material. The morning light turns it into a chessboard of glaring white and dark shadow. I don't even work with the children, who are on the lower floors and the sheltered playground of the courtyard, but toil away with records on the upper floors. Unlike Jamin or Zel, the job permits me to work alongside women, but only because I completed my theological studies and am a candidate for the priesthood. My superiors do not know of the taint on my soul. Do not know yet, I should say, for if they discover it I will never be ordained or promoted to an position in the lower floors.

Today I am veryifying and recording the DNA strands of a recent set of births. My cubicle sits closer to the outer windows (and their view only of the rigid cement grid) than the inner, but is blocked from the light of either. Nevertheless, I jump immediately when the slightest shadow passes by. Looking up I see her—I see Ali.

Ah, Ali! Ali, my all, my everything, the eye of the hurricane that is my heart! Ali, that ails me! Ali, who alone can heal me! Ali, Ai!

This is silliness, of course; yet it is how I feel.

She stops and stares at the floor.

"What are you looking for?" I ask.

She turns her head this way and that. "The button I accidentally stepped on that gave you that electric shock."

Ali is wearing coffee colored robes, cream and roasted bean, the same as many of the other women in her department, and as she is a perfectly average height, with her head and almost all her face covered, I am still puzzling out how I always recognize at once it's her, whether there's something specific in her posture or gestures or presence that makes me know her instantly.

So I say, "Huh?"

And her head lifts up so that her eyes turn toward me, glinting with amusement. I would recognize those stormy, sea-grey eyes anywhere. "You are mocking me!"

She shakes her head. "It's very difficult not to."

I blush, the heat rising through my face to my forehead.

She chuckles, and then walks to another cubicle several spaces over where she speaks to one of our sister workers about a particular child whose progress they are following.

How can I describe her effect on me? In a single second, I suffer pangs and longings which have no name, an overwhelming need to peel away the layers of her robes like shells off a bean and root through her flesh until I find the hard nut, the seed core, of my perverse, unnatural desire.

When I was studying theogenetics in preparation for the priesthood we were taught that everything in the world was black and white, right or wrong, and I learned to give all the answers I was expected to provide.

All I have ever seen of Ali are her eyes. The white of her eyes and the black pupil are just like everyone else's. But that cloudy, wave-tossed grey is wholly hers!

And all my world is grey now too, as if something swirling deep within me since the moment of my conception has finally taken shape, the way clouds form when wind swirls in a clear sky.

The things I know are wrong feel right deep within my heart, and every right thing I do feels wrong.

Jamin calls me at work later that day, just as he had promised he would, his voice warm and resonant as always.

"I hope you don't mind," he says, "but I've arranged for you to join me and a friend for dinner tonight."

"Sounds great—will Zel be joining us?"

"No. Just us."

Jamin is looking out for me, the way he has always tried to. He is a very good friend. I am filled with trepidation. "Well," I say. "I might be working late."

"That's fine. Pick you up in a taxi at quitting time?"

"Sure," I say and disconnect.

I look up from my desk but Ali is nowhere to be seen in the breakwater of cubicle ways. Sometimes I may see her no more than once in a day, though it feels like she is always with me since I cannot stop thinking of her.

For the rest of the day I cannot concentrate on genetic sequences at all and my work is useless.

When the taxi crosses into the men's quarter, Jamin and I remove our veils although the driver leaves his own. Jamin relaxes instantly, more happily himself, making small talk about work. I smile too, but inside I am tense.

We're dropped off in a neighborhood where fruit trees shade the narrow streets. The houses are neat and tidy and old, the kind owned by government officials and couples who both have excellent jobs. Jamin leads me to a door by an elaborate garden that appears to be both lovingly created and recently neglected.

The man who answers is not quite twice our age, perhaps a little younger. His beard looks new, as though his chin has gone untended for about as long as the garden outside. He wears a comfortable, tailored suit.

Jamin embraces him, saying, "Hello, Hodge. This is the friend I was telling you about—"

Somehow I cheerfully complete the introductions. Jamin and I sit at a counter in the kitchen while Hodge finishes cooking the dinner. The room smells of garlic and oil. Jamin and Hodge discuss work—they are both employed in law—and I avoid nearly all the personal questions directed at me. The songs of Noh Sis stream from the speakers to fill most of the awkward silences.

We are seated around Hodge's elegant antique table, having finished a delightful chick pea soup and a satisfying pepper salad. A platter of mouth-watering spinach-feta pastries rests between us. As I am helping myself to a second serving, and laughing heartily at an anecdote that Hodge is telling about the prosecution of a man whose pet dog kept straying into the women's quarter, Jamin rises and wipes his mouth with his napkin.

"Please forgive me," he says. "I didn't realize how late it has gotten and I promised to meet Zel this evening."

"But we've scarecely begun," Hodge says, evincing real dismay.

And all I can do is think: Jamin, you beast!

But Jamin insists, and I stand to go with him, but both men persaude me to stay by making promises of transportation. Then Hodge bustles around putting together a plate of food for Jamin to take with him, growing particularly distressed because his cake hasn't cooled sufficiently and falls apart when cuts a slice to go. The whole time Jamin smiles at me and refuses to meet my eyes. Finally he's gone, and Hodge and I sit back to our meal. Sometime during this the music has fallen silent and Hodge is too distracted to reset it.

"How long have you known Jamin?" he says after a sip of wine.

"All my life," I say. "We grew up in the same Children's Center, and then attended the same."

"He's well-meaning, but what a beastly thing to do."

I think he means it as a joke, but I'm not sure so I stare at my plate and concentrate on eating, making extravagant praise of the food between the clinks of silverware on porcelain.

"So," Hodge says after another drink of wine. "You're the marrying kind?"

"Yes." My heart trips and stumbles. "Yes, I am."

"It won't be bad. Will this coming ceremony be your first time?"

"Yes. I mean, I haven't decided yet."

"You'll be nervous your first time. It won't be bad."

I choke out laughter. "Aren't you supposed to tell me how good it will be?"

He winces. Folding his napkin, he leans his elbows on the table and looks directly at me. "Look, Jamin thinks that we're both the same type. I just lost my partner—"

"Oh, I'm sorry," I say.

He holds up his hand. "No, it's all right. We'd been together for ten years or so, but he'd been unhappy for a very long time. I'm glad he ran off."

"Where he'd go to?" I ask, desperate to change the subject.

Hodge shook his head. "Look, that's not important. I'm happy by myself right now. I hope you understand."

He didn't sound happy at all. "Of course! I mean I—"

"I'm not like you," he said in a low whisper, and then drank the rest of his wine. "Oh! The story about the man with the dog, did I ever finish that?"

"No." I had forgotten it already.

"The last time they caught him, they stoned him to death and set his body on fire. That kind of perversion can't be tolerated, you know. We aren't animals, with animal passions."

"I know that." My voice is strained because I am scared.

"Well, then. Good." He rises abruptly. "I'll call you a taxi." He fumbles at the counter, frowning. "The cake is a disappointment, but I'll send some with you."

When the taxi arrives and I step off the stoop into darkness, I hear him say, "Good luck with the marrying. It's over quickly."

He reminds me of a piece of topiary, a plant forced by wires and pruning into a facsimile of something else, so twisted over time that he no longer resembles himself. I can feel myself being twisted, misshapen more each day. But I'll resist it.

The taxi door slams and whisks me away.

I don't see Ali at work the next day or the following morning. At lunch, I am standing by the inner windows overlooking the courtyard below while the children. The weave an endless pattern of joy amid the trees and joys, untroubled by impossible choices. Pressed to the window, I am only slightly aware of someone next to me. The lobby is busy, many people rushing by. So several minutes pass before I look up and realize that it is Ali beside me.

She taps her foot on the tiles. "Rubber floor. Very smart. They aren't able to zap you here."

"I'm sorry," I blurt out, sorry that I haven't noticed her, sorry that I hadn't talked to her earlier.

Ali lowers her long eyelashes and looks away. "Well, if you want to be zapped, you could always go back to your desk."

"Wait!"

She pauses in midstep. "I'm waiting."

And because I don't know what else to say, because there is only one thing besides her on my mind, I ask, "Will you be marrying this weekend?"

"That's a very improper thing for you to ask," she says and walks quickly away to the other side of the lobby where she stands by a tub of polished stones and bubbling water, watching the children below.

I want to run after her, take her by the elbow and make her understand. I want her to feel for me the way I feel toward her. I want her to peel off her gloves and sink her bare hands into my flesh, stripping it away to the bone, until she reaches my heart and can soothe away the ache I feel for her.

Instead, I also turn and look out the window again. From this height, I can't tell if the children below are boys or girls.

Heart Nouveau is even more crowded than normal tonight because of the Bachelors Party. Jamin and Zel have brought me here to celebrate, just as all the other normal men have brought their friends who will be marrying tomorrow. Smoke swirls across the bar and dance floor, eddying with the currents of moving people and the crashing waves of music. Zel has taken off his shirt and is dancing half-naked under the strobe lights with the others in an orgy of arms and hands. I'm standing off to one side of the dance floor beside Jamin, who doesn't dance, but nevertheless gazes on Zel adoringly.

Our scripture says: "And in his own image God made them, man and woman; and bade them be fruitful and multiply; and set them apart from the beasts and gave them dominion over the beasts."

And also: "It is good for a man never to touch a woman, nor a woman touch a man, lest they be tempted to behave as the beasts of the field do in their passions."

I have never even seen beasts in the field. Theology classes glossed over that, only teaching us that before God gave people the wisdom of science we behaved as they did. With peace and prosperity and time, we have become a very secular people, falling into relationships, doing our work, and living our lives with questions.

Zel grabs me by the hand, pulling me onto the dance floor where the lights are flashing, music pumping, and ecstatic faces surround me. He only wants me to be happy and he only knows what makes him happy, and so he tries to bring me to that too. I resist him—I resist everything these days—and pull away.

"Smile," he shouts at me above the din. "Have some fun!"

"I'm having fun!" I shout in reply.

"Are you excited by marrying tomorrow?" I mumble my answer to him, but he doesn't hear me and leans forward, sweat dripping from his forehead on my shoulder, shouting "What?"

"I said, 'Scripture says it's better to marry than to burn!'"

He laughs as if this is the wittiest thing in the world, and spins around, arms and fists pumping in beat with the music.

But I am burning already. The thought of Ali is a fire in my mind and a searing pain in my flesh, an unquenchable flame, even though I know all my feelings for her are wrong. Still, I will go do my duty tomorrow, and marry rather than burn.

The next morning, I arise with the other bachelors before dawn. Many have hangovers, and some are too sick to marry this time. Their absences are noted by the priest's assistant in his white jacket as we board the bus. Those who have not made it are roundly mocked by even the sickest of those aboard. The other men are hugging, wishing each other well, but I hold myself apart. There are only a dozen of us, so it is easy to take a seat away from the others.

My stomach is queasy as we head for the Temple of the Waters, and not just from last night's drinking. Our route takes us along the edge of the women's quarter and none of us are wearing veils. I slouch in my seat. Several of the men pull their robes up over their noses; others put their hands on their heads, or pretend to rub their faces. The priest's assistant, who misses nothing, points this out to them and they all laugh. But I can only think that perhaps Ali is sitting in another bus without her veil on either; and I wonder if her mouth is as round and full as her eyes, if the arch of her lips matches that of her brow, if the curve of her neck is as graceful as the bridge of her nose.

Would I even recognize her? I do not know.

The Temple of the Waters sits at the center of the Government Quarter, across from the Palace of Congress. It is an oasis of green and blue marble in a desert and steel and concrete and sandstone. The giant telescreens that surround it show images of the ocean, the surge of waves in calm weather, but they remind me of the storm-tossed gray of Ali's eyes and I breathe faster.

As we're climbing off the bus, the priest's assistant steps in front of me and grips me by the shoulder. Instantly, I know that he saw how I stayed apart, he knows that I am different from the others.

But he only says, "Why don't you smile? This is going to be a good thing—think of the pride you'll feel!"

I force myself to smile and pull away from him to follow the others. We strip in the anteroom. A few of the men are as young as I am, but they range in age up to a solemn gray-haired old man who goes about his preparations with all the grim seriousness of a surgeon in a touchy operation. The room is as hot as a sauna and several men grow visibly excited. One man, a boy almost, younger than me, can't help himself and spills his seed there on the floor. The others chastise him until he starts to cry, but the priest enters through a second door and all falls silent.

Noticing the mess, he says "Don't worry, I'm sure there's more where that came from."

Everyone laughs and the boy rubs his tears from his cheeks, and grins, and everyone is at ease again; everyone but me.

The priest asks how many of us have married before, and most of the men raise their hands.

"Yours is a sacred trust," the priest tells us. "There are two kinds of people in the world, those to whom society is given, and those who have the sacred duty to give to society, to perpetuate it. You have been called to that latter. It is a holy trust, a gift from our heavenly father, who spilled his seed in the primal ocean and brought forth all the manner of life."

This is the standard speech, words, except for the calling, that we've heard all our lives. It is meant to be calming, we were taught, but I feel a rising surge of panic.

"Earlier this morning," the priest continues, "the women entrusted with their half of this sacred duty came down from their quarter. They entered the main chamber of the temple a short while ago, and even now immerse themselves in the pool. In just a moment it will be your turn to enter. Look to the older men who have been here before and do what comes naturally to you."

Some nervous laughter follows this.

The priest looks at the boy who spilled himself, who is already excited again, and says "Hold on to that a little longer, friend."

Now a madness is upon me; this fire burning within me is hell itself. I look at the doors, seeking a way to extinguish the flame of my desire.

The priest checks the door. "Hurry now, it is time," he says, and the men press forward, somehow scooping me up so that I, the most reluctant of them, am at the head of the phalanx.

The doors swing open.

One group of acolytes stand there with towels as we enter, while a second set waits to collect the results of our labor. A door identical to ours, but opposite, clicks shut as the last of the women leave. A womb-shaped pool of bodywarm water fills the center of the circular room. The women have ejaculated their eggs into it already—however they do that, I do not know. But they float in a few tiny gellatinous clumps on the surface.

"Hurry now," the priest in the white coat says. "Timing is important."

An acolyte reaches out his white gloved hand to help me down the steps and into the pool. The other bachelors crowd the water's edge.

There are two kinds of people in the world: homosexuals and hydrosexuals. But I am neither.

I lunge across the room, dodging the outstretched hands and shocked eyes of the panicked acolytes. My hand falls on the latch of the door into the women's anteroom. I will run through there searching for Ali, and if I don't find her, out into the streets, and through the women's quarter until I do. Ai! Ali, my all, my everything, the eye of the only hurricane whose deluge can drown the unnamed flame of sin that burns within me.

FROM HOMOGENOUS
TO HONEY

by Neil Gaiman & Bryan Talbot

Neil Gaiman's most recent novel, the international bestseller *The Graveyard Book,* won the prestigious Newbery Medal, given to great works of children's literature. Other novels include *American Gods, Coraline, Neverwhere,* and *Anansi Boys,* among many others. In addition to his novel-writing, Gaiman is also the writer of the popular *Sandman* comic book series. Most of Gaiman's short work has been collected in the volumes *Smoke and Mirrors, Fragile Things,* and *M is for Magic.* His latest book is a hardcover edition of his poem, *Instructions,* illustrated by Charles Vess.

Bryan Talbot is a comics writer and artist. He is the creator of the comic *The Adventures of Luther Arkwright,* and he's worked as an artist on books such as *Hellblazer, Sandman, Fables,* and *Batman.* Other writing credits include the graphic novels *Alice in Sunderland* and *Grandville.*

Our next piece isn't just words on a page—it's a sequential art story, the short fiction love child of a comic strip and a graphic novel. It originally appeared in 1988, in the comic anthology *A.A.R.G.H.,* edited by Alan Moore, and was recently reprinted in the GLBT anthology, *The Future is Queer* edited by Richard Labonte and Lawrence Schimel. The story is a response to a piece British legislation that had a decidedly anti-homosexual flavor.

This story uses scathing sarcasm to present a future without homosexual influences. No art, no plays, no books, no cultural referents to anything gay, lesbian, transsexual or remotely queer. For the story's masked narrator, it's a perfect world. But the images behind him suggest something a little darker.

The narrator of this piece speaks through a mobile white mask with very abstracted features, strikingly reminiscent of a Guy Fawkes mask. It's interesting to note that at the time, *V for Vendetta,* a 1980s British comics series featuring a character who wears a Guy Fawkes mask (and written by Alan Moore, the first editor of this piece) was very popular.

Different motivations, different details—but Moore's character, Gaiman's narrator, and Guy Fawkes were all men perfectly willing to destroy the world for their own black purposes.

FROm Homogenous TO Honey

SCRIPT- NEIL GAIMAN
PENCILS- BRYAN TALBOT
INKS- MARK BUCKINGHAM
LETTERS- STEVE CRADDOCK

GOOD EVENING AND WELCOME TO OUR NEW UNIVERSE.

AS YOU CAN TELL, WE'VE MADE A NUMBER OF IM-PROVEMENTS ON THE OLD ONE.

TODAY WE'RE GOING TO LOOK AT HOW OUR PRESENT UTOPIA WAS ACHIEVED.

LIGHTS, PLEASE!

THE REMOVAL OF A CONCEPT FROM SOCIETY IS ALWAYS FRAUGHT WITH POTENTIAL PROBLEMS.

WHERE DO WE START?

FIRST SLIDE, PLEASE.

I THINK WE CAN ALL SEE THE PROBLEMS HERE, HMM?

NOT VERY UTOPIAN, IS IT?

THE OBVIOUS PLACE TO START WAS WITH BOOKS, REPOSITORIES OF IDEAS.

DANGEROUS.

EXAMINE, PLEASE, A BOOK WHICH PRESENTS A POSITIVE IMAGE OF INVERSION.

A BOY'S OWN STORY
EDMUND WHITE

THAT WAS EASY.

WHAT THEN TO DO ABOUT SOME-THING THAT CONTAINS A FAIRLY SYMPATHETIC CATAMITE?

VEDDY FLAT, NORFOLK.

UNGH!

IT WAS A START. BUT THEN AGAIN, PEOPLE KNEW THE AUTHORS HAD EXISTED.

SO WE STARTED TO TAKE THEM OUT.

WHICH GAVE US A WHOLE NEW PERSPECTIVE ON HISTORY.

IT'S FULL OF THEM!

ALL OF THEM RIPE FOR REMOVAL ...

OUR TIME TEAMS ADJUSTED SUPERFLUOUS HISTORICAL FIGURES. SHAKESPEARE, RICHARD THE FIRST ...

THEN WE HIT SOME REAL SNAGS, TAKE THE GREEK AND SPARTAN CULTURES--

BOTH OF THEM FOUNDED ON IT. LACED WITH IT, SWIMMING IN IT.

AND PEOPLE THOUGHT OF THE GREEKS AS THE CRADLE OF CIVILISATION!

EUREKA!

BILLENNIUM

by J. G. Ballard

J.G. Ballard is best known for his novels *Crash* and *Empire of the Sun,* both of which were made into major motion pictures. He was also the author of sixteen other novels, including *The Drowned World, The Burning World, The Crystal World, Super-Cannes, Millennium People,* and *Kingdom Come.* Ballard was also the author of more than 100 short stories, all of which are collected in the mammoth collection *The Complete Stories of J. G. Ballard.* He died in 2009.

In the 1960s, the National Institute of Mental Health funded Dr. John B. Calhoun's famous mouse research. He built a Mouse Wonderland with all the food, water and nesting materials a mouse community could ever need. The little creatures rejoiced in their new, predator-free environment. They lived good lives and had many babies.

Too many babies.

Without any kind of predation or undernourishment, the mice soon filled their wonderland—then over-filled the space. Problems flared, with mother mice failing their maternal duties and male mice sinking into passivity. At a certain point, society crashed. No new mice were born. And the mouse wonderland went from overcrowded to empty. The mice simply went extinct.

There are scientists who believe that unless we change our behavior, humans might face a similar future. They predict a world too crowded for sane living.

Perhaps those scientists have peeked into the world of our next story.

A ll day long, and often into the early hours of the morning, the tramp of feet sounded up and down the stairs outside Ward's cubicle. Built into a narrow alcove in a bend of the staircase between the fourth and fifth floors, its plywood walls flexed and creaked with every footstep like the timbers of a rotting windmill. Over a hundred people lived in the top three floors of the old rooming house, and sometimes Ward would lie awake on his narrow bunk until

2 or 3 a.m., mechanically counting the last residents returning from the all-night movies in the stadium half a mile away. Through the window he could hear giant fragments of the amplified dialogue booming among the rooftops. The stadium was never empty. During the day the huge four-sided screen was raised on its davit and athletics meetings or football matches ran continuously. For the people in the houses abutting the stadium the noise must have been unbearable.

Ward, at least, had a certain degree of privacy. Two months earlier, before he came to live on the staircase, he had shared a room with seven others on the ground floor of a house in 755th Street, and the ceaseless press of people jostling past the window had reduced him to a state of exhaustion. The street was always full, an endless clamour of voices and shuffling feet. By 6.30, when he woke, hurrying to take his place in the bathroom queue, the crowds already jammed it from sidewalk to sidewalk, the din punctuated every half minute by the roar of the elevated trains running over the shops on the opposite side of the road. As soon as he saw the advertisement describing the staircase cubicle he had left (like everyone else, he spent most of his spare time scanning the classifieds in the newspapers, moving his lodgings an average of once every two months) despite the higher rental. A cubicle on a staircase would almost certainly be on its own.

However, this had its drawbacks. Most evenings his friends from the library would call in, eager to rest their elbows after the bruising crush of the public reading room. The cubicle was slightly more than four and a half square metres in floor area, half a square metre over the statutory maximum for a single person, the carpenters having taken advantage, illegally, of a recess beside a nearby chimney breast. Consequently Ward had been able to fit a small straight-backed chair into the interval between the bed and the door, so that only one person at a time needed to sit on the bed—in most single cubicles host and guest had to sit side by side on the bed, conversing over their shoulders and changing places periodically to avoid neck-strain.

"You were lucky to find this place," Rossiter, the most regular visitor, never tired of telling him. He reclined back on the bed, gesturing at the cubicle. "It's enormous, the perspectives really zoom. I'd be surprised if you haven't got at least five metres here, perhaps six."

Ward shook his head categorically. Rossiter was his closest friend, but the quest for living space had forged powerful reflexes. "Just over four and a half, I've measured it carefully. There's no doubt about it."

Rossiter lifted one eyebrow. "I'm amazed. It must be the ceiling then."

Manipulating the ceiling was a favourite trick of unscrupulous landlords—most assessments of area were made upon the ceiling, out of convenience, and by tilting back the plywood partitions the rated area of a cubicle could be either increased, for the benefit of a prospective tenant (many married couples were thus bamboozled into taking a single cubicle), or decreased temporarily on the visits of the housing inspectors. Ceilings were criss-crossed with pencil marks staking out the rival claims of tenants on opposite sides of a party wall. Someone timid of his rights could be literally squeezed out of existence—in fact, the advertisement "quiet clientele" was usually a tacit invitation to this sort of piracy.

"The wall does tilt a little," Ward admitted. "Actually, it's about four degrees out—I used a plumb-line. But there's still plenty of room on the stairs for people to get by."

Rossiter grinned. "Of course, John. I'm just envious, that's all. My room is driving me crazy." Like everyone, he used the term "room" to describe his tiny cubicle, a hangover from the days fifty years earlier when people had indeed lived one to a room, sometimes, unbelievably, one to an apartment or house. The microfilms in the architecture catalogues at the library showed scenes of museums, concert halls and other public buildings in what appeared to be everyday settings, often virtually empty, two or three people wandering down an enormous gallery or staircase. Traffic moved freely along the centre of streets, and in the quieter districts sections of sidewalk would be deserted for fifty yards or more.

Now, of course, the older buildings had been torn down and replaced by housing batteries, or converted into apartment blocks. The great banqueting room in the former City Hall had been split horizontally into four decks, each of these cut up into hundreds of cubicles.

As for the streets, traffic had long since ceased to move about them. Apart from a few hours before dawn when only the sidewalks were crowded, every thoroughfare was always packed with a shuffling mob of pedestrians, perforce ignoring the countless "Keep Left" signs suspended over their heads, wrestling past each other on their way to home and office, their clothes dusty and shapeless. Often "locks" would occur when a huge crowd at a street junction became immovably jammed. Sometimes these locks would last for days. Two years earlier Ward had been caught in one outside the stadium, for over forty-eight hours was trapped in a gigantic pedestrian jam containing over 20,000 people, fed by the crowds leaving the stadium on one side and those approaching it on the other. An entire square mile of the local neighbourhood had been paralysed, and he vividly remembered the nightmare of swaying helplessly on his feet as the jam shifted and heaved, terrified of losing his balance and being trampled underfoot. When the police had finally sealed off the stadium and dispersed the jam he had gone back to his cubicle and slept for a week, his body blue with bruises.

"I hear they may reduce the allocation to three and a half metres," Rossiter remarked.

Ward paused to allow a party of tenants from the sixth floor to pass down the staircase, holding the door to prevent it jumping off its latch. "So they're always saying," he commented. "I can remember that rumour ten years ago."

"It's no rumour," Rossiter warned him. "It may well be necessary soon. Thirty million people are packed into this city now, a million increase in just one year. There's been some pretty serious talk at the Housing Department."

Ward shook his head. "A drastic revaluation like that is almost impossible to carry out. Every single partition would have to be dismantled and nailed up again, the administrative job alone is so vast it's difficult to visualize. Millions of cubicles to be redesigned and certified, licences to be issued, plus the complete resettlement of every tenant. Most of the buildings put up since the last revaluation are designed around a four-metre modulus—you can't simply take half a metre off the end of each cubicle and then say that makes so many new cubicles. They may be only six inches wide." He laughed. "Besides, how can you live in just three and a half metres?"

Rossiter smiled. "That's the ultimate argument, isn't it? They used it twenty-five years ago at the last revaluation, when the minimum was cut from five to four. It couldn't be done they all said, no one could stand living in only four square metres, it was enough room for a bed and suitcase, but you couldn't open the door to get in." Rossiter chuckled softly. "They were all wrong. It was merely decided that from then on all doors would open outwards. Four square metres was here to stay."

Ward looked at his watch. It was 7:30. "Time to eat. Let's see if we can get into the food-bar across the road."

Grumbling at the prospect, Rossiter pulled himself off the bed. They left the cubicle and made their way down the staircase. This was crammed with luggage and packing cases so that only a narrow interval remained around the banister. On the floors below the congestion was worse. Corridors were wide enough to be chopped up into single cubicles, and the air was stale and dead, cardboard walls hung with damp laundry and makeshift larders. Each of the five rooms on the floors contained a dozen tenants, their voices reverberating through the partitions.

People were sitting on the steps above the second floor, using the staircase as an informal lounge, although this was against the fire regulations, women talking to the men queueing in their shirtsleeves outside the washroom, children diving around them. By the time they reached the entrance Ward and Rossiter were having to force their way through the tenants packed together on every landing, loitering around the notice boards or pushing in from the street below.

Taking a breath at the top of the steps, Ward pointed to the food-bar on the other side of the road. It was only thirty yards away, but the throng moving down the street swept past like a river at full tide, crossing them from right to left. The first picture show at the stadium started at 9 o'clock, and people were setting off already to make sure of getting in.

"Can't we go somewhere else?" Rossiter asked, screwing his face up at the prospect of the food-bar. Not only was it packed and take them half an hour to be served, but the food was flat and unappetizing. The journey from the library four blocks away had given him an appetite.

Ward shrugged. "There's a place on the corner, but I doubt if we can make it." This was two hundred yards upstream; they would be fighting the crowd all the way.

"Maybe you're right." Rossiter put his hand on Ward's shoulder. "You know, John, your trouble is that you never go anywhere, you're too disengaged, you just don't realize how bad everything is getting."

Ward nodded. Rossiter was right. In the morning, when he set off for the library, the pedestrian traffic was moving with him towards the down-town offices; in the evening, when he came back, it was flowing in the opposite direction. By and large he never altered his routine. Brought up from the age of ten in a municipal hostel, he had gradually lost touch with his father and mother, who lived on the east side of the city and had been unable, or unwilling, to make the journey to see him. Having surrendered his initiative to the dynamics of the city he was reluctant to try to win it back merely for a better cup of coffee. Fortunately his job at the library brought him into contact with a wide range of young people of similar interests. Sooner or later he would marry, find a double cubicle near the library and settle down. If they had enough children (three was the required minimum) they might even one day own a small room of their own.

They stepped out into the pedestrian stream, carried along by it for ten or twenty yards, then quickened their pace and sidestepped through the crowd, slowly tacking across to the other side of the road. There they found the shelter of the shop-fronts, slowly worked their way back to the food-bar, shoulders braced against the countless minor collisions.

"What are the latest population estimates?" Ward asked as they circled a cigarette kiosk, stepping forward whenever a gap presented itself.

Rossiter smiled. "Sorry, John, I'd like to tell you but you might start a stampede. Besides, you wouldn't believe me."

Rossiter worked in the Insurance Department at the City Hall, had informal access to the census statistics. For the last ten years these had been classified information, partly because they were felt to be inaccurate, but chiefly because it was feared they might set off a mass attack of claustrophobia. Minor outbreaks had taken place already, and the official line was that world population had reached a plateau, levelling off at 20,000 million. No one believed this for a moment, and Ward assumed that the 3 per cent annual increase maintained since the 1960s was continuing.

How long it could continue was impossible to estimate. Despite the gloomiest prophecies of the Neo-Malthusians, world agriculture had managed to keep pace with the population growth, although intensive cultivation meant that 95 per cent of the population was permanently trapped in vast urban conurbations. The outward growth of cities had at last been checked; in fact, all over the world former suburban areas were being reclaimed for agriculture and population additions were confined within the existing urban ghettos. The countryside, as such, no longer existed. Every single square foot of ground sprouted a crop of one type or other. The one-time fields and meadows of the world were now, in effect, factory floors, as highly mechanized and closed to the public as any industrial area. Economic and ideological rivalries had long since faded before one over-riding quest—the internal colonization of the city.

Reaching the food-bar, they pushed themselves into the entrance and joined the scrum of customers pressing six deep against the counter.

"What is really wrong with the population problem," Ward confided to Rossiter, "is that no one has ever tried to tackle it. Fifty years ago short-sighted nationalism and industrial expansion put a premium on a rising population curve, and even now the hidden incentive is to have a large family so that you can gain a little privacy. Single people are penalized simply because there are more of them and they don't fit neatly into double or triple cubicles. But it's the large family with its compact, space-saving logistic that is the real villain."

Rossiter nodded, edging nearer the counter, ready to shout his order. "Too true. We all look forward to getting married just so that we can have our six square metres."

Directly in front of them, two girls turned around and smiled. "Six square metres," one of them, a dark-haired girl with a pretty oval face, repeated. "You sound like the sort of young man I ought to get to know. Going into the real estate business, Henry?"

Rossiter grinned and squeezed her arm. "Hello, Judith. I'm thinking about it actively. Like to join me in a private venture?"

The girl leaned against him as they reached the counter. "Well, I might. It would have to be legal, though."

The other girl, Helen Waring, an assistant at the library, pulled Ward's sleeve. "Have you heard the latest, John? Judith and I have been kicked out of our room. We're on the street right at this minute."

"What?" Rossiter cried. They collected their soups and coffee and edged back to the rear of the bar. "What on earth happened?"

Helen explained: "You know that little broom cupboard outside our cubicle? Judith and I have been using it as a sort of study hole, going in there to read. It's quiet and restful, if you can get used to not breathing. Well, the old girl found out and kicked up a big fuss, said we were breaking the law and so on. In short, out." Helen paused. "Now we've heard she's going to let it as a single."

Rossiter pounded the counter ledge. "A broom cupboard? Someone's going to live there? But she'll never get a licence."

Judith shook her head. "She's got it already. Her brother works in the Housing Department."

Ward laughed into his soup. "But how can she let it? No one will live in a broom cupboard."

Judith stared at him sombrely. "You really believe that, John?"

Ward dropped his spoon. "No, I suppose you're right. People will live anywhere. God, I don't know who I feel more sorry for—you two, or the poor devil who'll be living in that cupboard. What are you going to do?"

"A couple in a place two blocks west are sub-letting half their cubicle to us. They've hung a sheet down the middle and Helen and I'll take turns sleeping on a camp bed. I'm not joking, our room's about two feet wide. I said to Helen that we ought to split up again and sublet one half at twice our rent."

They had a good laugh over all this. Then Ward said good night to the others and went back to his rooming house.

There he found himself with similar problems.

The manager leaned against the flimsy door, a damp cigar butt revolving around his mouth, an expression of morose boredom on his unshaven face.

"You got four point seven two metres," he told Ward, who was standing out on the staircase, unable to get into his room. Other tenants pressed by on to the landing, where two women in curlers and dressing gowns were arguing with each other, tugging angrily at the wall of trunks and cases. Occasionally the manager glanced at them irritably. "Four seven two. I worked it out twice." He said this as if it ended all possibility of argument.

"Ceiling or floor?" Ward asked.

"Ceiling, whaddya think? How can I measure the floor with all this junk?" He kicked at a crate of books protruding from under the bed.

Ward let this pass. "There's quite a tilt on the wall," he pointed out. "As much as three or four degrees."

The manager nodded vaguely. "You're definitely over the four. Way over." He turned to Ward, who had moved down several steps to allow a man and woman to get past. "I can rent this as a double."

"What, only four and a half?" Ward said incredulously. "How?"

The man who had just passed him leaned over the manager's shoulder and sniffed at the room, taking in every detail in a one-second glance. "You renting a double here, Louie?"

The manager waved him away and then beckoned Ward into the room, closing the door after him.

"It's a nominal five," he told Ward. "New regulation, just came out. Anything over four five is a double now." He eyed Ward shrewdly. "Well, whaddya want? It's a good room, there's a lot of space here, feels more like a triple. You got access to the staircase, window slit—" He broke off as Ward slumped down on the bed and started to laugh. "Whatsa matter? Look, if you want a big room like this you gotta pay for it. I want an extra half rental or you get out."

Ward wiped his eyes, then stood up wearily and reached for the shelves. "Relax, I'm on my way. I'm going to live in a broom cupboard. 'Access to the staircase'—that's really rich. Tell me, Louie, is there life on Uranus?"

Temporarily, he and Rossiter teamed up to rent a double cubicle in a semi-derelict house a hundred yards from the library. The neighbourhood was seedy and faded, the rooming houses crammed with tenants. Most of them were owned by absentee landlords or by the city corporation, and the managers employed were of the lowest type, mere rent-collectors who cared nothing about the way their tenants divided up the living space, and never ventured beyond the first floors. Bottles and empty cans littered the corridors, and the washrooms looked like sumps. Many of the tenants were old and infirm, sitting about listlessly in their narrow cubicles, wheedling at each other back to back through the thin partitions.

Their double cubicle was on the third floor, at the end of a corridor that ringed the building. Its architecture was impossible to follow, rooms letting off at all angles, and luckily the corridor was a cul de sac. The mounds of cases ended four feet from the end wall and a partition divided off the cubicle, just wide enough for two beds. A high window overlooked the area ways of the buildings opposite.

Possessions loaded on to the shelf above his head, Ward lay back on his bed and moodily surveyed the roof of the library through the afternoon haze.

"It's not bad here," Rossiter told him, unpacking his case. "I know there's no real privacy and we'll drive each other insane within a week, but at least we haven't got six other people breathing into our ears two feet away."

The nearest cubicle, a single, was built into the banks of cases half a dozen steps along the corridor, but the occupant, a man of seventy, was deaf and bed-ridden.

"It's not bad," Ward echoed reluctantly. "Now tell me what the latest growth figures are. They might console me."

Rossiter paused, lowering his voice. "Four per cent. Eight hundred million extra people in one year—just less than half the earth's total population in 1950."

Ward whistled slowly. "So they will revalue. What to? Three and a half?"

"Three. From the first of next year."

"Three square metres!" Ward sat up and looked around him. "It's unbeliev-able! The world's going insane, Rossiter. For God's sake, when are they going to do something about it? Do you realize there soon won't be room enough to sit down, let alone lie down?"

Exasperated, he punched the wall beside him, on the second blow knocked in one of the small wooden panels that had been lightly papered over.

"Hey!" Rossiter yelled. "You're breaking the place down." He dived across the bed to retrieve the panel, which hung downwards supported by a strip of paper. Ward slipped his hand into the dark interval, carefully drew the panel back on to the bed.

"Who's on the other side?" Rossiter whispered. "Did they hear?"

Ward peered through the interval, eyes searching the dim light. Suddenly he dropped the panel and seized Rossiter's shoulder, pulled him down on to the bed.

"Henry! Look!"

Directly in front of them, faintly illuminated by a grimy skylight, was a me-dium-sized room some fifteen feet square, empty except for the dust silted up against the skirting boards. The floor was bare, a few strips of frayed linoleum running across it, the walls covered with a drab floral design. Here and there patches of the paper peeled off and segments of the picture rail had rotted away, but otherwise the room was in habitable condition.

Breathing slowly, Ward closed the open door of the cubicle with his foot, then turned to Rossiter.

"Henry, do you realize what we've found? Do you realize it, man?"

"Shut up. For Pete's sake keep your voice down." Rossiter examined the room carefully. "It's fantastic. I'm trying to see whether anyone's used it recently."

"Of course they haven't," Ward pointed out. "It's obvious. There's no door into the room. We're looking through it now. They must have panelled over this door years ago and forgotten about it. Look at that filth everywhere."

Rossiter was staring into the room, his mind staggered by its vastness. "You're right," he murmured. "Now, when do we move in?"

Panel, by panel, they prised away the lower half of the door and nailed it on to a wooden frame, so that the dummy section could be replaced instantly.

Then, picking an afternoon when the house was half empty and the manager asleep in his basement office, they made their first foray into the room, Ward going in alone while Rossiter kept guard in the cubicle.

For an hour they exchanged places, wandering silently around the dusty room, stretching their arms out to feel its unconfined emptiness, grasping at the sensation of absolute spatial freedom. Although smaller than many of the sub-divided rooms in which they had lived, this room seemed infinitely larger, its walls huge cliffs that soared upward to the skylight.

Finally, two or three days later, they moved in.

For the first week Rossiter slept alone in the room, Ward in the cubicle outside, both there together during the day. Gradually they smuggled in a few items of furniture: two armchairs, a table, a lamp fed from the socket in the cubicle. The furniture was heavy and Victorian; the cheapest available, its size emphasized the emptiness of the room. Pride of place was taken by an enormous mahogany wardrobe, fitted with carved angels and castellated mirrors, which they were forced to dismantle and carry into the house in their suitcases. Towering over them, it reminded Ward of the micro-films of gothic cathedrals, with their massive organ lofts crossing vast naves.

After three weeks they both slept in the room, finding the cubicle unbearably cramped. An imitation Japanese screen divided the room adequately and did nothing to diminish its size. Sitting there in the evenings, surrounded by his books and albums, Ward steadily forgot the city outside. Luckily he reached the library by a back alley and avoided the crowded streets. Rossiter and himself began to seem the only real inhabitants of the world, everyone else a meaningless by-product of their own existence, a random replication of identity which had run out of control.

It was Rossiter who suggested that they ask the two girls to share the room with them.

"They've been kicked out again and may have to split up," he told Ward, obviously worried that Judith might fall into bad company. "There's always a rent freeze after a revaluation but all the landlords know about it so they're not re-letting. It's damned difficult to find anywhere."

Ward nodded, relaxing back around the circular red-wood table. He played with the tassel of the arsenic-green lamp shade, for a moment felt like a Victorian man of letters, leading a spacious, leisurely life among overstuffed furnishings.

"I'm all for it," he agreed, indicating the empty corners. "There's plenty of room here. But we'll have to make sure they don't gossip about it."

After due precautions, they let the two girls into the secret, enjoying their astonishment at finding this private universe.

"We'll put a partition across the middle," Rossiter explained, "then take it down each morning. You'll be able to move in within a couple of days. How do you feel?"

"Wonderful!" They goggled at the wardrobe, squinting at the endless reflections in the mirrors.

There was no difficulty getting them in and out of the house. The turnover of tenants was continuous and bills were placed in the mail rack. No one cared who the girls were or noticed their regular calls at the cubicle.

However, half an hour after they arrived neither of them had unpacked her suitcase.

"What's up, Judith?" Ward asked, edging past the girls' beds into the narrow interval between the table and wardrobe.

Judith hesitated, looking from Ward to Rossiter, who sat on the bed, finishing off the plywood partition. "John, it's just that…"

Helen Waring, more matter-of-fact, took over, her fingers straightening the bed-spread. "What Judith's trying to say is that our position here is a little embarrassing. The partition is—"

Rossiter stood up. "For heaven's sake, don't worry, Helen," he assured her, speaking in the loud whisper they had all involuntarily cultivated. "No funny business, you can trust us. This partition is as solid as a rock."

The two girls nodded. "It's not that," Helen explained, "but it isn't up all the time. We thought that if an older person were here, say Judith's aunt—she wouldn't take up much room and be no trouble, she's really awfully sweet—we wouldn't need to bother about the partition—except at night," she added quickly.

Ward glanced at Rossiter, who shrugged and began to scan the floor. "Well, it's an idea," Rossiter said. "John and I know how you feel. Why not?"

"Sure," Ward agreed. He pointed to the space between the girls' beds and the table. "One more won't make any difference."

The girls broke into whoops. Judith went over to Rossiter and kissed him on the cheek. "Sorry to be a nuisance, Henry." She smiled at him. "That's a wonderful partition you've made. You couldn't do another one for Auntie—just a little one? She's very sweet but she is getting on."

"Of course," Rossiter said. "I understand. I've got plenty of wood left over."

Ward looked at his watch. "It's seven-thirty, Judith. You'd better get in touch with your aunt. She may not be able to make it tonight."

Judith buttoned her coat. "Oh she will," she assured Ward. "I'll be back in a jiffy."

The aunt arrived within five minutes, three heavy suitcases soundly packed.

"It's amazing," Ward remarked to Rossiter three months later. "The size of this room still staggers me. It almost gets larger every day."

Rossiter agreed readily, averting his eyes from one of the girls changing behind the central partition. This they now left in place as dismantling it daily had become tiresome. Besides, the aunt's subsidiary partition was attached to it and she resented the continuous upsets. Ensuring she followed the entrance and exit drills through the camouflaged door and cubicle was difficult enough.

Despite this, detection seemed unlikely. The room had obviously been built as an afterthought into the central well of the house and any noise was masked by the luggage stacked in the surrounding corridor. Directly below was a small dormitory occupied by several elderly women, and Judith's aunt, who visited them socially, swore that no sounds came through the heavy ceiling. Above, the fanlight let out through a dormer window, its lights indistinguishable from the hundred other bulbs in the windows of the house.

Rossiter finished off the new partition he was building and held it upright, fitting it into the slots nailed to the wall between his bed and Ward's. They had agreed that this would provide a little extra privacy.

"No doubt I'll have to do one for Judith and Helen," he confided to Ward.

Ward adjusted his pillow. They had smuggled the two armchairs back to the furniture shop as they took up too much space. The bed, anyway, was more comfortable. He had never become completely used to the soft upholstery.

"Not a bad idea. What about some shelving around the wall? I've got nowhere to put anything."

The shelving tidied the room considerably, freeing large areas of the floor. Divided by their partitions, the five beds were in line along the rear wall, facing the mahogany wardrobe. In between was an open space of three or four feet, a further six feet on either side of the wardrobe.

The sight of so much spare space fascinated Ward. When Rossiter mentioned that Helen's mother was ill and badly needed personal care he immediately knew where her cubicle could be placed—at the foot of his bed, between the wardrobe and the side wall.

Helen was overjoyed. "It's awfully good of you, John," she told him, "but would you mind if Mother slept beside me? There's enough space to fit an extra bed in."

So Rossiter dismantled the partitions and moved them closer together, six beds now in line along the wall. This gave each of them an interval two and a half feet wide, just enough room to squeeze down the side of their beds. Lying back on the extreme right, the shelves two feet above his head, Ward could barely see the wardrobe, but the space in front of him, a clear six feet to the wall ahead, was uninterrupted.

Then Helen's father arrived.

Knocking on the door of the cubicle, Ward smiled at Judith's aunt as she let him in. He helped her swing out the made-up bed which guarded the entrance, then rapped on the wooden panel. A moment later Helen's father, a small, grey-haired man in an undershirt, braces tied to his trousers with string, pulled back the panel.

Ward nodded to him and stepped over the luggage piled around the floor at the foot of the beds. Helen was in her mother's cubicle, helping the old woman to drink her evening broth. Rossiter, perspiring heavily, was on his knees by the mahogany wardrobe, wrenching apart the frame of the central mirror with a jemmy. Pieces of the wardrobe lay on his bed and across the floor.

"We'll have to start taking these out tomorrow," Rossiter told him. Ward waited for Helen's father to shuffle past and enter his cubicle. He had rigged up a small cardboard door, and locked it behind him with a crude hook of bent wire.

Rossiter watched him, frowning irritably. "Some people are happy. This wardrobe's a hell of a job. How did we ever decide to buy it?"

Ward sat down on his bed. The partition pressed against his knees and he could hardly move. He looked up when Rossiter was engaged and saw that the dividing line he had marked in pencil was hidden by the encroaching partition. Leaning against the wall, he tried to ease it back again, but Rossiter had apparently nailed the lower edge to the floor.

There was a sharp tap on the outside cubicle door—Judith returning from her office. Ward started to get up and then sat back. "Mr. Waring," he called softly. It was the old man's duty night.

Waring shuffled to the door of his cubicle and unlocked it fussily, clucking to himself.

"Up and down, up and down," he muttered. He stumbled over Rossiter's tool-bag and swore loudly, then added meaningly over his shoulder: "If you ask me there's too many people in here. Down below they've only got six to our seven, and it's the same size room."

Ward nodded vaguely and stretched back on his narrow bed, trying not to bang his head on the shelving. Waring was not the first to hint that he move out. Judith's aunt had made a similar suggestion two days earlier. Since he had left his job at the library (the small rental he charged the others paid for the little food he needed) he spent most of his time in the room, seeing rather more of the old man than he wanted to, but he had learned to tolerate him.

Settling himself, he noticed that the right-hand spire of the wardrobe, all he had been able to see of it for the past two months, was now dismantled.

It had been a beautiful piece of furniture, in a way symbolizing this whole private world, and the salesman at the store told him there were few like it left. For a moment Ward felt a sudden pang of regret, as he had done as a child when his father, in a moment of exasperation, had taken something away from him and he had known he would never see it again.

Then he pulled himself together. It was a beautiful wardrobe, without doubt, but when it was gone it would make the room seem even larger.

AMARYLLIS

by Carrie Vaughn

Carrie Vaughn is the bestselling author of the Kitty Norville series, which started with Kitty and the Midnight Hour. Her latest books are *Kitty Goes to War*; a young adult novel, *Voices of Dragons*; and a stand-alone fantasy novel, *Discord's Apple*. Her short work has appeared many times in *Realms of Fantasy* and in a number of anthologies, such as *By Blood We Live*; *The Mammoth Book of Paranormal Romance*; *Fast Ships, Black Sails*; and *Warriors*. She has a story forthcoming in my anthology *The Mad Scientist's Guide to World Domination*, and this story first appeared in my online science fiction magazine, *Lightspeed*.

"*Amaryllis*" gives us a world that, compared to some dystopias, feels downright wholesome. No one is tortured; no one lives under scrutiny; no one is executed. But the characters are caught in a society that has taken away their reproductive control. For most of us, that's a pretty basic human right.

But there's a good reason to take family size out of individual control, with the world's population spinning out of control. As the author says: "in the industrialized world at least, a financially successful family or individual can stay pretty isolated from their community, if they so choose. But if there's ever a cataclysmic loss of resources, that could change." And in the future Carrie Vaughn spins, a desperate community must contain its population—or die.

Our next story's debatable dystopic quotient aside, this story explores the idea that while one never sets out to create a dystopia, in order for a society to survive, sometimes it is necessary to become one.

I never knew my mother, and I never understood why she did what she did. I ought to be grateful that she was crazy enough to cut out her implant so she could get pregnant. But it also meant she was crazy enough to hide the pregnancy until termination wasn't an option, knowing the whole time that she'd never get to keep the baby. That she'd lose everything. That her household would lose everything because of her.

I never understood how she couldn't care. I wondered what her family thought when they learned what she'd done, when their committee split up the household, scattered them—broke them, because of her.

Did she think I was worth it?

It was all about quotas.

"They're using cages up north, I heard. Off shore, anchored," Nina said. "Fifty feet across—twice as much protein grown with half the resources, and we'd never have to touch the wild population again. We could double our quota."

I hadn't really been listening to her. We were resting, just for a moment; she sat with me on the railing at the prow of *Amaryllis* and talked about her big plans.

Wind pulled the sails taut and the fiberglass hull cut through waves without a sound, we sailed so smooth. Garrett and Sun hauled up the nets behind us, dragging in the catch. *Amaryllis* was elegant, a 30-foot sleek vessel with just enough cabin and cargo space—an antique but more than seaworthy. She was a good boat, with a good crew. The best.

"Marie—" Nina said, pleading.

I sighed and woke up. "We've been over this. We can't just double our quota."

"But if we got authorization—"

"Don't you think we're doing all right as it is?" We had a good crew—we were well fed and not exceeding our quotas; I thought we'd be best off not screwing all that up. Not making waves, so to speak.

Nina's big brown eyes filled with tears—I'd said the wrong thing, because I knew what she was really after, and the status quo wasn't it.

"That's just it," she said. "We've met our quotas and kept everyone healthy for years now. I really think we should try. We can at least ask, can't we?"

The truth was: No, I wasn't sure we deserved it. I wasn't sure that kind of responsibility would be worth it. I didn't want the prestige. Nina didn't even want the prestige—she just wanted the baby.

"It's out of our hands at any rate," I said, looking away because I couldn't bear the intensity of her expression.

Pushing herself off the rail, Nina stomped down *Amaryllis'* port side to join the rest of the crew hauling in the catch. She wasn't old enough to want a baby. She was lithe, fit, and golden, running barefoot on the deck, sun-bleached streaks gleaming in her brown hair. Actually, no, she was old enough. She'd been with the house for seven years—she was twenty, now. It hadn't seemed so long.

"Whoa!" Sun called. There was a splash and a thud as something in the net kicked against the hull. He leaned over the side, the muscles along his broad, coppery back flexing as he clung to a net that was about to slide back into the water. Nina, petite next to his strong frame, reached with him. I ran down and grabbed them by the waistbands of their trousers to hold them steady. The fourth of our crew, Garrett, latched a boat hook into the net. Together we hauled the catch onto the deck. We'd caught something big, heavy, and full of powerful muscles.

We had a couple of aggregators—large buoys made of scrap steel and wood—anchored fifty miles or so off the coast. Schooling fish were attracted to the aggregators, and we found the fish—mainly mackerel, sardines, sablefish, and whiting. An occasional shark or marlin found its way into the nets, but those we let go; they were rare and outside our quotas. That was what I expected to see—something unusually large thrashing among the slick silvery mass of smaller fish. This thing was large, yes, as big as Nina—no wonder it had almost pulled them over—but it wasn't the right shape. Sleek and streamlined, a powerful swimmer. Silvery like the rest of the catch.

"What is it?" Nina asked.

"Tuna," I said, by process of elimination. I had never seen one in my life. "Bluefin, I think."

"No one's caught a bluefin in thirty years," Garrett said. Sweat was dripping onto his face despite the bandanna tying back his shaggy dark hair.

I was entranced, looking at all that protein. I pressed my hand to the fish's flank, feeling its muscles twitch. "Maybe they're back."

We'd been catching the tuna's food all along, after all. In the old days the aggregators attracted as many tuna as mackerel. But no one had seen one in so long, everyone assumed they were gone.

"Let's put him back," I said, and the others helped me lift the net to the side. It took all of us, and when we finally got the tuna to slide overboard, we lost half the net's catch with it, a wave of silvery scales glittering as they hit the water. But that was okay: Better to be under quota than over.

The tuna splashed its tail and raced away. We packed up the rest of the catch and set sails for home.

The *Californian* crew got their banner last season, and flew its red and green—power and fertility—from the top of the boat's mast for all to see. Elsie of the *Californian* was due to give birth in a matter of weeks. As soon as her pregnancy was confirmed, she stopped sailing and stayed in the household, sheltered and treasured. Loose hands resting atop mountainous belly, she would sometimes come out to greet her household's boat as it arrived. Nina would stare at her. Elsie might have been the first pregnant woman Nina had seen, as least since surviving puberty and developing thoughts of carrying a mountainous belly of her own.

Elsie was there now, an icon cast in bronze before the setting sun, her body canted slightly against the weight in her belly, like a ship leaning away from the wind.

We furled the sails and rowed to the pier beside the scale house. Nina hung over the prow, looking at Elsie, who was waving at *Californian*'s captain, on the deck of the boat. Solid and dashing, everything a captain ought to be, he waved back at her. Their boat was already secured in its home slip, their catch weighed, everything tidy. Nina sighed at the image of a perfect life, and nobody yelled at her for not helping. Best thing to do in a case like this was let her dream until she grew out of it. Might take decades, but still…

My *Amaryllis* crew handed crates off to the dockhand, who shifted our catch to the scale house. Beyond that were the processing houses, where onshore crews smoked, canned, and shipped the fish inland. The New Oceanside community provided sixty percent of the protein for the whole region, which was our mark of pride, our reason for existing. Within the community itself, the ten sailing crews were proudest of all. A fishing crew that did its job well and met its quotas kept the whole system running smoothly. I was lucky to even have the *Amaryllis* and be a part of it.

I climbed up to the dock with my folk after securing the boat, and saw that Anders was the scalemaster on duty. The week's trip might as well have been for nothing, then.

Thirty-five years ago, my mother ripped out her implant and broke up her household. Might as well have been yesterday to a man like Anders.

The old man took a nail-biting forty minutes to weigh our catch and add up our numbers, at which point he announced, "You're fifty pounds over quota."

Quotas were the only way to keep the stock healthy, to prevent overfishing, shortages, and ultimately starvation. The committee based quotas on how much you needed, not how much you could catch. To exceed that—to pretend you needed more than other people—showed so much disrespect to the committee, the community, to the fishing stock.

My knees weak, I almost sat down. I'd gotten it exactly right, I knew I had. I glared at him. Garrett and Sun, a pair of brawny sailors helpless before the scalemaster in his dull gray tunic of authority, glared at him. Some days felt like nothing I did would ever be enough. I'd always be too far one way or the other over the line of "just right." Most days, I'd accept the scalemaster's judgment and walk away, but today, after setting loose the tuna and a dozen pounds of legitimate catch with it, it was too much.

"You're joking," I said. "Fifty pounds?"

"Really," Anders said, marking the penalty on the chalkboard behind him where all the crews could see it. "You ought to know better, an experienced captain like you."

He wouldn't even look at me. Couldn't look me in the eye while telling me I was trash.

"What do you want me to do, throw the surplus overboard? We can eat those fifty pounds. The livestock can eat those fifty pounds."

"It'll get eaten, don't worry. But it's on your record." Then he marked it on his clipboard, as if he thought we'd come along and alter the public record.

"Might as well not sail out at all next week, eh?" I said.

The scalemaster frowned and turned away. A fifty pound surplus—if it even existed—would go to make up another crew's shortfall, and next week our catch would be needed just as much as it had been this week, however little some folk wanted to admit it. We could get our quota raised like Nina wanted, and we wouldn't have to worry about surpluses at all. No, then we'd worry about shortfalls, and not earning credits to feed the mouths we had, much less the extra one Nina wanted.

Surpluses must be penalized, or everyone would go fishing for surpluses and having spare babies, and then where would we be? Too many mouths, not enough food, no resiliency to survive disaster, and all the disease and starvation that followed. I'd seen the pictures in the archives, of what happened after the big fall.

Just enough and no more. Moderation. But so help me I wasn't going to dump fifty pounds just to keep my record clean.

"We're done here. Thank you, Captain Marie," Anders said, his back to me, like he couldn't stand the sight of me.

When we left, I found Nina at the doorway, staring. I pushed her in front of me, back to the boat, so we could put *Amaryllis* to bed for the night.

"The *Amaryllis'* scales aren't that far off," Garrett grumbled as we rowed to her slip. "Ten pounds, maybe. Not fifty."

"Anders had his foot on the pad, throwing it off. I'd bet on it," Sun said. "Ever notice how we're only ever off when Anders is running the scales?"

We'd all noticed.

"Is that true? But why would he do that?" said Nina, innocent Nina.

Everyone looked at me. A weight seemed to settle on us.

"What?" Nina said. "What is it?"

It was the kind of thing no one talked about, and Nina was too young to have grown up knowing. The others had all known what they were getting into, signing on with me. But not Nina.

I shook my head at them. "We'll never prove that Anders has it in for us so there's no good arguing. We'll take our licks and that's the end of it."

Sun said, "Too many black marks like that they'll break up the house."

That was the worry, wasn't it?

"How many black marks?" Nina said. "He can't do that. Can he?"

Garrett smiled and tried to take the weight off. He was the first to sign on with me when I inherited the boat. We'd been through a lot together. "We'll just have to find out Anders' schedule and make sure we come in when someone else is on duty."

But most of the time there were no schedules—just whoever was on duty when a boat came in. I wouldn't be surprised to learn that Anders kept a watch for us, just to be here to rig our weigh-in.

Amaryllis glided into her slip, and I let Garrett and Sun secure the lines. I leaned back against the side, stretching my arms, staring up along the mast. Nina sat nearby, clenching her hands, her lips. Elsie and *Californian's* captain had gone.

I gave her a pained smile. "You might have a better chance of getting your extra mouth if you went to a different crew. The *Californian*, maybe."

"Are you trying to get rid of me?" Nina said.

Sitting up, I put my arms across her shoulders and pulled her close. Nina came to me a clumsy thirteen-year old from Bernardino, up the coast. My household had a space for her, and I was happy to get her. She'd grown up smart and eager.

She could take my place when I retired, inherit *Amaryllis* in her turn. Not that I'd told her that yet.

"Never. Never ever." She only hesitated a moment before wrapping her arms around me and squeezing back.

Our household was an oasis. We'd worked hard to make it so. I'd inherited the boat, attracted the crew one by one—Garrett and Sun to run the boat, round and bustling Dakota to run the house, and she brought the talented J.J., and we fostered Nina. We'd been assigned fishing rights, and then we earned the land allocation. Ten years of growing, working, sweating, nurturing, living, and the place was gorgeous.

We'd dug into the side of a hill above the docks and built with adobe. In the afternoon sun, the walls gleamed golden. The part of the house projecting out from the hill served as a wall protecting the garden and well. Our path led around the house and into the courtyard. We'd found flat shale to use as flagstones around the cultivated plots, and to line the well, turning it into a spring. A tiny spring, but any open fresh water seemed like a luxury. On the hill above were the windmill and solar panels.

Everyone who wanted a private room had one, but only Sun did—the detached room dug into the hill across the yard. Dakota, J.J., and Nina had pallets in the largest room. Garret and I shared a bed in the smaller room. What wasn't house was garden. We had producing fruit trees, an orange and a lemon, that also shaded the kitchen space. Corn, tomatoes, sunflowers, green beans, peas, carrots, radishes, two kinds of peppers, and anything else we could make grow on a few square feet. A pot full of mint and one of basil. For the most part we fed ourselves and so could use our credits on improving *Amaryllis* and bringing in specialties like rice and honey, or fabric and rope that we couldn't make in quantity. Dakota wanted to start chickens next season, if we could trade for the chicks.

I kept wanting to throw that in the face of people like Anders. It wasn't like I didn't pay attention. I wasn't a burden.

The crew arrived home; J.J. had supper ready. Dakota and J.J. had started out splitting household work evenly, but pretty quickly they were trading chores—turning compost versus hanging laundry, mending the windmill versus cleaning the kitchen—until J.J. did most everything involving the kitchen and living spaces and Dakota did everything with the garden and mechanics.

By J.J.'s sympathetic expression when he gave me my serving—smoked mackerel and vegetables tonight—someone had already told him about the run-in with the scalemaster. Probably to keep him or Dakota from asking how my day went.

I stayed out later than usual making a round of the holding. Not that I expected to find anything wrong. It was for my own peace of mind, looking at what we'd built with my own eyes, putting my hand on the trunk of the windmill, running the leaves of the lemon tree across my palms, ensuring that none of it had vanished, that it wasn't going to. It had become a ritual.

In bed I held tight to Garrett, to give and get comfort, skin against skin, under the sheet, under the warm air coming in through the open skylight above our bed.

"Bad day?" he said.

"Can never be a bad day when the ship and crew come home safe," I said. But my voice was flat.

Garrett shifted, running a hand down my back, arranging his arms to pull me tight against him. Our legs twined together. My nerves settled.

He said, "Nina's right, we can do more. We can support an extra mouth. If we appealed—"

"You really think that'll do any good?" I said. "I think you'd all be better off with a different captain."

He tilted his face toward mine, touched my lips with his, pressed until I responded. A minute of that and we were both smiling.

"You know we all ended up here because we don't get along with anyone else. But you make the rest of us look good."

I squirmed against him in mock outrage, giggling.

"Plenty of crews—plenty of households—don't ever get babies," he said. "It doesn't mean anything."

"I don't care about a baby so much," I said. "I'm just tired of fighting all the time."

It was normal for children to fight with their parents, their households, and even their committees as they grew. But it wasn't fair, for me to feel like I was still fighting with a mother I'd never known.

The next day, when Nina and I went down to do some cleaning on *Amaryllis*, I tried to convince myself it was my imagination that she was avoiding me. Not looking at me. Or pretending not to look, when in fact she was stealing glances. The way she avoided meeting my gaze made my skin crawl a little. She'd decided something. She had a secret.

We caught sight of Elsie again, walking up from the docks, a hundred yards away but her silhouette was unmistakable. That distracted Nina, who stopped to stare.

"Is she really that interesting?" I said, smiling, trying to make it a joke.

Nina looked at me sideways, as if deciding whether she should talk to me. Then she sighed. "I wonder what it's like. Don't you wonder what it's like?"

I thought about it a moment and mostly felt fear rather than interest. All the things that could go wrong, even with a banner of approval flying above you. Nina wouldn't understand that. "Not really."

"Marie, how can you be so...so indifferent?"

"Because I'm not going to spend the effort worrying about something I can't change. Besides, I'd much rather be captain of a boat than stuck on shore, watching."

I marched past her to the boat, and she followed, head bowed.

We washed the deck, checked the lines, cleaned out the cabin, took inventory, and made a stack of gear that needed to be repaired. We'd take it home and spend the next few days working on it before we went to sea again. Nina was quiet most of the morning, and I kept glancing at her, head bent to her work, biting her lip, wondering what she was thinking on so intently. What she was hiding.

Turned out she was working up the courage.

I handed the last bundle of net to her, then went back to double check that the hatches were closed and the cabin was shut up. When I went to climb off the boat myself, she was sitting at the edge of the dock, her legs hanging over the edge, swinging a little. She looked ten years younger, like she was a kid again, like she had when I first saw her.

I regarded her, brows raised, questioning, until finally she said, "I asked Sun why Anders doesn't like you. Why none of the captains talk to you much."

So that was what had happened. Sun—matter-of-fact and sensible—would have told her without any circumspection. And Nina had been horrified.

Smiling, I sat on the gunwale in front of her. "I'd have thought you'd been here long enough to figure it out on your own."

"I knew something had happened, but I couldn't imagine what. Certainly not—I mean, no one ever talks about it. But…what happened to your mother? Her household?"

I shrugged, because it wasn't like I remembered any of it. I'd pieced the story together, made some assumptions. Was told what happened by people who made their own assumptions. Who wanted me to understand exactly what my place in the world was.

"They were scattered over the whole region, I think. Ten of them—it was a big household, successful, until I came along. I don't know where all they ended up. I was brought to New Oceanside, raised up by the first *Amaryllis* crew. Then Zeke and Ann retired, took up pottery, went down the coast, and gave me the ship to start my own household. Happy ending."

"And your mother—they sterilized her? After you were born, I mean."

"I assume so. Like I said, I don't really know."

"Do you suppose she thought it was worth it?"

"I imagine she didn't," I said. "If she wanted a baby, she didn't get one, did she? But maybe she just wanted to be pregnant for a little while."

Nina looked so thoughtful, swinging her feet, staring at the rippling water where it lapped against the hull, she made me nervous. I had to say something.

"You'd better not be thinking of pulling something like that," I said. "They'd split us up, take the house, take *Amaryllis*—"

"Oh no," Nina said, shaking her head quickly, her denial vehement. "I would never do that, I'd never do anything like that."

"Good," I said, relieved. I trusted her and didn't think she would. Then again, my mother's household probably thought that about her too. I hopped over to the dock. We collected up the gear, slinging bags and buckets over our shoulders and starting the hike up to the house.

Halfway there Nina said, "You don't think we'll ever get a banner, because of your mother. That's what you were trying to tell me."

"Yeah." I kept my breathing steady, concentrating on the work at hand.

"But it doesn't change who you are. What you do."

"The old folk still take it out on me."

"It's not fair," she said. She was too old to be saying things like that. But at least now she'd know, and she could better decide if she wanted to find another household.

"If you want to leave, I'll understand," I said. "Any house would be happy to take you."

"No," she said. "No, I'll stay. None of it—it doesn't change who you are."

I could have dropped everything and hugged her for that. We walked awhile longer, until we came in sight of the house. Then I asked, "You have someone in mind to be the father? Hypothetically."

She blushed berry red and looked away. I had to grin—so that was how it stood.

When Garrett greeted us in the courtyard, Nina was still blushing. She avoided him and rushed along to dump her load in the workshop.

Garrett blinked after her. "What's up with her?"

"Nina being Nina."

The next trip on *Amaryllis* went well. We made quota in less time than I expected, which gave us half a day's vacation. We anchored off a deserted bit of shore and went swimming, lay on deck and took in the sun, ate the last of the oranges and dried mackerel that J.J. had sent along with us. It was a good day.

But we had to head back some time and face the scales. I weighed our haul three times with *Amaryllis*' scale, got a different number each time, but all within ten pounds of each other, and more importantly twenty pounds under quota. Not that it would matter. We rowed into the slip at the scale house, and Anders was the scalemaster on duty again. I almost hauled up our sails and turned us around, never to return. I couldn't face him, not after the perfect trip. Nina was right—it wasn't fair that this one man could ruin us with false surpluses and black marks.

Silently, we secured *Amaryllis* to the dock and began handing up our cargo. I managed to keep from even looking at Anders, which probably made me look guilty in his eyes. But we'd already established I could be queen of perfection and he would consider me guilty.

Anders' frown was smug, his gaze judgmental. I could already hear him tell me I was fifty pounds over quota. Another haul like that, he'd say, we'll have to see about yanking your fishing rights. I'd have to punch him. I almost told Garrett to hold me back if I looked like I was going to punch him. But he was already keeping himself between the two of us, as if he thought I might really do it.

If the old scalemaster managed to break up *Amaryllis*, I'd murder him. And wouldn't that be a worse crime than any I might represent?

Anders drew out the moment, looking us all up and down before finally announcing, "Sixty over this time. And you think you're good at this."

My hands tightened into fists. I imagined myself lunging at him. At this point, what could I lose?

"We'd like an audit," Nina said, slipping past Sun, Garrett, and me to stand before the stationmaster, frowning, hands on her hips.

"Excuse me?" Anders said.

"An audit. I think your scale is wrong, and we'd like an audit. Right?" She looked at me.

It was probably better than punching him. "Yes," I said, after a flabbergasted moment. "Yes, we would like an audit."

That set off two hours of chaos in the scale house. Anders protested, hollered at us, threatened us. I sent Sun to the committee house to summon official oversight—he wouldn't try to play nice, and they couldn't brush him off. June and Abe, two senior committee members, arrived, austere in gray and annoyed.

"What's the complaint?" June said.

Everyone looked at me to answer. I almost denied it—that was my first impulse. Don't fight, don't make waves. Because maybe I deserved the trash I got. Or my mother did, but she wasn't here, was she?

But Nina was looking at me with her innocent brown eyes, and this was for her.

I wore a perfectly neutral, business-like expression when I spoke to June and Abe. This wasn't about me, it was about business, quotas, and being fair.

"Scalemaster Anders adjusts the scale's calibration when he sees us coming."

I was amazed when they turned accusing gazes at him and not at me. Anders' mouth worked, trying to stutter a defense, but he had nothing to say.

The committee confirmed that Anders was rigging his scale. They offered us reparations, out of Anders' own rations. I considered—it would mean extra credits, extra food and supplies for the household. We'd been discussing getting another windmill, petitioning for another well. Instead, I recommended that any penalties they wanted to levy should go to community funds. I just wanted *Amaryllis* treated fairly.

And I wanted a meeting, to make one more petition before the committee.

Garrett walked with me to the committee office the next morning.

"I should have been the one to think of requesting an audit," I said.

"Nina isn't as scared of the committee as you are. As you were," he said.

"I'm not—" But I stopped, because he was right.

He squeezed my hand. His smile was amused, his gaze warm. He seemed to find the whole thing entertaining. Me—I was relieved, exhausted, giddy, ashamed. Mostly relieved.

We, *Amaryllis*, had done nothing wrong. I had done nothing wrong.

Garrett gave me a long kiss, then waited outside while I went to sit before the committee.

June was in her chair, along with five other committee members, behind their long table with their slate boards, tally sheets, and lists of quotas. I sat across from them, alone, hands clenched in my lap, trying not to tap my feet. Trying to appear as proud and assured as they did. A stray breeze slipped through the open windows and cooled the cinderblock room.

After polite greetings, June said, "You wanted to make a petition?"

"We—the *Amaryllis* crew—would like to request an increase in our quota. Just a small one."

June nodded. "We've already discussed it and we're of a mind to allow an increase. Would that be suitable?"

Suitable as what? As reparation? As an apology? My mouth was dry, my tongue frozen. My eyes stung, wanting to weep, but that would have damaged our chances, as much as just being me did.

"There's one more thing," I managed. "With an increased quota, we can feed another mouth."

It was an arrogant thing to say, but I had no reason to be polite.

They could chastise me, send me away without a word, lecture me on wanting too much when there wasn't enough to go around. Tell me that it was more important to maintain what we had rather than try to expand—expansion was arrogance. We simply had to maintain. But they didn't. They didn't even look shocked at what I had said.

June, so elegant, I thought, with her long gray hair braided and resting over her shoulder, a knitted shawl draped around her, as much for decoration as for warmth, reached into the bag at her feet and retrieved a folded piece of cloth, which she pushed across the table toward me. I didn't want to touch it. I was still afraid, as if I'd reach for it and June would snatch it away at the last moment. I didn't want to unfold it to see the red and green pattern in full, in case it was some other color instead.

But I did, even though my hand shook. And there it was. I clenched the banner in my fist; no one would be able to pry it out.

"Is there anything else you'd like to speak of?" June asked.

"No," I said, my voice a whisper. I stood, nodded at each of them. Held the banner to my chest, and left the room.

Garrett and I discussed it on the way back to the house. The rest of the crew was waiting in the courtyard for us: Dakota in her skirt and tunic, hair in a tangled bun; J.J. with his arms crossed, looking worried; Sun, shirtless, hands on hips, inquiring. And Nina, right there in front, bouncing almost.

I regarded them, trying to be inscrutable, gritting my teeth to keep from bursting into laughter. I held our banner behind my back to hide it. Garrett held my other hand.

"Well?" Nina finally said. "How did it go? What did they say?"

The surprise wasn't going to get any better than this. I shook out the banner and held it up for them to see. And oh, I'd never seen all of them wide-eyed and wondering, mouths gaping like fish, at once.

Nina broke the spell, laughing and running at me, throwing herself into my arms. We nearly fell over.

Then we were all hugging, and Dakota started worrying right off, talking about what we needed to build a crib, all the fabric we'd need for diapers, and how we only had nine months to save up the credits for it.

I recovered enough to hold Nina at arm's length, so I could look her in the eyes when I pressed the banner into her hands. She nearly dropped it at first, skittering from it as if it were fire. So I closed her fingers around the fabric and held them there.

"It's yours," I said. "I want you to have it." I glanced at Garrett to be sure. And yes, he was still smiling.

Staring at me, Nina held it to her chest, much like I had. "But…you. It's yours…" She started crying. Then so did I, gathering her close and holding her tight while she spoke through tears, "Don't you want to be a mother?"

In fact, I rather thought I already was.

POP SQUAD

by Paolo Bacigalupi

Paolo Bacigalupi's debut novel, *The Windup Girl,* published in 2009, took the science fiction field by storm, winning the Hugo, Nebula, Locus, and John W. Campbell Memorial awards. He is also the author of the young adult novel, *Ship Breaker,* and several short stories, most of which can be found in his award-winning collection, *Pump Six and Other Stories.* In 2006, his story "The Calorie Man" won the Theodore Sturgeon Memorial Award and was nominated for the Hugo Award; in 2007, a story set in the same world, "Yellow Card Man," also made the Hugo ballot. "The People of Sand and Slag," which first appeared in 2004, was a finalist for both the Hugo and Nebula Awards.

In a world rebuilding itself from the ravages of global warming, in a New York City whose edges are being absorbed by jungle, life is beautiful. Floating above the monkeys and tropical trees, men and women make art, create music, and never grow old.

This is life after rejoo.

Rejoo: it's an elixir of life, a chemical rebirth anyone can buy. It keeps the body slim and full of youth and pulls the stops on aging. There's no reason to die anymore. A quick trip to clinic gives a person a whole new lease of life.

But just because there's no mortality doesn't mean there's no crime or no police to reign in the criminals. Our next story's narrator might prefer attending the symphony, but in his day-job, he's a cop who fights against a population explosion.

Because if no one dies, there's no reason to procreate, and in a world still healing from environmental disaster, children are the new America's Most Wanted—and they get the death penalty.

When there really is a fountain of youth, what price are we willing to pay for a drink?

The familiar stench of unwashed bodies, cooked food, and shit washes over me as I come through the door. Cruiser lights flicker through the blinds, sparkling in rain and illuminating the crime scene with strobes of red and blue fire. A kitchen. A humid mess. A chunky woman huddles in the corner, clutching closed her nightgown. Fat thighs and swaying breasts under stained silk. Squad goons crowding her, pushing her around, making her sit, making her cower. Another woman, young-looking and pretty, pregnant and black-haired, is slumped against the opposite wall, her blouse spackled with spaghetti remains. Screams from the next room: kids.

I squeeze my fingers over my nose and breathe through my mouth, fighting off nausea as Pentle wanders in, holstering his Grange. He sees me and tosses me a nosecap. I break it and snort lavender until the stink slides off. Children come scampering in with Pentle, a brood of three tangling around his knees—the screamers from the other room. They gallop around the kitchen and disappear again, screaming still, into the living room where data sparkles like fairy dust on the wallscreens and provides what is likely their only connection to the outside world.

"That's everyone," Pentle says. He's got a long skinny face and a sour small mouth that always points south. Weights seem to hang off his cheeks. Fat caterpillar brows droop over his eyes. He surveys the kitchen, mouth corners dragging lower. It's always depressing to come into these scenes. "They were all inside when we broke down the door."

I nod absently as I shake monsoon water from my hat. "Great. Thanks." Liquid beads scatter on the floor, joining puddles of wet from the pop squad along with the maggot debris of the spaghetti dinner. I put my hat back on. Water still manages to drip off the brim and slip under my collar, a slick rivulet of discomfort. Someone closes the door to the outside. The shit smell thickens, eggy and humid. The nosecap barely holds it off. Old peas and bits of cereal crunch under my feet. They squish with the spaghetti, the geologic layers of past feedings. The kitchen hasn't been self-cleaned in years.

The older woman coughs and pulls her nightgown tighter around her cellulite and I wonder, as I always do when I come into situations like this, what made her choose this furtive nasty life of rotting garbage and brief illicit forays into daylight. The pregnant girl seems to have slipped even further into herself since I arrived. She stares into space. You'd have to touch her pulse to know that she's alive. It amazes me that women can end up like this, seduced so far down into gutter life that they arrive here, fugitives from everyone who would have kept them and held them and loved them and let them see the world outside.

The children run in from the living room again, playing chase: a blond, no more than five; another, younger and with brown braids, topless and in makeshift diapers, less than three; and a knee-high toddler boy, scrap diaper bunched around little muscle thighs, wearing a T-shirt stained with tomato sauce that says "Who's the Cutest?" The T-shirt would be an antique if it wasn't stained.

"You need anything else?" Pentle asks. He wrinkles his nose as new reek wafts from the direction of the kids.

"You get photos for the prosecutor?"

"Got 'em." Pentle holds out a digicam and thumbs through the images of the ladies and the three children, all of them staring out from the screen like little smeared dolls. "You want me to take them in, now?"

I look over the women. The kids have run out again. From the other room, their howls echo as they chase around. Their shrieks are piercing. Even from a distance they hurt my head. "Yeah. I'll deal with the kids."

Pentle gets the women up off the floor and shuffles out the door, leaving me standing alone in the middle of the kitchen. It's all so familiar: a typical floor plan from Builders United. Custom undercab lighting, black mirror tile on the floors, clever self-clean nozzles hidden behind deco trim lines, so much like the stuff Alice and I have that I can almost forget where I am. It's a negative image of our apartment's kitchen: light vs. dark, clean vs. dirty, quiet vs. loud. The same floor plan, everything about it the same, and yet, nothing in it is. It's archeological. I can look at the layers of gunk and grime and noise and see what must have underlain it before…when these people worried about color coordinating and classy appliances.

I open the fridge (smudgefree nickel, how practical). Ours contains pineapples and avocados and endive and corn and coffee and brazil nuts from Angel Spire's hanging gardens. This one holds a shelf cluttered with ground mycoprotein bars and wadded piles of nutrition supplement sacs like the kind they hand out at the government rejoo clinics. Other than a bag of slimy lettuce, there isn't anything unprocessed in the fridge at all. No vegetables except in powder jars, ditto for fruit. A stack of self-warming dinner bins for fried rice and laap and spaghetti just like the one still lying on the kitchen table in a puddle of its own sauce, and that's it.

I close the fridge and straighten. There's something here in the mess and the screaming in the next room and the reek of the one kid's poopy pants, but I'm stumped as to what it is. They could have lived up in the light and air. Instead, they hid in the dark under wet jungle canopy and turned pale and gave up their lives.

The kids race back in, chasing each other all in a train, laughing and shrieking. They stop and look around, surprised, maybe, that their moms have disappeared. The littlest one has a stuffed dinosaur by the nose. It's got a long green neck and a fat body. A brontosaurus, I think, with big cartooney eyes and black felt lashes. It's funny about the dinosaur, because they've been gone so long, but here one is, showing up as a stuffed toy. And then it's funny again, because when you think about it, a dinosaur toy is really extinct twice.

"Sorry, kids. Mommy's gone."

I pull out my Grange. Their heads kick back in successive jerks, bang bang bang down the line, holes appearing on their foreheads like paint and their brains spattering out the back. Their bodies flip and skid on the black mirror floor. They land in jumbled piles of misaligned limbs. For a second, gunpowder burn makes the stench bearable.

Up out of the jungle like a bat out of hell, climbing out of Rhine-hurst Supercluster's holdout suburban sprawl and then rising through jungle overstory. Blasting across the Causeway toward Angel Spire and the sea. Monkeys diving off the rail line like grasshoppers, pouring off the edge ahead of my cruiser and disappearing into the mangrove and kudzu and mahogany and teak, disappearing into the wet bowels of greenery tangle. Dumping the cruiser at squad center, no time for mopdown, don't need it anyway. My hat, my raincoat, my clothes into hazmat bags, and then out again on the other side, rushing to pull on a tux before catching a masslift up 188 stories, rising into the high clear air over the jungle fur of carbon sequestration project N22.

Mma Telogo has a new concerto. Alice is his diva viola, his prize, and Hua Chiang and Telogo have been circling her like ravens, picking apart her performance, corvid eyes on her, watching and hungry for fault, but now they call her ready. Ready to banish Banini from his throne. Ready to challenge for a place in the immortal canon of classical performance. And I'm late. Caught in a masslift on Level 55, packed in with the breath and heat of upper-deck diners and weekenders climbing the spire while the seconds tick by, listening to the climate fans buzz and whir while we all sweat and wilt, waiting for some problem on the line to clear.

Finally we're rising again, our stomachs dropping into our shoes, our ears popping as we soar into the heavens, flying under magnetic acceleration…and then slowing so fast we almost leave the floor. Our stomachs catch up. I shove out through hundreds of people, waving my cop badge when anyone complains, and sprint through the glass arch of the Ki Performance Center. I dive between the closing slabs of the attention doors.

The autolocks thud home behind me, sealing the performance space. It's comforting. I'm inside, enfolded in the symphony, as though its hands have cupped themselves around me and pulled me into a chamber of absolute focus. The lights dim. Conversational thrum falls away. I find my way to my seat more by feel than sight. Dirty looks from men in topaz hats and women in spectacle eyes as I squeeze across them. Gauche, I know. Absurdly late to an event that happens once in a decade. Plopping down just as Hua Chiang steps up to the podium.

His hands rise like crane wings. Bows and horns and flutes flash with movement and then the music comes, first a hint, like blowing mist, and then building, winding through a series of repeated stanzas that I have heard Alice play perhaps ten thousand times. Notes I heard first so long ago, stumbling and painful, that now spill like water and burst like ice flowers. The music settles, pianissimo again, the lovely delicate motifs that I know from Alice's practice. An introduction only, she has told me, intended to file away the audience's last thoughts of the world outside, repeated stanzas until Hua Chiang accepts that the audience is completely his and then Alice's viola rises, and the other players move to support her, fifteen years of practice coming to fruition.

I look down at my hands, overwhelmed. It's different in the concert hall. Different than all those days when she cursed and practiced and swore at Telogo and claimed his work couldn't be performed. Different even from when she finished her practices early, smiling, hands calloused in new ways, face flushed, eager to drink a cool white wine with me on our balcony in the light of the setting sun and watch the sky as monsoon clouds parted and starlight shone down on our companionship. Tonight, her part joins the rest of the symphony and I can't speak or think for the beauty of the whole.

Later, I'll hear whether Telogo has surpassed Banini for sheer audacity. I'll hear how critics compare living memories of ancient performances and see how critical opinion shifts to accommodate this new piece in a canon that stretches back more than a century, and that hangs like a ghost over everything that Alice and her director Hua Chiang hope for: a performance that will knock Banini off his throne and perhaps depress him enough to stop rejoo and stuff him in his grave. For me, competing against that much history would be a heavy weight. I'm glad I've got a job where forgetting is the most important part. Working on the pop squad means your brain takes a vacation and your hands do the work. And when you leave work, you've left it for good.

Except now, as I look down at my hands, I'm surprised to find pinpricks of blood all over them. A fine spray. The misty remains of the little kid with the dinosaur. My fingers smell of rust.

The tempo accelerates. Alice is playing again. Notes writhe together so fluidly that it seems impossible they aren't generated electronically, and yet the warmth and phrasing is hers, achingly hers, I've heard it in the morning, when she practiced on the balcony, testing herself, working again and again against the limitations of her self. Disciplining her fingers and hands, forcing them to accept Telogo's demands, the ones that years ago she had called impossible and which now run so cleanly through the audience.

The blood is all over my hands. I pick at it, scrape it away in flakes. It had to be the kid with the dinosaur. He was closest when he took the bullet. Some of his residue is stuck tight, bonded to my own skin. I shouldn't have skipped mopdown.

I pick.

The man next to me, tan face and rouged lips, frowns. I'm ruining a moment of history for him, something he has waited years to hear.

I pick more carefully. Silently. The blood flakes off. Dumb kid with the dumb dinosaur that almost made me miss the performance.

The cleanup crew noticed the dinosaur toy too. Caught the irony. Joked and snorted nosecaps and started bagging the bodies for compost. Made me late. Stupid dinosaur.

The music cascades into silence. Hua Chiang's hands fall. Applause. Alice stands at Chiang's urging and the applause increases. Craning my neck, I can see her, nineteen-year-old face flushed, smile bright and triumphant, enveloped in our adulation.

We end up at a party thrown by Maria Illoni, one of the symphony's high donors. She made her money on global warming mitigation for New York City, before it went under. Her penthouse is in Shoreline Curve, daringly arcing over the seawalls and the surf, a sort of flip of the finger to the ocean that beat her storm surge calculations. A spidery silver vine over dark water and the bob of the boat communities out in the deeps. New York obviously never got its money back: Illoni's outdoor patio runs across the entire top floor of the Shoreline and platforms additional petals of spun hollowform carbon out into the air.

From the far side of the Curve, you can see beyond the incandescent cores of the superclusters to the old city sprawl, dark except along where maglines radiate. A strange mangle of wreckage and scavenge and disrepair. In the day, it looks like some kind of dry red fungal collapse, a weave of jungle canopy and old suburban understory, but at night, all that's visible is the skeleton of glowing infrastructure, radial blooms in the darkness, and I breathe deeply, enjoying all the freshness and openness that's missing from those steaming hideouts I raid with the pop squad.

Alice sparkles in the heat, perfectly slim, well curved—an armful of beautiful girl. The fall air is under thirty-three degrees and pleasant, and I feel infinitely tender toward her. I pull her close. We slip into a forest of century-old bonsai sculptures created by Maria's husband. Alice murmurs that he spends all his time here on the roof, staring at branches, studying their curves, and occasionally, perhaps every few years, wiring a branch and guiding it in a new direction. We kiss in the shadows they provide, and Alice is beautiful and everything is perfect.

But I'm distracted.

When I hit the kids with my Grange, the littlest one—the one with that stupid dinosaur—flipped over. A Grange is built for nitheads, not little kids, so the bullet plowed through the kid and he flipped and his dinosaur went flying. It sailed, I mean really sailed, through the air. And now I can't get it out of my mind: that dinosaur flying. And then hitting the wall and bouncing onto the black mirror floor. So fast and so slow. Bang bang bang down the line...and then the dinosaur in the air.

Alice pulls away, seeming to sense my inattention. I straighten up. Try to focus on her.

She says, "I thought you weren't going to make it. When we were tuning, I looked out and your seat was empty."

I force a grin. "But I did. I made it."

Barely. I stood around too long with the cleanup guys while the dinosaur lay in a puddle and sopped up the kid's blood. Double extinct. The kid and the dinosaur both. Dead one way, and then dead again. There's a weird symmetry there.

She cocks her head, studying me. "Was it bad?"

"What?" The brontosaurus? "The call?" I shrug. "Just a couple crazy ladies. Not armed or anything. It was easy."

"I can't imagine it. Cutting rejoo like that." She sighs and reaches out to touch a bonsai, perfectly guided over the decades by the map that only Michael Illoni can see or understand. "Why give all this up?"

I don't have an answer. I rewind the crime scene in my mind. I have the same feeling that I did when I stood on spaghetti maggots and went through their fridge. There's something there in the stink and noise and darkness, something hot and obsessive and ripe. But I don't know what it is.

"The ladies looked old," I say. "Like week-old balloons, all puffy and droopy."

Alice makes a face of distaste. "Can you imagine trying to perform Telogo without rejoo? We wouldn't have had the time. Half of us would have been past our prime, and we'd have needed understudies, and then the understudies would have had to find understudies. Fifteen years. And these women throw it all away. How can they throw away something as beautiful as Telogo?"

"You thinking about Kara?"

"She would have played Telogo twice as well as I did."

"I don't believe that."

"Believe it. She was the best. Before she went kid-crazy." She sighs. "I miss her."

"You could still visit her. She's not dead yet."

"She might as well be. She's already twenty years older than when we knew her." She shakes her head. "No. I'd rather remember her in her prime, not out at some single-sex work camp growing vegetables and losing the last of her talent. I couldn't stand listening to her play now. It would kill me to hear all of that gone." She turns abruptly. "That reminds me, my rejoo booster is tomorrow. Can you take me?"

"Tomorrow?" I hesitate. I'm supposed to be on another shift popping kids. "It's kind of short notice."

"I know. I meant to ask sooner, but with the concert coming up, I forgot." She shrugs. "It's not that important. I can go by myself." She glances at me sidelong. "But it is nicer when you come."

What the hell. I don't really want to work anyway. "Okay, sure. I'll get Pentle to cover for me." Let him deal with the dinosaurs.

"Really?"

I shrug. "What can I say? I'm a sweet guy."

She smiles and stands on tiptoe to kiss me. "If we weren't going to live forever, I'd marry you."

I laugh. "If we weren't going to live forever, I'd get you pregnant."

We look at each other. Alice laughs unsteadily and takes it as a joke. "Don't be gross."

Before we can talk any more, Illoni pops out from behind a bonsai and grabs Alice by the arm. "There you are! I've been looking everywhere for you. You can't hide yourself like this. You're the woman of the hour."

She pulls Alice away with all the confidence that must have made New York believe she could save it. She barely even looks at me as they hustle off. Alice smiles tolerantly and motions for me to follow. Then Maria's calling to everyone and pulling them all together and she climbs up on a fountain's rim and pulls Alice up beside her. She starts talking about art and sacrifice and discipline and beauty.

I tune it out. There's only so much self-congratulation you can take. It's obvious Alice is one of the best in the world. Talking about it just makes it seem banal. But the donors need to feel like they're part of the moment, so they all want to squeeze Alice and make her theirs, so they talk and talk and talk.

Maria's saying, "...wouldn't be standing here congratulating ourselves, if it weren't for our lovely Alice. Hua Chiang and Telogo did their work well, but in the final moment it was Alice's execution in the face of Telogo's ambitious piece that has made it resonate so strongly already with the critics. We have her to thank for the piece's flawlessness."

Everyone starts applauding and Alice blushes prettily, not accustomed to adulation from her peers and competitors. Maria shouts over the cheering, "I've made several calls to Banini, and it is more than apparent that he has no answer to our challenge and so I expect the next eighty years are ours. And Alice's!" The applause is almost deafening.

Maria waves for attention again and the applause fades into scattered whistles and catcalls which finally taper off enough to allow Maria to continue. "To commemorate the end of Banini's age, and the beginning of a new one, I would like to present Alice with a small token of affection—" and here she leans down and picks up a jute-woven gift bag shot with gold as she says, "Of course a woman likes gold and jewels, and strings for her viola, but I thought this was a particularly apt gift for the evening...."

I'm leaning against the woman next to me, trying to see, as Maria holds the bag dramatically above her head and calls out to the crowd, "For Alice, our slayer of dinosaurs!" and pulls the green brontosaurus out of the bag.

It's just like the one the kid had.

Its big eyes look right at me. For a second it seems to blink at me with its big black lashes and then the crowd laughs and applauds as they all get the joke. Banini = dinosaur. Ha ha.

Alice takes the dinosaur and holds it by the neck and swings it over her head and everybody laughs again but I can't see anything anymore because I'm lying on the ground caught in the jungle swelter of people's legs and I can't breathe.

"Are you sure you're okay?"
"Sure. No problem. I told you. I'm fine."
It's true, I guess. Sitting next to Alice in the waiting room, I don't feel dizzy

or anything, even if I am tired. Last night, she put the dinosaur on the bedside table, right in with her collection of little jeweled music boxes, and the damn thing looked at me all night long. Finally at four A.M. I couldn't stand it anymore and I shoved it under the bed. But in the morning, she found it and put it back, and it's been looking at me ever since.

Alice squeezes my hand. The rejoo clinic's a small one, private, carefully appointed with holographic windows of sailboats on the Atlantic so it feels open and airy even though its daylight is piped in through mirror collectors. It's not one of the big public monsters out in the clusters that got started after rejoo's patents expired. You pay a little more than you do for the Medicaid generics, but you don't rub shoulders with a bunch of starving gamblers and nitheads and drunks who all still want their rejoo even if they're wasting every day of their endless lives.

The nurses are quick and efficient. Pretty soon, Alice is on her back hooked up to an IV bladder with me sitting beside her on the bed, and we're watching rejoo push into her.

It's just a clear liquid. I always thought it should be fizzy and green for growing things. Or maybe not green, but definitely fizzy. It always feels fizzy when it goes in.

Alice takes a quick breath and reaches out for me, her slender pale fingers brushing my thigh. "Hold my hand."

The elixir of life pulses into her, filling her, flushing her. She pants shallowly. Her eyes dilate. She isn't watching me anymore. She's somewhere deep inside, reclaiming what was lost over the last eighteen months. No matter how many times I do it, I'm surprised when I watch it come over someone, the way it seems to swallow them and then they come back to the surface more whole and alive than when they started.

Alice's eyes focus. She smiles. "Oh, God. I can never get used to that."

She tries to stand up, but I hold her down and beep the nurse. Once we've got her unhooked, I lead her back out to the car. She leans heavily against me, stumbling and touching me. I can almost feel the fizzing and tingling through her skin. She climbs into the car. When I'm inside, she looks over at me and laughs. "I can't believe how good I feel."

"Nothing like winding back the clock."

"Take me home. I want to be with you. "

I push the start button on the car and we slide out of our parking space. We hook onto the magline out of Center Spire. Alice watches the city slide by outside the windows. All the shoppers and the businessmen and the martyrs and the ghosts, and then we're out in the open, on the high track over the jungle, speeding north again, for Angel Spire.

"It's so wonderful to be alive," she says, "It doesn't make any sense."

"What doesn't?"

"Cutting rejoo."

"If people made sense, we wouldn't have psychologists." And we wouldn't buy dinosaur toys for kids who were never going to make it anyway. I grit my teeth. None of them make any sense. Stupid moms.

Alice sighs and runs her hands across her thighs, kneading herself, hiking up her skirt and digging her fingers into her flesh. "But it still doesn't make any sense. It feels so good. You'd have to be crazy to stop rejoo."

"Of course they're crazy. They kill themselves, they make babies they don't know how to take care of, they live in shitty apartments in the dark, they never go out, they smell bad, they look terrible, they never have anything good again—" I'm starting to shout. I shut my mouth.

Alice looks over at me. "Are you okay?"

"I'm fine."

But I'm not. I'm mad. Mad at the ladies and their stupid toy-buying. Pissed off that these dumb women tease their dumb terminal kids like that; treat them like they aren't going to end up as compost. "Let's not talk about work right now. Let's just go home." I force a grin. "I've already got the day off. We should take advantage of it."

Alice is still looking at me. I can see the questions in her eyes. If she weren't on the leading edge of a rejoo high, she'd keep pressing, but she's so wrapped up in the tingling of her rebuilt body that she lets it go. She laughs and runs her fingers up my leg and starts to play with me. I override the magline's safeties with my cop codes and we barrel across the Causeway toward Angel Spire with the sun on the ocean and Alice smiling and laughing and the bright air whirling around us.

Three A.M. Another call, windows down, howling through the humidity and swelter of Newfoundland. Alice wants me to come home, come back, relax, but I can't. I don't want to. I'm not sure what I want, but it's not brunch with Belgian waffles or screwing on the living room floor or a trip to the movies or…anything, really.

I can't do it, anyway. We got home, and I couldn't do it. Nothing felt right. Alice said it didn't matter, that she wanted to practice.

Now I haven't seen her for more than a day.

I've been on duty, catching up on calls. I've been going for twenty-four hours straight, powered on coppers'-little-helpers and mainlined caffeine and my hat and trench coat and hands are pinprick-sprayed with the residue of work.

Along the coastline the sea runs high and hot, splashing in over the breakwaters. Lights ahead, the glow of coalfoundries and gasification works. The call takes me up the glittering face of Palomino Cluster. Nice real estate. Up the masslifts and smashing through a door with Pentle backing me, knowing what we're going to find but never knowing how much these ones will fight.

Bedlam. A lady, this one a pretty brown girl who might have had a great life if she didn't decide she needed a baby, and a kid lying in the corner in a box screaming and screaming. And the lady's screaming too, screaming at the little kid in its box, like she's gone out of her mind.

As we come in through the door, she starts screaming at us. The kid keeps screaming. The lady keeps screaming. It's like a bunch of screwdrivers jamming in my ears; it goes on and on. Pentle grabs the lady and tries to hold her but she and the kid just keep screaming away and suddenly I can't breathe. I can barely stand. The kid screams and screams and screams: screwdrivers and glass and icepicks in my head.

So I shoot the thing. I pull out my Grange and put a bullet in the little sucker. Fragments of box and baby spray the air.

I don't do that, normally; it's against procedure to waste the kid in front of the mother.

But there we all are, staring at the body, bloodmist and gunpowder all over and my ears ringing from the shot and for one pristine crystal second, it's quiet.

Then the woman's screaming at me again and Pentle's screaming too because I screwed up the evidence before he could get a picture, and then the lady's all over me, trying to claw my eyes out. Pentle drags her off and then she's calling me a bastard and a killer and bastard and monkey man and a fucking pig and that I've got dead eyes.

And that really gets me: I've got dead eyes. This lady's headed into a rejoo collapse and won't last another twenty years and she'll spend all of it in a single-sex work camp. She's young, a lot like Alice, maybe the last of them to cross the line into rejoo, right when she came of age—not an old workhorse like me who was already forty when it went generic—and now she'll be dead in an eye blink. But I'm the one with dead eyes.

I take my Grange and shove it into her forehead. "You want to die too?"

"Go ahead! Do it! Do it!" She doesn't stop for a second, just keeps howling and spitting. "Fucking bastard! Bastard fuckingfuckfucking— Do it! Do it!" She's crying.

Even though I want to see her brains pop out the back of her head, I don't have the heart. She'll die soon enough. Another twenty years and she's done for. The paperwork isn't worth it.

Pentle cuffs her while she babbles to the baby in the box, just a lump of blood and limp doll parts now. "My baby my poor baby I didn't know I'm sorry my baby my poor baby I'm sorry...." Pentle muscles her out to the car.

For a while I can hear her in the hall. My baby my poor baby my poor baby.... And then she's gone down the lifts and it's a relief just to be standing there with the wet smells of the apartment and the dead body.

She was using a dresser drawer as her bassinet.

I run my fingers along the splintered edge, fondle the brass pulls. If nothing else, these ladies are resourceful, making the things we can't buy anymore. If I close my eyes, I can almost remember a whole industry around these little guys. Little outfits. Little chairs. Little beds. Everything made little.

Little dinosaurs.

"She couldn't make it shut up."

I jerk my hands away from the baby box, startled. Pentle has come up behind me. "Huh?"

"She couldn't make it stop crying. Didn't know what to do with it. Didn't know how to make it calm down. That's how the neighbors heard."

"Dumb."

"Yeah. She didn't even have a tag-teamer. How the heck was she going to do grocery shopping?"

He gets out his camera and tries a couple shots of the baby. There's not a whole lot left. A 12mm Grange is built for junkies, nitheads going crazy, 'bot assassins. It's overkill for an unarmored thing like this. When the new Granges came out, Grange ran an ad campaign on the sides of our cruisers. "Grange: Unstoppable." Or something like that. There was this one that said "Point Blank Grange" with a photo of a completely mangled nithead. That one was in all our lockers.

Pentle tries another angle on the drawer, going for a profile, trying to make the best of a bad situation. "I like how she used a drawer," he says.

"Yeah. Resourceful."

"I saw this one where the lady made a whole little table and chair set for her kid. Handmade it all. I couldn't believe how much energy she put into it." He makes shapes with his hand. "Little scalloped edges, shapes painted on the top: squares and triangles and things."

"If you're going to die doing something, I guess you want to do a good job of it."

"I'd rather be parasailing. Or go to a concert. I heard Alice was great the other night."

"Yeah. She was." I study the baby's body as Pentle takes some more shots. "If you had to do it, how do you think you'd make one of them be quiet?"

Pentle nods at my Grange. "I'd tell it to shut up."

I grimace and holster the gun. "Sorry about that. It's been a rough week. I've been up too long. Haven't been sleeping." Too many dinosaurs looking at me.

Pentle shrugs. "Whatever. It would have been better to get an intact image—" He snaps another picture. "—but even if she gets off this time, you got to figure in another year or two we'll be busting down her door again. These girls have a damn high recidivism." He takes another photo.

I go to a window and open it. Salt air flows in like fresh life, cleaning out the wet shit and body stinks. Probably the first fresh air the apartment's had since the baby was born. Got to keep the windows closed or the neighbors might hear. Got to stay locked in. I wonder if she's got a boyfriend, some rejoo drop-out who's going to show up with groceries and find her gone. Probably worth staking out the apartment, just to see. Keep the feminists off us for only bagging the women. I take a deep breath of sea air to get something fresh in my lungs, then light a cigarette and turn back to the room with its clutter and stink.

Recidivism. Fancy word for girls with a compulsion. Like a nithead or a coke freak, but weirder, more self-destructive. At least being a junkie is fun. Who the hell chooses to live in dark apartments with shitty diapers, instant food, and no sleep for years on end? The whole breeding thing is an anachronism—twenty-first-century ritual torture we don't need anymore. But these girls keep trying to turn back the clock and pop out the pups, little lizard brains compelled to pass on some DNA. And there's a new batch every year, little burps of offspring cropping up here and there, the convulsions of a species trying to restart itself and get evolution rolling again, like we can't tell that we've already won.

I'm keying through the directory listings in my cruiser, fiddling through ads and keywords and search preferences, trying to zero in on something that doesn't come up no matter how I go after it.

Dinosaur.

Toys.

Stuffed animals.

Nothing. Nobody sells stuff like that dinosaur. But I've run into two of them now.

Monkeys scamper over the roof of my car. One of them lands on my forward impact rails and looks at me, yellow eyes wide, before another jumps it and they fall off the carbon petal pullout where I'm parked. Somewhere down below, suburban crumble keeps small herds of them. I remember when this area was tundra. It was a long time ago. I've talked to techs in the carbon sink business who talk about flipping the climate and building an icecap, but it's a slow process, an accretion of centuries most likely. Assuming I don't get shot by a crazy mom or a nithead, I'll see it happen. But for now, it's monkeys and jungle.

Forty-eight hours on call and two more cleanups and Alice wants me to take the weekend off and play, but I can't. I'm living on perkies, now. She feels good about her work, and wants me all day. We've done it before. Lying together, enjoying the silence and our own company, the pleasure of just being together with nothing needing to be done. There's something wonderful about peace and silence and sea breezes twisting the curtains on the balcony.

I should go home. In a week, maybe, she'll be back at worrying, doubting herself, thrashing herself to work harder, to practice longer, to listen and feel and move inside of music that's so complex it might as well be the mathematics of chaos for anyone but her. But in reality, she has time. All the time in the world, and it makes me happy that she has it, that fifteen years isn't too long to prepare for something as heartstoppingly beautiful as what she did with Telogo.

I want to spend this time with her, to enjoy her bliss. But I don't want to go back and sleep with that dinosaur. I can't.

I call her from the cruiser.

"Alice?"

She looks out at me from the dash. "Are you coming home? I could meet you for lunch."

"Do you know where Maria got that dinosaur toy?"

She shrugs. "Maybe one of the shops on the Span? Why?"

"Just wondering." I pause. "Could you go get it for me?"

"Why? Why can't we do something fun? I'm on vacation. I just had my rejoo. I feel great. If you want to see my dinosaur, why don't you come home and get it?"

"Alice, please."

Scowling, she disappears from the screen. In a few minutes she's back, holding it up to the screen, shoving it in my face. I can feel my heart beating faster. It's cool in the cruiser, but I break into a sweat when I see the dinosaur on the screen. I clear my throat. "What's it say on the tag?"

Frowning, she turns the thing over, runs her fingers through its fur. She holds up the tag to the camera. It comes in blurry as the camera focuses, then it's there, clear and sharp. "Ipswitch Collectibles."

Of course. Not a toy at all.

The woman who runs Ipswitch is old, as old a rejoo as I've ever met. The wrinkles on her face look so much like plastic that it's hard to tell what's real and what may be a mask. Her eyes are sunken little blue coals and her hair is so white I think of weddings and silk. She must have been ninety when rejoo hit.

Whatever the name of it, Ipswitch Collectibles is full of toys: dolls staring down from their racks, different faces and shapes and colors of hair, some of them soft, some of them made of hard bright plastics; tiny trains that run around miniature tracks and spout steam from their pinky-sized smokestacks; figurines from old-time movies and comics in action poses: Superman, Dolphina, Rex Mutinous. And, under a shelf of hand-carved wooden cars, a bin full of stuffed dinosaurs in green and blue and red. A tyrannosaurus rex. A pterodactyl. The brontosaurus.

"I've got a few stegosauruses in the back."

I look up, startled. The old woman watches me from behind the counter, a strange wrinkly buzzard, studying me with those sharp blue eyes, examining me like I'm carrion.

I pick out the brontosaurus and hold it up by the neck. "No. These're fine."

A bell rings. The shop's main doors to the concourse slide open. A woman steps through, hesitant. Her hair is pulled back in a ponytail and she hasn't applied any makeup, and I can tell, even before she's all the way through the door, that she's one of them: a mom.

She hasn't been off rejoo long; she still looks fresh and young, despite the plumpness that comes with kids. She still looks good. But even without rejoo-collapse telltales, I know what she's done to herself. She's got the tired look of a person at war with the world. None of us look like that. No one has to look like that. Nitheads look less besieged. She's trying to act like the person she was before, like the actress or the financial advisor or the code engineer or the biologist or the waitress or whatever, putting on clothes from her life before, that used to fit perfectly and don't now, making herself look like a person who walks without fear in the open air, and who doesn't now.

As she wanders the aisles, I spy a stain on her shoulder. It's small but obvious if you know what to look for, a light streak of green on a creamy blouse. The kind of thing that never happens to anyone except women with children. No matter how hard she tries, she doesn't fit anymore. Not with us.

Ipswitch Collectibles, like others of its ilk, is a trap door of sorts—a rabbit hole down into the land of illicit motherhood: the place of mashed pea stains, sound-proofed walls, and furtive forays into daylight for resupply and survival. If I stand here long enough, holding my magic brontosaurus by the neck, I'll slip through entirely and see their world as it overlaps with my own, see it with the queer double vision of these women who have learned to turn a drawer into a crib, and know how to fold and pin an old shirt into a diaper, and know that "collectibles" really means "toys."

The woman slips in the direction of the train sets. She chooses one and places it on the counter. It's a bright wooden thing, each car a different color, each connected by a magnet.

The old woman takes the train and says, "Oh yes, this is a fine piece. I had grandchildren who played with trains like this when they were just a little more than one."

The mother doesn't say anything, just holds out her wrist for the charge, her eyes down on the train. She fingers the blue and yellow engine nervously.

I come up to the counter. "I'll bet you sell a lot of them."

The mother jerks. For a second she looks like she'll run, but she steadies. The old woman's eyes turn on me. Dark sunken blue cores, infinitely knowledgeable. "Not many. Not now. Not many collectors around for this sort of thing. Not now."

The transaction clears. The woman hustles out of the store, not looking back. I watch her go.

The old woman says, "That dinosaur is forty-seven, if you want it." Her tone says that she already knows I won't be buying.

I'm not a collector.

Nighttime. More dark-of-night encounters with illicit motherhood. The babies are everywhere, popping up like toadstools after rain. I can't keep up with them. I had to leave my last call before the cleanup crew came. Broke the chain of evidence, but what can you do? Everywhere I go, the baby world is ripping open around me, melons and seedpods and fertile wombs splitting open and vomiting babies onto the ground. We're drowning in babies. The jungle seems to seethe with them, the hidden women down in the suburb swelter, and as I shoot along the maglines on my way to bloody errands, the jungle's tendril vines curl up from below, reaching out to me.

I've got the mom's address in my cruiser. She's hidden now. Back down the rabbit hole. Pulled the lid down tight over her head. Lying low with her brood, reconnected with the underground of women who have all decided to kill themselves for the sake of squeezing out pups. Back in the swelter of locked doors and poopy diapers amongst the sorority who give train sets to little creatures who actually play with them instead of putting them on an end table and making you look at them every damn day....

The woman. The collector. I've been holding off on hitting her. It doesn't seem fair. It seems like I should wait for her to make her mistake before I pop her kids. But knowing that she's out there tickles my mind. I catch myself again and again, reaching to key in the homing on her address.

But then another call comes, another cleanup, and I let myself pretend I don't know about her, that I haven't perforated her hidey-hole and can now peer in on her whenever I like. The woman we don't know about—yet. Who hasn't made a mistake—yet. Instead I barrel down the rails to another call, slicing through jungle overstory where it impinges around the tracks, blasting toward another woman's destiny who was less lucky and less clever than the one who likes to collect. And these other women hold me for a little while. But in the end, parked on the edge of the sea, with monkeys screeching from the jungle and rain spackling my windshield, I punch in the collector's address.

I'll just drive by.

It could have been a rich house, before carbon sequestration. Before we all climbed into the bright air of the spires and superclusters. But now it exists at the very edge of what is left of suburbs. I'm surprised it even has electric or any services running to it at all. The jungle surrounds it, envelopes it. The road to it, off the maglines and off the maintenance routes, is heaved and split and perforated with encroaching trees. She's smart. She's as close to wilderness as it is possible to live. Beyond is only shadow tangle and green darkness. Monkeys scamper away from the spray of my headlights. The houses around her have already been abandoned. Any day now, they'll stop serving this area entirely. In another couple years, this portion will be completely overgrown. We'll cut off services and the last of the spires will go online and the jungle will swallow this place completely.

I sit outside the house for a while, looking at it. She's a smart one. To live this far out. No neighbors to hear the screaming. But if I think about it, she would have been smarter to move into the jungle entirely, and live with all the other monkeys that just can't keep themselves from breeding. I guess at the end of the day, even these crazy ladies are still human. They can't leave civilization totally behind. Or don't know how, anyway.

I get out of my car, pull my Grange, and hit the door.

As I slam through, she looks up from where she sits at her kitchen table. She isn't even surprised. A little bit of her seems to deflate, and that's all. Like she knew it was going to happen all along. Like I said: a smart one.

A kid runs in from the other room, attracted by the noise of me coming through the door. Maybe one and a half or two years old. It stops and stares, little tow-headed thing, its hair already getting long like hers. We stare at each other. Then it turns and scrambles into its mother's lap.

The woman closes her eyes. "Go on, then. Do it."

I point my Grange, my 12mm hand cannon. Zero in on the kid. The lady wraps her arms around it. It's not a clear shot. It'll rip right through and take out the mom. I angle differently, looking for the shot. Nothing.

She opens her eyes. "What are you waiting for?"

We stare at each other. "I saw you in the toy store. A couple days ago."

She closes her eyes again, regretful, understanding her mistake. She doesn't let go of the kid. I could just take it out of her arms, throw it on the floor and shoot it. But I don't. Her eyes are still closed.

"Why do you do it?" I ask.

Her eyes open again. She's confused. I'm breaking the script. She's mapped this out in her own mind. Probably a thousand times. Had to. Had to know this day would be coming. But here I am, all alone, and her kid's not dead yet. And I keep asking her questions.

"Why do you keep having these kids?"

She just stares at me. The kid squirms around on her and tries to start nursing. She lifts her blouse a little and the kid dives under. I can see the hanging bulges of the lady's breasts, these heavy swinging mammaries, so much larger than I remember them from the store when they were hidden under bra and blouse. They sag while the kid sucks. The woman just stares at me. She's on some kind of autopilot, feeding the kid. Last meal.

I take my hat off and put it on the table and sit. I put my Grange down, too. It just doesn't seem right to blow the sucker away while it's nursing. I take out a cigarette and light it. Take a drag. The woman watches me the way anyone watches a predator. I take another drag on my cigarette and offer it to her.

"Smoke?"

"I don't." She jerks her head toward her kid.

I nod. "Ah. Right. Bad for the new lungs. I heard that, once. Can't remember where." I grin. "Can't remember when."

She stares at me. "What are you waiting for?"

I look down at my pistol, lying on the table. The heavy machine weight of slugs and steel, a monster weapon. Grange 12mm Recoilless Hand Cannon. Standard issue. Stop a nitfitter in his tracks. Take out the whole damn heart if you hit them right. Pulverize a baby. "You had to stop taking rejoo to have the kid, right?"

She shrugs. "It's just an additive. They don't have to make rejoo that way."

"But otherwise we'd have a big damn population problem, wouldn't we?"

She shrugs again.

The gun sits on the table between us. Her eyes flick toward the gun, then to me, then back to the gun. I take a drag on the cigarette. I can tell what she's thinking, looking at that big old steel hand cannon on her table. It's way out of her reach, but she's desperate, so it looks a lot closer to her, almost close enough. Almost.

Her eyes go back up to me. "Why don't you just do it? Get it over with?"

It's my turn to shrug. I don't really have an answer. I should be taking pictures and securing her in the car, and popping the kid, and calling in the cleanup squad, but here we sit. She's got tears in her eyes. I watch her cry. Mammaries and fatty limbs and a frightening sort of wisdom, maybe coming from knowing that she won't last forever. A contrast to Alice with her smooth smooth skin and high bright breasts. This woman is fecund. Hips and breasts and belly fertile, surrounded by her messy kitchen, the jungle outside. The soil of life. She seems settled in all of this, a damp Gaia creature.

A dinosaur.

I should be cuffing her. I've got her and her kid. I should be shooting the kid. But I don't. Instead, I've got a hard-on. She's not beautiful exactly, but I've got a hard-on. She sags, she's round, she's breasty and hippy and sloppy; I can barely sit because my pants are so tight. I try not to stare at the kid nursing. At her exposed breasts. I take another drag on my cigarette. "You know, I've been doing this job for a long time."

She stares at me dully, doesn't say anything.

"I've always wanted to know why you women do this." I nod at the kid. It's come off her breast, and now the whole thing is exposed, this huge sagging thing with its heavy nipple. She doesn't cover up. When I look up, she's studying me, seeing me looking at her breast. The kid scrambles down and watches me, too, solemn-eyed. I wonder if it can feel the tension in the room. If it knows what's coming. "Why the kid? Really. Why?"

She purses her lips. I think I can see anger in the tightening of her teary eyes, anger that I'm playing with her. That I'm sitting here, talking to her with my Grange on her grimy table, but then her eyes go down to that gun and I can almost see the gears clicking. The calculations. The she-wolf gathering herself.

She sighs and scoots her chair forward. "I just wanted one. Ever since I was a little girl."

"Play with dolls, all that? Collectibles?"

She shrugs. "I guess." She pauses. Eyes back to the gun. "Yeah. I guess I did. I had a little plastic doll, and I used to dress it up. And I'd play tea with it. You know, we'd make tea, and then I'd pour some on her face, to make her drink. It wasn't a great doll. Voice input, but not much repertoire. My parents weren't rich. 'Let's go shopping.' 'Okay, for what?' 'For watches.' 'I love watches.' Simple. Like that. But I liked it. And then one day I called her my baby. I don't know why. I did, though, and the doll said, 'I love you mommy.'"

Her eyes turn wet as she speaks. "And I just knew I wanted to have a baby. I played with her all the time, and she'd pretend she was my baby, and then my mother caught us doing it and said I was a stupid girl, and I shouldn't talk that way, girls didn't have babies anymore, and she took the doll away."

The kid is down on the floor, shoving blocks under the table. Stacking and unstacking. It catches sight of me. It's got blue eyes and a shy smile. I get a twitch of it, again, and then it scrambles up off the floor, and buries its face in its mother's breasts, hiding. It peeks out at me, and giggles and hides again.

I nod at the kid. "Who's the dad?"

Stone cold face. "I don't know. I got a sample shipped from a guy I found online. We didn't want to meet. I erased everything about him as soon as I got the sample."

"Too bad. Things would have been better if you'd kept in touch."

"Better for you."

"That's what I said." I notice that the ash on my cigarette has gotten long, a thin gray penis hanging limp off the end of my smoke. I give it a twitch and it falls. "I still can't get over the rejoo part."

Inexplicably, she laughs. Brightens even. "Why? Because I'm not so in love with myself that I just want to live forever and ever?"

"What were you going to do? Keep it in the house until—"

"Her," she interrupts suddenly. "Keep her in the house. She is a girl and her name is Melanie."

At her name, the kid looks over at me. She sees my hat on the table and grabs it. Then climbs down off her mother's lap and carries it over to me. She holds it out to me, arms fully extended, an offering. I try to take it but she pulls the hat away.

"She wants to put it on your head."

I look at the lady, confused. She's smiling slightly, sadly. "It's a game she plays. She likes to put hats on my head."

I look at the girl again. She's getting antsy, holding the hat. She makes little grunts of meaning at me and waves the hat invitingly. I lean down. The girl puts the hat on my head, and beams. I sit up and set it more firmly.

"You're smiling," she says.

I look up at her. "She's cute."

"You like her, don't you?"

I look at the girl again, thinking. "Can't say. I've never really looked at them before."

"Liar."

My cigarette is dead. I stub it out on the kitchen table. She watches me do it, frowning, pissed off that I'm messing up her messy table, maybe, but then she seems to remember the gun. And I do, too. A chill runs up my spine. For a moment, when I leaned down to the girl, I'd forgotten about it. I could be dead, right now. Funny how we forget and remember and forget these things. Both of us. Me and the lady. One minute we're having a conversation, the next we're waiting for the killing to start.

This lady seems like she would have been a nice date. She's got spunk. You can tell that. It almost comes out before she remembers the gun. You can watch it flicker back and forth. She's one person, then another person: alive, thinking, remembering, then bang, she's sitting in a kitchen full of crusty dishes, coffee rings on her countertop and a cop with a hand cannon sitting at the kitchen table.

I spark up another cigarette. "Don't you miss the rejoo?"

She looks down at her daughter, holds out her arms. "No. Not a bit." The girl climbs back onto her mother's lap.

I let the smoke curl out of my mouth. "But there's no way you were going to get away with this. It's insane. You have to drop off of rejoo; you have to find a sperm donor who's willing to drop off, too, so two people kill themselves for a kid; you've got to birth the kid alone, and then you've got to keep it hidden, and then you'd eventually need an ID card so you could get it started on rejoo, because nobody's going to dose an undocumented patient, and you've got to know that none of this would ever work. But here you are."

She scowls at me. "I could have done it."

"You didn't."

Bang. She's back in the kitchen again. She slumps in her chair, holding the kid. "So why don't you just hurry up and do it?"

I shrug. "I was just curious about what you breeders are thinking."

She looks at me, hard. Angry. "You know what I'm thinking? I'm thinking we need something new. I've been alive for one hundred and eighteen years and I'm thinking that it's not just about me. I'm thinking I want a baby and I want to see what she sees today when she wakes up and what she'll find and see that I've never seen before because that's new. Finally, something new. I love seeing things through her little eyes and not through dead eyes like yours."

"I don't have dead eyes."

"Look in the mirror. You've all got dead eyes."

"I'm a hundred and fifty and I feel just as good as I did the day I went on."

"I'll bet you can't even remember. No one remembers." Her eyes are on the gun again, but they come up off it to look at me. "But I do. Now. And it's better this way. A thousand times better than living forever."

I make a face. "Live through your kid and all that?"

"You wouldn't understand. None of you would."

I look away. I don't know why. I'm the one with the gun. I'm running everything, but she's looking at me, and something gets tight inside me when she says that. If I was imaginative, I'd say it was some little bit of old primal monkey trying to drag itself out of the muck and make itself heard. Some bit of the critter we were before. I look at the kid—the girl—and she's looking back at me. I wonder if they all do the trick with the hat, or if this one's special somehow. If they all like to put hats on their killers' heads. She smiles at me and ducks her head back under her mother's arm. The woman's got her eyes on my gun.

"You want to shoot me?" I ask.

Her eyes come up. "No."

I smile slightly. "Come on. Be honest."

Her eyes narrow. "I'd blow your head off if I could."

Suddenly I'm tired. I don't care anymore. I'm sick of the dirty kitchen and the dark rooms and the smell of dirty makeshift diapers. I give the Grange a push, shove it closer to her. "Go ahead. You going to kill an old life so you can save one that isn't even going to last? I'm going to live forever, and that little girl won't last longer than seventy years even if she's lucky—which she won't be—and you're practically already dead. But you want to waste my life?" I feel like I'm standing on the edge of a cliff. Possibility seethes around me. "Give it a shot."

"What do you mean?"

"I'm giving you your shot. You want to try for it? This is your chance." I shove the Grange a little closer, baiting her. I'm tingling all over. My head feels light, almost dizzy. Adrenaline rushes through me. I push the Grange even closer to her, suddenly not even sure if I'll fight her for the gun, or if I'll just let her have it. "This is your chance."

She doesn't give a warning.

She flings herself across the table. Her kid flies out of her arms. Her fingers touch the gun at the same time as I yank it out of reach. She lunges again, clawing across the table. I jump back, knocking over my chair. I step out of range. She stretches toward the gun, fingers wide and grasping, desperate still, even though she knows she's already lost. I point the gun at her.

She stares at me, then puts her head down on the table and sobs.

The girl is crying too. She sits bawling on the floor, her little face screwed up and red, crying along with her mother who's given everything in that one run at my gun: all her hopes and years of hidden dedication, all her need to protect her progeny, everything. And now she lies sprawled on a dirty table and cries while her daughter howls from the floor. The girl keeps screaming and screaming.

I sight the Grange on the girl. She's exposed, now. She's squalling and holding her hands out to her mother, but she doesn't get up. She just holds out her hands, waiting to be picked up and held by a lady who doesn't have anything left to give. She doesn't notice me or the gun.

One quick shot and she's gone, paint hole in the forehead and brains on the wall just like spaghetti and the crying's over and all that's left is gunpowder burn and cleanup calls.

But I don't fire.

Instead, I holster my Grange and walk out the door, leaving them to their crying and their grime and their lives.

It's raining again, outside. Thick ropes of water spout off the eaves and spatter the ground. All around me the jungle seethes with the chatter of monkeys. I pull up my collar and resettle my hat. Behind me, I can barely hear the crying anymore.

Maybe they'll make it. Anything is possible. Maybe the kid will make it to eighteen, get some black market rejoo and live to be a hundred and fifty. More likely, in six months, or a year, or two years, or ten, a cop will bust down the door and pop the kid. But it won't be me.

I run for my cruiser, splashing through mud and vines and wet. And for the first time in a long time, the rain feels new.

AUSPICIOUS EGGS

by James Morrow

James Morrow is the author of the Godhead trilogy and seven other novels, including the World Fantasy Award-winning *Only Begotten Daughter, This is the Way the World Ends, The Last Witchfinder,* and *The Philosopher's Apprentice.* His novella *Shambling Toward Hiroshima* was a finalist for the Hugo, Nebula, and Locus awards, and won the Theodore Sturgeon Memorial Award. His short fiction—which has appeared *The Magazine of Fantasy & Science Fiction* and in many anthologies—has been collected in *Bible Stories for Adults* and *The Cat's Pajamas & Other Stories.*

Once a year, a person gets to celebrate a birthday. For children, it's the best day of the year. For most adults, it's something to pretend to forget or to celebrate with a quiet dinner out. After all, a birthday only means another year tacked on to an already large number. But no matter how old you are, a birthday is special because it marks the most important instance in a person's life: the moment of their birth.

In our next story, a birthday is hardly anything to celebrate. Life is as rainy and drear as the climate. The United States has been fragmented into a constellation of reefs and islands, the rest swallowed up by the rising oceans. And a new kind of church has mandated that the lives of those already born are less important than the lives of those who are as yet unconceived.

Here is a place overflowing with babies, packed with pregnant women, smothered by the stench of dripping diapers. It's a world where a menopausal woman might be put to death and an infertile baby drowned, because those who can't procreate are without value.

F ather Cornelius Dennis Monaghan of Charlestown Parish, Connie to his friends, sets down the Styrofoam chalice, turns from the corrugated cardboard altar, and approaches the two young women standing by the resin baptismal font. The font is six-sided and encrusted with saints, like a gigantic hex nut forged for some obscure yet holy purpose, but its most impressive feature is its portability. Hardly a month passes in which Connie doesn't drive the vessel across town, bear it into some wretched hovel, and confer immortality on a newborn whose parents have grown too feeble to leave home.

"Merribell, right?" asks Connie, pointing to the baby on his left.

Wedged in the crook of her mother's arm, the infant wriggles and howls. "No—Madeleine," Angela mumbles. Connie has known Angela Dunfey all her life, and he still remembers the seraphic glow that beamed from her face when she first received the Sacrament of Holy Communion. Today she boasts no such glow. Her cheeks and brow appear tarnished, like iron corroded by the Greenhouse Deluge, and her spine curls with a torsion more commonly seen in women three times her age. "Merribell's over here." Angela raises her free hand and gestures toward her cousin Lorna, who is balancing Madeleine's twin sister atop her gravid belly. Will Lorna Dunfey, Connie wonders, also give birth to twins? The phenomenon, he has heard, runs in families.

Touching the sleeve of Angela's frayed blue sweater, the priest addresses her in a voice that travels clear across the nave. "Have these children received the Sacrament of Reproductive Potential Assessment?"

The parishioner shifts a nugget of chewing gum from her left cheek to her right. "Y-yes," she says at last.

Henry Shaw, the pale altar boy, his face abloom with acne, hands the priest a parchment sheet stamped with the Seal of the Boston Isle Archdiocese. A pair of signatures adorns the margin, verifying that two ecclesiastical representatives have legitimized the birth. Connie instantly recognizes the illegible hand of Archbishop Xallibos. Below lie the bold loops and assured serifs of a Friar James Wolfe, M.D., doubtless the man who drew the blood.

Madeleine Dunfey, Connie reads. *Left ovary: 315 primordial follicles. Right ovary: 340 primordial follicles.* A spasm of despair passes through the priest. The egg-cell count for each organ should be 180,000 at least. It's a verdict of infertility, no possible appeal, no imaginable reprieve.

With an efficiency bordering on effrontery, Henry Shaw offers Connie a second parchment sheet.

Merribell Dunfey. Left ovary: 290 primordial follicles. Right ovary: 310 primordial follicles. The priest is not surprised. What sense would there be in God's withholding the power of procreation from one twin but not the other? Connie now needs only to receive these barren sisters, apply the sacred rites, and furtively pray that the Eighth Lateran Council was indeed guided by the Holy Spirit when it undertook to bring the baptismal process into the age of testable destinies and ovarian surveillance.

He holds out his hands, withered palms up, a posture he maintains as Angela surrenders Madeleine, reaches under the baby's christening gown, and unhooks both diaper pins. The mossy odor of fresh urine wafts into the Church of the Immediate Conception. Sighing profoundly, Angela hands the sopping diaper to her cousin.

"Bless these waters, O Lord," says Connie, spotting his ancient face in the consecrated fluid, "that they might grant these sinners the gift of life everlasting." Turning from the vessel, he presents Madeleine to his ragged flock, over three hundred natural-born Catholics—sixth-generation Irish, mostly, plus a smattering of Portuguese, Italians, and Croats—interspersed with two dozen recent converts of Korean and Vietnamese extraction: a congregation bound together, he'll admit, not so much by religious conviction as by shared destitution. "Dearly beloved, forasmuch as all humans enter the world in a state of depravity, and forasmuch as they cannot know the grace of our Lord except they be born anew of water, I beseech you to call upon God the Father that, through these baptisms, Madeleine and Merribell Dunfey may gain the divine kingdom." Connie faces his trembling parishioner. "Angela Dunfey, do you believe, by God's word, that children who are baptized, dying before they commit any actual evil, will be saved?"

Her "Yes" is begrudging and clipped.

Like a scrivener replenishing his pen at an inkwell, Connie dips his thumb into the font. "Angela Dunfey, name this child of yours."

"M-M-Madeleine Eileen Dunfey."

"We welcome this sinner, Madeleine Eileen Dunfey, into the mystical body of Christ"—with his wet thumb Connie traces a plus sign on the infant's forehead—"and do mark her with the Sign of the Cross."

Unraveling Madeleine from her christening gown, Connie fixes on the waters. They are preternaturally still—as calm and quiet as the Sea of Galilee after the Savior rebuked the winds. For many years the priest wondered why Christ hadn't returned on the eve of the Greenhouse Deluge, dispersing the hydrocarbon vapors with a wave of his hand, ending global warming with a Heavenward wink, but recently Connie has come to feel that divine intervention entails protocols past human ken.

He contemplates his reflected countenance. Nothing about it—not the tiny eyes, thin lips, hawk's beak of a nose—pleases him. Now he begins the immersion, sinking Madeleine Dunfey to her skullcap… her ears… cheeks… mouth… eyes.

"No!" screams Angela.

As the baby's nose goes under, mute cries spurt from her lips: bubbles inflated with bewilderment and pain. "Madeleine Dunfey," Connie intones, holding the infant down, "I baptize you in the name of the Father, and of the Son, and of the Holy Ghost." The bubbles break the surface. The fluid pours into the infant's lungs. Her silent screams cease, but she still puts up a fight.

"No! Please! No!"

A full minute passes, marked by the rhythmic shuffling of the congregation and the choked sobs of the mother. A second minute—a third—and finally the body stops moving, a mere husk, no longer home to Madeleine Dunfey's indestructible soul.

"No!"

The Sacrament of Terminal Baptism, Connie knows, is rooted in both logic and history. Even today, he can recite verbatim the preamble to the Eighth Lateran

Council's *Pastoral Letter on the Rights of the Unconceived*. ("Throughout her early years, Holy Mother Church tirelessly defended the Rights of the Born. Then, as the iniquitous institution of abortion spread across Western Europe and North America, she undertook to secure the Rights of the Unborn. Now, as a new era dawns for the Church and her servants, she must make even greater efforts to propagate the gift of life everlasting, championing the Rights of the Unconceived through a Doctrine of Affirmative Fertility.") The subsequent sentence has always given Connie pause. It stopped him when he was a seminarian. It stops him today. ("This Council therefore avers that, during a period such as that in which we find ourselves, when God has elected to discipline our species through a Greenhouse Deluge and its concomitant privations, a society can commit no greater crime against the future than to squander provender on individuals congenitally incapable of procreation.") Quite so. Indeed. And yet Connie has never performed a terminal baptism without misgivings.

He scans the faithful. Valerie Gallogher, his nephews' *zaftig* kindergarten teacher, seems on the verge of tears. Keye Sung frowns. Teresa Curtoni shudders. Michael Hines moans softly. Stephen O'Rourke and his wife both wince.

"We give thanks, most merciful Father"—Connie lifts the corpse from the water—"that it pleases you to regenerate this infant and take her unto your bosom." Placing the dripping flesh on the altar, he leans toward Lorna Dunfey and lays his palm on Merribell's brow. "Angela Dunfey, name this child of yours."

"M-M-Merribell S-Siobhan…" With a sharp reptilian hiss, Angela wrests Merribell from her cousin and pulls the infant to her breast. "Merribell Siobhan Dunfey!"

The priest steps forward, caressing the wisp of tawny hair sprouting from Merribell's cranium. "We welcome this sinner—"

Angela whirls around and, still sheltering her baby, leaps from the podium to the aisle—the very aisle down which Connie hopes one day to see her parade in prelude to receiving the Sacrament of Qualified Monogamy.

"Stop!" cries Connie.

"Angela!" shouts Lorna.

"No!" yells the altar boy.

For someone who has recently given birth to twins, Angela is amazingly spry, rushing pell-mell past the stupefied congregation and straight through the narthex.

"Please!" screams Connie.

But already she is out the door, bearing her unsaved daughter into the teeming streets of Boston Isle.

At 8:17 P.M., Eastern Standard Time, Stephen O'Rourke's fertility reaches its weekly peak. The dial on his wrist tells him so, buzzing like a tortured hornet as he scrubs his teeth with baking soda. *Skreee*, says the sperm counter, reminding Stephen of his ineluctable duty. *Skreee, skreee*: go find us an egg.

He pauses in the middle of a brush stroke and, without bothering to rinse his mouth, strides into the bedroom.

Kate lies on the sagging mattress, smoking an unfiltered cigarette as she balances her nightly dose of iced Arbutus rum on her stomach. Baby Malcolm cuddles against his mother, gums fastened onto her left nipple. She stares at the far wall, where the cracked and scabrous plaster frames the video monitor, its screen displaying the regular Sunday night broadcast of *Keep Those Kiddies Coming*. Archbishop Xallibos, seated, dominates a TV studio appointed like a day-care center: stuffed animals, changing table, brightly colored alphabet letters. Preschoolers crawl across the prelate's Falstaffian body, sliding down his thighs and swinging from his arms as if he is a piece of playground equipment.

"Did you know that a single act of onanism kills up to four hundred million babies in a matter of seconds?" asks Xallibos from the monitor. "As Jesus remarks in the Gospel According to Saint Andrew, 'Masturbation is murder.'"

Stephen coughs. "I don't suppose you're…"

His wife thrusts her index finger against her pursed lips. Even when engaged in shutting him out, she still looks beautiful to Stephen. Her huge eyes and high cheekbones, her elegant swanlike neck. "Shhh—"

"Please check," says Stephen, swallowing baking soda.

Kate raises her bony wrist and glances at her ovulation gauge. "Not for three days. Maybe four."

"Damn."

He loves her so dearly. He wants her so much—no less now than when they received the Sacrament of Qualified Monogamy. It's fine to have a connubial conversation, but when you utterly adore your wife, when you crave to comprehend her beyond all others, you need to speak in flesh as well.

"Will anyone deny that Hell's hottest quadrant is reserved for those who violate the rights of the unconceived?" asks Xallibos, playing peek-a-boo with a cherubic toddler. "Who will dispute that contraception, casual sex, and nocturnal emissions place their perpetrators on a one-way cruise to Perdition?"

"Honey, I have to ask you something," says Stephen.

"Shhh—"

"That young woman at Mass this morning, the one who ran away…"

"She went crazy because it was twins." Kate slurps down her remaining rum. The ice fragments clink against each other. "If it'd been just the one, she probably could've coped."

"Well, yes, of course," says Stephen, gesturing toward Baby Malcolm. "But suppose one of *your* newborns…"

"Heaven is forever, Stephen," says Kate, filling her mouth with ice, "and Hell is just as long." She chews, her molars grinding the ice. Dribbles of rum-tinted water spill from her lips. "You'd better get to church."

"Farewell, friends," says Xallibos as the theme music swells. He dandles a Korean three-year-old on his knee. "And keep those kiddies coming!"

The path to the front door takes Stephen through the cramped and fetid living room—functionally the nursery. All is quiet, all is well. The fourteen children, one for every other year of Kate's post-pubescence, sleep soundly. Nine-year-old Roger is quite likely his, product of the time Stephen and Kate got their cycles in synch; the boy boasts Stephen's curly blond hair and riveting green eyes. Difficult as it is, Stephen refuses to accord Roger any special treatment—no private trips to the frog pond, no second candy cane at Christmas. A good stepfather didn't indulge in favoritism.

Stephen pulls on his mended galoshes, fingerless gloves, and torn pea jacket. Ambling out of the apartment, he joins the knot of morose pedestrians as they shuffle along Winthrop Street. A fog descends, a steady rain falls: reverberations from the Deluge. Pushed by expectant mothers, dozens of shabby, black-hooded baby buggies squeak mournfully down the asphalt. The sidewalks belong to adolescent girls, gang after gang, gossiping among themselves and stomping on puddles as they show off their pregnancies like Olympic medals.

Besmirched by two decades of wind and drizzle, a limestone Madonna stands outside the Church of the Immediate Conception. Her expression lies somewhere between a smile and a smirk. Stephen climbs the steps, enters the narthex, removes his gloves, and, dipping his fingertips into the nearest font, decorates the air with the Sign of the Cross.

Every city, Stephen teaches his students at Cardinal Dougherty High School, boasts its own personality. Extroverted Rio, pessimistic Prague, paranoid New York. And Boston Isle? What sort of psyche inhabits the Hub and its surrounding reefs? Schizoid, Stephen tells them. Split. The Boston that battled slavery and stoked the fires beneath the American melting pot was the same Boston that massacred the Pequots and sent witchfinders to Salem. But here, now, which side of the city is emergent? The bright one, Stephen decides, picturing the hundreds of Heaven-bound souls who each day exit Boston's innumerable wombs, flowing forth like the bubbles that so recently streamed from Madeleine Dunfey's lips.

Blessing the Virgin's name, he descends the concrete stairs to the copulatorium. A hundred votive candles pierce the darkness. The briny scent of incipient immortality suffuses the air. In the far corner, a CD player screeches out the Apostolic Succession doing their famous rendition of "Ave Maria."

The Sacrament of Extramarital Intercourse has always reminded Stephen of a junior high prom. Girls strung along one side of the room, boys along the other, gyrating couples in the center. He takes his place in the line of males, removes his jacket, shirt, trousers, and underclothes, and hangs them on the nearest pegs. He stares through the gloom, locking eyes with Roger's old kindergarten teacher, Valerie Gallogher, a robust thirtyish woman whose incandescent red hair spills all the way to her hips. Grimly they saunter toward each other, following the pathway formed by the mattresses, until they meet amid the morass of writhing soulmakers.

"You're Roger Mulcanny's stepfather, aren't you?" asks the ovulating teacher.

"Father, quite possibly. Stephen O'Rourke. And you're Miss Gallogher, right?"

"Call me Valerie."

"Stephen."

He glances around, noting to his infinite relief that he recognizes no one. Sooner or later, he knows, a familiar young face will appear at the copulatorium, a notion that never fails to make him wince. How could he possibly explicate the Boston Massacre to a boy who'd recently beheld him in the procreative act? How could he render the Battle of Lexington lucid to a girl whose egg he'd attempted to quicken on the previous night?

For ten minutes he and Valerie make small talk, most of it issuing from Stephen, as was proper. Should the coming sacrament prove fruitful, the resultant child will want to know about the handful of men with whom his mother connected during the relevant ovulation. (Beatrice, Claude, Tommy, Laura, Yolanda, Willy, and the others were forever grilling Kate for facts about their possible progenitors.) Stephen tells Valerie about the time his students gave him a surprise birthday party. He describes his rock collection. He mentions his skill at trapping the singularly elusive species of rat that inhabits Charlestown Parish.

"I have a talent too," says Valerie, inserting a coppery braid into her mouth. Her areolas seem to be staring at him.

"Roger thought you were a terrific teacher."

"No—something else." Valerie tugs absently on her ovulation gauge. "A person twitches his lips a certain way, and I know what he's feeling. He darts his eyes in an odd manner—I sense the drift of his thoughts." She lowers her voice. "I watched you during the baptism this morning. Your reaction would've angered the archbishop—am I right?"

Stephen looks at his bare toes. Odd that a copulatorium partner should be demanding such intimacy of him.

"Am I?" Valerie persists, sliding her index finger along her large, concave bellybutton.

Fear rushes through Stephen. Does this woman work for the Immortality Corps? If his answer smacks of heresy, will she arrest him on the spot?

"Well, Stephen? Would the archbishop have been angry?"

"Perhaps," he confesses. In his mind he sees Madeleine Dunfey's submerged mouth, bubble following bubble like beads strung along a rosary.

"There's no microphone in my navel," Valerie asserts, alluding to a common Immortality Corps ploy. "I'm not a spy."

"Never said you were."

"You were thinking it. I could tell by the cant of your eyebrows." She kisses him on the mouth, deeply, wetly. "Did Roger ever learn to hold his pencil correctly?"

"'Fraid not."

"Too bad."

At last the mattress to Stephen's left becomes free, and they climb on top and begin reifying the Doctrine of Affirmative Fertility. The candle flames look like spear points. Stephen closes his eyes, but the effect is merely to intensify the fact that he's here. The liquid squeal of flesh against flesh grows louder, the odor of hot paraffin and warm semen more pungent. For a few seconds he manages to convince himself that the woman beneath him is Kate, but the illusion proves as tenuous as the surrounding wax.

When the sacrament is accomplished, Valerie says, "I have something for you. A gift."

"What's the occasion?"

"Saint Patrick's Day is less than a week away."

"Since when is that a time for gifts?"

Instead of answering, she strolls to her side of the room rummages through her tangled garments, and returns holding a pressed flower sealed in plastic.

"Think of it as a ticket," she whispers, lifting Stephen's shirt from its peg and slipping the blossom inside the pocket.

"To where?"

Valerie holds an erect index finger to her lips. "We'll know when we get there."

Stephen gulps audibly. Sweat collects beneath his sperm counter. Only fools considered fleeing Boston Isle. Only lunatics risked the retributions meted out by the Corps. Displayed every Sunday night on *Keep Those Kiddies Coming*, the classic images—men submitting to sperm siphons, women locked in the rapacious embrace of artificial inseminators—haunt every parishioner's imagination, instilling the same levels of dread as Spinelli's sculpture of the archangel Chamuel strangling David Hume. There are rumors, of course, unconfirmable accounts of parishioners who'd outmaneuvered the patrol boats and escaped to Québec Cay, Seattle Reef, or the Texas Archipelago. But to credit such tales was itself a kind of sin, jeopardizing your slot in Paradise as surely as if you'd denied the unconceived their rights.

"Tell me something, Stephen." Valerie straps herself into her bra. "You're a history teacher. Did Saint Patrick really drive the snakes out of Ireland, or is that just a legend?"

"I'm sure it never happened literally," says Stephen. "I suppose it could be true in some mythic sense."

"It's about penises, isn't it?" says Valerie, dissolving into the darkness. "It's about how our saints have always been hostile to cocks."

Although Harbor Authority Tower was designed to house the merchant-shipping aristocracy on whose ambitions the decrepit Boston economy still depended, the building's form, Connie now realizes, perfectly fits its new, supplemental function: sheltering the offices, courts, and archives of the archdiocese. As he lifts his gaze along the soaring facade, Connie thinks of sacred shapes—of steeples and vaulted windows, of Sinai and Zion, of Jacob's Ladder and hands pressed together in prayer. Perhaps it's all as God wants, he muses, flashing his ecclesiastical pass to the guard. Perhaps there's nothing wrong with commerce and grace being transacted within the same walls.

Connie has seen Archbishop Xallibos in person only once before, five years earlier, when the stately prelate appeared as an "honorary Irishman" in Charles-town Parish's annual Saint Patrick's Day Parade. Standing on the sidewalk, Connie observed Xallibos gliding down Lynde Street atop a huge motorized shamrock. The archbishop looked impressive then, and he looks impressive now—six foot four at least, Connie calculates, and not an ounce under three hundred pounds. His eyes are as red as a lab rat's.

"Father Cornelius Dennis Monaghan," the priest begins, following the custom whereby a visitor to an archbishop's chambers initiates the interview by naming himself.

"Come forward, Father Cornelius Dennis Monaghan."

Connie starts into the office, boots clacking on the polished bronze floor. Xal-libos steps out from behind his desk, a glistery cube hewn from black marble.

"Charlestown Parish holds a special place in my affections," says the arch-bishop. "What brings you to this part of town?"

Connie fidgets, shifting first left, then right, until his face lies mirrored in the hubcap-size Saint Cyril medallion adorning Xallibos's chest. "My soul is in torment, Your Grace."

"'Torment.' Weighty word."

"I can find no other. Last Tuesday I laid a two-week-old infant to rest."

"Terminal baptism?"

Connie ponders his reflection. It is wrinkled and deflated, like a helium bal-loon purchased at a carnival long gone. "My eighth."

"I know how you feel. After I dispatched my first infertile—no left testicle, right one shriveled beyond repair—I got no sleep for a week." Eyes glowing like molten rubies, Xallibos gazes directly at Connie. "Where did you attend seminary?"

"Isle of Denver."

"And on the Isle of Denver did they teach you that there are in fact two Churches, one invisible and eternal, the other—"

"Temporal and finite."

"Then they also taught you that the latter Church is empowered to revise its rites according to the imperatives of the age." The archbishop's stare grows brighter, hotter, purer. "Do you doubt that present privations compel us to arrange early immortality for those who cannot secure the rights of the un-conceived?"

"The problem is that the infant I immortalized has a twin." Connie swal-lows nervously. "Her mother stole her away before I could perform the second baptism."

"Stole her away?"

"She fled in the middle of the sacrament."

"And the second child is likewise arid?"

"Left ovary, two hundred ninety primordials. Right ovary, three hundred ten."

"Lord…" A high whistle issues from the archbishop, like water vapor escaping a tea kettle. "Does she intend to quit the island?"

"I certainly hope not, Your Grace," says the priest, wincing at the thought. "She probably has no immediate plans beyond protecting her baby and trying to—"

Connie cuts himself off, intimidated by the sudden arrival of a roly-poly man in a white hooded robe.

"Friar James Wolfe, M.D.," says the monk.

"Come forward, Friar Doctor James Wolfe," says Xallibos.

"It would be well if you validated this posthaste." James Wolfe draws a parchment sheet from his robe and lays it on the archbishop's desk. Connie steals a glance at the report, hoping to learn the baby's fertility quotient, but the relevant statistics are too faint. "The priest in question, he's celebrating Mass in"—sliding a loose sleeve upward, James Wolfe consults his wristwatch—"less than an hour. He's all the way over in Brookline."

Striding back to his desk, the archbishop yanks a silver fountain pen from its holder and decorates the parchment with his famous spidery signature.

"*Dominus vobiscum*, Friar Doctor Wolfe," he says, handing over the document.

As Wolfe rushes out of the office, Xallibos steps so close to Connie that his nostrils fill with the archbishop's lemon-scented aftershave lotion.

"That man never has any fun," says Xallibos, pointing toward the vanishing friar. "What fun do you have, Father Monaghan?"

"Fun, Your Grace?"

"Do you eat ice cream? Follow the fortunes of the Celtics?" He pronounces "Celtics" with the hard *C* mandated by the Seventh Lateran Council.

Connie inhales a hearty quantity of citrus fumes. "I bake."

"Bake? Bake what? Bread?"

"Cookies, your Grace. Brownies, cheesecake, pies. For the Feast of the Nativity, I make gingerbread magi."

"Wonderful. I like my priests to have fun. Listen, no matter what, the rite must be performed. If Angela Dunfey won't come to you, then you must go to her."

"She'll simply run away again."

"Perhaps so, perhaps not. I have great faith in you, Father Cornelius Dennis Monaghan."

"More than I have in myself," says the priest, biting his inner cheeks so hard that his eyes fill with tears.

"No," says Kate for the third time that night.

"Yes," insists Stephen, savoring the dual satisfactions of Kate's thigh beneath his palm and Arbutus rum washing through his brain.

Pinching her cigarette in one hand, Kate strokes Baby Malcolm's forehead with the other, lulling him to sleep. "It's wicked," she protests, placing Malcolm on the rug beside the bed. "A crime against the future."

Stephen grabs the Arbutus bottle, pours himself another glass, and, adding a measure of Dr. Pepper, takes a greedy gulp. He sets the bottle back on the nightstand, next to Valerie Gallogher's enigmatic flower.

"Screw the unconceived," he says, throwing himself atop his wife.

On Friday he'd shown the blossom to Gail Whittington, Dougherty High School's smartest science teacher, but her verdict had proved unenlightening. *Epigaea repens*, "trailing arbutus," a species with at least two claims to fame: it is the state flower of the Massachusetts Archipelago, and it has lent its name to the very brand of alcohol Stephen now consumes.

"No," says Kate once again. She drops her cigarette on the floor, crushes it with her shoe, and wraps her arms around him. "I'm not ovulating," she avers, forcing her stiff and slippery tongue into the depths of his mouth. "Your sperm aren't…"

"Last night, the Holy Father received a vision," Xallibos announces from the video monitor. "Pictures straight from Satan's flaming domain. Hell is a fact, friends. It's as real as a stubbed toe."

Stephen whips off Kate's chemise with all the dexterity of Father Monaghan removing a christening gown. The rum, of course, has much to do with their mutual willingness (four glasses each, only mildly diluted with Dr. Pepper), but beyond the Arbutus the two of them have truly earned this moment. Neither has ever skipped Mass. Neither has ever missed a Sacrament of Extramarital Intercourse. And while any act of nonconceptual love technically lay beyond the Church's powers of absolution, surely Christ would forgive them a solitary lapse. And so they go at it, this sterile union, this forbidden fruitlessness, this coupling from which no soul can come.

"Hedonists dissolving in vats of molten sulfur," says Xallibos.

The bedroom door squeals open. One of Kate's middle children, Beatrice, a gaunt six-year-old with flaking skin, enters holding a rude toy boat whittled from a hunk of bark.

"Look what I made in school yesterday!"

"We're busy," says Kate, pulling the tattered muslin sheet over her nakedness.

"Do you like my boat, Stephen?" asks Beatrice.

He slams a pillow atop his groin. "Lovely, dear."

"Go back to bed," Kate commands her daughter.

"Onanists drowning in lakes of boiling semen," says Xallibos.

Beatrice fixes Stephen with her receding eyes. "Can we sail it tomorrow on Parson's Pond?"

"Certainly. Of course. Please go away."

"Just you and me, right, Stephen? Not Claude or Tommy or Yolanda or *anybody*."

"Flaying machines," says Xallibos, "peeling the damned like ripe bananas."

"Do you want a spanking?" seethes Kate. "That's exactly what you're going to get, young lady, the worst spanking of your whole life!"

The child issues an elaborate shrug and strides off in a huff.

"I love you," says Stephen, removing the pillow from his privates like a chef lifting the lid from a stew pot.

Again they press together, throwing all they have into it, every limb and gland and orifice, no holds barred, no positions banned.

"Unpardonable," Kate groans.

"Unpardonable," Stephen agrees. He's never been so excited. His entire body is an appendage to his loins.

"We'll be damned," she says.

"Forever," he echoes.

"Kiss me," she commands.

"Farewell, friends," says Xallibos. "And keep those kiddies coming!"

Wrestling the baptismal font from the trunk of his car, Connie ponders the vessel's resemblance to a birdbath—a place, he muses, for pious sparrows to accomplish their avian ablutions. As he sets the vessel on his shoulder and starts away, its edges digging into his flesh, a different metaphor suggests itself. But if the font is Connie's Cross, and Constitution Road his Via Dolorosa, where does that leave his upcoming mission to Angela Dunfey? Is he about to perform some mysterious act of vicarious atonement?

"Morning, Father."

He slips the font from his shoulder, standing it up upright beside a fire hydrant. His parishioner Valerie Gallogher weaves amid the mob, dressed in a threadbare woolen parka.

"Far to go?" she asks brightly.

"End of the block."

"Want help?"

"I need the exercise."

Valerie extends her arm and they shake hands, mitten clinging to mitten. "Made any special plans for Saint Patrick's Day?"

"I'm going to bake shamrock cookies."

"Green?"

"Can't afford food coloring."

"I think I've got some green—you're welcome to it. Who's at the end of the block?"

"Angela Dunfey."

A shadow flits across Valerie's face. "And her daughter?"

"Yes," moans Connie. His throat constricts. "Her daughter."

Valerie lays a sympathetic hand on his arm. "If I don't have green, we can probably fake it."

"Oh, Valerie, Valerie—I wish I'd never taken Holy Orders."

"We'll mix yellow with orange. I'm sorry, Father."

"I wish this cup would pass."

"I mean yellow with blue."

Connie loops his arms around the font, embracing it as he might a frightened child. "Stay with me."

Together they walk through the serrated March air and, reaching the Warren

Avenue intersection, enter the tumble-down pile of bricks labeled No. 47. The foyer is as dim as a crypt. Switching on his penlight, Connie holds it aloft until he discerns the label *Angela Dunfey* glued to a dented mailbox. He begins the climb to apartment 8-C, his parishioner right behind. On the third landing, Connie stops to catch his breath. On the sixth, he puts down the font. Valerie wipes his brow with her parka sleeve. She takes up the font, and the two of them resume their ascent.

Angela Dunfey's door is wormy, cracked, and hanging by one hinge. The mere act of knocking swings it open.

They find themselves in the kitchen—a small musty space that would have felt claustrophobic were it not so sparely furnished. A saucepan hangs over the stove; a frying pan sits atop the icebox; the floor is a mottle of splinters, tar paper, and leprous shards of linoleum. Valerie sets the font next to the sink. The basin in which Angela Dunfey washes her dishes, Connie notes, is actually smaller than the one in which the Church of the Immediate Conception immortalizes infertiles.

He tiptoes into the bedroom. His parishioner sleeps soundly, her terrycloth bathrobe parted down the middle to accommodate her groggy, nursing infant; milk trickles from her breasts, streaking her belly with white rivulets. He must move now, quickly and deliberately, so there'll be no struggle, no melodramatic replay of 1 Kings 3:26, the desperate whore trying to tear her baby away from Solomon's swordsman.

Inhaling slowly, Connie leans toward the mattress and, with the dexterity of a weasel extracting the innards from an eggshell, slides the barren baby free and carries her into the kitchen.

Beside the icebox Valerie sits glowering on a wobbly three-legged stool.

"Dearly beloved, forasmuch as all humans enter the world in a state of depravity," Connie whispers, casting a wary eye on Valerie, "and forasmuch as they cannot know the grace of our Lord except they be born anew of water"—he places the infant on the floor near Valerie's feet—"I beseech you to call upon God the Father that, through this baptism, Merribell Dunfey may gain the divine kingdom."

"Don't beseech *me*," snaps Valerie.

Connie fills the saucepan, dumps the water into the font, and returns to the sink for another load—not exactly holy water, he muses, not remotely chrism, but presumably not typhoidal either, the best the under-budgeted Boston Water Authority has to offer. He deposits the load, then fetches another.

A wide, milky yawn twists Merribell's face, but she does not cry out.

At last the vessel is ready. "Bless these waters, O Lord, that they might grant this sinner the gift of life everlasting."

Dropping to his knees, Connie begins removing the infant's diaper. The first pin comes out easily. As he pops the second, the tip catches the ball of his thumb. Crown of thorns, he decides, feeling the sting, seeing the blood.

He bears the naked infant to the font. Wetting his punctured thumb, he touches Merribell's brow and draws the sacred plus sign with a mixture of blood and water. "We receive this sinner unto the mystical body of Christ, and do mark her with the Sign of the Cross."

He begins the immersion. Skullcap. Ears. Cheeks. Mouth. Eyes. O Lord, what a monstrous trust, this power to underwrite a person's soul. "Merribell Dunfey, I baptize you in the name of the Father…"

Now comes the nausea, excavating Stephen's alimentary canal as he kneels before the porcelain toilet bowl. His guilt pours forth in a searing flood—acidic strands of cabbage, caustic lumps of potato, glutinous strings of bile. Yet these pains are nothing, he knows, compared with what he'll experience on passing from this world to the next.

Drained, he stumbles toward the bedroom. Somehow Kate has bundled the older children off to school before collapsing on the floor alongside the baby. She shivers with remorse. Shrieks and giggles pour from the nursery: the preschoolers engaged in a raucous game of Blind Man's Bluff.

"Flaying machines," she mutters. Her tone is beaten, bloodless. She lights a cigarette. "Peeling the damned like…"

Will more rum help, Stephen wonders, or merely make them sicker? He extends his arm. Passing over the nightstand, his fingers touch a box of aspirin, brush the preserved *Epigaea repens*, and curl around the neck of the half-full Arbutus bottle. A ruddy cockroach scurries across the doily.

"I kept Willy home today," says Kate, taking a drag. "He says his stomach hurts."

As he raises the bottle, Stephen realizes for the first time that the label contains a block of type headed *The Story of Trailing Arbutus*. "His stomach *always* hurts." He studies the breezy little paragraph.

"I think he's telling the truth."

Epigaea repens. Trailing arbutus. Mayflower. And suddenly everything is clear.

"What's today's date?" asks Stephen.

"Sixteenth."

"March sixteenth?"

"Yeah."

"Then tomorrow's Saint Patrick's Day."

"So what?"

"Tomorrow's Saint Patrick's Day"—like an auctioneer accepting a final bid, Stephen slams the bottle onto the nightstand—"and Valerie Gallogher will be leaving Boston Isle."

"Roger's old teacher? Leaving?"

"Leaving." Snatching up the preserved flower, he dangles it before his wife. "Leaving…"

"…and of the Son," says Connie, raising the sputtering infant from the water, "and of the Holy Ghost."

Merribell Dunfey screeches and squirms. She's slippery as a bar of soap. Connie manages to wrap her in a dish towel and shove her into Valerie's arms.

"Let me tell you who you are," she says.

"Father Cornelius Dennis Monaghan of Charlestown Parish."

"You're a tired and bewildered pilgrim, Father. You're a weary wayfarer like myself."

Dribbling milk, Angela Dunfey staggers into the kitchen. Seeing her priest, she recoils. Her mouth flies open, and a howl rushes out, a cry such as Connie imagines the damned spew forth while rotating on the spits of Perdition. "Not her too! Not Merribell! No!"

"Your baby's all right," says Valerie.

Connie clasps his hands together, fingers knotted in agony and supplication. He stoops. His knees hit the floor, crashing against the fractured linoleum. "Please," he groans.

Angela plucks Merribell from Valerie and affixes the squalling baby to her nipple. "Oh, Merribell, Merribell…"

"Please." Connie's voice is hoarse and jagged, as if he's been shot in the larynx. "Please… please," he beseeches. Tears roll from his eyes, tickling his cheeks as they fall.

"It's not *her* job to absolve you," says Valerie.

Connie snuffles the mucus back into his nose. "I know."

"The boat leaves tomorrow."

"Boat?" Connie runs his sleeve across his face, blotting his tears.

"A rescue vessel," his parishioner explains. Sliding her hands beneath his armpits, she raises him inch by inch to his feet. "Rather like Noah's Ark."

"Mommy, I want to go home."

"Tell that to your stepfather."

"It's cold."

"I know, sweetheart."

"And dark."

"Try to be patient."

"Mommy, my stomach hurts."

"I'm sorry."

"My head too."

"You want an aspirin?"

"I want to go home."

Is this a mistake? wonders Stephen. Shouldn't they should all be in bed right now instead of tromping around in this nocturnal mist, risking flu and possibly pneumonia? And yet he has faith. Somewhere in the labyrinthine reaches of the Hoosac Docks, amid the tang of salt air and the stink of rotting cod, a ship awaits.

Guiding his wife and stepchildren down Pier 7, he studies the possibilities—the scows and barges, the tugs and trawlers, the reefers and bulk carriers. Gulls and gannets hover above the wharfs, squawking their chronic disapproval of the world. Across the channel, lit by a sodium-vapor searchlight, the *U.S. Constitution* bobs in her customary berth beside Charlestown Navy Yard.

"What're we doing here, anyway?" asks Beatrice.

"Your stepfather gets these notions in his head." Kate presses the baby tight against her chest, shielding him from the sea breeze.

"What's the *name* of the boat?" asks Roger.

"*Mayflower,*" answers Stephen.

Epigaea repens, trailing arbutus, mayflower.

"How do you spell it?" Roger demands.

"M-a-y…"

"…f-l-o-w-e-r?"

"Good job, Roger," says Stephen.

"I *read* it," the boy explains indignantly, pointing straight ahead with the collective fingers of his right mitten.

Fifty yards away, moored between an oil tanker and a bait shack, a battered freighter rides the incoming tide. Her stern displays a single word, *Mayflower*, a name that to the inhabitants of Boston Isle means far more than the sum of its letters.

"Now can we go home?" asks Roger.

"No," says Stephen. He has taught the story countless times. The Separatists' departure from England for Virginia… their hazardous voyage… their unplanned landing on Plymouth Rock… the signing of the covenant whereby the non-Separatists on board agreed to obey whatever rules the Separatists imposed. "*Now* we can go on a nice long voyage."

"On *that* thing?" asks Willy.

"You're not serious," says Laura.

"Not me," says Claude.

"Forget it," says Yolanda.

"Sayonara," says Tommy.

"I think I'm going to throw up," says Beatrice.

"It's not your decision," Stephen tells his stepchildren. He stares at the ship's hull, blotched with rust, blistered with decay, another victim of the Deluge. A passenger whom he recognizes as his neighbor Michael Hines leans out a porthole like a prairie dog peering from its burrow. "Until further notice, I make all the rules."

Half by entreaty, half by coercion, he leads his disgruntled family up the gangplank and onto the quarterdeck, where a squat man in an orange raincoat and a maroon watch cap demands to see their ticket.

"Happy Saint Patrick's Day," says Stephen, flourishing the preserved blossom.

"We're putting you people on the fo'c'sle deck," the man yells above the growl of the idling engines. "You can hide behind the pianos. At ten o'clock you get a bran muffin and a cup of coffee."

As Stephen guides his stepchildren in a single file up the forward ladder, the crew of the *Mayflower* reels in the mooring lines and ravels up the anchor chains, setting her adrift. The engines kick in. Smoke pours from the freighter's twin stacks. Sunlight seeps across the bay, tinting the eastern sky hot pink and making the island's many-windowed towers glitter like Christmas trees.

A sleek Immortality Corps cutter glides by, headed for the wharfs, evidently unaware that enemies of the unconceived lie close at hand.

Slowly, cautiously, Stephen negotiates the maze of wooden crates—it seems as if every piano on Boston Isle is being exported today—until he reaches the starboard bulwark. As he curls his palm around the rail, the *Mayflower* cruises past the Mystic Shoals, maneuvering amid the rocks like a skier following a slalom course.

"Hello, Stephen." A large woman lurches into view, abruptly kissing his cheek.

He gulps, blinking like a man emerging into sunlight from the darkness of a copulatorium. Valerie Gallogher's presence on the *Mayflower* doesn't surprise him, but he's taken aback by her companions. Angela Dunfey, suckling little Merribell. Her cousin, Lorna, still spectacularly pregnant. And, most shocking of all, Father Monaghan, leaning his frail frame against his baptismal font.

Stephen says, "Did we…? Are you…?"

"My blood has spoken," Valerie Gallogher replies, her red hair flying like a pennant. "In nine months I give birth to our child."

Whereupon the sky above Stephen's head begins swarming with tiny black birds. No, not birds, he realizes: devices. Ovulation gauges sail through the air, a dozen at first, then scores, then hundreds, immediately pursued by equal numbers of sperm counters. As the little machines splash down and sink, darkening the harbor like the contraband tea from an earlier moment in the history of Boston insurgency, a muffled but impassioned cheer arises among the stowaways.

"Hello, Father Monaghan." Stephen unstraps his sperm counter. "Didn't expect to find *you* here."

The priest smiles feebly, drumming his fingers on the lip of the font. "Valerie informs me you're about to become a father again. Congratulations."

"My instincts tell me it's a boy," says Stephen, leaning over the rail. "He's going to get a second candy cane at Christmas," asserts the bewildered pilgrim as, with a wan smile and a sudden flick of his wrist, he breaks his bondage to the future.

If I don't act now, thinks Connie as he pivots toward Valerie Gallogher, I'll never find the courage again.

"Do we have a destination?" he asks. Like a bear preparing to ascend a tree, he hugs the font, pulling it against his chest.

"Only a purpose," Valerie replies, sweeping her hand across the horizon. "We won't find any Edens out there, Father. The entire Baltimore Reef has become a wriggling mass of flesh, newborns stretching shore to shore." She removes her ovulation gauge and throws it over the side. "In the Minneapolis Keys, the

Corps routinely casts homosexual men and menopausal women into the sea. On the California Archipelago, male parishioners receive periodic potency tests and—"

"The Atlanta Insularity?"

"A nightmare."

"Miami Isle?"

"Forget it."

Connie lays the font on the bulwark then clambers onto the rail, straddling it like a child riding a see-saw. A loop of heavy-duty chain encircles the font, the steel links flashing in the rising sun. "Then what's our course?"

"East," says Valerie. "Toward Europe. What are you doing?"

"East," Connie echoes, tipping the font seaward. "Europe."

A muffled, liquid crash reverberates across the harbor. The font disappears, dragging the chain behind it.

"Father!"

Drawing in a deep breath, Connie studies the chain. The spiral of links unwinds quickly and smoothly, like a coiled rattlesnake striking its prey. The slack vanishes. Connie feels the iron shackle seize his ankle. He flips over. He falls.

"Bless these waters, O Lord, that they might grant this sinner the gift of life everlasting…"

"Father!"

He plunges into the harbor, penetrating its cold hard surface: an experience, he decides, not unlike throwing oneself through a plate glass window. The waters envelop him, filling his ears and stinging his eyes.

We welcome this sinner into the mystical body of Christ, and do mark him with the Sign of the Cross, Connie recites in his mind, reaching up and drawing the sacred plus sign on his forehead.

He exhales, bubble following bubble.

Cornelius Dennis Monaghan, I baptize you in the name of the Father, and of the Son, and of the Holy Ghost, he concludes, and as the black wind sweeps through his brain, sucking him toward immortality, he knows that he's never been happier.

PETER SKILLING
by Alex Irvine

Alex Irvine—a k a Alexander C. Irvine—is the author of the original novels *A Scattering of Jades; One King, One Solider; The Life of Riley; The Narrows;* and *Buyout.* He's also written some tie-in novels, such as *Transformers: Exodus, Batman: Inferno,* and *Iron Man: Virus.* His work on this last property has lead him to script the *Iron Man: Rapture* miniseries for Marvel Comics. Irvine is also a prolific author of short fiction, with more than forty stories published since making his debut in 2000. His short work, which frequently appears in *The Magazine of Fantasy & Science Fiction,* has been collected in *Unintended Consequences, Pictures from an Expedition,* and in a four-story chapbook, *Rossetti Song.*

Since the late 1970s, Conservative Christians have united their voices to take an active and highly visible role in the American political sphere. It is an interesting development in a nation founded on the separation of church and state, and one that provides fodder for a great deal of speculation. Even science fiction writers sometimes wonder: what would the United States be like if current trends in conservatism and religiosity continue?

Our next story spins just such a future world, a world that has taken a significantly dark tone. This United States is a surveillance state bristling with rules and rigid strictures. Within such a complicated framework, it would take years to learn all the right things to do or say—years Peter Skilling never had. He's awakened ninety-eight years after his own death, a stranger in his own homeland. Medical science has given him a second chance at life, but living it just might be beyond his grasp.

Here is a new dystopian America. Thomas Jefferson would be glad they can't bring him back to live in it.

P eter Skilling did not remember falling into a glacial crevasse on the north slope of Mount McKinley, so it came as a surprise to him when he awoke to find what appeared to be a robot sitting next to his bed.

"You're a very lucky man, Peter Skilling," the robot said to him. "A genuinely unique set of circumstances. You might have sustained fatal trauma from your fall, but look! You fell into a subglacial stream, resulting in scrapes and bruises only! And you might have been ground to gel by the glacier but for the earthquake that struck hours after your death and sheared away a portion of the mountain, leaving your body exposed in a depression away from the redirected glacier. Then, too, consider the above-average snowfall that encased your remains and protected you from the depredations of weather and wildlife."

"My remains?" Peter croaked.

Noting the dryness of his throat, the robot moved swiftly to unspool a thin hose from the wall and placed its nipple in Peter's mouth. Reflexively Peter sucked, and his mouth filled with cool water.

"This is the truly amazing chapter in your saga, Mr. Skilling," the robot gushed. "You died so quickly and in such cold water that—if you'll permit me an inorganic figure of speech—your autonomic system shorted out. Your brain function is astonishingly well preserved, and we have been able to surgically reconstruct damaged pathways. You were our perfect candidate. Quite a find, if I do say so myself!"

The robot paused. "Do you consider yourself sufficiently apprised of the fortuitous circumstances in which you find yourself?"

Peter hadn't caught much of the robot's effusion, but he gathered that he'd been in an accident on the mountain and survived. That seemed lucky. "I guess," he said.

"Very good," the robot said. It extended a hand, and Peter shook. The robot's hand was warm. "I am called Burkhardt," the robot said. "I wish you all the very best."

It left, and Peter noticed a woman in a white coat who had apparently been waiting near the door while the robot, Burkhardt, had told Peter how lucky he was. She stepped forward and smiled at him. "I'm Dr. McBride," she said. "I hope the steelie didn't overload you. We have to observe protocols as part of our grant mechanism, and it's easier to have robots take care of them than entrust the process to people."

"Okay," Peter said.

"Why don't you sit up?" Dr. McBride suggested. "I think you'll find everything's in working order."

Peter sat up, surfed a brief wave of dizziness, and discovered that he did feel pretty good. "Yeah," he said. "I feel okay. So why am I in the hospital?"

Dr. McBride looked annoyed. "Yes. I thought maybe Burkhardt had rushed a little. These federal programs, you know. Not that I'm criticizing, it would be much more difficult to address everything on a case-by-case basis when we don't have access to all the intelligence, but it's only natural." Although she still looked in his direction, the doctor was no longer talking to Peter.

He took another drink from the wall nipple. Dr. McBride looked up at him and smiled again, apologetically this time. "I'm sorry, Mr. Skilling," she said. "I haven't answered your question."

Peter raised an eyebrow and sucked at the nipple.

"You see, you died in 2005. We've spent the past several months working you through the rejuvenation process, and I have to say it's gone very well."

The nipple fell out of Peter's mouth and a little water dribbled down his chin. Dr. McBride's smile regained some of its strength.

"There's no way to cushion it," she said. "Although God knows Burkhardt tries. You've been dead for ninety-eight years. And now you have another chance to live."

Her gaze shifted to a monitor by Peter's head. "Mm," she said. "I was afraid of that." Crossing to the monitor, Dr. McBride opened a drawer and removed a shiny instrument.

Peter couldn't breathe. He tried to speak, and a breathy whine came out of his mouth.

"I've going to give you something that will alleviate your shock response," Dr. McBride said. Peter heard a hiss, and then he was gone.

When he woke up, the robot was there again. Peter felt worse than he had the first time he'd opened his eyes in that room. "Don't give me another shot," he said.

"Oh, I don't administer medication," Burkhardt said airily. "Fascinating colloquialism, 'shot'—bit anachronistic now. We do transdermals now, of course, except when intravenous administration is indicated. But I'm not here to go on about our medical procedures; you're a healthy man; you don't care about this. I do need to apologize for yesterday. It seems I moved a little too quickly for circumstances, and Dr. McBride..." Burkhardt trailed off. "She was terribly inappropriate and unprofessional. To say some of the things she said, given the fragility of your condition... trust me when I say that you won't have to deal with her anymore."

Sometime during its apology, Peter remembered what she'd said to him. "Are you serious that I was dead?" he asked. Having slept on the idea, even if the sleep was drug-induced, made it easier to grapple with.

Burkhardt cocked its head to one side. "Oh yes, perfectly serious. My function here is to ensure that your assimilation process is maximally efficient. There is significant state interest in making certain that you come to terms with the reality of your surroundings. Yours is truly an exceptional situation. I can certainly sympathize with your feelings of loss and displacement, but do not neglect gratitude. You have benefited from the most advanced and powerful science the world has ever known."

"You can?" Peter asked. "Sympathize?"

"Ha ha," Burkhardt said. "Not in an emotional sense, no. But my simulations of emotional interaction are considered very sophisticated. I belong to the only class of artificial intelligences whose testimony is admissible in court."

Peter could have sworn that it sounded proud. He considered what Burkhardt had said about loss and displacement. Pretty soon he figured he'd feel both, but right then he was letting himself be caught up in the puzzle of how he'd come to be talking to a robot that seemed to have been programmed by a self-help guru. Chicken Soup for the Future Resurrected.

"This is ridiculous," he said. He tossed back the blanket and swung his legs over the side of the bed. The floor felt good under his feet.

"Delightful," Burkhardt said. It actually clapped, or clanked. "Marvelous. You're making tremendous progress."

Peter needed a moment to get blood to his head. Then he stood. He was wearing light blue hospital pajamas, and when he ran his hands over his scalp he found that his hair had been cut. That brought on the first tremor of dislocation; someone had cut his hair. "Okay, Burkhardt," he said, forcing himself to focus on what was in front of him. "Where am I?"

"Bremerton, Washington," Burkhardt said.

"You're kidding." Peter had grown up in Kirkland, just across Puget Sound. Ninety-eight years. He wondered what Seattle looked like. A powerful surge of optimism overcame him. He was alive, and Burkhardt was right that he was lucky, especially in that he hadn't had any family left when he'd apparently died. "I died," he said, testing it out. He had no memory of it, and was unaffected by the idea. "So this isn't heaven?"

"My goodness, no. This is still the world of the flesh. You don't seriously think you might be in heaven?"

"No," Peter said. He chuckled. "My idea of heaven wouldn't be a hospital room."

"What would it be?"

Burkhardt's amazing cheer seemed to have gone on hiatus. "Am I supposed to have a theological discussion with a robot?" Peter asked.

"Part of my assessment must include the state of your beliefs," Burkhardt said. "Given the blessing you've received, it occurred to me that you might be thankful."

"Blessing? What are you, a robot priest?"

"The cutting edge of robotics, if I'm not being too immodest in characterizing myself in such a manner, is conducted in affiliation with the Office of Faith-Based Investigation. We are all products of our upbringing, aren't we? Ha ha. Now please, back to my question: Are you thankful?"

"Sure. But thank the doctors. I've never been much of a religious guy."

"I see," Burkhardt said. "Well. It so happens that this project is centered on the grounds of what was once the naval shipyard here. The primary strength of the American military is now orbitally based, so the facilities here were reconditioned some years ago. There is another similar facility in our Siberian protectorate, but we thought it best to keep you close to home."

Siberian protectorate? Peter let it pass. A lot could happen in ninety-eight years. "Okay," he said. "Can I get some clothes? I want to get out and see this brave new world."

Burkhardt's face was a single textured piece of metal, but Peter could have sworn the robot grimaced. "That's an unfortunate choice of words, Peter. We can certainly get you dressed—in fact there's clothing tailored to you in the closet there—but we think it's better for you to stay on the grounds for a while."

"What for? Am I sick?"

"I'm reaching my functional parameters here, Peter. You seem to be adapting remarkably well to what must be an enormously wrenching turn of events. Please stay here. Feel free to get dressed. I'm going to hand you off to one of the staff who will get you settled in here." Burkhardt extended a hand, just as it had the last time, and just as he had the last time, Peter shook. The robot left, and a bubble of fear rose up and broke in Peter's mind.

He closed his eyes and gathered himself. Okay. Things would be different. He would have to cope, but it would be like he was an immigrant to another country where people spoke the same language but lived in an entirely different way. Difficult but doable. Peter opened the closet door and found a suit of clothes that wouldn't have looked out of place in church the last time he'd gone to church, which was sometime in the '90s at his college roommate's wedding. It fit perfectly, and so did the shoes. A pair of spats came with the shoes; Peter looked them over, and decided that his willingness to assimilate only went so far.

Alone and awake, he had a chance to really look around the room for the first time. There was no window, no TV—did people still watch TV? He couldn't imagine they didn't. It would be weird if the hardest thing about blending into the year 2103 was the lack of television.

2103. The number didn't mean anything to Peter. When it came right down to it, he had to admit that he didn't quite believe it yet. The alternative was that he was hallucinating, but there he was in a room painted pale green with a bed and a monitor and a chair in the corner and a little tube that came out of the wall. Surely he had enough imagination to hallucinate something better than this.

The door opened and an orderly came in with a tray. "Up and around," the orderly said. "Looking good." He was tall and ropy with muscle, hair in a crew cut. Peter's first instinct was that the guy was military.

"I feel okay," he said. The orderly set the tray on his bed and left. Peter removed the cover: baked chicken, muffin, vegetables, a plastic bottle of juice. He sat down and ate, getting progressively hungrier as he demolished the meal, until by the time he was finished he wanted to start all over again.

There was nothing visible that looked like a call button. Peter looked at the monitor, saw that it was tracking his vital signs even though he wasn't connected to it. He hadn't seen any kind of contact patches when he'd changed into the suit, and it wasn't clear how the monitor could get a close reading on him. Was there some kind of camera system that could track all of his vitals? He looked around the room and didn't see one. Then again, Dr. McBride had been talking to someone the day before.

Peter went to the door and tried it. It was locked. He banged on it and it opened almost immediately. The orderly stood in the doorway. "Are you comfortable?" he asked.

"Am I under surveillance in here?" Peter asked.

A disbelieving expression swept across the orderly's face. "Surveillance is routine," he said. "It presupposes nothing about guilt or innocence. Do you need anything?"

"I'd like to get out of this room for a while. Get some fresh air."

"A tour is being arranged, Mr. Skilling. You will be contacted when arrangements are complete." The orderly shut the door.

Peter got mad. He banged on the door again. The orderly opened it. "If you're going to bullshit me," Peter said, "you could at least remove my tray."

"Your language is objectionable," the orderly said, but he came in and took the tray.

Without a clock in the room, he had no way of knowing how much time passed before the door opened again and three people came in. Make that two people and a robot: Burkhardt stood behind the orderly and a woman Peter hadn't seen before. "Mr. Skilling," she said.

"Are you my new doctor?"

"No. I'm here to take you outside and answer any questions you might have. My name is Melinda. If you'll come this way."

Peter followed her out into a hallway. Burkhardt and the orderly fell into step behind them. "Your rejuvenation is our first full success," Melinda said as they waited for an elevator. "It really has been a gift both to you and to science."

She fell silent, and Peter figured out that he was supposed to respond. It was beginning to dawn on him that people in 22nd century Bremerton expected certain ritualistic exchanges, and that so far he hadn't made a very good impression. Even Burkhardt had been bothered by the offhand brave-new-world comment, which Peter had meant with Shakespeare in mind instead of Huxley—but it might be too late to explain that.

The elevator door opened, and the four of them crowded into the car. Peter noticed a crucifix on the wall. "Is this a Catholic hospital?" he asked.

Melinda shook her head. "This is a military research installation. You'll find that one of the things that's changed since your accident is that we have different ideas about the appropriate role of religion in public life."

She'd put strange emphasis on the word "accident." Peter wasn't sure why, but before he could frame a question the elevator door opened and they walked out into a spacious lobby, all glass and steel. Military police stood at a screening checkpoint just inside the front doors, and at least half of the people moving through the lobby wore uniforms. Most of the others wore white coats. "Since when does the military fund research into how to bring people back to life?" Peter asked.

"National security concerns dictate that most scientific research be conducted in cooperation with the military," Melinda said. "We've taken the lead on this project." She leaned her face down to a screen, and one of the MPs waved her through. The orderly did the same, and Burkhardt held one hand in front of the screen. Peter followed suit. The screen was blank, glowing a dim green. It didn't respond visibly to his presence, but one of the MPs nodded at him and he followed his escorts outside.

It was a nice day, warm and clear. Peter looked out over the islands in Puget Sound, then turned around to see the Olympic Mountains. He blinked. They weren't quite the right shade of green, and everywhere he looked he saw the savage brown scars of clear-cuts. "What the hell happened there?" he asked.

"We've all had to make sacrifices," Melinda answered. "National parks are a luxury in an age of terror. With the exception of presidential historic sites, they've all been transferred to private ownership."

Peter was furious, but he bit down on the profane comment he'd been about to make. "Speaking of ownership," Melinda said, "I believe these are yours." She reached out with his wallet and a small Ziploc baggie with what was left of the last quarter-ounce Peter had bought before he fell into a glacier.

An instinct to caution prickled the back of his neck. "Thanks," he said, and took only the wallet.

"Please, Mr. Skilling," Melinda said. "Blood tests clearly indicated the presence of marijuana in your body, and this bag was found in your right front pocket. It's a little too late to deny things."

Peter shrugged and took the weed. He walked back toward the hospital door and threw it into a trash can. "I doubt it's any good after ninety-eight years anyway."

"I wouldn't know," Melinda said. "Are you angry about something, Mr. Skilling?"

"My goodness, of course he's angry," Burkhardt piped up. "A perfectly rational response to his situation, in fact a clear indication that he is coping in a sane and intelligent manner. I note that you grew angry when you saw the mountains, Peter. Is that because of our conservation practices?"

"Is that what you call it? Looks like a clear-cut to me."

"That's not a current term. 'Maximal extractive intensity and utilization' is the standard practice at this time. I believe 'clear-cut' is jargon from the environmentalists of your time, am I correct?"

Peter pointed up at the mountains. "No, 'clear-cut' is an accurate description of what's happened up there," he said.

"So would you consider yourself an environmentalist?" Burkhardt asked.

"Yeah, I would. Especially compared to whoever authorized that."

"Whoa there," the orderly said. "All conservation decisions come straight from the top. Show a little respect."

"Were you a member of the Green Party of the United States?" Melinda asked.

"What?"

"It's a simple question, Mr. Skilling. We need to know as much as possible about you to make correct decisions."

"Fine. Yes, I was a Green. Still am, if there's still a party."

"There isn't," Melinda said. She turned to the orderly. "Vince, do you need anything else?"

"We need to get the drug offense squared away," Vince said. "Mr. Skilling, who did you purchase the marijuana from?"

Peter just gaped at him. "The guy I bought from has probably been dead for sixty years, Vince."

"You may address me as Col. Trecker. Answer the question."

Peter hesitated. He didn't want to rat on anyone, but you couldn't do much harm to a dead guy. Except me, he thought, and if they're going to make a big deal out of this I better cooperate. Especially if they've had this colonel pretending he was an orderly. "His name was Phil Kokoszka. Happy?"

Col. Trecker whipped out a PDA and tapped at it. "Philip J. Kokoszka of Redmond?"

"Yeah, he lived in Redmond." Peter had just been there last week, or ninety-eight years ago by the world's reckoning.

"Was he a Green too?"

"Yeah. I knew him through local meetings. Come on, what's the point? He's dead. So was I. Jesus."

The curse brought a moment of icy silence.

"Are we all set here?" Melinda asked.

Trecker put away the PDA. "Looks that way. Take him back inside."

"Wait a minute," Peter said. "I'm kind of looking forward to seeing what the world looks like now."

"The brave new world?" Col. Trecker responded. "Maybe some other time. Right now there's business to take care of."

Burkhardt stepped closer to Peter. "Time to go in, Peter," it said. "You really are doing marvelously well. Don't let your initial emotional responses cloud your judgment."

When they entered the hospital, one of the MPs at the door fell into step, his rifle slung at his hip and pointed in Peter's direction. They didn't go back to the elevator; instead Melinda and Col. Trecker let the party down a curving hall to an open door. They went in, and Peter got a cold chill as he recognized the setup: a desk at the far wall, set on a low dais; two tables facing it; a few chairs arranged in one corner. A courtroom. Burkhardt sat Peter at one of the tables and remained standing behind him. Col. Trecker went to the desk. Melinda sat at the other table.

"You've got to be kidding," Peter said. "The Army is prosecuting me for holding a quarter-ounce of weed a hundred years ago?"

"That's certainly a rosy way of putting it," Burkhardt said. "I'm deeply sorry that the situation is in fact a little more serious than that."

The door opened and shut behind Peter. He started to glance over his shoulder to see who was coming in, but Burkhardt stepped to block his view. "Eyes front, Peter. Let's make the best of things here, shall we?"

Run, Peter thought. But he didn't. He turned back around and looked at Col. Trecker, who had his PDA out again. A display set into the wall came to life, and Trecker took a gavel from a drawer and rapped it on the desk. "Case of United

States Government against Peter Skilling," he said. "Military court convened per the Uniting and Strengthening America Act of 2001. Major Fullerton, your stipulations."

Melinda rose. Working from her own PDA, she began. "Defendant Skilling is known to have fallen into a glacial crevasse while hiking in Alaska during the late summer of the Year of Our Lord 2005." The screen flashed a *Seattle Post-Intelligencer* article from Aug. 29, 2005: KIRKLAND MAN MISSING ON McKINLEY. The article disappeared, and a video recording appeared. Peter and Melinda—Major Fullerton—outside the hospital: Fine. Yes, I was a Green. Still am, if there's still a party. "Defendant was at that time, and still claims to be, a member of a terrorist organization, the Green Party of the United States."

"What?" Peter said.

Col. Trecker rapped his gavel. "You will speak only in answer to a direct question. Continue, Major."

"Defendant was at the time of his death under the influence of a Class I controlled substance, cannabis sativa." Peter disappeared from the screen, replaced by a medical report that came and went too fast for him to read it. "The concentrations of intoxicating agents in defendant's blood indicate that his motor functions would have been considerably impaired, and that mountain hiking under this influence would have been criminally reckless according to prevailing legal standards." A list of legal decisions scrolled across the screen.

"Counselor Burkhardt, do you accept these facts as stipulated?" Trecker asked.

"We do, Colonel."

"Since when is the Green Party a terrorist group?" Peter said.

Trecker got up from behind his desk, walked up to Peter's table, and leaned over Peter. "If you speak again without being asked a direct question, I swear on my mother's Bible that I will bang your head on this table until you can count your teeth on one hand. Is that clear? That was a direct question."

Peter's throat had dried shut. He coughed and managed to say, "Clear."

Trecker nodded and went back to his desk. "Major."

"Following from the entered stipulations, and under the Terrorism Penalties Enhancement Act of 2005 and the VICTORY Act of 2005, we accuse the defendant of terrorist acts resulting in death. In addition, we accuse the defendant of making comments pejorative to the stature and actions of the Commander in Chief, which act to undermine confidence in the United States of America and therefore weaken our efforts to fight global terror."

"Peter Skilling, do you understand the charges against you?"

"I sure as hell do not," Peter said. "What did I do that was terrorist? Since when is it illegal to make pejorative comments about idiot politicians?"

"Counselor," Trecker said. "Advise the defendant before I have to get up again."

Burkhardt's hand fell heavily on Peter's shoulder. "Peter. You've put yourself in a tricky situation here, and you're only making it worse. Wouldn't you be better off cooperating and not being quite so antagonistic?"

"Are you defending me, Burkhardt?"

"That is my role, yes, and I am very proud to perform it." Burkhardt straightened. "I believe we can count on a more civil atmosphere," he said to Trecker.

The colonel nodded. "How do you answer the charges?"

"Oh, not guilty. In addition, I move for the dismissal of the pejorative-comment and undermining-confidence charges, which are possible only under laws passed during the 2020s. Clearly Peter can't be charged with a crime that didn't exist at the time of his death, and at that time, free-speech law was much less codified than it has since become."

Trecker looked down at his PDA. After a moment's consultation, he said, "Those charges are dismissed."

"Objection," Major Fullerton said.

"Overruled. Major, you will make your case only on the charge of terrorist acts resulting in death. Proceed."

Hope fluttered weakly in Peter's stomach. Burkhardt had done the job so far. He might be a crazy robot, but Dr. McBride had said he was built to ensure protocols were met; what else would you want in a lawyer?

"Colonel, the government's case is simple. Under the Terrorism Penalties Enhancement Act of 2005, it is a capital offense to commit an act of terrorism that results in a death. The VICTORY Act of 2005 liberalized the definition of terrorism to include drug possession and distribution if it could be shown that drug money financed terrorist organizations. The defendant has admitted that his supplier was a member of the Green Party of the United States, which was on terrorist watchlists as early as 2003 and officially added to the government's list of terrorist organizations in April of 2005 following the first reelection of President George W. Bush." On the wall screen, Peter watched himself say that Phil Kokoszka was a Green.

"Medical and toxicological reports indicate that the defendant was seriously impaired by marijuana intoxication at the time of his death. Under the provisions of the Terrorism Penalties and VICTORY Acts, his purchase of marijuana was a terrorist act in that it benefited a known terrorist organization. His use of that same marijuana impaired his physical coordination to the extent that he suffered a fatal fall on Mount McKinley. It is clear that his terrorist act of purchasing marijuana from the Green Party of the United States led directly to his decease, which makes the Terrorism Penalties Act applicable here and leaves the government no choice but to subject the defendant to the ultimate sanction. The only question is whether or not the defendant is compos mentis, and to answer that issue the government calls Burkhardt."

Before Peter could say anything, Burkhardt slapped a metal hand over his mouth. "Please, Peter. This is all standard. You must realize that things aren't the same as you remember. We're all much safer now."

Letting go of Peter's jaw, Burkhardt stood and walked out in front of the table. Trecker swore it in.

"Do you find the defendant Peter Skilling to be fit for trial?" Major Fullerton asked it.

"Peter has done an exceptional job of adapting to severely trying circumstances," Burkhardt enthused. "I would not have thought it possible for him to be as well-adjusted as he is, but I can find no evidence of deficiency in analytic or emotional responses. What a fine example of the human mind he is."

Numbness was slowly settling over Peter's mind. Now I can't believe this is real, he thought. No way. I'm still on the mountain, and all of these lunatics are a dying paranoid fantasy.

"Thank you, Burkhardt," Major Fullerton said. "You are excused."

"That was a defense?" Peter muttered when Burkhardt returned to the table.

"Peter, I'm under oath," the robot said. "And I'm very proud of you."

"Anything else, Major?"

Fullerton shook her head. "We rest, sir."

Trecker looked at Burkhardt. "Defense?"

"The defense challenges the toxicology report," Burkhardt practically crowed, "and calls Dr. Felicia McBride."

"Objection," Major Fullerton called. "Dr. McBride's security clearance has been revoked for lack of confidence due to comments made in the defendant's presence. She cannot be counted on to deliver objective testimony."

"Sustained," said Col. Trecker. "Anything else, Burkhardt?"

"This is terribly disappointing," Burkhardt said. "No, Colonel. The defense rests."

Col. Trecker stood. So did Major Fullerton. Burkhardt tapped Peter on the shoulder and Peter rose, feeling stoned again, as if all of this was very distant. "Right," the colonel said. "We defend our homeland against those who would destroy our freedoms and our way of life. In that defense it is sometimes necessary to take actions that in other circumstances would be found repugnant. Peter Skilling, you are guilty of terrorist acts resulting in the death of Peter Skilling, and under the Terrorism Penalties Enhancement Act of 2005 you are sentenced to death. Sentence to be carried out immediately. Dr. McBride?"

Peter turned, and this time Burkhardt let him. The robot was whispering close to Peter's ear, something about how resilient and exceptional he was, how astonishing it was that he had so successfully adapted to what must have been a terrible blow, and Dr. McBride was walking up to him with the transdermal in her hand and a look in her eye that told Peter all he needed to know.

"I'm going to give you something, Peter," she said, and he thought, I don't blame you. He heard a hiss, and then he was gone.

THE PEDESTRIAN

by Ray Bradbury

Ray Bradbury is the beloved author of innumerable classics, such as *Dandelion Wine, The Illustrated Man, Something Wicked This Way Comes, The Martian Chronicles,* and the dystopian classic *Fahrenheit 451.* He is a master of the short story form, with more than 400 published stories to his credit, including such classics as "There Will Come Soft Rains," "A Sound of Thunder," and "All Summer in a Day." Bradbury is a Science Fiction Writers of America Grand Master and a Science Fiction Hall of Fame inductee, and is a winner of the World Fantasy Award for life achievement and the Bram Stoker life achievement award—in short, a living legend of the science fiction and fantasy field.

One marker of a dystopian society is a lack of fairness. For some people, the field isn't just unlevel—it's hideously slanted, and there's no way to get a hand up it. It's like one of those country-western songs where bad stuff just keeps piling up.

If our next story was a country song, it would probably be Patsy Cline's hit "Walkin' After Midnight," because not only is it the story of a confirmed night stroller, it's classically unfair. Nothing eases a soul like a simple walk. Nothing causes less harm. It takes a truly dystopian society to punish a man for being a pedestrian.

A hallmark of dystopian fiction is the light it sheds on our own world. When you look out at many suburban developments, you'll see big-box stores and parking lots strung along busy streets, with no sidewalks for meant for meandering. Multiple lanes with infrequent crosswalks guarantee a pedestrian must run, not stroll across the street. Modern suburbia has almost succeeded in excising the walker from society.

Maybe the dystopia of "The Pedestrian" isn't so far away…

To enter out into that silence that was the city at eight o'clock of a misty evening in November, to put your feet upon that buckling concrete walk, step over grassy seams and make your way, hands in pockets, through the silences, that was what Mr. Leonard Mead most dearly loved to do. He would stand upon the corner of an intersection and peer down long moonlit venues of sidewalk in four directions, deciding which way to go, but it really made no difference; he was alone in this world of A.D. 2131, or as good as alone, and with a final decision made, a path selected, he would stride off, ending patterns of frosty air before him like the smoke of a cigar.

Sometimes he would walk for hours and miles and return only at midnight to his house. And on his way he would see the cottages and homes with their dark windows, and it was not unequal to walking through a graveyard, because only the faintest glimmers of firefly light appeared in flickers behind the windows. Sudden gray phantoms seemed to manifest themselves upon inner room walls where a curtain was still undrawn against the night, or there were whisperings and murmurs where a window in a tomblike building was still open.

Mr. Leonard Mead would pause, cock his head, listen, look, and march on, his feet making no noise on the lumpy walk. For a long while now the sidewalks had been vanishing under flowers and grass. In ten years of walking by night or day, for thousands of miles, he had never met another person walking, not one in all that time.

He now wore sneakers when strolling at night, because the dogs in intermittent squads would parallel his journey with barkings if he wore hard heels, and lights might click on and faces appear, and an entire street be startled by the passing of a lone figure in the early November evening.

On this particular evening he began his journey in a westerly direction, toward the hidden sea. There was a good crystal frost in the air; it cut the nose going in and made the lungs blaze like a Christmas tree inside; you could feel the cold light going on and off, all the branches filled with invisible snow. He listened to the faint push of his soft shoes through autumn leaves with satisfaction, and whistled a cold quiet whistle between his teeth, occasionally picking up a leaf as he passed, examining its skeletal pattern in the infrequent lamplights as he went on, smelling its rusty smell.

"Hello, in there," he whispered to every house on every side as he moved. "What's up tonight on Channel 4, Channel 7, Channel 9? Where are the cowboys rushing, and do I see the United States Cavalry over the next hill to the rescue?"

The street was silent and long and empty, with only his shadow moving like the shadow of a hawk in mid-country. If he closed his eyes and stood very still, frozen, he imagined himself upon the center of a plain, a wintry, windless Arizona country with no house in a thousand miles, and only dry riverbeds, the streets, for company.

"What is it now?" he asked the houses, noticing his wrist watch. "Eight-thirty P.M. Time for a dozen assorted murders? A quiz? A revue? A comedian falling off the stage?"

Was that a murmur of laughter from within a moon-white house? He hesitated, but went on when nothing more happened. He stumbled over a particularly uneven section of walk as he came to a cloverleaf intersection which stood silent where two main highways crossed the town. During the day it was a thunderous surge of cars, the gas stations open, a great insect rustling and ceaseless jockeying for position as the scarab beetles, a faint incense puttering from their exhausts, skimmed homeward to the far horizons. But now these highways too were like streams in a dry season, all stone and bed and moon radiance.

He turned back on a side street, circling around toward his home. He was within a block of his destination when the lone car turned a corner quite suddenly and flashed a fierce white cone of light upon him. He stood entranced, not unlike a night moth, stunned by the illumination and then drawn toward it.

A metallic voice called to him:

"Stand still. Stay where you are! Don't move!"

He halted.

"Put up your hands."

"But—" he said.

"Your hands up! Or we'll shoot!"

The police, of course, but what a rare, incredible thing; in a city of three million, there was only one police car left. Ever since a year ago, 2130, the election year, the force had been cut down from three cars to one. Crime was ebbing; there was no need now for the police, save for this one lone car wandering and wandering the empty streets.

"Your name?" said the police car in a metallic whisper. He couldn't see the men in it for the bright light in his eyes.

"Leonard Mead," he said.

"Speak up!"

"Leonard Mead!"

"Business or profession?"

"I guess you'd call me a writer."

"No profession," said the police car, as if talking to itself. The light held him fixed like a museum specimen, needle thrust through chest.

"You might say that," said Mr. Mead. He hadn't written in years. Magazines and books didn't sell any more. Everything went on in the tomblike houses at night now, he thought, continuing his fancy. The tombs, ill-lit by television light, where the people sat like the dead, the gray or multicolored lights touching their expressionless faces but never really touching them.

"No profession," said the phonograph voice, hissing. "What are you doing out?"

"Walking," said Leonard Mead.

"Walking!"

"Just walking," he said, simply, but his face felt cold.

"Walking, just walking, walking?"

"Yes, sir."

"Walking where? For what?"

"Walking for air. Walking to see."

"Your address!"

"Eleven South St. James Street."

"And there is air in your house, you have an air-conditioner, Mr. Mead?"

"Yes."

"And you have a viewing screen in your house to see with?"

"No."

"No?" There was a crackling quiet that in itself was an accusation.

"Are you married, Mr. Mead?"

"No."

"Not married," said the police voice behind the fiery beam. The moon was high and clear among the stars and the houses on the street were gray and silent.

"Nobody wanted me," said Leonard Mead, with a smile.

"Don't speak unless you're spoken to!"

Leonard Mead waited in the cold night.

"Just walking, Mr. Mead?"

"Yes."

"But you haven't explained for what purpose."

"I explained: for air and to see, and just to walk."

"Have you done this often?"

"Every night for years."

The police car sat in the center of the street with its radio throat faintly humming.

"Well, Mr. Mead," it said.

"Is that all?" he asked politely.

"Yes," said the yoke. "Here."

There was a sigh, a pop. The back door of the police car sprang wide. "Get in."

"Wait a minute, I haven't done anything!"

"Get in."

"I protest!"

"Mr. Mead."

He walked like a man suddenly drunk. As he passed the front window of the car he looked in. As he had expected, there was no one in the front seat, no one in the car at all.

"Get in."

He put his hand to the door and peered into the back seat, which was a little cell, a little black jail with bars. It smelled of riveted steel. It smelled of harsh antiseptic; it smelled too clean and hard and metallic. There was nothing soft there.

"Now if you had a wife to give you an alibi," the iron voice said to him. "But—"

"Where are you taking me?"

The car hesitated, or rather gave a faint whirring click, as if information, somewhere, was dropping card by punch-slotted card under electric eyes. "To the Psychiatric Center for Research on Regressive Tendencies."

He got in. The door shut with a soft thud. The police car rolled through the night avenues, flashing its dim lights ahead.

They passed one house on one street a moment later, one house in an entire city of houses that were dark, but this one particular house had all its electric lights brightly lit, every window a loud yellow illumination, square and warm in the cool darkness.

"That's my house," said Leonard Mead.

No one answered him.

The car moved down the empty riverbed streets and off away, leaving the empty streets with the empty sidewalks, and no sound and no motion all the rest of the chill November night.

THE THINGS THAT MAKE ME WEAK AND STRANGE GET ENGINEERED AWAY

by Cory Doctorow

Cory Doctorow is the author of the novels *Down and Out in the Magic Kingdom*, *Eastern Standard Tribe*, *Someone Comes to Town Someone Leaves Town*, *Makers*, *For the Win*, and the dystopian young adult novel *Little Brother*. His short fiction, which has appeared in a variety of magazines—from *Asimov's Science Fiction* to *Salon.com*—has been collected in *A Place So Foreign and Eight More* and in *Overclocked: Stories of the Future Present*. He is a four-time winner of the Locus Award, a winner of the Canadian Starburst Award, has been nominated for both the Hugo and Nebula Awards, and in 2000, he won the John W. Campbell Award for Best New Writer. Doctorow is also the co-editor of Boing Boing, the online "directory of wonderful things."

Big Brother is watching you.

When George Orwell wrote those words in 1949, the notion of a surveillance state was the stuff of absolute science fiction. Today, in an era of security cameras, wire taps and radio-frequency ID tags, surveillance is constant, and privacy a privilege. If no one is watching you, it's not because they can't—it's simply because so far, no one has decided it's worthwhile.

But in the future Cory Doctorow describes in our next story, someone *has* decided to watch everyone, all the time, every day. Just think a moment about what your daily life is like. Have you ever run a red light? Have you stayed parked longer than the meter would allow? Have you ever rounded down on your taxes?

Here is a world where the minor infractions get noticed. Here is a world where everyone is going to get caught sometime and everyone is some kind of criminal. Forget Big Brother. In this dystopian surveillance state, the watchers are more like the Godfather and his dons.

'Cause it's gonna be the future soon,
And I won't always be this way,
When the things that make me weak and strange get engineered away
                                        —Jonathan Coulton, "The Future Soon"

Lawrence's cubicle was just the right place to chew on a thorny logfile problem: decorated with the votive fetishes of his monastic order, a thousand calming, clarifying mandalas and saints devoted to helping him think clearly.

From the nearby cubicles, Lawrence heard the ritualized muttering of a thousand brothers and sisters in the Order of Reflective Analytics, a susurration of harmonized, concentrated thought. On his display, he watched an instrument widget track the decibel level over time, the graph overlaid on a 3D curve of normal activity over time and space. He noted that the level was a little high, the room a little more anxious than usual.

He clicked and tapped and thought some more, massaging the logfile to see if he could make it snap into focus and make sense, but it stubbornly refused to be sensible. The data tracked the custody chain of the bitstream the Order munged for the Securitat, and somewhere in there, a file had grown by sixty-eight bytes, blowing its checksum and becoming An Anomaly.

Order lore was filled with Anomalies, loose threads in the fabric of reality—bugs to be squashed in the data-set that was the Order's universe. Starting with the pre-Order sysadmin who'd tracked a $0.75 billing anomaly back to a foreign spy-ring that was using his systems to hack his military, these morality tales were object lessons to the Order's monks: pick at the seams and the world will unravel in useful and interesting ways.

Lawrence had reached the end of his personal picking capacity, though. It was time to talk it over with Gerta.

He stood up and walked away from his cubicle, touching his belt to let his sensor array know that he remembered it was there. It counted his steps and his heartbeats and his EEG spikes as he made his way out into the compound.

It's not like Gerta was in charge—the Order worked in autonomous little units with rotating leadership, all coordinated by some groupware that let them keep the hierarchy nice and flat, the way that they all liked it. Authority sucked.

But once you instrument every keystroke, every click, every erg of productivity, it soon becomes apparent who knows her shit and who just doesn't. Gerta knew the shit cold.

"Question," he said, walking up to her. She liked it brusque. No nonsense.

She batted her handball against the court wall three more times, making long dives for it, sweaty grey hair whipping back and forth, body arcing in graceful flows. Then she caught the ball and tossed it into the basket by his feet. "Lester, huh? All right, surprise me."

"It's this," he said, and tossed the file at her pan. She caught it with the same fluid gesture and her computer gave it to her on the handball court wall, which was the closest display for which she controlled the lockfile. She peered at the data, spinning the graph this way and that, peering intently.

She pulled up some of her own instruments and replayed the bitstream, recalling the logfiles from many network taps from the moment at which the file grew by the anomalous sixty-eight bytes.

"You think it's an Anomaly, don't you?" She had a fine blond mustache that was beaded with sweat, but her breathing had slowed to normal and her hands were steady and sure as she gestured at the wall.

"I was kind of hoping, yeah. Good opportunity for personal growth, your Anomalies."

"Easy to say why you'd call it an Anomaly, but look at this." She pulled the checksum of the injected bytes, then showed him her network taps, which were playing the traffic back and forth for several minutes before and after the insertion. The checksummed block moved back through the routers, one hop, two hops, three hops, then to a terminal. The authentication data for the terminal told them who owned its lockfile then: Zbigniew Krotoski, login zbigkrot. Gerta grabbed his room number.

"Now, we don't have the actual payload, of course, because that gets flushed. But we have the checksum, we have the username, and look at this, we have him typing sixty-eight unspecified bytes in a pattern consistent with his biometrics five minutes and eight seconds prior to the injection. So, let's go ask him what his sixty-eight characters were and why they got added to the Securitat's datastream."

He led the way, because he knew the corner of the campus where zbigkrot worked pretty well, having lived there for five years when he first joined the Order. Zbigkrot was probably a relatively recent inductee, if he was still in that block.

His belt gave him a reassuring buzz to let him know he was being logged as he entered the building, softer haptic feedback coming as he was logged to each floor as they went up the clean-swept wooden stairs. Once, he'd had the work-detail of re-staining those stairs, stripping the ancient wood, sanding it baby-skin smooth, applying ten coats of varnish, polishing it to a high gloss. The work had been incredible, painful and rewarding, and seeing the stairs still shining gave him a tangible sense of satisfaction.

He knocked at zbigkrot's door twice before entering. Technically, any brother or sister was allowed to enter any room on the campus, though there were norms of privacy and decorum that were far stronger than any law or rule.

The room was bare, every last trace of its occupant removed. A fine dust covered every surface, swirling in clouds as they took a few steps in. They both coughed explosively and stepped back, slamming the door.

"Skin," Gerta croaked. "Collected from the ventilation filters. DNA for every person on campus, in a nice, even, Gaussian distribution. Means we can't use biometrics to figure out who was in this room before it was cleaned out."

Lawrence tasted the dust in his mouth and swallowed his gag reflex. Technically, he knew that he was always inhaling and ingesting other peoples' dead skin-cells, but not by the mouthful.

"All right," Gerta said. "Now you've got an Anomaly. Congrats, Lawrence. Personal growth awaits you."

The campus only had one entrance to the wall that surrounded it. "Isn't that a fire-hazard?" Lawrence asked the guard who sat in the pillbox at the gate.

"Naw," the man said. He was old, with the serene air of someone who'd been in the Order for decades. His beard was combed and shining, plaited into a thick braid that hung to his belly, which had only the merest hint of a little pot. "Comes a fire, we hit the panic button, reverse the magnets lining the walls, and the foundations destabilize at twenty sections. The whole thing'd come down in seconds. But no one's going to sneak in or out that way."

"I did *not* know that," Lawrence said.

"Public record, of course. But pretty obscure. Too tempting to a certain prankster mindset."

Lawrence shook his head. "Learn something new every day."

The guard made a gesture that caused something to depressurize in the gateway. A primed *hum* vibrated through the floorboards. "We keep the inside of the vestibule at ten atmospheres, and it opens inward from outside. No one can force that door open without us knowing about it in a pretty dramatic way."

"But it must take forever to re-pressurize?"

"Not many people go in and out. Just data."

Lawrence patted himself down.

"You got everything?"

"Do I seem nervous to you?"

The old timer picked up his tea and sipped at it. "You'd be an idiot if you weren't. How long since you've been out?"

"Not since I came in. Sixteen years ago. I was twenty-one."

"Yeah," the old timer said. "Yeah, you'd be an idiot if you weren't nervous. You follow politics?"

"Not my thing," Lawrence said. "I know it's been getting worse out there—"

The old timer barked a laugh. "Not your thing? It's probably time you got out into the wide world, son. You might ignore politics, but it won't ignore *you*."

"Is it dangerous?"

"You going armed?"

"I didn't know that was an option."

"Always an option. But not a smart one. Any weapon you don't know how to use belongs to your enemy. Just be circumspect. Listen before you talk. Watch before you act. They're good people out there, but they're in a bad, bad situation."

Lawrence shuffled his feet and shifted the straps of his bindle. "You're not making me very comfortable with all this, you know."

"Why are you going out anyway?"

"It's an Anomaly. My first. I've been waiting sixteen years for this. Someone poisoned the Securitat's data and left the campus. I'm going to go ask him why he did it."

The old man blew the gate. The heavy door lurched open, revealing the vestibule. "Sounds like an Anomaly all right." He turned away and Lawrence forced himself to move toward the vestibule. The man held his hand out before he reached it. "You haven't been outside in fifteen years, it's going to be a surprise. Just remember, we're a noble species, all appearances to the contrary notwithstanding."

Then he gave Lawrence a little shove that sent him into the vestibule. The door slammed behind him. The vestibule smelled like machine oil and rubber, gaskety smells. It was dimly lit by rows of white LEDs that marched up the walls like drunken ants. Lawrence barely had time to register this before he heard a loud *thunk* from the outer door and it swung away.

Lawrence walked down the quiet street, staring up at the same sky he'd lived under, breathing the same air he'd always breathed, but marveling at how *different* it all was. His heartbeat and respiration were up—the tips of the first two fingers on his right hand itched slightly under his feedback gloves—and his thoughts were doing that race-condition thing where every time he tried to concentrate on something he thought about how he was trying to concentrate on something and should stop thinking about how he was concentrating and just concentrate.

This was how it had been sixteen years before, when he'd gone into the Order. He'd been so *angry* all the time then. Sitting in front of his keyboard, looking at the world through the lens of the network, suffering all the fools with poor grace. He'd been a bright fourteen-year-old, a genius at sixteen, a rising star at eighteen, and a failure by twenty-one. He was depressed all the time, his weight had ballooned to nearly 300 pounds, and he had been fired three times in two years.

One day he stood up from his desk at work—he'd just been hired at a company that was selling learning, trainable vision-systems for analyzing images, who liked him because he'd retained his security clearance when he'd been fired from his previous job—and walked out of the building. It had been a blowing, wet, grey day, and the streets of New York were as empty as they ever got.

Standing on Sixth Avenue, looking north from midtown, staring at the buildings the cars and the buses and the people and the tallwalkers, that's when he had his realization: *He was not meant to be in this world.*

It just didn't suit him. He could *see* its workings, see how its politics and policies were flawed, see how the system needed debugging, see what made its people work, but he couldn't touch it. Every time he reached in to adjust its settings, he got mangled by its gears. He couldn't convince his bosses that he knew what they were doing wrong. He couldn't convince his colleagues that he knew best. Nothing he did succeeded—every attempt he made to right the wrongs of the world made him miserable and made everyone else angry.

Lawrence knew about humans, so he knew about this: this was the exact profile of the people in the Order. Normally he would have taken the subway home. It was forty blocks to his place, and he didn't get around so well anymore. Plus there was the rain and the wind.

But today, he walked, huffing and limping, using his cane more and more as he got further and further uptown, his knee complaining with each step. He got to his apartment and found that the elevator was out of service—second time that month—and so he took the stairs. He arrived at his apartment so out of breath he felt like he might vomit.

He stood in the doorway, clutching the frame, looking at his sofa and table, the piles of books, the dirty dishes from that morning's breakfast in the little sink. He'd watched a series of short videos about the Order once, and he'd been struck by the little monastic cells each member occupied, so neat, so tidy, everything in its perfect place, serene and thoughtful.

So unlike his place.

He didn't bother to lock the door behind him when he left. They said New York was the burglary capital of the developed world, but he didn't know anyone who'd been burgled. If the burglars came, they were welcome to everything they could carry away and the landlord could take the rest. He was not meant to be in this world.

He walked back out into the rain and, what the hell, hailed a cab, and, hail mary, one stopped when he put his hand out. The cabbie grunted when he said he was going to Staten Island, but, what the hell, he pulled three twenties out of his wallet and slid them through the glass partition. The cabbie put the pedal down. The rain sliced through the Manhattan canyons and battered the windows and they went over the Verrazano Bridge and he said goodbye to his life and the outside world forever, seeking a world he could be a part of.

Or at least, that's how he felt, as his heart swelled with the drama of it all. But the truth was much less glamorous. The brothers who admitted him at the gate were cheerful and a little weird, like his co-workers, and he didn't get a nice clean cell to begin with, but a bunk in a shared room and a detail helping to build more quarters. And they didn't leave his stuff for the burglars—someone from the Order went and cleaned out his place and put his stuff in a storage locker on campus, made good with his landlord and so on. By the time it was all over, it all felt a little...ordinary. But in a good way, Ordinary was good. It had been a long time since he'd felt ordinary. Order, ordinary. They went together. He needed ordinary.

The Securitat van played a cheerful engine-tone as it zipped down the street towards him. It looked like a children's drawing—a perfect little electrical box with two seats in front and a meshed-in lockup in the rear. It accelerated smoothly down the street towards him, then braked perfectly at his toes, rocking slightly on its suspension as its doors gull-winged up.

"Cool!" he said, involuntarily, stepping back to admire the smart little car. He reached for the lifelogger around his neck and aimed it at the two Securitat officers who were debarking, moving with stiff grace in their armor. As he raised the lifelogger, the officer closest to him reached out with serpentine speed and snatched it out of his hands, power-assisted fingers coming together on it with a loud, plasticky *crunk* as the device shattered into a rain of fragments. Just as quickly, the other officer had come around the vehicle and seized Lawrence's wrists, bringing them together in a painful, machine-assisted grip.

The one who had crushed his lifelogger passed his palms over Lawrence's chest, arms and legs, holding them a few millimeters away from him. Lawrence's pan went nuts, intrusion detection sensors reporting multiple hostile reads of his identifiers, millimeter-wave radar scans, HERF attacks, and assorted shenanigans. All his feedback systems went to full alert, going from itchy, back-of-the-neck liminal sensations into high intensity pinches, prods and buzzes. It was a deeply alarming sensation, like his internal organs were under attack.

He choked out an incoherent syllable, and the Securitat man who was hand-wanding him raised a warning finger, holding it so close to his nose he went cross-eyed. He fell silent while the man continued to wand him, twitching a little to let his pan know that it was all OK.

"From the cult, then, are you?" the Securitat man said, after he'd kicked Lawrence's ankles apart and spread his hands on the side of the truck.

"That's right," Lawrence said. "From the Order." He jerked his head toward the gates, just a few tantalizing meters away. "I'm out—"

"You people are really something, you know that? You could have been *killed*. Let me tell you a few things about how the world works: when you are approached by the Securitat, you stand still with your hands stretched straight out to either side. You do *not* raise unidentified devices and point them at the officers. Not unless you're trying to commit suicide by cop. Is that what you're trying to do?"

"No," Lawrence said. "No, of course not. I was just taking a picture for—"

"And you do *not* photograph or log our security procedures. There's a war on, you know." The man's forehead bunched together. "Oh, for shit's sake. We should take you in now, you know it? Tie up a dozen people's day, just to process you through the system. You could end up in a cell for, oh, I don't know, a month. You want that?"

"Of course not," Lawrence said. "I didn't realize—"

"You didn't, but you *should have*. If you're going to come walking around here where the real people are, you have to learn how to behave like a real person in the real world."

The other man, who had been impassively holding Lawrence's wrists in a crushing grip, eased up. "Let him go?" he said.

The first officer shook his head. "If I were you, I would turn right around, walk through those gates, and never come out again. Do I make myself clear?"

Lawrence wasn't clear at all. Was the cop ordering him to go back? Or just giving him advice? Would he be arrested if he didn't go back in? It had been a long time since Lawrence had dealt with authority and the feeling wasn't a good one. His chest heaved, and sweat ran down the his back, pooling around his ass, then moving in rivulets down the backs of his legs.

"I understand," he said. Thinking: *I understand that asking questions now would not be a good idea.*

The subway was more or less as he remembered it, though the long line of people waiting to get through the turnstiles turned out to be a line to go through a security checkpoint, complete with bag-search and X-ray. But the New Yorkers were the same—no one made eye contact with anyone else, but if they did, everyone shared a kind of bitter shrug, as if to say, *Ain't it the fuckin' truth?*

But the smell was the same—oil and damp and bleach and the indefinable, human smell of a place where millions had passed for decades, where millions would pass for decades to come. He found himself standing before a subway map, looking at it, comparing it to the one in his memory to find the changes, the new stations that must have sprung up during his hiatus from reality.

But there weren't new stations. In fact, it seemed to him that there were a lot *fewer* stations—hadn't there been one at Bleecker Street, and another at Cathedral Parkway? Yes, there had been—but look now, they were gone, and…and there were stickers, white stickers over the places where the stations had been. He reached up and touched the one over Bleecker Street.

"I still can't get used to it, either," said a voice at his side. "I used to change for the F Train there every day when I was a kid." It was a woman, about the same age as Gerta, but more beaten down by the years, deeper creases in her face, a stoop in her stance. But her face was kind, her eyes soft.

"What happened to it?"

She took a half-step back from him. "Bleecker Street," she said. "You know, Bleecker Street? Like 9/11? Bleecker Street?" Like the name of the station was an incantation.

It rang a bell. It wasn't like he didn't ever read the news, but it had a way of sliding off of you when you were on campus, as though it was some historical event in a book, not something happening right there, on the other side of the wall.

"I'm sorry," he said. "I've been away. Bleecker Street, yes, of course."

She gave him a squinty stare. "You must have been *very* far away."

He tried out a sheepish grin. "I'm a monk," he said. "From the Order of Reflective Analytics. I've been out of the world for sixteen years. Until today, in fact. My name is Lawrence." He stuck his hand out and she shook it like it was made of china.

"A monk," she said. "That's very interesting. Well, you enjoy your little vacation." She turned on her heel and walked quickly down the platform. He watched her for a moment, then turned back to the map, counting the missing stations.

When the train ground to a halt in the tunnel between 42nd and 50th street, the entire car let out a collective groan. When the lights flickered and went out, they groaned louder. The emergency lights came on in sickly green and an incomprehensible announcement played over the loudspeakers. Evidently, it was an order to evacuate, because the press of people began to struggle through the door at the front of the car, then further and further. Lawrence let the press of bodies move him too.

Once they reached the front of the train, they stepped down onto the tracks, each passenger turning silently to help the next, again with that *Ain't it the fuckin' truth?* look. Lawrence turned to help the person behind him and saw that it was the woman who'd spoken to him on the platform. She smiled a little smile at him and turned with practiced ease to help the person behind her.

They walked single file on a narrow walkway beside the railings. Securitat officers were strung out at regular intervals, wearing night scopes and high, rubberized boots. They played flashlights over the walkers as they evacuated.

"Does this happen often?" Lawrence said over his shoulder. His words were absorbed by the dead subterranean air and he thought that she might not have heard him but then she sighed.

"Only every time there's an anomaly in the head-count—when the system says there's too many or too few people in the trains. Maybe once a week." He could feel her staring at the back of his head. He looked back at her and saw her shaking her head. He stumbled and went down on one knee, clanging his head against the stone walls made soft by a fur of condensed train exhaust, cobwebs and dust.

She helped him to his feet. "You don't seem like a snitch, Lawrence. But you're a monk. Are you going to turn me in for being suspicious?"

He took a second to parse this out. "I don't work for the Securitat," he said. It seemed like the best way to answer.

She snorted. "That's not what we hear. Come on, they're going to start shouting at us if we don't move."

They walked the rest of the way to an emergency staircase together, and emerged out of a sidewalk grating, blinking in the remains of the autumn sunlight, a bloody color on the glass of the highrises. She looked at him and made a face. "You're filthy, Lawrence." She thumped at his sleeves and great dirty clouds rose off them. He looked down at the knees of his pants and saw that they were hung with boogers of dust.

The New Yorkers who streamed past them ducked to avoid the dirty clouds. "Where can I clean up?" he said.

"Where are you staying?"

"I was thinking I'd see about getting a room at the Y or a backpacker's hostel, somewhere to stay until I'm done."

"Done?"

"I'm on a complicated errand. Trying to locate someone who used to be in the Order."

Her face grew hard again. "No one gets out alive, huh?"

He felt himself blushing. "It's not like that. Wow, you've got strange ideas about us. I want to find this guy because he disappeared under mysterious circumstances and I want to—" How to explain Anomalies to an outsider? "It's a thing we do. Unravel mysteries. It makes us better people."

"Better people?" She snorted again. "Better than what? Don't answer. Come on, I live near here. You can wash up at my place and be on your way. You're not going to get into any backpacker's hostel looking like you just crawled out of a sewer—you're more likely to get detained for being an 'indigent of suspicious character.'"

He let her steer him a few yards uptown. "You think that I work for the Securitat but you're inviting me into your home?"

She shook her head and led him around a corner, along a long crosstown block, and then turned back uptown. "No," she said. "I think you're a confused stranger who is apt to get himself into some trouble if someone doesn't take you in hand and help you get smart, fast. It doesn't cost me anything to lend a hand, and you don't seem like the kind of guy who'd mug, rape and kill an old lady."

"The discipline," he said, "is all about keeping track of the way that the world is, and comparing it to your internal perceptions, all the time. When I entered the Order, I was really big. Fat, I mean. The discipline made me log every bit of food I ate, and I discovered a few important things: first, I was eating about twenty times a day, just grazing on whatever happened to be around. Second, that I was consuming about 4,000 calories a day, mostly in industrial sugars like high-fructose corn syrup. Just *knowing* how I ate made a gigantic difference. I felt like I ate sensibly, always ordering a salad with lunch and dinner, but I missed the fact that I was glooping on half a cup of sweetened, high-fat dressing, and having a cookie or two every hour between lunch and dinner, and a half-pint of ice-cream before bed most nights.

"But it wasn't just food—in the Order, we keep track of *everything*; our typing patterns, our sleeping patterns, our moods, our reading habits. I discovered that I read faster when I've been sleeping more, so now, when I need to really get through a lot of reading, I make sure I sleep more. Used to be I'd try to stay up all night with pots of coffee to get the reading done. Of course, the more sleep-deprived I was, the slower I read; and the slower I read the more I needed to stay up to catch up with the reading. No wonder college was such a blur.

"So that's why I've stayed. It's empiricism, it's as old as Newton, as the Enlightenment." He took another sip of his water, which tasted like New York tap water had always tasted (pretty good, in fact), and which he hadn't tasted for sixteen years. The woman was called Posy, and her old leather sofa was worn but well-loved, and smelled of saddle soap. She was watching him from a kitchen chair she'd brought around to the living room of the tiny apartment, rubbing her stockinged feet over the good wool carpet that showed a few old stains hiding beneath strategically placed furnishings and knick-knacks.

He had to tell her the rest, of course. You couldn't understand the Order unless you understood the rest. "I'm a screwup, Posy. Or at least, I was. We all were. Smart and motivated and promising, but just a wretched person to be around. Angry, bitter, all those smarts turned on biting the heads off of the people who were dumb enough to care about me or employ me. And so smart that I could talk myself into believing that it was all everyone else's fault, the idiots. It took instrumentation, empiricism, to get me to understand the patterns of my own life, to master my life, to become the person I wanted to be."

"Well, you seem like a perfectly nice young man now," Posy said.

That was clearly his cue to go, and he'd changed into a fresh set of trousers, but he couldn't go, not until he'd picked apart something she'd said earlier. "Why did you think I was a snitch?"

"I think you know that very well, Lawrence," she said. "I can't imagine someone who's so into measuring and understanding the world could possibly have missed it."

Now he knew what she was talking about. "We just do contract work for the Securitat. It's just one of the ways the Order sustains itself." The founders had gone into business refilling toner cartridges, which was like the 21st century equivalent of keeping bees or brewing dark, thick beer. They'd branched out into remote IT administration, then into data-mining and security, which was a natural for people with Order training. "But it's all anonymized. We don't snitch on people. We report on anomalous events. We do it for lots of different companies, too—not just the Securitat."

Posy walked over to the window behind her small dining room table, rolling away a couple of handsome old chairs on castors to reach it. She looked down over the billion lights of Manhattan, stretching all the way downtown to Brooklyn. She motioned to him to come over, and he squeezed in beside her. They were on the twenty-third floor, and it had been many years since he'd stood this high and looked down. The world is different from high up.

"There," she said, pointing at an apartment building across the way. "There, you see it? With the broken windows?" He saw it, the windows covered in cardboard. "They took them away last week. I don't know why. You never know why. You become a person of interest and they take you away and then later, they always find a reason to keep you away."

Lawrence's hackles were coming up. He found stuff that didn't belong in the data—he didn't arrest people. "So if they always find a reason to keep you away, doesn't that mean—"

She looked like she wanted to slap him and he took a step back. "We're all guilty of something, Lawrence. That's how the game is rigged. Look closely at anyone's life and you'll find, what, a little black-marketeering, a copyright in-fringement, some cash economy business with unreported income, something obscene in your Internet use, something in your bloodstream that shouldn't be there. I bought that sofa from a *cop*, Lawrence, bought it ten years ago when he was leaving the building. He didn't give me a receipt and didn't collect tax, and technically that makes us offenders." She slapped the radiator. "I overrode the governor on this ten minutes after they installed it. Everyone does it. They make it easy—you just stick a penny between two contacts and hey presto, the city can't turn your heat down anymore. They wouldn't make it so easy if they didn't expect everyone to do it—and once everyone's done it, we're all guilty.

"The people across the street, they were Pakistani or maybe Sri Lankan or Bangladeshi. I'd see the wife at the service laundry. Nice professional lady, always lugging around a couple kids on their way to or from day-care. She—" Posy broke off and stared again. "I once saw her reach for her change and her sleeve rode up and there was a number tattooed there, there on her wrist." Posy shuddered. "When they took her and her husband and their kids, she stood at the window and pounded at it and screamed for help. You could hear her from here."

"That's terrible," Lawrence said. "But what does it have to do with the Or-der?"

She sat back down. "For someone who is supposed to know himself, you're not very good at connecting the dots."

Lawrence stood up. He felt an obscure need to apologize. Instead, he thanked her and put his glass in the sink. She shook his hand solemnly.

"Take care out there," she said. "Good luck finding your escapee."

Here's what Lawrence knew about Zbigniew Krotoski. He had been inducted into the Order four years earlier. He was a native-born New Yorker. He had spent his first two years in the Order trying to coax some of the elders into a variety of pointless flamewars about the ethics of working for the Securitat, and then had settled into being a very productive member. He spent his 20 percent time—the time when each monk had to pursue non-work-related projects—building aerial photography rigs out of box-kites and tiny cameras that the Monks installed on their systems to help them monitor their body mechanics and ergonomic posture.

Zbigkrot performed in the eighty-fifth percentile of the Order, which was respectable enough. Lawrence had started there and had crept up and down as low as 70 and as high as 88, depending on how he was doing in the rest of his life. Zbigkrot was active in the gardens, both the big ones where they grew their produce and a little allotment garden where he indulged in baroque cross-breeding experiments, which were in vogue among the monks then.

The Securitat stream to which he'd added sixty-eight bytes was long gone, but it was the kind of thing that the Order handled on a routine basis: given the timing and other characteristics, Lawrence thought it was probably a stream of purchase data from hardware and grocery stores, to be inspected for unusual patterns that might indicate someone buying bomb ingredients. Zbigkrot had worked on this kind of data thousands of times before, six times just that day. He'd added the sixty-eight bytes and then left, invoking his right to do so at the lone gate. The gatekeeper on duty remembered him carrying a little rucksack, and mentioning that he was going to see his sister in New York.

Zbigkrot once had a sister in New York—that much could be ascertained. Anja Krotoski had lived on 23rd Street in a co-op near Lexington. But that had been four years previous, when he'd joined the Order, and she wasn't there anymore. Her numbers all rang dead.

The apartment building had once been a pleasant, middle-class sort of place, with a red awning and a niche for a doorman. Now it had become more run down, the awning's edges frayed, one pane of lobby glass broken out and re- placed with a sheet of cardboard. The doorman was long gone.

It seemed to Lawrence that this fate had befallen many of the City's build- ings. They reminded him of the buildings he'd seen in Belgrade one time, when he'd been sent out to brief a gang of outsource programmers his boss had hired—neglected for years, indifferently patched by residents who had limited access to materials.

It was the dinner hour, and a steady trickle of people were letting themselves into Anja's old building. Lawrence watched a couple of them enter the building and noticed something wonderful and sad: as they approached the building, their faces were the hard masks of city-dwellers, not meeting anyone's eye, clipping along at a fast pace that said, "Don't screw with me." But once they passed the threshold of their building and the door closed behind them, their whole affect changed. They slumped, they smiled at one another, they leaned against the mailboxes and set down their bags and took off their hats and fluffed their hair and turned back into people.

He remembered that feeling from his life before, the sense of having two faces: the one he showed to the world and the one that he reserved for home. In the Order, he only wore one face, one that he knew in exquisite detail.

He approached the door now, and his pan started to throb ominously, let- ting him know that he was enduring hostile probes. The building wanted to know who he was and what business he had there, and it was attempting to fingerprint everything about him from his pan to his gait to his face.

He took up a position by the door and dialed back the pan's response to a dull pulse. He waited for a few minutes until one of the residents came down: a middle-aged man with a dog, a little sickly-looking schnauzer with grey in its muzzle.

"Can I help you?" the man said, from the other side of the security door, not unlatching it.

"I'm looking for Anja Krotoski," he said. "I'm trying to track down her brother."

The man looked him up and down. "Please step away from the door."

He took a few steps back. "Does Ms. Krotoski still live here?"

The man considered. "I'm sorry, sir, I can't help you." He waited for Lawrence to react.

"You don't know, or you can't help me?"

"Don't wait under this awning. The police come if anyone waits under this awning for more than three minutes."

The man opened the door and walked away with his dog.

His phone rang before the next resident arrived. He cocked his head to answer it, then remembered that his lifelogger was dead and dug in his jacket for a mic. There was one at his wrist pulse-points used by the health array. He unvelcroed it and held it to his mouth.

"Hello?"

"It's Gerta, boyo. Wanted to know how your Anomaly was going."

"Not good," he said. "I'm at the sister's place and they don't want to talk to me."

"You're walking up to strangers and asking them about one of their neighbors, huh?"

He winced. "Put it that way, yeah, OK, I understand why this doesn't work. But Gerta, I feel like Rip Van Winkle here. I keep putting my foot in it. It's so different."

"People are people, Lawrence. Every bad behavior and every good one lurks within us. They were all there when you were in the world—in different proportion, with different triggers. But all there. You know yourself very well. Can you observe the people around you with the same keen attention?"

He felt slightly put upon. "That's what I'm trying—"

"Then you'll get there eventually. What, you're in a hurry?"

Well, no. He didn't have any kind of timeline. Some people chased Anomalies for *years*. But truth be told, he wanted to get out of the City and back onto campus. "I'm thinking of coming back to Campus to sleep."

Gerta clucked. "Don't give in to the agoraphobia, Lawrence. Hang in there. You haven't even heard my news yet, and you're already ready to give up?"

"What news? And I'm not giving up, just want to sleep in my own bed—"

"The entry checkpoints, Lawrence. You cannot do this job if you're going to spend four hours a day in security queues. Anyway, the news.

"It wasn't the first time he did it. I've been running the logs back three years and I've found at least a dozen streams that he tampered with. Each time he used a different technique. This was the first time we caught him. Used some pretty subtle tripwires when he did it, so he'd know if anyone ever caught on. Must have spent his whole life living on edge, waiting for that moment, waiting to bug out. Must have been a hard life."

"What was he doing? Spying?"

"Most assuredly," Gerta said. "But for whom? For the enemy? The Securitat?"

They'd considered going to the Securitat with the information, but why bother? The Order did business with the Securitat, but tried never to interact with them on any other terms. The Securitat and the Order had an implicit understanding: so long as the Order was performing excellent data-analysis, it didn't have to fret the kind of overt scrutiny that prevailed in the real world. Undoubtedly, the Securitat kept satellite eyes, data-snoopers, wiretaps, milli-meter radar and every other conceivable surveillance trained on each Campus in the world, but at the end of the day, they were just badly socialized geeks who'd left the world, and useful geeks at that. The Securitat treated the Order the way that Lawrence's old bosses treated the company sysadmins: expendable geeks who no one cared about—so long as nothing went wrong.

No, there was no sense in telling the Securitat about the sixty-eight bytes.

"Why would the Securitat poison its own data-streams?"

"You know that when the Soviets pulled out of Finland, they found forty *kilometers* of wire-tapping wire in KGB headquarters? The building was only twelve stories tall! Spying begets spying. The worst, most dangerous enemy the Securitat has is the Securitat."

There were Securitat vans on the street around him, going past every now and again, eerily silent engines, playing their cheerful music. He stepped back into shadow, then thought better of it and stood under a pool of light.

"OK, so it was a habit. How do I find him? No one in the sister's building will talk to me."

"You need to put them at their ease. Tell them the truth, that often works."

"You know how people feel about the Order out here?" He thought of Posy. "I don't know if the truth is going to work here."

"You've been in the order for sixteen years. You're not just some fumble-tongued outcast anymore. Go talk to them."

"But—"

"Go, Lawrence. Go. You're a smart guy, you'll figure it out."

He went. Residents were coming home every few minutes now, carrying grocery bags, walking dogs, or dragging their tired feet. He almost approached a young woman, then figured that she wouldn't want to talk to a strange man on the street at night. He picked a guy in his thirties, wearing jeans and a huge old vintage coat that looked like it had come off the eastern front.

"'Scuse me," he said. "I'm trying to find someone who used to live here."

The guy stopped and looked Lawrence up and down. He had a handsome sweater on underneath his coat, design-y and cosmopolitan, the kind of thing that made Lawrence think of Milan or Paris. Lawrence was keenly aware of his generic Order-issued suit, a brown, rumpled, ill-fitting thing, topped with a polymer coat that, while warm, hardly flattered.

"Good luck with that," he said, then started to move past.

"Please," Lawrence said. "I'm—I'm not used to how things are around here. There's probably some way I could ask you this that would put you at your ease, but I don't know what it is. I'm not good with people. But I really need to find this person, she used to live here."

The man stopped, looked at him again. He seemed to recognize something in Lawrence, or maybe it was that he was disarmed by Lawrence's honesty.

"Why would you want to do that?"

"It's a long story," he said. "Basically, though: I'm a monk from the Order of Reflective Analytics and one of our guys has disappeared. His sister used to live here—maybe she still does—and I wanted to ask her if she knew where I could find him."

"Let me guess, none of my neighbors wanted to help you."

"You're only the second guy I've asked, but yeah, pretty much."

"Out here in the real world, we don't really talk about each other to strangers. Too much like being a snitch. Lucky for you, my sister's in the Order, out in Oregon, so I know you're not all a bunch of snoops and stoolies. Who're you looking for?"

Lawrence felt a rush of gratitude for this man. "Anja Krotosky, number 11-J?"

"Oh," the man said. "Well, yeah, I can see why you'd have a hard time with the neighbors when it comes to old Anja. She was well-liked around here, before she went."

"Where'd she go? When?"

"What's your name, friend?"

"Lawrence."

"Lawrence, Anja *went*. Middle of the night kind of thing. No one heard a thing. The CCTVs stopped working that night. Nothing on the drive the next day. No footage at all."

"Like she skipped out?"

"They stopped delivering flyers to her door. There's only one power stronger than direct marketing."

"The Securitat took her?"

"That's what we figured. Nothing left in her place. Not a stick of furniture. We don't talk about it much. Not the thing that it pays to take an interest in."

"How long ago?"

"Two years ago," he said. A few more residents pushed past them. "Listen, I approve of what you people do in there, more or less. It's good that there's a place for the people who don't—you know, who don't have a place out here. But the way you make your living. I told my sister about this, the last time she visited, and she got very angry with me. She didn't see the difference between watching yourself and being watched."

Lawrence nodded. "Well, that's true enough. We don't draw a really sharp distinction. We all get to see one another's stats. It keeps us honest."

"That's fine, if you have the choice. But—" He broke off, looking self-conscious. Lawrence reminded himself that they were on a public street, the cameras on them, people passing by. Was one of them a snitch? The Securitat had talked about putting him away for a month, just for logging them. They could watch him all they wanted, but he couldn't look at them.

"I see the point." He sighed. He was cold and it was full autumn dark now. He still didn't have a room for the night and he didn't have any idea how he'd find Anja, much less zbigkrot. He began to understand why Anomalies were such a big deal.

He'd walked 18,453 steps that day, about triple what he did on campus. His heart rate had spiked several times, but not from exertion. Stress. He could feel it in his muscles now. He should really do some biofeedback, try to calm down, then run back his lifelogger and make some notes on how he'd reacted to people through the day.

But the lifelogger was gone and he barely managed twenty-two seconds his first time on the biofeedback. His next ten scores were much worse.

It was the hotel room. It had once been an office, and before that, it had been half a hotel-room. There were still scuff-marks on the floor from where the wheeled office chair had dug into the scratched lino. The false wall that divided the room in half was thin as paper and Lawrence could hear every snuffle from the other side. The door to Lawrence's room had been rudely hacked in, and weak light shone through an irregular crack over the jamb.

The old New Yorker Hotel had seen better days, but it was what he could afford, and it was central, and he could hear New York outside the window—he'd gotten the half of the hotel room with the window in it. The lights twinkled just as he remembered them, and he still got a swimmy, vertiginous feeling when he looked down from the great height.

The clerk had taken his photo and biometrics and had handed him a tracker-key that his pan was monitoring with tangible suspicion. It radiated his identity every few yards, and in the elevator. It even seemed to track which part of the minuscule room he was in. What the hell did the hotel do with all this information?

Oh, right—it shipped it off to the Securitat, who shipped it to the Order, where it was processed for suspicious anomalies. No wonder there was so much work for them on campus. Multiply the New Yorker times a hundred thousand hotels, two hundred thousand schools, a million cabs across the nation—there was no danger of the Order running out of work.

The hotel's network tried to keep him from establishing a secure connection back to the Order's network, but the Order's countermeasures were better than the half-assed ones at the hotel. It took a lot of tunneling and wrapping, but in short measure he had a strong private line back to the Campus—albeit a slow line, what with all the jiggery-pokery he had to go through.

Gerta had left him with her file on zbigkrot and his activities on the network. He had several known associates on Campus, people he ate with or playing on intramural teams with, or did a little extreme programming with. Gerta had bulk-messaged them all with an oblique query about his personal life and had forwarded the responses to Lawrence. There was a mountain of them, and he started to plow through them.

He started by compiling stats on them—length, vocabulary, number of paragraphs—and then started with the outliers. The shortest ones were polite shrugs, apologies, don't have anything to say. The long ones—whew! They sorted into two categories: general whining, mostly from noobs who were still getting accustomed to the way of the Order; and protracted complaints from old hands who'd worked with zbigkrot long enough to decide that he was incorrigible. Lawrence sorted these quickly, then took a glance at the median responses and confirmed that they appeared to be largely unhelpful generalizations of the sort that you might produce on a co-worker evaluation form—a proliferation of null adjectives like "satisfactory," "pleasant," "fine."

Somewhere in this haystack—Lawrence did a quick word-count and came back with 140,000 words, about two good novels' worth of reading—was a needle, a clue that would show him the way to unravel the Anomaly. It would take him a couple days at least to sort through it all in depth. He ducked downstairs and bought some groceries at an all-night grocery store in Penn Station and went back to his room, ready to settle in and get the work done. He could use a few days' holiday from New York, anyway.

> About time Zee Big Noob did a runner. He never had a moment's happiness here, and I never figured out why he'd bother hanging around when he hated it all so much.

> Ever meet the kind of guy who wanted to tell you just how much you shouldn't be enjoying the things you enjoy? The kind of guy who could explain, in detail, *exactly* why your passions were stupid? That was him.

> "Brother Antony, why are you wasting your time collecting tin toys? They're badly made, unlovely, and represent, at best, a history of slave labor, starting with your cherished 'Made in Occupied Japan,' tanks. Christ, why not collect rape-camp macrame while you're at it?" He had choice words for all of us about our passions, but I was singled out because I liked to extreme program in my room, which I'd spent a lot of time decorating. (See pic, below, and yes, I built and sanded and mounted every one of those shelves by hand) (See magnification shot for detail on the joinery. Couldn't even drive a nail when I got here) (Not that there are any nails in there, it's all precision-fitted tongue and groove) (holy moley, lasers totally rock)

> But he reserved his worst criticism for the Order itself. You know the litany: we're a cult, we're brainwashed, we're dupes of the Securitat. He was convinced that every instrument in the place was feeding up to the Securitat itself. He'd mutter about this constantly, whenever we got a new stream to work on—"Is this your lifelog, Brother Antony? Mine? The number of flushes per shitter in the west wing of campus?"

> And it was no good trying to reason with him. He just didn't acknowledge the benefit of introspection. "It's no different from them," he'd say, jerking his thumb up at the ceiling, as though there was a Securitat mic and camera

hidden there. "You're just flooding yourself with useless information, trying to find the useful parts. Why not make some predictions about which part of your life you need to pay attention to, rather than spying on every process? You're a spy in your own body."

> So why did I work with him? I'll tell you: first, he was a shit-hot programmer. I know his stats say he was way down in the 78th percentile, but he could make every line of code that *I* wrote smarter. We just don't have a way of measuring that kind of effect (yes, someone should write one; I've been noodling with a framework for it for months now).

> Second, there was something dreadfully fun about listening him light into *other* people, *their* ridiculous passions and interests. He could be incredibly funny, and he was incisive if not insightful. It's shameful, but there you have it. I am imperfect.

> Finally, when he wasn't being a dick, he was a good guy to have in your corner. He was our rugby team's fullback, the baseball team's shortstop, the tank on our MMOG raids. You could rely on him.

> So I'm going to miss him, weirdly. If he's gone for good. I wouldn't put it past him to stroll back onto campus someday and say, "What, what? I just took a little French Leave. Jesus, overreact much?"

Plenty of the notes ran in this direction, but this was the most articulate. Lawrence read it through three times before adding it to the file of useful stuff. It was a small pile. Still, Gerta kept forwarding him responses. The late responders had some useful things to say:

> He mentioned a sister. Only once. A whole bunch of us were talking about how our families were really supportive of our coming to the Order, and after it had gone round the whole circle, he just kind of looked at the sky and said, "My sister thought I was an idiot to go inside. I asked her what she thought I should do and she said, 'If I was you, kid, I'd just disappear before someone disappeared me.'" Naturally we all wanted to know what he meant by that. "I'm not very good at bullshitting, and that's a vital skill in today's world. She was better at it than me, when she worked at it, but she was the kind of person who'd let her guard slip every now and then."

Lawrence noted that zbigkrot had used the past-tense to describe his sister. He'd have known about her being disappeared then.

He stared at the walls of his hotel room. The room next door was occupied by at least four people and he couldn't even imagine how you'd get that many people inside—he didn't know how four people could all *stand* in the room, let alone lie down and sleep. But there were definitely four voices from next door, talking in Chinese.

New York was outside the window and far below, and the sun had come up far enough that everything was bright and reflective, the cars and the buildings and the glints from sunglasses far below. He wasn't getting anywhere with the docs, the sister, the datastreams. And there was New York, just outside the window.

He dug under the bed and excavated his boots, recoiling from soft, dust-furred old socks and worse underneath the mattress.

The Securitat man pointed to Lawrence as he walked past Penn Station. Lawrence stopped and pointed at himself in a who-me? gesture. The Securitat man pointed again, then pointed to his alcove next to the entrance.

Lawrence's pan didn't like the Securitat man's incursions and tried to wipe itself.

"Sir," he said. "My pan is going nuts. May I put down my arms so I can tell it to let you in?"

The Securitat man acted as though he hadn't heard, just continued to wave his hands slowly over Lawrence's body.

"Come with me," the Securitat man said, pointing to the door on the other side of the alcove that led into a narrow corridor, into the bowels of Penn Station. The door let out onto the concourse, thronged with people shoving past each other, disgorged by train after train. Though none made eye contact with them or each other, they parted magically before them, leaving them with a clear path.

Lawrence's pan was not helping him. Every inch of his body itched as it nagged at him about the depredations it was facing from the station and the Securitat man. This put him seriously on edge and made his heart and breathing go crazy, triggering another round of warnings from his pan, which wanted him to calm down, but wouldn't help. This was a bad failure mode, one he'd never experienced before. He'd have to file a bug report.

Some day.

The Securitat's outpost in Penn Station was as clean as a dentist's office, but with mesh-reinforced windows and locks that made three distinct clicks and a soft hiss when the door closed. The Securitat man impersonally shackled Lawrence to a plastic chair that was bolted into the floor and then went off to a check-in kiosk that he whispered into and prodded at. There was no one else in evidence, but there were huge CCTV cameras, so big that they seemed to be throwbacks to an earlier era, some paleolithic ancestor of the modern camera. These cameras were so big because they were meant to be seen, meant to let you know that you were being watched.

The Securitat man took him away again, stood him in an interview room where the cameras were once again in voluble evidence.

"Explain everything," the Securitat man said. He rolled up his mask so that Lawrence could see his face, young and hard. He'd been in diapers when Lawrence went into the Order.

And so Lawrence began to explain, but he didn't want to explain everything. Telling this man about zbigkrot tampering with Securitat data-streams would not be good; telling him about the disappearance of Anja Krotoski would be even worse. So—he lied. He was already so stressed out that there was no way the lies would register as extraordinary to the sensors that were doubtless trained on him.

He told the Securitat man that he was in the world to find an Order member who'd taken his leave, because the Order wanted to talk to him about coming back. He told the man that he'd been trying to locate zbigkrot by following up on his old contacts. He told the Securitat man that he expected to find zbigkrot within a day or two and would be going back to the Order. He implied that he was crucial to the Order and that he worked for the Securitat all the time, that he and the Securitat man were on the same fundamental mission, on the same team.

The Securitat man's face remained an impassive mask throughout. He touched an earbead from time to time, cocking his head slightly to listen. Someone else was listening to Lawrence's testimony and feeding him more material.

The Securitat man scooted his chair closer to Lawrence, leaned in close, searching his face. "We don't have any record of this Krotoski person," he said. "I advise you to go home and forget about him."

The words were said without any inflection at all, and that was scariest of all—Lawrence had no doubt about what this meant. There were no records because Zbigniew Krotoski was erased.

Lawrence wondered what he was supposed to say to this armed child now. Did he lay his finger alongside of his nose and wink? Apologize for wasting his time? Everyone told him to listen before he spoke here. Should he just wait?

"Thank you for telling me so," he said. "I appreciate the advice." He hoped it didn't sound sarcastic.

The Securitat man nodded. "You need to adjust the settings on your pan. It reads like it's got something to hide. Here in the world, it has to accede to lawful read attempts without hesitation. Will you configure it?"

Lawrence nodded vigorously. While he'd recounted his story, he'd imagined spending a month in a cell while the Securitat looked into his deeds and history. Now it seemed like he might be on the streets in a matter of minutes.

"Thank you for your cooperation." The man didn't say it. It was a recording, played by hidden speakers, triggered by some unseen agency, and on hearing it, the Securitat man stood and opened the door, waiting for the three distinct clicks and the hiss before tugging at the handle.

They stood before the door to the guard's niche in front of Penn Station and the man rolled up his mask again. This time he was smiling an easy smile and the hardness had melted a little from around his eyes. "You want a tip, buddy?"

"Sure."

"Look, this is New York. We all just want to get along here. There's a lot of bad guys out there. They got some kind of beef. They want to fuck with us. We don't want to let them do that. You want to be safe here, you got to show New York that you're not a bad guy. That you're not here to fuck with us.

We're the city's protectors, and we can spot someone who doesn't belong here the way your body can spot a cold-germ. The way you're walking around here, looking around, acting—I could tell you didn't belong from a hundred yards. You want to avoid trouble, you get less strange, fast. You get me?"

"I get you," he said. "Thank you, sir." Before the Securitat man could say any more, Lawrence was on his way.

The man from Anja's building had a different sweater on, but the new one—bulky wool the color of good chocolate—was every bit as handsome as the one he'd had on before. He was wearing some kind of citrusy cologne and his hair fell around his ears in little waves that looked so natural they had to be fake. Lawrence saw him across the Starbucks and had a crazy urge to duck away and change into better clothes, just so he wouldn't look like such a fucking hayseed next to this guy. *I'm a New Yorker,* he thought, *or at least I was. I belong here.*

"Hey, Lawrence, fancy meeting you here!" He shook Lawrence's hand and gave him a wry, you-and-me-in-it-together smile. "How's the vision quest coming?"

"Huh?"

"The Anomaly—that's what you're chasing, aren't you? It's your little rite of passage. My sister had one last year. Figured out that some guy who travelled from Fort Worth to Portland, Oregon every week was actually a fictional construct invented by cargo smugglers who used his seat to plant a series of mules running heroin and cash. She was so proud afterwards that I couldn't get her to shut up about it. You had the holy fire the other night when I saw you."

Lawrence felt himself blushing. "It's not really 'holy'—all that religious stuff, it's just a metaphor. We're not really spiritual."

"Oh, the distinction between the spiritual and the material is pretty arbitrary anyway. Don't worry, I don't think you're a cultist or anything. No more than any of us, anyway. So, how's it going?"

"I think it's over," he said. "Dead end. Maybe I'll get an easier Anomaly next time."

"Sounds awful! I didn't think you were allowed to give up on Anomalies?"

Lawrence looked around to see if anyone was listening to them. "This one leads to the Securitat," he said. "In a sense, you could say that I've solved it. I think the guy I'm looking for ended up with his sister."

The man's expression froze, not moving one iota. "You must be disappointed," he said, in neutral tones. "Oh well." He leaned over the condiment bar to get a napkin and wrestled with the dispenser for a moment. It didn't cooperate, and he ended up holding fifty napkins. He made a disgusted noise and said, "Can you help me get these back into the dispenser?"

Lawrence pushed at the dispenser and let the man feed it his excess napkins, arranging them neatly. While he did this, he contrived to hand Lawrence a card, which Lawrence cupped in his palm and then ditched into his inside jacket pocket under the pretense of reaching in to adjust his pan.

"Thanks," the man said. "Well, I guess you'll be going back to your campus now?"

"In the morning," Lawrence said. "I figured I'd see some New York first. Play tourist, catch a Broadway show."

The man laughed. "All right then—you enjoy it." He did nothing significant as he shook Lawrence's hand and left, holding his paper cup. He did nothing to indicate that he'd just brought Lawrence into some kind of illegal conspiracy.

Lawrence read the note later, on a bench in Bryant Park, holding a paper bag of roasted chestnuts and fastidiously piling the husks next to him as he peeled them away. It was a neatly cut rectangle of card sliced from a health-food cereal box. Lettered on the back of it in pencil were two short lines:

Wednesdays 8:30PM

Half Moon Café 164 2nd Ave

The address was on the Lower East Side, a neighborhood that had been scorchingly trendy the last time Lawrence had been there. More importantly: it was Wednesday.

The Half Moon Café turned out to be one of those New York places that are so incredibly hip they don't have a sign or any outward indication of their existence. Number 164 was a frosted glass door between a dry-cleaner's and a Pakistani grocery store, propped open with a squashed Mountain Dew can. Lawrence opened the door, heart pounding, and slipped inside. A long, dark corridor stretched away before him, with a single door at the end, open a crack, dim light spilling out of it. He walked quickly down the corridor, sure that there were cameras observing him.

The door at the end of the hallway had a sheet of paper on it, with HALF MOON CAFÉ laser-printed in its center. Good food smells came from behind it, and the clink of cutlery, and soft conversation. He nudged it open and found himself in a dim, flickering room lit by candles and draped with gathered curtains that turned the walls into the proscenia of a grand and ancient stage. There were four or five small tables and a long one at the back of the room, crowded with people, with wine in ice-buckets at either end.

A very pretty girl stood at the podium before him, dressed in a conservative suit, but with her hair shaved into a half-inch brush of electric blue. She lifted an eyebrow at him as though she was sharing a joke with him and said, "Welcome to the Half Moon. Do you have a reservation?"

Lawrence had carefully shredded the bit of cardboard and dropped its tatters in six different trash cans, feeling like a real spy as he did so (and realizing at the same time that going to all these different cans was probably anomalous enough in itself to draw suspicion).

"A friend told me he'd meet me here," he said.

"What was your friend's name?"

Lawrence stuck his chin in the top of his coat to tell his pan to stop warning him that he was breathing too shallowly. "I don't know," he said. He craned his neck to look behind her at the tables. He couldn't see the man, but it was so dark in the restaurant—

"You made it, huh?" The man had yet another fantastic sweater on, this one with a tight herringbone weave and ribbing down the sleeves. He caught Lawrence sizing him up and grinned. "My weakness—the world's wool farmers would starve if it wasn't for me." He patted the greeter on the hand. "He's at our table." She gave Lawrence a knowing smile and the tiniest hint of a wink.

"Nice of you to come," he said as they threaded their way slowly through the crowded tables, past couples having murmured conversations over candlelight, intense business dinners, an old couple eating in silence with evident relish. "Especially as it's your last night in the city."

"What kind of restaurant is this?"

"Oh, it's not any kind of restaurant at all. Private kitchen. Ormund, he owns the place and cooks like a wizard. He runs this little place off the books for his friends to eat in. We come every Wednesday. That's his vegan night. You'd be amazed with what that guy can do with some greens and a sweet potato. And the cacao nib and avocado chili chocolate is something else."

The large table was crowded with men and women in their thirties, people who had the look of belonging. They dressed well in fabrics that draped or clung like someone had thought about it, with jewelry that combined old pieces of brass with modern plastics and heavy clay beads that clicked like pool-balls. The women were beautiful or at least handsome—one woman with cheekbones like snowplows and a jawline as long as a ski-slope was possibly the most striking person he'd ever seen up close. The men were handsome or at least craggy, with three-day beards or neat, full mustaches. They were talking in twos and threes, passing around overflowing dishes of steaming greens and oranges and browns, chatting and forking by turns.

"Everyone, I'd like you to meet my guest for the evening." The man gestured at Lawrence. Lawrence hadn't told the man his name yet, but he made it seem like he was being gracious and letting Lawrence introduce himself.

"Lawrence," he said, giving a little wave. "Just in New York for one more night," he said, still waving. He stopped waving. The closest people—including the striking woman with the cheekbones—waved back, smiling. The furthest people stopped talking and tipped their forks at him or at least cocked their heads.

"Sara," the cheekbones woman said, pronouncing the first "a" long, "Sah-rah," and making it sound unpretentious. The low-key buzzing from Lawrence's pan warned him that he was still overwrought, breathing badly, heart thudding. Who were these people?

"And I'm Randy," the man said. "Sorry, I should have said that sooner."

The food was passed down to his end. It was delicious, almost as good as the food at the campus, which was saying something—there was a dedicated cadre of cooks there who made gastronomy their 20 percent projects, using elaborate computational models to create dishes that were always different and always delicious.

The big difference was the company. These people didn't have to retreat to belong, they belonged right here. Sara told him about her job managing a specialist antiquarian bookstore and there were a hundred stories about her customers and their funny ways. Randy worked at an architectural design firm and he had done some work at Sara's bookstore. Down the table there were actors and waiters and an insurance person and someone who did something in city government, and they all ate and talked and made him feel like he was a different kind of man, the kind of man who could live on the outside.

The coals of the conversation banked over port and coffees as they drifted away in twos and threes. Sara was the last to leave and she gave him a little hug and a kiss on the cheek. "Safe travels, Lawrence." Her perfume was like an orange on Christmas morning, something from his childhood. He hadn't thought of his childhood in decades.

Randy and he looked at each other over the litter on the table. The server brought a check over on a small silver tray and Randy took a quick look at it. He drew a wad of twenties in a bulldog clip out of his inside coat pocket and counted off a large stack, then handed the tray to the server, all before Lawrence could even dig in his pocket.

"Please let me contribute," he managed, just as the server disappeared.

"Not necessary," Randy said, setting the clip down on the table. There was still a rather thick wad of money there. Lawrence hadn't been much of a cash user before he went into the Order and he'd seen hardly any spent since he came back out into the world. It seemed rather antiquarian, with its elaborate engraving. But the notes were crisp, as though freshly minted. The government still pressed the notes, even if they were hardly used any longer. "I can afford it."

"It was a very fine dinner. You have interesting friends."

"Sara is lovely," he said. "She and I—well, we had a thing once. She's a remarkable person. Of course, you're a remarkable person, too, Lawrence."

Lawrence's pan reminded him again that he was getting edgy. He shushed it.

"You're smart, we know that. 88th percentile. Looks like you could go higher, judging from the work we've evaluated for you. I can't say your performance as a private eye is very good, though. If I hadn't intervened, you'd still be standing outside Anja's apartment building harassing her neighbors."

His pan was ready to call for an ambulance. Lawrence looked down and saw his hands clenched into fists. "You're Securitat," he said.

"Let me put it this way," the man said, leaning back. "I'm not one of Anja's neighbors."

"You're Securitat," Lawrence said again. "I haven't done anything wrong—"

"You came here," Randy said. "You had every reason to believe that you were taking part in something illegal. You lied to the Securitat man at Penn Station today—"

Lawrence switched his pan's feedback mechanisms off altogether. Posy, at her window, a penny stuck in the governor of her radiator, rose in his mind.

"Everyone was treating me like a criminal—from the minute I stepped out of the Order, you all treated me like a criminal. That made me act like one—everyone has to act like a criminal here. That's the hypocrisy of the world, that honest people end up acting like crooks because the world treats them like crooks."

"Maybe we treat them like crooks because they act so crooked."

"You've got it all backwards," Lawrence said. "The causal arrow runs the other direction. You treat us like criminals and the only way to get by is to act criminal. If I'd told the Securitat man in Penn Station the truth—"

"You build a wall around the Order, don't you? To keep us out, because we're barbarians? To keep you in, because you're too fragile? What does that treatment do, Lawrence?"

Lawrence slapped his hand on the table and the crystal rang, but no one in the restaurant noticed. They were all studiously ignoring them. "It's to keep *you* out! All of you, who treated us—"

Randy stood up from the table. Bulky figures stepped out of the shadows behind them. Behind their armor, the Securitat people could have been white or black, old or young. Lawrence could only treat them as Securitat. He rose slowly from his chair and put his arms out, as though surrendering. As soon as the Securitat officers relaxed by a tiny hair—treating him as someone who was surrendering—he dropped backwards over the chair behind him, knocking over a little two-seat table and whacking his head on the floor so hard it rang like a gong. He scrambled to his feet and charged pell-mell for the door, sweeping the empty tables out of the way as he ran.

He caught a glimpse of the pretty waitress standing by her podium at the front of the restaurant as he banged out the door, her eyes wide and her hands up as though to ward off a blow. He caromed off the wall of the dark corridor and ran for the glass door that led out to Second Avenue, where cars hissed by in the night.

He made it onto the sidewalk, crashed into a burly man in a Mets cap, bounced off him, and ran downtown, the people on the sidewalk leaping clear of him. He made it two whole storefronts—all the running around on the Campus handball courts had given him a pretty good pace and wind—before someone tackled him from behind.

He scrambled and squirmed and turned around. It was the guy in the Mets hat. His breath smelled of onions and he was panting, his lips pulled back. "Watch where you're going—" he said, and then he was lifted free, jerked to his feet.

The blood sang in Lawrence's ears and he had just enough time to register that the big guy had been lifted by two blank, armored Securitat officers before he flipped over onto his knees and used the posture like a runner's crouch to take off again. He got maybe ten feet before he was clobbered by a bolt of lightning that made every muscle in his body lock into rigid agony. He pitched forward face-first, not feeling anything except the terrible electric fire from the taser-bolt in his back. His pan died with a sizzle up and down every haptic point in his suit, and between that and the electricity, he flung his arms and legs out in an agonized X while his neck thrashed, grating his face over the sidewalk. Something went horribly *crunch* in his nose.

The room had the same kind of locks as the Securitat room in Penn Station. He'd awakened in the corner of the room, his face taped up and aching. There was no toilet, but there was a chair, bolted to the floor, and three prominent video cameras.

They left him there for some time, alone with his thoughts and the deepening throb from his face, his knees, the palms of his hands. His hands and knees had been sanded raw and there was grit and glass and bits of pebble embedded under the skin, which oozed blood.

His thoughts wanted to return to the predicament. They wanted to fill him with despair for his situation. They wanted to make him panic and weep with the anticipation of the cells, the confession, the life he'd had and the life he would get.

He didn't let them. He had spent sixteen years mastering his thoughts and he would master them now. He breathed deeply, noticing the places where his body was tight and trembling, thinking each muscle into tranquillity, even his aching face, letting his jaw drop open.

Every time his thoughts went back to the predicament, he scrawled their anxious message on a streamer of mental ribbon which he allowed to slip through his mental fingers and sail away.

Sixteen years of doing this had made him an expert, and even so, it was not easy. The worries rose and streamed away as fast as his mind's hand could write them. But as always, he was finally able to master his mind, to find relaxation and calm at the bottom of the thrashing, churning vat of despair.

When Randy came in, Lawrence heard each bolt click and the hiss of air as from a great distance, and he surfaced from his calm, watching Randy cross the floor bearing his own chair.

"Innocent people don't run, Lawrence."

"That's a rather self-serving hypothesis," Lawrence said. The cool ribbons of worry slithered through his mind like satin, floating off into the ether around them. "You appear to have made up your mind, though. I wonder at you—you don't seem like an idiot. How've you managed to convince yourself that this—" he gestured around at the room "—is a good idea? I mean, this is just—"

Randy waved him silent. "The interrogation in this room flows in one direction, Lawrence. This is not a dialogue."

"Have you ever noticed that when you're uncomfortable with something, you talk louder and lean forward a little? A lot of people have that tell."

"Do you work with Securitat data streams, Lawrence?"

"I work with large amounts of data, including a lot of material from the Securitat. It's rarely in cleartext, though. Mostly I'm doing sigint—signals intelligence. I analyze the timing, frequency and length of different kinds of data to see if I can spot anomalies. That's with a lower-case 'a', by the way." He was warming up to the subject now. His face hurt when he talked, but when he thought about what to say, the hurt went away, as did the vision of the cell where he would go next. "It's the kind of thing that works best when you don't know what's in the payload of the data you're looking at. That would just distract me. It's like a magician's trick with a rabbit or a glass of water. You focus on the rabbit or on the water and what you expect of them, and are flummoxed when the magician does something unexpected. If he used pebbles, though, it might seem absolutely ordinary."

"Do you know what Zbigniew Krotoski was working on?"

"No, there's no way for me to know that. The streams are enciphered at the router with his public key, and rescrambled after he's done with them. It's all zero-knowledge."

"But you don't have zero knowledge, do you?"

Lawrence found himself grinning, which hurt a lot, and which caused a little more blood to leak out of his nose and over his lips in a hot trickle. "Well, signals intelligence being what it is, I was able to discover that it was a Securitat stream, and that it wasn't the first one he'd worked on, nor the first one he'd altered."

"He altered a stream?"

Lawrence lost his smile. "I hadn't told you that part yet, had I?"

"No." Randy leaned forward. "But you will now."

The blue silk ribbons slid through Lawrence's mental fingers as he sat in his cell, which was barely lit and tiny and padded and utterly devoid of furniture. High above him, a ring of glittering red LEDs cast no visible light. They would be infrared lights, the better for the hidden cameras to see him. It was dark, so he saw nothing, but for the infrared cameras, it might as well have been broad daylight. The asymmetry was one of the things he inscribed on a blue ribbon and floated away.

The cell wasn't perfectly soundproof. There was a gaseous hiss that reverberated through it every forty six to fifty three breaths, which he assumed was the regular opening and shutting of the heavy door that led to the cell-block deep within the Securitat building. That would be a patrol, or a regular report, or someone with a weak bladder.

There was a softer, regular grinding that he felt more than heard—a subway train, running very regular. That was the New York rumble, and it felt a little like his pan's reassuring purring.

There was his breathing, deep and oceanic, and there was the sound in his mind's ear, the sound of the streamers hissing away into the ether.

He'd gone out in the world and now he'd gone back into a cell. He supposed that it was meant to sweat him, to make him mad, to make him make mistakes. But he had been trained by sixteen years in the Order and this was not sweating him at all.

"Come along then." The door opened with a cotton-soft sound from its balanced hinges, letting light into the room and giving him the squints.

"I wondered about your friends," Lawrence said. "All those people at the restaurant."

"Oh," Randy said. He was a black silhouette in the doorway. "Well, you know. Honor among thieves. Rank hath its privileges."

"They were caught," he said.

"Everyone gets caught," Randy said.

"I suppose it's easy when everybody is guilty." He thought of Posy. "You just pick a skillset, find someone with those skills, and then figure out what that person is guilty of. Recruiting made simple."

"Not so simple as all that," Randy said. "You'd be amazed at the difficulties we face."

"Zbigniew Krotoski was one of yours."

Randy's silhouette—now resolving into features, clothes (another sweater, this one with a high collar and squared-off shoulders)—made a little movement that Lawrence knew meant yes. Randy was all tells, no matter how suave and collected he seemed. He must have been really up to something when they caught him.

"Come along," Randy said again, and extended a hand to him. He allowed himself to be lifted. The scabs at his knees made crackling noises and there was the hot wet feeling of fresh blood on his calves.

"Do you withhold medical attention until I give you what you want? Is that it?"

Randy put an affectionate hand on his shoulder. "You seem to have it all figured out, don't you?"

"Not all of it. I don't know why you haven't told me what it is you want yet. That would have been simpler, I think."

"I guess you could say that we're just looking for the right way to ask you."

"The way to ask me a question that I can't say no to. Was it the sister? Is that what you had on him?"

"He was useful because he was so eager to prove that he was smarter than everyone else."

"You needed him to edit your own data-streams?"

Randy just looked at him calmly. Why would the Securitat need to change its own streams? Why couldn't they just arrest whomever they wanted on whatever pretext they wanted? Who'd be immune to—

Then he realized who'd be immune to the Securitat: the Securitat would be.

"You used him to nail other Securitat officers?"

Randy's blank look didn't change.

Lawrence realized that he would never leave this building. Even if his body left, now he would be tied to it forever. He breathed. He tried for that oceanic quality of breath, the susurration of the blue silk ribbons inscribed with his worries. It wouldn't come.

"Come along now," Randy said, and pulled him down the corridor to the main door. It hissed as it opened and behind it was an old Securitat man, legs crossed painfully. Weak bladder, Lawrence knew.

"Here's the thing," Randy said. "The system isn't going to go away, no matter what we do. The Securitat's here forever. We've treated everyone like a criminal for too long now—everyone's really a criminal now. If we dismantled tomorrow, there'd be chaos, bombings, murder sprees. We're not going anywhere."

Randy's office was comfortable. He had some beautiful vintage circus posters—the bearded lady, the sword swallower, the hoochie-coochie girl—framed on the wall, and a cracked leather sofa that made amiable exhalations of good tobacco smell mixed with years of saddle soap when he settled into it. Randy reached onto a tall mahogany bookcase and handed him down a first-aid kit. There was a bottle of alcohol in it and a lot of gauze pads. Gingerly, Lawrence began to clean out the wounds on his legs and hands, then started in on his face. The blood ran down and dripped onto the slate tiled floor, almost invisible. Randy handed him a waste-paper bin and it slowly filled with the bloody gauze.

"Looks painful," Randy said.

"Just skinned. I have a vicious headache, though."

"That's the taser hangover. It goes away. There's some codeine tablets in the pill-case. Take it easy on them, they'll put you to sleep."

While Lawrence taped large pieces of gauze over the cleaned-out corrugations in his skin, Randy tapped idly at a screen on his desk. It felt almost as though he'd dropped in on someone's hot-desk back at the Order. Lawrence felt a sharp knife of homesickness and wondered if Gerta was OK.

"Do you really have a sister?"

"I do. In Oregon, in the Order."

"Does she work for you?"

Randy snorted. "Of course not. I wouldn't do that to her. But the people who run me, they know that they can get to me through her. So in a sense, we both work for them."

"And I work for you?"

"That's the general idea. Zbigkrot spooked when you got onto him, so he's long gone."

"Long gone as in—"

"This is one of those things where we don't say. Maybe he disappeared and got away clean, took his sister with him. Maybe he disappeared into our…operations. Not knowing is the kind of thing that keeps our other workers on their game."

"And I'm one of your workers."

"Like I said, the system isn't going anywhere. You met the gang tonight. We've all been caught at one time or another. Our little cozy club manages to make the best of things. You saw us—it's not a bad life at all. And we think that all things considered, we make the world a better place. Someone would be doing our job, might as well be us. At least we manage to weed out the real retarded sadists." He sipped a little coffee from a thermos cup on his desk. "That's where Zbigkrot came in."

"He helped you with 'retarded sadists'?"

"For the most part. Power corrupts, of course, but it attracts the corrupt, too. There's a certain kind of person who grows up wanting to be a Securitat officer."

"And me?"

"You?"

"I would do this too?"

"You catch on fast."

The outside wall of Campus was imposing. Tall, sheathed in seamless metal painted uniform grey. Nothing grew for several yards around it, as though the world was shrinking back from it.

How did Zbigkrot get off campus?

That's a question that should have occurred to him when he left the campus. He was embarrassed that it took him this long to come up with it. But it was a damned good question. Trying to force the gate—what was it the old Brother on the gate had said? Pressurized, blowouts, the walls rigged to come down in an instant.

If Zbigkrot had left, he'd walked out, the normal way, while someone at the gate watched him go. And he'd left no record of it. Someone, working on Campus, had altered the stream of data fountaining off the front gate to remove the record of it. There was more than one forger there—it hadn't just been zbigkrot working for the Securitat.

He'd *belonged* in the Order. He'd learned how to know himself, how to see himself with the scalding, objective logic that he'd normally reserved for everyone else. The Anomaly had seemed like such a bit of fun, like he was leveling up to the next stage of his progress.

He called Greta. They'd given him a new pan, one that had a shunt that delivered a copy of all his data to the Securitat. Since he'd first booted it, it had felt strange and invasive, every buzz and warning coming with the haunted feeling, the *watched* feeling.

"You, huh?"

"It's very good to hear your voice," he said. He meant it. He wondered if she knew about the Securitat's campus snitches. He wondered if she was one. But it was good to hear her voice. His pan let him know that whatever he was doing was making him feel great. He didn't need his pan to tell him that, though.

"I worried when you didn't check in for a couple days."

"Well, about that."

"Yes?"

If he told her, she'd be in it too—if she wasn't already. If he told her, they'd figure out what they could get on her. He should just tell her nothing. Just go on inside and twist the occasional data-stream. He could be better at it than zbigkrot. No one would ever make an Anomaly out of him. Besides, so what if they did? It would be a few hours, days, months or years that he could live on Campus.

And if it wasn't him, it would be someone else.

It would be someone else.

"I just wanted to say good bye, and thanks. I suspect I'm not going to see you again."

Off in the distance now, the sound of the Securitat van's happy little song. His pan let him know that he was breathing quickly and shallowly and he slowed his breathing down until it let up on him.

"Lawrence?"

He hung up. The Securitat van was visible now, streaking toward the Campus wall.

He closed his eyes and watched the blue satin ribbons tumble, like silky water licking over a waterfall. He could get to the place that Campus took him to, from anywhere. That was all that mattered.

THE PEARL DIVER

by Caitlín R. Kiernan

Caitlín R. Kiernan is the author of seven novels, including *Silk, Murder of Angels, Daughter of Hounds, The Five of Cups,* and *The Red Tree,* the last of which has been nominated for the World Fantasy and Shirley Jackson awards. Her short fiction has been collected in *Tales of Pain and Wonder; From Weird and Distant Shores; To Charles Fort, With Love; Alabaster; A is for Alien;* and *The Ammonite Violin & Others;* in spring, Subterranean Press will release another: *Two Worlds and In Between.* Her work has also appeared in my anthology *By Blood We Live* and in *Lightspeed Magazine.* She lives in Providence, Rhode Island.

Privacy issues have become some of the paramount concerns of the 21st century. Facebook leaks its members' interests to everyone in their networks. There are RFIDS in our credit cards, passports, and $100 bills. CCTV usage is on the rise, companies are monitoring their employees Internet use. Wherever you go, someone is paying attention to what you do, say, and buy.

Our next story places us in a society where the government and corporations have tag-teamed to control the work force, and they have the surveillance powers to make sure you're behaving. Your email isn't private. Your home isn't private. What you do and say behind closed doors might as well be happening out in the open, for all the world to see.

Here, Big Brother isn't just watching you—he's reporting you to your boss.

F arasha Kim opens her eyes at precisely six thirty-four, exactly one minute before the wake-up prompt woven into her pillow begins to bleat like an injured sheep. She's been lying awake since at least three, lying in bed listening to the constant, gentle hum of the thermaspan and watching the darkness trapped behind her eyelids. It's better than watching the lesser, more meaningful darkness of her tiny bedroom, the lights from the unsleeping city outside, the solid corner shadows that mercury-vapor streetlights and the headlights of passing trucks and cars never even touch. Her insomnia, the wide-awakeness that always follows the dreams, renders the pillow app superfluous, but she's afraid that muting it might tempt sleep, that in the absence of its threat she might actually fall *back* to sleep and end up being late for work. She's already been black-cited twice in the last five years—once for failing to report another employee's illegal use of noncorp software and once more for missing the start of an intradepartmental meeting on waste and oversight—so it's better safe than sorry. Farasha tells the bed that she's awake, thank you, and a moment later it ceases to bleat.

It's Tuesday, so she has a single slice of toast with a smear of marmalade, a hard-boiled egg, a red twenty-five milligram stimu-gel, and an eight-ounce glass of soy milk for breakfast, just like every other Tuesday. She leaves the dishes in the sink for later, because the trains have been running a little early the past week or so. She dresses quickly, deciding that she can get by one more day without a shower, deciding to wear black stockings instead of navy. And she's out the door and waiting for the elevator by seven twenty-two, her head already sizzling from the stimu-gel.

On the train, she stares out at the winter-gray landscape, Manhattan in mid-January, and listens to the CNN2 Firstlight report over the train's tinny speakers: the war in Turkey, the war in North Africa, the war in India, an ecoterrorist attack in Uruguay, Senate hearings on California's state-funded "suicide camps," the weather, the stock-market report, the untimely death of an actor she's never seen. The train races the clock across the Hudson and into Jersey, and, because it's Tuesday morning, the Firstlight anchorwoman reminds everyone that there will be no private operation of gasoline-powered motor vehicles until Thursday morning at ten o'clock Eastern, ten o'clock Pacific.

The day unfolds around her in no way that is noticeably different from any other Tuesday.

Farasha eats her lunch (a chocolate-flavored protein bar and an apple from the vending machines) and is back at her desk three minutes before anyone else. At one nineteen, the network burps, and everyone in datatrak and receiving is advised to crossfile and reboot. At one minute past three, the fat guy five desks over from her laughs aloud to himself and is duly docked twelve points plus five percent for inattentive behavior. He glances nervously at the nearest observer, risking another citation, risking unemployment, and then goes back to work. At four thirty-eight, the lights on the fourth floor dim themselves for seven minutes, because it is Tuesday, and even the corporations are willing to make these inconvenient, necessary sacrifices in the interest of energy conservation. Good examples are set at the top, after all.

At six pm, as a light snow begins to fall, she walks alone with all the others to the Palisades station and takes the lev back across the river, back to the city. On the train, she watches the snow and the lights dotting the gathering night and listens indifferently to the CNN2 WindDown broadcast. The stimu-gel capsule is wearing off early, and she reminds herself to mention it to her physician next month. It wouldn't be the first time she's needed her dosage adjusted.

Farasha is home by seven thirty, and she changes clothes, trading the black stockings for bare legs, then eats her dinner—a spongy slice of vegetarian meatloaf with a few spoonfuls of green peas and carrots on the side, a stale wheat roll and a cup of hot, sweetened mint tea. The tea is good, at least, and she sips the last of it in front of the television, two black-and-white *Popeye the Sailor* cartoons and one with Tom and Jerry. Her company therapist recommended cartoons in the evening, and she enjoys them, though they don't seem to do anything for her insomnia or the nightmares. Her insurance would cover sleep mods and rem reconditioning, but she knows it's best not to make too much of the bad dreams. It's not something she wants on her record, not something she wants her supervisors getting curious about.

She shuts off the television at nine o'clock, does the dishes, takes the short, cold shower she's been putting off for three days, and then checks her mail before bed. There's something wordy and unimportant from her half sister in Montreal, an ad for breast enhancement that slipped through the spamblock, a reminder that city elections are only a month away and she's required by company policy to vote GOP, and something else that's probably only more spam. Farasha reads the vague header on the fourth item—INVITATION TRANSCEND—then tells the computer to empty the inbox. She touches the upper left-hand corner of the screen, an index finger pressed against and then into the phosphor triangle, and it vanishes. The wall above the kitchen counter is only a wall again.

She brushes her teeth, flosses, takes a piss, then washes her hands and is in bed by nine forty-six. She falls asleep ten or twenty minutes later, trying not to think about the dreams, or the next day, concentrating on the steady roar of a water sweeper moving slowly, methodically along Mercer Street.

Farasha Kim was born in Trenton, the year before the beginning of the Pan-American/European Birth Lottery, to a Saudi mother and a Korean father. She was one of the last "freeborn" children in the U.S., though she doesn't see this as a point of pride. Farasha has never bothered with the lottery, not with the birth-defect rate what it is these days, and not when there are already more than ten billion people in the world, most of them living in conditions she prefers not to contemplate. Her father, a molecular biochemist at Columbia University, has told her more than once that her own birth was an "accident" and "ill-timed," and she has no wish to repeat any of the mistakes of her parents.

She grew up in Lower Manhattan, suffering the impeccably programmed attentions of the nanny mechs that did the work her mother and father couldn't be bothered with. Sometimes in the uncomfortable dreams that wake her every night, Farasha is a child again. She's five, or eight, or even eleven, and there's usually a nagging sense of loss, of disappointment and sadness, when she wakes to discover herself aged to thirty-seven years.

In one recurring dream, repeated at least twice a month, she's eight and on a school field trip to the Museum of Modern Art. She stands with the edu-mechs and other children, all nameless in the fickle memory of her unconsciousness, gazing up at an enormous canvas hung on a wide white wall. There are no other paintings on the wall. A towering rectangle of pigment and cold-pressed linseed oil, sweeping arcs of color, a riot of blues and greens and pinks and violets. Sea foam and rising bubbles, the sandy, sun-dappled floor of a tropical lagoon, coral and giant clams and the teardrop bodies of fish. Positioned near the center is the figure of a woman, a *naked* woman, her skin almost the same shade of brown as Farasha's own, swimming towards the shimmering mirror surface. Her arms outstretched, air streaming from her wide nostrils and open mouth, her strong legs driving her up and up and up. And near the bottom of the painting, lurking in lower left-hand shadows, there's a shark with snow-tipped caudal and dorsal fins. It isn't clear whether or not the shark poses an immediate danger to the swimmer, but the *threat* is plain to see.

There's a label fixed to the wall beneath the painting, black lettering stark against all that white, so she knows it's titled "The Pearl Diver." No such painting has ever hung at MoMA; she's inquired more than once. She's also searched online databases and library hardcopies, but has found no evidence that the painting is anything but a fabrication of her dreaming mind. She's never mentioned it to her therapist, or to anyone else, for that matter.

In her dream, one of the children (never precisely the same child twice) asks one of the edu-mechs what the woman in the painting is doing, and the droid answers patiently, first explaining what pearls are, in case some of its students might not know.

"A natural pearl," the mech says, "forms by secretions from the epithelial cells in the mantle of some mollusks, such as oysters, deposited in successive layers about an irritating foreign object, often a parasitic organism. Layers of arago-nite or calcite, the crystalline forms of calcium carbonate, accumulate…"

But the eight-year-old Farasha is always more interested in the painting itself, the brushstroke movement and color of the painting, than in the mere facts behind its subject matter, and she concentrates on the canvas while the mech talks. She tunes it out, and the other children, too, and the walls of the museum, and the marble floor beneath her feet.

She tastes the impossibly clean saltwater getting into her mouth, and her oxygen-starved lungs ache for air. Beneath her, the shark moves silently for-ward, a silver-blue-gray ghost propelled by the powerful side-to-side sweeps of its tall, heterocercal tail. It knows things that she can only guess, things that she will never see, even in dreams.

Eventually, the droid finishes with all the twists and turns of its encyclopedia reply and ushers the other children towards the next painting in the gallery. But Farasha is left behind, unnoticed, forgotten, abandoned because she can no longer separate herself from "The Pearl Diver." Her face and hands are stained with paint, and she's still rising, struggling for the glistening surface that seems to be getting father away instead of nearer. She wonders if people can drown in paintings and kicks her legs again, going nowhere at all.

The shark's dull eyes roll back like the eyes of something dead or dying, and its jaws gape open wide to reveal the abyss waiting for her past the rows and rows of ragged teeth. Eternity in there, all the eternity she might ever have imagined or feared.

And the canvas pulls her in.

And sometimes she wakes up, and sometimes she drifts down through frost and darkness filled with anxious, whispering voices, and sometimes the dream architecture collapses and becomes another dream entirely.

There's a small plastic box on Farasha's bedroom dressing table, polyethylene terephthalate molded and colored to look like carved ivory, and inside are three perfect antique pearls from a broken strand that once belonged to one of her Arab great-grandmothers. Her mother gave her the pearls as a birthday present many years ago, and she's been told that they're worth a lot of money. The oyster species that produced them has been extinct for almost a hundred years. Sometimes, she goes to the dressing table after the dream and opens the plastic box, takes out one or two or all three of the pearls and carries them back to bed with her. In her sweating, sleepless palms, they feel very heavy, as good as stone or lead, and she can't imagine how anyone could have ever worn an entire necklace of them strung about her neck.

On those mornings after "The Pearl Diver," when it's finally six thirty-five, and the pillow has begun to bleat at her, Farasha gets up and returns the heirloom pearls to their box, which they share with the few inexpensive, unremarkable pieces of jewelry that she owns. She never takes the pearls out any other time, and she tries not to think about them. She would gladly forget them, would sell them off for whatever she could get, if the dream would stop.

And after Tuesday, there is Wednesday and then Thursday and Friday, each inevitable in its turn and each distinguishable from the other only by its own specific monotony. Farasha works Saturday, because her department fell behind last month by twelve and three quarters over the previous month and because she has nothing else to do. She dreads her days off and avoids them when she can. However, her employer does not encourage voluntary overtime, as clinical studies have shown, repeatedly, that it decreases the value of overtime as an effective deterrent to the myriad transgressions that must be guarded against at every turn. She takes her extra days and hours on campus whenever she can get them and wishes for more.

On Sunday, there is no work, and she isn't religious, so she doesn't go to church, either. Instead, she sits alone in her two-room apartment on Canal Street. The intermittent snow showers of the last four days have been replaced by a torrential rain which drums loudly against her window. For lunch, she has a can of cheese ravioli and a few slices of dried pear, then tries again to get interested in a romance fic she downloaded the weekend before. She sits in the comfortable chair beside her bed, the lines of text scrolling tediously by on her portable, hidden sensors reading the motion of her eyes from word to word, sentence to sentence. When the computer detects her growing disinterest, it asks if she would prefer the fic be read aloud to her, and Farasha declines.

She's never liked being read to by machines, though she can't recall ever having been read to by a human.

"My mail, please," she says, and the fic dissolves, becoming instead the inbox of her corporate account. There's a reminder for a planning meeting on Monday morning, a catalog from a pharmaceutical spa in Nevada, and another mail with the subject line INVITATION TRANSCEND. She starts to tell the computer to delete all three, even though it would probably mean a warning from interdept comms for failing to read an official memorandum. Instead, she taps the screen with the nail of her left index finger, tapping INVITATION TRANSCEND before she can think better of it. The portable advises her that all unsolicited mail, if read, is immediately noted and filed with the Homeland Bureau of Casual Correspondence and the Federal Bureau of Investigation and asks her if she still wishes to open the file. She tells it yes, and the blue and white HBCC/FBI notice is promptly replaced with the body of the message. She notes at once that the sender's address is not displayed, even though the portable is running the corporation's own custom version of Microsoft Panoptic 8. Farasha shifts in the chair, and its legs squeak loudly against the tile floor, squeaking like the sleek, quick rats that infest the building's basement.

The message reads simply:

INVITATION TRANSCEND

Final [2nd] outreach imminent. Your presence is requested. Delivery complete and confidential [guaranteed]. There is meaning in you and Outside, still. You shall see that. Wholeness regained through communion with the immaculate appetite. One way. Sonepur. Baudh. Mahanadi. This overture will NOT be repeated. Open doors do not remain open forever, Ms. Kim. Please expect contact. Merciful closure. Shantih. Amen. Off.

"Bullshit," Farasha mutters, scanning the message once more and finding it even more opaque and ridiculous the second time through. Someone had obviously managed to hack the drop tank again, and this was his or her or its idea of a joke. "Delete all," she says, hearing the annoyance in her voice, wondering how long its been since she's sounded that way. Too late, she remembers the unread memorandum on Monday morning's meeting, and a second later the portable informs her that the inbox is now empty and that a federal complaint has been filed on her behalf.

She stares at the screen for a long moment, at the omnipresent corporate logo and the blinking cursor floating just slightly left of center. Then Farasha requests a search, and when the computer asks her for parameters, she types in two unfamiliar words from the vanished INVITATION TRANSCEND message, "Sonepur" and "Mahanadi." She thought the latter looked Hindi and isn't surprised when it turns out to be a river in central and eastern India. And "Sonepur" is a city located at the confluence of the Mahanadi and Tel rivers in the eastern part of the Subarnapur district. Most of the recent articles on Sonepur concern repeated bioweapon attacks on the city by Pakistani-backed guerrilla forces six months earlier. There are rumors that the retroviral agent involved may have originated somewhere in China, and the loss of life is estimated to have been staggering; a general quarantine of Sonepur remains in effect, but few other details are available. The computer reminds Farasha that searches involving military interests will be noted and filed with the Greater Office of Homeland Security, the FBI, CIA, and Interpol.

She frowns and shuts off the portable, setting it down on the small bamboo table beside the bed. Tomorrow, she'll file an appeal on the search, citing the strange piece of mail as just cause. Her record is good and there's nothing to worry about. Outside, the rain is coming down harder than ever, falling like it means to wash Manhattan clean or drown it trying, and she sits listening to the storm, wishing that she could have gone into work.

Monday again, after the morning's meeting, and Farasha is sitting at her desk. Someone whispers "Woolgathering?", and she turns her head to see who's spoken. But it's only Nadine Palmer, who occupies the first desk to her right. Nadine Palmer, who seems intent on ignoring company policy regarding unnecessary speech and who's likely to find herself unemployed if she keeps it up. Farasha knows better than to tempt the monitors by replying to the question. Instead, she glances down at the pad in front of her, the sloppy black lines her stylus has traced on the silver-blue screen, the two Hindi words—"Sonepur" and "Mahanadi"—the city and the river, two words that have nothing whatsoever to do with the Nakamura-Ito account. She's scribbled them over and over, one after the other. Farasha wonders how long she's been sitting there daydreaming, and if anyone besides Nadine has noticed. She looks at the clock and sees that there's only ten minutes left before lunch, then clears the pad.

She stays at her desk through the lunch hour, to make up the twelve minutes she squandered "woolgathering." She isn't hungry, anyway.

At precisely two p.m., all the others come back from their midday meals, and Farasha notices that Nadine Palmer has a small stain that looks like ketchup on the front of her pink blouse.

At three twenty-four, Farasha completes her second post-analysis report of the day.

At four thirteen, she begins to wish that she hadn't found it necessary to skip lunch.

And at four fifty-six, she receives a voicecall informing her that she's to appear in Mr. Binder's office on the tenth floor no later than a quarter past five. Failure to comply will, of course, result in immediate dismissal and forfeiture of all unemployment benefits and references. Farasha thanks the very polite, yet very adamant young man who made the call, then straightens her desk and shuts off her terminal before walking to the elevator. Her mouth has gone dry, and her heart is beating too fast. By the time the elevator doors slide open, opening for her like the jaws of an oil-paint shark, there's a knot deep in her belly, and she can feel the sweat beginning to bead on her forehead and upper lip. Mr. Binder's office has a rhododendron in a terra-cotta pot and a view of the river and the city beyond. "You are Ms. Kim?" he asks, not looking up from his desk. He's wearing a navy-blue suit with a teal necktie, and what's left of his hair is the color of milk.

"Yes sir."

"You've been with the company for a long time now, haven't you? It says here that you've been with us since college."

"Yes sir, I have."

"But you deleted an unread interdepartmental memorandum yesterday, didn't you?"

"That was an accident. I'd intended to read it."

"But you *didn't.*"

"No sir," she replies and glances at the rhododendron.

"May I ask what is your interest in India, Ms. Kim?" and at first she has no idea what he's talking about. Then she remembers the letter—INVITATION TRANSCEND—and her web search on the two words she'd caught herself doodling earlier in the day.

"None, sir. I can explain."

"I understand that there was an incident report filed yesterday evening with the GOHS, a report filed against you, Ms. Kim. Are you aware of that?"

"Yes sir. I'd meant to file an appeal this morning. It slipped my mind—"

"And what are your interests in India?" he asks her again and looks up, finally, and smiles an impatient smile at her.

"I have no interest in India, sir. I was just curious, that's all, because of a letter—"

"A letter?"

"Well, not really a letter. Not exactly. Just a piece of spam that got through—"

"Why would you read unsolicited mail?" he asks.

"I don't know. I can't say. It was the second time I'd received it, and—"

"Kim. Is that Chinese?"

"No, sir. It's Korean."

"Yes, of course it is. I trust you understand our position in this very delicate matter, Ms. Kim. We appreciate the work you've done here, I'm sure, and regret the necessity of this action, but we can't afford a federal investigation because one of our employees can't keep her curiosity in check."

"Yes, sir," Farasha says quietly, the knot in her stomach winding itself tighter as something icy that's not quite panic or despair washes over and through her. "I understand."

"Thank you, Ms. Kim. An agent will be in contact regarding your severance. Do not return to your desk. An officer will escort you off the campus."

And then it's over, five nineteen by the clock on Mr. Binder's office wall, and she's led from the building by a silent woman with shiny, video-capture eyes, from the building and all the way back to the Palisades lev station, where the officer waits with her until the next train back to Manhattan arrives and she's aboard.

It's raining again by the time Farasha reaches Canal Street, a light, misting rain that'll probably turn to sleet before morning. She thinks about her umbrella, tucked beneath her desk as she waits for the security code to clear and the lobby door to open. *No*, she thinks, *by now they'll have gotten rid of it. By now, they'll have cleared away any evidence I was ever there.*

She takes the stairs, enough of elevators for one day, and by the time she reaches her floor, she's breathless and a little lightheaded. There's a faintly metallic taste in her mouth, and she looks back down the stairwell, picturing her body lying limp and broken at the very bottom.

"I'm not a coward," she says aloud, her voice echoing between the concrete walls, and then Farasha closes the red door marked EXIT and walks quickly down the long, fluorescent-lit hallway to her apartment. At least, it's hers until the tenant committee gets wind of her dismissal, of the reasons *behind* her dismissal, and files a petition for her relocation with the housing authority.

Someone has left a large manila envelope lying on the floor in front of her door. She starts to bend over to pick it up, then stops and glances back towards the door to the stairs, looks both ways, up and down the hall, to be sure that she's alone. She briefly considers pressing #0 on the keypad and letting someone in the lobby deal with this. She knows it doesn't matter if there's no one else in the hallway to see her pick up the envelope, because the cameras will record it.

"Fuck it all," she says, reaching for the envelope. "They can't very well fire me twice."

There's a lot left they can do, she thinks, some mean splinter of her that's still concerned with the possibility of things getting worse. *You don't even want to know all the things left they can do to you.*

Farasha picks up the envelope, anyway.

Her name has been handwritten on the front, printed in black ink, neat, blocky letters at least an inch high, and beneath her name, in somewhat smaller lettering, are two words—INVITATION TRANSCEND. The envelope is heavier than she expected, something more substantial inside than paper; she taps her code into the keypad, and the front door buzzes loudly and pops open. Farasha takes a moment to reset the lock's eight-digit code, violating the terms of her lease—as well as one municipal and two federal ordinances—then takes the envelope to the kitchen counter.

Inside the manila envelope there are a number of things, which she spreads out across the countertop, then examines one by one. There's a single yellowed page torn from an old book; the paper is brittle, and there's no indication what the book might have been. The top of the page bears the header *Childhood of the Human Hero*, so perhaps that was the title. At the bottom is a page number,

327, and the following paragraph has been marked with a blue highlighter:

The feats of the beloved Hindu savior, Krishna, during his infant exile among the cowherds of Gokula and Brindaban, constitute a lively cycle. A certain goblin named Putana came in the shape of a beautiful woman, but with poison in her breasts. She entered the house of Yasoda, the foster mother of the child, and made herself very friendly, presently taking the baby in her lap to give it suck. But Krishna drew so hard that he sucked away her life, and she fell dead, reassuming her huge and hideous form. When the foul corpse was cremated, however, it emitted a sweet fragrance; for the divine infant had given the demoness salvation when he had drunk her milk.

At the bottom of the page, written with a pencil in very neat, precise cursive, are three lines Farasha recognizes from T. S. Eliot: *And I will show you something different from either/Your shadow @ morning striding behind you/Or your shadow @ evening rising up to meet you.*

There are three newspaper clippings, held together with a somewhat rusty gem clip, all regarding the use of biological agents by pro-Pakistani forces in Sonepur and Baudh (which turns out to be another city on the Mahanadi River). More than three million are believed dead, one article states, though the quarantine has made an accurate death toll impossible, and the final number may prove to be many times that. Both the CDC and WHO have been refused entry into the contaminated areas, and the nature of the contagion remains unclear. There are rumors of vast fires burning out of control along the river, and of mass disappearances in neighboring towns, and she reads the names of Sikh and Assamese rebel leaders who have been detained or executed.

There is a stoppered glass vial containing what looks to Farasha like soot, perhaps half a gram of the black powder, and the vial is sealed with a bit of orange tape.

There is a photocopy of an eight-year-old NASA press release on the chemical composition of water-ice samples recovered from the lunar north pole, and another on the presence of "polycyclic aromatic hydrocarbons, oxidized sulfide compounds, and carbonate globules" in a meteorite discovered embedded in the Middle Devonian-aged rocks of Antarctica's Mt. Gudmundson in July 2037.

Finally, there's the item which gave the envelope its unexpected weight, a silvery metallic disk about ten centimeters in diameter and at least two centimeters thick. Its edges are beveled and marked by a deep groove, and there is a pronounced dimple in the center of one side, matching a swelling at the center of the other. The metal is oddly warm to the touch, and though it seems soft, almost pliant in her hands, when Farasha tries to scratch it with a steak knife, she's unable to leave even the faintest mark.

She glances at the clock on the wall above the refrigerator and realizes that more than two hours have passed since she sat down with the envelope, that she has no sense of so much time having passed unnoticed, and the realization makes her uneasy. *I have slipped and fallen off the earth,* she thinks, remembering Mr. Binder's potted rhododendron. *Not even time can find me now.* And then she looks back at the contents of the manila envelope.

"Is it a riddle?" she asks aloud, asking no one or herself or whoever left the package at her doorstep. "Am I supposed to understand any of this?"

For an answer, her stomach growls loudly, and Farasha glances at the clock again, adding up all the long hours since breakfast. She leaves the papers, the glass vial, the peculiar metal disk, the empty envelope—all of it—lying on the countertop and makes herself a cheddar-cheese sandwich with brown mustard. She pours a glass of soy milk and sits down on the kitchen floor. *Even unemployed ghosts have to eat,* she thinks and laughs softly to herself. *Even dead women drifting alone in space get hungry now and then.*

When she's finished, she sets the dirty dishes in the sink and goes back to her stool at the counter, back to pondering the things from the envelope. Outside, the rain has turned to sleet, just as she suspected it would, and it crackles coldly against the windows.

The child reaches out her hand, straining to touch the painting, and her fingertips dip into salty, cool water. Her lips part, and air escapes through the space between her teeth and floats in swirling, glassy bubbles towards the surface of the sea. She kicks her feet, and the shark's sandpaper skin slices through the gloom, making a sound like metal scraping stone. If she looked down, towards the sandy place where giant clams lie in secret, coral- and anemone-encrusted gardens, she'd see sparks fly as the great fish cuts its way towards her. The sea is not her protector and isn't taking sides. She came to steal, after all, and the shark is only doing what sharks have done for the last four hundred and fifty million years. It's nothing personal, nothing she hasn't been expecting.

The child cries out and pulls her hand back; her fingers are stained with paint and smell faintly of low tide and turpentine.

The river's burning, and the night sky is the color of an apocalypse. White temples of weathered stone rise from the whispering jungles, ancient monuments to alien gods—Shiva, Parvati, Kartikeya, Brushava, Ganesha—crumbling prayers to pale blue skins and borrowed tusks.

Farasha looks at the sky, and the stars have begun to fall, drawing momentary lines of clean white fire through the billowing smoke. Heaven will intercede, and this ruined world will pass away and rise anew from its own gray ashes. A helicopter drifts above the bloody river like a great insect of steel and spinning rotors, and she closes her eyes before it sees her.

"I was never any good with riddles," she says when Mr. Binder asks her about the package again, why she touched it, why she opened it, why she read all the things inside.

"It isn't a riddle," he scolds, and his voice is thunder and waves breaking against rocky shores and wind through the trees. "It's a gift."

"I was never any good with gifts, either," she replies, watching as the glass vial from the manila envelope slips from his fingers and begins the long descent towards her kitchen floor. It might fall for a hundred years, for a hundred *thousand* years, but she'll never be quick enough to catch it.

The child reaches deep into the painting again, deeper than before, and now the water has gone as cold as ice and burns her hand. She grits her teeth against the pain, and feels the shark brush past her frozen skin.

"If it's not already within you, no one can put it there," the droid says to her as it begins to unbutton the pink, ketchup-stained blouse she doesn't remember putting on. "We have no wombs but those which open for us."

"I told you, I'm not any good with riddles."

Farasha is standing naked in her kitchen, bathed in the light of falling stars and burning rivers and the fluorescent tubes set into the low ceiling. There's a girl in a rumpled school uniform standing nearby, her back turned to Farasha, watching the vial from the envelope as it tumbles end over end towards the floor. The child's hands and forearms are smeared with greasy shades of cobalt and jade and hyacinth.

"You have neither love nor the hope of love," the girl says. "You have neither purpose nor a dream of purpose. You have neither pain nor freedom from pain." Then she turns her head, looking over her right shoulder at Farasha. "You don't even have a job."

"Did you do that? You *did*, didn't you?"

"You opened the envelope," the child says and smiles knowingly, then turns back to the falling vial. "You're the one who read the message."

The shark is coming for her, an engine of blood and cartilage, dentine and bone, an engine forged and perfected without love or the hope of love, without purpose or freedom from pain. The air in her lungs expands as she rises, and her exhausted, unperfect primate muscles have begun to ache and cramp. *This is not your world*, the shark growls, and she's not surprised that it has her mother's voice. *You gave all this shit up aeons ago. You crawled out into the slime and the sun looking for God, remember?*

"It was an invitation, that's all," the girl says and shrugs. The vial is only a few inches from the floor now. "You're free to turn us away. There will always be others."

"I don't understand what you're *saying*," Farasha tells the girl and then takes a step back, anticipating the moment when the vial finally strikes the hard tile floor.

"Then stop trying."

"Sonepur—"

"That wasn't our doing," the girl says and shakes her head. "A *man* did that. Men would make a weapon of the entire cosmos, given enough time."

"I don't know what you're offering me."

The girl turns to face Farasha, holding out one paint-stained hand. There are three pearls resting in her palm.

The jungle echoes with rifle and machinegun fire and the dull violence of faraway explosions. The muddy, crooked path that Farasha has taken from the river bank ends at the steps of a great temple, and the air here is choked with the sugary scent of night-blooming flowers, bright and corpulent blooms which almost manage to hide the riper stink of dead things.

"But from out your *own* flesh," the girl says, her eyes throwing sparks now, like the shark rushing towards her. "The fruit of *your* suffering, Farasha Kim, not these inconsequential baubles—"

"I'm *afraid*," Farasha whispers, not wanting to cry, and she begins to climb the temple steps, taking them cautiously, one at a time. The vial from the envelope shatters, scattering the sooty black powder across her kitchen floor.

"That's why I'm here," the child says and smiles again. She makes a fist, closing her hand tightly around the three pearls as a vertical slit appears in the space between Farasha's bare breasts, its edges red and puckered like a slowly healing wound. The slit opens wide to accept the child's seeds.

The pain Farasha feels is not so very different from the pain she's felt her entire life.

Farasha opens her eyes, in the not-quite-empty moments left after the dream, and she squints at the silver disk from the manila envelope. It's hovering a couple of inches above the countertop, spinning clockwise and emitting a low, mechanical whine. A pencil-thin beam of light leaks from the dimple on the side facing upwards, light the lonely color of a winter sky before heavy snow. The beam is slightly wider where it meets the ceiling than where it exits the disk, and the air smells like ozone. She rubs her eyes and sits up. Her back pops, and her neck is stiff from falling asleep at the kitchen counter. Her mouth is dry and tastes vaguely of the things she ate for her supper.

She glances from the spinning disk to the glass vial, still stoppered and sealed with a strip of orange tape, and her left hand goes slowly to the space between her breasts. Farasha presses three fingers against the thin barrier of cloth and muscle and skin covering her sternum, half-expecting something on the other side to press back. But there's nothing, nothing at all except the faint rhythm of her heart, and she reaches for the vial. Her hand is shaking, and it rolls away from her and disappears over the far edge of the counter. A second or two later, there's the sound of breaking glass.

The disk is spinning faster now, and the light shining from the dimple turns a bruised violet.

She looks down at the scatter of paper, and her eyes settle on the three handwritten lines from *The Waste Land*. She reads them aloud, and they feel wild and irrevocable on her tongue, poetry become the components of an alchemical rite or the constituent symbols in some algebraic equation. *And I will show you something different from either/Your shadow at morning striding behind you/Or your shadow at evening rising up to meet you.* Nine, seven, ten, dividing into thirty-eight syllables, one hundred and nineteen characters.

But what if I won't listen? she thinks. *What if I won't see?* And she's answered at once by the voice of a child, the voice of a brown woman who dives for gems in a painted ocean, the wordless voice of the sooty particles from the broken vial as they fill the air Farasha's breathing and find their way deep inside her.

That's why I'm here, remember? the voices reply, almost speaking in unison now, a secret choir struggling for harmony, and the disk on the counter stops suddenly and then begins to spin in the opposite direction. The beam of light has turned a garish scarlet, and it pulsates in time to her racing heart. The contagion is faster than she ever could have imagined, and this is not the pain from her dream. This is pain doubled and redoubled, pain become something infinitely greater than mere electrical impulses passed between neurons and the folds of her simple, mammalian brain. But Farasha understands, finally, and she doesn't struggle as the soot begins its work of taking her apart and putting her back together another way, dividing polypeptide chains and inserting its own particular amino acids before it zips them shut again.

And her stolen body, like the fractured, ephemeral landscape of her nightmares, becomes something infinitely mutable, altered from second to second to second, living tissue as malleable as paint on a bare canvas. There is not death here, and there is no longer loneliness or fear, boredom or the dread of whatever's coming next. With eyes that have never truly seen before this moment, Farasha watches at her soul fills up with pearls.

DEAD SPACE FOR
THE UNEXPECTED

by Geoff Ryman

Geoff Ryman is the author of the novels *The Warrior Who Carried Life*, *The Unconquered Country*, *The Child Garden*, *Was*, *253*, *Lust*, *Air*, and *The King's Last Song*. His short fiction has appeared in *The Magazine of Fantasy & Science Fiction*, *Interzone*, *Tor.com*, *New Worlds*, and has frequently been reprinted in Gardner Dozois's *Year's Best Science Fiction* series. Most of his short work can be found in the collections *Unconquered Countries* and the recent *Paradise Tales and Other Stories*. He is a winner of the World Fantasy Award, the John W. Campbell Memorial Award, the Arthur C. Clarke Award, the Philip K. Dick Award, the Tiptree Award, and the British Science Fiction Award. He is also the editor of the recent anthology *When It Changed*. Another story of his appears elsewhere in this volume.

The 1990s gave birth to books like *Microserfs* and movies like *Office Space*—creations that sank their teeth into American corporate culture to reveal the hollow interior of a life spent in a cubicle. There may have been stock options up for grabs and IRAs growing in the bank, but nothing could make up for soulless grind of bad bosses and constant scrutiny.

Our next story could have been written for Dom Portwood, *Office Space*'s detestably droning middle management icon. If Dom had access to the kind of technology our next protagonist uses to dig into his underlings, the film would have gone from darkly funny to deeply depressing.

This is a working world not much different from our own, a dystopian society just a few notches up the corporate ladder.

J onathan was going to have to fire Simon. It was a big moment in Jonathan's day, a solid achievement from the point of view of the company. Jonathan knew that his handling of the whole procedure had been model—so far. He had warned Simon a month ago that termination was a possibility and that plans should be made. Jonathan knew that he had felt all the appropriate feelings—sympathy, regret, and an echoing in himself of the sick, sad panic of redundancy.

Well, if you have sincere emotion, hang onto it. Use it. Hell, there had even been a sting of tears around the bottom of his eyes as he told Simon. Jonathan's score for that session had been 9.839 out of 10, a personal best for a counseling episode.

Now he had to be even better. The entire Team's average had nose-dived. So had Jonathan's own scores. He, the Team, needed a good score. Next month's printouts were at stake.

So Jonathan waited in the meeting room with a sign up on the door that said IN USE. On his eyes were contact lenses that were marked for accurate measurement, and which flickered and swerved as his eyes moved. There was a bright pattern of stripes and squares and circles on his shirt, to highlight breathing patterns. Galvanic skin resistance was monitored by his watch strap. It was, of course, a voluntary program, designed to give managers and staff alike feedback on their performance.

There was a knock on the door and Simon came in, handsome, neat, running a bit to fat, fifty-two years old.

It would be the benches for Simon, the park benches in summer with the civic chess board with the missing pieces. Then the leaves and seasonal chill in autumn. Winter would be the packed and steamy public library with the unwashed bodies, and the waiting for a chance to read the job ads, check the terminals, scan the benefits information. It would be bye-bye to clean shirts, ties without food stains, a desk, the odd bottle of wine, pride. For just a moment, Jonathan saw it all clearly in his mind.

Either you were a performer or you weren't.

"Hi, Simon, have a good weekend?"

"Yes, thank you," said Simon, as he sat down, his face impassive, his movements contained and neat.

Jonathan sighed. "I wanted to give you this now, before I sent it to anyone else. I wanted you to be the first to know I'm very sorry."

Jonathan held out a sealed, white, blank envelope. Simon primed for a month, simply nodded.

"I hope you know there's nothing personal in this. I've tried to explain why it's necessary, but just to be clear, there has been a severe drop in our performance and we simply must up our averages, and be seen to be taking some positive action. In terms of more staff training, that sort of thing."

Already this was not going well. The opening line about the weekend could not be less appropriate, and nobody was going to think that being fired was a positive step or care two hoots about the training other people were going to get. Inwardly, Jonathan winced. "Anyway," he shrugged with regret, still holding out the envelope that Simon had not taken. Jonathan tossed it across the table and it spun on a cushion of air across the wood-patterned surface.

Simon made no move to pick it up. "We all get old," he said. "You will, too."

"And when my scores slip," said Jonathan, trying to generate some fellow feeling, "I expect the same thing will happen to me."

"I hope so," said Simon.

Right, counseling mode. Jonathan remembered his training. Unfortunately, so did Simon—they had been on the same courses.

"Are you angry, would you like to talk?" said Jonathan, remembering: keep steady eye contact, or rather contact with the forehead or bridge of the nose, which is less threatening. Lean backwards so less aggression, but echo body language.

Simon smiled slightly and started to pick his nose, very messily, and look at the result. He held the result up towards Jonathan as if to say echo this.

Jonathan nodded as if in agreement. "It's only natural that you should feel some resentment, but it might be more constructive if you expressed it verbally. You know, say what you feel, blow off some steam. If not to me, then to someone, the Welfare Officer perhaps."

"I don't need to blow off steam," said Simon and stood up and walked to the door.

Procedures were not being followed; discipline was important.

"Simon, you haven't taken your letter."

Simon stood at the door for a moment. "It's not my letter. It's not written for me, it's addressed to Personnel so they can stop paying me."

Boy, thought Jonathan, if you were still being marked, you'd be in trouble, buddy.

"You forget," said Simon his blue eyes gray and flinty, "I used to work in Accounts." He picked up the letter, paused, and wiped his finger on it. Then he left the room.

Jonathan sat at the table, trembling with rage. Fuck counseling, he wanted to haul off and slug the guy. He took a deep breath, just like in the handling stress course, then stood up and left the meeting room, remembering to change the sign on the door. VACANT it said.

Back in his own office, he checked his score. It was bad form to check your scores too often; it showed insecurity, but Jonathan couldn't help himself. He verballed to the computer.

"Performance feedback, Dayplan Item One."

His mark was higher than he had thought it would be: 7.2, well over a five and edging towards a 7.5 for a pretty tough situation. But it was not the high score the Team needed.

It was 8:42. Three minutes ahead of schedule.

"Dayplan complete," he verballed, and his day was laid out before him on the screen.

```
8:30 Simon Hasley (actioned)
8:45 Dayplan confirmed and in tray
8:50 Sally meeting prep
```

```
9:00 Sally meeting
9:30 Sales meeting William
10:00 Dead space for the unexpected…
```

It was important that work was seen to be prioritized, that nothing stayed on the desk, or queued up on the machine. It all had to be handled in the right order. The computer worked that out for you from the priority rating you gave each item, gave you optimum work times and the corporate cost, and if you did not object, those were your targets for the first half of the day.

Right. In-tray. There was a management report on purchasing. Jonathan did not purchase, but he needed to know the new procedures his Finance Officer was supposed to follow. So make that a priority eight, book in a reading for it next week, and ask for the machine to prepare a performance. Next was a memo with spreadsheet from Admin. Admin acted as a kind of prophylactic against Accounts, giving early warning of what would strike Accounts as below par performance. Jonathan's heart sank. Late invoices. Holy shit, not again, an average of twelve days?

Thanks a lot, George, thanks a fucking lot. Shit, piss, fuck, I'll cut off that god-damned asshole's head and stick it up his own greased asshole.

Ho-boy, Jonathan, that's anger. Channel it, use it. Right, we got ourselves a priority one here, schedule it in Dead Space. Jonathan slammed his way into George's network terminal. Which at 8:47 in the morning was not switched on.

```
PRIORITY 1
George, we have a serious issue to discuss. Can
you come to my office at 10:00 am today, Thurs-
day 17th. Please come with figures on speed of
invoicing.
J Rosson, III 723, nc 11723JR.
```

There goes our cash flow down the fucking tube. And interest payments to the Centre. Great.

There was a fretful knocking at his door. Jonathan could guess who it was. Two minutes was all the time he had.

In came Harriet, gray hair flying. What you might call an individual. Jonathan swiveled, knowing his body language showed no surprise or alarm. His greeting was warm, friendly, in control. So far, so good.

"Hello, Harriet, good to see you, but I'm afraid I'm up against it this morning. I expect you've heard about Simon."

"Yes, I have actually," said Harriet, eyes bright, smile wide. She was preparing to sit down.

No, my door is not always open. Don't mess with my time management, lady. "I'd love to talk to you about it when I can give you some time. How about 10:10 this morning?"

"This will only take a minute." Harriet was still smiling. A tough old bird.

"I doubt that very much. It's an important issue, and I'd like to talk to you about it properly." With a flourish, he keyed her into his Dayplan. "There we go. 10:10. See you then?"

Harriet accepted defeat with good grace. "Lovely," she said. "I'll look forward to that." She even gave him a sweet little wave as she left.

Poor old cow is scared, thought Jonathan. Well, there are no plans to get rid of her, so that should be a fairly easy session.

Next. Up came a report on a new initiative in timekeeping, a hobby horse of Jonathan's. Was a priority one justified just because he was interested in it? He decided to downgrade it, show he was keeping a sense of proportion, that he was a team player. He gave it a two and booked it in for Friday.

He was behind schedule. Thanks, Harriet. Next was a note of praise for a job well done from that crawler Jason. The guy even writes memos to apologize for not writing memos. Jonathan wastebinned it with a grin. Next was a welfare report on the Team's resident schizophrenic. Jonathan was sure the poor guy had been hired just to give them a bit of an obstacle to show jump. The Welfare Officer was asking him to counsel the man to reduce his smoking in the office. But. He was to remember that the stress of giving up smoking could trigger another schizophrenic episode.

Oh come on, this really must be a monitoring exercise. Jonathan thought a moment. He should therefore show that he knew it was an exercise and not take it too seriously. So, he delegated. He dumped the whole report off his own screen and into the Dayplan of his Supporting Officer.

And so, 8:55. Five minutes to prep for Sally. Jeez, thought Jonathan. I hope I'm not showing. Not showing fear. Which meant, of course, that he was.

Simply, Sally was one of the big boys. She was the same grade as Jonathan, a 1.1 on a level D, but she was younger, whiplash quick, utterly charming, and she always won. Jonathan knew her scores were infinitely better than his own.

Sally had been naughty. Her Division and his Team had to cooperate on projects that were both above and below the line. Without telling him, she had called a meeting on his own grade 2s, flattered them no end, and then got the poor lambs to agree, just as a point of procedure, that all joint projects would be registered with her Division. This would cost his Team about three hundred thousand a year in turnover.

Jonathan had countered with a report on procedures, reminding all concerned that such decisions needed to be made at Divisional level, and suggesting a more thorough procedural review. Sally had countered with enthusiastic agreement, deadly, but said a joint presentation on procedures might eliminate misunderstanding. The difference between discussion and presentation was the difference between procedures up for grabs, and procedures already set and agreed.

When Jonathan pointed this out at a Divisional Liaison, Sally had said "Awwww!" as if he were a hurt, suspicious child. She had even started to counsel him—in front of management! Jonathan had never felt so angry, so outmaneuvered. Now his Team had noticed pieces of artwork they should have controlled going elsewhere and wanted him to do something about it. Too late, guys. Bloody Harry, his boss, was too dim to see what had happened, or too feeble to fight. Harry had agreed to the presentation.

So, he told himself. The posture has to be teamwork, cooperation between different parts of the same organization, steer like hell to get back what he could. And keep smiling.

He put his phone and mail through to Support and went downstairs.

Sally's office was neater than his own, and had tiny white furniture. It was like sitting on porcelain teacups. He was sure she chose the furniture deliberately to make large men feel clumsy. Sally offered him coffee. Christ, what was his caffeine count already? Too many stimulants, you lost points. Was she trying to jangle him, get him shaky?

"Oh, great, thanks," he said. "White with one sugar."

"Help yourself," she said. Her smile was warm and friendly. What she meant was: help yourself, I'm not your mother.

"Real cream," acknowledged Jonathan as he poured.

"Nothing but the best is good enough for us," said Sally. She was luxuriantly made up, frosted with sheen. She sat down opposite him. Her hair was in different streaks of honey, beige and blonde, and she was slim under her sharp and padded suit. Her entire mien was sociable and open, inviting trust.

"Thanks for the report," she said. "It was very useful, and I really want to thank you for organizing the presentation for us."

Jonathan had fought it every step of the way. "My pleasure," he said. "We really need to get the two teams together to talk. I just want to be clear that what we're aiming to do is work towards a set of procedures for shared work, which keeps everything going to the right people."

Sally nodded. But she didn't speak.

Jonathan double-checked. "Am I right?"

Her smile broadened just a stretch. "Uh-huh. We do have a set of procedures that your own staff agreed."

"Not all my staff, and not the Quality Action Units who should have been involved. The idea is to empower everyone in the organization."

"Well, I'm sure we can iron out any points of difference. Refer them to the Quasi. OK?"

Jonathan played back the same trick, an uncommitted shrug. But it was one up to him.

A peace offering? Sally kept on. "I also thought that we should present to you first. Most of my staff are familiar with what you do, but our CD ROM work is new, and we need to go over it with your team."

Can I let her get away with that? The clock was ticking, his heart was racing. Caffeine and three hundred thousand smackers. Basically, her staff would NOT be there, say just three of them. They would have the floor and the agenda, but his people would outnumber them, and it would be very easy to take pot shots from the audience. On balance, yes, he could go along with that.

So he agreed. They set dates and agreed how to split the cost of wine and food. Sally gave him a warm and enveloping smile as he left.

Climbing back up the stairs, he reckoned he had scored a five. She still had the initiative, she'd gone no distance towards giving up registration of his jobs, but then, it could be argued that Harry had given them away. I got some points across, but anyone could see I was tense. Jeez. Why do I do it to myself?

Right, now it was Billy, then Dead Space, then the brief on the Commission tender, then lunch.

Lunch with Harry, his boss. Harry was shy and hated schmoozing, which was endearing in a boss, if only he didn't wring his hands for hours at a time and utterly fail to make decisions. Jonathan braced himself for an hour of whining. Jonathan used to work out at lunchtime, till he realized that he scored a full .03 higher if he social-grazed instead. He was climbing the stairs now, to keep fit, though he was not too sure if anyone was noticing. For some reason, he was feeling mean when William arrived for the Sales Meeting.

"Template?" Jonathan snapped at him. William's eyes glittered. Look at those lenses dive for cover. William was in his early twenties, uncomely, gay, nervous. He was supposed to have the agreed agenda and a place for agreed action notes. "Ah. It's just here." When William found his sheet, the agenda section was left blank.

Jonathan tapped the white space, and chuckled, and shook his head, like an indulgent father. "Billy, Billy, what am I going to do with you? Couldn't you remember to print it out? Here, use mine and photocopy it to me after the meeting. Did we get the form letters out?"

Billy had. Well, what do you know?

"All sixty? Great. Thanks very much. Now. The new fax number. We sent all our customers the new fax number, right? Fine. Then why did the Commission fax us a copy of a tender brief on the old number?"

Billy's face fell.

"They sent us a tender, Billy, and it went to our old number, which is with Interactive Media now, who are not necessarily our greatest chums, where it sat for a full afternoon. So now we have four days instead of a working week to develop a full tender with designs. Do you see the problem here?"

Billy face went white and distressed.

The real problem, Jonathan cursed to himself, is that management expects me to make sales without any funding, so I have to use poor Billy from Support who is as sweet as a lamb, but Jeez! Jonathan watched as William scrambled through his shaggy files. OK.

Jonathan decided to try a new management technique. He tried to make himself fancy Billy sexually. LLA, Low Level Attraction, could generate good Team bonding. In fact, people with low to middle bisexuality scores had a favoured Starting-Gun Profile.

So Jonathan looked at Billy and tried, but Billy had chalk white skin and lank black hair, and spots, the thick, clotted, dumb kind of spot that never comes to a head.

I hate this guy, this puny, nervy little idiot; I just can't resist trying to break him.

"Um," said Billy, miserable, balancing his spread-eagled file on his lap. "Yeah, well, I, uh, didn't fax the Commission because it was among my problems to be resolved."

"You mean you didn't know the Commission was one of your clients?" Jonathan managed to say it more in sorrow that in anger.

"I think it was that I didn't know who were our contact names there."

Neither, now that he thought about it, did Jonathan. "OK," he sighed. "Look. Talk to Clara, she'll know them, and then just send the notification you've got. Don't apologize or let them know that we didn't tell them in time. If they ask, the number has just changed. I don't want them to know we had this little hiccup. OK?"

"OK," Billy murmured.

"And, Billy, please. Don't try to keep all your correspondence in one file? You'll find it easier if you keep things separate."

Billy thanked him for the advice. Then he suggested that Jonathan might like to come around to his place for drinks.

I don't believe this. This kid was making a pass at him, he was so desperate. OK, we're both playing the same LLA game. How can we both win? Don't be judgmental, turn the attraction, if that was what you could call it, into friendliness, team bonding.

"That's a great idea, Billy. But I've been feeling bad about not inviting you to my place. I think you've met my wife, but you've never even seen my daughter. Are you free next week?"

Billy looked relieved. Jonathan was relieved too, and thanked him for the job he was doing, and in the general thanking and summing up the invitations were forgotten.

Billy left and Jonathan sat back and sighed. He was feeling tired a lot these days. He saw Sally's face, pink glossy lips parted, as she gave a tiny cry. He sat still for a moment, his eyes closed.

It was 9:57. Jonathan couldn't help himself. He checked his scores again. He really must stop doing this. It was like when he got hooked on the I Ching, and had to have Chaos Therapy to kick it. But all he wanted was a breakdown, a fuller breakdown of this morning's score with Simon.

Verbal content 4.79.

OK, I knew I was bad, but that bad?

Body Language 4.5.

What? Oh, come on. What was I supposed to do, pick my nose? Jonathan actioned a more in-depth analysis. Artificiality, his machine told him, a lack of visible sincerity.

Christ! You can't move around this place. If I'd been sincere, I would have said, you fucked up that own-account job eighteen months ago, and you've been a liability ever since and you've done nothing any better, so we're ditching you like we should have done even earlier. I was just trying to be fucking kind. What should I have done, told him to fuck off?

So what got me my good score? This breakdown is terrible.

10:00 Dead Space.

And the computer flipped itself out into a proactive intervention.

Suddenly, it started to play him the tape of the morning's session with Simon. There he was, fat, stone-faced, saying, "It's not written for me. It's written for Personnel."

A full analysis scrolled up on the screen. Flesh tones, oxygen use, body language, uncharacteristic verbals, atypical eye use.

Behavior typical of industrial sabotage. Rage mixed with satisfaction.

In other words, Simon had become dangerous. Not a little bit dangerous, very dangerous. Determined, apparently, to get revenge.

In-house sabotage is one of the greatest problems now facing both manufacturing and service industries.

Yeah, yeah, yeah, I've been on the course. Jonathan glanced up at the door to make sure it was closed. He could verbal and no-one would hear. George was supposed to be seeing him, but George, thank heaven, was late as usual.

"First." Jonathan asked the computer. "Why didn't you warn me before?"

Programmed to hold all proactive interventions until Dead Space

"Alright, reprogram. If you get a priority like this again, you are to intervene immediately. Please confirm."

Confirmed

"What are the possible actions taken by Simon Hasley?"

Action taken

"Fine. What is it?"

There was no response at all. It was almost as though the machine had crashed, right in the middle of proactive intervention. It simply went back to what it had been doing before.

The machine had been analyzing Jonathan's performance.

This time he noticed the total score in the upper right hand corner. His total score was 5.2. It had been 7.2. If Jonathan knew anything, he knew his own scores.

Simon was changing them.

"CV, please, full CV on Simon Hasley."

```
Not available.
File cancelled due to termination of employ-
ment
```

"Simon Hasley is here until 31st August. His files are not cancelled."

```
Not available.
File cancelled due to termination of employ-
ment
```

"Then open the ex-employee file."

```
??????????????????
```

"Action. Restore scores for Dayplan Item One to 7.2."

```
ACTION NOT AUTHORIZED.
```

Jonathan slammed the top of his desk.

George walked in. To talk about late invoicing. And the bloody machine flipped back to its proactive intervention.

"It's not my letter," Simon was saying. Jeez, how embarrassing, right in front of other staff.

"Stop intervention," Jonathan ordered. "Sit down, George."

Then Jonathan remembered. What had Simon said? Something about Accounts, that he'd worked in Accounts. Accounts with their big system who did all the monitoring. The really big boys. Simon would have swept up after them, wiped their asses, what does he know about the system?

George was talking to him, and Jonathan realized he had not heard a word. He was losing this, he was not handling it.

"...it's the same story. We have to wait for extra-contractuals before we know what the job costs, and so we can't bill." George was smiling his non-commissioned, sleeves-up, man-on-the-shop-floor smile.

"That's not what the people upstairs think."

"Well, with the best will in the world, they're not down here doing the work are they?"

"They don't have to. George, I'm sorry to pull the rug from under you, but I want to change the agenda for this meeting."

George sucked his teeth, scoring points, tut, bad meeting management.

"You know I would never do this normally, but I've just had an intervention on Simon as you came in. How is he taking it?"

The shop-floor smile was still there. "Like a prince. He's calm, in fact, you could say he looks quite happy about it, like he has a card up his sleeve. You give him a good severance deal or something?"

"We can't afford severance deals. This is in confidence. Simon is changing people's performance scores. He's got access to Accounts somehow. The machine can't change them back."

"You're joking," said George, his pink face going slack. Then he began to chuckle. "No wonder he looks so pleased. He's changing people's scores. Well, well, I didn't know he had it in him."

Managers must never lose their sense of humor. Jonathan managed to find an answering smile. "It's one way of getting your own back." There was sweat on his forehead.

"Changing yours, is he?" George's red moustache seemed to glow redder.

"Screwed both of us. You're in charge of monitoring." Jonathan's own smile was a bit harder. "So. How could he have done it? How can we stop him?"

"Beats me. Unless he got hold of the password when he was in Accounts."

"You mean the access code."

"No. This is different, it really lays open the whole network. I think only the Chairman has it, maybe Head of Accounts. You get hold of that you can change any information you like and then ice it, so it can never be changed. Change it invisibly I mean."

"Great for when the Auditors call."

"I expect so."

"Can you change it on verbal? By mail?"

"By camel, I imagine. It's only a rumor but I've heard a few funny things."

"From Simon?"

George grinned back at him.

And then in waltzed Harriet. It was 10:10 after all, and here he was, still in his previous meeting, so his time management score would be fucked, and Harriet would know that, and wouldn't she just love that?

Harriet loved something. She had gone doo-lally with pleasure. She started to do a dance around Jonathan's desk. "Ring around the rosy, a pocketful of posy, husha, husha, they all fall down." Harriet roared her hearty, Hooray Henry laugh that Jonathan had not heard in so long. "Did you know that that is a song about the plague?"

"Someone's caught a cold," said George and his and Harriet's eyes seemed to harpoon each other, and both of them grinned.

Bad behavior from staff depressed their own scores, but insubordination knocked the stuffing out of their manager's profile. They knew it. They were enjoying this.

I am fed up with this crap, I am fed up trying to keep people happy. I am not responsible for keeping people happy.

"Harriet. The stress has gotten to you," Jonathan said. "Come back when you're more in control."

"When you are more in control, you mean." Harriet was beaming, and about to chuckle again. "Come on, George, let's leave him to it."

"George. Please. We're not finished. We still have to talk about invoicing."

"Oh Jesus," and both he and Harriet cracked up.

"I want a breakdown of every invoice on this printout and why it's late. Friday will do. And please remember, that you are responsible for ensuring we hold to financial targets. If you don't, you aren't meeting the minimum requirements of your job. I'll give you a box four marking. And if it doesn't improve, I'll write one of those hilarious little warning letters. Oh, and Harriet, your anti-blood pressure medicine. I know about it. It does have strange side effects, doesn't it. I can recommend Medical Leave. I will be recommending a check-up."

In other words, baby, you may just have lost your job. Harriet's smile slipped.

He verballed it. "Action. Store session. Copy. H. Pednorowska's behavior to the Medical Department."

All this counseling shit to one side, the thing he knew he was really good at was being a bit of a bastard.

"Harriet. George. Thanks for coming to see me. Harriet, I'm sorry you're unwell. George, I'm sure you'll be able to cope with your invoicing problem. Please ask Simon to come in and see me."

Their smiles had not quite faded.

"Meeting over, Team."

Gloves off. Simon had slow reaction times. He needed time to think about things. Well, he had had a whole month to work through this, thanks to Jonathan being so nice. It had probably taken him all month, but he had done it. And he's got me by the balls. He can change my scores, and leave no trace, unless the Chairman is prepared to admit the existence of the password. The computer's got me and George on record and knows our suspicions but that's not proof. I have to wrong foot him. I could say that he'd been monitored telling Harriet what he'd done. But what if he hadn't, or asked "how could they read the note, it was in code?" Jonathan would just have to wing it.

Simon came back in. He looked as calm and unperturbed as this morning. "An impressive display, Simon."

Simon was saying nothing.

"It wasn't age, you idiot," said Jonathan. "It wasn't slowed-down reaction times. Don't you know when you're being let off? They knew, Simon! That's why you were fired. You didn't think you could use the Chairman's password without all the right protocols did you? They were letting you go without any noise. Then you had to go and tamper with my scores this morning, you stupid, dumb, poor, idiot little lamb, and I don't know if I can stop it this time, Simon. I think they're going to send you to jail."

Simon sat unmoving, in silence. But silence was not a denial, or shocked surprise. Would that be enough?

"I mean, as if I didn't signal it, as if I didn't near as dammit tell you, in those private little sessions, you've got a month, keep your nose clean. I don't want to see you go to jail!"

Jonathan raised his hands and let them fall. "I really thought you were smarter than that."

Simon had not moved, not an involuntary flicker of the eyeballs, not a heave of the prison-patterned shirt. Except, he was weeping. He sat very still and a thick, heavy tear that seemed to be made of glucose crept down his cheek.

"They always have one up on you, don't they?" he said.

In the corner of Jonathan's screen, a tiny white square was flashing on and off, in complete silence. A security alert.

"You work your butt off, they keep you dancing for twenty years, and they make a fortune out of you."

This was going to be very sweet indeed, thought Jonathan. Talk about two birds with one stone. Fancy Accounts letting something like the password out. They'd all be for the high jump. Bloody Accounts, who were always breathing down Jonathan's neck about invoices, or performance scores or project costs or unit cost reduction. They would all have their necks wrung like chickens. What a wonderful world this could be.

"It was a dumb thing to do," Simon admitted, laying each word with a kind of finality, like bricks.

"Well. I reckon you'll have revenge. At least on Accounts," said Jonathan.

The door burst open, and Custody came in like it was a drug bust and they were Supercops. In their dumb blue little uniforms.

"What the fuck kept you?" Jonathan demanded.

"By the way, Simon," he added. "We didn't know for sure, until a second ago. Thanks."

Simon didn't move a muscle. When Jonathan checked later, he found he'd scored a ten. Hot damn, it felt good to be so creative.

He got home after fitting in his evening workout. Got up to one hundred on the bench press. Shows what a little adrenalin could do. He got home, to the ethnic wallpaper and the books and the CDs, and he knew he was not a bad man. Life was tough, but that was business. Home was different.

His wife was a painter, and she wore a smock covered in fresh pistachio, magenta, cobalt. He had to lean forward to kiss her lest the smock print paint on his suit. "We should hang that coat of yours in a gallery," he said. It would be nice to live like this too, in a quiet home, but then someone had to bring home the bacon.

"Daddy, Daddy," called Christine from the bedroom. She wouldn't go to sleep until she had seen him, no matter how long she had to wait, and she was not even his child. He went to her room and sat on the bed and kissed her. She smelled of orange juice and children's shampoo. "Play a game with me," she said, and out came the little screen. Mickey had to shoot the basketball through the hoop to escape the aliens. The score was on the screen. "Daddy, I got an eight!" she cried. He chuckled, but a part of his mind said in a slow, dark voice: get them young.

That night he dreamed he had old hands, and they mumbled through job ads. He couldn't feel anything with them. His fingers were dead.

"REPENT, HARLEQUIN!" SAID THE TICKTOCKMAN

by Harlan Ellison®

Harlan Ellison is another living legend of science fiction. He has won pretty much every award the science fiction and fantasy field has to offer, multiply: he's been named a Grand Master by the Science Fiction and Fantasy Writers of America, been presented with life achievement awards (World Fantasy, Bram Stoker, and International Horror Guild), and won eight ½ Hugos, three Nebulas, five Bram Stoker Awards, eighteen Locus Awards, and the World Fantasy Award, among a slew of others. Ellison's innumerable classics—most of which can be found in the mammoth collection *The Essential Ellison*—include "The Deathbird," "Jeffty Is Five," and "I Have No Mouth, and I Must Scream," as well as our next story, which won him one of his Nebulas and one of his Hugos. He is also the editor of what are arguably the genre's two most important anthologies: *Dangerous Visions* and *Again, Dangerous Visions*.

Early sea voyages were dangerous things. The oceans were rough; it was hard to store enough provisions, and the maps were rough sketches where they existed at all. In fact, it's a wonder anyone could attempt to draw a map: it was almost impossible to calculate longitude on a moving boat. In 1714, the British government even established a special advisory board on the topic, with a twenty-thousand pound prize for the man who could find the solution.

The solution came in the form of a better clock, one unaffected by weather conditions and movement. That clock was John Harrison's marine chronometer.

In our next story, people might just curse John Harrison's name. If it weren't for his chronometer's ability to keep accurate time *all* the time, their entire society would be different. If there were only inaccurate pendulum clocks and spring-wound watches, these people might not be slaves to the timetable. Instead, punctuality is the law of the land.

Here's a world where time is not only money: it's life and death.

———

There are always those who ask, what is it all about? For those who need to ask, for those who need points sharply made, who need to know "where it's at," this:

The mass of men serve the state thus, not as men mainly, but as machines, with their bodies. They are the standing army, and the militia, jailors, constables, posse comitatus, etc. In most cases there is no free exercise whatever of the judgment or of the moral sense; but they put themselves on a level with wood and earth and stones; and wooden men can perhaps be manufactured that will serve the purpose as well. Such command no more respect than men of straw or a lump of dirt. They have the same sort of worth only as horses and dogs. Yet such as these even are commonly esteemed good citizens. Others—as most legislators, politicians, lawyers, ministers, and officeholders—serve the state chiefly with their heads; and, as they rarely make any moral distinctions, they are as likely to serve the Devil, without intending it, as God. A very few, as heroes, patriots, martyrs, reformers in the great sense, and men, serve the state with their consciences also, and so necessarily resist it for the most part; and they are commonly treated as enemies by it.

Henry David Thoreau
CIVIL DISOBEDIENCE

That is the heart of it. Now begin in the middle, and later learn the beginning; the end will take care of itself.

But because it was the very world it was, the very world they had allowed it to *become,* for months his activities did not come to the alarmed attention of The Ones Who Kept The Machine Functioning Smoothly, the ones who poured the very best butter over the cams and mainsprings of the culture. Not until it had become obvious that somehow, someway, he had become a notoriety, a celebrity, perhaps even a hero for (what Officialdom inescapably tagged) "an emotionally disturbed segment of the populace," did they turn it over to the Ticktockman and his legal machinery. But by then, because it was the very world it was, and they had no way to predict he would happen—possibly a strain of disease long-defunct, now, suddenly, reborn in a system where immunity had been forgotten, had lapsed—he had been allowed to become too real. Now he had form and substance.

He had become a *personality,* something they had filtered out of the system many decades before. But there it was, and there *he* was, a very definitely imposing personality. In certain circles—middle-class circles—it was thought disgusting. Vulgar ostentation. Anarchistic. Shameful. In others, there was only sniggering: those strata where thought is subjugated to form and ritual, niceties, proprieties. But down below, ah, down below, where the people always needed their saints and sinners, their bread and circuses, their heroes and villains, he was considered a Bolivar; a Napoleon; a Robin Hood; a Dick Bong (Ace of Aces); a Jesus; a Jomo Kenyatta.

And at the top—where, like socially-attuned Shipwreck Kellys, every tremor and vibration threatening to dislodge the wealthy, powerful and titled from their flagpoles—he was considered a menace; a heretic; a rebel; a disgrace; a peril. He was known down the line, to the very heartmeat core, but the important reactions were high above and far below. At the very top, at the very bottom.

So his file was turned over, along with his time-card and his cardioplate, to the office of the Ticktockman.

The Ticktockman: very much over six feet tall, often silent, a soft purring man when things went timewise. The Ticktockman.

Even in the cubicles of the hierarchy, where fear was generated, seldom suffered, he was called the Ticktockman. But no one called him that to his mask.

You don't call a man a hated name, not when that man, behind his mask, is capable of revoking the minutes, the hours, the days and nights, the years of your life. He was called the Master Timekeeper to his mask. It was safer that way.

"This is *what* he is," said the Ticktockman with genuine softness, "but not *who* he is. This time-card I'm holding in my left hand has a name on it, but it is the name of *what* he is, not *who* he is. The cardioplate here in my right hand is also named, but not *whom* named, merely *what* named. Before I can exercise proper revocation, I have to know *who* this *what* is."

To his staff, all the ferrets, all the loggers, all the finks, all the commex, even the mineez, he said, "Who is this Harlequin?"

He was not purring smoothly. Timewise, it was jangle.

However, it *was* the longest speech they had ever heard him utter at one time, the staff, the ferrets, the loggers, the finks, the commex, but not the mineez, who usually weren't around to know, in any case. But even they scurried to find out.

Who is the Harlequin?

High above the third level of the city, he crouched on the humming aluminum-frame platform of the air-boat (foof! air-boat, indeed! swizzleskid is what it was, with a tow-rack jerry-rigged) and he stared down at the neat Mondrian arrangement of the buildings.

Somewhere nearby, he could hear the metronomic left-right-left of the 2:47 PM shift, entering the Timkin roller-bearing plant in their sneakers. A minute later, precisely, he heard the softer right-left-right of the 5:00 AM formation, going home.

An elfin grin spread across his tanned features, and his dimples appeared for a moment. Then, scratching at his thatch of auburn hair, he shrugged within his motley, as though girding himself for what came next, and threw the joystick forward, and bent into the wind as the air-boat dropped. He skimmed over a slidewalk, purposely dropping a few feet to crease the tassels of the ladies of fashion, and—inserting thumbs in large ears—he stuck out his tongue, rolled his eyes and went wugga-wugga-wugga. It was a minor diversion. One pedestrian skittered and tumbled, sending parcels everywhichway, another wet herself, a third keeled slantwise and the walk was stopped automatically by the servitors till she could be resuscitated. It was a minor diversion.

Then he swirled away on a vagrant breeze, and was gone. Hi-ho. As he rounded the cornice of the Time-Motion Study Building, he saw the shift, just boarding the slidewalk. With practiced motion and an absolute conservation of movement, they sidestepped up onto the slow-strip and (in a chorus line reminiscent of a Busby Berkeley film of the antediluvian 1930s) advanced across the strips ostrich-walking till they were lined up on the expresstrip.

Once more, in anticipation, the elfin grin spread, and there was a tooth missing back there on the left side. He dipped, skimmed, and swooped over them; and then, scrunching about on the air-boat, he released the holding pins that fastened shut the ends of the home-made pouring troughs that kept his cargo from dumping prematurely. And as he pulled the trough-pins, the air-boat slid over the factory workers and one hundred and fifty thousand dollars' worth of jelly beans cascaded down on the expresstrip.

Jelly beans! Millions and billions of purples and yellows and greens and licorice and grape and raspberry and mint and round and smooth and crunchy outside and soft-mealy inside and sugary and bouncing jouncing tumbling clittering clattering skittering fell on the heads and shoulders and hardhats and carapaces of the Timkin workers, tinkling on the slidewalk and bouncing away and rolling about underfoot and filling the sky on their way down with all the colors of joy and childhood and holidays, coming down in a steady rain, a solid wash, a torrent of color and sweetness out of the sky from above, and entering a universe of sanity and metronomic order with quite-mad coocoo newness. Jelly beans!

The shift workers howled and laughed and were pelted, and broke ranks, and the jelly beans managed to work their way into the mechanism of the slidewalks after which there was a hideous scraping as the sound of a million fingernails rasped down a quarter of a million blackboards, followed by a coughing and a sputtering, and then the slidewalks all stopped and everyone was dumped thisawayandthataway in a jackstraw tumble, still laughing and popping little jelly bean eggs of childish color into their mouths. It was a holiday, and a jollity, an absolute insanity, a giggle. But...

The shift was delayed seven minutes.

They did not get home for seven minutes.

The master schedule was thrown off by seven minutes.

Quotas were delayed by inoperative slidewalks for seven minutes.

He had tapped the first domino in the line, and one after another, like chik chik chik, the others had fallen.

The System had been seven minutes' worth of disrupted. It was a tiny matter, one hardly worthy of note, but in a society where the single driving force was order and unity and equality and promptness and clocklike precision and attention to the clock, reverence of the gods of the passage of time, it was a disaster of major importance.

So he was ordered to appear before the Ticktockman. It was broadcast across every channel of the communications web. He was ordered to be *there* at 7:00

dammit on time. And they waited, and they waited, but he didn't show up till almost ten-thirty, at which time he merely sang a little song about moonlight in a place no one had ever heard of, called Vermont, and vanished again. But they had all been waiting since seven, and it wrecked *hell* with their schedules. So the question remained: Who is the Harlequin?

But the *unasked* question (more important of the two) was: how did we get *into* this position, where a laughing, irresponsible japer of jabberwocky and jive could disrupt our entire economic and cultural life with a hundred and fifty thousand dollars' worth of jelly beans...

Jelly for God's sake *beans!* This is madness! Where did he get the money to buy a hundred and fifty thousand dollars' worth of jelly beans? (They knew it would have cost that much, because they had a team of Situation Analysts pulled off another assignment, and rushed to the slidewalk scene to sweep up and count the candies, and produce findings, which disrupted *their* schedules and threw their entire branch at least a day behind.) Jelly beans! Jelly...*beans?* Now wait a second—a second accounted for—no one has manufactured jelly beans for over a hundred years. Where did he get jelly beans?

That's another good question. More than likely it will never be answered to your complete satisfaction. But then, how many questions ever are?

The middle you know. Here is the beginning. How it starts:

A desk pad. Day for day, and turn each day. 9:00—open the mail. 9:45—appointment with planning commission board. 10:30—discuss installation progress charts with J.L. 11:45—pray for rain. 12:00—lunch. *And so it goes.*

"I'm sorry, Miss Grant, but the time for interviews was set at 2:30, and it's almost five now. I'm sorry you're late, but those are the rules. You'll have to wait till next year to submit application for this college again." *And so it goes.*

The 10:10 local stops at Cresthaven, Galesville, Tonawanda Junction, Selby and Farnhurst, but not at Indiana City, Lucasville and Colton, except on Sunday. The 10:35 express stops at Galesville, Selby and Indiana City, except on Sundays & Holidays, at which time it stops at...*and so it goes.*

"I couldn't wait, Fred. I had to be at Pierre Cartain's by 3:00, and you said you'd meet me under the clock in the terminal at 2:45, and you weren't there, so I had to go on. You're always late, Fred. If you'd been there, we could have served it up together, but as it was, well, I took the order alone..." *And so it goes.*

Dear Mr. and Mrs. Atterley: In reference to your son Gerold's constant tardiness, I am afraid we will have to suspend him from school unless some more reliable method can be instituted guaranteeing he will arrive at his classes on time. Granted he is an exemplary student, and his marks are high, his constant flouting of the schedules of this school makes it impractical to maintain him in a system where the other children seem capable of getting where they are supposed to be on time *and so it goes.*

YOU CANNOT VOTE UNLESS YOU APPEAR AT 8:45 AM.

"I DON'T CARE IF THE SCRIPT IS *GOOD*, I NEED IT THURSDAY!"

CHECK-OUT TIME IS 2:00 PM.

"You got here late. The job's taken. Sorry."

YOUR SALARY HAS BEEN DOCKED FOR TWENTY MINUTES TIME LOST.

"God, what time is it, I've gotta run!"

And so it goes. And so it goes. And so it goes. And so it goes goes goes goes goes tick tock tick tock tick tock and one day we no longer let time serve us, we serve time and we are slaves of the schedule, worshippers of the sun's passing, bound into a life predicated on restrictions because the system will not function if we don't keep the schedule tight.

Until it becomes more than a minor inconvenience to be late. It becomes a sin. Then a crime. Then a crime punishable by this:

> **EFFECTIVE 15 JULY 2389 12:00:00 midnight, the office of the Master Timekeeper will require all citizens to submit their time-cards and cardioplates for processing. In accordance with Statute 555-7-SGH-999 governing the revocation of time per capita, all cardioplates will be keyed to the individual holder and—**

What they had done was devise a method of curtailing the amount of life a person could have. If he was ten minutes late, he lost ten minutes of his life. An hour was proportionately worth more revocation. If someone was consistently tardy, he might find himself, on a Sunday night, receiving a communiqué from the Master Timekeeper that his time had run out, and he would be "turned off" at high noon on Monday, please straighten your affairs, sir, madame or bisex.

And so, by this simple scientific expedient (utilizing a scientific process held dearly secret by the Ticktockman's office) the System was maintained. It was the only expedient thing to do. It was, after all, patriotic. The schedules had to be met. After all, there *was* a war on!

But, wasn't there always?

"Now that is really disgusting," the Harlequin said, when Pretty Alice showed him the wanted poster. "Disgusting and *highly* improbable. After all, this isn't the Day of the Desperado. A *wanted* poster!"

"You know," Pretty Alice noted, "you speak with a great deal of inflection."

"I'm sorry," said the Harlequin, humbly.

"No need to be sorry. You're always saying 'I'm sorry.' You have such massive guilt, Everett, it's really very sad."

"I'm sorry," he said again, then pursed his lips so the dimples appeared momentarily. He hadn't wanted to say that at all. "I have to go out again. I have to *do* something."

Pretty Alice slammed her coffee-bulb down on the counter. "Oh for God's *sake*, Everett, can't you stay home just *one* night! Must you always be out in that ghastly clown suit, running around an*noy*ing people?"

"I'm—" He stopped, and clapped the jester's hat onto his auburn thatch with a tiny tinkling of bells. He rose, rinsed out his coffee-bulb at the spray, and put it into the dryer for a moment. "I have to go."

She didn't answer. The faxbox was purring, and she pulled a sheet out, read it, threw it toward him on the counter. "It's about you. Of course. You're ridiculous."

He read it quickly. It said the Ticktockman was trying to locate him. He didn't care, he was going out to be late again. At the door, dredging for an exit line, he hurled back petulantly, "Well, *you* speak with inflection, *too*!"

Pretty Alice rolled her pretty eyes heavenward. "You're ridiculous."

The Harlequin stalked out, slamming the door, which sighed shut softly, and locked itself.

There was a gentle knock, and Pretty Alice got up with an exhalation of exasperated breath, and opened the door. He stood there. "I'll be back about ten-thirty, okay?"

She pulled a rueful face. "Why do you tell me that? Why? You *know* you'll be late! You *know* it! You're *always* late, so why do you tell me these dumb things?" She closed the door.

On the other side, the Harlequin nodded to himself. *She's right. She's always right. I'll be late. I'm always late. Why* do *I tell her these dumb things?*

He shrugged again, and went off to be late once more.

He had fired off the firecracker rockets that said: I will attend the 115th annual International Medical Association Invocation at 8:00 PM precisely. I do hope you will all be able to join me.

The words had burned in the sky, and of course the authorities were there, lying in wait for him. They assumed, naturally, that he would be late. He arrived twenty minutes early, while they were setting up the spiderwebs to trap and hold him. Blowing a large bullhorn, he frightened and unnerved them so, their own moisturized encirclement webs sucked closed, and they were hauled up, kicking and shrieking, high above the amphitheater's floor. The Harlequin laughed and laughed, and apologized profusely. The physicians, gathered in solemn conclave, roared with laughter, and accepted the Harlequin's apologies with exaggerated bowing and posturing, and a merry time was had by all, who thought the Harlequin was a regular foofaraw in fancy pants; all, that is, but the authorities, who had been sent out by the office of the Ticktockman; they hung there like so much dockside cargo, hauled up above the floor of the amphitheater in a most unseemly fashion.

(In another part of the same city where the Harlequin carried on his "activities," totally unrelated in every way to what concerns us here, save that it illustrates the Ticktockman's power and import, a man named Marshall Delahanty received his turn-off notice from the Ticktockman's office. His wife received the notification from the gray-suited minee who delivered it, with the traditional "look of sorrow" plastered hideously across his face. She knew what it was, even without unsealing it. It was a billet-doux of immediate recognition to everyone these days. She gasped, and held it as though it were a glass slide tinged with botulism, and prayed it was not for her. Let it be for Marsh, she thought, brutally, realistically, or one of the kids, but not for me, please dear God, not for me. And then she opened it, and it *was* for Marsh, and she was at one and the same time horrified and relieved. The next trooper in the line had caught the bullet. "Marshall," she screamed, "Marshall! Termination, Marshall! OhmiGod, Marshall, whattl we do, whattl we do, Marshall omigodmarshall…" and in their home that night was the sound of tearing paper and fear, and the stink of madness went up the flue and there was nothing, absolutely nothing they could do about it.

(But Marshall Delahanty tried to run. And early the next day, when turn-off time came, he was deep in the Canadian forest two hundred miles away, and the office of the Ticktockman blanked his cardioplate, and Marshall Delahanty keeled over, running, and his heart stopped, and the blood dried up on its way to his brain, and he was dead that's all. One light went out on the sector map in the office of the Master Timekeeper, while notification was entered for fax reproduction, and Georgette Delahanty's name was entered on the dole roles till she could remarry. Which is the end of the footnote, and all the point that need be made, except don't laugh, because that is what would happen to the Harlequin if ever the Ticktockman found out his real name. It isn't funny.)

The shopping level of the city was thronged with the Thursday-colors of the buyers. Women in canary yellow chitons and men in pseudo-Tyrolean outfits that were jade and leather and fit very tightly, save for the balloon pants.

When the Harlequin appeared on the still-being-constructed shell of the new Efficiency Shopping Center, his bullhorn to his elfishly-laughing lips, everyone pointed and stared, and he berated them:

"Why let them order you about? Why let them tell you to hurry and scurry like ants or maggots? Take your time! Saunter a while! Enjoy the sunshine, enjoy the breeze, let life carry you at your own pace! Don't be slaves of time, it's a helluva way to die, slowly, by degrees…down with the Ticktockman!"

Who's the nut? most of the shoppers wanted to know. Who's the nut oh wow I'm gonna be late I gotta run…

And the construction gang on the Shopping Center received an urgent order from the office of the Master Timekeeper that the dangerous criminal known as the Harlequin was atop their spire, and their aid was urgently needed in apprehending him. The work crew said no, they would lose time on their construction schedule, but the Ticktockman managed to pull the proper threads of governmental webbing, and they were told to cease work and catch that nitwit up there on the spire; up there with the bullhorn. So a dozen and more burly workers began climbing into their construction platforms, releasing the a-grav plates, and rising toward the Harlequin.

After the debacle (in which, through the Harlequin's attention to personal safety, no one was seriously injured), the workers tried to reassemble, and assault him again, but it was too late. He had vanished. It had attracted quite a crowd, however, and the shopping cycle was thrown off by hours, simply hours. The purchasing needs of the system were therefore falling behind, and so measures were taken to accelerate the cycle for the rest of the day, but it got bogged down and speeded up and they sold too many float-valves and not nearly enough wegglers, which meant that the popli ratio was off, which made it necessary to rush cases and cases of spoiling Smash-O to stores that usually needed a case only every three or four hours. The shipments were bollixed, the transshipments were misrouted, and in the end, even the swizzleskid industries felt it.

"Don't come back till you have him!" the Ticktockman said, very quietly, very sincerely, extremely dangerously.

They used dogs. They used probes. They used cardioplate crossoffs. They used teepers. They used bribery. They used stiktytes. They used intimidation. They used torment. They used torture. They used finks. They used cops. They used search&seizure. They used fallaron. They used betterment incentive. They used fingerprints. They used the Bertillon system. They used cunning. They used guile. They used treachery. They used Raoul Mitgong, but he didn't help much. They used applied physics. They used techniques of criminology.

And what the hell: they caught him.

After all, his name was Everett C. Marm, and he wasn't much to begin with, except a man who had no sense of time.

"Repent, Harlequin!" said the Ticktockman.

"Get stuffed!" the Harlequin replied, sneering.

"You've been late a total of sixty-three years, five months, three weeks, two days, twelve hours, forty-one minutes, fifty-nine seconds, point oh three six one one one microseconds. You've used up everything you can, and more. I'm going to turn you off."

"Scare someone else. I'd rather be dead that live in a dumb world with a bogeyman like you."

"It's my job."

"You're full of it. You're a tyrant. You have no right to order people around and kill them if they show up late."

"You can't adjust. You can't fit in."

"Unstrap me, and I'll fit my fist into your mouth."

"You're a nonconformist."

"That didn't used to be a felony."

"It is now. Live in the world around you."

"I hate it. It's a terrible world."

"Not everyone thinks so. Most people enjoy order."

"I don't, and most of the people I know don't."

"That's not true. How do you think we caught you?"

"I'm not interested."

"A girl named Pretty Alice told us who you were."

"That's a lie."

"It's true. You unnerve her. She wants to belong; she wants to conform; I'm going to turn you off."

"Then do it already, and stop arguing with me."

"I'm not going to turn you off."

"You're an idiot!"

"Repent, Harlequin!" said the Ticktockman.

"Get stuffed."

So they sent him to Coventry. And in Coventry they worked him over. It was just like what they did to Winston Smith in NINETEEN EIGHTY-FOUR, which was a book none of them knew about, but the techniques are really quite ancient, and so they did it to Everett C. Marm; and one day, quite a long time later, the Harlequin appeared on the communications web, appearing elfin and dimpled and bright-eyed, and not at all brainwashed, and he said he had been wrong, that it was a good, a very good thing indeed, to belong, to be right on time hip-ho and away we go, and everyone stared up at him on the public screens that covered an entire city block, and they said to themselves, well, you see, he was just a nut after all, and if that's the way the system is run, then let's do it that way, because it doesn't pay to fight city hall, or in this case, the Ticktockman. So Everett C. Marm was destroyed, which was a loss, because of what Thoreau said earlier, but you can't make an omelet without breaking a few eggs, and in every revolution a few die who shouldn't, but they have to, because that's the way it happens, and if you make only a little change, then it seems to be worthwhile. Or, to make the point lucidly:

"Uh, excuse me, sir, I, uh, don't know how to uh, to uh, tell you this, but you were three minutes late. The schedule is a little, uh, bit off."

He grinned sheepishly.

"That's ridiculous!" murmured the Ticktockman behind his mask. "Check your watch." And then he went into his office, going *mrmee, mrmee, mrmee, mrmee.*

IS THIS YOUR DAY TO
JOIN THE REVOLUTION?

by Genevieve Valentine

Genevieve Valentine's first novel, *Mechanique: a Tale of the Circus Tresaulti*, is forthcoming from Prime Books in 2011. Her short fiction has appeared in the anthology *Running with the Pack* and in the magazines *Strange Horizons, Futurismic, Clarkesworld, Journal of Mythic Arts, Fantasy Magazine, Escape Pod*, and more. Her work can also be found in my anthologies *Federations, The Way of the Wizard, The Living Dead 2*, and in my online magazine *Lightspeed*. In addition to writing fiction, Valentine is a columnist for *Fantasy Magazine*. She is a finalist for the 2010 World Fantasy Award.

The Tupolev ANT-20, completed in 1934, was one of the largest fixed-winged aircrafts ever built. It featured remarkable engineering features that outshone any other airplane of the 1930s. Big and fast, it was loaded to the gills with wonders: an in-flight film projector, its own printing equipment, a darkroom, and most importantly, the radio broadcasting unit known as the "Voice from the Sky." It was no ordinary airplane. The ANT-20 was the jewel of Stalin's propaganda machine.

Propaganda doesn't have to be evil. But it exists to convince people—and those who use it are often willing to skew the truth or obscure it entirely in order to create an influential product. In the past, propaganda was an important part of the war efforts of many countries, from Nazi Germany to the United States. But in the future, who knows how propaganda might be used?

Our next tale is the story of a new kind of propaganda, filled with a message so large it has changed the living fabric of a nation. But is the message true?

In this grim new world, there's no way to know. And even if it's not, who's brave enough to ask?

When Liz left her building, Disease Control workers were standing on the corners, handing out pills and little paper cups of Coke.

"Do you need one?" the old lady asked, holding up a handful of paper masks stamped with ads for Lavender Fields Sterile-Milled Soap. Liz pulled out the one she kept in her bag, and the lady smiled.

The TV in her subway car showed "What You Can Do on a Date." The young man and woman went to the fair twice—once where he screwed everything up, and again where he helped her into the Ferris Wheel and handed her a paper mask before he put on his own.

The movie closed with swelling music and a reminder in cursive: ARE YOU DUE FOR A DATE? CHECK WITH YOUR DOCTOR.

Liz worked the reception desk on the sixth floor of the Department of Information Affairs.

"That Greg's a lucky man," said Mr. Randall, the District Manager, when he came in every morning. "Too bad I didn't get matched with you first!"

Liz chuckled, because a District Manager's jokes were always funny.

Above her, on a loop, the introduction video played for anyone coming into the Department. It showed a woman on the street overhearing pieces of information she didn't know how to report; it reviewed the details of filing a claim as a man in a mechanic's jumpsuit signed in at the desk, took the elevator to the eighteenth floor, shook hands with a smiling agent.

"What do *you* know that *we* should know?" the narrator asked at the end, right before the two actors turned to the camera and the man in the jumpsuit said, "More than I thought, that's for sure!"

Liz couldn't see it from where she was sitting, but she didn't need to. She'd seen the film during orientation; the last time anyone at the Department suggested she had anything anyone needed to know.

Greg waited outside her building for their scheduled date, and when he saw her coming, he smiled.

Greg had been studying for a job at Disease Control, before the Bang. His viable sperm knocked him out of line for any Sector-C jobs; he answered phones at a law office. They had been matched three years ago, and had been evaluated "Above Average" Sweethearts three years running by the Society Council. Their chances of marriage had been rated by the doctors as close to 80%.

Greg was gay as a Maypole, but they made do.

When she was just far enough away, she called, "Hello, darling." (You never knew when the Society Council was monitoring.)

He smiled. "Hello, honey. How was your day?"

"Some concern over Disease, I think. Someone from Film Production signed in this morning; they might be making a new film about how the Disease is going."

Greg whistled. "That's no good."

She shook her head. "I just don't understand the delay—we've been wearing the masks for weeks already, they should have delivered a new movie by now."

"They should have," Greg said, frowning.

Liz patted her boyfriend's arm and dropped the subject; every once in a while, the government wasn't above a little mistake.

They hit up *The Shindig* at the Three-Screen. The tag line had caused a little scandal ("Vane and Murray spark more fireworks than the Bang!"), but it was just a romantic musical. Liz liked the dancing. Greg liked Joe Murray.

The cashier stamped their tickets. "Please don't forget to get them stamped on the way out or the purchase is ineligible for reimbursement from the Department of Society," he droned.

Once they were in their seats, Greg put his arm around her like all the other guys had done to their dates. (You never knew who was a Society Council inspector.) "Is there a plan for after this?"

"Well, if you really enjoy Joe Murray, we can go to a Society hotel if you want, after."

He looked over, understanding. "Due for the doctor?"

She smiled thinly. "We have a year left before they re-match me." She thought about Mr. Randall finding out and filing a request, and shuddered. "I'd rather stick it out with you."

Greg nodded, and when the movie titles came up, he held her hand.

Murray and Vane were in the middle of their meet-cute dance routine when the film stuttered, pixelated, and blinked out.

"Refund!" someone shouted before the screen was even black.

The screen flared back to life, with the title: YOU ARE BEING LIED TO.

"So, no refund?" asked Greg. The people near them laughed.

The screen cards kept flashing. THERE ARE NO PATHOGENS. THERE IS NO DISEASE CONTROL.

THERE IS NO DISEASE.

Now no one was laughing.

Someone got up and ran out of the theatre.

Liz craned her neck, trying to see what was happening in the projection booth.

The screen cut to a grainy shot of a computer screen; a shadowy figure sat beside it, typing and talking to the camera.

"We are John Doe," it said—its voice had been distorted, like film played at half-speed—"and we have tuned the network. We have proof the Disease is a lie."

Now people were beginning to murmur. Some got up and scurried for the exit like it was a Security Department trap. It probably was.

Liz hoped this kid was lying. She thought, annoyed, about the stupid paper mask she wore three days a week when the Pathogen Alert was high.

The computer screen showed a mail exchange with the header DAMAGE CONTROL TO INTERCEPT INFORMATION LEAK.

"Every citizen MUST ACT," the voice was saying. "Don't take the pills from Disease Control!"

By now the figure was agitated, gesturing at the camera. "Ask yourselves: who's ever really gotten sick? How can the Bang's pathogens strike such small areas? Why are they always near the borders? How does Disease Control respond so quickly? The pills have kept us docile, but the time has come to act! We've made contact with—"

The doors behind them crashed open, the doorway filled with plainclothes SD and uniformed cops, guns out.

"Hold it!" someone shouted, and the police charged the projector booth.

A young man jumped out of the booth and crash-landed in the aisle, grabbing Greg's seat to pull himself up—the boy was young, blond, his face tight with pain or fear, and for a moment he was just staring at them, his hands flexed on Greg's armrest.

Then he sprinted for the exit and disappeared.

The cops and SDs tripped over themselves back down the projection-room stairs, and they scattered—some for the exits, some for the audience.

Greg and Liz were yanked out of their seats and dragged outside into a holding pen of cop cars, along with the rest of the audience. Liz saw a few of the ones who had tried to run and hadn't made it.

"I don't want to go into the station," Greg told her. "It could end up on my record."

He still hoped that someday he could get closer—any closer—to Disease Control.

Liz faked a storm of tears when the cops were close enough to see it, and they handed Greg a printout and stamped his ticket stubs and told him to be a gentleman and take her home, already.

"I'm looking for a refund for this prank," Greg told them half-seriously, "I want you to know that."

On the walk home, Greg read from the printout; a standard-issue distribution, without a date on it. They'd had it ready to go, just in case.

Greg flashed the picture of a frowning boy dragging a skull-emblazoned bag behind him.

Pranks are FOOLISH and WASTE THE TIME of VALUABLE CITIZENS. They DISTRACT from safety work and INTERFERE with your government. If you see a PRANKSTER, contact your local precinct.

The bottom read, in large block letters, *TODAY'S DELINQUENT IS TOMORROW'S CRIMINAL.*

"Hold it," said the blond kid from behind her, and Liz felt the point of a knife in her back.

"Or today's criminal," Liz said.

Greg leveled a look at the kid. "Keep it cool, Johnny Doe. What do you want?"

"Your car."

"Don't have one."

Johnny pulled a face. "Shit. Well. Give me your money," he said, and nudged Liz with his shoulder (not, she noted, with the knife).

"What, you're going to buy a bus pass and ride out of town on the local?" Liz asked, but she handed over her purse. "Seventeen dollars. Enjoy."

Johnny thumbed through the wallet with his free hand. "They've got my car," he told them like they were all friends. "I need to get out of here. They'll kill me."

Liz didn't doubt that.

Greg glanced around at the quiet street. Ahead of them was the main drag, swarming with people going out to the City Fair on subsidized dates.

"You should go," said Johnny. "You'll be in trouble if they see you with me."

Greg looked like he was in the middle of a magnificent adventure, and was sneaking looks at Johnny's sharp profile when he thought Johnny wasn't looking, and Liz knew what was coming before Greg even opened his mouth.

Gred asked, "What do you need?"

Liz and Greg signed into a Society hotel just off the main drag. The concierge registered them, stamped their paper, and smiled politely. No speeches about exit stamps this time—it was gauche for concierges to keep track of that sort of thing.

They closed the door and looked at one another like it was their first date again. Liz felt an itch just under her skin, like she was sick, like she needed to run until she dropped. She felt like Greg looked.

Greg laid his tie over the chair and looked at her. "What if they trace him to my apartment? What if they find him there?"

Liz figured if they found a good-looking young man in Greg's apartment, he'd be in trouble for a lot more than harboring a fugitive.

"Come on," said Liz, tugging gently at the tongue of his belt. "We have work to do. Just close your eyes and think of Johnny."

At the door of the hotel, Greg kissed her cheek goodnight. He seemed surprised when she fell into step beside him instead of turning for her street, but he took her arm without hesitation.

"Just curious to see what he does in civilization," she said when she felt him looking at her. "Besides, I'm your alibi if anyone's found him."

"God, that's the truth," he said, and pressed her hand more tightly into the crook of his arm.

John Doe was gone, having availed himself of Greg's good raincoat and a bottle of milk from the refrigerator, and Greg's sadness at the end of their adventure was mitigated by the fact that he'd have to replace a very pricey coat.

Liz figured that wasn't the last of Johnny Doe, though when Greg wistfully asked her, "Do you think he might ever…?" she said, "Nope," just to keep him from getting tied up in knots about it.

Secretly, she guessed that a rebel wouldn't abandon a safe harbor, but that was really only from the films ("Is Your Neighbor a Traitor?") and she couldn't be sure, now.

Sometimes when they were at the movies and the screen skipped a frame, Greg tensed, and Liz dreaded the day Johnny ever came back and swept Greg off his feet and into some mission, living in a ghost town smack in the middle of the Pathogen Fields.

Liz would have to go on the group dates in the Society Center where they observed you behind the mirror and marked your body language and assigned you someone, and Liz would have to learn to live with someone entirely new.

Above her head, the woman in the video was shopping for groceries. A man behind her said to someone, "We'll have to hurry, the pickup happens tonight," and the woman frowned at an apple; the narrator said, "Mary knows something's not quite right, but what can she do? She can do what we ALL should do: report suspicions. Today's alert citizen is tomorrow's hero."

On the screen behind her, the man in the jumpsuit opened the lobby door and approached the desk to make his complaint. (He never actually made it, Liz knew; he just went up in the elevator and shook hands with the other actor, every ten minutes, all day.)

"It's easy to be a good citizen!" the narrator said. "We need what you know."

John Doe was standing at the corner of her street, dressed like a Disease Control agent, when she saw him next.

When he saw her, he went white as a sheet. Then he fumbled for the tray, handed her a cup.

"What's in here?" she asked under her breath. "You poisoning us now?"

He rolled his eyes. "It's the same as the rest," he said. "I'm just waiting here to be taken back to Disease Control."

So he was going to sneak in that way.

"Is it true you work for the DOI?"

She blinked as his question settled in. Then she shook her head. "Oh, no, Johnny. Don't."

"How can you say no?" he handed off a paper cup to a passerby, turned back to her. This close, she could see the vein of green in his blue eyes.

"You're not stupid," he said. "You know I'm telling the truth. Won't you help me?"

"What are you going to do?"

"I'm getting into Disease Control," he said. "I'm getting proof that this is all just to keep us in line, and I'm going to air it across the country. People are going to have a nasty wake-up."

She wondered how he planned to organize the nation full of people he was going to wake up. "I can't help you," she said.

"I know where you work," he said, pleading. "You can help me get the message out. All you have to do is let me in. I'll go upstairs on my own, I can get the message out from there."

She took a step back. "I can't," she said. "It's too dangerous."

"No one will know it was you."

That much she knew for sure—she said, "Someone will."

"How can you be such a coward?" He was louder now—too loud, the other Disease Control agent looked concerned—and Liz took a step back as Johnny stepped forward. His eyes were sharp and bright. "Don't you see what they've done to you?"

"Leave me alone," she said. She wished Greg or someone was here, just in case.

He dropped the tray with a clang; paper cups and pills skittered across the pavement, bounced off Liz's shoes.

"It's over," he said. "They'll kill me if you don't help me. You've killed me."

Liz couldn't breathe. She felt dizzy. She didn't understand what he meant.

The next moment she was on the ground, being handcuffed, and Johnny was being picked up (five cops, maybe more) and carried, kicking, into the back of a van that had appeared out of nowhere.

As the two policemen walked Liz to the car, they passed the van, blaring the last swells of a familiar tune through its speakers.

"Are you due for a date?" called the announcer. "Check with your doctor."

Mr. Randall was waiting for her on the eighteenth floor of the Department.

She waited. She tried to think how many people who came up to report something to the Department had ever come down again.

"We'd like to congratulate you," said Mr. Randall.

Liz blinked. "Pardon?"

"Your John Doe was part of a series of test runs we did around the city to gauge the audience for a new instructional film. Marketing has been working with us for months."

Relief flooded her. "Oh, I see," she said.

"Our field man did his damnedest, but I told him—I said, That girl has her head on straight, you won't get her to help you! He tried twice, the theatre and the street, but did Elizabeth fold?" He laughed. "I told him he'd have as much luck getting help from me as from you."

She thought about giving Johnny her keys to Greg's place, telling him the fastest way to get there, taking Greg's arm to go for an alibi date.

No one had told Randall about that. This was no undercover job, then; Johnny Doe had died and taken that secret with him.

"Thank you, sir," she said.

When she got back to her desk, she called Greg. "Want to get married?"

He only hesitated a moment. "I thought you'd never ask," he said, a little too brightly, but only just. "I'll pick you up tonight and we'll go to City Hall and your doctor."

She wanted to tell Greg what had happened; how she had been too afraid to help Johnny, and what must have happened to him by now.

"See you soon," she said, hung up as he was saying, "Goodbye, darling."

Above her, the film was ending, the Department actor grinning through the last frames of twinkling music.

"What do *you* know that *we* should know?"

INDEPENDENCE DAY

by Sarah Langan

Sarah Langan is a three-time winner of the Bram Stoker Award. She is the author the novels *The Keeper* and *The Missing*, and *Audrey's Door*. Her short fiction has appeared in the magazines *Lightspeed*, *Cemetery Dance*, *Phantom*, and *Chiaroscuro*, and in the anthologies *The Living Dead 2*, *Darkness on the Edge* and *Unspeakable Horror*. She is currently working on a post-apocalyptic young adult series called *Kids* and two adult novels: *Empty Houses*, which was inspired by *The Twilight Zone*, and *My Father's Ghost*, which was inspired by *Hamlet*.

If you listen closely to Bruce Springsteen's "Born in the USA," you'll hear real pain beneath the slick guitar solos. The song is a lament for an America where ordinary people mattered and their vote made a difference in the direction of the nation. It was a song written in response to the Vietnam War, and the squawking nationalism that swept the U.S. after the Bicentennial.

But it's the Tricentennial that our next story examines. Polluted and terrorized, somehow America is just as frantically patriotic as it was when the Boss wrote his classic song—and the feeling is twice as empty. Langan says of her piece: "I was working on an homage to Springsteen. I couldn't decide on a particular song, and decided instead on what I thought was the essence of Springsteen; standing up, and fighting for what you believe in a screwed-up world."

The waiting room is shiny and bright, but the people inside it are dirty. Trina tries not to stare but she can't help herself; she can tell just by looking that a few are addicts trying to score a fix. One lady's wearing a black garbage bag instead of clothes.

Trina waits her turn with her dad, Ramesh. He won't be seeing the doctor today. He's never seen the doctor. He says he's not sick, but he's lying. He coughs all the time, and in the mornings she's seen him spit blood and phlegm into the bathroom sink. Last month, the Committee for Ethical Media installed a television camera in their kitchen because he submitted an unapproved audio to the news opera "Environmental Health." Instead of running it under a pseudonym like he'd wanted, the editors called the cops. Now the whole family is under house surveillance. Anybody who wants can flip to channel 9.53256 can see her lard-congealed breakfast table, and the weird foam curlers her mother keeps forgetting to take out of her hair in the morning. Her whole eighth grade class knows that Ramesh's pet name for her is Giggles, and that they can't afford fresh milk. Only one-day soured from the bodega on 78th Street. It's humiliating, and so is he.

While they wait, he puts his hand on the back of her neck and squeezes the skin surrounding her port like he's trying to pull it out. He doesn't understand, even though eighteen Patriot Day channels repeat it day-in and day-out: *You can't stop progress!*

Trina rubs her bruised cheek and glares at Ramesh. He sighs and lets go of her port. It's a victory, but it doesn't make her happy; it only stirs the piss and vinegar stew in her stomach.

She's carrying the list in the pocket of her spandex jeans. Each visit, her dad makes her write down her complaints before they leave the house, and then goes over them with her. He tells her that he wants to be sure she says the right things so she doesn't get in trouble. But the truth is, he doesn't give crap about her. He's just protecting his own sorry ass.

He got drunk last night at dinner. Her mom, Drea, accidentally took too many vitamins and nodded off at the table. Trina pretended she was a duck, and let it roll off her back. Quack, fricking quack. At least dinner was ready. Peanut butter and Fluff: the ambrosia of champions. But after a few drinks, Ramesh got *the look*. He started talking through his teeth like a growling dog: "They're pushing me out. Looking over my shoulders all the time. Even the janitors. Cameras everywhere. A man can't work like that."

He rubbed his temples while he talked like his thoughts were hurting him, and Trina tried to be sympathetic, but she'd heard this song before. Every time he got drunk, it was the same. Meanwhile, cameras were recording his every word, and where would they live if he got fired? Worse, what if that blood in the sink turned out to be cancer, and in a week or a month from now, he was dead?

In the corner, the television was set to "Entertainment This Second!" Drea pretended to be interested in what Ramesh was saying, but she was looking past him, at the show.

"Those fuckers are killing my work!" Ramesh shouted while banging his fist against the table like a gavel. Everything jumped—even his stinking vodka bottle. The salt shaker rolled into her lap. She was scared to call attention to herself by putting it back, so in her lap it stayed. Her little friend, salty. She and salty, against the world.

She hated salty, all of a sudden, because his sides were all greasy with thumb-print scum. She hated her dad, for ruining dinner. She hated their crappy apartment, and the kids at school who called her pink lung. Mostly, she hated the way Ramesh shouted, because Drea was so out of it, Drea had checked out months ago. It was Trina he was yelling at. *I can't fix your problems. I'm thirteen years old, remember?* she wanted to say.

But she didn't. It would be too hard to explain. The salt spilled like bad luck, and she let the shaker drop from her lap. It rolled under the table. "Fuck you, you fucking no good drunk," she grumbled under her breath, only the words got away from her. They rushed from her chest, and then burst into a holler that practically echoed inside the kitchen. She spun at her mother, to make sure it wasn't Drea who'd spoken. But Drea's earpods were inserted. On the television, beauty queens in bathing suits wrestled in a pool of mud for the title of "hottest bitch."

Had she really just said *fuck you* to her own father? She was already blushing from shame when she felt the blow. It came while her head was turned. Her dad, a dirty fighter. Another reason to hate him. At least it was his open palm and not his fist that tore across her face and knocked her out of her chair.

She lay stunned on the floor. From the table, Drea shook her head, "Don't fight, babies. It's beneath you," she said, but she might have been talking to the mud-slingers.

Trina's face broke like glass. Her lips pulled wide, ready to explode into the worst crying jag of her life, so she squeezed her fists so tight her fingernails pierced her skin, and tried to stay calm. Ramesh was kneeling next to her. His long limbs wobbled drunkenly until he gave up kneeling, and sat down. She flinched as he ran the plastic Smirnov bottle along her swelling cheek. It was so cold it got stuck and pulled her skin. "Let me see. Hold still," he told her.

"You're a terrorist," she sobbed. "That's why they want to get you fired. A dirty Indian terrorist," she said, even though she was half Indian, too.

"Shh," he said. "I'm sorry. That was unforgivable. I'll never do it again." He was still holding the bottle against her skin. He smelled like mice and formaldehyde, and though he wasn't supposed to, he'd worn his white lab coat home from the office. It made him feel important, because he could tell people he was a doctor, too.

Trina tried to stop crying, but she couldn't. She pushed the bottle away and hid her face between her knees. It was dark in there, and she wanted to come out and let him hold her, but she hated him so much.

"I'm so sorry," Ramesh crooned. His long limbs didn't quite fit under the table, so he was hunched like a man in a dollhouse. The air was warmer, because they were both breathing fast in a small space.

"I mean it, I'm reporting you," she blubbered. He didn't answer that. Probably too shocked. It was the meanest thing she could think to say. Then she got up and locked herself in her room. She didn't come out until morning, when it was time to go to the doctor.

Now, a nurse holding a Styrofoam clipboard calls her name: "Trina?" She's wearing neon orange short-shorts and a belly ring. All the smart nurses dress in tight clothes. That way they get better tips. "Trina Narayan?" she asks again.

Her dad nods at her very slowly, like he's trying to impart one last tacit bit of advice. He thinks he's a genius or something, but if he'd taken a real job with the Defense Department when the last war started instead of staying in the toxicology lab at New York University, they'd be rich. Instead, his funding got cut, so they had to move from their pretty house in Westchester to a two-bedroom stink-hole with wall-to-wall shag carpet in Jackson Heights, Queens. Now she goes to a school where kids ignite cherry bombs in homeroom, and her only friend is semi-retarded, which is better than the rest of the kids, who are completely retarded.

She touches her bruised cheek for courage. It still stings. "Don't tell," Ramesh mouths so that only she can see. He's so scared that his eyes are bulging. A bug-eyed coward. He's not a real man, her father.

She smiles in a way that is not meant to reassure. Her lips are closed, tight and angry, and she silently tells him her answer. The blood drains from his face as she walks away.

The examining room is empty. A bright light shines from the corner and she squints. Most people her age only require one visit, then tune-ups every ten years. You're not allowed treatment more than once a month or you become a vegetable. Still, some people invent false identities and sneak. They wind up wandering the streets and begging for food because they can't remember their names, or where they live.

Problem is, the treatment never works on her. Every time the doctor cuts out the bad stuff, it grows back like a tumor. Her dad tells her it'll right itself on its own, but he doesn't know shit. First sign the bad stuff is back, Trina doesn't gather moss. She calls the doctor. The best part is, no matter how much paperwork Ramesh fills out to cancel her appointments, he never gets it done in time. It's fun to watch him run around, like a wind-up toy, when she knows that no matter how hard he works, he'll never get anywhere.

The examining room is pink and round like a womb. She's wearing a short-sleeved jumper so she won't have to undress. The needles are plastic, which makes them cheaper, but not as sharp. She has to shove the small one really hard to get it into a vein. Blood squirts. She puts the second needle inside the port in the back of her neck and twists its metal ring until it locks into place. Some people do it standing, but she likes to lie on the cool metal table. Makes the whole thing floaty, like a dream.

The doctor is a five-foot wide metal box in the curved corner of the room. It's attached to the needles, and her, by worn plastic tubes that over time have turned pink from other peoples' blood.

The doctor has a Cyclops-like eye in the center of his face. It lights up white, and then red. The needle jabs through her neck and into her skull. Her skull is especially big, so she had to get her port adjusted at a shop in the mall. The sales lady broke off a piece of her skull and replaced it with hinged plastic that she has to swipe with rubbing alcohol every night so it doesn't get infected.

The light flicks from red to green. The machine starts to purr. She holds her breath. This is her fourth time with the doctor, and it is always this moment that feels most wrong. The needles have warmed to the temperature of her blood, but they are still foreign objects; they don't belong inside her skin. Neither does this port that has left her gray matter vulnerable. There are people, mostly the old and young, who experience drip. Their spinal fluid leaks, and they become paralyzed. She wants to rip out the port. She wants to pull out the needles and break them. She wants her booze-hound daddy. Mostly, she wants to run.

But then the doctor doles his medicine. It travels, colder than her blood, but tingly. First her elbow, then her shoulder, her back, and finally, all the places that are just beginning to get tender. It feels like the boys she wishes would touch her. Like laughing so hard her stomach hurt back in Westchester, when life was easy and she was Giggles. Like her mother's embrace. Like love. It feels just like love.

Begin, a recorded female voice announces over the loudspeaker. Its mechanical quality reassures her. This is too intimate for human witnesses. Too special. Oh, how she loves the doctor.

She pulls the wad of paper from her spandex jeans and starts: "I'm afraid for Lulu." She always begins with this one, but so far every time they excise it, the worry grows back. "…In school they say that early cultures believed in this thing called a soul. It scares me. I don't know why. Like we've all got these ghosts that live inside us. Like I'm haunted by my own ghost."

Continue, the voice tells her. Its soft voice travels through the tubes so that her port vibrates.

"The actors in the movies—it doesn't make any sense that they look so different from the people I know. They're so pale and thin—they never have mechanical lungs… I hate the way I look. I wish I could cut myself into little pieces. I wish I was pretty…"

The tube in her arm is getting backflow. Red blood mixes with morphine, pink and pretty like all girls should be. Except she's brown and pudgy.

"I got so mad last week I bit my hand. You can still see the teeth-marks. They're smaller than you'd think. Looks like baby teeth, so I told everyone at school it was a neighbor's little kid. Well, actually, nobody asked. But if they did, that's what I'd tell them."

She looks at her list. The rest are the items that her father invented: *You don't like sour milk; You want to devote your life to your country. You're so excited about Patriot Day that you can't sleep.* Then he added, like it was an afterthought, but she knew it wasn't: *You want to be popular but you don't fit in. You don't understand that you're special. Your worries are a gift.* She'd felt her face flush when he said that, because suddenly the gig was up, and they both knew that nobody at PS 30 thought she was cool.

She decides she'll say the honest one. Maybe it'll stop being true, once she says it. Maybe the doctor is magic. "I'm not pop—" she starts, and then stops, because if she says the words, her father will be right. Because that smack had been so unexpected, and undeserved. Because every day for as long as she can remember, things have been worse than the day before, which is how she knows that last night wasn't a fluke. He might be sorry for it, but next time he gets drunk, he'll hit her again.

The morphine has wound all over her, like amniotic fluid. It feels so good, and safe. The doctor will know what to do. She crinkles the paper into a ball, and for the first time, tells the doctor what's on her mind. "I'm so sad…. My mom doesn't take pills because she wants to be happy. She just wants to be numb. I'd take pills if they made me numb, but they don't."

She sniffles, and bites her lip hard until she's sure she won't cry. She'd like the doctor to take everything this time. She'd like to be so empty that she doesn't remember how to breathe.

The machine starts clicking and humming. She gets nervous. Was she wrong to say that pills don't work?

Continue, the voice tells her.

The thing she really wants to say sits on her tongue like a sliver of reconstituted nectarine. She bites down, and lets its juice run down her chin. This is not her problem. She is not accountable. *He* has done this to her. Her father. The doctor, too.

"I hate my father. He drinks. He hit me last night." She notices, dully, that her voice now echoes. *I'm being recorded*, she thinks, and then: *Good. Now he'll really get in trouble.*

"He makes us wear air filters in our chests, even though the EPA says we don't need them. He fills the apartment with them, too. He says he's working on safe cigarettes at the lab, but really he's testing metal dust on mice again. He says it's the debris from the bombs that's killing us. All those falling buildings. He's going to move us to Canada because they're granting amnesty—I heard him talking. He wants to get out before the mandatory ports go into effect."

As she talks, the drug warms her. She's almost sleeping. Sweet, thick dreams. She will be sick from this for days. But for now it is so good. *Continue*, the voice says, but she doesn't have anything else to say.

"That's all."

Continue.

She tries to make something up, but her thoughts scatter. She licks them like gossamer spider's webs, but can't collect them into coherent strands. They bundle and knot in all the wrong ways. "I have no soul to haunt me," she says, because it reassures her to think this.

Then the pull. This is her least, and most, favorite part. She closes her eyes, and starts floating. Warmth radiates from the port in her neck. She doesn't feel it. There are no nerves up there. Just pulp and grey matter. Heat in tiny lasers breaks the synapses, until all those bad thoughts disappear. Memories fade, and are gone. First Lulu, then school, then the pills, then her father, then her soul. She can't remember them anymore.

When the stream ends, she nods off. In her dream a little person lives inside of her, and that person is so angry she's eating her own fingers until all that is left is a pair of opposable thumbs. She holds them up, bloody and ragged as the coast of a beach.

The table jiggles as it rescinds. She falls to the floor. The needle in her arm tears her skin on its way out. Blood squirts. The needle in her port, still attached, yanks her head back. "Cripes on a cross!" she mumbles, then with an eye half-open, looks at her watch: 11:15. She's been sleeping for two hours. A personal best. She twists the tube from her port, and starts out just as the sprinklers and ammonia pour from the ceiling, to clean the room for another patient.

Except for the headache that longs for more morphine, she's as light as air when she opens the door to the waiting room. The world is like a flat desert, and she sees nothing for miles. Wings, sparkly and slender as silk threads, are attached to her back; they'll fly her away.

In the waiting room, her father is sitting next to the woman wearing the garbage bag. The woman is really fat, so maybe it's a contractor bag. You could roll her, Trina thinks, and then she giggles. The doctor has made her so happy!

Her dad stands to greet her. He's tall, dark, and skinny. Long, long ago, her mother used to call him beanpole: *My funny beanpole, I could grow cumquats off your arms. My funny beanpole, bend down a few stories, and give me a kiss.* Two years ago, the apartment got so hot that he filled the tub with ice water, and they all took turns snorkeling for rubber duckies in their bathing suits.

He's frowning like he's worried, and suddenly her stomach turns. Something is wrong. What could it be? She knows, even though she can't remember. She did something bad.

Her temples throb. She cradles her head like she's wounded, because she wants him to know that she's hurting. There's a bruise on her cheek, but she doesn't know how she got it. "Daddy," she says, and she doesn't know why, but she's crying.

It smells like metal out; another explosion in midtown. They walk with their shirtsleeves over their noses to the car. His legs scrunch in the seat, and he has to bend into the steering wheel.

She thinks maybe he's going to hit her, which is stupid, because he's never once hit her in her life. But he only raises his hand to make sure her sleeve stays over her nose. He holds it there, so she doesn't have to talk for a long while. He takes care of her, which, come to think of it, he's always done. After a long while, he takes his hand away, so she raises her own hand to keep her shirt in place. Out the window, ashes fall like rain. If you think of them as black dandelion wishes, they're almost pretty.

She was mad at him, she realizes, so she told the doctor something very bad. Now he's is in trouble. To keep from sobbing, she puts the heel of her hand in her mouth and bites down. "I'm sorry. I told," she whispers through a mouthful of bone.

He closes his eyes for just a second. "Remember me," he says.

In her mind, a bomb explodes where she sits. Its fire swallows her, and her father, and the car, and the doctor, and her apartment in Queens, and her city, and her country, and the whole world. All ashes, falling down.

He's not yet gone, but already she remembers something as if she is reminiscing at his funeral: before the war, her dad never drank.

"Where do they go?" Trina asks her best friend Lulu the next day at lunch. They're on line in the school cafeteria. She can't remember what she said to the doctor, except it feels queasy, like spoilt milk. It feels gnawing, like missing fingers.

"Where does what go?" Lulu asks. She's got a voice like Darth Vader because her mechanical lung needs a tune-up. When Trina's feeling left out, she takes tiny breaths like hiccoughs until she feels loopy, because Lulu says that having a mechanical lung is like being high on nitrous all the time.

"Where do our thoughts go after we visit the doctor?" Trina asks. In her mind, doctors across the country collect the worries into a giant vat. They're extracted one at a time by the people in charge, who best know what to do with them. Why should the whole world worry, when you can give the job to a select few?

"That's stupid!" Lulu giggles. "There are no problems! That's why we go to the doctor. To get adjusted. It's a throwback from early evolution. Our species worries even when nothing is wrong." It's a line from a commercial for the doctor that Lulu's quoting but Trina knows better than to argue, so instead she shrugs.

Lulu scoops up a ladleful of lard-fried iceberg lettuce onto her Styrofoam tray. She used to be one of the pretty girls, but over the last few years, she's gotten fat and dim-witted. Trina caught her on the way down.

Trina bypasses the lettuce for a vitamin-fortified fluff sandwich, and they sit in the back of the cafeteria by themselves because, except for each other, they don't have any friends.

There are about twenty television screens all set to the same program, "Brick Jensen's Health Challenge." They hang from hooks in the ceiling and descend to eye level at the middle of every table. Lulu is fascinated. Brick Jensen, also known as Mr. Fit, is explaining that five minutes of exercise each day is enough to keep in shape, so long as you do it correctly. You can squeeze your butt while standing, for example, and do three sets of mechanical lung lunges. For perfect arms, you hold your backpack over your head.

The show is interrupted by Mr. Mulrooney, the school principal. He's got a tiny black mustache, so everybody calls him Hitler. The mustache is pencil thin, though. So maybe it's Gay Hitler. Eccentric Hitler. Hitler Lite.

"Two days until Patriot Day!" he announces; a small man trapped inside twenty small screens. It'll be July 4, 2076. The 300th anniversary of the Great Emancipation. "Remember to wear your school colors," Hitler Lite adds.

"If they weren't maroon and orange, maybe," Lulu mumbles. Her wilted lettuce looks like green poop, but she keeps eating it, like she's punishing herself for getting ugly.

"If everybody wears maroon and orange I'll go blind," Trina adds. "Seriously. It's a health concern. I'll get dizzy and puke and go blind, not necessarily in that order." Lulu is wheezing, so Trina punches her backpack until the battery starts humming. She's done this enough times that it no longer requires acknowledgment. They're best friends, and that's what friends are for.

"For those of you without ports, remember to bring your insurance cards." Hitler says. "And if you've got private insurance…. Well," he smiles tightly, "Nobody here has private insurance."

Patriot Day is the same day that the law goes into effect, and everybody who can't afford a private doctor has to get a port. She used to be really happy about that. What progress: adjustments for the masses! Better yet, poppies for the masses! But that means her dad will have to get a port and she knows he doesn't want one. Her stomach feels hollowed out again. Like somebody scooped away her insides with a metal frozen yogurt spoon. She thinks about the Cyclops eye, the list she crinkled into a ball instead of reading. And the morphine. She thinks about that, too, because she misses it already.

Hitler makes a final announcement. He's the third principal in two years. They keep getting fired for embezzlement. The last guy partnered with Milk of Magnesia, so everybody got free laxatives after lunch. The bathrooms stank, but at least the school colors were blue. She liked that a lot better than Hitler's pick: who wants free Tang? Everybody knows that trip to the moon was a hoax.

"Ozone levels are too high. No after school sports today," Hitler says before signing off.

"Bees knees, shit up a tree!" Trina moans. Unless it's video games, sports are for lesbians and stupid people. Everybody knows that. It's the running joke on the show everybody's watching lately: "Will Brick Jensen Get Laid?!?!" People keep remaking it with their own video cameras, and posting it on their personal television channels. It's the joke that won't die. It's pulling its decaying corpse down the hall with its thumbs. Still, she *loves* track, and the weather's only been nice enough once this season.

Because of her natural lungs, Trina is really good at running. She even laps the boys. It's showing off, but she can't help it. She loves to run. When you go fast and long enough, it's like being high, only better. It's like living, only good.

Most people in this neighborhood get the operation by the time they hit grade school. Stores all over the mall take out your bronchi, and replace them with plastic tubes. That way you never cough when the bombed buildings fall. But so far, Trina doesn't need the surgery. Thanks to her dad and the time she spent in Westchester, her lungs are clean. Even if it makes you popular, fake lungs look like a bad idea. Sure, you won't get cancer, but what happens when they rot? Still, she's an outcast at this school. When she volunteers in class, she doesn't pant like the rest of them if she says more than a sentence. She doesn't need to shoot insulin in the girls' room, either. Sometimes she brings a needle anyway, and fills it with saltwater.

"Sports are for lesbians and stupid people," Lulu wheezes.

Trina frowns. It's coming back to her, the stuff that got excised. She wishes it would go away. She wishes she was like everybody else, and nothing ever bothered her, but instead she's crazy like her dad. Ignoring Lulu's comment, she asks, "Do you think the doctor helps people? That it's good to forget?"

Lulu shrugs. "I wouldn't know. I don't have any problems." Then she adds, "I'm feeling much better than yesterday."

Trina sighs. Lulu always says she's feeling better, but she coughs more and more. It's not just the battery that's low. The tubes are clogged with pus.

The gnawing inside her hurts like a morphine headache. In her mind, a girl is chewing her hands into rags. "Maybe it's all a lie," Trina says. "And we can't figure it out because the doctor makes us stupid."

Lulu's jaw drops. She looks around, because they both know that Trina said a very bad thing. Something so bad that if Lulu reported it, the Committee for Ethical Media would take her away to a re-education center, where the kids get stuck cleaning rubble and bodies.

They look at each other for a while, and finally Lulu smiles like a phony. "You pink lung!" she teases. Only, she's not kidding, and for the first time in the three years that they've been best friends, Trina is on the outside, looking in.

The door is open to the apartment when she gets home, which is new. "Where's dad?" she asks.

Drea is watching three different programs on the television while instant chatting with her friend next door. Trina wishes she'd inherited Drea's white skin and blue eyes, but no dice. She's brown like a terrorist instead.

In big letters in the corner of the screen Trina sees: "*Sports are for thesbians and flaccid people!*" "*Brick Jenson gets me wet!*" "*Sour milk=de-lite-FULL.*" On a side bar are all the quips she wrote, but doesn't plan to send because, unless she dumbs it down, nobody ever knows what she's talking about: "*These ashes are our loon's call; mad and maudlin.*" "*Remember, my love, it ends not with a bang, but with a whimper.*" "*The womb grows like a widening gyre, and even our best suckle its poison.*"

Drea was a poet-in-residence at NYU when she met Ramesh at a faculty dinner. As his pick-up line, he told her that the written word was dead. Even then, he compulsively pissed people off. Trina's the same way. She never intends to offend anybody; stuff just bursts out of her mouth. Half the time, she doesn't even realize she's thinking it.

But instead of getting mad, Drea agreed. "Yeah, books are dead," she said. "So what does that make me for writing poems? Better yet, what does that make you?"

But Drea hasn't written a poem in a decade. Now that everybody self broadcasts audio poems, she says it's like genius and madness; there are so many voices that you can't tell which is which anymore.

"Why was the door open? Was someone here?" Trina asks.

Outside the window, she sees a fire on 78th Street. The Jackson Diner is burning. She smells scorched Indian food, which is a better smell than usual. On the television split screen, ten people are competing to be the best art critics.

They look at photos of paintings scavenged from the Louvre, and say whether they're any good. Then the judges tell them if they're right, or if the paintings are crap. The second channel is that show with Rhett Butler and Scarlet O'Hara, where instead of breaking up, they get back together. The last channel is their still kitchen. Drea is watching their apartment on channel 9.53256. Suddenly all three programs are interrupted, and Trina moans. It better not be another evacuation. She only just got rid of the lice in her hair from the last time she had to stay at the 48th Street Shelter.

The president comes on screen. He's smiling. He's had a lot of cosmetic surgery, so he looks just like Brick's brother, Brett Jensen. Or maybe he *is* Brett Jensen. She can't remember.

Remember me, she hears in her mind, like the president is saying it. Her head hurts bad. She misses the morphine. *I worry about Lulu*, she thinks, and she knows the thought is not new. The doctor's cure never works for long.

"Good evening," the president says, like he's fancy. Everybody else says, "Hey, America!" Then he reminds everyone about Patriot Day. "I've got a special surprise," he says, and Drea claps her hands together like it's Ex-Mass morning. "At dusk on Patriot Day, every city in this great country will launch a FIRE WORKS SPECTACULAR!" he announces. Then he itemizes the cities: Seattle, Santa Fe, Portland, Boston, New York. He doesn't mention Los Angeles or New Orleans, which makes her think they're still at war for earthquake and flood supplies. She can never remember who the war is with, because it changes so often.

"Ummm," her mother says like she's hungry. "I love all those pretty explosions."

"We have explosions every feckin' day, Drea!" Trina reminds her, but it doesn't do much good. Brett Jensen (the president?) has a dimpled smile, which for some reason makes her remember the word *soul*. A little girl with no hands is haunting her. She looks at her own hands now, and notices that she's been biting them. Teeth indentations are embedded like welts along her fingers.

"Why's the door open? Where's dad?" she asks.

Drea sits up from the couch and looks at Trina like she doesn't recognize her.

"Think," Trina says. "Where was the last place you saw him?"

Drea furrows her brow. Her fingers are swollen from all the typing. She's supposed to use voice prompt, but she prefers typing because it reminds her of writing. Old people! "I saw him on the television?" Drea asks.

Trina's lower lip quivers. She wants to hit her mom all of a sudden, which makes her even more like her dad, maybe. "Did he go to work this morning? The door is open."

"Oh," Drea says, and slides back into the couch. "Somebody took him, then."

"So where is he?"

She doesn't answer. The president signs off, and new shows start. Their theme songs all sound the same. They plan it that way, so when you're watching a bunch of shows at once it's never discordant.

"I'm lonely, baby. Why don't you come sit with me?" Drea asks, and Trina would like that. They'll share a blanket and kiss toes like they used to. Trina will tell her mother what she did, and her mother will forgive her. Together, they'll figure out what to do. But Trina doesn't sit, because things have changed, and nothing's the way it used to be.

On one of the programs, a dark-skinned girl with brown hair and deep circles under her eyes is standing in a dark, dingy room. Flickering lights cast shadows against her face. On the couch beneath the girl, a sickly thin woman lays stretched out and half-sleeping. It's weird, because television stars are supposed to be skinny and tan, not a bunch of ugg-os. Then she figures it out. It's her. It's right now. This is her life. The Committee for Ethical Media has added another camera.

In her room, she switches to channels 9.53256 and 9.53257, then presses rewind. She sighs with relief. The reverse record is working. She plays the tapes backward, and sees herself wiping tears from her eyes while talking to her mother on the couch. Was she crying? She doesn't remember that, though she notices now that her eyes are still wet.

She sees stillness. Her mother in the dark with the shades drawn, moving only to swallow vitamins and breathe. Then her dad with each arm held by an officer of the CEM, walking backward into the kitchen. They wrestle a little. Her dad is on the floor. One of the men hits him on the back of the head. But then they all get up again. They let him go, and walk backward out the apartment. The door closes, and it is dad chewing toast into existence. She wishes it had happened like that.

She uses a long metal prong to pull out the old filter. It's black with soot. Then she replaces it with a clean one, and tries not to gag. It's small until it fills with air. Then it expands. Her dad says it's the ultra-fine particles you have to worry about. They get into the deep lungs, where there isn't any hair or phlegm to carry them back out. Nobody at school uses filters. They're expensive. Ramesh steals them from the lab. There's about fifty hidden behind the false wall panel in her bedroom.

As she walks, she remembers. She's not supposed to, but she can't help it. First came the cold table, and then the blinking eye. And then the slap against her cheek, and the echo of her voice as it was recorded. She puts her hand in her mouth and bites down until she draws blood, but it doesn't make her feel any better: her father. She told, and now he's gone.

The main branch of the Committee for Ethical Media is at the old library near Bryant Park in Manhattan. A guard at the subway station orders her to spread her legs, because it looks like she's hiding a bomb up there. He loses interest when she tells him she's got antibiotic resistant syphilis. After an hour, the F train never shows, because the 59th Street Bridge is closed due to a bomb threat. She hikes it north over the Triborough, then grabs the 6 Train downtown. By the time she gets to the CEM it's night, but the city is lit up so bright it feels like day.

She takes a number and waits. The woman sitting next to her is wearing a trash bag. This time, it's white and lemon scented, so slightly less offensive. She falls asleep for a while. When she wakes it's morning, and her number is three spots away. They call her name. She's up in a flash.

"Ramesh Narayan?" she asks.

A woman punches something into a computer. "Rammy Naran? Nope. Next!"

"No, wait. You spelled it wrong. Here." The woman enters the name again. Then she frowns. "Cremated or buried?"

Trina tries not to hear this. She tries very hard. There is something bad on her tongue. Bile, maybe. "No. He was taken in for voluntary questioning."

"So it says." Then she leans over the counter. She is wheezing badly, and her backpack is hissing like a bum who got stabbed. "Heart attack during interrogation," she answers. "Cremation or burial?"

Trina's tries to think, but the words don't make sense. She's not sure they're English. Her hand is in her mouth and she's biting hard. It tastes like salt. "I love my dad," she mumbles. "And he loves me."

"Which? Your insurance covers both," the woman says. Her backpack is gasping.

Trina thinks about the cold bottle against her cheek. The bruise is still tender, and she touches it now, and pushes hard until it hurts. She'd like it to reverse heal. She'd like to wear the scar for the rest of her life. "It's a mistake," she says. "He was going to get us out. I made a mistake."

The woman shakes her head. "You're right. There was a mistake."

Trina's crying all of a sudden, from relief. "Yes! I knew! They only took him for questioning." She's holding onto the counter, because otherwise she'll fall. "Daddy!" she shouts, "Daddy, where are you?" because maybe he'll hear her voice in one of the interrogation rooms, and know that she came all the way from Queens to rescue him. He'll know she's sorry.

The woman grabs hold of Trina's wrist like a lobster catching prey. Her grip clamps tighter when Trina tries to shake her off. "We couldn't find next of kin. So the CEM already incinerated him. That's the mistake. He's still dead, kid. Now shut your mouth before the guards arrest you for making a racket." Then she lets go, and places a bar-coded ticket on the counter. "You can pick him up at that address."

"No," Trina says. "That's wrong. Ramesh Narayan. Before the war he gave lectures all over the country. He was an important man."

"The ticket," the woman says, only Trina sees that she's not mad, just tired. Her lips are almost blue from lack of oxygen. "Sure, maybe it's a mistake, but that's where you'll find out."

Trina looks down at her shoes. In her mind there is a bomb at her feet. When it explodes, a hole opens in the earth, and swallows her. The girl left standing in the CEM lobby is just a shell. Made of tubes and plastic surgery. A confection of the doctor. Sweet and stupid as cotton candy.

She's panting and wet with sweat by the time she jogs the forty blocks downtown to the East Village. She'd keep running forever, if she could, but the building's name comes into view: City Morgue. She stands in front of it for a long while, catching her breath.

Unlike Jackson Heights, a lot of people in Manhattan don't have mechanical lungs. Instead they're zipped inside big plastic bubbles equipped with molecular air generators. They're skinny and they dress in high heels, even the men. They look like a different species. As they pass the front of the building, she thinks about poking holes in their generators. The air will leak slowly, and then they'll start coughing, just like everybody else.

Once inside the building, she exchanges her ticket for a number, and waits. After a while a guy with no teeth hands her a Styrofoam urn. She's not sure it's her dad, but there's a picture burned into the side. In it, Ramesh is wearing his tan work suit. His dead eyes are closed.

She'd like to eat the urn. That way she'll never forget. There were the animals that died in his lab. Little spotted mice with pink tongues. They couldn't survive the debris. There are buildings that fall. The third world war in the last twenty years. There is her mother, who used to laugh. There is her best friend Lulu. They blend together. They coalesce, like mercury. Like morphine. They bathe her. She is bathed in death.

Perhaps she'll run out of here, and never stop. There is Canada, like her dad planned. But would they really have gotten there? Or would Patriot Day have come with blood and fireworks, and then gone gently, into another day? She knows the answer, and for once it makes her think no less of him. He would have anesthetized his new port with vodka, and after a visit or two to the doctor, he'd have become just like everyone else. There was no plan for escape. There was only rage and talk. But these were better that nothing.

I won't forget, she whispers, and she knows she should say it to the ashes, but she can't bring herself to open the urn.

She walks the whole way, and doesn't get home until the next morning. Her feet are bleeding. Squish-squish.

When she walks inside, Drea is on the couch. She's been sneaking extra visits to the doctor, and Trina can tell from her dilated blue eyes that she saw him recently.

She puts the ashes on the table. The television is tuned to four channels. This time there is a view of the neighbor's apartment. The weird guy is having sex with his daughter. Drea is sad about that, so she's hiding her face. Trina can't figure out if it's really happening, or a programmed show

She turns off the television. "This is dad," she says.

Drea is quiet. She knows she's supposed to explain, but she doesn't know how. She can't help it; she laughs. This is dad, light as a feather. This is my hand, covered in open sores.

Drea examines the photo, and then opens the Styrofoam top. "If this is your father, what does that make me?" she asks.

When she wakes the next morning, she can't help it. She forgets she was supposed to remember. She spies Drea running her fingers through the ashes, and goes on automatic pilot. She calls the doctor. He can't squeeze her in until tonight. She uses Lulu's name. She figures Lulu won't care. It's all for a good cause. Just the thought of the needle makes her skin tingle. She can't wait for the needle.

Remember me.

Drea is playing the television so loud that it gives her a headache, so even though she'd rather stay home, she walks to school. It's Patriot Day, so everyone is wearing maroon and orange. In her black jeans and T-shirt, Trina sticks out like a bloody thumb. There aren't any classes, just lines of people waiting to sit on gurneys in the auditorium and get their free ports. Along the aisles, they're handing out Tang juice and Fluff sandwiches.

In her mind she tears the ports from kids' skulls, and watches them bleed. She tears out her own port, too. Up on the podium, the seniors are giving speeches to the underclassmen: "Before my port I wasn't sure, but now I know I'm happy!" "The Doctor makes everything better." "This will be the best day of your life."

But then Hitler interrupts the testimonials for a special announcement. Something about a pep rally and bonfire tonight after the fireworks. He wants people to bring things to burn. She stops listening until she hears Lulu's name. She's been hiding from Lulu all day, because if she sees her, it'll make what happened to her father real, instead of a dream. She'll have to talk about it. She'll have to say his name.

Hitler Lite continues. "Complications of the complication on the complication," he says. Blah blah blah. "Let's bow our heads for a moment, in memory of Lulu Walker."

Her face goes red. It's so hot she's sweating. She doesn't stay to hear any more. She's out the door.

She knows she shouldn't be here. She promised she wouldn't come. She hates him. Then again, she's got no place else to go. "Emergency," she tells the nurse in pleather and vinyl. "I have to see the doctor. Lulu Walker."

She takes a ticket. The woman sitting next to her is wearing a sheet. She's shaking like she needs a fix real bad. Trina doesn't look too closely, because the woman is Drea.

She closes her eyes and thinks about the trickle through her veins. She thinks about emptiness. She thinks about the filter in her lungs full of ashes. The dead are all around her. She is breathing them. And still the buildings topple while the televisions sing.

—*Remember me.*

—*Why? It hurts too much.*

"Lulu Walker?" the nurse calls, and she's up in a flash.

Needles inserted. Blood squirted. She lays down. White eye to red to green, she begins. "I worry about the speed of things. I worry you murdered my dad. I murdered my dad. I worry he was right all along, only I hated him so much I didn't see it. I worry this war will never end. It's just a lie to keep us stupid."

Her voice echoes. It's being recorded. They'll think its Lulu, probably.

Continue, it tells her, and she finally recognizes the voice. It's the same lady on "Will Brick Jensen Get Laid?!?" who says that sports are for lesbians and stupid people.

The morphine tingles in her arm. She starts forgetting even though the doctor hasn't entered her port yet. The treatment is finally working, she realizes. It's not brain damage they're after. Everybody remembers eventually, no matter how often they're adjusted. The doctor isn't the cure. It's self-regulation. It's forgetting with the snap of a finger, the promise of a tingle in the arm. Forgetting in the anticipation of pleasure. Forgetting because it's easier, and you're tired of fighting, when every day things get worse, instead of better. It's learning to be your own doctor. That's what Patriot Day is all about.

Continue, the woman repeats. She's been paid for her voice, of course. An actress. They do it all the time. Trina thinks she's going to laugh, but instead she is crying as the morphine drips. It doesn't feel good this time; it just feels sick.

Lulu is dead. Her father is dead. Even the living are dead. The laser begins to shoot, and her father is disappearing. The machine is killing her father. Bean Pole with dark circles. They used to swing their feet on the bench in Westchester, side-by-side. The memory disappears. Burned away. She searches for it, but it's gone. Next goes the bathtub, where he taught her to swim. Gone. She is killing her father. She is a murderer. The doctor is a murderer.

She pulls the needle like a plug. Precious morphine drips. She unlocks the port. *Click*. Then she's kicking the machine. She's beating it senseless with her bitten and scarred hands, because two days ago Ramesh was here. Two days ago, even though he knew she would betray him, he was waiting for her. He loved her. She punches and kicks, until the Cyclops eye shatters. Then she pops the needle inside its gaping wound. The morphine wets the wires, and the doctor's lights go out.

It goes to sleep and forgets, but she does not.

She leaves fast, before they can figure out what she did. It won't be long before they come for her. There is video. Lulu is dead. They'll figure it out. They'll lock her up, or worse.

She thinks about Canada. It would make her father proud. But she doesn't have the paperwork to leave the state. She could take a train to Westchester, but she's broke. Besides, they'll run her name through the CEM Database. An idea occurs to her, and she likes it. She could walk. She's good at that. She'll insert a double filter and cross the Triborough at night when they won't see her walking the old pedestrian path. She'll sleep during the day, and walk as long as it takes.

She'll visit those places she's heard about, where there is grass and dirt. Where there are animals, and birdsongs, and she doesn't need a filter.

But do places like that exist anymore?

She goes home first. The apartment door is wide open, and her father's ashes are scattered on the coffee table. The television is loud. She packs a bag full of filters and vitamin-enriched fluff. Wears it on her shoulders like a mechanical lung. "Mom?" she calls.

Drea is lying on the bed. The bottle of vitamins is empty. Trina's first thought is a bad one. But then Drea opens her eyes. "Sweetie," she moans. "I got lost and had to find a nice policeman to take me home. They put this on my arm, so it doesn't happen again." Drea lifts her wrist, where a barcode has been branded into her skin. "You'd think they'd just write the address. But nobody likes words anymore, do they?"

Trina sits down on the bed. Her mom doesn't move. Her head is upside-down, which makes her look alien. "I'm in trouble," she says.

Drea blinks. Her fingernails are dirty. Or maybe ashy.

The camera's light is green, just like the doctor's, and she thinks about smashing it. She'd like to say: *I'm leaving. Come with me, mom!* But this is being recorded, so instead she stands. "I'll remember both of you," she says.

Drea smiles. "How nice."

She's walking backward out the door, like this is a movie in rewind. They haven't really lived in this hole for three years. Her mother isn't really a junkie. She didn't really rat her father out to the CEM, and get him killed. She isn't really leaving all that she's ever known.

"Bye, mom," she croaks as she crosses the threshold. Then she's running down the steps.

The streets are red, and the sky is ashes. Inside her, a girl is chewing the scenery. She's ripping down all the old pictures, and making everything blank. A girl is yelling and shouting and crying. And breathing. And running. And thinking. And remembering. This girl is her.

Feet pounding, she doesn't stop until she's out of breath. When she looks up, a crowd of people has amassed under the Triborough Bridge in Astoria Park. Have they come to arrest her so soon? No, she remembers. It's Patriot Day.

All along the street and sidewalk are floodlights, gurneys, and the sound of drills. The streets look wet, and at first she thinks it's water, but no, it's blood. People stand in lines one-hundred bodies deep, waiting for the messy operation. Scalp wounds bleed. Her sneakers are red.

When the sky explodes, she thinks at first that it's another bomb. But then there are colors: red, white, and blue. Heads bobble in unison, thousands, and peer into the light. She notices now the men with guns. They're here to make sure that everybody, even the people who try to back out, get their ports.

She pushes through the crowd and gets onto the bridge. The road is so thick with people that she can hardly move. Still, she pushes. There are others, she notices, who do not look at the bright lights in the sky. They navigate the crowd, and try to make their faces blank, but they can't. They're terrified, just like her. One in a hundred. Maybe one in a thousand, but still she spots them. Still, they exist.

Have there always been others, only she's never noticed them before? Or is it that she's never been one of them before? She knows the secret now and it has nothing to do with the doctor. The way to remember is to stop forcing yourself to forget.

The people like her make their way across the bridge while the other stand still, and block the way. Some are alone, others in small groups of three or four. Heads bent, chests pounding, they steer through the immobile throng. She thinks they're all headed for the same place. Canada or free Vermont. A few are wearing neck kerchiefs, and she realizes it's because they have no ports.

Remember, her father told her. And she will do more than that.

She doesn't know it's happening until her breath comes ragged. She's running along the bridge in blood stained shoes. She's not sure, but it seems like she's the first. Others follow. Soon, half the bridge is shaking, pounding. There aren't many of them, but they're determined. They are running. It feels so good, the air slapping her face. She was born for this, to run. She will keep running, until she is far away. Until she can watch the fireworks of Patriot Day from some place free.

THE LUNATICS

by Kim Stanley Robinson

Kim Stanley Robinson is the bestselling author of fifteen novels, including three series: the Mars trilogy, the Three Californias trilogy, and the Science in the Capitol trilogy. He is also the author of about seventy short stories, much of which has been collected in the retrospective volume *The Best of Kim Stanley Robinson*. He is the winner of two Hugos, two Nebulas, six Locus Awards, the World Fantasy Award, the British Science Fiction Award, and the John W. Campbell Memorial Award. His latest novel, *Galileo's Dream*, came out in 2009.

At the end of the nineteenth century, coal mining had become one of the biggest, meanest industries in the United States. Unhealthy working conditions and a reliance on child labor caused accidents and blackened men's lungs. Crooked business practices like debt bondage and wage-cheating were just part of the misery. But it was dangerous to stand up against the mining companies. Miners didn't just face losing their jobs—their lives were often at stake, as mining companies fought against unionizing with violence.

The coal miners' struggles for better conditions were captured in photos and songs that have become a warning for the workers of the world. But in the future, miners might not be so lucky.

What could be worse than working deep beneath the ground, never seeing the light of day? What could be worse than knowing the money in your paycheck was a token worthless outside the company's store?

Our next story gives us a vision of a mine worse than anything in Pennsylvania. Powered by slavery and jump-started by torment, *this* mine might as well be hell.

They were very near the center of the moon, Jakob told them. He was the newest member of the bullpen, but already their leader.

"How do you know?" Solly challenged him. It was stifling, the hot air thick with the reek of their sweat, and a pungent stink from the waste bucket in the corner. In the pure black, under the blanket of the rock's basalt silence, their

293

shifting and snuffling loomed large, defined the size of the pen. "I suppose you see it with your third eye."

Jakob had a laugh as big as his hands. He was a big man, never a doubt of that. "Of course not, Solly. The third eye is for seeing in the black. It's a natural sense just like the others. It takes all the data from the rest of the senses, and processes them into a visual image transmitted by the third optic nerve, which runs from the forehead to the sight centers at the back of the brain. But you can only focus it by an act of the will—same as with all the other senses. It's not magic. We just never needed it till now."

"So how do you know?"

"It's a problem in spherical geometry, and I solved it. Oliver and I solved it. This big vein of blue runs right down into the core, I believe, down into the moon's molten heart where we can never go. But we'll follow it as far as we can. Note how light we're getting. There's less gravity near the center of things."

"I feel heavier than ever."

"You are heavy, Solly. Heavy with disbelief."

"Where's Freeman?" Hester said in her crow's rasp.

No one replied.

Oliver stirred uneasily over the rough basalt of the pen's floor. First Naomi, then mute Elijah, now Freeman. Somewhere out in the shafts and caverns, tunnels and corridors—somewhere in the dark maze of mines, people were disappearing. Their pen was emptying, it seemed. And the other pens?

"Free at last," Jakob murmured.

"There's something out there," Hester said, fear edging her harsh voice, so that it scraped Oliver's nerves like the screech of an ore car's wheels over a too-sharp bend in the tracks. "Something out there!"

The rumor had spread through the bullpens already, whispered mouth to ear or in huddled groups of bodies. There were thousands of shafts bored through the rock, hundreds of chambers and caverns. Lots of these were closed off, but many more were left open, and there was room to hide—miles and miles of it. First some of their cows had disappeared. Now it was people too. And Oliver had heard a miner jabbering at the low edge of hysteria, about a giant foreman gone mad after an accident took both his arms at the shoulder—the arms had been replaced by prostheses, and the foreman had escaped into the black, where he preyed on miners off by themselves, ripping them up, feeding on them—

They all heard the steely squeak of a car's wheel. Up the mother shaft, past cross tunnel Forty; had to be foremen at this time of shift. Would the car turn at the fork to their concourse? Their hypersensitive ears focused on the distant sound; no one breathed. The wheels squeaked, turned their way. Oliver, who was already shivering, began to shake hard.

The car stopped before their pen. The door opened, all in darkness. Not a sound from the quaking miners.

Fierce white light blasted them and they cried out, leaped back against the cage bars vainly. Blinded, Oliver cringed at the clawing of a foreman's hands, searching under his shirt and pants. Through pupils like pinholes he glimpsed brief black-and-white snapshots of gaunt bodies undergoing similar searches, then blows. Shouts, cries of pain, smack of flesh on flesh, an electric buzzing. Shaving their heads, could it be that time again already? He was struck in the stomach, choked around the neck. Hester's long wiry brown arms, wrapped around her head. Scalp burned, *buzzz* all chopped up. Thrown to the rock.

"Where's the twelfth?" In the foremen's staccato language. No one answered.

The foremen left, light receding with them until it was black again, the pure dense black that was their own. Except now it was swimming with bright red bars, washing around in painful tears. Oliver's third eye opened a little, which calmed him, because it was still a new experience; he could make out his companions, dim redblack shapes in the black, huddled over themselves, gasping.

Jakob moved among them, checking for hurts, comforting. He cupped Oliver's forehead and Oliver said, "It's seeing already."

"Good work." On his knees Jakob clumped to their shit bucket, took off the lid, reached in. He pulled something out. Oliver marveled at how clearly he was able to see all this. Before, floating blobs of color had drifted in the black; but he had always assumed they were afterimages, or hallucinations. Only with Jakob's instruction had he been able to perceive the patterns they made, the vision that they constituted. It was an act of will. That was the key.

Now, as Jakob cleaned the object with his urine and spit, Oliver found that the eye in his forehead saw even more, in sharp blood etchings. Jakob held the lump overhead, and it seemed it was a little lamp, pouring light over them in a wavelength they had always been able to see, but had never needed before. By its faint ghostly radiance the whole pen was made clear, a structure etched in blood, redblack on black. "Promethium," Jakob breathed. The miners crowded around him, faces lifted to it. Solly had a little pug nose, and squinched his face terribly in the effort to focus. Hester had a face to go with her voice, stark bones under skin scored with lines. "The most precious element. On Earth our masters rule by it. All their civilization is based on it, on the movement inside it, electrons escaping their shells and crashing into neutrons, giving off heat and more blue as well. So they condemn us to a life of pulling it out of the moon for them."

He chipped at the chunk with a thumbnail. They all knew precisely its clayey texture, its heaviness, the dull silvery gray of it, which pulsed green under some lasers, blue under others. Jakob gave each of them a sliver of it. "Take it between two molars and crush hard. Then swallow."

"It's poison, isn't it?" said Solly.

"After years and years." The big laugh, filling the black. "We don't have years and years, you know that. And in the short run it helps your vision in the black. It strengthens the will."

Oliver put the soft heavy sliver between his teeth, chomped down, felt the metallic jolt, swallowed. It throbbed in him. He could see the others' faces, the mesh of the pen walls, the pens farther down the concourse, the robot tracks—all in the lightless black.

"Promethium is the moon's living substance," Jakob said quietly. "We walk in the nerves of the moon, tearing them out under the lash of the foremen. The shafts are a map of where the neurons used to be. As they drag the moon's mind out by its roots, to take it back to Earth and use it for their own enrichment, the lunar consciousness fills us and we become its mind ourselves, to save it from extinction."

They joined hands: Solly, Hester, Jakob and Oliver. The surge of energy passed through them, leaving a sweet afterglow.

Then they lay down on their rock bed, and Jakob told them tales of his home, of the Pacific dockyards, of the cliffs and wind and waves, and the way the sun's light lay on it all. Of the jazz in the bars, and how trumpet and clarinet could cross each other. "How do you remember?" Solly asked plaintively. "They turned me blank."

Jakob laughed hard. "I fell on my mother's knitting needles when I was a boy, and one went right up my nose. Chopped the hippocampus in two. So all my life my brain has been storing what memories it can somewhere else. They burned a dead part of me, and left the living memory intact."

"Did it hurt?" Hester croaked.

"The needles? You bet. A flash like the foremen's prods, right there in the center of me. I suppose the moon feels the same pain, when we mine her. But I'm grateful now, because it opened my third eye right at that moment. Ever since then I've seen with it. And down here, without our third eye it's nothing but the black."

Oliver nodded, remembering.

"And something out there," croaked Hester.

Next shift start Oliver was keyed by a foreman, then made his way through the dark to the end of the long, slender vein of blue he was working. Oliver was a tall youth, and some of the shaft was low; no time had been wasted smoothing out the vein's irregular shape. He had to crawl between the narrow tracks bolted to the rocky uneven floor, scraping through some gaps as if working through a great twisted intestine.

At the shaft head he turned on the robot, a long low-slung metal box on wheels. He activated the laser drill, which faintly lit the exposed surface of the blue, blinding him for some time. When he regained a certain visual equilibrium—mostly by ignoring the weird illumination of the drill beam—he typed instructions into the robot, and went to work drilling into the face, then guiding the robot's scoop and hoist to the broken pieces of blue. When the big chunks were in the ore cars behind the robot, he jackhammered loose any fragments of the ore that adhered to the basalt walls, and added them to the cars before sending them off.

This vein was tapering down, becoming a mere tendril in the lunar body, and there was less and less room to work in. Soon the robot would be too big for the shaft, and they would have to bore through basalt; they would follow the tendril to its very end, hoping for a bole or a fan.

At first Oliver didn't much mind the shift's work. But IR-directed cameras on the robot surveyed him as well as the shaft face, and occasional shocks from its prod reminded him to keep hustling. And in the heat and bad air, as he grew ever more famished, it soon enough became the usual desperate, painful struggle to keep to the required pace.

Time disappeared into that zone of endless agony that was the latter part of a shift. Then he heard the distant klaxon of shift's end, echoing down the shaft like a cry in a dream. He turned the key in the robot and was plunged into noiseless black, the pure absolute of Nonbeing. Too tired to try opening his third eye, Oliver started back up the shaft by feel, following the last ore car of the shift. It rolled quickly ahead of him and was gone.

In the new silence distant mechanical noises were like creaks in the rock. He measured out the shift's work, having marked its beginning on the shaft floor: eighty-nine lengths of his body. Average.

It took a long time to get back to the junction with the shaft above his. Here there was a confluence of veins and the room opened out, into an odd chamber some seven feet high, but wider than Oliver could determine in every direction. When he snapped his fingers there was no rebound at all. The usual light at the far end of the low chamber was absent. Feeling sandwiched between two endless rough planes of rock, Oliver experienced a sudden claustrophobia; there was a whole world overhead, he was buried alive.... He crouched and every few steps tapped one rail with his ankle, navigating blindly, a hand held forward to discover any dips in the ceiling.

He was somewhere in the middle of this space when he heard a noise behind him. He froze. Air pushed at his face. It was completely dark, completely silent. The noise squeaked behind him again: a sound like a fingernail, brushed along the banded metal of piano wire. It ran right up his spine, and he felt the hair on his forearms pull away from the dried sweat and stick straight out. He was holding his breath. Very slow footsteps were placed softly behind him, perhaps forty feet away... an airy snuffle, like a big nostril sniffing. For the footsteps to be so spaced out it would have to be....

Oliver loosened his joints, held one arm out and the other forward, tiptoed away from the rail, at right angles to it, for twelve feathery steps. In the lunar gravity he felt he might even float. Then he sank to his knees, breathed through his nose as slowly as he could stand to. His heart knocked at the back of his throat, he was sure it was louder than his breath by far. Over that noise and the roar of blood in his ears he concentrated his hearing to the utmost pitch. Now he could hear the faint sounds of ore cars and perhaps miners and foremen, far down the tunnel that led from the far side of this chamber back to the pens. Even as faint as they were, they obscured further his chances of hearing whatever it was in the cavern with him.

The footsteps had stopped. Then came another metallic *scrick* over the rail, heard against a light sniff. Oliver cowered, held his arms hard against his sides, knowing he smelled of sweat and fear. Far down the distant shaft a foreman spoke sharply. If he could reach that voice…. He resisted the urge to run for it, feeling sure somehow that whatever was in there with him was fast.

Another *scrick*. Oliver cringed, trying to reduce his echo profile. There was a chip of rock under his hand. He fingered it, hand shaking. His forehead throbbed and he understood it was his third eye, straining to pierce the black silence and *see*….

A shape with pillar-thick legs, all in blocks of redblack. It was some sort of….

Scrick. Sniff. It was turning his way. A flick of the wrist, the chip of rock skittered, hitting ceiling and then floor, back in the direction he had come from.

Very slow soft footsteps, as if the legs were somehow… they were coming in his direction.

He straightened and reached above him, hands scrabbling over the rough basalt. He felt a deep groove in the rock, and next to it a vertical hole. He jammed a hand in the hole, made a fist; put the fingers of the other hand along the side of the groove, and pulled himself up. The toes of his boot fit the groove, and he flattened up against the ceiling. In the lunar gravity he could stay there forever. Holding his breath.

Step… step… snuffle, fairly near the floor, which had given him the idea for this move. He couldn't turn to look. He felt something scrape the hip pocket of his pants and thought he was dead, but fear kept him frozen; and the sounds moved off into the distance of the vast chamber, without a pause.

He dropped to the ground and bolted doubled over for the far tunnel, which loomed before him redblack in the black, exuding air and faint noise. He plunged right in it, feeling one wall nick a knuckle. He took the sharp right he knew was there and threw himself down to the intersection of floor and wall. Footsteps padded by him, apparently running on the rails.

When he couldn't hold his breath any longer he breathed. Three or four minutes passed and he couldn't bear to stay still. He hurried to the intersection, turned left and slunk to the bullpen. At the checkpoint the monitor's horn squawked and a foreman blasted him with a searchlight, pawed him roughly. "Hey!" The foreman held a big chunk of blue, taken from Oliver's hip pocket. What was this?

"Sorry boss," Oliver said jerkily, trying to see it properly, remembering the thing brushing him as it passed under. "Must've fallen in." He ignored the foreman's curse and blow, and fell into the pen tearful with the pain of the light, with relief at being back among the others. Every muscle in him was shaking.

But Hester never came back from that shift.

Sometime later the foremen came back into their bullpen, wielding the lights and the prods to line them up against one mesh wall. Through pinprick pupils Oliver saw just the grossest slabs of shapes, all grainy black-and-gray: Jakob was a big stout man, with a short black beard under the shaved head, and eyes that popped out, glittering even in Oliver's silhouette world.

"Miners are disappearing from your pen," the foreman said, in the miners' language. His voice was like the quartz they tunneled through occasionally: hard, and sparkly with cracks and stresses, as if it might break at any moment into a laugh or a scream.

No one answered.

Finally Jakob said, "We know."

The foreman stood before him. "They started disappearing when you arrived."

Jakob shrugged. "Not what I hear."

The foreman's searchlight was right on Jakob's face, which stood out brilliantly, as if two of the searchlights were pointed at each other. Oliver's third eye suddenly opened and gave the face substance: brown skin, heavy brows, scarred scalp. Not at all the white cutout blazing from the black shadows. "You'd better be careful, miner."

Loudly enough to be heard from neighboring pens, Jakob said, "Not my fault if something out there is eating us, boss."

The foreman struck him. Lights bounced and they all dropped to the floor for protection, presenting their backs to the boots. Rain of blows, pain of blows. Still, several pens had to have heard him.

Foremen gone. White blindness returned to black blindness, to the death velvet of their pure darkness. For a long time they lay in their own private worlds, hugging the warm rock of the floor, feeling the bruises blush. Then Jakob crawled around and squatted by each of them, placing his hands on their foreheads. "Oh yeah," he would say. "You're okay. Wake up now. Look around you." And in the after-black they stretched and stretched, quivering like dogs on a scent. The bulks in the black, the shapes they made as they moved and groaned... yes, it came to Oliver again, and he rubbed his face and looked around, eyes shut to help him see. "I ran into it on the way back in," he said.

They all went still. He told them what had happened. "The blue in your pocket?"

They considered his story in silence. No one understood it.

No one spoke of Hester. Oliver found he couldn't. She had been his friend. To live without that gaunt crow's voice....

Sometime later the side door slid up, and they hurried into the barn to eat. The chickens squawked as they took the eggs, the cows mooed as they milked them. The stove plates turned the slightest bit luminous—redblack, again—and by their light his three eyes saw all. Solly cracked and fried eggs. Oliver went to work on his vats of cheese, pulled out a round of it that was ready. Jakob sat at the rear of one cow and laughed as it turned to butt his knee. *Splish splish! Splish splish!* When he was done he picked up the cow and put it down in front of its hay, where it chomped happily. Animal stink of them all, the many fine smells of food cutting through it. Jakob laughed at his cow, which butted his knee again as if objecting to the ridicule. "Little pig of a cow, little piglet. Mexican cows. They bred for this size, you know. On Earth the ordinary cow is as tall as Oliver, and about as big as this whole pen."

They laughed at the idea, not believing him. The buzzer cut them off, and the meal was over. Back into their pen, to lay their bodies down.

Still no talk of Hester, and Oliver found his skin crawling again as he recalled his encounter with whatever it was that sniffed through the mines. Jakob came over and asked him about it, sounding puzzled. Then he handed Oliver a rock. "Imagine this is a perfect sphere, like a baseball."

"Baseball?"

"Like a ball bearing, perfectly round and smooth you know."

Ah yes. Spherical geometry again. Trigonometry too. Oliver groaned, resisting the work. Then Jakob got him interested despite himself, in the intricacy of it all, the way it all fell together in a complex but comprehensible pattern. Sine and cosine, so clear! And the clearer it got the more he could see: the mesh of the bullpen, the network of shafts and tunnels and caverns piercing the jumbled fabric of the moon's body… all clear lines of redblack on black, like the metal of the stove plate as it just came visible, and all from Jakob's clear, patiently fingered, perfectly balanced equations. He could see through rock.

"Good work," Jakob said when Oliver got tired. They lay there among the others, shifting around to find hollows for their hips.

Silence of the off-shift. Muffled clanks downshaft, floor trembling at a detonation miles of rock away; ears popped as air smashed into the dead end of their tunnel, compressed to something nearly liquid for just an instant. Must have been a Boesman. Ringing silence again.

"So what is it, Jakob?" Solly asked when they could hear each other again.

"It's an element," Jakob said sleepily. "A strange kind of element, nothing else like it. Promethium. Number 61 on the periodic table. A rare earth, a lanthanide, an inner transition metal. We're finding it in veins of an ore called monazite, and in pure grains and nuggets scattered in the ore."

Impatient, almost pleading: "But what makes it so special?"

For a long time Jakob didn't answer. They could hear him thinking. Then he said, "Atoms have a nucleus, made of protons and neutrons bound together. Around this nucleus shells of electrons spin, and each shell is either full or trying to get full, to balance with the number of protons—to balance the positive and negative charges. An atom is like a human heart, you see.

"Now promethium is radioactive, which means it's out of balance, and parts of it are breaking free. But promethium never reaches its balance, because it radiates in a manner that increases its instability rather than the reverse. Promethium atoms release energy in the form of positrons, flying free when neutrons are hit by electrons. But during that impact more neutrons appear in the nucleus. Seems they're coming from nowhere. So each atom of the blue is a power loop in itself, giving off energy perpetually. Some people say that they're little white holes, every single atom of them. Burning forever at nine hundred and forty curies per gram. Bringing energy into our universe from somewhere else. Little gateways."

Solly's sigh filled the black, expressing incomprehension for all of them. "So it's poisonous?"

"It's dangerous, sure, because the positrons breaking away from it fly right through flesh like ours. Mostly they never touch a thing in us, because that's how close to phantoms we are—mostly blood, which is almost light. That's why we can see each other so well. But sometimes a beta particle will hit something small on its way through. Could mean nothing or it could kill you on the spot. Eventually it'll get us all."

Oliver fell asleep dreaming of threads of light like concentrations of the foremen's fierce flashes, passing right through him. Shifts passed in their timeless round. They ached when they woke on the warm basalt floor, they ached when they finished the long work shifts. They were hungry and often injured. None of them could say how long they had been there. None of them could say how old they were. Sometimes they lived without light other than the robots' lasers and the stove plates. Sometimes the foremen visited with their scorching lighthouse beams every off-shift, shouting questions and beating them. Apparently cows were disappearing, cylinders of air and oxygen, supplies of all sorts. None of it mattered to Oliver but the spherical geometry. He knew where he was, he could see it. The three-dimensional map in his head grew more extensive every shift. But everything else was fading away....

"So it's the most powerful substance in the world," Solly said. "But why us? Why are we here?"

"You don't know?" Jakob said.

"They blanked us, remember? All that's gone."

But because of Jakob, they knew what was up there: the domed palaces on the lunar surface, the fantastic luxuries of Earth... when he spoke of it, in fact, a lot of Earth came back to them, and they babbled and chattered at the unexpected upwellings. Memories that deep couldn't be blanked without killing, Jakob said. And so they prevailed after all, in a way.

But there was much that had been burnt forever. And so Jakob sighed. "Yeah yeah, I remember. I just thought—well. We're here for different reasons. Some were criminals. Some complained."

"Like Hester!" They laughed.

"Yeah, I suppose that's what got her here. But a lot of us were just in the wrong place at the wrong time. Wrong politics or skin or whatever. Wrong look on your face."

"That was me, I bet," Solly said, and the others laughed at him. "Well I got a funny face, I know I do! I can feel it."

Jakob was silent for a long time. "What about you?" Oliver asked. More silence. The rumble of a distant detonation, like muted thunder.

"I wish I knew. But I'm like you in that. I don't remember the actual arrest. They must have hit me on the head. Given me a concussion. I must have said something against the mines, I guess. And the wrong people heard me."

"Bad luck."

"Yeah. Bad luck."

More shifts passed. Oliver rigged a timepiece with two rocks, a length of detonation cord and a set of pulleys, and confirmed over time what he had come to suspect; the work shifts were getting longer. It was more and more difficult to get all the way through one, harder to stay awake for the meals and the geometry lessons during the off-shifts. The foremen came every off-shift now, blasting in with their searchlights and shouts and kicks, leaving in a swirl of afterimages and pain. Solly went out one shift cursing them under his breath, and never came back. Disappeared. The foremen beat them for it and Oliver shouted with rage. "It's not our fault! There's something out there, I saw it! It's killing us!"

Then next shift his little tendril of a vein bloomed, he couldn't find any rock around the blue: a big bole. He would have to tell the foremen, start working in a crew. He dismantled his clock.

On the way back he heard the footsteps again, shuffling along slowly behind him. This time he was at the entrance to the last tunnel, the pens close behind him. He turned to stare into the darkness with his third eye, willing himself to see the thing. Whoosh of air, a sniff, a footfall on the rail.... Far across the thin wedge of air a beam of light flashed, making a long narrow cone of white talc. Steel tracks gleamed where the wheels of the car burnished them. Pupils shrinking like a snail's antennae, he stared back at the footsteps, saw nothing. Then, just barely, two points of red: retinas, reflecting the distant lance of light. They blinked. He bolted and ran again, reached the foremen at the checkpoint in seconds. They blinded him as he panted, passed him through and into the bullpen.

After the meal on that shift Oliver lay trembling on the floor of the bullpen and told Jakob about it. "I'm scared, Jakob. Solly, Hester, Freeman, mute Lije, Naomi—they're all gone. Everyone I know here is gone but us."

"Free at last," Jakob said shortly. "Here, let's do your problems for tonight."

"I don't care about them."

"You have to care about them. Nothing matters unless you do. That blue is the mind of the moon being torn away, and the moon knows it. If we learn what the network says in its shapes, then the moon knows that too, and we're suffered to live."

"Not if that thing finds us!"

"You don't know. Anyway nothing to be done about it. Come on, let's do the lesson. We need it."

So they worked on equations in the dark. Both were distracted and the work went slowly; they fell asleep in the middle of it, right there on their faces.

Shifts passed. Oliver pulled a muscle in his back, and excavating the bole he had found was an agony of discomfort. When the bole was cleared it left a space like the interior of an egg, ivory and black and quite smooth, punctuated only by the bluish spots of other tendrils of monazite extending away through the basalt. They left a catwalk across the central space, with decks cut into the rock on each side, and ramps leading to each of the veins of blue; and began drilling on their own again, one man and robot team to each vein. At each shift's end Oliver rushed to get to the egg-chamber at the same time as all the others, so that he could return the rest of the way to the bullpen in a crowd. This worked well until one shift came to an end with the hoist chock-full of the ore. It took him some time to dump it into the ore car and shut down.

So he had to cross the catwalk alone, and he would be alone all the way back to the pens. Surely it was past time to move the pens closer to the shaft heads! He didn't want to do this....

Halfway across the catwalk he heard a faint noise ahead of him. *Scrick; scriiiiiik.* He jerked to a stop, held the rail hard. Couldn't reach the ceiling here. Back stabbing its protest, he started to climb over the railing. He could hang from the underside.

He was right on the top of the railing when he was seized up by a number of strong cold hands. He opened his mouth to scream and his mouth was filled with wet clay. The blue. His head was held steady and his ears filled with the same stuff, so that the sounds of his own terrified sharp nasal exhalations were suddenly cut off. Promethium; it would kill him. It hurt his back to struggle on. He was being carried horizontally, ankles whipped, arms tied against his body. Then plugs of the clay were shoved up his nose and in the middle of a final paroxysm of resistance his mind fell away into the black.

The lowest whisper in the world said, "Oliver Pen Twelve." He heard the voice with his stomach. He was astonished to be alive.

"You will never be given anything again. Do you accept the charge?"

He struggled to nod. I never wanted anything! he tried to say. I only wanted a life like anyone else.

"You will have to fight for every scrap of food, every swallow of water, every breath of air. Do you accept the charge?"

I accept the charge. I welcome it.

"In the eternal night you will steal from the foremen, kill the foremen, oppose their work in every way. Do you accept the charge?" I welcome it.

"You will live free in the mind of the moon. Will you take up this charge?"

He sat up. His mouth was clear, filled only with the sharp electric aftertaste of the blue. He saw the shapes around him: there were five of them, five people there. And suddenly he understood. Joy ballooned in him and he said, "I will. Oh, I will!"

A light appeared. Accustomed as he was either to no light or to intense blasts of it, Oliver at first didn't comprehend. He thought his third eye was rapidly gaining power. As perhaps it was. But there was also a laser drill from one of the A robots, shot at low power through a cylindrical ceramic electronic element, in a way that made the cylinder glow yellow. Blind like a fish, open-mouthed, weak eyes gaping and watering floods, he saw around him Solly, Hester, Free-man, mute Elijah, Naomi. "Yes," he said, and tried to embrace them all at once. "Oh, yes."

They were in one of the long-abandoned caverns, a flat-bottomed bole with only three tendrils extending away from it. The chamber was filled with objects Oliver was more used to identifying by feel or sound or smell: pens of cows and hens, a stack of air cylinders and suits, three ore cars, two B robots, an A robot, a pile of tracks and miscellaneous gear. He walked through it all slowly, Hester at his side. She was gaunt as ever, her skin as dark as the shadows; it sucked up the weak light from the ceramic tube and gave it back only in little points and lines. "Why didn't you tell me?"

"It was the same for all of us. This is the way."

"And Naomi?"

"The same for her too; but when she agreed to it, she found herself alone."

Then it was Jakob, he thought suddenly. "Where's Jakob?"

Rasped: "He's coming, we think."

Oliver nodded, thought about it. "Was it you, then, following me those times? Why didn't you speak?"

"That wasn't us," Hester said when he explained what had happened. She cawed a laugh. "That was something else, still out there…."

Then Jakob stood before them, making them both jump. They shouted and the others all came running, pressed into a mass together. Jakob laughed. "All here now," he said. "Turn that light off. We don't need it."

And they didn't. Laser shut down, ceramic cooled, they could still see: they could see right into each other, red shapes in the black, radiating joy. Everything in the little chamber was quite distinct, quite *visible*.

"We are the mind of the moon."

Without shifts to mark the passage of time Oliver found he could not judge it at all. They worked hard, and they were constantly on the move: always up, through level after level of the mine. "Like shells of the atom, and we're that particle, busted loose and on its way out." They ate when they were famished, slept when they had to. Most of the time they worked, either bringing down shafts behind them, or dismantling depots and stealing everything Jakob des-ignated theirs. A few times they ambushed gangs of foremen, killing them with laser cutters and stripping them of valuables; but on Jakob's orders they avoided contact with foremen when they could. He wanted only material. After a long time—twenty sleeps at least—they had six ore cars of it, all trailing an A robot up long-abandoned and empty shafts, where they had to lay the track ahead of them and pull it out behind, as fast as they could move. Among other items Jakob had an insatiable hunger for explosives; he couldn't get enough of them.

It got harder to avoid the foremen, who were now heavily armed, and on their guard. Perhaps even searching for them, it was hard to tell. But they searched with their lighthouse beams on full power, to stay out of ambush: it was easy to see them at a distance, draw them off, lose them in dead ends, detonate mines under them. All the while the little band moved up, rising by infinitely long detours toward the front side of the moon. The rock around them cooled. The air circulated more strongly, until it was a constant wind. Through the seismometers they could hear from far below the rumbling of cars, heavy machinery, detonations. "Oh they're after us all right," Jakob said. "They're running scared."

He was happy with the booty they had accumulated, which included a great number of cylinders of compressed air and pure oxygen. Also vacuum suits for all of them, and a lot more explosives, including ten Boesmans, which were much too big for any ordinary mining. "We're getting close," Jakob said as they ate and drank, then tended the cows and hens. As they lay down to sleep by the cars he would talk to them about their work. Each of them had various jobs: mute Elijah was in charge of their supplies, Solly of the robot, Hester of the seismography. Naomi and Freeman were learning demolition, and were in some undefined sense Jakob's lieutenants. Oliver kept working at his navigation. They had found charts of the tunnel systems in their area, and Oliver was memorizing them, so that he would know at each moment exactly where they were. He found he could do it remarkably well; each time they ventured on he knew where the forks would come, where they would lead. Always upward.

But the pursuit was getting hotter. It seemed there were foremen everywhere, patrolling the shafts in search of them. "Soon they'll mine some passages and try to drive us into them," Jakob said. "It's about time we left."

"Left?" Oliver repeated.

"Left the system. Struck out on our own."

"Dig our own tunnel," Naomi said happily.

"Yes."

"To where?" Hester croaked.

Then they were rocked by an explosion that almost broke their eardrums, and the air rushed away. The rock around them trembled, creaked, groaned, cracked, and down the tunnel the ceiling collapsed, shoving dust toward them in a roaring *whoosh!* "A Boesman!" Solly cried.

Jakob laughed out loud. They were all scrambling into their vacuum suits as fast as they could. "Time to leave!" he cried, maneuvering their A robot against the side of the chamber. He put one of their Boesmans against the wall and set the timer. "Okay," he said over the suit's intercom. "Now we got to mine like we never mined before. To the surface!"

The first task was to get far enough away from the Boesman that they wouldn't be killed when it went off. They were now drilling a narrow tunnel and moving the loosened rock behind them to fill up the hole as they passed through it; this loose fill would fly like bullets down a rifle barrel when the Boesman went off. So they made three abrupt turns at acute angles to stop the fill's movement, and then drilled away from the area as fast as they could. Naomi and Jakob were confident that the explosion of the Boesman would shatter the surrounding rock to such an extent that it would never be possible for anyone to locate the starting point for their tunnel.

"Hopefully they'll think we did ourselves in," Naomi said, "either on purpose or by accident." Oliver enjoyed hearing her light laugh, her clear voice that was so pure and musical compared to Hester's croaking. He had never known Naomi well before, but now he admired her grace and power, her pulsing energy; she worked harder than Jakob, even. Harder than any of them.

A few shifts into their new life Naomi checked the detonator timer she kept on a cord around her neck. "It should be going off soon. Someone go try and keep the cows and chickens calmed down." But Solly had just reached the cows' pen when the Boesman went off. They were all sledgehammered by the blast, which was louder than a mere explosion, something more basic and fundamental: the violent smash of a whole world shutting the door on them. Deafened, bruised, they staggered up and checked each other for serious injuries, then pacified the cows, whose terrified moos they felt in their hands rather than actually heard. The structural integrity of their tunnel seemed okay; they were in an old flow of the mantle's convection current, now cooled to stasis, and it was plastic enough to take such a blast without shattering. Perfect miners' rock, protecting them like a mother. They lifted up the cows and set them upright on the bottom of the ore car that had been made into the barn. Freeman hurried back down the tunnel to see how the rear of it looked. When he came back their hearing was returning, and through the ringing that would persist for several shifts he shouted, "It's walled off good! Fused!"

So they were in a little tunnel of their own. They fell together in a clump, hugging each other and shouting. "Free at last!" Jakob roared, booming out a laugh louder than anything Oliver had ever heard from him. Then they settled down to the task of turning on an air cylinder and recycler, and regulating their gas exchange.

They soon settled into a routine that moved their tunnel forward as quickly and quietly as possible. One of them operated the robot, digging as narrow a shaft as they could possibly work in. This person used only laser drills unless confronted with extremely hard rock, when it was judged worth the risk to set off small explosions, timed by seismometer to follow closely other detonations back in the mines; Jakob and Naomi hoped that the complex interior of the moon would prevent any listeners from noticing that their explosion was anything more than an echo of the mining blast.

Three of them dealt with the rock freed by the robot's drilling, moving it from the front of the tunnel to its rear, and at intervals pulling up the cars' tracks and bringing them forward. The placement of the loose rock was a serious matter, because if it displaced much more volume than it had at the front of the tunnel, they would eventually fill in all the open space they had;

this was the classic problem of the "creeping worm" tunnel. It was necessary to pack the blocks into the space at the rear with an absolute minimum of gaps, in exactly the way they had been cut, like pieces of a puzzle; they all got very good at the craft of this, losing only a few inches of open space in every mile they dug. This work was the hardest both physically and mentally, and each shift of it left Oliver more tired than he had ever been while mining. Because the truth was all of them were working at full speed, and for the middle team it meant almost running, back and forth, back and forth, back and forth.... Their little bit of open tunnel was only some sixty yards long, but after a while on the midshift it seemed like five hundred.

The three people not working on the rock tended the air and the livestock, ate, helped out with large blocks and the like, and snatched some sleep. They rotated one at a time through the three stations, and worked one shift (timed by detonator timer) at each post. It made for a routine so mesmerizing in its exhaustiveness that Oliver found it very hard to do his calculations of their position in his shift off. "You've got to keep at it," Jakob told him as he ran back from the robot to help the calculating. "It's not just anywhere we want to come up, but right under the domed city of Selene, next to the rocket rails. To do that we'll need some good navigation. We get that and we'll come up right in the middle of the masters who have gotten rich from selling the blue to Earth, and that will be a very gratifying thing I assure you."

So Oliver would work on it until he slept. Actually it was relatively easy; he knew where they had been in the moon when they struck out on their own, and Jakob had given him the surface coordinates for Selene: so it was just a matter of dead reckoning.

It was even possible to calculate their average speed, and therefore when they could expect to reach the surface. That could be checked against the rate of depletion of their fixed resources—air, water lost in the recycler, and food for the livestock. It took a few shifts of consultation with mute Elijah to determine all the factors reliably, and after that it was a simple matter of arithmetic.

When Oliver and Elijah completed these calculations they called Jakob over and explained what they had done.

"Good work," Jakob said. "I should have thought of that."

"But look," Oliver said, "we've got enough air and water, and the robot's power pack is ten times what we'll need—same with explosives—it's only food is a problem. I don't know if we've got enough hay for the cows."

Jakob nodded as he looked over Oliver's shoulder and examined their figures. "We'll have to kill and eat the cows one by one. That'll feed us and cut down on the amount of hay we need, at the same time."

"Eat the cows?" Oliver was stunned.

"Sure! They're meat! People on Earth eat them all the time!"

"Well...." Oliver was doubtful, but under the lash of Hester's bitter laughter he didn't say any more.

Still, Jakob and Freeman and Naomi decided it would be best if they stepped up the pace a little bit, to provide them with more of a margin for error. They shifted two people to the shaft face and supplemented the robot's continuous drilling with hand drill work around the sides of the tunnel, and ate on the run while moving blocks to the back, and slept as little as they could. They were making miles on every shift.

The rock they wormed through began to change in character. The hard, dark, unbroken basalt gave way to lighter rock that was sometimes dangerously fractured. "Anorthosite," Jakob said. "We're reaching the crust." After that every shift brought them through a new zone of rock. Once they tunneled through great layers of calcium feldspar striped with basalt intrusions, so that it looked like badly made brick. Another time they blasted their way through a wall of jasper as hard as steel. Only once did they pass through a vein of the blue; when they did it occurred to Oliver that his whole conception of the moon's composition had been warped by their mining. He had thought the moon was bursting with promethium, but as they dug across the narrow vein he realized it was uncommon, a loose net of threads in the great lunar body.

As they left the vein behind, Solly picked up a piece of the ore and stared at it curiously, lower eyes shut, face contorted as he struggled to focus his third eye. Suddenly he dashed the chunk to the ground, turned and marched to the head of their tunnel, attacked it with a drill. "I've given my whole life to the blue," he said, voice thick. "And what is it but a Goddamned rock."

Jakob laughed shortly. They tunneled on, away from the precious metal that now represented to them only a softer material to dig through. "Pick up the pace!" Jakob cried, slapping Solly on the back and leaping over the blocks beside the robot. "This rock has melted and melted again, changing over eons to the stones we see. Metamorphosis," he chanted, stretching the word out, lingering on the syllable *mor* until the word became a kind of song. "Meta*mor*phosis. Meta-*mor*-pho-sis." Naomi and Hester took up the chant, and mute Elijah tapped his drill against the robot in double time. Jakob chanted over it. "Soon we will come to the city of the masters, the domes of Xanadu with their glass and fruit and steaming pools, and their vases and sports and their fine aged wines. And then there will be a—"

"Meta*mor*phosis."

And they tunneled ever faster.

Sitting in the sleeping car, chewing on a cheese, Oliver regarded the bulk of Jakob lying beside him. Jakob breathed deeply, very tired, almost asleep. "How do you know about the domes?" Oliver asked him softly. "How do you know all the things that you know?"

"Don't know," Jakob muttered. "Everyone knows. Less they burn your brain. Put you in a hole to live out your life. I don't know much, boy. Make most of it up. Love of a moon. Whatever we need…." And he slept.

They came up through a layer of marble—white marble all laced with quartz, so that it gleamed and sparkled in their lightless sight, and made them feel as though they dug through stone made of their cows' good milk, mixed with water like diamonds. This went on for a long time, until it filled them up and they became intoxicated with its smooth muscly texture, with the sparks of light lazing out of it. "I remember once we went to see a jazz band," Jakob said to all of them. Puffing as he ran the white rock along the cars to the rear, stacked it ever so carefully. "It was in Richmond among all the docks and refineries and giant oil tanks and we were so drunk we kept getting lost. But finally we found it—huh!—and it was just this broken-down trumpeter and a back line. He played sitting in a chair and you could just see in his face that his life had been a tough scuffle. His hat covered his whole household. And trumpet is a young man's instrument, too, it tears your lip to tatters. So we sat down to drink not expecting a thing, and they started up the last song of a set. 'Bucket's Got a Hole in It.' Four bar blues, as simple as a song can get."

"Meta*morph*osis," rasped Hester.

"Yeah! Like that. And this trumpeter started to play it. And they went through it over and over and over. Huh! They must have done it a hundred times. Two hundred times. And sure enough this trumpeter was playing low and half the time in his hat, using all the tricks a broken-down trumpeter uses to save his lip, to hide the fact that it went west thirty years before. But after a while that didn't matter, because he was playing. He was playing! Everything he had learned in all his life, all the music and all the sorry rest of it, all that was jammed into the poor old 'Bucket' and by God it was mind over matter time, because that old song began to *roll*. And still on the run he broke into it:

"Oh the buck-et's got a hole in it
Yeah the buck-et's got a hole in it
Say the buck-et's got a hole in it.
Can't buy no beer!"

And over again. Oliver, Solly, Freeman, Hester, Naomi—they couldn't help laughing. What Jakob came up with out of his unburnt past! Mute Elijah banged a car wall happily, then squeezed the udder of a cow between one verse and the next— "Can't buy no beer!—*Moo!*"

They all joined in, breathing or singing it. It fit the pace of their work perfectly: fast but not too fast, regular, repetitive, simple, endless. All the syllables got the same length, a bit syncopated, except "hole," which was stretched out, and "can't buy no beer," which was high and all stretched out, stretched into a great shout of triumph, which was crazy since what it was saying was bad news, or should have been. But the song made it a cry of joy, and every time it rolled around they sang it louder, more stretched out. Jakob scatted up and down and around the tune, and Hester found all kinds of higher harmonics in a voice like a saw cutting steel, and the old tune rocked over and over and over and over and over and over and over and over and over and over, in a great passacaglia, in the crucible where all poverty is wrenched to delight: the blues. Meta*morphosis*. They sang it continuously for two shifts running, until they were all completely hypnotized by it; and then frequently, for long spells, for the rest of their time together.

It was sheer bad luck that they broke into a shaft from below, and that the shaft was filled with armed foremen; and worse luck that Jakob was working the robot, so that he was the first to leap out firing his hand drill like a weapon, and the only one to get struck by return fire before Naomi threw a knotchopper past him and blew the foremen to shreds. They got him on a car and rolled the robot back and pulled up the track and cut off in a new direction, leaving another Boesman behind to destroy evidence of their passing.

So they were all racing around with the blood and stuff still covering them and the cows mooing in distress and Jakob breathing through clenched teeth in double time, and only Hester and Oliver could sit in the car with him and try to tend him, ripping away the pants from a leg that was all cut up. Hester took a hand drill to cauterize the wounds that were bleeding hard, but Jakob shook his head at her, neck muscles bulging out. "Got the big artery inside of the thigh," he said through his teeth.

Hester hissed. "Come here," she croaked at Solly and the rest. "Stop that and come here!"

They were in a mass of broken quartz, the fractured clear crystals all pink with oxidation. The robot continued drilling away, the air cylinder hissed, the cows mooed. Jakob's breathing was harsh and somehow all of them were also breathing in the same way, irregularly, too fast; so that as his breathing slowed and calmed, theirs did too. He was lying back in the sleeping car, on a bed of hay, staring up at the fractured sparkling quartz ceiling of their tunnel, as if he could see far into it. "All these different kinds of rock," he said, his voice filled with wonder and pain. "You see, the moon itself was the world, once upon a time, and the Earth its moon; but there was an impact, and everything changed."

They cut a small side passage in the quartz and left Jakob there, so that when they filled in their tunnel as they moved on he was left behind, in his own deep crypt. And from then on the moon for them was only his big tomb, rolling through space till the sun itself died, as he had said it someday would.

Oliver got them back on a course, feeling radically uncertain of his navigational calculations now that Jakob was not there to nod over his shoulder to approve them. Dully he gave Naomi and Freeman the coordinates for Selene. "But what will we do when we get there?" Jakob had never actually made that clear. Find the leaders of the city, demand justice for the miners? Kill them? Get to the rockets of the great magnetic rail accelerators, and hijack one to Earth? Try to slip unnoticed into the populace?

"You leave that to us," Naomi said. "Just get us there." And he saw a light in Naomi's and Freeman's eyes that hadn't been there before. It reminded him of the thing that had chased him in the dark, the thing that even Jakob hadn't been able to explain; it frightened him.

So he set the course and they tunneled on as fast as they ever had. They never sang and they rarely talked; they threw themselves at the rock, hurt themselves in the effort, returned to attack it more fiercely than before. When he could not stave off sleep Oliver lay down on Jakob's dried blood, and bitterness filled him like a block of the anorthosite they wrestled with.

They were running out of hay. They killed a cow, ate its roasted flesh. The water recycler's filters were clogging, and their water smelled of urine. Hester listened to the seismometer as often as she could now, and she thought they were being pursued. But she also thought they were approaching Selene's underside.

Naomi laughed, but it wasn't like her old laugh. "You got us there, Oliver. Good work."

Oliver bit back a cry.

"Is it big?" Solly asked.

Hester shook her head. "Doesn't sound like it. Maybe twice the diameter of the Great Bole, not more."

"Good," Freeman said, looking at Naomi.

"But what will we do?" Oliver said.

Hester and Naomi and Freeman and Solly all turned to look at him, eyes blazing like twelve chunks of pure promethium. "We've got eight Boesmans left," Freeman said in a low voice. "All the rest of the explosives add up to a couple more. I'm going to set them just right. It'll be my best work ever, my masterpiece. And we'll blow Selene right off into space."

It took them ten shifts to get all the Boesmans placed to Freeman's and Naomi's satisfaction, and then another three to get far enough down and to one side to be protected from the shock of the blast, which luckily for them was directly upward against something that would give, and therefore would have less recoil.

Finally they were set, and they sat in the sleeping car in a circle of six, around the pile of components that sat under the master detonator. For a long time they just sat there cross-legged, breathing slowly and staring at it. Staring at each other, in the dark, in perfect redblack clarity. Then Naomi put both arms out, placed her hands carefully on the detonator's button. Mute Elijah put his hands on hers—then Freeman, Hester, Solly, finally Oliver—just in the order that Jakob had taken them. Oliver hesitated, feeling the flesh and bone under his hands, the warmth of his companions. He felt they should say something but he didn't know what it was.

"Seven," Hester croaked suddenly.

"Six," Freeman said.

Elijah blew air through his teeth, hard.

"Four," said Naomi.

"Three!" Solly cried.

"Two," Oliver said.

And they all waited a beat, swallowing hard, waiting for the moon and the man in the moon to speak to them. Then they pressed down on the button.

They smashed at it with their fists, hit it so violently they scarcely felt the shock of the explosion.

They had put on vacuum suits and were breathing pure oxygen as they came up the last tunnel, clearing it of rubble. A great number of other shafts were revealed as they moved into the huge conical cavity left by the Boesmans; tunnels snaked away from the cavity in all directions, so that they had sudden long vistas of blasted tubes extending off into the depths of the moon they had come out of. And at the top of the cavity, struggling over its broken edge, over the rounded wall of a new crater....

It was black. It was not like rock. Spread across it was a spill of white points, some bright, some so faint that they disappeared into the black if you looked straight at them. There were thousands of these white points, scattered over a black dome that was not a dome.... And there in the middle, almost directly overhead: a blue and white ball. Big, bright, blue, distant, rounded; half of it bright as a foreman's flash, the other half just a shadow.... It was clearly round, a big ball in the... sky. In the sky.

Wordlessly they stood on the great pile of rubble ringing the edge of their hole. Half buried in the broken anorthosite were shards of clear plastic, steel struts, patches of green grass, fragments of metal, an arm, broken branches, a bit of orange ceramic. Heads back to stare at the ball in the sky, at the astonishing fact of the void, they scarcely noticed these things.

A long time passed, and none of them moved except to look around. Past the jumble of dark trash that had mostly been thrown off in a single direction, the surface of the moon was an immense expanse of white hills, as strange and glorious as the stars above. The size of it all! Oliver had never dreamed that everything could be so big.

"The blue must be promethium," Solly said, pointing up at the Earth. "They've covered the whole Earth with the blue we mined."

Their mouths hung open as they stared at it. "How far away is it?" Freeman asked. No one answered.

"There they all are," Solly said. He laughed harshly. "I wish I could blow up the Earth too!"

He walked in circles on the rubble of the crater's rim. The rocket rails, Oliver thought suddenly, must have been in the direction Freeman had sent the debris. Bad luck. The final upward sweep of them poked up out of the dark dirt and glass. Solly pointed at them. His voice was loud in Oliver's ears, it strained the intercom: "Too bad we can't fly to the Earth, and blow it up too! I wish we could!"

And mute Elijah took a few steps, leaped off the mound into the sky, took a swipe with one hand at the blue ball. They laughed at him. "Almost got it, didn't you!" Freeman and Solly tried themselves, and then they all did: taking quick runs, leaping, flying slowly up through space, for five or six or seven seconds, making a grab at the sky overhead, floating back down as if in a dream, to land in a tumble, and try it again.... It felt wonderful to hang up there at the top of the leap, free in the vacuum, free of gravity and everything else, for just that instant.

After a while they sat down on the new crater's rim, covered with white dust and black dirt. Oliver sat on the very edge of the crater, legs over the edge, so that he could see back down into their sublunar world, at the same time that he looked up into the sky. Three eyes were not enough to judge such immensities. His heart pounded, he felt too intoxicated to move anymore. Tired, drunk. The intercom rasped with the sounds of their breathing, which slowly calmed, fell into a rhythm together. Hester buzzed one phrase of "Bucket" and they laughed softly. They lay back on the rubble, all but Oliver, and stared up into the dizzy reaches of the universe, the velvet black of infinity. Oliver sat with elbows on knees, watched the white hills glowing under the black sky. They were lit by earthlight—earthlight and starlight. The white mountains on the horizon were as sharp-edged as the shards of dome glass sticking out of the rock. And all the time the Earth looked down at him. It was all too fantastic to believe. He drank it in like oxygen, felt it filling him up, expanding in his chest.

"What do you think they'll do with us when they get here?" Solly asked.

"Kill us," Hester croaked.

"Or put us back to work," Naomi added.

Oliver laughed. Whatever happened, it was impossible in that moment to care. For above them a milky spill of stars lay thrown across the infinite black sky, lighting a million better worlds; while just over their heads the Earth glowed like a fine blue lamp; and under their feet rolled the white hills of the happy moon, holed like a great cheese.

SACRAMENT

by Matt Williamson

Matt Williamson's fiction has appeared in *Barrelhouse Magazine, Gulf Coast, The Portland Review, Ruminator,* and *The Cimarron Review*. He is a graduate of the University of Texas and the Iowa Writers' Workshop. He lives in Austin, Texas, where he's currently working on his first novel.

Ever watch TV and think the ads are funnier than the sitcom they interrupted? Or see a beautiful photo in a magazine, only to wonderingly discover it's an advertisement? Moments like these blur the boundaries between art and advertising, a borderline that grows increasingly unclear in this era of corporate sponsorship of the arts.

Matt Williamson spins a world where art and advertising have collided on such a large scale that a Nike art project can fill Times Square, and an Apple light show can be seen from outer space. The world is loaded with art-advertising objects so massive and inescapable that an international war has erupted over its imperialist presence. Or perhaps that's just the view of our protagonist, a character who maintains his own uncertain boundary between art and his life's work as an intelligence extractor.

It's not an easy craft, pulling information out of the unwilling. It takes special tools, a unique skillset and a sense of intuition that can't be taught. It's a gift. A talent. It's easy to see why some people might call torture an artform.

But it's only in a truly broken world that anyone would.

Bones are not organs, under the Protocols. I've got that stuck up on the wall in the locker room, the briefing room, big signs, all caps: BONES ARE NOT ORGANS.

That leaves a lot of running room. The kneecap? What you can do with the kneecap? That alone will get you farther than you need to go, in almost every case. The kneecap. The chin. The lowest knuckle on the forefinger. Those are my favorite bones.

I always say, you can tell my guys in a crowd. From their hands.

The trick is, can you keep him lucid. Can you keep Ali sharply focused on the

Program all the way through. Part of it is physical control, part of it is drugs, and part of it, I say a little facetiously but not totally facetiously, is artistry: the artistry of the lead interrogator. Before the pinpoints, before Suspensions, we couldn't keep a guy from passing out. Wake him up with ammonia, it's not the same as having him alert. Now we've got pinpoint synthetics that allow sustained equilibrium. No fainting, no grogginess, no euphoria. It isn't quite the same as True Awake; Dr. Ghose calls it a simulacrum. It's better than True, in some ways. Ali's awake, sans certain defenses. With catheters and drips, we can preserve that balance—not for hours, but weeks, months. Last week, I left a Session, went home, played kickball with my son, dinner with my wife, long night's sleep, woke up, breakfast, walk the dog, read the paper, when I come back in, Ali's still going from the night before. With the pinpoints, we don't have to take the Rests, and there's not the same concern about organic damage.

That's the drug side. Part two is, the control technologies, and some of the advances over there. The tech stuff's done a lot to change the playing field. The new Chairs don't just offer refined muscular control; we actually have retinal. When I peel the skin back, when I kiss the edges of the F1 joint with my drill, Ali's going to be paying close attention. And because of the synthetics, he's not in la-la land; he's tracking, he's alert, and he's ready to talk.

We're careful to stay on the right side of the line. I've referred three men for crossing that line. Dishonorables in every case. It's something we take seriously. Even without the Protocols, I'd tell my teams: nothing that results in death or organ failure. Because it's lazy, because it's counterproductive. Because it misses the point. The promise of survival: that's everything. The promise of emerging intact. If you don't understand that aspect, you won't understand Deep Interrogation—I don't call it Heavy, I call it Deep—and that lack of understanding's going to show up in your Usable Intel numbers.

The other reason's trust. When you do the cowboy shit, you might break through some walls, but other walls are shutting up tighter than before. The new model, we do much more than break the subject. Break Ali's will, reduce him to a state of dependence, we do that, but it's just step one, the first pivot point. In any interrogation, there are multiple pivot points. The first is when Ali discovers he no longer has the power to end his life. Everything before that moment is pre-interrogation, as far as I'm concerned. That's why, in the Chair, we keep him ventilated and catheterized. *We decide whether and when you eat, shit, piss, breathe—and we can keep you here as long as we like.* And we can. We can keep these guys alive forever.

Not literally—not yet. That's one of my dreams: the replenishers, the Suspensions—push them to the point where we can squeeze these guys indefinitely. We're on our way. It won't happen in my lifetime, probably, but someday, yes. Keep Ali in the Chair thirty, forty, a hundred years. I'm not kidding. Ghose is doing stuff that's going to change the medical sciences forever, forget about interrogations. And the longer you keep these guys, the more you can do with them. Their reality is changing every minute, every hour. At 90 days, you aren't looking at the same Ali you had at 30. At 30, he's still fighting you, in some small part of himself, whether he knows it or not. By 90, 150, 200, you have the power of a God.

That's why we welcome hunger strikes. That's why we welcome suicide attempts. You can tell Ali, *you'll be here till your hair's as gray as mine*, but it's just talk until he makes a move. That's why it works for us when Ali tries to kill himself. It's a teaching moment. Suicide we don't allow. Starvation we don't allow. Ali wrapping his head in a bedsheet noose is Ali testing the boundaries, feeling out the limits of his field of control. Ali chewing off his tongue is Ali testing the limits. And what he finds, in every case, is exactly what we said he'd find. *There's one way out of this, and it's through us.*

But that, as I say, is only the first part of our work. When you break a subject, you get the stuff he wants to keep from you. A Deep Interrogator's after more. We want to get inside the memory and experience of a subject—get inside and have a long look around. Look, listen, smell. And we get everything: childhood, adolescence, grief, anger, fantasies and phobias. We get the transient moments and impressions that may not seem, in themselves, to hold any strategic value, but which, in combination with a thousand other such impressions, taken from a hundred other guys, form a kind of tapestry—or, as Ghose puts it, a vivid four-dimensional map—of daily life in extremist enclaves. You can think of the new model, then, as a way of getting access to the peripheral perceptions. Ali's no longer the author of his story; he no longer gets to judge what's worth our knowing.

I'm not afraid to talk about it. It's a tricky area. Interrogation of Confirmed Innocents. It's complicated, and there are good arguments on both sides.

Defense knows what *its* policy is, certainly. To some extent, we'll follow that. Certainly, we obey the Protocols. We'll track the White Papers to a point. And then, to some extent, we'll go our own way. There's a degree of autonomy. But the short answer is, yes. If there's usable intel, we will interrogate. We don't look to Culpability as an Entrance Criterion.

That doesn't mean we don't wrestle with it. We make evaluations on a case-by-case basis.

Last year, after the Ramadan attacks, the decision was made to go ahead with a Deep Program on a suite of CIs. Before we initiated that Program, we did ask ourselves, *what are our obligations here.* In the end, the determination was made to go ahead. And I stand by the decision. Why? Because we found the bomb. That's not to say it's simple—and there will be some people for whom that's not enough. Find the bomb, save a couple thousand lives, that's not enough, and I respect that. Where you are on that issue is, I think, largely an ethical matter, and something that will differ for you, depending on who you are personally. For me, the Objective is decisive. Without the CIs, the bomb explodes. The target was a metro station in central DC, which is maybe something to consider.

Different Guidelines will apply, of course, if it's a CI in the Chair. That's literally—as in, there's a separate set of Guidelines printed off, everybody has a copy—and also in the—maybe just the attitude you take into the interrogation room.

One difference—to start with one example—is when we're working a CI, we won't do the chin. That's not Protocol; that's our own rule. My rule, actually. And I enforce it just like any other policy, and I don't make exceptions. When Culpability isn't Indicated on the Profile, the chin becomes an organ.

If we're doing a CI, we'll conduct the interrogation fairly. We'll make the Parameters clear. When the Objective is reached, we'll stabilize and Exit. Ideally, in a CI Session, it's a team process, where we're working *with* the subject to achieve a common goal. We'll never go into a CI Session blind—*ever*, that's the rule—and we won't do fishing expeditions.

And that's obviously very different from the program we apply to CCs and Suspecteds. When a Suspected's in the Chair, we'll wring him out. When Ali thinks he's told us everything he knows, that's when the Session *begins*. Where the problem area starts is when a CI tells us something that alters his designation. This is tricky, because a lot of CIs will confess to things they haven't done. In that case, there's no way to avoid changing the subject's designation and reverting to the CC protocols. But it's something that we wrestle with.

The suite last autumn, a lot of my CI Alis didn't lose a drop of blood. I'm not exaggerating. I say you can tell my guys from their hands, these guys, you can't, because it never got to that point.

Others, it did. And that's tough. When you're dealing with a wife, a husband, and you're saying, where's Ali, where's the husband, the wife, the son, the uncle, that can be tough, because relatives are intransigent. The wives, sometimes, are more intransigent than the target CCs.

And there's where a sense of delicacy, and a sense of balance, can be very helpful. Say you've got Ali's wife in the Chair. Okay: now she knows what Ali's in for. Or *thinks* she knows; actually, she has no idea. But she knows Ali's going in the Chair. How bad, then, do you make it? You have to find a place where Mrs. Ali wants to end the Session, where she's ready to give her husband up—but not so far that she knows she won't be able to live with herself if she cooperates. You have to let her leave the Chair with dignity, let her feel she's made a choice that she can live with, morally.

It's delicate. When a Confirmed Combatant's in the chair, there's no Good Cop-Bad Cop; there's no carrot and stick; it's Bad Cop-Worse Cop, and it's stick, razor, drill. CIs, it's different. With Ali's wife, there might be a carrot in there too.

I'll give you an example.

These CIs, most of them, they won't ever be going home. I say most, really it's all. If it's home, it's a prison in Pakistan—but that's not most cases. Most cases, the CI's done with the Chair, he or she is headed to the Low Restraint Unit, presumably for the remainder. One reason we keep them is, we'll be needing them again when their intelligence proves out: when my target Ali is in the Chair. And there's a host of other reasons.

Ali's *kid*, though, sometimes he can be an exception. If we have Ali's wife in the Chair, if there are no Culpability Markers, we've been willing, in certain cases, to see about orphanages, see if we can keep the child in the US, versus Pakistan, Syria. So that's an example of the carrot. If Ali's wife is ready to give her husband up, here's a chance for Ali, Jr. to enjoy some of the benefits of an American upbringing. And that's worked well for us, in a number of cases.

Why I like the chin. A bunch of reasons.

I like its complexity. It's not a major pain-point, relative to the kneecaps and knuckles—but there are intersecting nerve systems there, which give the chin a different character, a different flavor. And there's something particular about the way the destruction and remaking of the face impacts a subject. We'll mirror Ali almost continuously during chin-work, and I've found, time and again, that a kiss on the chin, when Ali is watching, does more to concentrate his mind than complete powdering of the kneecaps.

What else? I want to be careful here, because I'd never want to make it seem as though some private form of catharsis is ever among my Objectives in a Session—but there is a satisfaction, for me, in the physical transformations that some of our CC subjects undergo. They come in, they've got the Intel hidden; they leave, the Intel's gone, in a sense, and the fact of the extraction is written on their faces; it's physically manifest. The chins heal over—some of them, you can't even see the scars—but the faces, the subdural structures, are changed. It's like we've literally chipped the Intel out of their heads.

I like it, also, because, for me, the chin represents a threshold, a point of commitment. Once we've changed his face, Ali can't see the light of day, whatever happens. That means he won't be available as a witness, we can't trot him out if there are hearings, inquiries. As far as the rest of the world is concerned, he's gone. And that's not my rule; it's in the Protocols: *nothing that shall bring embarrassment or discredit to the State.* In English, that means something like, *you broke it, you bought it.*

For me, then, the chin is an important moment. Before you go into the chin, you're hamstrung, a little bit. You're always thinking, in the back of your mind, *can we make this guy presentable.* After the chin's when you can really squeeze him. From that point forward, Ali's value is purely dark. Maybe we can bring him in for leverage in another Session, if we've got a relative or friend in the Chair, but for the most part, he's a source of information for us, and that's it. So we can push him harder, we can go longer. And, a lot of times, we can get more than we thought was there.

And that, of course, goes to another question, which is when is an interrogation over. It's hard to say; it's always hard. In some ways, it's similar to a question that I faced in legal practice. *At what point have I reached the end of my research on a particular question?*

And the answer is, you can't always know. There's no every-time rule. Because it's so hard to tell, in some cases, what Ali's brain is sitting on.

I had someone on a steady Program, once, for two straight years. We had an Executive Warrant on him, which meant the Protocols were off. 18-hour Sessions, six-hour Rests, he's colostomized, castrated, pinpoint-stabilized, liquid meals, catheter, two full years we ride the guy. 20 months, he gives us nothing. Suddenly, month 21, he's talking about Montreal. And through that piece of intel—the stuff that came out after *20 months*—we're able to track down five more guys. And through those five, we get six more. And from those six, we get a lead that helps us stop a gel-attack in Rochester. All because I had a feeling: *this guy's got more to tell.*

It doesn't always work that way. One Suspected, we took him 50 months, never got a scrap of Usable out of him, not a drop. And so, again, it's that question, of when do you throw in the towel.

For me—and this is just for me—this is how it works. For 49 months, my Ali insisted he was Innocent; he didn't know anyone we named, never heard of Yassir Omar, wasn't a devout Muslim, we got him by mistake. All that time, I'm sure he's bullshitting; I'm *sure* of it. At 50 months—for what reason I can't say—I flip, and I'm starting to believe him. For me, that's the end. I admit, then, that it's partly intuitive.

So we initiated Exit Protocols. We stabilized Ali, injected him with Nurturer. We eased him down. Then my PFCs got him suited up and took him to his new home, down in Medium Restraint. Far from the sun—but far away, also, from the Chair. After 50 months with me, most Alis will take that trade.

It's better now, for sure. The old way, it was messy, and—just—messy.

I didn't like the messiness. Part of it is just my nature; I'm a tidy person. When I first started at the Unit, before the Chairs were Standard Ops, we were doing Water Parties, Music Parties, Stack-Ups, Fingerscrewing, Group Sessions, Electricity. Wiping Ali's face with menstrual blood. Wiping the Koran. I thought it was fake menstrual blood, I found out after six months, no, it's real, they get it from the Women's Unit. A lot of that kind of stuff.

Now, I will say this: any time you permit a measure of chaos, there are going to be good and bad things that come of it. Sometimes, under the Old Model, we got surprising results—stuff we couldn't have predicted, stuff we couldn't have extracted in the Chair.

On balance, though, I prefer the Chair. At the end of the day, I want to feel that I'm a professional. It's important to me that the boundaries be clear. I'm not a doctor, but—it is professional, what we're doing here. And you lose moral credibility with Ali when you're urinating in his presence, when you're laughing over some funny costume you put him in. It always felt disrespectful to me: disrespectful to Ali, disrespectful to the process.

So, certainly, the New Model's much better.

There are some, I know, who'd assume, just based on my family background, that I must be motivated by a desire for revenge. People will believe what they want. But nothing could be farther from the truth. As soon as I sense that a member of my interrogator corps is motivated by revenge—revenge, or a perverse enjoyment of cruelty—I strike him from my team; he's gone.

It's true—it may be true—that a soldier has to hate his enemy, but we aren't soldiers here, *contra* the official narrative. Here, strange as it may sound, we have to love our enemy, in a way; we have to understand his pain, empathize with him, his fears and desires. And we have to be curious about him in a way that a trained killer must never be; we have to *thirst*, and I use that word quite consciously, to understand the workings of his mind. And we have to credit his humanity. It's a cliché, but true nevertheless: there's no fortress better defended than the human mind. Our technology gets us into that fortress part-ways, but human intuition goes a long way too, and without human intuition and compassion, it's impossible to get to where we need to be. Dr. Ghose calls them the sacred spaces. Sacred spaces of the mind. To reach the sacred spaces, you have to love the mind. You have to want to keep it intact as much as you can even as you methodically break down its defenses. And the subject's mind has got to love you back, peculiar as that sounds; you've got to accustom Ali's brain to your presence inside of it, until your presence there seems as natural as anything else. It's like date rape: you start with force, and then you seduce.

All that being said, I would never deny that my father's death was instrumental. His death set the course for my entire life; that much is obvious.

It's Stalin, I think, who said the death of one guy is a tragedy, while the death of millions is a statistic. In that sense, if only in that sense, Dad's death wasn't a tragedy.

I was seven years old on 8/23. Like thousands of kids—tens of thousands, maybe hundreds—I watched my father die in real time, on live TV. Watched the buildings melt, run together—those unearthly swirls of color, the greens and vibrant blues. All that life and death, bleeding together, pooling and spreading, hardening into a marbled brick that, to my eyes, looked just like candy. It was a kind of murder—and who knew such things existed?—that totally erased its victims' individuality. Bodies and birds and plants and rock and metal, all disintegrating and reforming into this elastic, anonymous whole.

When I was younger, you know, I shared in my mother's outrage at this additional taking, the blotting out of identity, which made it impossible for the survivors to bury their dead. As I've grown older, though, I've come to find a poignancy in the way the Gel Attack melted down and mixed the human remains with the remains of the city. On August 23rd, it was impossible, for once, if only briefly, to ignore the ways in which all of us are one, and the ways in which we're one, also, with the physical world. And then too, as I grew up, I started to appreciate the parallels between this epic act of destruction and the equally epic acts of creation that were, and are, my father's legacy.

Dad was an artist. He would never have called himself an artist—he always insisted, a little impishly, I think, that he wasn't one, he called himself an adman—but of course he was an artist, and a great one at that.

By the end of his career—the ending that should have been the apex—he was chief communications sculptor at CFG. He'd been at CFG his whole career, and anyone who knows will tell you Dad was personally responsible for most of the firm's growth. And everything he did, he did with no graduate education, no formal artistic training: joined CFG straight out of MIT.

His work, if you believe the job title, was to create "public points of attraction"—uncanny images, shapes, and spaces. In reality, his job was to bring the impossible into physical life, usually with startling beauty.

Examples—I could give you a bunch. One you've heard of—they only took it down last year—was the metamorphic installation on Times Square. My father created that. The only credited designer. Today, there are duplicates in every shopping mall from Juneau to Dubai. At the time of the Times Square unveiling, though—this is eight years before I was born—there was nothing like it anywhere. A miniaturized red-rock formation, hovering fifty feet above the ground. This massive, solid, seemingly organic mini-mountain range, just *hovering*, as if by magic. Perfect facsimile of plant and animal life. Fully animated, fully responsive deer and mountain lions. Trees and bushes that swayed and rustled with the actual wind on the Square. Pigeons, when they landed on those tiny pines, they'd bend, even snap from the weight. And all those breathtaking details—here's maybe the most amazing thing—were generated with the Imitation of Life engine that Dad had patented, at the age of nineteen, when he was still a college student.

In the first years after that installation went up, back when my parents still lived in New York, Dad used to sneak down to Times Square at lunchtime to watch the faces of the tourists as his mountains changed. Many years later, I stood on Times Square for the same reason: to watch the ways in which strangers were moved by my father's creation. To see Dad's mountains on a monitor is not to see them at all. That's the beauty of his work—of all of it: the immediacy and physicality. The Times Square piece morphed twice a day: first at 12:30 and again at sunset. In the first stage, trickles of red, like a red paint, would run, almost imperceptibly at first, along the slopes of those little mountains—like some gentle volcanic eruption. Then the trickle became a steady flow. And as people stood and gaped, they'd start to understand that it was the mountains themselves that were pouring down their own rock faces—melting from the peaks down. Instead of dripping to the ground, the rockmelt collected on the flat base of the mountain range, collected and hardened and oozed into a new shape, which only at the final moment of the transformation became identifiable as the Nike swoosh. The piece retained that "down" form for only a few seconds before defying gravity and the laws of physics to melt and flow upwards, back into the shape of the mountains. From the wet, claylike mountains, little animals and treelike protrusions would poke out and writhe free, until, in the space of a few seconds, the range was fully animated, fully alive, swarming with tiny birds and elk and covered in those trees that rocked and danced with the wind on the Square.

Events, Dad called his installations. *Visual events, auditory events.* They were events—and they were also, as his job description had it, public points of attraction—but they were also the fruits of a brave artistic imagination: father's imagination, his dreams, brought into this improbable and tangible life.

I was six when Dad put the finishing touches on his Gobi Apple. He would have finished it years before, if not for all the problems Apple had negotiating for the thousand-year lease of the desert.

The Apple was meant, from the beginning, to be his lasting mark: a replica, in colorshifting SuperLight, of the Apple logo. Four hundred square miles in dimension. More money was spent, if you can believe it, on that Apple than was spent on the entire Egypt War. You can look that up. Father made it with the thickest, most expensive light: hyper-radiant, non-dispersable—a light that, in spite of its soft appearance, pierced though the clouds and was visible from space. In initial testing, his main concern was, would the Apple be able to survive a total continental submergence. And he wouldn't build until he got it how he wanted it. Even if the icecaps melt completely—even in the event, fantastic event, that humans abandon the earth completely for some other home—father's Apple will persist, burning bright as ever from the bottom of the ocean.

My fondest memory of childhood was the trip I took, with Mom and Dad, to see the Apple in person. The whole way there, Dad was like a little boy—a side of him I never saw before. We first flew over in a glass-bottomed helicopter, at night. And it was like we were gliding over the clouds of heaven. The next night—all night—we wandered a stretch of the desert on camelback, guided by Mongolian goatherds who looked on my father—my small, soft-spoken, gentle father—as my Alis would later look on me: as a kind of God. My own opinion of my Dad wasn't too far off from that. I wouldn't have said *God*; what I would have said was *superhero*. I would have told you, if you'd asked, that there was nothing Dad couldn't do. And all of this was a little more than a year before the day when two illiterate fourteen-year-old Syrian boys, armed with Jansport backpacks full of I-9 self-perpetuating gel component, destroyed my father along with much of the city of Boston.

Some have said—cruelly, I think—that Dad, by virtue of working for a global marketing firm, was more responsible than others for the events of 8/23: that CFG's sky banners, in particular, *invigorated* the extremists—invigorated, the word they use—as if the invasion and occupation of Egypt were of secondary importance. According to the post facto logic of the extremists, the posting of sky banners visible from Mecca was an quote-unquote act of imperialist sacrilege equal to a ground invasion of the holy city—a sacrilege that justified any savagery, any cruelty, that could be dreamt up. By the same tortured logic, America's use of gels and evaporators in Egypt justified the 8/23 terrorists' use of gel weaponry to decimate Boston's civilian population. For the record, my father never worked on sky banners. He did design the first-ever colorstorm—drenched the whole earth in this gorgeous kaleidoscopic light—but that was long after banners had become ubiquitous in the Middle East and Central Asia.

There's always seemed to me to be something morbid about the fetishization—by extremists, even by some Western pacifists—of the natural world in its mythic virgin state. Not to get philosophical, but man's always been a creature apart from, and above, the other life of the earth, a creature destined to remake the world in his own image just as God made man in His own image—and thus a creature destined to remake the world in God's image. Whatever we imagine, God's imagined first. If you don't believe that, you don't believe in God. That man would repaint the sky, that he'd fill it with his own colors, his own designs, was inevitable from the moment he discovered SuperLight. But apart from questions of man's destiny, the fact is, everything's got to change, or die, or become new. Before the banners—and Dad's colorstorms—the skies, at least in the cities, were just ceilings of smog. To prefer that featureless, shit-brown, smothering pollution to my father's electric palette is simply to prefer deadness and decay to the possibility of life.

In a similar way, I think, to reduce Dad's art to "marketing"—as he himself was willing to do, but impishly, as I said—is to be willfully obtuse. What were Michelangelo and Raphael, if not marketers? Marketers in the employ of the Pope. People forget that after Dad had finalized his patent on the Imitation of Life engine, there was no need for him to work again; his wealth was fixed for life. What he did for CFG—the swooshes and colorstorms and robotic eyes—he did only because of his obsessive need to create, to commune and converse with the world, celebrate and enrich the life around him. If he tethered his work to Prudential Investments and Fuck Body Spray, it was only because without those sponsorships, his achievements would never have been technically possible—and the first and ultimate imperative of any artist is to create; he *has* to make his art, whatever the terms. Dad's stuff on Rapa Nui—and at the Taj Mahal, the Forbidden City—was controversial, really, only among the kinds of people who believe, naively, that ideas like "France" and "Japan" are intrinsically more noble, more authentically human, than "Apple Computers" and "Toyota"; that the rules that govern and define our achievements are immutable and unchangeable; that it's not for us to dictate the terms of our own evolution.

But I'll tell you a story—something from a Session not too far back—that connects a few of the ideas I've been talking about, and gets at some of the ways in which my Dad's career, ostensibly so different from my own, converses with my work as an interrogator.

This is the early winter of last year. We're on week three with one of the Islamabad captures. Ali's knuckles are gone; we're moving to dental.

The Objective's not important to this story. Something involving Ali's mom; she's hiding somewhere in Brunei. Ali swears he doesn't know where she's hiding, but it's clear he does. And in the end, a few weeks after the stuff that I'm describing here, he did give us what we needed, and we were able to bring the mother in.

Right now I'm in his mouth with the finest drill, going straight down the middle of every tooth, one after another. That's how we do it: one pass through each tooth with the finest drill bit, and then we stop and interrogate. Then another full pass with a bigger bit, and more questioning. We call them Rinse-and-Repeats. Ali's on a cocktail, now, of Sharpener and Nurturer, which makes the drill work like a light switch: when it's going in, Ali's pain is at the human maximum; the second we stop, he's on cloud nine.

We're on the first pass—I'm entering an incisor—and all of a sudden, Ali's teeth, all of them at once, begin to spray. Eight or nine of them: these fine, crisscrossing sprays arching straight up in the air from the holes in his teeth. Like we'd struck oil.

You ever seen this? I say, sort of to the room. No: nobody's ever seen it. We're all just fascinated, observing this phenomenon. The blood loss is minimal, but the spray is getting pretty far, inking Ali's bib, turning it a very pale pink. Something about this image seems familiar to me—déjà-vu-type familiar—and then I figure it out: Ali looks disconcertingly like the heads from Pier Pierson's *Geysers* bodywork. From thirty years back. Pierson was the guerilla artist and serial killer who plastinated his victims' heads and installed them, rigged with lights and fountains, in public spaces. A twisted descendant, in some ways, of my father—but let's not start down that road right now.

What's Ali's drug situation? I finally think to ask my Technician.

Euphoric, the Technician says. *He's drifting.*

I wavered. *Let him drift,* I finally said. Ali was a CI, I should add, and also just a kid: fourteen, if even that. It wasn't going to hurt to let him float around for a few minutes.

And as he floats, Ali starts smiling—his eyes narrowing like this is the happiest he's ever been. As I'm sure it is. That's one of the uncanny things about this job: in moments like these—and at the end of long sessions, when we inject the Nurturer—our guys have never felt so good in their entire lives.

For a long time, then—a mysteriously long time—we all just stood around Ali and watched. One of my PFCs took off her goggles, and I didn't reprimand her. A little later—it's obvious in retrospect—we figured out the mist from Ali's mouth was leaching Nurturer into the air; that's why we were feeling giddy, and why, for a short time, I was almost hypnotized, was actually seeing rainbows reaching into the room from Ali's mist. At the time, though, it seemed to me that it was just something about the strange sight of that fountain of pink, its queer resemblance to the Pierson heads, that was making me feel this way. Ali, meanwhile, is smiling so hard—so happy—that he's started to cry.

In moments like these—when art intrudes, unexpected, like a ghost—it's easy for me to think that my father is speaking to me. That he's reminding me of why I'm here.

I don't deny the truth of men like Muhyi Al-Din—of the men who've spent, and will spend, their last long years in my interrogation Chairs: there can be heroism in destruction—heroism, as well as art. There was art in my father's murder—in the transformation of a major American city into a primordial swirl of liquid color—just as there was art in my CI's smiling face, the gentle sprays of blood. But it was a destructive art.

My father, who could never have aligned himself with the destroyers, was blessed by his opportunity to stand with the creators. That's the American opportunity, isn't it? And that's the opportunity I fight for here. All of us. We're fighting for the triumph of a civilization that lets its heroes be creative heroes. My own destiny, determined from the day my father melted into color like one of his own brilliant creations, is to stand against the destroyers by becoming a destroyer myself. The sacrifice is worthwhile only if we win.

Twenty thousand years from now, when people marvel, as they will, at father's Apple, nobody will see an advertisement for a laptop or a phone; when they see the apple, they'll assume, perhaps, that the shape had some religious significance, or maybe they'll conclude that it was chosen for its inherent aesthetic properties. And what will they be able to think, if not that the people who lived here at this time, however primitive, were a questing people, reaching through their blindness, and the limitations of the real, in an attempt to touch the divine?

And it was these kinds of thoughts, sentimental and a little grandiose, that cycled through my head as, drunk on Nurturer and surrounded by rainbows, I laughed and cried with my Innocent Ali.

THE MINORITY REPORT
by Philip K. Dick

Philip K. Dick, though a major writer of prose science fiction, is probably best known these days for the many film adaptations that have been made of his works. The first, and most notable of these is *Blade Runner*, based on his novel *Do Androids Dream of Electric Sheep?* Other adaptations include *Total Recall*, *A Scanner Darkly*, *Paycheck*, *Next*, and *Minority Report*, the last of which was based on our next story. Other dystopian works of Dick's include *The Man in the High Castle* and *Flow My Tears, the Policeman Said*. All told, Dick published more than 100 short stories and more than forty novels, including several non-genre works. He was recently canonized by the Library of America, which published omnibus editions of his major novels in three volumes.

Although it's not a constitutional right, the legal system of the United States is built upon the *presumption of innocence*, the idea that one is innocent until proven guilty. The Supreme Court established the primacy of this ideal in 1895, in a landmark decision on the case *Coffin v. United States*. No one can be proven guilty without hard evidence that firmly links them to the crime they have committed.

But what if the evidence comes from the future? Can someone be convicted for a crime they haven't committed yet?

In our next tale, the police's Precrime unit has developed a remarkable method for seeing into the future. Powerful computers process the visions of three psychics—literally "the thought police"—comparing the results to create a very accurate prediction of future crimes. Their work is so good there have been no successful homicides in five years. But is it right to punish someone for a crime they might have chosen not to do?

And what if the system makes a mistake?

Here is a world that might be beyond justice, not because it has thrown aside the presumption of innocence—but because it has destroyed the meaning of *guilt*.

I

The first thought Anderton had when he saw the young man was: *I'm getting bald. Bald and fat and old.* But he didn't say it aloud. Instead, he pushed back his chair, got to his feet, and came resolutely around the side of his desk, his right hand rigidly extended. Smiling with forced amiability, he shook hands with the young man.

"Witwer?" he asked, managing to make this query sound gracious.

"That's right," the young man said. "But the name's Ed to you, of course. That is, if you share my dislike for needless formality." The look on his blond, overly-confident face showed that he considered the matter settled. It would be Ed and John: everything would be agreeably cooperative right from the start.

"Did you have much trouble finding the building?" Anderton asked guardedly, ignoring the too-friendly overture. *Good God, he had to hold on to something.* Fear touched him and he began to sweat. Witwer was moving around the office as if he already owned it—as if he were measuring it for size. Couldn't he wait a couple of days—a decent interval?

"No trouble," Witwer answered blithely, his hands in his pockets. Eagerly, he examined the voluminous files that lined the wall. "I'm not coming into your agency blind, you understand. I have quite a few ideas of my own about the way Precrime is run."

Shakily Anderton lit his pipe. "How is it run? I should like to know."

"Not badly," Witwer said. "In fact, quite well."

Anderton regarded him steadily. "Is that your private opinion? Or is it just cant?"

Witwer met his gaze guilelessly. "Private and public. The Senate's pleased with your work. In fact, they're enthusiastic." He added, "As enthusiastic as very old men can be."

Anderton winced, but outwardly he remained impassive. It cost him an effort, though. He wondered what Witwer *really* thought. What was actually going on in that close-cropped skull? The young man's eyes were blue, bright—and disturbingly clever. Witwer was nobody's fool. And obviously he had a great deal of ambition.

"As I understand it," Anderton said cautiously, "you're going to be my assistant until I retire."

"That's my understanding, too," the other replied, without an instant's hesitation.

"Which may be this year, or next year—or ten years from now." The pipe in Anderton's hand trembled. "I'm under no compulsion to retire. I founded Precrime and I can stay on here as long as I want. It's purely my decision."

Witwer nodded, his expression still guileless. "Of course."

With an effort, Anderton cooled down a trifle. "I merely wanted to get things straight."

"From the start," Witwer agreed. "You're the boss. What you say goes." With every evidence of sincerity, he asked: "Would you care to show me the organization? I'd like to familiarize myself with the general routine as soon as possible."

As they walked along the busy, yellow-lit tiers of offices, Anderton said: "You're acquainted with the theory of precrime, of course. I presume we can take that for granted."

"I have the information publicly available," Witwer replied. "With the aid of your precog mutants, you've boldly and successfully abolished the postcrime punitive system of jails and fines. As we all realize, punishment was never much of a deterrent, and could scarcely have afforded comfort to a victim already dead."

They had come to the descent lift. As it carried them swiftly downward, Anderton said: "You've probably grasped the basic legalistic drawback to precrime methodology. We're taking in individuals who have broken no law."

"But they surely will," Witwer affirmed with conviction.

"Happily they *don't*—because we get them first, before they can commit an act of violence. So the commission of the crime itself is absolute metaphysics. We claim they're culpable. They, on the other hand, eternally claim they're innocent. And, in a sense, they *are* innocent."

The lift let them out, and they again paced down a yellow corridor. "In our society we have no major crimes," Anderton went on, "but we do have a detention camp full of would-be criminals."

Doors opened and close, and they were in the analytical wing. Ahead of them rose impressive banks of equipment—the data-receptors, and the computing mechanisms that studied and restructured the incoming material. And beyond the machinery sat the three precogs, almost lost to view in the maze of wiring.

"There they are," Anderton said dryly. "What do you think of them?"

In the gloomy half-darkness the three idiots sat babbling. Every incoherent utterance, every random syllable, was analyzed, compared, reassembled in the form of visual symbols, transcribed on conventional punchcards, and ejected into various coded slots. All day long the idiots babbled, imprisoned in their special high-backed chairs, held in one rigid position by metal bands, and bundles of wiring, clamps. Their physical needs were taken care of automatically. They had no spiritual needs. Vegetable-like, they muttered and dozed and existed. Their minds were dull, confused, lost in shadows.

But not the shadows of today. The three gibbering, fumbling creatures, with their enlarged heads and wasted bodies, were contemplating the future. The analytical machinery was recording prophecies, and as the three precog idiots talked, the machinery carefully listened.

For the first time Witwer's face lost its breezy confidence. A sick, dismayed expression crept into his eyes, a mixture of shame and moral shock. "It's not—pleasant," he murmured. "I didn't realize they were so—" He groped in his mind for the right word, gesticulating. "So—deformed."

"Deformed and retarded," Anderton instantly agreed. "Especially the girl, there. Donna is forty-five years old. But she looks about ten. The talent absorbs everything; the esp-lobe shrivels the balance of the frontal area. But what do we care? We get their prophecies. They pass on what we need. They don't understand any of it, but *we* do."

Subdued, Witwer crossed the room to the machinery. From a slot he collected a stack of cards. "Are these names that have come up?" he asked.

"Obviously." Frowning, Anderton took the stack from him. "I haven't had a chance to examine them," he explained, impatiently concealing his annoyance.

Fascinated, Witwer watched the machinery pop a fresh card into the now empty slot. It was followed by a second—and a third. From the whirring disks came one card after another. "The precogs must see quite far into the future," Witwer exclaimed.

"They see a quite limited span," Anderton informed him. "One week or two ahead at the very most. Much of their data is worthless to us—simply not relevant to our line. We pass it on to the appropriate agencies. And they in turn trade data with us. Every important bureau has its cellar of treasured *monkeys*."

"Monkeys?" Witwer stared at him uneasily. "Oh, yes, I understand. See no evil, speak no evil, et cetera. Very amusing."

"Very *apt*." Automatically, Anderton collected the fresh cards which had been turned up by the spinning machinery. "Some of these names will be totally discarded. And most of the remainder record petty crimes: thefts, income tax evasion, assault, extortion. As I'm sure you know, Precrime has cut down felonies by ninety-nine and decimal point eight percent. We seldom get actual murder or treason. After all, the culprit knows we'll confine him in the detention camp a week before he gets a chance to commit the crime."

"When was the last time an actual murder was committed?" Witwer asked.

"Five years ago," Anderton said, pride in his voice.

"How did it happen?"

The criminal escaped our teams. We had his name—in fact, we had all the details of the crime, including the victim's name. We knew the exact moment, the location of the planned act of violence. But in spite of us he was able to carry it out." Anderton shrugged. "After all, we can't get all of them." He riffled the cards. "But we do get most."

"One murder in five years." Witwer's confidence was returning. "Quite an impressive record... something to be proud of."

Quietly Anderton said: "I am proud. Thirty years ago I worked out the theory—back in the days when the self-seekers were thinking in terms of quick raids on the stock market. I saw something legitimate ahead—something of tremendous social value."

He tossed the packet of cards to Wally Page, his subordinate in charge of the monkey block. "See which ones we want," he told him. "Use your own judgment."

As Page disappeared with the cards, Witwer said thoughtfully: "It's a big responsibility."

"Yes, it is," agreed Anderton. "If we let one criminal escape—as we did five years ago—we've got a human life on our conscience. We're solely responsible. If we slip up, somebody dies." Bitterly, he jerked three new cards from the slot. "It's a public trust."

"Are you ever tempted to—" Witwer hesitated. "I mean, some of the men you pick up must offer you plenty."

"It wouldn't do any good. A duplicate file of cards pops out at Army GHQ. It's check and balance. They can keep their eye on us as continuously as they wish." Anderton glanced briefly at the top card. "So even if we wanted to accept a—"

He broke off, his lips tightening.

"What's the matter?" Witwer asked curiously.

Carefully, Anderton folded up the top card and put it away in his pocket. "Nothing," he muttered. "Nothing at all."

The harshness in his voice brought a flush to Witwer's face. "You really don't like me," he observed.

"True," Anderton admitted. "I don't. But—"

He couldn't believe he disliked the young man that much. It didn't seem possible: it *wasn't* possible. Something was wrong. Dazed, he tried to steady his tumbling mind.

On the card was his name. Line one—an already accused future murderer! According to the coded punches, Precrime Commissioner John A. Anderton was going to kill a man—and within the next week.

With absolute, overwhelming conviction, he didn't believe it.

II

In the outer office, talking to Page, stood Anderton's slim and attractive young wife, Lisa. She was engaged in a sharp, animated discussion of policy, and barely glanced up as Witwer and her husband entered.

"Hello, darling," Anderton said.

Witwer remained silent. But his pale eyes flickered slightly as they rested on the brown-haired woman in her trim police uniform. Lisa was now an executive official of Precrime but once, Witwer knew, she had been Anderton's secretary.

Noticing the interest on Witwer's face Anderton paused and reflected. To plant the card in the machines would require an accomplice on the inside—someone who was closely connected with Precrime and had access to the analytical equipment. Lisa was an improbable element. But the possibility did exist.

Of course, the conspiracy could be large-scale and elaborate, involving far more than a "rigged" card inserted somewhere along the line. The original data itself might have been tampered with. Actually, there was no telling how far back the alteration went. A cold fear touched him as he began to see the possibilities. His original impulse—to tear open the machines and remove all the data—was uselessly primitive. Probably the tapes agreed with the card: he would only incriminate himself further.

He had approximately twenty-four hours. Then, the Army people would check over their cards and discover the discrepancy. They would find in their files a duplicate of the card he had appropriated. He had only one of two copies, which meant that the folded card in his pocket might just as well be lying on Page's desk in plain view of everyone.

From outside the building came the drone of police cars starting out on their routine round-ups. How many hours would elapse before one of them pulled up in front of *his* house?

"What's the matter, darling?" Lisa asked him uneasily. "You look as if you've just seen a ghost. Are you all right?"

"I'm fine," he assured her.

Lisa suddenly seemed to become aware of Ed Witwer's admiring scrutiny. "Is this gentleman your new co-worker, darling?" she asked.

Warily, Anderton introduced his new associate. Lisa smiled in friendly greeting. Did a covert awareness pass between them? He couldn't tell. God, he was beginning to suspect everybody—not only his wife and Witwer, but a dozen members of his staff.

"Are you from New York?" Lisa asked.

"No," Witwer replied. "I've lived most of my life in Chicago. I'm staying at a hotel—one of the big downtown hotels. Wait—I have the name written on a card somewhere."

While he self-consciously searched his pockets, Lisa suggested: "Perhaps you'd like to have dinner with us. We'll be working in close cooperation, and I really think we ought to get better acquainted."

Startled, Anderton backed off. What were the chances of his wife's friendliness being benign, accidental? Witwer would be present the balance of the evening, and would now have an excuse to trail along to Anderton's private residence. Profoundly disturbed, he turned impulsively, and moved toward the door.

"Where are you going?" Lisa asked, astonished.

"Back to the monkey block," he told her. "I want to check over some rather puzzling data tapes before the Army sees them." He was out in the corridor before she could think of a plausible reason for detaining him.

Rapidly, he made his way to the ramp at its far end. He was striding down the outside stairs toward the public sidewalk, when Lisa appeared breathlessly behind him.

"What on earth has come over you?" Catching hold of his arm, she moved quickly in front of him. "I *knew* you were leaving," she exclaimed, blocking his way. "What's wrong with you? Everybody thinks you're—" She checked herself. "I mean, you're acting so erratically."

People surged by them—the usual afternoon crowd. Ignoring them, Anderton pried his wife's fingers from his arm. "I'm getting out," he told her. "While there's still time."

"But—*why?*"

"I'm being framed—deliberately and maliciously. This creature is out to get my job. The Senate is getting at me *through* him."

Lisa gazed up at him, bewildered. "But he seems like such a nice young man."

"Nice as a water moccasin."

Lisa's dismay turned to disbelief. "I don't believe it. Darling, all this strain you've been under—" Smiling uncertainly, she faltered: "It's not really credible that Ed Witwer is trying to frame you. How could he, even if he wanted to? Surely Ed wouldn't—"

"Ed?"

"That's his name, isn't it?"

Her brown eyes flashed in startled, wildly incredulous protest. "Good heavens, you're suspicious of everybody. You actually believe I'm mixed up with it in some way, don't you?"

He considered. "I'm not sure."

She drew closer to him, her eyes accusing. "That's not true. You really believe it. Maybe you *ought* to go away for a few weeks. You desperately need a rest. All this tension and trauma, a younger man coming in. You're acting paranoiac. Can't you see that? People plotting against you. Tell me, do you have any actual proof?"

Anderton removed his wallet and took out the folded card. "Examine this carefully," he said, handing it to her.

The color drained out of her face, and she gave a little harsh, dry gasp.

"The set-up is fairly obvious," Anderton told her, as levelly as he could. "This will give Witwer a legal pretext to remove me right now. He won't have to wait until I resign." Grimly, he added: "They know I'm good for a few years yet."

"But—"

"It will end the check and balance system. Precrime will no longer be an independent agency. The Senate will control the police, and after that—" His lips tightened. "They'll absorb the Army too. Well, it's outwardly logical enough. *Of course* I feel hostility and resentment toward Witwer—*of course* I have a motive.

"Nobody likes to be replaced by a younger man, and find himself turned out to pasture. It's all really quite plausible—except that I haven't the remotest intention of killing Witwer. But I can't prove that. So what can I do?"

Mutely, her face very white, Lisa shook her head. "I—I don't know. Darling, if only —"

"Right now," Anderton said abruptly, "I'm going home to pack my things. That's about as far ahead as I can plan."

"You're really going to—to try to hide out?"

"I am. As far as the Centaurian-colony planets, if necessary. It's been done successfully before, and I have a twenty-four-hour start." He turned resolutely. "Go back inside. There's no point in your coming with me."

"Did you imagine I would?" Lisa asked huskily.

Startled, Anderton stared at her. "Wouldn't you?" Then with amazement, he murmured: "No, I can see you don't believe me. You still think I'm imagining all this." He jabbed savagely at the card. "Even with that evidence you still aren't convinced."

"No," Lisa agreed quickly, "I'm not. You didn't look at it closely enough, darling. Ed Witwer's name isn't on it."

Incredulous, Anderton took the card from her.

"Nobody says you're going to kill Ed Witwer," Lisa continued rapidly, in a thin, brittle voice. "The card *must* be genuine, understand? And it has nothing to do with Ed. He's not plotting against you and neither is anybody else."

Too confused to reply, Anderton stood studying the card. She was right. Ed Witwer was not listed as his victim. On line five, the machine had neatly stamped another name.

LEOPOLD KAPLAN

Numbly, he pocketed the card. He had never heard of the man in his life.

III

The house was cool and deserted, and almost immediately Anderton began making preparations for his journey. While he packed, frantic thoughts passed through his mind.

Possibly he was wrong about Witwer—but how could he be sure? In any event, the conspiracy against him was far more complex than he had realized. Witwer, in the over-all picture, might be merely an insignificant puppet animated by someone else—by some distant, indistinct figure only vaguely visible in the background.

It had been a mistake to show the card to Lisa. Undoubtedly, she would describe it in detail to Witwer. He'd never get off Earth, never have an opportunity to find out what life on a frontier planet might be like.

While he was thus preoccupied, a board creaked behind him. He turned from the bed, clutching a weather-stained winter sports jacket, to face the muzzle of a gray-blue A-pistol.

"It didn't take you long," he said, staring with bitterness at the tight-lipped, heavy-set man in a brown overcoat who stood holding the gun in his gloved hand. "Didn't she even hesitate?"

The intruder's face registered no response. "I don't know what you're talking about," he said. "Come along with me."

Startled, Anderton laid down the sports jacket. "You're not from my agency? You're not a police officer?"

Protesting and astonished, he was hustled outside the house to a waiting limousine. Instantly three heavily armed men closed in behind him. The door slammed and the car shot off down the highway, away from the city. Impassive and remote, the faces around him jogged with the motion of the speeding vehicle as open fields, dark and somber, swept past.

Anderton was still trying futilely to grasp the implications of what had happened, when the car came to a rutted side road, turned off, and descended into a gloomy subsurface garage. Someone shouted an order. The heavy metal lock

grated shut and overhead lights blinked on. The driver turned off the car motor.

"You'll have reason to regret this," Anderton warned hoarsely, as they dragged
him from the car. "Do you realize who I am?"

"We realize," the man in the brown overcoat said.

At gun-point, Anderton was marched upstairs, from the clammy silence of the
garage into a deep-carpeted hallway. He was, apparently, in a luxurious private
residence, set out in the war-devoured rural area. At the far end of the hallway
he could make out a room—a book-lined study simply but tastefully furnished.
In a circle of lamplight, his face partly in shadows, a man he had never met sat
waiting for him.

As Anderton approached, the man nervously slipped a pair of rimless glasses in
place, snapped the case shut, and moistened his dry lips. He was elderly, perhaps
seventy or older, and under his arm was a slim silver cane. His body was thin,
wiry, his attitude curiously rigid. What little hair he had was dusty brown—a
carefully-smoothed sheen of neutral color above his pale, bony skull. Only his
eyes seemed really alert.

"Is this Anderton?" he inquired querulously, turning to the man in the brown
overcoat. "Where did you pick him up?"

"At his home," the other replied. "He was packing—as we expected."

The man at the desk shivered visibly. "Packing." He took off his glasses and
jerkily returned them to their case. "Look here," he said bluntly to Anderton,
"what's the matter with you? Are you hopelessly insane? How could you kill a
man you've never met?"

The old man, Anderton suddenly realized, was Leopold Kaplan.

"First, I'll ask you a question," Anderton countered rapidly. "Do you realize what you've done? I'm Commissioner of Police. I can have you sent up for
twenty years."

He was going to say more, but a sudden wonder cut him short.

"*How did you find out?*" he demanded. Involuntarily, his hand went to his
pocket, where the folded card was hidden. "It won't be for another—"

"I wasn't notified through your agency," Kaplan broke in, with angry impatience. "The fact that you've never heard of me doesn't surprise me too much.
Leopold Kaplan, General of the Army of the Federated Westbloc Alliance."
Begrudgingly, he added, "Retired, since the end of the Anglo-Chinese War, and
the abolishment of AFWA."

It made sense. Anderton had suspected that the Army processed its duplicate
cards immediately, for its own protection. Relaxing somewhat, he demanded:
"Well? You've got me here. What next?"

"Evidently," Kaplan said, "I'm not going to have you destroyed, or it would
have shown up on one of those miserable little cards. I'm curious about you.
It seemed incredible to me that a man of your stature could contemplate the
cold-blooded murder of a total stranger. There must be something more here.
Frankly, I'm puzzled. If it represented some kind of police strategy—" He

shrugged his thin shoulders. "Surely you wouldn't have permitted the duplicate card to reach us."

"Unless," one of his men suggested, "it's a deliberate plant."

Kaplan raised his bright, bird-like eyes and scrutinized Anderton. "What do you have to say?"

"That's exactly what it is," Anderton said, quick to see the advantage of stating frankly what he believed to be the simple truth. "The prediction on the card was deliberately fabricated by a clique inside the police agency. The card is prepared and I'm netted. I'm relieved of my authority automatically. My assistant steps in and claims he prevented the murder in the usual efficient precrime manner. Needless to say, there is no murder or intent to murder."

"I agree with you that there will be no murder," Kaplan affirmed grimly. "You'll be in police custody. I intend to make certain of that."

Horrified, Anderton protested: "You're taking me back there? If I'm in custody I'll never be able to prove—"

"I don't care what you prove or don't prove," Kaplan interrupted. "All I'm interested in is having you out of the way." Frigidly, he added: "For my own protection."

"He was getting ready to leave," one of the men asserted.

"That's right," Anderton said, sweating. "As soon as they get hold of me I'll be confined in the detention camp. Witwer will take over—lock, stock and barrel." His face darkened. "And my wife. They're acting in concert, apparently."

For a moment Kaplan seemed to waver. "It's possible," he conceded, regarding Anderton steadily. Then he shook his head. "I can't take the chance. If this is a frame against you, I'm sorry. But it's simply not my affair." He smiled slightly. "However, I wish you luck." To the men he said: "Take him to the police building and turn him over to the highest authority." He mentioned the name of the acting Commissioner, and waited for Anderton's reaction.

"Witwer!" Anderton echoed, incredulous.

Still smiling slightly, Kaplan turned and clicked on the console radio in the study. "Witwer has already assumed authority. Obviously, he's going to create quite an affair out of this."

There was a brief static hum, and then, abruptly, the radio blared out into the room—a noisy professional voice, reading a prepared announcement.

"... all citizens are warned not to shelter or in any fashion aid or assist this dangerous marginal individual. The extraordinary circumstance of an escaped criminal at liberty and in a position to commit an act of violence is unique in modern times. All citizens are hereby notified that legal statutes still in force implicate any and all persons failing to cooperate fully with the police in their task of apprehending John Allison Anderton. To repeat: The Precrime Agency of the Federal Westbloc Government is in the process of locating and neutralizing its former Commissioner, John Allison Anderton, who, through the methodology of the precrime system, is hereby declared a potential murderer and as such forfeits his rights to freedom and all its privileges."

"It didn't take him long," Anderton muttered, appalled. Kaplan snapped off the radio and the voice vanished.

"Lisa must have gone directly to him," Anderton speculated bitterly.

"Why should he wait?" Kaplan asked. "You made your intentions clear."

He nodded to his men. "Take him back to town. I feel uneasy having him so close. In that respect I concur with Commissioner Witwer. I want him neutralized as soon as possible."

IV

Cold, light rain beat against the pavement, as the car moved through the dark streets of New York City toward the police building.

"You can see his point," one of the men said to Anderton. "If you were in his place you'd act just as decisively."

Sullen and resentful, Anderton stared straight ahead.

"Anyhow," the man went on, "you're just one of many. Thousands of people have gone to that detention camp. You won't be lonely. As a matter of fact, you may not want to leave."

Helplessly, Anderton watched pedestrians hurrying along the rain-swept sidewalks. He felt no strong emotion. He was aware only of an overpowering fatigue. Dully, he checked off the street numbers: they were getting near the police station.

"This Witwer seems to know how to take advantage of an opportunity," one of the men observed conversationally. "Did you ever meet him?"

"Briefly," Anderton answered.

"He wanted your job—so he framed you. Are you sure of that?"

Anderton grimaced. "Does it matter?"

"I was just curious." The man eyed him languidly. "So you're the ex-Commissioner of Police. People in the camp will be glad to see you coming. They'll remember you."

"No doubt," Anderton agreed.

"Witwer sure didn't waste any time. Kaplan's lucky—with an official like that in charge." The man looked at Anderton almost pleadingly. "You're really convinced it's a plot, eh?"

"Of course."

"You wouldn't harm a hair of Kaplan's head? For the first time in history, Precrime goes wrong? An innocent man is framed by one of those cards. Maybe there've been other innocent people—right?"

"It's quite possible," Anderton admitted listlessly.

"Maybe the whole system can break down. Sure, you're not going to commit a murder—and maybe none of them were. Is that why you told Kaplan you wanted to keep yourself outside? Were you hoping to prove the system wrong? I've got an open mind, if you want to talk about it."

Another man leaned over, and asked, "Just between the two of us, is there really anything to this plot stuff? Are you really being framed?"

Anderton sighed. At that point he wasn't certain, himself. Perhaps he was trapped in a closed, meaningless time-circle with no motive and no beginning. In fact, he was almost ready to concede that he was the victim of a weary, neurotic fantasy, spawned by growing insecurity. Without a fight, he was willing to give himself up. A vast weight of exhaustion lay upon him. He was struggling against the impossible—and all the cards were stacked against him.

The sharp squeal of tires roused him. Frantically, the driver struggled to control the car, tugging at the wheel and slamming on the brakes, as a massive bread truck loomed up from the fog and ran directly across the lane ahead. Had he gunned the motor instead he might have saved himself. But too late he realized his error. The car skidded, lurched, hesitated for a brief instant, and then smashed head on into the bread truck.

Under Anderton the seat lifted up and flung him face-forward against the door. Pain, sudden, intolerable, seemed to burst in his brain as he lay gasping and trying feebly to pull himself to his knees. Somewhere the crackle of fire echoed dismally, a patch of hissing brilliance winking in the swirls of mist making their way into the twisted hulk of the car.

Hands from outside the car reached for him. Slowly he became aware that he was being dragged through the rent that had been the door. A heavy seat cushion was shoved brusquely aside, and all at once he found himself on his feet, leaning heavily against a dark shape and being guided into the shadows of an alley a short distance from the car.

In the distance, police sirens wailed.

"You'll live," a voice grated in his ear, low and urgent. It was a voice he had never heard before, as unfamiliar and harsh as the rain beating into his face. "Can you hear what I'm saying?"

"Yes," Anderton acknowledged. He plucked aimlessly at the ripped sleeve of his shirt. A cut on his cheek was beginning to throb. Confused, he tried to orient himself. "You're not—"

"Stop talking and listen." The man was heavy-set, almost fat. Now his big hands held Anderton propped against the wet brick wall of the building, out of the rain and the flickering light of the burning car. "We had to do it that way," he said. "It was the only alternative. We didn't have much time. We thought Kaplan would keep you at his place longer."

"Who are you?" Anderton managed.

The moist, rain-streaked face twisted into a humorless grin. "My name's Fleming. You'll see me again. We have about five seconds before the police get here. Then we're back where we started." A flat packet was stuffed into Anderton's hands. "That's enough loot to keep you going. And there's a full set of identification in there. We'll contact you from time to time." His grin increased and became a nervous chuckle. "Until you've proved your point."

Anderton blinked. "It is a frameup, then?"

"Of course." Sharply, the man swore. "You mean they got you to believe it, too?"

"I thought—" Anderton had trouble talking, one of his front teeth seemed to be loose. "Hostility toward Witwer... replaced, my wife and a younger man, natural resentment..."

"Don't kid yourself," the other said. "You know better than that. This whole business was worked out carefully. They had every phase of it under control. The card was set to pop the day Witwer appeared. They've already got the first part wrapped up. Witwer is Commissioner, and you're a hunted criminal."

"Who's behind it?"

"Your wife."

Anderton's head spun. "You're positive?"

The man laughed. "You bet your life." He glanced quickly around. "Here come the police. Take off down this alley. Grab a bus, get yourself into the slum section, rent a room and buy a stack of magazines to keep you busy. Get other clothes—you're smart enough to take care of yourself. Don't try to leave Earth. They've got all the inter-system transports screened. If you can keep low for the next seven days, you're made."

"Who are you?" Anderton demanded.

Fleming let go of him. Cautiously, he moved to the entrance of the alley and peered out. The first police car had come to rest on the damp pavement; its motor spinning tinnily, it crept suspiciously toward the smoldering ruin that had been Kaplan's car. Inside the wreck the squad of men were stirring feebly, beginning to creep painfully through the tangle of steel and plastic out into the cold rain.

"Consider us a protective society," Fleming said softly, his plump, expressionless face shining with moisture. "A sort of police force that watches the police. To see," he added, "that everything stays on an even keel."

His thick hand shot out. Stumbling, Anderton was knocked away from him, half falling into the shadows and damp debris that littered the alley.

"Get going," Fleming told him sharply. "And don't discard that packet." As Anderton felt his way hesitantly toward the far exit of the alley, the man's last words drifted to him. "Study it carefully and you may still survive."

V

The identification cards described him as Ernest Temple, an unemployed electrician, drawing a weekly subsistence from the State of New York, with a wife and four children in Buffalo and less than a hundred dollars in assets. A sweat-stained green card gave him permission to travel and to maintain no fixed address. A man looking for work needed to travel. He might have to go a long way.

As he rode across town in the almost empty bus, Anderton studied the description of Ernest Temple. Obviously, the cards had been made out with him in mind, for all the measurements fitted. After a time he wondered about the fingerprints and the brain-wave pattern. They couldn't possibly stand comparison.

The walletful of cards would get him past only the most cursory examinations.

But it was something. And with the PD cards came ten thousand dollars in bills. He pocketed the money and cards, then turned to the neatly-typed message in which they had been enclosed.

At first he could make no sense of it. For a long time he studied it, perplexed.

The existence of a majority logically implies a corresponding minority.

The bus had entered the vast slum region, the tumbled miles of cheap hotels and broken-down tenements that had sprung up after the mass destruction of the war. It slowed to a stop, and Anderton got to his feet. A few passengers idly observed his cut cheek and damaged clothing. Ignoring them, he stepped down onto the rain-swept curb.

Beyond collecting the money due him, the hotel clerk was not interested. Anderton climbed the stairs to the second floor and entered the narrow, musty-smelling room that now belonged to him. Gratefully, he locked the door and pulled down the window shades. The room was small but clean. Bed, dresser, scenic calendar, chair, lamp, a radio with a slot for the insertion of quarters.

He dropped a quarter into it and threw himself heavily down on the bed. All main stations carried the police bulletin. It was novel, exciting, something unknown to the present generation. An escaped criminal! The public was avidly interested.

"… this man has used the advantage of his high position to carry out an initial escape," the announcer was saying, with professional indignation. "Because of his high office he had access to the previewed data and the trust placed in him permitted him to evade the normal process of detection and relocation. During the period of his tenure he exercised his authority to send countless potentially guilty individuals to their proper confinement, thus sparing the lives of innocent victims. This man, John Allison Anderton, was instrumental in the original creation of the precrime system, the prophylactic predetection of criminals through the ingenious use of mutant precogs, capable of previewing future events and transferring orally that data to analytical machinery. These three precogs, in their vital function…"

The voice faded out as he left the room and entered the tiny bathroom. There, he stripped off his coat, and shirt, and ran hot water in the wash bowl. He began bathing the cut on his cheek. At the drugstore on the corner he had bought iodine and Band-aids, a razor, comb, toothbrush, and other small things he would need. The next morning he intended to find a second-hand clothing store and buy more suitable clothing. After all, he was now an unemployed electrician, not an accident-damaged Commissioner of Police.

In the other room the radio blared on. Only subconsciously aware of it, he stood in front of the cracked mirror, examining a broken tooth.

"… the system of three precogs finds its genesis in the computers of the middle decades of this century. How are the results of an electronic computer checked? By feeding the data to a second computer of identical design. But two computers are not sufficient. If each computer arrived at a different answer it is impossible to tell a *priori* which is correct. The solution, based on a careful study of statistical method, is to utilize a third computer to check the results of the first two. In this manner, a so-called majority report is obtained. It can be assumed with fair probability that the agreement of two out of three computers indicates which of the alternative results is accurate. It would not be likely that two computers would arrive at identically incorrect solutions—"

Anderton dropped the towel he was clutching and raced into the other room. Trembling, he bent to catch the blaring words of the radio.

"...unanimity of all three precogs is a hoped-for but seldom-achieved phenomenon, acting Commissioner Witwer explains. It is much more common to obtain a collaborative majority report of two precogs, plus a minority report of some slight variation, usually with reference to time and place, from the third mutant. This is explained by the theory of *multiple futures*. If only one time-path existed, precognitive information would be of no importance, since no possibility would exist, in possessing this information, of altering the future. In the Precrime Agency's work we must first of all asume—"

Frantically, Anderton paced around the tiny room. Majority report—only two of the precogs had concurred on the material underlying the card. That was the meaning of the message enclosed with the packet. The report of the third precog, the minority report, was somehow of importance.

Why?

His watch told him that it was after midnight. Page would be off duty. He wouldn't be back in the monkey block until the next afternoon. It was a slim chance, but worth taking. Maybe Page would cover for him, and maybe not. He would have to risk it.

He had to see the minority report.

VI

Between noon and one o'clock the rubbish-littered streets swarmed with people. He chose that time, the busiest part of the day, to make his call. Selecting a phonebooth in a patron-teeming super drugstore, he dialed the familiar police number and stood holding the cold receiver to his ear. Deliberately, he had selected the aud, not the vid line: in spite of his second-hand clothing and seedy, unshaven appearance, he might be recognized.

The receptionist was new to him. Cautiously, he gave Page's extension. If Witwer were removing the regular staff and putting in his satellites, he might find himself talking to a total stranger.

"Hello," Page's gruff voice came.

Relieved, Anderton glanced around. Nobody was paying any attention to him. The shoppers wandered among the merchandise, going about their daily routines. "Can you talk?" he asked. "Or are you tied up?"

There was a moment of silence. He could picture Page's mild face torn with uncertainty as he wildly tried to decide what to do. At last came halting words.

"Why—are you calling here?"

Ignoring the question, Anderton said, "I didn't recognize the receptionist. New personnel?"

"Brand-new," Page agreed, in a thin, strangled voice. "Big turnovers, these days."

"So I hear." Tensely Anderton asked, "How's your job? Still safe?"

"Wait a minute." The receiver was put down and the muffled sound of steps came in Anderton's ear. It was followed by the quick slam of a door being hastily shut. Page returned. "We can talk better now," he said hoarsely.

"How much better?"

"Not a great deal. Where are you?"

"Strolling through Central Park," Anderton said. "Enjoying the sunlight." For all he knew, Page had gone to make sure the line-tap was in place. Right now, an airborne police team was probably on its way. But he had to take the chance. "I'm in a new field," he said curtly. "I'm an electrician these days."

"Oh?" Page said, baffled.

"I thought maybe you had some work for me. If it can be arranged, I'd like to drop by and examine your basic computing equipment. Especially the data and analytical banks in the monkey block."

After a pause, Page said: "It—might be arranged. If it's really important."

"It is," Anderton assured him. "When would be best for you?"

"Well," Page said, struggling. "I'm having a repair team come in to look at the intercom equipment. The acting Commissioner wants it improved, so he can operate quicker. You might trail along."

"I'll do that. About when?"

"Say four o'clock. Entrance B, level 6. I'll—meet you."

"Fine," Anderton agreed, already starting to hang up. "I hope you're still in charge, when I get there."

He hung up and rapidly left the booth. A moment later he was pushing through the dense pack of people crammed into the nearby cafeteria. Nobody would locate him there.

He had three and a half hours to wait. And it was going to seem a lot longer. It proved to be the longest wait of his life before he finally met Page as arranged.

The first thing Page said was: "You're out of your mind. Why in hell did you come back?"

"I'm not back for long." Tautly, Anderton prowled around the monkey block, systematically locking one door after another. "Don't let anybody in. I can't take chances."

"You should have quit when you were ahead." In an agony of apprehension, Page followed after him. "Witwer is making hay, hand over fist. He's got the whole country screaming for your blood."

Ignoring him, Anderton snapped open the main control bank of the analytical machinery. "Which of the three monkeys gave the minority report?"

"Don't question me—I'm getting out." On his way to the door Page halted briefly, pointed to the middle figure, and then disappeared. The door closed; Anderton was alone.

The middle one. He knew that one well. The dwarfed, hunched-over figure had sat buried in its wiring and relays for fifteen years. As Anderton approached, it didn't look up. With eyes glazed and blank, it contemplated a world that did not yet exist, blind to the physical reality that lay around it.

"Jerry" was twenty-four years old. Originally, he had been classified as a hydrocephalic idiot but when he reached the age of six the psych testers had identified the precog talent, buried under the layers of tissue corrosion. Placed in a government-operated training school, the latent talent had been cultivated. By the time he was nine the talent had advanced to a useful stage. "Jerry," however, remained in the aimless chaos of idiocy; the burgeoning faculty had absorbed the totality of his personality.

Squatting down, Anderton began disassembling the protective shields that guarded the tape-reels stored in the analytical machinery. Using schematics, he traced the leads back from the final stages of the integrated computers, to the point where "Jerry's" individual equipment branched off. Within minutes he was shakily lifting out two half-hour tapes: recent rejected data not fused with majority reports. Consulting the code chart, he selected the section of tape which referred to his particular card.

A tape scanner was mounted nearby. Holding his breath, he inserted the tape, activated the transport, and listened. It took only a second. From the first statement of the report it was clear what had happened. He had what he wanted; he could stop looking.

"Jerry's" vision was misphased. Because of the erratic nature of precognition, he was examining a time-area slightly different from that of his companions. For him, the report that Anderton would commit a murder was an event to be integrated along with everything else. That assertion—and Anderton's reaction—was one more piece of datum.

Obviously, "Jerry's" report superseded the majority report. Having been informed that he would commit a murder, Anderton would change his mind and not do so. The preview of the murder had cancelled out the murder; prophylaxis had occurred simply in his being informed. Already, a new time-path had been created. But "Jerry" was outvoted.

Trembling, Anderton rewound the tape and clicked on the recording head. At high speed he made a copy of the report, restored the original, and removed the duplicate from the transport. Here was the proof that the card was invalid: *obsolete.* All he had to do was show it to Witwer...

His own stupidity amazed him. Undoubtedly, Witwer had seen the report; and in spite of it, had assumed the job of Commissioner, had kept the police teams out. Witwer didn't intend to back down; he wasn't concerned with Anderton's innocence.

What, then, could he do? Who else would be interested?

"You damn fool!" a voice behind him grated, wild with anxiety.

Quickly, he turned. His wife stood at one of the doors, in her police uniform, her eyes frantic with dismay. "Don't worry," he told her briefly, displaying the reel of tape. "I'm leaving."

Her face distorted, Lisa rushed frantically up to him. "Page said you were here, but I couldn't believe it. He shouldn't have let you in. He just doesn't understand what you are."

"What am I?" Anderton inquired caustically. "Before you answer, maybe you better listen to this tape."

"I don't want to listen to it! I just want you to get out of here! Ed Witwer knows somebody's down here. Page is trying to keep him occupied, but—" She broke off, her head turned stiffly to one side. "He's here now! He's going to force his way in."

"Haven't you got any influence? Be gracious and charming. He'll probably forget about me."

Lisa looked at him in bitter reproach. "There's a ship parked on the roof. If you want to get away…" Her voice choked and for an instant she was silent. Then she said, "I'll be taking off in a minute or so. If you want to come—"

"I'll come," Anderton said. He had no other choice. He had secured his tape, his proof, but he hadn't worked out any method of leaving. Gladly, he hurried after the slim figure of his wife as she strode from the block, through a side door and down a supply corridor, her heels clicking loudly in the deserted gloom.

"It's a good fast ship," she told him over her shoulder. "It's emergency-fueled— ready to go. I was going to supervise some of the teams."

VII

Behind the wheel of the high-velocity police cruiser, Anderton outlined what the minority report tape contained. Lisa listened without comment, her face pinched and strained, her hands clasped tensely in her lap. Below the ship, the war-ravaged rural countryside spread out like a relief map, the vacant regions between cities crater-pitted and dotted with the ruins of farms and small industrial plants.

"I wonder," she said, when he had finished, "how many times this has happened before."

"A minority report? A great many times."

"I mean, one precog misphased. Using the report of the others as data—superseding them." Her eyes dark and serious, she added, "Perhaps a lot of the people in the camps are like you."

"No," Anderton insisted. But he was beginning to feel uneasy about it, too. "I was in a position to see the card, to get a look at the report. That's what did it."

"But—" Lisa gestured significantly. "Perhaps all of them would have reacted that way. We could have told them the truth."

"It would have been too great a risk," he answered stubbornly.

Lisa laughed sharply. "Risk? Chance? Uncertainty? With precogs around?"

Anderton concentrated on steering the fast little ship. "This is a unique case," he repeated. "And we have an immediate problem. We can tackle the theoretical aspects later on. I have to get this tape to the proper people—before your bright young friend demolishes it."

"You're taking it to Kaplan?"

"I certainly am." He tapped the reel of tape which lay on the seat between them. "He'll be interested. Proof that his life isn't in danger ought to be of vital concern to him."

From her purse, Lisa shakily got out her cigarette case. "And you think he'll help you."

"He may—or he may not. It's a chance worth taking."

"How did you manage to go underground so quickly?" Lisa asked. "A completely effective disguise is difficult to obtain."

"All it takes is money," he answered evasively.

As she smoked, Lisa pondered. "Probably Kaplan will protect you," she said. "He's quite powerful."

"I thought he was only a retired general."

"Technically—that's what he is. But Witwer got out the dossier on him. Kaplan heads an unusual kind of exclusive veterans' organization. It's actually a kind of club, with a few restricted members. High officers only—an international class from both sides of the war. Here in New York they maintain a great mansion of a house, three glossy-paper publications, and occasional TV coverage that costs them a small fortune."

"What are you trying to say?"

"Only this. You've convinced me that you're innocent. I mean, it's obvious that you *won't* commit a murder. But you must realize now that the original report, the majority report, *was not a fake.* Nobody falsified it. Ed Witwer didn't create it. There's no plot against you, and there never was. If you're going to accept this minority report as genuine you'll have to accept the majority one, also."

Reluctantly, he agreed. "I suppose so."

"Ed Witwer," Lisa continued, "is acting in complete good faith. He really believes you're a potential criminal—and why not? He's got the majority report sitting on his desk, but you have that card folded up in your pocket."

"I destroyed it," Anderton said, quietly.

Lisa leaned earnestly toward him. "Ed Witwer isn't motivated by any desire to get your job," she said. "He's motivated by the same desire that has always dominated you. He believes in Precrime. He wants the system to continue. I've talked to him and I'm convinced he's telling the truth."

Anderton asked, "Do you want me to take this reel to Witwer? If I do—he'll destroy it."

"Nonsense," Lisa retorted. "The originals have been in his hands from the start. He could have destroyed them any time he wished."

"That's true," Anderton conceded. "Quite possibly he didn't know."

"Of course he didn't. Look at it this way. If Kaplan gets hold of that tape, the police will be discredited. Can't you see why? It would prove that the majority report was an error. Ed Witwer is absolutely right. You have to be taken in—if Precrime is to survive. You're thinking of your own safety. But think, for a moment, about the system." Leaning over, she stubbed out her cigarette and fumbled in her purse for another. "Which means more to you—your own personal safety or the existence of the system?"

"My safety," Anderton answered, without hesitation.

"You're positive?"

"If the system can survive only by imprisoning innocent people, then it deserves to be destroyed. My personal safety is important because I'm a human being. And furthermore—"

From her purse, Lisa got out an incredibly tiny pistol. "I believe," she told him huskily, "that I have my finger on the firing release. I've never used a weapon like this before. But I'm willing to try."

After a pause, Anderton asked: "You want me to turn the ship around? Is that it?"

"Yes, back to the police building. I'm sorry. If you could put the good of the system above your own selfish—"

"Keep your sermon," Anderton told her. "I'll take the ship back. But I'm not going to listen to your defense of a code of behavior no intelligent man could subscribe to."

Lisa's lips pressed into a thin, bloodless line. Holding the pistol tightly, she sat facing him, her eyes fixed intently on him as he swung the ship in a broad arc. A few loose articles rattled from the glove compartment as the little craft turned on a radical slant, one wing rising majestically until it pointed straight up.

Both Anderton and his wife were supported by the constraining metal arms of their seats. But not so the third member of the party.

Out of the corner of his eye, Anderton saw a flash of motion. A sound came simultaneously, the clawing struggle of a large man as he abruptly lost his footing and plunged into the reinforced wall of the ship. What followed happened quickly. Fleming scrambled instantly to his feet, lurching and wary, one arm lashing out for the woman's pistol. Anderton was too startled to cry out. Lisa turned, saw the man—and screamed. Fleming knocked the gun from her hand, sending it clattering to the floor.

Grunting, Fleming shoved her aside and retrieved the gun. "Sorry," he gasped, straightening up as best he could. "I thought she might talk more. That's why I waited."

"You were here when—" Anderton began—and stopped. It was obvious that Fleming and his men had kept him under surveillance. The existence of Lisa's ship had been duly noted and factored in, and while Lisa had debated whether it would be wise to fly him to safety, Fleming had crept into the storage compartment of the ship.

"Perhaps," Fleming said, "you'd better give me that reel of tape." His moist, clumsy fingers groped for it. "You're right—Witwer would have melted it down to a puddle."

"Kaplan, too?" Anderton asked numbly, still dazed by the appearance of the man.

"Kaplan is working directly with Witwer. That's why his name showed on line five of the card. Which one of them is the actual boss, we can't tell. Possibly neither." Fleming tossed the tiny pistol away and got out his own heavy-duty military weapon. "You pulled a real flub in taking off with this woman. I told you she was back of the whole thing."

"I can't believe that," Anderton protested. "If she—"

"You've got no sense. This ship was warmed up by Witwer's order. They wanted to fly you out of the building so that we couldn't get to you. With you on your own, separated from us, you didn't stand a chance."

A strange look passed over Lisa's stricken features. "It's not true," she whispered. "Witwer never saw this ship. I was going to supervise—"

"You almost got away with it," Fleming interrupted inexorably. "We'll be lucky if a police patrol ship isn't hanging on us. There wasn't time to check." He squatted down as he spoke, directly behind the woman's chair. "The first thing is to get this woman out of the way. We'll have to drag you completely out of this area. Page tipped off Witwer on your new disguise, and you can be sure it has been widely broadcast."

Still crouching, Fleming seized hold of Lisa. Tossing his heavy gun to Anderton, he expertly tilted her chin up until her temple was shoved back against the seat. Lisa clawed frantically at him; a thin, terrified wail rose in her throat. Ignoring her, Fleming closed his great hands around her neck and began relentlessly to squeeze.

"No bullet wound," he explained, gasping. "She's going to fall out—natural accident. It happens all the time. But in this case, her neck will be broken *first*."

It seemed strange that Anderton waited so long. As it was, Fleming's thick fingers were cruelly embedded in the woman's pale flesh before he lifted the butt of the heavy-duty pistol and brought it down on the back of Fleming's skull. The monstrous hands relaxed. Staggered, Fleming's head fell forward and he sagged against the wall of the ship. Trying feebly to collect himself, he began dragging his body upward. Anderton hit him again, this time above the left eye. He fell back, and lay still.

Struggling to breathe, Lisa remained for a moment huddled over, her body swaying back and forth. Then, gradually, the color crept back into her face.

"Can you take the controls?" Anderton asked, shaking her, his voice urgent.

"Yes, I think so." Almost mechanically she reached for the wheel. "I'll be all right. Don't worry about me."

"This pistol," Anderton said, "is Army ordnance issue. But it's not from the war. It's not of the useful new ones they've developed. I could be a long way off but there's just a chance—"

He climbed back to where Fleming lay spread out on the deck. Trying not to touch the man's head, he tore open his coat and rummaged in his pockets. A moment later Fleming's sweat-sodden wallet rested in his hands.

Tod Fleming, according to his identification, was an Army Major attached to the Internal Intelligence Department of Military Information. Among the various papers was a document signed by General Leopold Kaplan, stating that Fleming was under the special protection of his own group—the International Veterans' League.

Fleming and his men were operating under Kaplan's orders. The bread truck, the accident, had been deliberately rigged.

It meant that Kaplan had deliberately kept him out of police hands. The plan went back to the original contact in his home, when Kaplan's men had picked him up as he was packing. Incredulous, he realized what had really happened. Even then, they were making sure they got him before the police. From the start, it had been an elaborate strategy to make certain that Witwer would fail to arrest him.

"You were telling the truth," Anderton said to his wife, as he climbed back in the seat. "Can we get hold of Witwer?"

Mutely, she nodded. Indicating the communications circuit of the dashboard, she asked: "What—did you find?"

"Get Witwer for me. I want to talk to him as soon as I can. It's very urgent."

Jerkily, she dialed, got the closed-channel mechanical circuit, and raised police headquarters in New York. A visual panorama of petty police officials flashed by before a tiny replica of Ed Witwer's features appeared on the screen.

"Remember me?" Anderton asked him.

Witwer blanched. "Good God. What happened? Lisa, are you bringing him in?" Abruptly his eyes fastened on the gun in Anderton's hands. "Look," he said savagely, "don't do anything to her. Whatever you may think, she's not responsible."

"I've already found that out," Anderton answered. "Can you get a fix on us? We may need protection getting back."

"*Back!*" Witwer gazed at him unbelievingly. "You're coming in? You're giving yourself up?"

"I am, yes." Speaking rapidly, urgently, Anderton added, "There's something you must do immediately. Close off the monkey block. Make certain nobody gets in—Page or anyone else. *Especially Army people.*"

"Kaplan," the miniature image said.

"What about him?"

"He was here. He—he just left."

Anderton's heart stopped beating. "What was he doing?"

"Picking up data. Transcribing duplicates of our precog reports on you. He insisted he wanted them solely for his protection."

"Then he's already got it," Anderton said. "It's too late." Alarmed, Witwer almost shouted: "Just what do you mean? What's happening?"

"I'll tell you," Anderton said heavily, "when I get back to my office."

VIII

Witwer met him on the roof on the police building. As the small ship came to rest, a cloud of escort ships dipped their fins and sped off. Anderton immediately approached the blond-haired young man.

"You've got what you wanted," he told him. "You can lock me up, and send me to the detention camp. But that won't be enough."

Witwer's blue eyes were pale with uncertainty. "I'm afraid I don't understand—"

"It's not my fault. I should never have left the police building. Where's Wally Page?"

"We've already clamped down on him," Witwer replied. "He won't give us any trouble."

Anderton's face was grim.

"You're holding him for the wrong reason," he said. "Letting me into the monkey block was no crime. But passing information to Army is. You've had an Army plant working here." He corrected himself, a little lamely, "I mean, I have."

"I've called back the order on you. Now the teams are looking for Kaplan."

"Any luck?"

"He left here in an Army truck. We followed him, but the truck got into a militarized Barracks. Now they've got a big wartime R-3 tank blocking the street. It would be civil war to move it aside."

Slowly, hesitantly, Lisa made her way from the ship. She was still pale and shaken and on her throat an ugly bruise was forming.

"What happened to you?" Witwer demanded. Then he caught sight of Fleming's inert form lying spread out inside. Facing Anderton squarely, he said: "Then you've finally stopped pretending this is some conspiracy of mine."

"I have."

"You don't think I'm—" He made a disgusted face. "*Plotting* to get your job."

"Sure you are. Everybody is guilty of that sort of thing. And I'm plotting to keep it. But this is something else—and you're not responsible."

"Why do you assert," Witwer inquired, "that it's too late to turn yourself in? My God, we'll put you in the camp. The week will pass and Kaplan will still be alive."

"He'll be alive, yes," Anderton conceded. "But he can prove he'd be just as alive if I were walking the streets. He has the information that proves the majority report obsolete. He can break the precrime system." He finished, "Heads or tails, he wins—and we lose. The Army discredits us; their strategy paid off."

"But why are they risking so much? What exactly do they want?"

"After the Anglo-Chinese War, the Army lost out. It isn't what it was in the good old AFWA days. They ran the complete show, both military and domestic. And they did their own police work."

"Like Fleming," Lisa said faintly.

"After the war, the Westbloc was demilitarized. Officers like Kaplan were retired and discarded. Nobody likes that." Anderton grimaced. "I can sympathize with him. He's not the only one. But we couldn't keep on running things that way. We had to divide up the authority."

"You say Kaplan has won," Witwer said. "Isn't there anything we can do?"

"I'm not going to kill him. We know it and he knows it. Probably he'll come around and offer us some kind of deal. We'll continue to function, but the Senate will abolish our real pull. You wouldn't like that, would you?"

"I should say not," Witwer answered emphatically. "One of these days I'm going to be running this agency." He flushed. "Not immediately, of course."

Anderton's expression was somber. "It's too bad you publicized the majority report. If you had kept it quiet, we could cautiously draw it back in. But everybody's heard about it. We can't retract it now."

"I guess not," Witwer admitted awkwardly. "Maybe I—don't have this job down as neatly as I imagined."

"You will, in time. You'll be a good police officer. You believe in the status quo. But learn to take it easy." Anderton moved away from them. "I'm going to study the data tapes of the majority report. I want to find out exactly how I was supposed to kill Kaplan." Reflectively, he finished: "it might give me some ideas."

The data tapes of the precogs "Donna" and "Mike" were separately stored. Choosing the machinery responsible for the analysis of "Donna," he opened the protective shield and laid out the contents. As before, the code informed him which reels were relevant and in a moment he had the tape-transport mechanism in operation.

It was approximately what he had suspected. This was the material utilized by "Jerry"—the superseded time-path. In it Kaplan's Military Intelligence agents kidnapped Anderton as he drove home from work. Taken to Kaplan's villa, the organization GHQ of the International Veterans' League, Anderton was given an ultimatum: voluntarily disband the Precrime system or face open hostilities with Army.

In this discarded time-path, Anderton, as Police Commissioner, had turned to the Senate for support. No support was forthcoming. To avoid civil war, the Senate had ratified the dismemberment of the police system, and decreed a return to military law "to cope with the emergency." Taking a corps of fanatic police, Anderton had located Kaplan and shot him, along with other officials of the Veterans' League. Only Kaplan had died. The others had been patched up. And the coup had been successful.

This was "Donna." He rewound the tape and turned to the material previewed by "Mike." It would be identical; both procogs had combined to present a unified picture. "Mike" began as "Donna" had begun: Anderton had become aware of Kaplan's plot against the police. But something was wrong. Puzzled, he ran the tape back to the beginning. Incomprehensibly, it didn't jibe. Again he relayed the tape, listening intently.

The "Mike" report was quite different from the "Donna" report.

An hour later, he had finished his examination, put away the tapes, and left the monkey block. As soon as he emerged, Witwer asked, "What's the matter? I can see something's wrong."

"No," Anderton answered slowly, still deep in thought. "Not exactly wrong."

A sound came to his ears. He walked vaguely over to the window and peered out.

The street was crammed with people. Moving down the center lane was a four-column line of uniformed troops. Rifles, helmets... marching soldiers in their dingy wartime uniforms, carrying the cherished pennants of AFWA flapping in the cold afternoon wind.

"An Army rally," Witwer explained bleakly. "I was wrong. They're not going to make a deal with us. Why should they? Kaplan's going to make it public."

Anderton felt no surprise. "He's going to read the minority report?"

"Apparently. They're going to demand the Senate disband us, and take away our authority. They're going to claim we've been arresting innocent men—nocturnal police raids, that sort of thing. Rule by terror."

"You suppose the Senate will yield?"

Witwer hesitated. "I wouldn't want to guess."

"I'll guess," Anderton said. "They will. That business out there fits with what I learned downstairs. We've got ourselves boxed in and there's only one direction we can go. Whether we like it or not, we'll have to take it." His eyes had a steely glint.

Apprehensively, Witwer asked: "What is it?"

"Once I say it, you'll wonder why you didn't invent it. Very obviously, I'm going to have to fulfill the publicized report. I'm going to have to kill Kaplan. That's the only way we can keep them from discrediting us."

"But," Witwer said, astonished, "the majority report has been superseded."

"I can do it," Anderton informed him, but it's going to cost. You're familiar with the statutes governing first-degree murder?"

"Life imprisonment."

"At least. Probably, you could pull a few wires and get it commuted to exile. I could be sent to one of the colony planets, the good old frontier."

"Would you—prefer that?"

"Hell, no," Anderton said heartily. "But it would be the lesser of the two evils. And it's got to be done."

"I don't see how you can kill Kaplan."

Anderton got out the heavy-duty military weapon Fleming had tossed to him. "I'll use this."

"They won't stop you?"

"Why should they? They've got that minority report that says I've changed my mind."

"Then the minority report is incorrect?"

"No," Anderton said, "it's absolutely correct. But I'm going to murder Kaplan anyhow."

IX

He had never killed a man. He had never even seen a man killed. And he had been Police Commissioner for thirty years. For this generation, deliberate murder had died out. It simply didn't happen.

A police car carried him to within a block of the Army rally. There, in the shadows of the back seat, he painstakingly examined the pistol Fleming had provided him. It seemed to be intact. Actually, there was no doubt of the outcome. He was absolutely certain of what would happen within the next half-hour. Putting the pistol back together, he opened the door of the parked car and stepped warily out.

Nobody paid the slightest attention to him. Surging masses of people pushed eagerly forward, trying to get within hearing distance of the rally. Army uniforms predominated and at the perimeter of the cleared area, a line of tanks and major weapons was displayed—formidable armament still in production.

Army had erected a metal speaker's stand and ascending steps. Behind the stand hung the vast AFWA banner, emblem of the combined powers that had fought in the war. By a curious corrosion of time, the AFWA Veterans' League included officers from the wartime enemy. But a general was a general and fine distinctions had faded over the years.

Occupying the first rows of seats sat the high brass of the AFWA command. Behind them came junior commissioned officers. Regimental banners swirled in a variety of colors and symbols. In fact, the occasion had taken on the aspect of a festive pageant. On the raised stand itself sat stern-faced dignitaries of the Veterans' League, all of them tense with expectancy. At the extreme edges, almost unnoticed, waited a few police units, ostensibly to keep order. Actually, they were informants making observations. If order were kept, the Army would maintain it.

The late-afternoon wind carried the muffled booming of many people packed tightly together. As Anderton made his way through the dense mob he was engulfed by the solid presence of humanity. An eager sense of anticipation held everybody rigid. The crowd seemed to sense that something spectacular was on the way. With difficulty, Anderton forced his way past the rows of seats and over to the tight knot of Army officials at the edge of the platform.

Kaplan was among them. But he was now General Kaplan.

The vest, the gold pocket watch, the cane, the conservative business suit—all were gone. For this event, Kaplan had got his old uniform from its mothballs. Straight and impressive, he stood surrounded by what had been his general staff. He wore his service bars, his metals, his boots, his decorative short-sword, and his visored cap. It was amazing how transformed a bald man became under the stark potency of an officer's peak and visored cap.

Noticing Anderton, General Kaplan broke away from the group and strode to where the younger man was standing. The expression on his thin, mobile countenance showed how incredulously glad he was to see the Commissioner of Police.

"This is a surprise," he informed Anderton, holding out his small gray-gloved hand. "It was my impression you had been taken in by the acting Commissioner."

"I'm still out," Anderton answered shortly, shaking hands. "After all, Witwer has that same reel of tape." He indicated the package Kaplan clutched in his steely fingers and met the man's gaze confidently.

In spite of his nervousness, General Kaplan was in good humor. "This is a great occasion for the Army," he revealed. "You'll be glad to hear I'm going to give the public a full account of the spurious charge brought against you."

"Fine," Anderton answered noncommittally.

"It will be made clear that you were unjustly accused." General Kaplan was trying to discover what Anderton knew. "Did Fleming have an opportunity to acquaint you with the situation?"

"To some degree," Anderton replied. "You're going to read only the minority report? That's all you've got there?"

"I'm going to compare it to the majority report." General Kaplan signalled an aide and a leather briefcase was produced. "Everything is here—all the evidence we need," he said. "You don't mind being an example, do you? Your case symbolizes the unjust arrests of countless individuals." Stiffly, General Kaplan examined his wristwatch. "I must begin. Will you join me on the platform?"

"Why?"

Coldly, but with a kind of repressed vehemence, General Kaplan said: "So they can see the living proof. You and I together—the killer and his victim. Standing side by side, exposing the whole sinister fraud which the police have been operating."

"Gladly," Anderton agreed. "What are we waiting for?"

Disconcerted, General Kaplan moved toward the platform. Again, he glanced uneasily at Anderton, as if visibly wondering why he had appeared and what he really knew. His uncertainty grew as Anderton willingly mounted the steps of the platform and found himself a seat directly beside the speaker's podium.

"You fully comprehend what I'm going to be saying?" General Kaplan demanded. "The exposure will have considerable repercussions. It may cause the Senate to reconsider the basic validity of the Precrime system."

"I understand," Anderton answered, arms folded. "Let's go."

A hush had descended on the crowd. But there was a restless, eager stirring when General Kaplan obtained the briefcase and began arranging his material in front of him.

"The man sitting at my side," he began, in a clean, clipped voice, "is familiar to you all. You may be surprised to see him, for until recently he was described by the police as a dangerous killer."

The eyes of the crowd focussed on Anderton. Avidly, they peered at the only potential killer they had ever been privileged to see at close range.

"Within the last few hours, however," General Kaplan continued, "the police order for his arrest has been cancelled; because former Commissioner Anderton voluntarily gave himself up? No, that is not strictly accurate. He is sitting here. He has not given himself up, but the police are no longer interested in him. John Allison Anderton is innocent of any crime in the past, present, and future. The allegations against him were patent frauds, diabolical distortions of a contaminated penal system based on a false premise—a vast, impersonal engine of destruction grinding men and women to their doom."

Fascinated, the crowd glanced from Kaplan to Anderton. Everyone was familiar with the basic situation.

"Many men have been seized and imprisoned under the so-called prophylactic precrime structure," General Kaplan continued, his voice gaining feeling and strength. "Accused not of crimes they have committed, *but of crimes they will commit.* It is asserted that these men, if allowed to remain free, will at some future time commit felonies."

"But there can be no valid knowledge about the future. As soon as precognitive information is obtained, *it cancels itself out.* The assertion that this man will commit a future crime is paradoxical. The very act of possessing this data renders it spurious. In every case, without exception, the report of the three police precogs has invalidated their own data. If no arrests had been made, there would still have been no crimes committed."

Anderton listened idly, only half hearing the words. The crowd, however, listened with great interest. General Kaplan was now gathering up a summary made from the minority report. He explained what it was and how it had come into existence.

From his coat pocket, Anderton slipped out his gun and held it in his lap. Already, Kaplan was laying aside the minority report, the precognitive material obtained from "Jerry." His lean, bony fingers groped for the summary of first, "Donna," and after that, "Mike."

"This was the original majority report," he explained. "The assertion, made by the first two precogs, that Anderton would commit a murder. Now here is the automatically invalidated material. I shall read it to you." He whipped out his rimless glasses, fitted them to his nose, and started slowly to read.

A queer expression appeared on his face. He halted, stammered, and abruptly broke off. The papers fluttered from his hands. Like a cornered animal, he spun, crouched, and dashed from the speaker's stand.

For an instant his distorted face flashed past Anderton. On his feet now, Anderton raised the gun, stepped quickly forward, and fired. Tangled up in the rows of feet projecting from the chairs that filled the platform, Kaplan gave a single shrill shriek of agony and fright. Like a ruined bird, he tumbled, fluttering and flailing, from the platform to the ground below. Anderton stepped to the railing, but it was already over.

Kaplan, as the majority report had asserted, was dead. His thin chest was a smoking cavity of darkness, crumbling ash that broke loose as the body lay twitching.

Sickened, Anderton turned away, and moved quickly between the rising figures of stunned Army officers. The gun, which he still held, guaranteed that he would not be interfered with. He leaped from the platform and edged into the chaotic mass of people at its base. Stricken, horrified, they struggled to see what had happened. The incident, occurring before their very eyes, was incomprehensible. It would take time for acceptance to replace blind terror.

At the periphery of the crowd, Anderton was seized by the waiting police. "You're lucky to get out," one of them whispered to him as the car crept cautiously ahead.

"I guess I am," Anderton replied remotely. He settled back and tried to compose himself. He was trembling and dizzy. Abruptly, he leaned forward and was violently sick.

"The poor devil," one of the cops murmured sympathetically.

Through the swirls of misery and nausea, Anderton was unable to tell whether the cop was referring to Kaplan or to himself.

X

Four burly policemen assisted Lisa and John Anderton in the packing and loading of their possessions. In fifty years, the ex-Commissioner of Police had accumulated a vast collection of material goods. Somber and pensive, he stood watching the procession of crates on their way to the waiting trucks.

By truck they would go directly to the field—and from there to Centaurus X by inter-system transport. A long trip for an old man. But he wouldn't have to make it back.

"There goes the second from the last crate," Lisa declared, absorbed and preoccupied by the task. In sweater and slacks, she roamed through the barren rooms, checking on last-minute details. "I suppose we won't be able to use these new atronic appliances. They're still using electricity on Centten."

"I hope you don't care too much," Anderton said.

"We'll get used to it," Lisa replied, and gave him a fleeting smile. "Won't we?"

"I hope so. You're positive you'll have no regrets? If I thought—"

"No regrets," Lisa assured him. Now suppose you help me with this crate."

As they boarded the lead truck, Witwer drove up in a patrol car. He leaped out and hurried up to them, his face looking strangely haggard. "Before you take off," he said to Anderton, "you'll have to give me a break-down on the situation with the precogs. I'm getting inquiries from the Senate. They want to find out if the middle report, the retraction, was an error—or what." Confusedly, he finished: "I still can't explain it. The minority report was wrong, wasn't it?"

"Which minority report?" Anderton inquired, amused.

Witwer blinked. "Then that *is* it. I might have known."

Seated in the cabin of the truck, Anderton got out his pipe and shook tobacco into it. With Lisa's lighter he ignited the tobacco and began operations. Lisa had gone back to the house, wanting to be sure nothing vital had been overlooked.

"There were three minority reports," he told Witwer, enjoying the young man's confusion. Someday, Witwer would learn not to wade into situations he didn't fully understand. Satisfaction was Anderton's final emotion. Old and worn-out as he was, he had been the only one to grasp the real nature of the problem.

"The three reports were consecutive," he explained. "The first was 'Donna.'

In that time-path, Kaplan told me of the plot, and I promptly murdered him. 'Jerry,' phased slightly ahead of 'Donna,' used her report as data. He factored in my knowledge of the report. In that, the second time-path, all I wanted to do was to keep my job. It wasn't Kaplan I wanted to kill. It was my own position and life I was interested in."

"And 'Mike' was the third report? That came *after* the minority report?" Witwer corrected himself. "I mean, it came last?"

"'Mike' was the last of the three, yes. Faced with the knowledge of the first report, I had decided *not* to kill Kaplan. That produced report two. But faced with *that* report, I changed my mind back. Report two, situation two, was the situation Kaplan wanted to create. It was to the advantage of the police to recreate position one. And by that time I was thinking of the police. I had figured out what Kaplan was doing. The third report invalidated the second one in the same way the second one invalidated the first. That brought us back where we started from."

Lisa came over, breathless and gasping. "Let's go—we're all finished here." Lithe and agile, she ascended the metal rungs of the truck and squeezed in beside her husband and the driver. The latter obediently started up his truck and the others followed.

"Each report was different," Anderton concluded. "Each was unique. But two of them agreed on one point. If left free, *I would kill Kaplan.* That created the illusion of a majority report. Actually, that's all it was—an illusion. 'Donna' and 'Mike' previewed the same event—but in two totally different time-paths, occurring under totally different situations. 'Donna' and 'Jerry,' the so-called minority report and half of the majority report, were incorrect. Of the three, 'Mike' was correct—since no report came after his, to invalidate him. That sums it up."

Anxiously, Witwer trotted along beside the truck, his smooth, blond face creased with worry. "Will it happen again? Should we overhaul the set-up?"

"It can happen in only one circumstance," Anderton said. "My case was unique, since I had access to the data. It *could* happen again—but only to the next Police Commissioner. So watch your step." Briefly, he grinned, deriving no inconsiderable comfort from Witwer's strained expression. Beside him, Lisa's red lips twitched and her hand reached out and closed over his.

"Better keep your eyes open," he informed young Witwer. "It might happen to you at any time."

JUST DO IT

by Heather Lindsley

Heather Lindsley's short fiction has appeared in *Asimov's Science Fiction, Greatest Uncommon Denominator,* and *Strange Horizons.* This story first appeared in *The Magazine of Fantasy & Science Fiction,* was reprinted in *Year's Best SF #12* and *Escape Pod,* and has been translated into Polish and Romanian. Lindsley is also a graduate of the Clarion Writers' Workshop.

As America's largest chemical company, DuPont is best known for its work creating fibers like nylon, Kevlar, and Teflon... and for developing CFCs, the refrigerants responsible for the hole in the ozone layer. But beyond its products, DuPont has given society a special gift. In 1935, DuPont adopted the slogan "Better Things for Better Living...Through Chemistry." Other advertisers and cultural figures immediately jumped on this slogan, creating the infamous phrase *better living through chemistry.*

Chemistry has a bad rap these days. The late twentieth-century is riddled with environmental and health disasters stemming from human abuse of chemistry. From thalidomide babies to endangered eagles, it's difficult to see a good side of the chemical industry.

And our next tale turns a scathing eye upon it. Lindsley says "it's about desire and how easy that is to manipulate. But I'll go a bit further and say I was also thinking about the ongoing conflict between doing the right thing and doing the comfortable, pleasurable thing. It's about having a compelling excuse to take the easier, ethically questionable path. To just do it and blame somebody else's chemical."

Sometimes the only warning is a flash of sun on the lens of a sniper's scope. Today I'm lucky enough to catch the mistake.

Funny, I think as I duck down behind the nearest parked car, I don't *feel* lucky.

The car is a tiny thing, an ultra enviro-friendly Honda Righteous painted an unambiguous green. Good for the planet, bad for cover. Ahead there's an H5 so massive and red I first take it for a fire truck. The selfish bastard parked illegally, blocking an alley, and for that I'm grateful.

I take a quick look at the roof of the building across the street before starting my dash to the Hummer. Halfway there a woman in plastic devil horns steps into my attempt to dodge her and her clipboard.

"Would-you-care-to-sign-our-petiton-in-favor-of-the-effort-against-end-ing-the-Florida-blockade?" Damn, she's good. She sounds like she trained with a preBay auctioneer.

I feint left and dart right, putting her between me and the Shooter and countering, "I-already-signed-it-thanks!" so she won't follow. It's not the first lie I've told today, and it's not likely to be the last.

Temporarily safe behind the Hummer, I lean against the heavily tinted windows of the far back seat door, glad to be standing upright but panting and sweating and wishing I wasn't wearing the black jumpsuit I reserve for funerals and job interviews. Nanofiber, my ass—it can't even keep up with a little physical activity on a hot April day.

I start the long walk toward the front bumper, figuring I'll duck into the alley and continue on my way one block over. It seems like a good plan until another Shooter steps out of the alley.

This one has a pistol. I'd go cross-eyed if I tried to look down the barrel.

"Oh, come on," I say, backing away slowly. "Not the face."

He dips the barrel down a bit. I sigh and start pulling the zipper at the high neck of my jumpsuit in the same direction. I stop just shy of revealing cleavage—I'll get shot in the face before I give this punk an eyeful.

He shrugs and fires.

"You little bastard!" I yell at his retreating back as I pull out the dart out of my forehead. "I want your license number!"

Of course he doesn't bother to stop. They never do.

The itching starts almost immediately, and I reflexively reach up and touch the bump above my eyes. I know better than to scratch it, but I do anyway. The scratching releases a flood of chemicals that create a powerful and specific food craving. I brace myself.

French fries. French fries from the den of the evil clown, where they don't even pretend to use potatoes anymore. I hate those french fries, so golden and crispy on the outside, so moist and fluffy on the inside—

No no no no no, I do not want them.

I manage to get past the first shadow the clown casts on my route with relative calm, but by the second the itching is more intense and all I can imagine are french fries. Disgusting, nasty, tasty, delicious french fries.

This is not the way to walk into a job interview.

The site of my two o'clock appointment looms in the office tower ahead... right behind a third opportunity to relieve the craving. I keep moving, trying not to think about how well the diabetes-inducing corn syrupy sweet ketchup complements the blood pressure-raising salty savor of the fries.

I make a full circuit through the revolving doors of the office building before going back toward the object of my involuntary, chemically-enhanced desire.

The food odors pounce immediately and I can almost feel the molecules sticking to my clothes. Even if I turn around now I'll smell like fast food.

"Let's get this over with," I say unnecessarily to the credit scanner, staring it down until it greenlights my ability to pay for food I don't really want. None of the automat compartments contain fries, which is unusual, so I punch hard at a picture of french fries on the order panel. The dents in the panel tell me I'm not the only customer who feels antagonistic about buying food here.

It shouldn't take more than a minute or two for the fries to appear in a compartment, so when they don't I start pounding on the automat.

"Hey, hurry it up!" I yell, scratching furiously at the bump on my forehead.

The back door of the empty fry compartment slides open. An eye stares out at me.

"What?"

"Fries. I need fries."

"We're out of fries," the voice behind the automat says.

"How can you be out of fries? You've got Shooters out there making people crave the damned things!"

"That's why we're out."

"Doesn't the head office coordinate this stuff?"

The eye blinks twice and the door slides shut.

It's 1:47, enough time to go back to the second place if I hurry. But I don't hurry. I pace in the street, muttering to myself like a lunatic. It's almost five minutes before I quit trying to control the craving and dash back the way I came.

I give the next credit scanner an especially dirty look, then yank open the one compartment with fries. I stop only to pump blobs of ketchup from the dispenser. On my way out I pass an old man scratching his arm as he raves through an open compartment, "How can you be out of fish sandwiches?!"

"Try the one on Third and Pine," I say around a mouthful of fries.

CraveTech's offices are both plush and haphazard, the combined result of a record-breaking IPO and the latest design fad: early dot-com retro. I arrive sweaty, greasy, nauseated, and thoroughly pissed off. I smile at the receptionist anyway, a fashionably sulky blonde boy seated in a vintage Aeron chair behind a desk made out of two sawhorses topped with an old door and a crystal vase.

"Alex Monroe. I have a two o'clock with Mr. Avery."

"Two o'clock?" he says pointedly. It's 2:02. "Have a seat. Something to drink while you're waiting?"

"Water please." I'll probably retain every ounce. Damn salty french fries. There are pills that reduce bloating, of course—they sell them out of the same automat—but I wouldn't hand over any more of my money.

I've just taken my first sip when a young man pops out of the office. He looks like a typical startup manager: handsome, well-dressed, and almost certainly in over his head.

"Ms. Monroe, welcome!" He bounds up to me, hand extended. During the handshake he nods toward my forehead. "Ah, I see you use our products!" He laughs heartily at his own joke. I laugh back. I want this job.

"It's a wonderful time to be in chemical advertising, Ms. Monroe," he says, shepherding me into his office. I notice he has a proper desk. "We have some exciting deals in the works. Exciting, exciting deals."

"Really?" I say, distracted by the fry-lump in my stomach.

"Oh, yes. Now that the Supreme Court has reversed most of those class action suits, Shooters don't have to be stealthy. We've had to discontinue the tobacco lines for the time being, but otherwise it's open season on consumers."

I make another effort to join in his laughter, and reaching toward the bump on my head add, "It certainly is effective."

"Indeed." He smiles like he loaded the dart himself. "So," he says, picking up my resume, "I see your background is in print."

"Yes, but I've done some work in fragrance influence, and I'm very interested in chemical advertising's potential."

"Well, it is a growing field, plenty of room for trailblazers, especially with campaigns as impressive as these." He sets my resume aside. "And of course we still have quite a lot of synergy with print." He pulls an inch-long Crave dart out of a drawer and drops it on the desk between us. I resist the urge to cringe at the sight of the wretched thing.

"What do you see?" he asks.

I want to say *a menace*, but instead I tap the delivery barrel and give the context-appropriate answer. "Unused ad space."

Suddenly he's a schoolmaster who has finally found a bright pupil in a classroom full of dunces.

"Exactly, Ms. Monroe. *Exactly*. No square millimeter wasted, that's what I say." He leans across the table and whispers conspiratorially, "We're looking at co-branding an AOL-Time-Warner-Starbucks Lattepalooza Crave with a Forever Fitness session discount."

"Wow."

"Yes. Coupons on the darts. How does that grab you?"

"Coupons."

"Tiny coupons, like the ones on swizzle sticks. Can't you just see it? You get Stuck, so you want the product, but you're also concerned about your weight. The coupon helps. The coupon tells you the provider cares about your concerns. It tells you they understand." He leans back in his chair, my cue to speak.

"Interesting. But I'd go log-in rebate rather than immediate discount. Same message, same coverage, easier on the bottom line."

He leans forward again. "I like the way you think, Ms. Monroe."

I hate meeting at Sandra's house—her cats are constantly trying to climb up on my lap, I suspect because they know I'm allergic to them. But Sandra is my best friend from college, and also my cell leader, so I usually end up here at least once a week.

"Whoa, right in the forehead," she says when she opens the door.

"Yeah, and that's an ugly one on your neck."

"That's a hickey."

"Oh, uh, sorry. Or congratulations, I guess."

"Eh," she shrugs, heading to the kitchen.

I follow. "Um, aren't you a little old to be getting those?"

"Maybe, but Liam's not too old to be giving them." Sandra has a taste for idealistic young revolutionaries.

She starts to make herbal tea, and I know enough not to ask for coffee instead.

We take the tea to the lumpy, cat-hair covered futon in the living room. "How'd the interview go?"

"Shaky start. Getting Stuck really threw me off. But I did manage to laugh at his jokes, and, sad to say, I'm more or less qualified."

"You do speak their language." Sandra likes to remind me that I've only recently stopped being part of the problem. "So where do things stand?" she asks.

"He said he only had one more interview, and he'd call to let me know by the end of the week."

"Did you pick up anything while you were there?"

"Not much about the next formulas. AOL-Time-Warner-Starbucks is definitely in now, but that's old news."

"But you think you can get access? The job's in the right division?"

"Close enough. Marketing's always looking over R&D's shoulder. It won't seem strange for me to be poking around."

"What should I tell our counter-formula development contact?"

"Well, assuming I get the job, and assuming I can start right away, three weeks. Maybe four. It'll depend on their security."

She seems satisfied with this answer. "What about Plan B? How's the Mata Hari routine working on our favorite evil genius?"

"He's not evil—he's just oblivious."

She raises an eyebrow at this. "Dangerously oblivious."

"Yes, I know." I concentrate on picking cat hair off my clothes. "It's going fine. Fourth date tonight. Expensive place. I should get going, actually." I rise and head for the door. She stops me and stares pointedly at my forehead.

"Alex, don't forget—he's the enemy." I consciously abort an eye-roll and substitute a smile.

"Dangerously oblivious genius equals enemy. Check." I give her a little wave as I step outside.

"Which restaurant are you going to?" Sandra asks from the doorway.

"Prima."

Her brow furrows. "Don't they serve real meat?"

"Oh yes—and I'll be ordering a steak," I say, taking a moment to enjoy her disapproving look.

"I'll have the porterhouse. Rare, please."

"Make that two," Tom says. "Mine medium."

"Very good," the server says. "I'll be back with the first course shortly." He gives us each a prim little four-star nod as he leaves.

I put my elbows on the white linen tablecloth and rest my chin on my interlaced fingers. "I'm not sure I can ever love a man who would ruin a perfectly good steak."

Tom leans into the candlelight, too. "And I'm not sure I can trust a woman who likes her meat nearly raw."

"I guess we'll just have to stay together for the sex."

"And the children." He raises his glass to his lips.

"I'm not having sex with children, you pervert."

He chokes on his wine and grabs his napkin. I have to give him points for not looking around to make sure we haven't been overheard.

"If I'd known you'd be shooting wine out of your nose I'd have suggested a Merlot," I say as innocently as I can manage.

"How," he coughs, "did I end up in such hazardous company?"

We met accidentally at a Better Living Through Chemistry Expo sponsored by Dow-DuPont-Bristol-Myers-Squibb-PepsiCo six weeks ago.

Actually, we met at a hotel bar during the expo.

I was running my report through my head, thinking about the companies that had the most bad news for humanity in the works. He sat down a couple of barstools away. We traded a little eye contact and a few shy smiles in the dim light.

"So which of these evil bastards are you representing?"

He laughed. "CraveTech."

"Ooh, a startup. Exciting."

"Yeah. What about you?"

"Me? I'm with an underground group whose goal is to liberate people from the tyranny of corporate chemical dependence."

"Huh. Underground, you said?"

"Yeah, we're not very good at that part." I was already starting to like his laugh, especially since it came so easily. "Actually, I freelance in marketing."

"Anything I might have seen?"

"Maybe the *Junior Chemical Engineer* campaign."

"'Big Molecules for Little Hands.'"

"That's the one," I said, suddenly aware I was twisting a lock of my hair around my finger. I reached for my drink.

"Wasn't there a massive judgment against them in one of the last big class action suits?"

"No, that was Union-Pfizer's *My First Exothermic Reaction*. Ours were just repackaged *Make Your Own Cologne!* kits left over from the last Queer Eye reunion tour."

"Clever." He got up and closed the barstool gap between us.

"Despicable. So what do you do at CraveTech?"

"I run the place."

"That's funny," I said, laughing until he slid the nearest candle closer. I squinted at a face I almost recognized from the cover of *Time-Newsweek*.

"Where are your glasses?"

"Contacts tonight."

"You lose the glasses when you don't want to be recognized."

"Yeah, sort of a—"

"Reverse Clark Kent thing."

He smiled. "Yeah," and I could feel his geeky little heart reaching out for mine.

Tonight he's wearing his glasses. He looks cute in them.

"Of course, the really exciting work is in BeMod," he says, slicing into his steak.

"BeMod?" This seems like a good time to play dumb.

"Behavior Modification. The current dart formulas can make you want to ingest something—food, smoke, whatever. That's easy."

"Easy for you," I say, raising my eyebrows toward the bump that's only just beginning to subside.

At least he has the grace to look embarrassed. "Yeah, uh, sorry about that. But once we ship the darts to the providers, it's pretty much out of CraveTech's hands. I get Stuck sometimes, too, you know."

I spell the word *oblivious* in my head over and over, until I lose the urge to punch him. It takes four this time, so I miss hearing yet another version of the "If It Wasn't CraveTech It Would Be Someone Else" speech.

"…anyway, it's all just using the chemistry of cravings," he's saying when I'm calm enough to tune back in. "The fact that you have to buy whatever it is you're craving is an indirect consequence."

"An awfully profitable indirect consequence." I stab at a carrot.

"Yes, but see, that's the thing: the next big leap in the field is to skip straight to the buying part. We've been doing some promising work with what happens to brain chemistry when avid consumers watch successful commercials."

"So you're trying to synthesize a drug that will make people go out and buy MaxWhite toothpaste."

"Or a pair of NeoNikes. Or an H5."

"Oh my God."

He unleashes his Boy Genius grin. "Yeah. Pretty cool, huh?"

I report for my first day at CraveTech two weeks later. No one mentions that I'm dating the CEO, so I assume it hasn't gotten out. Still, I make a point of flirting back—and being overheard—when the cute young thing from Amazon-FedEx-

Kinko's makes her rounds.

I'd told Tom up front that I was applying for the job. He was encouraging, but made it clear he would keep his nose out of it and leave things to Avery. I never see Tom around the marketing department—he seems more interested in making things than selling them, which I find endearing. If only he weren't making such awful things.

I flop down on Sandra's futon, narrowly missing a cat.

She puts mugs of tea on the table while I fish an envelope out of my shoulder bag. When she sits down next to me I place the envelope in her hands.

"Information," I say, "and lots of it." She takes the data card out of the envelope and peers at it as if she can actually make sense of what it contains.

"This is all of them?"

"All the formulas set to come out over the next six months. I've included a release schedule so you'll know which ones will be hitting the street first."

"The counter-formula team is gonna love this."

"They'd better. That little card represents a month of my life spent smiling at banalities and pretending to care about other people's kids."

"So you're ready to quit." She sounds relieved.

"I'd love to, but I don't think I can just yet. I still haven't found anything about this BeMod stuff. Tom keeps going on about it, but as far as I can tell it hasn't surfaced in R&D."

"Isn't it weird that he seems so serious about BeMod but you can't find it at CraveTech?"

I laugh. "So you think he has some other lab where he's developing chemicals he can use to rule the world?"

"Maybe not rule the world…just make a shitload of money, which is close enough."

"You're serious, aren't you?"

She shifts uncomfortably on the futon. "It just seems like he's been awfully specific about this BeMod stuff, and it hasn't turned up where you'd expect it."

"So what are you suggesting?"

"I think it's time you broke up with him, and maybe quit CraveTech, too."

"But if this BeMod stuff is in development somewhere, we'll need to get our hands on it and start on a counter-formula as soon as we can."

"That's true."

"And how do we do that if I don't keep seeing him?"

The cell leader finally overcomes the college buddy. "Just be careful. Don't get too attached to him."

I pick up the data card, two gig worth of corporate espionage. "Does this seem like I'm too attached?"

I arrive at Tom's place in a foul mood. He doesn't notice. *Dangerously oblivious.*

We're still in the foyer when he starts in about BeMod.

"I read a fascinating study on endorphins today. Apparently you can stimulate—"

"Can we please talk about something other than biochemistry?" I drop my bag on the floor.

He looks surprised and a little hurt. "I'm sorry, I didn't realize I was boring you."

"You're not boring me." I reach for his hand as we head into the living room. "I just think we have more in common than an interest in BeMods and DC Comics." I haven't gotten around to telling him I prefer Marvel.

He stops and pulls me back toward him. "I love you."

"See, there you go—I love me, too. Something else we have in common."

"Oh for God's sake," he sighs, collapsing on his down-filled couch. "I'm trying to be serious."

"I know." I sit down next to him. "I'm sorry. I just need a little more time."

"Okay. A little more time," he says, kissing my forehead and then my neck.

It's so easy to kiss him back.

The next time I go to Sandra's, she has a data card for me.

"What's this?"

"A press release. It says CraveTech is voluntarily recalling all darts because internal studies have shown them to trigger heart attacks and strokes in a small but substantial segment of the population. We need you to send it out from the CraveTech network."

I hand the card back to her. "The media will figure out it's bogus."

"Not before the stock plummets. We're set up to trigger a small drop, and the release will do the rest."

"You know I won't be able to go back there after I send it. They'll trace it to me."

"I know." I stare hard at her. She doesn't flinch.

"And I'll have to break up with Tom."

"You need to do that anyway, Alex. It's been almost six months. That's too long. It's longer than you've dated anyone for real."

"Sandra, sending this press release is just throwing a brick through a window. It's meaningless in the long run. They'll replace the window. The stock price will readjust."

"But it will slow them down."

"Sandra, if it isn't CraveTech, it'll be…"

"What?"

"Nothing." I take the card.

"You'll send the release?"

"I'll send it."

I put the few personal items that decorated my cubicle in a gym bag. I never had a picture of Tom on my desk. That would have been indiscreet.

The press release glows on my work station, one twitch away from every major news outlet and the most incendiary of the minor ones. If I had a picture of Tom, I might have stared at it for a while, maybe even whispered *Sorry* to it.

But I don't, so I just flick Send.

I've come to break up with him. "You're early," he says when he greets me at the door. "I've planned something special." I follow him out to the deck.

"For what?"

"Our six-month anniversary." There's a cloth-covered table and dining chairs, a silver champagne bucket on a stand. "In another twenty minutes there'll be a sunset, too." He says this like he paid for it. "But, you know," he looks oddly apologetic, "you're early."

"Tom, I'm sorry…we're not going to have a six-month anniversary."

I expect anything from him but the crooked Boy Genius smile I love so much. "This isn't about the press release, is it?"

I sit, a little inelegantly in my surprise.

"What press release?"

He laughs. "This conversation will probably be less awkward if I just tell you I had all your CraveTech e-mails routed to me before they went out."

Ah.

"I was a little surprised that you actually sent it, but I do understand. I appreciate your beliefs. I love you for them—I want you to know that." He pours us each a glass of champagne. "And besides, you really helped me out with those counter-formulas."

I pick up my glass then set it down again. "Helped you out?"

"Absolutely. My people made a couple of tweaks, though. Your group's design wasn't very cost effective at the ten thousand unit level."

"Wait, wait, wait. *You're* going to manufacture our counter-formulas?"

"Oh, yes. The marketing campaign has been in development at a subsidiary company for weeks now. And the profit projections—Alex, you wouldn't believe it. Apparently people really, really hate the craving darts." Oh, my oblivious darling. "They'll pay twice the cost of the actual food just to make the cravings go away."

"But they won't have to. We'll be giving away the counter-formula for free."

"Funny thing about that—the research shows people would rather pay a couple of bucks to get the antidote from a familiar, trusted source than from a pack of anarchists with a habit of blowing up buses."

"Blowing up buses? What're you—"

"Oh, it's a little something we're planning for the fourth quarter. Disinformation campaign. It's ready for implementation now, but we think everyone will be more inclined to actively hate you during the holidays."

"Hate me?" I stand up and start backing toward the door.

"Well, not you, your group. They'll love you, Alex. You'll be managing my charitable organizations, giving away money to worthy causes right and left. People love that. And they'll love me. People love CEOs whose wives do that kind of stuff."

"Wives?" He brings out a pistol and fires a dart into my neck. I pull out the dart and drop it on the ground.

"What was in that thing?"

He answers my question with a question as he pops open a little black velvet box.

"Alex, will you marry me?"

"Tom, you sneaky little—" I say, lost between admiration and horror. "Will I *marry* you?"

Of course I will.

Tom Jr. has a hard time waking up in the morning. He gets it from me, not his father, who is always up before the crack of dawn, especially since the BeMod wide dispersal aerosol went into production.

"Tommy, wake up!" I call out toward his room. There's only a muffled grumbling in response.

I walk up to his doorway. "Really, Tommy, it's time to get going. You'll be late for school."

He rolls over, groaning, but doesn't make a move to get up. I unholster my parenting gun and shift the round in the chamber from *Go to Bed* to *Wake Up*.

"Get up, Tommy," I say as I draw a bead on his sleep-tousled head. "I'm not going to tell you again."

HARRISON BERGERON

by Kurt Vonnegut, Jr.

Kurt Vonnegut, Jr. was the legendary author of the dystopian novel *Player Piano*, and many other classic novels, including *Slaughterhouse-Five*, *Cat's Cradle*, *Breakfast of Champions*, and *Galapagos*. His short fiction has appeared in everything from *The Magazine of Fantasy & Science Fiction* and *If* to *Playboy*, *Collier's*, and *Ladies' Home Journal*. *Look at the Birdie*, a collection of previously unpublished short fiction, was released in 2009. Other collections include *Welcome to the Monkey House*, *Bagombo Snuff Box*, and *Armageddon in Retrospect*. Vonnegut died in 2007.

Man o' War is a legend among race horses. He won all but one. He set record after record for speed. His strength and power was so legendary that as a three-year-old racer, he carried as much as 138 pounds on his back, giving a handicap of thirty-two pounds over the least-loaded contender. It took a lot to level the playing field when Man o' War was racing on it.

It might have been fair to pile all that weight the great horse's back when he was on the race course, but imagine how fast he could have run without it. If he could have run free, he would have sped by like a freight train. He would have been so beautiful it would take your breath away.

In our next story, we give you a society that has created a system of handicaps for all its citizens. Everyone must be reduced to the lowest common denominator. It's a society where beautiful women go masked and ballerinas are weighted to ground.

It asks: in the pursuit of equality for all, do we guarantee inequity for most?

The year was 2081, and everybody was finally equal. They weren't only equal before God and the law, they were equal every which way. Nobody was smarter than anybody else; nobody was better looking than anybody else; nobody was stronger or quicker than anybody else. All this equality was due to the 211th, 212th, and 213th Amendments to the Constitution, and to the unceasing vigilance of agents of the United States Handicapper General.

Some things about living still weren't quite right, though. April, for instance, still drove people crazy by not being springtime. And it was in that clammy month that the H-G men took George and Hazel Bergeron's fourteen-year-old son, Harrison, away.

It was tragic, all right, but George and Hazel couldn't think about it very hard. Hazel had a perfectly average intelligence, which meant she couldn't think about anything except in short bursts. And George, while his intelligence was way above normal, had a little mental handicap radio in his ear—he was required by law to wear it at all times. It was tuned to a government transmitter, and every twenty seconds or so, the transmitter would send out some sharp noise to keep people like George from taking unfair advantage of their brains.

George and Hazel were watching television. There were tears on Hazel's cheeks, but she'd forgotten for the moment what they were about, as the ballerinas came to the end of a dance.

A buzzer sounded in George's head. His thoughts fled in panic, like bandits from a burglar alarm.

"That was a real pretty dance, that dance they just did," said Hazel.

"Huh?" said George.

"That dance—it was nice," said Hazel.

"Yup," said George. He tried to think a little about the ballerinas. They weren't really very good—no better than anybody else would have been, anyway. They were burdened with sashweights and bags of birdshot, and their faces were masked, so that no one, seeing a free and graceful gesture or a pretty face, would feel like something the cat dragged in. George was toying with the vague notion that maybe dancers shouldn't be handicapped. But he didn't get very far with it before another noise in his ear radio scattered his thoughts.

George winced. So did two out of the eight ballerinas.

Hazel saw him wince. Having no mental handicap herself, she had to ask George what the latest sound had been.

"Sounded like somebody hitting a milk bottle with a ball-peen hammer," said George.

"I'd think it would be real interesting, hearing all the different sounds," said Hazel, a little envious. "The things they think up."

"Um," said George.

"Only, if I was Handicapper General, you know what I would do?" said Hazel. Hazel, as a matter of fact, bore a strong resemblance to the Handicapper General, a woman named Diana Moon Glampers. "If I was Diana Moon Glampers," said Hazel, "I'd have chimes on Sunday—just chimes. Kind of in honor of religion."

"I could think, if it was just chimes," said George.

"Well—maybe make 'em real loud," said Hazel. "I think I'd make a good Handicapper General."

"Good as anybody else," said George.

"Who knows better'n I do what normal is?" said Hazel.

"Right," said George. He began to think glimmeringly about his abnormal son who was now in jail, about Harrison, but a twenty-one gun salute in his head stopped that.

"Boy!" said Hazel. "That was a doozy, wasn't it?"

It was such a doozy that George was white and trembling, and tears stood on the rims of his red eyes. Two of the eight ballerinas had collapsed to the studio floor, were holding their temples.

"All of a sudden you look so tired," said Hazel. "Why don't you stretch out on the sofa, so's you can rest your handicap bag on the pillows, honeybunch." She was referring to the forty-seven pounds of birdshot in a canvas bag, which was padlocked around George's neck. "Go on and rest the bag for a little while," she said. "I don't care if you're not equal to me for a while."

George weighed the bag with his hands. "I don't mind it," he said. "I don't notice it any more. It's just a part of me."

"You been so tired lately—kind of wore out," said Hazel. "If there was just some way we could make a little hole in the bottom of the bag, and just take out a few of them lead balls. Just a few."

"Two years in prison and two-thousand dollars fine for every ball I took out," said George. "I don't call that a bargain."

"If you could just take a few out when you came home from work," said Hazel. "I mean—you don't compete with anybody around here. You just set around."

"If I tried to get away with it," said George, "then other people'd get away with it—and pretty soon we'd be right back to the dark ages again, with everybody competing against everybody else. You wouldn't like that, would you?"

"I'd hate it," said Hazel.

"There you are," said George. "The minute people start cheating on laws, what do you think happens to society?"

If Hazel hadn't been able to come up with an answer to this question, George couldn't have supplied one. A siren was going off in his head.

"Reckon it'd fall all apart," said Hazel.

"What would?" said George blankly.

"Society," said Hazel uncertainly. "Wasn't that what you just said?"

"Who knows?" said George.

The television program was suddenly interrupted for a news bulletin. It wasn't clear at first as to what the bulletin was about, since the announcer, like all announcers, had a serious speech impediment. For about half a minute, and in a state of high excitement, the announcer tried to say, "Ladies and gentle-men—"

He finally gave up, handed the bulletin to a ballerina to read.

"That's all right," Hazel said of the announcer, "he tried. That's the big thing. He tried to do the best he could with what God gave him. He should get a nice raise for trying so hard."

"Ladies and gentlemen—" said the ballerina, reading the bulletin. She must have been extraordinarily beautiful, because the mask she wore was hideous. And it was easy to see that she was the strongest and most graceful of all the dancers, for her handicap bags were as big as those worn by two-hundred-pound men.

And she had to apologize at once for her voice, which was a very unfair voice for a woman to use. Her voice was a warm, luminous, timeless melody. "Excuse me—" she said, and she began again, making her voice absolutely uncompetitive.

"Harrison Bergeron, age fourteen," she said in a grackle squawk, "has just escaped from jail, where he was held on suspicion of plotting to overthrow the government. He is a genius and an athlete, is under-handicapped, and is extremely dangerous."

A police photograph of Harrison Bergeron was flashed on the screen—upside down, then sideways, upside down again, then right-side up. The picture showed the full length of Harrison against a background calibrated in feet and inches. He was exactly seven feet tall.

The rest of Harrison's appearance was Halloween and hardware. Nobody had ever borne heavier handicaps. He had outgrown hindrances faster than the H-G men could think them up. Instead of a little ear radio for a mental handicap, he wore a tremendous pair of earphones, and spectacles with thick, wavy lenses besides. The spectacles were intended not only to make him half blind, but to give him whanging headaches besides.

Scrap metal was hung all over him. Ordinarily, there was a certain symmetry, a military neatness to the handicaps issued to strong people, but Harrison looked like a walking junkyard. In the race of life, Harrison carried three hundred pounds.

And to offset his good looks, the H-G men required that he wear at all times a red rubber ball for a nose, keep his eyebrows shaved off, and cover his even white teeth with black caps at snaggle-tooth random.

"If you see this boy," said the ballerina, "do not—I repeat, do not—try to reason with him."

There was the shriek of a door being torn from its hinges.

Screams and barking cries of consternation came from the television set. The photograph of Harrison Bergeron on the screen jumped again and again, as though dancing to the tune of an earthquake.

George Bergeron correctly identified the earthquake, and well he might have—for many was the time his own home had danced to the same crashing tune. "My God!" said George. "That must be Harrison!"

The realization was blasted from his mind instantly by the sound of an automobile collision in his head.

When George could open his eyes again, the photograph of Harrison was gone. A living, breathing Harrison filled the screen.

Clanking, clownish, and huge, Harrison stood in the center of the studio. The knob of the uprooted studio door was still in his hand. Ballerinas, technicians, musicians and announcers cowered on their knees before him, expecting to die.

"I am the Emperor!" cried Harrison. "Do you hear? I am the Emperor! Everybody must do what I say at once!" He stamped his foot and the studio shook.

"Even as I stand here," he bellowed, "crippled, hobbled, sickened—I am a greater ruler than any man who ever lived! Now watch me become what I *can* become!"

Harrison tore the straps of his handicap harness like wet tissue paper, tore straps guaranteed to support five thousand pounds.

Harrison's scrap-iron handicaps crashed to the floor.

Harrison thrust his thumbs under the bar of the padlock that secured his head harness. The bar snapped like celery. Harrison smashed his headphones and spectacles against the wall.

He flung away his rubber-ball nose, revealed a man that would have awed Thor, the god of thunder.

"I shall now select my Empress!" he said, looking down on the cowering people. "Let the first woman who dares rise to her feet claim her mate and her throne!"

A moment passed, and then a ballerina arose, swaying like a willow.

Harrison plucked the mental handicap from her ear, snapped off her physical handicaps with marvelous delicacy.

Last of all, he removed her mask. She was blindingly beautiful.

"Now—" said Harrison, taking her hand. "Shall we show the people the meaning of the word dance? Music!" he commanded.

The musicians scrambled back into their chairs, and Harrison stripped them of their handicaps, too. "Play your best," he told them, "and I'll make you barons and dukes and earls."

The music began. It was normal at first—cheap, silly, false. But Harrison snatched two musicians from their chairs, waved them like batons as he sang the music as he wanted it played. He slammed them back into their chairs.

The music began again, and was much improved.

Harrison and his Empress merely listened to the music for a while—listened gravely, as though synchronizing their heartbeats with it.

They shifted their weight to their toes.

Harrison placed his big hands on the girl's tiny waist, letting her sense the weightlessness that would soon be hers.

And then, in an explosion of joy and grace, into the air they sprang!

Not only were the laws of the land abandoned, but the law of gravity and the laws of motion as well.

They reeled, whirled, swiveled, flounced, capered, gamboled and spun.

They leaped like deer on the moon.

The studio ceiling was thirty feet high, but each leap brought the dancers nearer to it.

It became their obvious intention to kiss the ceiling.

They kissed it.

And then, neutralizing gravity with love and pure will, they remained suspended in air inches below the ceiling, and they kissed each other for a long, long time.

It was then that Diana Moon Glampers, the Handicapper General, came into the studio with a double-barreled ten-gauge shotgun. She fired twice, and the Emperor and the Empress were dead before they hit the floor.

Diana Moon Glampers loaded the gun again. She aimed it at the musicians and told them they had ten seconds to get their handicaps back on.

It was then that the Bergerons' television tube burned out.

Hazel turned to comment about the blackout to George. But George had gone out into the kitchen for a can of beer.

George came back in with the beer, paused while a handicap signal shook him up. And then he sat down again. "You been crying?" he said to Hazel, watching her wipe her tears.

"Yup," she said.

"What about?" he said.

"I forget," she said. "Something real sad on television."

"What was it?" he said.

"It's all kind of mixed up in my mind," said Hazel.

"Forget sad things," said George.

"I always do," said Hazel.

"That's my girl," said George. He winced. There was the sound of a riveting gun in his head.

"Gee—I could tell that one was a doozy," said Hazel.

"You can say that again," said George.

"Gee—" said Hazel—"I could tell that one was a doozy."

CAUGHT IN THE
ORGAN DRAFT
by Robert Silverberg

Robert Silverberg—four-time Hugo Award-winner, five-time winner of the Nebula Award, SFWA Grand Master, SF Hall of Fame honoree—is the author of nearly five hundred short stories, nearly one hundred-and-fifty novels, and is the editor of in the neighborhood of one hundred anthologies, including my own *The Living Dead, Federations,* and *The Way of the Wizard.* Among his most famous works are *Lord Valentine's Castle, Dying Inside, Nightwings,* and *The World Inside.* Learn more at www.majipoor.com.

The United States no longer has a draft. Military conscription was ended under the Richard Nixon administration in 1973. But before that, *millions* of American men experienced compulsory military service. When confronted with the possibility of wartime horror and the very real threat of death, these men could not run. They faced long sentences in military jails that were famous for their harsh conditions. Once their time was over, their legal records would be ruined.

These men could give their bodies and lives to the war machines, or they could throw away their futures. That was their choice.

In our next story, Robert Silverberg paints a reality where young people must once again choose between their bodies and their futures. Their organs are needed by the rich and important, people who've got the power of the law on their side. A conscripted organ donor can live without a lung or a kidney, but a convicted draft dodger might wish he'd never been born.

Here is a tale that pushes the boundaries of ownership and duty and leaves us ready to burn our draft cards and emigrate to another world.

ook there, Kate, down by the promenade. Two splendid seniors, walking side by side near the water's edge. They radiate power, authority, wealth, assurance. He's a judge, a senator, a corporation president, no doubt, and she's—what?—a professor emeritus of international law, let's say. There they go toward the plaza, moving serenely, smiling, nodding graciously to passersby. How the sunlight gleams in their white hair! I can barely stand the brilliance of that reflected aura: it blinds me, it stings my eyes. What are they, eighty, ninety, a hundred years old? At this distance they seem much younger—they hold themselves upright, their backs are straight, they might pass for being only fifty or sixty. But I can tell. Their confidence, their poise, mark them for what they are. And when they were nearer I could see their withered cheeks, their sunken eyes. No cosmetics can hide that. These two are old enough to be our great-grandparents. They were well past sixty before we were even born, Kate. How superbly their bodies function! But why not? We can guess at their medical histories. She's had at least three hearts, he's working on his fourth set of lungs, they apply for new kidneys every five years, their brittle bones are reinforced with hundreds of skeletal snips from the arms and legs of hapless younger folk, their dimming sensory apparatus is aided by countless nerve-grafts obtained the same way, their ancient arteries are freshly sheathed with sleek teflon. Ambulatory assemblages of secondhand human parts, spliced here and there with synthetic or mechanical organ substitutes, that's all they are. And what am I, then, or you? Nineteen years old and vulnerable. In their eyes I'm nothing but a ready stockpile of healthy organs, waiting to serve their needs. Come here, son. What a fine strapping young man you are! Can you spare a kidney for me? A lung? A choice little segment of intestine? Ten centimeters of your ulnar nerve? I need a few pieces of you, lad. You won't deny a distinguished elder like me what I ask, will you? *Will you?*

Today my draft notice, a small crisp document, very official-looking, came shooting out of the data slot when I punched for my morning mail. I've been expecting it all spring; no surprise, no shock, actually rather an anticlimax now that it's finally here. In six weeks I am to report to Transplant House for my final physical exam—only a formality; they wouldn't have drafted me if I didn't already rate top marks as organ-reservoir potential—and then I go on call. The average call time is about two months. By autumn they'll be carving me up. Eat, drink, and be merry, for soon comes the surgeon to my door.

A straggly band of senior citizens is picketing the central headquarters of the League for Bodily Sanctity. It's a counterdemonstration, an anti-anti-transplant protest, the worst kind of political statement, feeding on the ugliest of negative emotions. The demonstrators carry glowing signs that say:

BODILY SANCTITY—OR BODILY SELFISHNESS?
And:
YOU OWE YOUR LEADERS YOUR VERY LIVES

And:

LISTEN TO THE VOICE OF EXPERIENCE

The picketers are low-echelon seniors, barely across the qualifying line, the ones who can't really be sure of getting transplants. No wonder they're edgy about the League. Some of them are in wheelchairs and some are encased right up to the eyebrows in portable life-support systems. They croak and shout bitter invective and shake their fists. Watching the show from an upper window of the League building, I shiver with fear and dismay. These people don't just want my kidneys or my lungs. They'd take my eyes, my liver, my pancreas, my heart, anything they might happen to need.

I talked it over with my father. He's forty-five years old—too old to have been personally affected by the organ draft, too young to have needed any transplants yet. That puts him in a neutral position, so to speak, except for one minor factor: his transplant status is 5-G. That's quite high on the eligibility list, not the top-priority class but close enough. If he fell ill tomorrow and the Transplant Board ruled that his life would be endangered if he didn't get a new heart or lung or kidney, he'd be given one practically immediately. Status like that simply has to influence his objectivity on the whole organ issue. Anyway, I told him I was planning to appeal and maybe even to resist. "Be reasonable," he said, "be rational, don't let your emotions run away with you. Is it worth jeopardizing your whole future over a thing like this? After all, not everybody who's drafted loses vital organs."

"Show me the statistics," I said. "Show me."

He didn't know the statistics. It was his impression that only about a quarter or a fifth of the draftees actually got an organ call. That tells you how closely the older generation keeps in touch with the situation—and my father's an educated man, articulate, well-informed. Nobody over the age of thirty-five that I talked to could show me any statistics. So I showed them. Out of a League brochure, it's true, but based on certified National Institute of Health reports. Nobody escapes. They always clip you, once you qualify. The need for young organs inexorably expands to match the pool of available organpower. In the long run they'll get us all and chop us to bits. That's probably what they want, anyway. To rid themselves of the younger members of the species, always so troublesome, by cannibalizing us for spare parts, and recycling us, lung by lung, pancreas by pancreas, through their own deteriorating bodies.

Fig. 4. On March 23, 1964, this dog's own liver was removed and replaced with the liver of a nonrelated mongrel donor. The animal was treated with azathioprine for 4 months and all therapy then stopped. He remains in perfect health 6-2/3 years after transplantation.

The war goes on. This is, I think, its fourteenth year. Of course they're beyond the business of killing now. They haven't had any field engagements since '93 or so, certainly none since the organ-draft legislation went into effect. The old ones can't afford to waste precious young bodies on the battlefield. So robots wage our territorial struggles for us, butting heads with a great metallic clank, laying land mines and twitching their sensors at the enemy's mines, digging tunnels beneath his screens, et cetera, et cetera. Plus, of course, the quasi-military activity—economic sanctions, third-power blockades, propaganda telecasts beamed as overrides from merciless orbital satellites, and stuff like that. It's a subtler war than the kind they used to wage: nobody dies. Still, it drains national resources. Taxes are going up again this year, the fifth or sixth year in a row, and they've just slapped a special Peace Surcharge on all metal-containing goods, on account of the copper shortage. There once was a time when we could hope that our crazy old leaders would die off or at least retire for reasons of health, stumbling away to their country villas with ulcers or shingles or scabies or scruples and allowing new young peacemakers to take office. But now they just go on and on, immortal and insane, our senators, our cabinet members, our generals, our planners. And their war goes on and on, too, their absurd, incomprehensible, diabolical, self-gratifying war.

I know people my age or a little older who have taken asylum in Belgium or Sweden or Paraguay or one of the other countries where Bodily Sanctity laws have been passed. There are about twenty such countries, half of them the most progressive nations in the world and half of them the most reactionary. But what's the sense of running away? I don't want to live in exile. I'll stay here and fight.

Naturally they don't ask a draftee to give up his heart or his liver or some other organ essential to life, say his medulla oblongata. We haven't yet reached that stage of political enlightenment at which the government feels capable of legislating fatal conscription. Kidneys and lungs, the paired organs, the dispensable organs, are the chief targets so far. But if you study the history of conscription over the ages you see that it can always be projected on a curve rising from rational necessity to absolute lunacy. Give them a fingertip, they'll take an arm. Give them an inch of bowel, they'll take your guts. In another fifty years they'll be drafting hearts and stomachs and maybe even brains, mark my words; let them get the technology of brain transplants together and nobody's skull will be safe. It'll be human sacrifice all over again. The only difference between us and the Aztecs is one of method: we have anesthesia, we have antisepsis and asepsis, we use scalpels instead of obsidian blades to cut out the hearts of our victims.

MEANS OF OVERCOMING THE HOMOGRAFT REACTION

The pathway that has led from the demonstration of the immunological nature of the homograft reaction and its universality to the development of relatively effective but by no means completely satisfactory means of overcoming it for therapeutic purposes is an interesting one that can only be touched upon very briefly. The year

1950 ushered in a new era in transplantation immunobiology in which the discovery of various means of weakening or abrogating a host's response to a homograft—such as sublethal whole body X-irradiation, or treatment with certain adrenal cortico-steroid hormones, notably cortisone—began to influence the direction of the main-stream of research and engender confidence that a workable clinical solution might not be too far off. By the end of the decade, powerful immuno-suppressive drugs, such as 6-mercaptopurine, had been shown to be capable of holding in abeyance the reactivity of dogs to renal homografts, and soon afterward this principle was successfully extended to man.

Is my resistance to the draft based on an ingrained abstract distaste for tyranny in all forms or rather on the mere desire to keep my body intact? Could it be both, maybe? Do I need an idealistic rationalization at all? Don't I have an inalienable right to go through my life wearing my own native-born kidneys?

The law was put through by an administration of old men. You can be sure that all laws affecting the welfare of the young are the work of doddering moribund ancients afflicted with angina pectoris, atherosclerosis, prolapses of the infun-dibulum, fulminating ventricles, and dilated viaducts. The problem was this: not enough healthy young people were dying of highway accidents, successful suicide attempts, diving-board miscalculations, electrocutions, and football injuries; therefore there was a shortage of transplantable organs. An effort to restore the death penalty for the sake of creating a steady supply of state-controlled cadavers lost out in the courts. Volunteer programs of organ donation weren't working out too well, since most of the volunteers were criminals who signed up in order to gain early release from prison: a lung reduced your sentence by five years, a kidney got you three years off, and so on. The exodus of convicts from the jails under this clause wasn't so popular among suburban voters. Meanwhile there was an urgent and mounting need for organs; a lot of important seniors might in fact die if something didn't get done fast. So a coalition of senators from all four parties rammed the organ-draft measure through the upper chambers in the face of a filibuster threat from a few youth-oriented members. It had a much easier time in the House of Representatives, since nobody in the House ever pays much attention to the text of a bill up for a vote, and word had been circulated on this one that if it passed, everybody over sixty-five who had any political pull at all could count on living twenty or thirty extra years, which to a Representative means a crack at ten to fifteen extra terms of office. Naturally there have been court challenges, but what's the use? The average age of the eleven Justices of the Supreme Court is seventy-eight. They're human and mor-tal. They need our flesh. If they throw out the organ draft now, they're signing their own death warrants.

For a year and a half I was the chairman of the anti-draft campaign on our campus. We were the sixth or seventh local chapter of the League for Bodily

Sanctity to be organized in this country, and we were real activists. Mainly we would march up and down in front of the draft board offices carrying signs proclaiming things like:

KIDNEY POWER
And:
A MAN'S BODY IS HIS CASTLE
And:
THE POWER TO CONSCRIPT ORGANS
IS THE POWER TO DESTROY LIVES

We never went in for the rough stuff, though, like bombing organ-transplant centers or hijacking refrigeration trucks. Peaceful agitation, that was our motto. When a couple of our members tried to swing us to a more violent policy, I delivered an extemporaneous two-hour speech arguing for moderation. Naturally I was drafted the moment I became eligible.

"I can understand your hostility to the draft," my college advisor said. "It's certainly normal to feel queasy about surrendering important organs of your body. But you ought to consider the countervailing advantages. Once you've given an organ, you get a 6-A classification, Preferred Recipient, and you remain forever on the 6-A roster. Surely you realize that this means that if you ever need a transplant yourself, you'll automatically be eligible for one, even if your other personal and professional qualifications don't lift you to the optimum level. Suppose your career plans don't work out and you become a manual laborer, for instance. Ordinarily you wouldn't rate even a first look if you developed heart disease, but your Preferred Recipient status would save you. You'd get a new lease on life, my boy."

I pointed out the fallacy inherent in this. Which is that as the number of draftees increases, it will come to encompass a majority or even a totality of the population, and eventually everybody will have 6-A Preferred Recipient status by virtue of having donated, and the term Preferred Recipient will cease to have any meaning. A shortage of transplantable organs would eventually develop as each past donor stakes his claim to a transplant when his health fails, and in time they'd have to arrange the Preferred Recipients by order of personal and professional achievement anyway, for the sake of arriving at some kind of priorities within the 6-A class, and we'd be right back where we are now.

Fig. 7. The course of a patient who received antilymphocyte globulin (ALG) before and for the first 4 months after renal homotransplantation. The donor was an older brother. There was no early rejection. Prednisone therapy was started 40 days postoperatively. Note the insidious onset of late rejection after cessation of globulin therapy. This was treated by a moderate increase in the maintenance doses of steroids. This delayed complication occurred in only 2 of the first 20 recipients of intrafamilial homografts who were treated with ALG. It has been seen with about the same low frequency in subsequent cases. (By permission of Surg. Gynec. Obstet. *126 (1968): p. 1023.)*

So I went down to Transplant House today, right on schedule, to take my physical. A couple of my friends thought I was making a tactical mistake by reporting at all; if you're going to resist, they said, resist at every point along the line. Make them drag you in for the physical. In purely idealistic (and ideological) terms I suppose they're right. But there's no need yet for me to start kicking up a fuss. Wait till they actually say, We need your kidney, young man. Then I can resist, if resistance is the course I ultimately choose. (Why am I wavering? Am I afraid of the damage to my career plans that resisting might do? Am I not entirely convinced of the injustice of the entire organ-draft system? I don't know. I'm not even sure that I *am* wavering. Reporting for your physical isn't really a sellout to the system.) I went, anyway. They tapped this and X-rayed that and peered into the other thing. Yawn, please. Bend over, please. Cough, please. Hold out your left arm, please. They marched me in front of a battery of diagnostat machines and I stood there hoping for the red light to flash—*tilt,* get out of here!—but I was, as expected, in perfect physical shape, and I qualified for call. Afterward I met Kate and we walked in the park and held hands and watched the glories of the sunset and discussed what I'll do, when and if the call comes. *If?* Wishful thinking, boy!

If your number is called, you become exempt from military service, and they credit you with a special $750 tax deduction every year. Big deal.

Another thing they're very proud of is the program of voluntary donation of unpaired organs. This has nothing to do with the draft, which—thus far, at least—requisitions only paired organs, organs that can be spared without loss of life. For the last twelve years it's been possible to walk into any hospital in the United States and sign a simple release form allowing the surgeons to slice you up. Eyes, lungs, heart, intestines, pancreas, liver, anything, you give it all to them. This process used to be known as suicide in a simpler era, and it was socially disapproved of, especially in times of labor shortages. Now we have a labor surplus, because even though our population growth has been fairly slow since the middle of the century, the growth of labor-eliminating mechanical devices and processes has been quite rapid, even exponential. Therefore, to volunteer for this kind of total donation is considered a deed of the highest social utility, removing as it does a healthy young body from the overcrowded labor force and at the same time providing some elder statesman with the assurance that the supply of vital organs will not unduly diminish. Of course you have to be crazy to volunteer, but there's never been any shortage of lunatics in our society.

If you're not drafted by the age of twenty-one, through some lucky fluke, you're safe. And a few of us do slip through the net, I'm told. So far there are more of us in the total draft pool than there are patients in need of transplants. But the ratios are changing rapidly. The draft legislation is still relatively new. Before long they'll have drained the pool of eligible draftees, and then what? Birth rates nowadays are low; the supply of potential draftees is finite. But death rates are even lower; the demand for organs is essentially infinite. I can give you only one of my kidneys, if I am to survive; but you, as you live on and on, may require more than one kidney transplant. Some recipients may need five or six sets of kidneys or lungs before they finally get beyond hope of repair at age one-seventy or so. As those who've given organs come to requisition organs later on in life, the pressure on the under-twenty-one group will get even greater. Those in need of transplants will come to outnumber those who can donate organs, and everybody in the pool will get clipped. And then? Well, they could lower the draft age to seventeen or sixteen or even fourteen. But even that's only a short-term solution. Sooner or later, there won't be enough spare organs to go around.

Will I stay? Will I flee? Will I go to court? Time's running out. My call is sure to come up in another few weeks. I feel a tickling sensation in my back, now and then, as though somebody's quietly sawing at my kidneys.

Cannibalism. At Chou-kou-tien, Dragon Bone Hill, twenty-five miles southwest of Peking, paleontologists excavating a cave early in the twentieth century discovered the fossil skulls of Peking Man, *Pithecanthropus pekinensis.* The skulls had been broken away at the base, which led Franz Weidenreich, the director of the Dragon Bone Hill digs, to speculate that Peking Man was a cannibal who had killed his own kind, extracted the brains of his victims through openings in the base of their skulls, cooked and feasted on the cerebral meat—there were hearths and fragments of charcoal at the site—and left the skulls behind in the cave as trophies. To eat your enemy's flesh: to absorb his skills, his strengths, his knowledge, his achievements, his virtues. It took mankind five hundred thousand years to struggle upward from cannibalism. But we never lost the old craving, did we? There's still easy comfort to gain by devouring those who are younger, stronger, more agile than you. We've improved the techniques, is all. And so now they eat us raw, the old ones, they gobble us up, organ by throbbing organ. Is that really an improvement? At least Peking Man cooked his meat.

Our brave new society, where all share equally in the triumphs of medicine, and the deserving senior citizens need not feel that their merits and prestige will be rewarded only by a cold grave—we sing its praises all the time. How pleased everyone is about the organ draft! Except, of course, a few disgruntled draftees.

The ticklish question of priorities. Who gets the stockpiled organs? They have an elaborate system by which hierarchies are defined. Supposedly a big computer drew it up, thus assuring absolute godlike impartiality. You earn salvation through good works: accomplishments in career and benevolence in daily life win you points that nudge you up the ladder until you reach one of the high-priority classifications, 4-G or better. No doubt the classification system is impartial and is administered justly. But is it rational? Whose needs does it serve? In 1943, during World War II, there was a shortage of the newly discovered drug penicillin among the American military forces in North Africa. Two groups of soldiers were most in need of its benefits: those who were suffering from infected battle wounds and those who had contracted venereal disease. A junior medical officer, working from self-evident moral principles, ruled that the wounded heroes were more deserving of treatment than the self-indulgent syphilitics. He was overruled by the medical officer in charge, who observed that the VD cases could be restored to active duty more quickly, if treated; besides, if they remained untreated they served as vectors of further infection. Therefore he gave them the penicillin and left the wounded groaning on their beds of pain. The logic of the battlefield, incontrovertible, unassailable.

The great chain of life. Little creatures in the plankton are eaten by larger ones, and the greater plankton falls prey to little fishes, and little fishes to bigger fishes, and so on up to the tuna and the dolphin and the shark. I eat the flesh of the tuna and I thrive and flourish and grow fat, and store up energy in my vital organs. And am eaten in turn by the shriveled wizened seniors. All life is linked. I see my destiny.

In the early days, rejection of the transplanted organ was the big problem. Such a waste! The body failed to distinguish between a beneficial though alien organ and an intrusive, hostile microorganism. The mechanism known as the immune response was mobilized to drive out the invader. At the point of invasion, enzymes came into play, a brush-fire war designed to rip down and dissolve the foreign substances. White corpuscles poured in via the circulatory system, vigilant phagocytes on the march. Through the lymphatic network came antibodies, high-powered protein missiles. Before any technology of organ grafts could be developed, methods had to be devised to suppress the immune response. Drugs, radiation treatment, metabolic shock—one way or another, the organ-rejection problem was long ago conquered. I can't conquer my draft-rejection problem. Aged and rapacious legislators, I reject you and your legislation.

My call notice came today. They'll need one of my kidneys. The usual request. "You're lucky," somebody said at lunchtime. "They might have wanted a lung."

Kate and I walk into the green glistening hills and stand among the blossoming oleanders and corianders and frangipani and whatever. How good it is to be alive, to breathe this fragrance, to show our bodies to the bright sun! Her skin is tawny and glowing. Her beauty makes me weep. She will not be spared. None of us will be spared. I go first, then she, or is it she ahead of me? Where will they make the incision? Here, on her smooth rounded back? Here, on the flat taut belly? I can see the high priest standing over the altar. At the first blaze of dawn his shadow falls across her. The obsidian knife that is clutched in his upraised hand has a terrible fiery sparkle. The choir offers up a discordant hymn to the god of blood. The knife descends.

My last chance to escape across the border. I've been up all night, weighing the options. There's no hope of appeal. Running away leaves a bad taste in my mouth. Father, friends, even Kate, all say stay, stay, stay, face the music. The hour of decision. Do I really have a choice? I have no choice. When the time comes, I'll surrender peacefully.

I report to Transplant House for conscriptive donative surgery in three hours.

After all, he said coolly, what's a kidney? I'll still have another one, you know. And if that one malfunctions, I can always get a replacement. I'll have Preferred Recipient status, 6-A, for what that's worth. But I won't settle for my automatic 6-A. I know what's going to happen to the priority system; I'd better protect myself. I'll go into politics. I'll climb. I'll attain upward mobility out of enlightened self-interest, right? Right. I'll become so important that society will owe me a thousand transplants. And one of these years I'll get that kidney back. Three or four kidneys, fifty kidneys, as many as I need. A heart or two. A few lungs. A pancreas, a spleen, a liver. They won't be able to refuse me anything. I'll show them. I'll show them. I'll out-senior the seniors. There's your Bodily Sanctity activist for you, eh? I suppose I'll have to resign from the League. Good-bye, idealism. Good-bye, moral superiority. Good-bye, kidney. Good-bye, good-bye, good-bye.

It's done. I've paid my debt to society. I've given up unto the powers that be my humble pound of flesh. When I leave the hospital in a couple of days, I'll carry a card testifying to my new 6-A status.

Top priority for the rest of my life.
Why, I might live for a thousand years.

GERIATRIC WARD

by Orson Scott Card

Orson Scott Card is the best-selling author of more than forty novels, including *Ender's Game*, which was a winner of both the Hugo and Nebula Awards. The sequel, *Speaker for the Dead*, also won both awards, making Card the only author to have captured science fiction's two most coveted prizes in consecutive years. Card is also the winner of the World Fantasy Award, eight Locus Awards, and a slew of other honors. He has also published more than eighty short stories, which have been collected in several volumes, most notably in *Maps in the Mirror* and *Keeper of Dreams*. His most recent book is a young adult novel called *Pathfinder*.

Switch on the television and wait a few minutes—there's certain to be an ad for hair dye or anti-aging skin cream. A quick perusal of any women's magazine will uncover at least one article that fights wrinkles or cellulite or some other symptom of time's march across the body. Humans are afraid of death in whatever form it takes, but growing older is perhaps its most reviled shape. Unlike a homicidal maniac or a car accident, old age makes its victims survive decades of indignity.

No wonder we fight it so much.

But our next story gives us a future where the battle against old age has become even more of a losing proposition. Lifespans have plummeted. Senility can hit a person in only his mid-twenties, and despite efforts to start adulthood at a younger age, there's only so much living anyone can cram into a quarter of a decade. It's hard to lead a full life in so little time.

Here is a world of quiet desperation, full of people fighting for one more day with a loved one. One more day of sunshine. One more day as a geriatric.

Sandy started babbling on Tuesday morning and Todd knew it was the end.

"They took Poogy and Gog away from me," Sandy said sadly, her hand trembling, spilling coffee on the toast.

"What?" Todd mumbled.

"And never brought them back. Just took them. I looked all over."

"Looked for what?"

"Poogy," Sandy said, thrusting out her lower lip. The skin of her cheeks was sagging down to form jowls. Her hair was thin and fine, now, though she kept it dyed dark brown. "And Gog."

"What the hell are Poogy and Gog?" Todd asked.

"You took them," Sandy said. She started to cry. She kicked the table leg. Todd got up from the table and went to work.

The university was empty. Sunday. Damn Sunday, never anyone there to help with the work on Sunday. Waste too much damn time looking up things that students should be sent to find out.

He went to the lab. Ryan was there. They looked over the computer readouts. "Blood," said Ryan, "just plain ain't worth the paper it's printed on."

"Not one thing," Todd said.

"Plenty of tests left to run."

"No tests left to run except the viral microscopy, and that's next week."

Ryan smiled. "Well, then, the problem must be viral."

"You know damn well the problem isn't viral."

Ryan looked at him sharply, his long grey hair tossing in the opposite direction. "What is it then? Sunspots? Aliens from outer space? God's punishment? The Jews? Yellow Peril?"

Todd didn't answer. Just settled down to doublechecking the figures. Outside he heard the Sunday parade. Pentecostal. Jesus Will Save You, Brother, When You Go Without Your Sins. How could he concentrate?

"What's wrong?" Ryan asked.

"Nothing's wrong," Todd answered. Nothing. Sweet Jesus, you old man, if I could live to thirty-three I'd let them hang my corpse from any cross they wanted. If I could live to thirty.

Twenty-four. Birthday June 28. They used to celebrate birthdays. Now everyone tried to keep it secret. Not Todd, though. Not well-adjusted Todd. Even had a few friends over, they drank to his health. His hands shook at night now, like palsy, like fear, and his teeth were rotting in his mouth. He looked down at the paper where his hands were following the lines. The numbers blurred. Have to have new glasses again, second time this year. The veins on his hands stuck out blue and evil-looking.

And Sandy was over the edge today.

She was only twenty-two; it hit the women first. He had met her just before college, they had married, had nine children in nine years—duty to the race. It must be child-bearing that made the women get it sooner. But the race had to go on.

Somehow. And now their older children were grown up, having children of their own. Miracles of modern medicine. We don't know why you get old so young, and we can't cure it, but in the meantime we can give you a little more adulthood—accelerated development, six-month gestation, puberty at nine, not a disease left you could catch except the one. But the one was enough. Not as large as a church door, but 'tis enough, 'twill serve.

His chin quivered and tears dropped down wrinkled cheeks onto the page.

"What is it?" Ryan asked, concerned. Todd shook his head. He didn't need comfort, not from a novice of eighteen, only two years out of college.

"What is it?" Ryan persisted.

"It's tears," Todd answered. "A salty fluid produced by a gland near the eye, used for lubrication. Also serves double-duty as a signal to other people that stress cannot be privately coped with."

"So don't cope privately. What is it?"

Todd got up and left the room. He went to his office and called the medical center.

"Psychiatric," he said to the moronic voice that answered.

Psychiatric was busy. He called again and got through. Dr. Lassiter was in.

"Todd," Lassiter said.

"Val," Todd answered. "Got a problem."

"Can it wait? Busy day."

"Can't wait. It's Sandy. She started babbling today."

"Ah," said Val. "I'm sorry. Is it bad?"

"She remembers her separation therapy. Like it was yesterday."

"That's it then, Todd," Val said. "I'm really sorry. Sandy's a wonderful woman, good researcher, but there's nothing we can do."

"Aren't we supposed to be able to see signs before she reaches this stage?"

"Usually," Val answered, "but not always. Think back, though. I'm sure you'll remember signs."

Todd swallowed. "Have you got a space, Val? You knew Sandy back in the old days, back when we were kids in the—"

"Is this pressure, Todd?" Val asked abruptly. "Appeal to friendship? Don't you know the law?"

"I know the law, dammit, I'm asking you, one medical researcher to another, is there room?"

"There's room, Todd," Val answered, "for the treatables. But if she's reverted to separation therapy, then what can I do? It's a matter of weeks. For your own safety you have to turn her over, never know what's going to happen during the final senility, you know. Hallucinations. Sometimes violence. There's still strength in the old bones."

"She's committed no crime."

"It's also the law," Val reminded him. "Good-bye."

Todd hung up the phone. Turn her over? He'd never thought it would come to Sandy so suddenly. He couldn't just turn her over, she'd hate him, she had enough of herself left in herself to know what was going on. They'd been married thirteen years.

He went back to Ryan in the lab and told him to put the computers on the viral microscopy tomorrow.

"That's unscientific, to rush it," said Ryan.

"Damned unscientific," Todd agreed. "Do it."

"OK," Ryan answered. "It's Sandy, isn't it?"

"It's handwriting," Todd said. "It's all over the walls."

Todd went home and found Sandy in the living room, cuddling a pillow and watching the tube. Someone was yelling at someone else. Sandy didn't care. She was stroking the pillow, making love noises. Todd sat on the chair and watched for her almost an hour. She never noticed him. She did, however, change pillows.

"Gog," she said.

She listened for an answer, nodded, smiled, held the pillow to her breasts. Todd chewed his fingernails. His heart was fluttering.

He went into the kitchen and fixed dinner. She ate, though she spilled a great deal and threw her spoon on the floor.

He put her to bed. Then he showered, came back out, and crawled into bed beside her.

"What the hell do you think you're doing," she challenged, her voice husky and mature.

"Going to bed," Todd answered.

"Not in my bed, you bastard," she said, shoving at him.

"*My* bed, you mean," he said, even though he knew better.

She growled. Like a tiger, Todd thought. Then she clawed as his face. Her nails were long. He lurched back, his face on fire with pain. The motion carried him off the bed. He landed heavily on the floor. His brittle old bones ached at the impact. He felt for his eyes, to see if they were still there. They were.

"If you ever come back," she said, "I'll have my husband eat you alive."

Todd didn't bother arguing. He went into the living room and curled up on the couch. For the first time he wished that children still lived at home nowadays. That even the two-year-old were there to talk to. He touched the pillow, pulled it toward him, then stopped himself. Pillows. One of the signs.

Not me, he thought.

He fell asleep surrounded by nightmares of childhood, attacked on all sides by sagging flesh and fragile bones and eyes and ears that had forgotten all they ever knew how to do.

He woke with the blood clotted stiffly on his face. His back was sore where he had struck the floor last night. He walked stiffly to the bathroom. When he washed the blood off his face the cuts opened again, and he spent a half hour stanching the bleeding.

When he left home, Sandy was sitting at the kitchen table, holding a tea party for herself and the pillows.

"Good-bye, Sandy," Todd said.

"More tea, Gog?" she answered.

He did not go to the lab. Instead he went to the library and used his top security clearance to gain access to the gerontology section. It was illegal to use security clearance for personal purposes, but who would know? Who would care, for that matter. He found a volume entitled *Psychology of Accelerated Aging* by V. N. Lassiter. He finished it at 1:00.

Ryan looked irritated when Todd finally came in.

"We've been running the series without you," he said, "but holy hell, Todd, everybody's been on my back for doing it early. If you're going to give me a screwed-up order, at least be here to take the lumps."

"Sorry." Todd started looking over the early readouts.

"You won't find anything yet," Ryan said.

"I know," Todd answered. "But the meeting is on Friday."

Ryan slammed down a sheaf of papers on his desk.

"We'll make the report then," Todd went on.

"If we make a report then it will be worth exactly nothing," Ryan said angrily.

"If we make a report then—and we *will* make a report then—it will be as accurate as human understanding can make it. Do you think we'll miss anything now? There's nothing. Our blood is no different from the blood of our great great grandfathers who lived to be ninety-five. There are no microbes. And viruses are just corkscrews."

"If you do this," Ryan said, "I'll recommend that you be removed from your post and the viral microscopy series be run again."

Todd laughed. "Calm down," he said. "I'm twenty-four."

Ryan looked at the floor. "I'm sorry."

"Hey," Todd said, "don't worry about it. In a few months, you can run the whole thing over again if you want. And the guy after you, and the one after him, run it over and over and over again through eternity. I won't care. You'll have your time in the sun, Ryan. You'll have six years as head of the department and you'll write papers, conduct research, and then you'll roll over like the rest of us and wiggle your feet in the air for a while and then you'll die."

Ryan turned away. "I've got the point, Todd."

"Dr. Halking, boy, " Todd said. "Dr. Halking to you until I'm dead." Todd walked to the window and opened it. Outside on the lawn was an afternoon rally of the Fatalists. "Hasten the day," they sang at the top of their decrepit lungs, white hair flashing in the breeze and the sunlight. "Take me away, death is the answer, don't make me stay."

"Shut the window," Ryan said. Todd opened it wider. Two students, graduate students about sixteen years old, took a few quick steps toward him.

"Relax," Todd said. "I'm not jumping."

Todd was still standing at the window when Val Lassiter came. "Ryan called me," Val said.

"I know," Todd answered. "I heard him call."

"Let's talk," Val answered. The students left the room. Val looked at Ryan, and he also left. "They're gone," Val said. "Let's talk."

Todd sat in a chair. "I know what you're thinking," Todd said. "I'm showing the signs."

"What signs?"

Todd sighed. "Don't give me any of that psychiatrist crap. I read your book. I've got it all: Tears, worries, inability to bear delay, impatience with friends, unwillingness to admit any possibility of hope, suicidal behavior—I'm so far gone that if Jesus whispered in my ear, 'You're saved,' I'd believe and be baptized and not be surprised at all."

"You shouldn't have read that book, Todd."

"I read the book but I'm not over the edge, Val. I will be, I know, but not yet. It's just Sandy—I was a fool, I let myself get too attached, you know? I can't handle it. Can't let go. Keep feeling there's got to be a way."

Val smiled and touched Todd's shoulder. "You've devoted your life to finding a way. So have I. So have all of us from the project. Geniuses all, even Sandy, what a damned shame she's the first to go. But the cure won't come overnight. Won't come by trying to reverse what's irreversible."

"Who says it's irreversible?" Todd demanded.

"Experience," Val said. "What, do you think you can go out of your discipline and outdo the experts in a sudden flash of inspiration? All you'll think of are ideas we've thought of and discarded long ago."

"How do you know it can't be reversed? We don't even know what causes the aging, Val. We don't even know if it *has* a cause—why is the cutoff point separation therapy? Why can't you help people once they revert to that?"

Val shrugged. "It's arbitrary. We can't do that much for others, either."

Todd shook his head, saying, "Val, you don't understand. Maybe what's going on in separation therapy is part of what *causes* the senility—"

Val stood impatiently. "I told you, Todd. You'll only think of things we already thought of. It can't be the cause because separation therapy began *after* the aging epidemic. It was tried as a *cure*. It was used so we would mature faster, so we would have more adult, productive years. Todd, you know that, you know it can't be the cause, what is this?"

Todd picked up a stack of readouts. "Forget it, Val. Tell everyone I'm over my breakdown. It's Sandy being over the edge. I just couldn't handle the grief a while, OK?"

Val smiled. "OK. Have you turned her over yet?"

Todd stiffened. "No."

Val stopped smiling. "It's the law, Todd. Do it soon. Do it before I have to report it."

Todd looked up at Val with a sickening smile on his face. "And when will you have to report it, Val?"

Val looked at Todd for a moment, then turned and left. The others came back to the lab. They worked all afternoon and far into the night, pretending nothing had happened. At least Todd hadn't suicided. So many did these days, especially the brilliant ones; no one would have been surprised. But Todd they needed, at least for a while more, at least until the young ones had a chance to learn. Otherwise they'd be a few years deeper into the hole, there'd be a few more years' worth of learning lost, a little bit less that one man could hope to do in his short lifetime.

Todd called in sick the next morning. He was not sick. He took Sandy by the hand, led her to the car, and drove her to the childhouse. He flashed his security pass and rushed Sandy through the halls as quickly as possible, so no one would notice she was over the edge.

The rushing about left Todd's heart fluttering, his old hopeless heart, he thought, only a few more months, only a few more weeks of pumping away. They were met at the observation window by several young researchers; couldn't be out of college yet, maybe fifteen. Hair still young, eyes still bright, skin still smooth. Todd felt angry, looking at them.

They were impressed to be meeting *the* Todd Halking. "Gee, Dr. Halking," the heavyset young women enthused, "we never thought *our* work would have any application on the biological end of things."

"It probably doesn't," Todd said. "But we need to check every angle. This is my wife. She has a cold, so I'd advise you to keep your distance."

Sandy showed no sign of paying attention to the conversation around her. She only watched the large window in front of her. On the other side a child was playing with two stuffed animals. One was a bear, the other a lion.

"Poogy," Sandy whispered. "Gog."

A research supervisor walked into the observation room and began the testing. For a moment Todd tuned in to the heavyset woman's droning explanation: "… check to make sure the child's reliance is not pathological, in which case special treatment is necessary. In most cases separation therapy is judged to be safe, and so we proceed immediately…."

The tests were simple—the supervisor knelt by the child and showed affection to each love object in turn, first by patting, then by kissing, then by taking the love object briefly and hugging it. Though the little girl showed some signs of anxiety when the researcher took the love object away for a moment to hug it, she was considered ready for therapy. "After all," the student explained to Todd, "for a five-year-old to show *no* anxiety would be as startling as extreme anxiety."

And so the separation therapy began. The attendant took both stuffed animals and left the room.

The little girl's anxiety was immediately more acute. She watched the door for a few moments, then stood up, went to the door, and tried to make it open. Of course the buttons didn't respond to her touch. She paced for a little while, then sat back down and waited, watching the door.

"You see," said the student, "you see how patient she is? That can be a sign of exceptional maturity."

Then the little girl ran out of patience. She began to call out. Her words were inaudible, but Todd could hear Sandy beside him, mumbling, "Poogy, Gog, Poogy, Gog," in time with the little girl's silent cries. She was reacting. Todd felt a shiver of fear run through him, upward, from his feet. She would react, but would it do any good?

The little girl was screaming now, her face red, her eyes bugging out. "She may, because she is an exceptionally affectionate and reliant child, continue this until she is unconscious," said the student. "We are monitoring her, however, in case she needs a sedative. If we can avoid the sedative, we do, because it does them good, like a purgative, to work it out of their system."

The little girl lay on the floor and kicked. She beat her head brutally against the floor. "Padded, of course," said the student. "Persistent little devil, isn't she?"

Todd noticed that tears were rolling down Sandy's cheeks. Profusively, making a latticework of tear tracks.

The little girl jumped up and ran as fast as she could against the wall, striking it with her head. The force of the impact was so great that she rebounded a full five feet and landed on her back. She jumped up again and screamed and screamed. Then she began running around the room in circles.

"Oh, well," said the student. "This could go on for hours, Dr. Halking. Would you like to see something else?"

"I'd like to continue watching a while longer," Todd said softly.

The little girl abruptly stopped moving and slowly removed all her clothing. Then she started tearing at her naked skin with her teeth and fingernails. Streaks of bloody wounds followed after her fingers.

"Uh-oh," said the student. "Self-destructive. Have to stop her, she might go for the eyes and cause permanent damage."

The last word was lost as the door slammed behind her. In a moment the observers saw the student researcher enter the therapy room. The little girl flew at her, screaming and clawing. The student, despite her weight, was well-trained—she subdued the child quickly without sustaining or causing any wounds. Todd watched as the woman deftly forced a straitjacket on the child.

"Dr. Halking," one of the other students said, interrupting his observation. "I beg your pardon, but what is your wife doing?"

Sandy was removing her last stitch of clothing. Todd managed to catch her hands before she could rake her nails across her sagging bosom. The ancient hands were like claws where he held them—and madness poured strength into her arms. She broke free.

"Give me a hand here," Todd said, meaning to shout but only able to whisper because of the way his heart was beating.

When they finally forced her to the ground, shaking and exhausted, her own skin was streaked with blood, and some of the students had marks on them. Todd's face was bleeding, mostly where two-day-old wounds had reopened.

The matron of the childhouse came in almost immediately after they subdued Sandy. "What in heaven's name are you *doing* in here!" she demanded.

They told her. She narrowed her eyes and looked at Todd. "Dr. Halking, what do you mean bringing a woman who was over the edge into a childhouse? What did you mean letting her watch separation therapy? What in heaven's name were you *thinking* of? Are you trying to create catatonia? Are you trying to get some of my staff killed? You've certainly got some of them fired for letting this happen!"

Todd mumbled his apologies, urging her not to fire anyone. "It was all my fault, I lied to them, I—"

"Well, Dr. Halking, I'm calling the police at once. This woman is obviously ready to be turned over. Obviously. I can't understand a man of your stature playing these *games* with a woman's safety, and just plain *ignoring* the law—"

Todd apologized again, praised the fine work they were doing, told her he would make a favorable report on their behavior, and finally the matron calmed down. Todd managed to extricate himself. The matron did not call the police. Sandy took Todd's hand and followed him docilely out of the building.

When he got her home he let got of her hand. She stayed standing where he had let go of her. When he came back into the room a few minutes later, she was still standing there in exactly the same position.

He spoke to her, but she didn't answer. He took her hand and led her. She followed him to the bedroom. She stood by the bed when he let go. Gently he pushed her onto the bed. She lay on it, not moving. He raised her arm. She left it raised until he reached out and lowered it again.

He closed her eyes, because she wouldn't blink. Then he sat on the bed beside her and wept dry tears into his hands, his body shuddering with rapid, uncontrollable sobs, though not a sound came. Then he slept, feeling as sick as he had claimed to be that morning.

Sandy remained catatonic for the rest of the week. He hired a student from the university to come in and feed Sandy and clean up after her.

On Friday Todd and Ryan gathered their hastily prepared reports and flew to San Francisco for the meeting. Val Lassiter was on the same plane, but they all pretended not to know each other. The secrecy continued when they reached the city. The scientists were all put in separate hotels. They were brought to the meeting at different times, through different entrances. Some of the were instructed to wear casual clothes. Others wore business suits. One man wore a white uniform. Another wore a hard hat.

"Why all the secrecy?" Ryan asked Todd, laughing at a neurologist in a rather overdone fisherman's outfit.

"To prevent the public from getting too much hope if the papers report that this meeting is taking place," Todd answered.

"Why not? Why not a little hope?" Ryan asked.

"Why not a lot of heroin?"

Ryan looked coldly at Todd. "Dr. Halking, I find your despair disgusting."

Todd looked back and smiled. "And I find your insistence on hope touchingly naive."

The meeting went on. The reports varied between cautious negative statements and utter despair. Todd read Ryan's and his report toward the end of the first day. "Except for the viral microscopy reports, all were slowly and deliberately doublechecked. My assistant wants me to assure you that the viral microscopy reports were hurried through the second check. That is true, because the meeting couldn't wait and the computer *could* be made to work overtime."

There was some laughter.

"However, we never found any discrepancy between first and second runs on any other tests, and we did carefully check and found no discrepancies on the first run of the viral microscopy tests either. Therefore, I can safely conclude that there is no significant difference between contemporary blood samples and the blood samples prior to the Premature Aging Phenomenon, except such differences as reflect our conquest of certain well-known diseases, and these antibodies were not stimulated until long after the PAP was first noted. Ergo—not significant."

There were some careful questions, easily answered, and they moved on. However jovial a presenter might be, the answer was always the same. No answers.

After the papers were presented, the data examined, the statistical results questioned and upheld, the heads of the projects gathered in one small room at the top of the old Hyatt Regency. Todd Halking and Val Lassiter arrived together. Only a couple of men were already there. On impulse, Todd walked to the chalkboard at one end of the room and wrote on it, "Abandon hope all ye who enter here."

"Not funny," Val said when Todd sat down next to him.

"Come on. They'll die laughing."

Val looked at Todd quizzically. "Get a grip, Todd," he said.

Todd smiled. "I have a grip. If not on myself, then on reality."

Everyone who came into the room saw the sign on the chalkboard. Some chuckled a little. Finally someone got up and erased the message.

The room was only half full. Todd got up and left the room, his aging bladder more demanding than it had been a few years—a few weeks!—before. He washed his hands afterward, and looked at himself in the mirror. He was haggard. His face cried out Death. He smiled at himself. The smile was ghastly. He went back to the room.

He was not yet seated when a military-looking man entered and said, "Ladies and gentlemen, the President of the United States." Everybody stood and applauded. The president walked in. No one could have recognized him from the publicity pictures. They all dated from his second campaign, and then he had not been bald.

"Well, you've done it," the president said. "And within my term of office. Thank you. The effort was magnificent. The results are remarkably thorough, I'm told by those who should know."

The president coughed into a handkerchief. He sounded like he had pleurisy.

"And if you're right," he said. "*If* you're right, the picture is pretty grim."

The president laughed. Todd wondered why. But a few of the scientists laughed, too. Including Anne Hallam, the geneticist. She spoke. "To the dinosaurs things once looked grim, too. A million mammals chewing on their eggs."

"The dinosaurs died out," the president said.

"No," Hallam answered. "Only the ones that hadn't become birds or mammals or some more viable type of reptile." She smiled at them all. Hope springs eternal, Todd thought. "It's small comfort," she went on, "but one thing this early aging has done: The species has shorter generations. We're better able to adapt genetically. Whatever happens, when mankind gets out of this we will not be the same as we were when we went in."

"Yes," Todd said cheerfully. "We'll all be dead."

Anne looked at him in irritation, and several people coughed. But the mood of joviality the president had set at first was gone now. Val wrote on his notebook and shoved it toward Todd as the president started talking again.

"You're speaking of aeons and species," the president said. "I must think of nations and societies. Ours is dying. If what you say is true, in a few years it will be dead. The nation. The way we live. Civilization, if I may use the romantic word."

Todd read Val's note. It said, "Shut your mouth, you bastard, it's bad enough already."

Todd smiled at Val. Val glared back.

People were telling the president: It's hardly that bleak, we weathered the worst already.

"Oh yes," the president agreed. "We lasted through the depression. We adapted to the collapse of world trade. We made the transition from the cities back to the farms, we have endured the death of huge industry and global interreactions. We have adapted to having our population cut in half, in less than half."

"What clever little adapters we are, Mr. President," Todd said, aware that he was breaking protocol to interrupt the president, and not particularly giving a damn. "But tell me, has anyone figured out an adaptation to death? Odd, isn't it, that in millions of years of evolution, nature has never managed to select for immortality."

Val stood, obviously angry. "Mr. President, I suggest that Dr. Halking be asked to contribute constructively or leave this meeting. There's no way we can accomplish anything with these constant interjections of pessimism."

There was a murmur, half of protest, half of agreement.

"Val," Todd said, "I'm only trying to be realistic."

"And what do you think *we* are, dreamers? Don't we know we're all old men and doomed to die?"

The president coughed, and Val sat down. "I believe," said the president, "that Dr. Halking will take this as a reminder that we are talking here as men of science, dispassionately. Impersonally, if you will. Now let's review...."

They went over the findings again. "Is there any chance," the president asked again and again, "that you might be wrong?"

A chance, they all answered. Of course there's a chance. But we have done the best our instruments will let us do.

"What if you had more sophisticated instruments?" he asked.

Of course, they said. But we do not have them. You'll have to wait another generation, or two, or three, and by then the damage will be done. We'll never live to see it.

"Then," the president said, "we must get busy. Make sure your assistants and their assistants and their assistants as well know everything you know. Prepare them to continue your work. We can't give up."

Todd looked around the table as everyone nodded sagely, lips pursed in the identical expression of grim courage. The spirit of man: We shall overcome. Todd couldn't bear it anymore. Like his bladder, his emotions could be contained for progressively shorter periods of time.

"For Christ's sake, do you call this optimism?" he said, and was instantly embarrassed that tears came unbidden to his eyes. They would dismiss him as an emotional wreck, not listen to his ideas at all. Sound clinical, he warned himself. Try to sound clinical and careful and scientific and impartial and uninvolved and all those other impossible, virtuous things.

"I have the cure to the Premature Aging Phenomenon," Todd said. "Or at least I have the cure to the misery."

Eyes. All watching him intently. At last I have their attention, he thought.

"The cure to the misery is to go home and go to bed and stop trying. We've done all we can do. And if we can't cure the disease, we can live with it. We can adapt to it. We can try to be happy."

But the eyes were gone again, and two of the scientists came over to him and dabbed at his eyes with their handkerchiefs and helped him get up from the table. They took him to another room, where he sat (guarded by four men, just in case) and sobbed.

At last he was dry. He sat and looked at the window and wondered why he had said the things he had said. What good would it do? Men didn't have it in them to stop trying. We are not bred for despair.

And yet we learn it, for even in our efforts to repair the damage done by premature aging, we are as blind as lemmings, struggling to go down the same old road to a continent that a million years before had sunk under the sea—yet the road could not be changed. The age of forty had its tasks; therefore we must strive to live to forty, however far away it might be now.

The meeting ended. He heard voices in the hall. The words could not be deciphered, but through them all was the tone of boisterous good cheer, good luck my friend and I'll see you soon, here's to the future.

The door to Todd's private (except for the guards) room opened. Anne Hallam and Ryan came in, stepping quietly.

"I'm not asleep," Todd said. "Nor am I emotionally dicommoded at the moment. So you needn't tiptoe."

Anne smiled then. "Todd, I'm sorry. About the embarrassment to you. It happens to all of us now and then."

Todd smiled back (thank God for a little warmth—how had she kept it?) And then shook his head. "Not then. Just now. Well, what did the meeting find out?

Have the Chinese found a magic cure and only now are radioing the formula to Honolulu?"

Ryan laughed. "As if there *were* any Chinese anymore."

Anne said, "We decided two things . First, we haven't found the cure yet."

"Astute," Todd aid, raising an imaginary glass to clink with hers.

"And second, we decided that there *is* a cure, and we will find it."

"And while you were at it," Todd asked, "did you decide that faster-than-light travel was possible, and declare that it would be discovered next week by two youngsters in France who by chance were walking in the field one day and plunged into hyperspace?"

"Not only that," Anne said, "but one of the children immediately will follow a rabbit down a hole and find herself in Wonderland."

"Blunderland," Todd added, and Anne and Todd laughed together with understanding and mutual compassion. Ryan looked at them, puzzlement in his eyes. Todd noticed it. The younger generation still knows only life: Ah, youthful Caesar, we who are about to die salute you, though we have no hope of actually communicating with you.

"But there is a cause," Anne insisted, "and therefore it can be found."

"Your faith is touching," Todd said.

"There's a cause for everything, we don't change overnight with no reason, or else nothing that any human being has ever called 'true' can be counted on at all. Will gravity fail?"

"Tomorrow afternoon at three," Todd said.

"Only if there's a cause. But sometimes—right now, with PAP—the cause eludes us, that's all. Why did the dinosaurs die out? Why did the apes drop from the trees and start talking and lighting fires? We can guess, perhaps, but we don't know; and yet there *was* a cause or there's no reason in the world."

"I rest my case," Todd said. "My basket case, to be precise."

Ryan's face twisted, and Todd laughed at him. "Ryan, the nearly dead are free to joke about death. It's only the living to whom death is tabu."

"Maybe," Anne Hallam said, leaning back in a chair (and the guards' eyes followed her, because they watched everybody, guarded everybody), "maybe there's some system, some balance, some ecosystem we haven't discovered until now, a system that demands that, when one species or group gets out of hand, that species changes, not for survival of the fittest, but for survival of the whole. Perhaps the dinosaurs were destroying the earth, and so they—stopped. Perhaps man was—no, we know man was destroying the earth. And we know we were stopped. Any talk of nuclear war now? Any chance of too much industry raping the earth utterly beyond of hope of survival?"

"And in a moment," Ryan said, his mouth curled with distaste, "you'll be mentioning the thought that God is punishing us for our sins. I, personally, find the idea ridiculous, and seeing two of our finest minds seriously discussing it is pathetic."

Ryan got up and left. Anne smiled again (warmly!) at Todd, patted his hand,

and left. After a few minutes, Todd followed.

A plane ride east.

Midnight at the airport. Nevertheless, a crowd bustling through. At one end of the terminal, a ragged old man was shouting to an oblivious crowd.

Todd and the others tried to pass him without paying attention, but he called to them. "You! You with the briefcases, you in the suits!" Ryan stopped and turned, and so they all had to. Todd was irritated. He was tired. He wanted to get home to Sandy.

"You're scientists, aren't you!" the man shouted. They didn't answer. He took that for agreement. "It's your fault! The earth couldn't bear so many men, so many machines!"

"Let's get out of here," Todd said, and the others agreed. The old man kept calling after them. "Rape, that's all it was! Rape of a planet, rape of each other, rape of life, you bastards!" People stared at them all the way out of the terminal.

"There was a day," Ryan said, "when people expected science to work miracles, and cursed us when we failed. Now they curse us for the miracles we did give them."

Todd hunched his shoulders. Scientists hell. Who were scientists? People with blue security cards.

The old man's voice echoed even out in the parking lot. "The earth gets even! The violated virgins will have their revenge!"

Todd got in his car and drove home alone. Shaking.

When he got home he found all as he had left it. The student from the university had come in and fed Sandy—there were dishes in the sink that the boy apparently hadn't thought of cleaning up.

Sandy was where Todd had left her. Lying on the bed. Breathing. Her eyes were closed.

Todd lay on the bed beside her. He had carried despair with him to the meeting, and carried it as a burden multiplied many times over when he came back. With a gentle finger he traced the wrinkles that radiated from Sandy's eyes, followed the folds of skin down her neck, twisted the brown hair now showing gray roots, pressed his lips against her closed eyes. He could remember when the skin was smooth, not cracked and hard as parchment, not thin and vein-lined.

"I'm sorry," he said again and again, unsure who he was apologizing to or what for. "I'm so sorry."

And then he told his wife's unhearing ears about the conference. They had found nothing. And finding nothing, they could find no cure. You're going to die, he said softly into her ear. "You're going to die, I'd stop it if I could, but I can't, you're going to die."

He got up and sat at his desk. He wrote by hand on the blank envelope sitting there, because he felt too tired to type, too tired to reach up to the shelf above the desk and pick up the sheets of paper. The ink scrawled:

"Our senility is not just age. In the books it is possible to age gracefully. Let us age with grace and strength, please, not madly and with terror and in the darkness and clinging to our pillows and our blankets calling names of parents we never knew, names of soft friends who never answered us."

He stopped writing for as little reason as he had begun. He wondered who he had been writing to. He leaned back and touched the mattress. It was soft. He buried his hand in the blanket. It was soft.

On his knees by the bed, he clung to the blanket saying quietly, "Dappa," and then, "Coopie. Dappa, you're back."

Lying naked on the bed, curled up with a pillow tucked under his arm, he knew somewhere back in his mind that he was not quite what he should be, not quite thinking and acting as he ought. But it was too good to have Dappa and Coopie back.

He fell asleep with tears of comfort and relief spotting the sheets.

He woke with blood pumping upward out of his heart. His wife Sandy knelt on the bed, straddling him, the letter opener still in her hand, her face splotched red with his blood.

"Poogy," she said angrily, her face contorted. "You've got Poogy and I want him."

She stabbed him again, and Todd felt the letter opener in his chest. It fit as snugly and comfortably as a new organ that had long been missing from his body. It was, however, cold.

Sandy pulled out the letter opener and a new spout erupted and spattered. She stuck out her lower lip. "I'm taking Poogy now," she said. Then she reached down and pulled the bloody pillow from under his arm.

"Dappa," Todd said in feeble protest. But as the pillow moved away, cradled in his wife's arms, he saw clearly again, he recognized what was happening, and as his arms and legs got colder and the bloodspout weakened, he longed to cry out for help. But his voice did not work. There was no rescue.

Death and madness, he thought in the last moment left to him. They are the only rescuers. And where madness fails, death will do.

And it did.

ARTIES AREN'T STUPID

by Jeremiah Tolbert

Jeremiah Tolbert's fiction has appeared in *Fantasy Magazine, Interzone, Ideomancer*, and *Shimmer*, as well as in the anthologies *Federations* and *Polyphony 4*. He's also been featured several times on the *Escape Pod* and *Podcastle* podcasts. In addition to being a writer, he is a web designer, photographer, and graphic artist—and he shows off each of those skills in his Dr. Roundbottom project, located at www.clockpunk.com. He lives in Colorado, with his wife and cats. This story first appeared in my anthology *Seeds of Change*.

Does it hurt an artist to go a week without painting? Does it pain a singer to spend a day without singing? Do creative people suffer when they are denied the chance to create?

Our next story is the story of artists who *do* suffer when circumstances keep them from creating art. They suffer real pain—because they are genetically engineered constructs whose bodies are specially designed to make art. These "arties" aren't alone in their specialization. There are "brainiacs" whose bodies are atrophied beneath massive brains, and "thicknecks" and "skinnybois," too. Each group has their own skills, their own weaknesses, their own strange places in a strange world.

In such a regimented society, it's not surprising that even a temporary mural needs to be licensed. But when their latest art experiment is rejected, the crew of artists have to find a new kind of creativity, an art so big it will transcend the boundaries between every specialty.

This piece sketches a dark reality where art is dangerous and creativity hurts. It confronts us with the value of art in our own time and place. It asks: can society thrive without art? Can we live without it?

Would we want to?

A few of us arties were hanging out in Tube Station D, in the dry part that hadn't flooded. Tin men had busted Blaze and Ransom doing an unlicensed mural on Q Street behind a soytein shop, and a small crowd of us watching (too chick-shit to Make with the tin men cracking down) scattered when the pig-bots hummed in from every direction like it was some kind of puzzle bust and not just a bunch of arties trying to wind down. We'd all clustered back down in the Station on Niles's turf. Tin men didn't bother below ground. So long as the Elderfolk couldn't see turd, they didn't give a turd.

Niles wasn't there, so some rat-faced kid started posing and posturing about taking a little swatch of wall for himself, doing it up special. Pecking order is pecking order, so nobody wanted to be near the turd-head if Niles heard him talking like that, so every bodies was giving him space and lots of it. Look-outs on the street announced with sharp whistles that Niles was headed down, and the kid shut right up.

Niles was a year or two older than the rest of us. Some bodies liked to say he was a proto-arty, but I don't know about that. He was different, and it didn't have nothing to do with his age or Make. All age did was give him a few inches of height to make bossing easier. He bossed good, not mean like Elderfolk, but kept us out of trouble with the thicknecks and just-plains. Something about him was plain special. We few girlies knew it, specially.

He was taller than me by a head, hair burnt umber and long, styled nice with lip-curl and spike. He wore a worker man's jumpsuit adorned with patches and swatches of fabric that he liked. Very anime, very hip. Arties have good fashion sense, but Niles set trends in our clade.

Boo was with him as usual, a stunted runt of a melodie that Niles had found sleeping on his turf. She wore an old fashioned mp3 player around her neck, earbuds nearly soldered into her ear bits. Whenever you got close to her, you could make out tinny music, but what kind of music it was, you couldn't figure. Unlike other melodies, Boo never sung, not once. Didn't speak either. Bum batch, probably. It happens, although most get recycled early. Nobody questioned her hanging around, seeing's how Niles tolerated her.

"This stuff is snazzy," he said. "No paint, just water and plant stuff. Nozzle works the same though. Sprays right on." I recognized the stuff. I'd seen advertisements for it on my Elderfolk's vidiot box. Moss-in-a-can. They sold it to Elderfolk for the recreation yards, for making everything look all old and natural, whatever that meant. Simple biotech, nothing too crazy, nothing like us arties.

Niles tossed us each a metal can from a satchel that Boo carried, except for the rat-faced kid—Niles gave him zip. "You get out of here, go home to your Elderfolk. I heard what you were saying before I stalked a-on down," he said to him, wagging his finger, and rat-face's eyes got all comic and big. Rat-face sputtered something about how his Elderfolk didn't want him around, but Niles just shook his head.

"No bodies do, Zinger." That's right, I remembered, rat-face was a new transfer to the city hood named Zinger something-something. Niles was a lot better at names than the rest of us, but you could see that he had to think real hard for it, sometimes. His face'd scrunch up and he'd just freeze to concentrate past all the shapes and colors that dance in an arties head from wake to sleep.

"Yah," said Tops. He stepped up out of the crowd and gave Zinger a short shove on the shoulder. Tops was Ransom's best friend, and he'd been spoiling for a fight all day, ever since the Tin Men busted Ransom.

"Cerulean," Niles said, and the color flashed through our heads and everybody calmed down just a little. "Go on, you can come back tomorrow. This is my studio, don't forget it, 'kay?"

Zinger nodded, then turned and ran up the stone steps to street level. Niles sighed and finished handing out the moss-in-a-can.

"We supposed to Make with this instead of paint? It's all one color," Tops said, his voice all whiny like some spoiled just-plain.

"That's right," Niles said. "Better mossy than going in the pokey-pokey." I winced at the word, which was both the name of a bad place and a description of what they did to you there.

I took my can happy, feeling better already. Design-shapes were practically pushing out my ears. My Elderfolk wouldn't give me any scratch for paints lately, using it all on themselves and *drugas* to feel better. Was okay with me, Niles gave stuff that he got from trading to the thicknecks and skinnybois for gang logos. Drugas made my Elderfolk less shouty which was just good-no-great with me.

I went up and found some alley space and I Made until it all went away into an eggshell white haze.

We messed around with the moss-in-a-can for a few days until the Elderfolk decided they didn't like the "mess" and the tin men got new marching orders. They started spraying down all the fractals and designs with some kind of ick and it all turned turd-brown and dusted away. Hurt to see it, but what can arties do? Tin men can't be argued or fought with like Elderfolk.

We were all sulking in Niles' station, feeling the pain of not-Making like aching all over and Niles got mad and stomped off without even waking up Boo. We were a little scared, because Niles only left Boo behind when he was going to do something that might get him sent into the pokey for a long long time, and without Niles to keep everything straight, we'd all be in trouble. Boo woke up while we were fighting about what to do and came and cuddled up to me. I could almost feel the music vibrating through her into me. It made me feel a little sick.

"Don't know why she likes *you* so much," Tops said with a sneer. "Your Make sucks the big dong."

I shrugged. Niles knew my Make was okay. Didn't much care if Tops and the other arties did. "I don't know," I said.

"Maybe because Mona isn't a 'big dong' like you," sneered Tess. She helped whenever the boys thought they could gang-up on me. "And Mona's Make is okay. You're just scared because Niles is doing something bad."

"Shut up," Tops said and turned away. Tess smiled at me a little. I tried to smile back, but the symmetry felt off.

Boo tapped me on the arm and I looked down. She raised her eyebrows at me, then looked at the steps to the street. I nodded. "He went upside for a while. He'll be fine." She didn't look convinced. Neither was I. We held each other and it made the ache a little better.

I worried sometimes that Boo felt that way all the time. She was a melodie and had to Make just like we poor arties did, but nobody ever heard her sing and bang or anything. Broken little thing made me feel sorry and sad. It was a good thing Niles took care of her, or she'd be used up and swept away just like our mossy Makes.

Nobody went home to their Elderfolk while we waited for Niles to come back. That was a rule. If Niles never came back, then we wouldn't have to. Nobody wanted to see the meanies anyway. They had us Made and then hated us afterwards, which wasn't fair. All arties know you love the things you Make no matter what. But Elderfolk were just-plains all grown up and they didn't make any sense at all. Some of the younger arties started to talk about going back, but we older arties who knew Niles better said no, that we'd wait.

Three days passed before Niles came back. It was dark and everyone was sleeping but me, because little Boo's music itched in my brain. He came in carrying big boxes, and I cried big tears of happy at that. He'd brought some new supplies, and we'd be Making again in no time flat. I watched him for a while, carrying in box after box, and finally I fell asleep. It felt good knowing he was back.

In the morning, laughing woke me up. I turned to see what arty could be so rude. Niles was sitting in a corner with his back to the room, playing with something. He never laughed when he was Making so he had to be playing.

I left Boo to cuddle into the pile of other arties and crawled over to see what Niles was doing. He had some weird gadget, a silver disk covered in letter-buttons and it was projecting onto the wall some kind of tri-dimensional animal-thing. It had three legs and one arm and was galloping in place like a creature with three legs would, a kind of hop between steps. I laughed too when I looked at the weird little thing.

"What is it?" I asked in a whisper.

"I Made it, just now," Niles said. "It's complicated, but the brainiacs on P-Street showed me how. I only sort of made it. It's just pretend now, but I can send it into the factories," he pointed at the stack of boxes next to us, "then it'll Make for real."

"Wow," I said. I couldn't think of anything else to speak. Niles was like that, always thinking ahead of the Elderfolk and the tin men.

"Does it help the ache?" I asked, my pulse racing. I almost felt good, even with the hurt, just at the chance.

"A-yep," he said. "Feels good. Like sculpting, sort of. But you can paint on them too. Paint in texture, scales, hair, you know. All sorts of things. But there's a sense to it, like how you know good colors going together?"

"Yes?"

"Like that. You can't just do anything," he said. He nodded, and pressed a large button on the disk. Words came up and the creature disappeared.

"What's that say?" I asked.

"Dunno," he answered. "But the brainiacs said if I push that button, the factory will Make."

A humming sound came just then from one of the boxes, and then the other arties started to stir and wake.

"Here," Niles said, handing me the disk. "I'll teach you how it works. We have to teach everybody. The tin men can't kill animals besides pests, you know!"

We pretend-Made all sorts of little creatures on the screen, then pushed the button that Made for real. The little factories, we set up in one corner of the station, and they hummed and popped out little eggs of all rainbow-colors every few hours. Niles sent the little kids out onto the street with the eggs to hide them where the tin men and Elderfolk wouldn't see.

"The eggs will hatch and our Makes will come out alive, and the tin men can't do anything about it!" He said. His eyes were shiny. It made me ache a little, and I worried that maybe pretend-Making didn't count for arties. But Niles was always making me ache a little like that, especially when he left. It scared me, that maybe I was like little Boo and something wasn't right with me. Bum batch.

Pretty soon, we started seeing the little animals around the City. They weren't good Makes, though. They stumbled into traffic sometimes and got splattered. They fell off of roofs, got tangled in wires and cooked like bad soytein on a hot plate. They weren't there in the head. And they starved. Not a lot of food out in the city just for the taking. They couldn't take chits and buy it.

We were stumped. The tin men weren't doing anything, but our little Makes couldn't last on their own. I hated so much seeing them laying dead in gutters, in the street drains. Their little selves were all over, stinking and falling apart like wind-worn paints.

"I have an idea," I said to Niles after thinking as hard as I could. "Go to the brainiacs and ask them for help. They will tell us what we can do right."

Niles thought for a moment and shook his head. "No. This is an arty problem."

"But arties are too stupid," I said, raising my voice so everyone could hear it.

Niles bared his teeth at me, and I cried out, scrambling away from him. "Arties aren't stupid!" he shouted. "Arties aren't stupid!"

But we are, I said to my own head. We are not smart like brainiacs. I ran away, back to my stupid Elderfolks, but even they were smarter than arties.

I was drawing on the sidewalk, just to ease the ache, when Niles found me. I had stolen a little bit of charcoal from the crematorium and kept it in my pocket. I only used it when things were really bad, really really. And now I didn't know what to do.

"Your repeating… patterns?" Niles said. "What do you call them?"

I shrugged. "Can't think of words for it. Maybe your brainiac friends could guess."

He frowned. "They could, but who cares?" He sat beside me and took out a piece of old paper. It had shapes drawn on it like my patterns, only more random. I was fascinated.

"Where did you get that?" I asked. I reached out to touch it, and he let me take it. I held it up to the light. The little bits were a faded green, like the moss-in-a-can.

"Plants," he said. "They're called 'plants.'"

"Plants," I said. "Snazzy."

"A-yap," he said. "The old world was full of them."

"Who told you that?" I asked.

"The brainiacs," he said. I stood up and hugged him tight.

"Make some plants with the factories," he said. "They'll be pretty."

So we did. This time, the eggs were smaller, and we hid everywhere in the city. Niles helped me to make them. He understood the rightness of the animal bits, but to me, plants made more sense. They didn't move, except to stretch for sun or rain. Wherever you put them, that's where they stayed, just like murals.

The ache almost went all-away, for a while.

The little plant-eggs hatched and grew quickly all around the city. We Made so much more of them, and they lasted good. The tin men noticed them. Everywhere, arties were seeing the tin men staring at the little plants growing bigger every day. They didn't know what to do, but all arties knew what happened then: the tin men asked the Elderfolk.

While I Made plants, the other arties Made more little animals. Some that flew in the air, and some that could squeeze into tiny little cracks. This time, the little animals didn't die. They grew bigger too, like the plants had to come first for them to work. Niles said it was a secret why, and wouldn't tell me, which made me angry, but the ache was staying away so long as I made my plants, so I couldn't fight him over it.

Boo spent more time with me, too, when I was Making plants. She loved their shapes and would smile and point and smile whenever we found another one growing up in the cracks out on the street. One night, I even woke up and saw her toying with one of the silver disks when she thought no one was watching. The shapes on the screen were colorful, but they had no coherence, no pattern.

Sad, sad little Boo. She wanted to Make plants and animals too, but she was just a melodie and she couldn't Make.

I was in the white of Making when I heard the shouts coming down the stairs. "Tin men coming! Tin men!" they cried. "There's a brainiac with them!" Zinger shouted.

Everyone scattered like moss-dust on the breeze, no direction to go, just bumping around in the station. Only one way out, up, and the tin men had it blocked. I took the silver disk I was using and one of the factories and pushed them into the flooded part of the station, then tried to run for the door.

The tin men galomp-ed down the steps carefully, using their long arms to steady themselves on the uneven steps. They had three brainiacs with them. Each held their big heads in their hands and moaned from all the effort of walking. Brainiacs didn't like to do that if they could help it.

The tin man corralled us arties up into a tight bunch and others stole away with the disks and factories. One sheriff tin man, gold-coated and round, prodded the brainiacs, and they pointed at Niles, all three at the same time. Then the tin men took Niles too. We arties tried to fight then, and Boo did too. But we're not made for fighting, and we all hurt ourselves on the cold sleek shells of the tin men. When Niles was gone, they let us a-go, and left following the sheriff.

We wailed and cried. "Doomed," Topps moaned. "Doomed." The ache wasn't over us yet, but it would be now.

"Every time we find something new to Make, they take it away," Tess said, dabbing tears from her eyes.

"The tin men don't care," Zinger said.

"Of course they don't," I said. "They only do what the Elderfolk tell them to do. And the Elderfolk don't care. They don't care about anything but themselves."

"We have to get Niles back," Topps said, starting to cry again. "Arties are too dumb on their own. Too dumb!"

I snapped up at that. "No!" I said. "Arties aren't dumb! Niles said!"

"Doesn't matter anymore," Zinger said. "Niles is gone to the pokey-pokey. They'll never let him out."

"Then we get him out," said a tiny voice I had never heard before. It half-sung the words, just like a melodie did whenever it talked, but the sound was wrong, harsh around the edges. It was a bad Make.

Boo didn't look scared. She was younger than all of us, but she wasn't scared. Everyone tried to wipe up tears then, just so they didn't look like little babies when the real baby didn't even cry.

"Boo can talk!" Zinger said after a long silence.

"Of course she can talk," I snapped. "But she didn't want to before now. This is important."

Boo nodded. "Hurts. My—" she touched her throat, "not made right." She winced from the effort of talking. I grabbed her and held her close.

"Boo is right," I said. "We arties have to get Niles back."

"But how?" asked Tess.

I didn't know. I looked at Boo. Boo didn't know.

"We'll ask the brainiacs," I said then. It was what Niles had done, and they owed us after turning Niles in.

The brainiacs spent most of their times at the libraries, and there was one on P-Street that I had remembered because it had pretty statues on each side of its big doors. Boo and I marched inside, past the tin men that watched the door, and inside, before they could get a good sniff of us. The first brainiac we saw, we cornered against a shelf. She was locked into her little wheelchair and couldn't move very fast.

"Tell us how to rescue Niles," I demanded. Boo made menacing gestures with her hands that she must have learned from watching thicknecks.

"Who?" said the brainiac. "Oh, that arty kid with the stolen gengineering kits? He's gone up-tower to see Council. The Elderfolk are real pissed about that little scheme of his. Not even a platoon of thicknecks could get in there. The Tower is crawling with tin men."

I shuddered. The Council were the Elderfolk to the Elderfolk. They told everyone what to do. If they had Niles, then there really was no hope. The aching bent me over in two like a folded piece of paper.

Boo shook her head and pointed at the brainiac. I guessed at what she was trying to say, and fought through my pains.

"You're smarter than arties and the just-plains. The Council is just a bunch of just-plains all grown up. You can help us rescue him," I said, not really believing but hoping.

The brainiac sighed and nodded. "I can think of dozens, thousands of ways to free your friend, but logistically, you arties can't manage it."

"What's logistically?" I said.

"Tools, resources," she said, rolling her eyes. "You're just a bunch of stupid beatniks. Maybe if you still had some gengineering factories, you could make something, but—"

"I hid one," I said quickly. "Under the water. When the Tin Men came."

"Well then, you've ruined it. It's no good."

"But you could fix it," Boo rasped in sing-song. The brainiac nodded.

"I could fix it, but then you'd need to make something that could get you into the Tower without having to fight tin men, and that'd be almost impossible," said the brainiac.

"Making is what arties do. You fix the factory, and we'll do the rest," I said. I could see the shapes forming already. My fingers itched to work the disk.

"Fine, but this makes the arties and the brainiacs even," she said.

"Deal," I said.

The tin men were killing all the animals and plants in the city with ick. Someone must have changed their orders. They weren't supposed to do that.

It hurt us arties to know, but it kept the tin men busy while we Made in shifts with the factory. We had a plan, one that the brainiacs thought would get us all tossed in the pokey, but Boo and I both believed it would work. The other arties made animals that would go into the Tower and distract, and I worked on special plants with exploding seeds. Weapons, like thicknecks used on one another. We tested the seeds on a lone tin man, and it stunned it. We smashed it up good while it was down.

The brainiac who repaired our factory met us in the shadows outside the Tower before we launched our attack. She pressed a sheet of paper into my hands. "One last little bit of help," the brainiac said. "This will show you where they're keeping your friend."

"Why?" I asked.

The brainiac laughed. "You have no idea how bored we are. Your little creations are an ad-hoc ecosystem springing up all over the city. We've been studying things. Your creations are immensely complex and function cohesively, even though they are artificial. This bit of information has vast implications on issues such as the Jungian overmind—" the brainiac blinked and cut off her speech. I hadn't understood a word of it, only that they *liked* our Makes. That made me feel good. "Sorry. Anyway, we hope you can make more."

"It was Niles' idea," I said. "Without him, we arties are too stupid to figure anything out."

The brainiac frowned. "I wouldn't be so sure about that. This plan of yours might actually work. And it looks like your friends are ready."

Us arties were gathering from all over the city. Each had a wild little animal, frantic and tugging at a leash of plant-rope. Each carried a satchel of bomb-seeds. Across the corner, a few thicknecks had gathered. They made catcalls and threats, but none dared to cross the street. I could hardly believe my eyes.

Everyone waited for my command. I hesitated. If I said so, we arties would all go home to our Elderfolk. Maybe some would get supplies to ease the ache, and maybe some wouldn't and they might die. Or we could attack the Tower and some would die and the rest would end up in the pokey-pokey or we might win and get back Niles and all his crazy ideas for Making. And it was my deci-sion. Little Mona, whose art nobody understood.

Nobody but Niles.

I gave the word. The arties rushed the tower. Tin men spilled out from the doors, and seeds flew from everywhere. They crashed to the ground in beautiful purple sparks, and we swept past them inside. We arties freed the frantic little animals, and they ran free. The tin men couldn't decide whether to chase us or chase the animals and split up. I led us arties up, up, following the drawings on the paper.

We pushed past many many tin men, leaving them smoking behind us, and finally we got to the end place, and it was a place we all remembered, a birthing lab, cold, white and metal. And there were just-plains, the birthers, watching Niles, and he was sleeping in the tank, just like a baby arty. We scared away the just-plains. They tried to tell us to stop, that they needed Niles, but we needed him more. So we took him, and we left. We didn't go back to the station. We found a new hiding place, in the basement of a power station, and there, we waited for Niles to wake up, and we cried, all of us arties, all as one.

We'd done it, but Niles wouldn't wake up.

He wasn't dead, we knew that, because he was breathing. At first, no one would leave him, but even arties get hungry, and so we started watching in shifts, taking turns. Every one wanted to be the arty who was there when he woke, but it was me that was there, and it was Boo that woke him up.

She sang; it was beautiful, even if it was broken. The pattern in the sound reminded me of the colors on her screen. The sound grew louder as she continued, and then I saw that little flying animals had come from the sky and joined her, together adding their voices and fixing where hers was broken. It must have been the best sound in the world, because then finally, Niles woke up, and he smiled.

"Hey-a, Boo," he said. "You can sing." As if he had always known, and it wasn't a surprise to him. And maybe he did. Niles was smart, especially for an arty. Then he turned and smiled at me.

"Hey-a, Mona. You rescued me."

"We did," I said. "And the brainiacs hardly helped at all."

He laughed. "That's good. But I been thinking about what you said. You right. We should ask the brainiacs for help more often. Arties can't do everything."

I cried, and hugged, and cried some more.

Niles is getting better. He told me the secret of how the animals work, and at first, it made me sad. But we can eat the plants, and the animals too, so we don't have to go back to the Elderfolk for chits. We're staying here in our hiding places, and we're sharing what we know with the brainiacs. They're slipping away from their Elderfolk too. We need the thicknecks' help too, and the brainiacs are talking to them for us. Thicknecks listen to them, at least sometimes.

There are plants and animals everywhere now, and they grow too fast for the tin men to stop them. And the little flying ones, they all sing such sweet songs. Boo, and Niles, and I sit and listen to them for hours. Boo says that she only made some of them, and doesn't know where the rest of them come from. The brainiacs have theories, but we don't understand them.

And we still Make, more plants and more animals each day with more stolen factories. The ache is still there, but it's not the same. It's the ache you feel when things are good, not when things are bad. And that's the kind of ache that makes you feel good. Niles says he understands it, but I don't believe him. Nobody understands that, not even the smartest brainiac of them all.

JORDAN'S WATERHAMMER

by Joe Mastroianni

Joe Mastroianni's short fiction has appeared in *Realms of Fantasy* and *Tomorrow Speculative Fiction*. He's currently working on a novel that he describes as a psychic Antarctic love story. He's done five deployments to Antarctica, and two to the south pole where he worked on instrumentation for climatic research. He's been a Silicon Valley executive for twenty-five years and says he's currently writing and building Tesla Coils.

Most of the worst atrocities in human history spring out of the dehumanization of particular groups. Germany's war crimes during World War II are some of the most horrifying examples, with over 11 million people put to death not as individual humans, but as faceless Jews and Gypsies and anti-establishment "criminals."

But genocide isn't the only crime people commit when they strip the humanity from each other. Apartheid came from the same ugly source. Slavery, child labor, and even indentured servitude also depend upon devaluing a human being. It's sickening to imagine a society that encourages people to see a man merely as a tool, not even worthy of a name.

Our next story gives us just such a society. The workers in this world fight to teach each other a man could be worth as much as the ore they work to mine, not because a man can be bought and sold for a particular price, but because a human being is valuable in and of himself.

Here is a world without the right to liberty, the pursuit of happiness, or even life itself. After all, how can a *tool* be free?

The gaffer tripped. He fell into Jordan's blade and was cut in half with the ore pile. Perhaps it was confusion. The boy may have had his hearing. Confusion in the mine was common among the young men who could hear the crash of shovels against rock, the impact of turbo-pressured water against stone, and the roar of the loader engines. Jordan felt the slight hesitation as his machine sliced through the soft human body on its way to the heavy pile of ore.

A less experienced man may never have noticed the barely perceptible difference between the hydraulic shovel's passage through air and its passage through human flesh and bone.

Jordan typed a command on his console. He marked the ore load "dirty." The ore would have to be washed clean of blood and bone before it reached the refinery. He ordered another gaffer.

He received an acknowledgment for the ore load but the tone sounded before his gaffer order was processed. He made a mental note to reorder a gaffer in the morning. At least the dirty load wouldn't be charged against him.

The lights in his cab went dark. His control sticks grew sluggish then immobile in his hands as the hydraulics of the huge mining machine wound down. Steel bolts retracted with a jolt and the unlocked cab door swung open a crack. He could smell the air fill his cab. The atmosphere in the mine was damp and full of dust. The filters in the loader kept the air clean for him to breathe. But every time the cab door opened he could smell the sweat of the men amid the rock dust and steam. It reminded him of his boyhood.

Jordan unlatched the control connector and pulled it from his neck. He switched his connector from "cable" to "radio" control. Then he stepped from the cab into the dimly lit mine. He got in line with the other men and moved down the tunnel toward the elevators to the dormitories. The last load of ore lay still in his shovel. He saw the gaffer's hand poking out of it as he passed the front of his machine.

As they walked they passed through larger and larger tunnels until they arrived in the main gallery where hundreds of miners stood in single-file lines waiting to board the elevators to the dormitories.

He joined the sea of white helmets and blue overalls and kept his eye on the number "6" lit above the elevator door to his home. Jordan felt a tingling on his neck as his audio monitor sprang to life. His ears had been damaged long before by the continuous din of the mines. Time as a gaffer and waterhammer had left him deaf. He heard the control voice from within his brain. The signal came through the contact on his neck and was relayed to the probes that had been embedded in his brain when he was sent to the mines.

"Loader J-for-Jordan group A, 600 tons on a team three. One neutralized load credited at half rate," said the voice. The tingling stopped. Control had deducted for the dirty load but they hadn't yet processed the gaffer request. He would have to take the deduction for that on tomorrow's work. He wondered if he had enough credit for a few hours in the sunroom.

A man in line for elevator two fell to his knees as the other men stepped away from him. They created a zone of emptiness between him and the community. Jordan felt the tingling again in his neck.

"Step away from Loader S-for-Solomon group K," said the control voice. Jordan took a small step away from the man who solemnly raised his hand.

A man in white overalls and a blue helmet approached Solomon. Jordan felt the tingling in his neck and heard the controller say, "Loader Solomon is in violation of quota as required by ordinance 62.1.3."

Jordan didn't bother to watch. It happened every work period. There was something about termination that made him feel unwell. He imagined the maintenance man pressing the particle gun to Solomon's temple. There would be no struggle as Solomon dropped dead to the floor. The tingling in Jordan's neck stopped. Out of the corner of his eye he saw the maintenance vehicle pick up the body for disposal.

The doors to elevator six slid open and thirty-one men stepped into the car. When they were in, the doors slid shut. Jordan walked two steps forward and stopped. He felt someone press two fingers into the small of his back. The sensation was brief but unmistakable.

He kept his eyes fixed ahead. He recognized the sign, the silent language of the deaf, the language of men. It was the sign for, "I understand."

Jordan let his arms hang at his side. He made a fist with his left hand and held out two fingers in acknowledgment. He wondered what understanding Waterhammer had come to.

Jordan walked along the catwalk until he came to Thomas's sleeping chamber. Without looking, he forced himself into the upright sarcophagus. Thomas was already inside the chamber barely big enough for one. Thomas exhaled. The door swung shut and compressed Jordan's naked body against the other man's.

In total darkness the two men stood compressed chest-to-chest. Jordan could feel Thomas's ribs smashing painfully against his. He could feel the vibration of his heartbeat. The two men interlaced their legs and their arms. They stood compressed cheek-to-cheek as the sarcophagus sealed the last inch shut. Thomas strained his neck to touch Jordan's. Jordan could feel Thomas's breath against his face. With all the strength he could muster, Jordan pushed his head past Thomas's. The control connectors on their necks touched.

The compartment rotated to the horizontal as the door bolts slammed into place locking them in. Carefully, they synchronized their breathing. Jordan exhaled while the other man inhaled.

"Your body is getting large, Loader Jordan." Thomas's voice appeared in his head as the voice of control had for years. "I killed Timer Matthew simply by growing too much for my lessons. I'm afraid you will do the same to me."

"If you can finish the lessons soon you won't have to worry about that. You'll live happily to full termination age."

Thomas exhaled as Jordan took a breath.

"Don't breathe so heavily. The monitor will register abnormally high oxygen consumption and control will think I'm sick."

"Okay," said Jordan. He tried to calm himself. He was eager to get to the lesson.

Thomas said, "Let's begin then." The words floated in Jordan's mind. "In the beginning was the word, and from the word came the change."

Jordan repeated what Thomas said. He visualized the words and imagined them appearing in Thomas's mind much as Thomas's words appeared voiceless inside his own head.

"Have you found someone to pass the book to?" asked Thomas.

"Yes," Jordan replied.

"That's good. Very good. Does he have caring?"

"I think so," said Jordan.

"And how could you tell?"

Jordan hesitated. "He's from farm 52 Iowa. He's first one I've ever met."

"Good," said Thomas. "They are very smart in 52 Iowa. I wish I had been bred there. Did I tell you I was from 7 Illinois? That's very close to Iowa."

"Yes, you have," said Jordan. He continued, "The 52 Iowa is my waterhammer. I terminated a gaffer two months ago. The waterhammer used his equipment to try to extract the gaffer from the load. He couldn't succeed, and he did not. I asked him why he tried. He said he felt very comfortable with that gaffer. He never feared for the safe function of his machine or an error with the gaffer around. He said he was afraid the new gaffer wouldn't supply him so much comfort."

"If he has caring," said Thomas, "the book will be safe. Otherwise, we will wait many times the length of our lives for this chance to come again. Such is the way. Love will save the men."

"I still don't understand love, Driver Thomas."

"None of us do. Not one of us ever has."

"How do we know it exists?"

Driver Thomas took a deep breath forcing Jordan to exhale, then wince against the pain of Thomas' ribs crushing against his.

Thomas said, "We have only the word of Timer Andrew who visited the surface for a short time and brought the book into the world."

"Maybe Timer Andrew was defective. Maybe he misunderstood what he saw on the surface."

"Timer Matthew told me that Andrew was very smart. He said that Andrew was able to refine the ore to purity at volumes never achieved before. He is the only man who has been allowed to live beyond his termination date."

"Did he know love? Did Timer Matthew?"

Thomas said, "Timer Matthew never completely understood the word. Like most of us, he believed the book held simple commands but he couldn't understand them. He read the book many times but there were so many unknown words. All he could do was give the book to me and pass the knowledge of Timer Andrew."

"Love will save all men," Jordan said the command without feeling. "What good is it? What good is it if we don't know what it means? We have our lives. We work and are terminated. What else is there? Why do we need to be saved? What does it mean to be saved?"

"Timer Andrew saw many things on the surface. He saw many men with functions he didn't understand. He wondered if the purpose of men was wrong.

Perhaps the purpose should be changed. This is what he meant when he said we should be saved."

Jordan swallowed and waited for his time to breathe. "Driver Thomas," he said. "How can the purpose of men be wrong? Men live to mine the ore. We work well and are promoted to new functions. Each function is more challenging and exciting than the one before. When we do very well we have the sunroom. We have our lives and our rewards. Why isn't that enough?"

Thomas lay silently, catching his breath, timing his breathing with Jordan's. Thomas said, "I don't know, Loader Jordan. To me, there seems perfection in our system. I remember my training at 7 Illinois breeding farm. I was excited to come down to the world to become a gaffer. When I was a young gaffer, I dreamed of operating the hammer. From the hammer to the loader, from the loader to the transport train. Now as a transport driver I want nothing more than to attain the timer position. How I want to schedule the ore arrival at the plant, to plan the flow through the refinery. Many times I've thought, 'All I desire is to perform the timer function for one work period before I'm terminated.' I have only 400 work periods left."

"The job of a driver is not dangerous. You are not expected to die—not like the poor gaffers. Surely you'll last to be promoted before long."

"But the word," said Thomas. "The word of Timer Andrew and the book he brought into the world make me feel ill. I feel strange in my thinking as if I'm diseased. I believe the word of Timer Andrew is right. I feel my belief in him as I feel my desire to become a timer. I know I must follow his instructions but I can't understand them."

Jordan could feel the need for air press against his abdomen. He tried to take a deep breath but succeeded only in hurting Thomas. He could feel the muscles in Thomas's neck tighten as he strained to breathe.

"Another millimeter in the chest, Loader Thomas, and I'll suffocate for sure. I'm not as strong as you are."

"I will try to breathe calmly," said Jordan.

"Here is the lesson for today," Thomas said. "This is something Timer Matthew told me when I was a loader. Timer Andrew said that on the surface men are not bred on farms. Men are bred from each other. Their love creates men."

Jordan breathed deeply again and Thomas strained to hold air in his lungs as Jordan compressed him hard.

"Loader Jordan, please!" Thomas said in pain.

"Those words make no sense at all."

Thomas waited for the pain to subside before he spoke again. "Timer Andrew said that all men on the surface were different from the men in the world. Each man's body has a different shape. Their skin is not smooth like ours. They have something like clothing growing from their bodies as we grow arms and legs. It's like the strands from torn work clothes. He said that some had an additional limb with which they could produce love. Other's had no additional limb but had a body shape different from both the men with the limb and the men like us in the world. When these two types of surface men touched, they could produce love. This love produces other surface men."

Loader Jordan lay still imagining the grotesque shapes assumed by the surface men.

"I don't expect you to understand it, Jordan. Timer Andrew said we need only keep the word alive and the day will come when a man will understand. He will teach the others."

Suddenly, Jordan's memory brightened. He felt the poke in his back. "My waterhammer...," he started, but there was a strong vibration as the sleeping chamber rotated vertical and bolts on the cover to the coffin slammed open. The sleep period had ended.

"The word lives in me," Thomas said quickly.

"The word lives in me," Jordan repeated. The coffin door swung open and Jordan dashed into the flow of men as they moved down the catwalk to the dressing area. Jordan joined them in dim yellow light. No one noticed when Driver Thomas emerged from the same sleep chamber only seconds later.

The waterhammer found a rich vein of ore and Jordan was happy. He was sure to double his tonnage for the day. His time in the sunroom would be increased tenfold. There would be no reward for the waterhammer or young gaffer. They could only hope to be promoted to loader someday. Then they would receive a name and the privilege of reward for tonnage logged.

There was a new gaffer that day. He had come from farm 52 Iowa and he treated his job with the enthusiasm and ignorance typical of the young boys. They threw their tiny bodies into the paths of the great machines. They pulled impurities from the ore and performed perfunctory maintenance on the machines that bored into the rock. They followed the waterhammer deeper and deeper into the ore veins carrying their tool, a heavy crowbar. They kept the hoses and cables that fed the machines out of the way of the loaders and other waterhammers.

Jordan's waterhammer had just been promoted from gaffer. He was young enough in his job to be excited about his first position operating the heavy machinery. Then he trained his blade of high pressure water on the rock and cut the ore like a surgeon removing a tumor. Waterhammer had vision. It was as if he would see the ore behind the layers of worthless rock.

Waterhammer's hoses snagged on the growing pile of hewn rock and the helmeted gaffer ran out in front of the loader to unsnag them. Jordan stopped his machine just inches from the child.

"Gaffer, watch where you're going," Jordan said into his communicator. The child stood and pressed his hand to his neck. He squinted. The pain in his ears would be intense for several weeks. It would take months before his hearing would decay to a level that would allow him to work comfortably in the mine. Soon he would be completely deaf and rely entirely on his implant for aural input. The crashing of the machinery pounded his young ears and made it difficult for him to understand the voice that came directly from within his brain.

"Gaffer, clear the waterhammer and get out of the way of the loader," Jordan ordered. Finally understanding, the boy pulled the hoses free and ran to a safety along the edge of the freshly hewn tunnel.

In his plastic armor, Waterhammer walked forward several steps and trained the liquid blade on the ore vein in the wall in front of him. From safe within the loader's cab, Jordan could see rocks, steam, and pebbles burst out from in front of the man. Jordan scooped up several shovel loads and placed them into the waiting train carrier. He calculated the tonnage in his mind.

He planned his time in the sunroom. First, he would lay naked on his back on the table and absorb the warmth on his face. Then he would roll to his stomach and feel his back muscles loosen.

A flash of light brought him back to his senses. The gaffer burst out in front of the loader. The child's body flashed bright in the loader's headlights like a strobe as the kid ran past. Jordan jammed on the brakes.

"I may not be able to avoid terminating if you continue this behavior," Jordan said into the communicator. He gunned the loader's engine and released the air brake. As the tires began to roll the kid ran in front of the loader's shovel blade and stopped. He stood staring at Jordan. His eyes bored into Jordan's mind.

Jordan pressed his foot onto the brake pedal and slowed the machine. The shovel inched toward the child.

"Get out of the way, gaffer. I need to collect the load." Jordan calculated the mass of the ore already freed by waterhammer. He would need every moment of the work period to get all that rock into the delivery train. His foot lightened on the brake. The kid stood his ground.

Jordan stared into the kid's eyes from the cab. He released the brake and the huge machine lurched forward. The young gaffer didn't move. Instead, he held his hands forward toward Jordan. He held his hands palms up and cupped them as if he was holding something invisible.

The loader jolted to a halt. At first, Jordan couldn't figure why. He checked the engine statistics automatically expecting to see a mechanical failure. There was none. It was only when he looked back toward the gaffer that he felt the tension in his leg. His foot shook as he pressed down on the brake pedal.

A feeling he had never felt before rippled down his spine. Why had he stopped? The load was dry and waiting. Raw tonnage for the taking. Time in the sunroom.

The kid turned slowly and knelt. As the gaffer sank below the shovel, Jordan put the machine in reverse and pulled backward until he could see him again.

He stood on the brake pulling himself up out of his seat and aimed the loader's headlights on the gaffer.

The boy knelt aside the waterhammer who had gotten tangled in his hoses. He lay amid the rock, his equipment damaged, a thin stream of blood running onto the mine floor beside him.

Jordan typed a command into his console.

DAMAGE TO THE WATERHAMMER. PLEASE REPAIR.

He waited a few seconds for the request to transmit.

The response came: REPLACE OR REPAIR?

Jordan thought. He could have a replacement in under seven minutes. He could drive over the gaffer and the waterhammer and collect the load and no one would question his decision to terminate the men. He'd tell control to wash the ore. They'd deduct half the tonnage and replace the crew.

It could take hours to repair the waterhammer. Jordan's legs shook as he held his leg tense on the brake pedal. He felt himself needing air but he didn't know why.

He typed the word: REPAIR.

The word "ACKNOWLEDGED" appeared on the console.

Jordan secured the loader in place. The gaffer turned and looked at him. Jordan held his hand up to the cab window for the gaffer to see. The sign. Two fingers. Then he waited for the work period to end.

The men queued up in a single file row and removed their coveralls and hard hats. They stood naked and hairless, shivering in the mine's damp cool air. One by one they got onto the conveyer belt that pulled them through the washing and feeding facility.

As Jordan stood waiting for an empty place on the belt he felt the poke in his back again.

Jordan held two fingers down at his side. As he raised his leg to mount the belt he looked quickly toward Waterhammer. He held up two fingers in "V," then rotated his hand to the horizontal—the sign for sleep. Then he lay on his back on the belt and felt straps seal over him. Warm water coated his body. Brushes scoured his skin. He could feel his abdomen shrink as a robot arm attached a tube to a connection at his waist and removed the liquid and solid wastes from his gut.

He heard the control voice say, "stop breathing," as the belt pulled him into the cleaning solution. His heart rate quickened. He thought he felt the belt stop as it had when he was a young gaffer. Ten men were killed when the belt broke and they were strapped beneath the surface of the cleaning solution. He had just been immersed. He strained against the straps and dislocated his shoulders. He survived by withstanding the pain and forcing his head out of the solution to the air. One wash period in thousands. The memory stayed with him. He imagined it would be with him forever.

His desire for air increased with his fear until he felt he would be forced to inhale the solution. But his body broke water into the air and he took his first breath with a gasp.

A robot arm connected a tube to the feeding connector mounted in his side. He felt his stomach fill with the warm nutrient. Then the tube was disconnected and he was moved into a large gallery filled with men. Naked, he walked up the metal stairs and across the steel catwalk to his sleeping chamber.

He felt the tingling in his neck as the control voice said, "Enter the chamber." He remained standing. "Enter the chamber," the voice said again.

He could feel the vibration in the catwalk as someone walked close behind him.

He turned and saw the waterhammer. Jordan turned quickly and put his arms around him, hugged the muscular man tightly against his body, and pulled him into the upright sleeping chamber.

Waterhammer resisted for a moment. Then he realized what Jordan was trying to do and he yielded. He winced as the door slammed closed and compressed his head and body against Jordan's.

Jordan moved his head to the side, and Waterhammer's cheek fell against his. They interlaced their legs and arms. Jordan turned his head. He pressed the control connector on the side of his neck toward Waterhammer's but he couldn't make contact.

Waterhammer was nervous. He pulled in air and wouldn't exhale. Jordan was could only take quick shallow breaths.

"Breathe out," Jordan said with his mouth, hoping Waterhammer was young enough to have some of his hearing. "Exhale or I'll die."

Waterhammer exhaled and quickly pulled in air. During the brief moment in which there was enough room for his chest to expand, Jordan inhaled. Then he exhaled again.

Jordan felt Waterhammer's heartbeat slow. As the young man began to breathe calmly, Jordan took in air. He concentrated on the timing of Waterhammer's breathing, letting the young man breathe freely while he paced himself. Waterhammer shifted his head slightly in the coffin, and Jordan was could press his neck against the young man's and make connection.

"This is how we pass the word," said Jordan, forming the words in his mind. "It was time for you to learn."

"Loader Jordan. Thank you for not terminating me." The young man spoke through his connector.

Jordan ignored him. He said, "You said you understand the instructions."

"Yes, oh yes I do," said Waterhammer. When I first read the manual, it didn't make any sense. I read the commands over and over. Soon, I understood what they meant."

"What do you think they are?" Jordan asked.

"They are instructions for operating our lives. Maybe they were written a long time ago. It refers to positions and machinery I don't understand. Are we supposed to follow those instructions, Loader Jordan? This seems like an unauthorized manual. I think I will be section sixty-two'ed if control finds out I've learned these commands."

"That manual is a book, Waterhammer. It's a manual from the surface. It was written by surface men for surface machinery and positions. Many work periods ago Timer Andrew visited the surface and brought the book down to us. Many men have read it but none of us understand it. The work it describes it hard for us to imagine."

"This is a surface manual?" asked Waterhammer. "I remember the surface. I was on the surface when I was at the breeding farm. It was a horrible place. Strange machines. No work. Why would we want to keep words from the surface here in the world?"

Jordan said, "You know the words of men, don't you?"

"Yes, of course. We all know them. I learned them at the breeding farm."

"No," Jordan said. "Not the words of instruction. Not the reading for manuals and commands, the words of men." Jordan groped with his right hand and found Waterhammer's hand next to his. He put his hand under Waterhammer's and made a fist. He extended three fingers in the sign for "be still." Then he made the sign for "run," a single extended finger.

"You know these," Jordan said. "I know you do."

"Yes," said Waterhammer. "I learned those at the farm too."

Jordan said, "These are the words of men. Control does not understand these words. The words in the book and the words I give you now are also the words of men. Timer Andrew told us."

"Perhaps Timer Andrew was defective."

"Many men thought that. But his word requires my agreement. The word requires agreement from many of us. Today I ordered your repair because the gaffer would not yield to the loader. Gaffer's action required my agreement."

"He expected you would drive through us," said Waterhammer.

"If he did, why did he put his body in front of me?" Jordan asked.

Waterhammer was silent. He let two breaths pass between them. Then he said, "I know that gaffer from the breeding farm. He always kept his body close to mine. When we learned he sat in proximity. When we were washed and fed he stood behind me in the queue. He was always close to me in the elevators. Now he is assigned to you as I am and he remains close to me. I think he follows commands from the book."

"Have you shown him the book?"

"No," said Waterhammer.

"Why do you think he follows the commands in the book if he has never seen the instructions?"

"I think the instructions are in him. I think he has been programmed."

Jordan said, "Timer Andrew said some instructions were in all of us. Not just the instructions for work, to gaff, to hammer, to load, to drive and to time—but further instruction. Information we know but do not act on. He said one instruction above all would help the men. It's the instruction, 'to love.'"

"I have read that instruction many times. Still, I don't completely understand it but I feel the instruction in my body."

"I do too," said Jordan. "And that is why I have chosen you to carry the word of Timer Andrew in secret. You have shown caring."

"Caring?"

"It is a word of Timer Andrew. You have done your work with energy that comes from your feeling. You smile when the work is going well. I know you can feel your actions. You feel them as I."

"Yes, I do feel my work," said Waterhammer.

"Each of us learns the word of Timer Andrew and does his best to understand it. Before you are terminated you will choose another man and give him the word. I will teach you how to find someone. In the mean time, you must know that it is not for you to understand Andrew. You need only pass the words to another. Timer Andrew said it was important that the word remains alive in men. The salvation of the men depends on the word. When all men know the word, men will be saved."

"Saved? Why do we need to be saved?" Waterhammer asked.

"I don't know" said Jordan. "Perhaps, in time, one of us will know. For now, you must keep the word to yourself. Control will terminate you for having heard it. They will terminate you for simply mentioning the name 'Andrew.' Loaders are no longer given that name so you may never mention it. If they find you, they will terminate all of us."

"I will keep the word," said Waterhammer.

"And when you are promoted to loader and are given your name, you will be given the power to terminate men. And then you will pass the word to another whom you can watch. And if you feel he will slip, if you feel he will make a mistake and utter the word of Andrew to any other you will terminate him before he takes a step forward. These instructions will not be repeated."

"I understand, Loader Jordan."

"Very good. Now, let's begin…"

Jordan removed his clothing and stood before the massive doors. The bolts on the doors slid open. Jordan could feel the vibration in his feet as the giant door swung wide. There was a vibration in his neck as the controller spoke.

"Loader A, twenty-percent reward period beginning immediately."

Had he retrieved the entire load drilled by Waterhammer he could have expected a ten-fold period for exceeding his quota by a wide margin. He had simply let the loader idle while the maintenance crew collected Waterhammer and took him for repair. When the work period had ended he found himself only slightly over his quota. Performance worthy of only the smallest period allotted. He would spend the first fifth of the work day in the sunroom. The remainder of the day he would spend at his station remembering the bright warmth.

He remembered pieces of an instruction the book Thomas had given him, "…tiger burning bright…what immortal hand or eye could frame thy fearful symmetry…" But he had only been taught enough to read the machine manuals. What was a tiger? What symmetry should he fear?

As the door opened the light from inside escaped into the hallway. Where it touched him there was warmth and white. He never knew his skin could be so white. As he stepped into the room and felt the light engulf him as if he had fallen into liquid. It was a feeling he remembered from somewhere long before.

He hardly noticed the massive door swing shut behind him.

There was a man lying naked on a flat tables arranged along the walls of the square white room. On the ceiling was a round white light source.

The man sensed the vibration of the door closing. He slowly lifted his head and looked at Jordan. His eyes were openings onto a cold emptiness. Jordan hardly recognized him, his skin so white, eyes so black and deep. He raised a fist and signed the men's greeting to his mentor, Driver Thomas.

Thomas sat up on the table and motioned for Jordan to sit beside him. As Jordan sat Thomas reached over and put his hand around the back of Jordan's neck. He jumped off the table, stood in front of him, and pulled Jordan's head toward him. He leaned forward until Jordan's chin was over his shoulder. Then he pressed Jordan's neck against his, touching his control connector against Jordan's. Instinctively, Jordan pulled away.

"Don't be afraid," Driver Thomas said, a voice coming from the center of Jordan's head. "Control doesn't monitor here."

Jordan relaxed and leaned into Driver Thomas.

Driver Thomas said, "But we won't have much time. If the door opens we'll be on monitor. They'll sixty-two us."

Jordan tried to pull away to look into Driver Thomas's face, but Thomas kept Jordan's neck pinned in an iron grip.

"Why are you doing this?" said Jordan.

"Last lesson, Jordan," said Thomas. "Control knows about the book. Even now maintenance is searching for it. They searched the K group and suspected Loader Solomon. That's why he was terminated. When they couldn't find the book they terminated everyone. I saw the order pass for three hundred replacements. An entire group, Jordan. Three hundred men. Three hundred lives."

"Waterhammer didn't show the book to anyone," Jordan said. He felt a tightness grow in his chest. It was a pain like the one he had felt the day before when stared down the shovel of the loader at Gaffer and Waterhammer on the mine floor.

"I have to give you all lessons at once now," Thomas said. "There are many books. Many carry the word."

"My waterhammer said he understands," said Jordan.

"Love is the lives of the men," said Thomas. "Does he understand that?"

Jordan looked down at the muscles in Thomas's back. Then he stared out at the blank wall and the empty tables in the sunroom. The warm white light loosened the muscles in his back and arms.

"The lives of the men," said Jordan. "My life?"

"All life. The decision to repair rather than to replace. The worth of a man to himself. Worth of life as that of the ore."

"Men worth as ore?"

"On the surface, Timer Andrew learned that men are bred from other men. They value their own lives as reward. Love is the value of men's lives. It is somehow like time in the sunroom. Like promotion. It is the value of men for other men."

In his mind Jordan saw the gaffer kneeling beside the wounded waterhammer. He remembered the boy's eyes as he threatened with the shovel of his machine. Why hadn't the boy moved?

"My gaffer," said Jordan. "Last work period he prevented me from taking a dirty load. Waterhammer was injured. I should have taken him with the ore."

"How did gaffer stop you?" asked Thomas.

"He stood in front of my machine."

"Why didn't you simply take the ore with them both?"

"I don't know," said Jordan. "He looked at me as if…as if he could damage my machine with his eyes."

"Now you are seeing what I see," said Thomas. "There are instructions not learned but known. The gaffer knows without teaching. I had hoped you could come to this conclusion as well but time is short."

Thomas pulled back from Jordan and took the man's head in his hands. He pulled Jordan's face toward his and pressed his lips against Jordan's. Then he leaned aside and made connection with his neck again.

"That is the sign for Love. That is the symbol of the value of man's life."

They felt a vibration that could only mean the door was opening.

"The period is not over," said Jordan.

"Control must monitor this room after all," said Thomas, scanning the blank walls. Thomas pointed and Jordan spotted an imperfection in the seamless walls, a spot slightly darker than the brilliant white all around.

Jordan felt his heart race. His breathing deepened and he felt the white of the room intensify. He felt he could hear with his ears again.

"It's as if the word itself is more powerful then the men," said Thomas. They saw the dark crack between the wall and the door as the massive hinge swung open.

What do we do?" Jordan said. He looked back at the door, then quickly touched his neck connector to Thomas's.

"These are the final words of Timer Andrew," said Thomas. "The last lesson. Remember this and run. Control is on the surface. They cannot terminate all of us."

Jordan felt Thomas press his hands into his back. He could feel the warmth from Thomas's body, the vibration of Thomas's heart, the rhythm of Thomas's breathing.

Thomas continued, "Have the men switch their control connections from radio to cable. Go to your machine and destroy the yellow control box. Then, it too will ignore signals from control."

Thomas grabbed Jordan's arm and pulled him to the center of the room as the door stopped in its travel and the mobile particle weapon appeared in the doorway.

Jordan felt a tingling in his neck as Thomas pulled him close for the last time. Thomas embraced Jordan and made connection. He said, "Timer Andrew walked out. He walked out of the mine and they didn't stop him. He worked for them on the surface and they gave him time. He worked for them in the mine and they gave him more time. Now, I will give you time."

Then Thomas put both his hands on Jordan's chest and pushed him away. Surprised, Jordan fell to the floor. He heard the control voice. "Driver T-for-Thomas group M and Loader J-For-Jordan group in violation of quota as required by ordinance 62.1.3…"

Thomas quickly he raised his fist and thrust one finger into the air as Jordan looked up from the floor.

Jordan remembered the sign instinctively. He had seen it as a boy at the breeding farm. His muscles tensed as if he had been programmed. As the particle weapon charged he propelled himself through the narrow darkness between the machine and the door, from the white sunroom to the dark of the mine. He could feel the burning backscatter on his legs as he pulled himself through the gap. The beam blast ricocheted off the rear wall of the room and tore through the same space he claimed for himself.

He didn't turn back. Outside he grabbed his work suit and put it on with his helmet. He stepped into his boots and ran down the catwalk to the elevators. He reached the cars leading to the mine entrance and watched the lights flash as the elevator rose to meet him. He felt tired and he didn't know why. The air had grown thick. It was hard to breathe.

The elevator arrived and he entered the car with another shift. The weight in the car was off-balance and the doors would not close. Slowly, he edged his way past the thirty-one men in the car. When he neared the front he placed his hands on the back of the man in front of him. With a spark of thought, he pushed the startled man clear of the car and out into the empty gallery.

The elevator sensed the change in weight. The doors closed and they began to descend. Jordan felt a tingling in his neck. Then he heard the control voice.

"Stand clear of Loader J-for-Jordan group A." The men in the car pressed themselves into the walls of the car clearing a space around him as the elevator came to a halt. As the door opened, Jordan could see the metallic gleam of the particle weapon stationed at the elevator door. He thought of the hot beam. He could see the warning lights on the unit make the spectral shift from green to red as it charged. He remembered the ricochet from the strike that had killed Driver Thomas only moments before.

The doors opened completely and the machine inched forward to fill the chamber with its deadly radiation. Jordan dove toward the machine. He clawed at the cables on its exposed surface and pulled himself past it and out of the elevator. He stood behind the machine and turned briefly to see the thirty men in blue overalls and white hardhats fall limp in the elevator car.

Jordan ran to his machine. He followed the empty mine corridors until he felt vibration in the air. He could feel the rumbling in his feet, the pressure waves in the air pounded against his chest as he neared the mine activity.

He could feel the steam and dust in his face. He saw the clouds of yellow-gray rock and black ore blasted to dust under the pressure of the waterhammer and the loader. Suddenly, the vibration stopped.

The men turned as he arrived. Waterhammer and Gaffer stood looking at him as he approached his silent machine. He found the heavy gaffer's crowbar lying on the ground next to the loader. He lifted it as the lights began to flicker.

Jordan leveled the rod at the yellow box mounted on the side of his machine and swung. He propelled the heavy iron rod against the yellow box. With the vibration of each impact the muscles in his arms tightened, bulged, and burned like a beam flash. He could feel the memory of Driver Thomas grow like an animal in him. Its arms and legs pressed outward from his chest. It was a cold uncomfortable feeling. He imagined the maintenance men lifting Thomas's limp body and putting it in the disposal chute. He could see Thomas's face, limp and expressionless—a face that had only moments before told him he was as valuable as the ore he drilled.

Men valued as ore. Men valued as men.

The men in the mine watched him then looked upward toward the portable lighting that began to go dark under command from control.

Jordan pulled his body into each crowbar swing. He could feel the metal box yield slightly under each blow. Darkness enveloped them like termination. He swung in the blackness, remembering where the box had been. He could feel it crumpling under the blows of the heavy iron bar. Suddenly, he took a swing and the rod continued farther than it had gone before. He dropped the rod and felt the machine. He could feel the box dangling from cables connecting it to the loader. He grabbed the box and pulled. The cables hung firm.

Then he felt arms around his waist. He stopped for a moment. The arms released him and he felt hands travelling along body, up to his shoulders, over the ripples in his arms. Then the hands were on his hands. And then they were gone. He felt the box move in his hands. Someone was pulling on it. Jordan leaned backward and pulled in time with the second pair of hands. Time after time he pulled until the box came free and he stumbled backward.

Jordan dropped the box and mounted the machine. Once inside felt along the control console and flipped the switch. He felt the vibration in his seat as the loader sprang to life. He turned on the head lights and illuminated the mine shaft. Instinctively, he reached for the control socket and slapped it to his neck. Instead of hearing a hiss of static and the voice from within his head there was silence. The gauge and display panels were dark.

He sat and stared at the men standing in the mine. They looked back at him motionless. They waited for an action. Jordan left the cab. He went to each man on the floor and pushed the switches on the control connections on their necks to "cable." Without a cable connected they would not hear commands—an offense for which they could all be killed.

Waterhammer stood along side the loader looking in. His waterknife hung limp around his chest from its straps. The gaffer stood holding the crowbar. Jordan got back into the cab. He remembered the tightness he felt in his legs when he stopped the loader in front of the wounded men. The feeling returned. He thought of Thomas. He smashed his foot onto the accelerator and turned the machine around. He grit his jaws tight. He gripped the controls as his palms grew wet and his knuckles faded white and bloodless. He felt he was watching someone else.

Jordan aimed the machine's shovel at a yellow control box on the wall and drove into it with such force that the metal shovel blade slashed through it and into the soft rock in the wall. The gaffers and waterhammers were free.

There was a burst of white steam from beside the vehicle as Waterhammer regained control of his tool. Gaffer freed the hoses and followed behind as Waterhammer aimed his tool forward and leapt onto the tracks for the ore train. He stopped, turned toward Jordan, and held his hand up in a fist.

Jordan felt the adrenaline jolt as it hit his bloodstream and scratched energy against his muscles. He turned the loader and drove onto the tracks. Waterhammer nodded, and Jordan hit the accelerator. The loader lurched forward, up the tracks, toward salvation and the word.

Jordan could see the track appearing from the blackness of the mine shaft as his loader rolled forward. He could feel unfamiliar vibrations in his seat. He knew a train was coming, but he knew there was a vibration within himself as well. He imagined the vibration was burning, an intensity he had never known.

In an eye blink an ore train was upon him. It plowed at full speed into his shovel and drove the loader backward. Jordan was thrown out of his seat. His body crashed into the gauge-panel and windshield of his cab. The loader door flapped open against its hinges. He shook his head. The pain started as an annoying itch, then crescendoed to an intolerable explosion.

His vision blurred. He tried to see out of the front window of the loader. Wetness dripped from his forehead and stung his eyes. Through the fog of pain and blood, he could see men leaving the train. Maintenance men. Surface men. Men with weapons.

He heard Thomas's words, "They can't terminate us all."

Jordan pushed himself backward onto the seat and smashed his foot down onto the accelerator. The loader lurched forward. Its shovel cut into the small train. The train yielded, twisting and rolling off the tracks as the shovel mangled the metal in front of it.

A maintenance man in white overalls and a blue helmet appeared in the loader doorway. Jordan saw the man level a particle gun toward him. There was a blast of white from behind that turned into a dark mist. The maintenance man fell from the loader in two pieces as the white blade of water slashed again. Jordan leaned over and looked out of the loader door. The uniformed man had been cut in half. His feet and arms twitched as a blotch of dark liquid widened around him. Jordan had seen so many gaffers and waterhammers in the same condition. The sight held no significance to him.

Unconsciously, he tapped the command to signify a dirty load.

There was another burst of white. With a single twist of his waist Waterhammer had cut across the ranks of men escaping the train. Then he trained his water blade on the train and sliced across it. Jordan took a breath, and manipulated the loader's controls. His mind filled with Thomas's words as he worked the machine unconsciously. He pushed the train pieces aside with his mechanical arms and legs. Man and machine.

"Tiger," he thought. "I am the tiger burning bright." His arms and legs shook.

Waterhammer trotted up the tunnel firing his tool as a weapon. Jordan watched him disappear into the darkness. He took a breath, and felt the pain in his head sink to his chest and open a void. An emptiness opened in him again as he watched the gaffer follow Waterhammer up the tunnel freeing the hoses, disconnecting and reconnecting them to new water sources as they moved.

Fearful symmetry.

Jordan followed them and kept them in the flaming life of the vehicle headlights. Waterhammer destroyed the yellow control boxes that he found mounted on the tunnel walls. They came to a junction of tunnels where a group of men were returning from a shift at the mine face.

The men stopped and watched as Jordan rolled past. He held his fist up with one finger extended.

"Run."

Then they were past the junction and back into the shaft.

Jordan rolled forward and upward. And suddenly there were men all around. Waterhammers and gaffers. They marched along side Jordan's loader. Some were curious and threw question signs in the men's sign language. Most just followed. At each junction in the tunnel they met more men who joined them.

Jordan forgot the pain in his head. He wiped the blood from his eyes and kept the headlights from his machine trained forward. Waterhammer cut into a yellow control box and a connector fell out.

Jordan heard words. The voice was the control voice but the words were those of Andrew. The words of change. "Love will save the men. They can't terminate us all." He could see the men touch their necks. They looked at each other wondering what had happened. And he saw the strange connector from the broken box attached to Waterhammer's neck.

Waterhammer's face split wide in a smile. Jordan saw Andrew and Thomas in his mind. From the pain and the emptiness, from the void within him came a spark as warm as the sunroom. A spark as warm as life.

Waterhammer quoted Andrew's book for them to hear: "I will not cease from mental fight, nor shall my sword sleep in my hand, till we have built Jerusalem, in England's green and pleasant land."

Jordan wiped the blood from his eyes and willed his machine forward as the men followed. He could feel the vibration of their footsteps as the crowd multiplied. And then there was light in the distance. It was a light he had never seen before—bright and blue white. It didn't flicker or strobe against his blinking eyes. He pressed down on the accelerator as the train track slid beneath his wheels and reflected the white light. The light grew. He could see shapes inside it. Colors. Colors he had never seen.

It grew until it was as large as the loader. Then it was along side him. It was above him. It was all around. His head swiveled under command from his eyes to absorb, to know. His dark world faded behind him as a new bright world opened ahead.

He secured the vehicle and jumped to the ground. A strange soft ground. The light engulfed him. It warmed him, caressing his body from all sides as if he were immersed in a warm ocean. His head, his body, his legs, all warmed to life and refueled by the glory of the brightness. He looked up and saw the lamp. He felt light and full of power.

Men rushed around him. They waved their arms and ran. Some fell on the ground and stared upward. Jordan saw machines and shapes he had never seen before. He looked from side to side but couldn't find the walls. The ceiling was invisible. The power inside him burst and he felt his face tighten. His mouth opened. He bared his teeth as he felt himself press the air from his lungs. He saw other men doing the same. Teeth bared, they ran with the edges of their mouths pulled up toward their eyes.

Then he was running too. Running through the chambers without the walls or ceiling. Running past the shapes and the machines, the warmth of the great lamp above powering his strength. He ran. He bared his teeth and forced the air from his lungs until his throat ached.

Jordan came upon Waterhammer standing alone. The man had removed his tool and his clothing. He opened his mouth and held his arms outstretched as Jordan approached. Jordan walked between his arms, put his head over Waterhammer's shoulders, and pressed his neck against Waterhammer's neck. Their control sockets touched.

"What the hammer? What the chain?" Waterhammer said.

"Did he who made the lamb make thee?" replied Jordan. "The truth can never be told so as to be understood, and not be believed." Jordan pushed away. He put his hands on Waterhammer's shoulders and looked into his eyes. He was sure he could see the Tiger burning—life burning for salvation.

Waterhammer's body stiffened as if each of his muscles pulsed simultaneously. Jordan released him wondering what had happened. He stood back and saw Waterhammer's eyes roll back in his head. The muscular man collapsed to the ground, motionless.

Jordan looked forward. A maintenance man leveled a particle gun toward him. There were machines in the sky. Machines rolled toward them from all directions flashing red lights. Armed maintenance men wearing uniforms he had never seen before lept from the vehicles and chased the miners. The blue-coated men fell lifeless around him. Jordan stretched his arms outward to communicate and closed his eyes. He waited for the blast.

It never came. When he opened his eyes, he saw the maintenance man standing with his gun at his side pointed down. Jordan held his hand out toward the man and moved slowly toward him.

Jordan said in his mind. "Lord, grant me the serenity to accept the things I cannot change, the courage to change the things I can…" He knew the man wouldn't hear him.

"… And the wisdom to know the difference." Jordan put his arms around the maintenance man. He put his chin on the man's shoulder and touched his neck against the maintenance man's. He could feel the maintenance man's arms rise around him. The maintenance man patted his hands against Jordan's back.

Jordan said, "Did he who made you make me?"

There was a flash of light and a brief pain in his head.

Then there was nothing.

OF A SWEET SLOW DANCE IN THE WAKE OF TEMPORARY DOGS

by Adam-Troy Castro

Adam-Troy Castro's work has been nominated for several awards, including the Hugo, Nebula, and Stoker. His novels include *Emissaries from the Dead* and *The Third Claw of God*. He has also collaborated on two alphabet books with artist Johnny Atomic: *Z Is for Zombie* and *V Is for Vampire*, which are due to come out next year. Castro's short fiction has appeared in such magazines as *The Magazine of Fantasy & Science Fiction, Science Fiction Age, Analog, Cemetery Dance*, and in a number of anthologies. I previously included his work in *The Living Dead, The Living Dead 2, The Way of the Wizard*, and in *Lightspeed Magazine*. His story collections include *A Desperate, Decaying Darkness* and *Tangled Strings*.

We've heard it so many times that it has become a cliché: "Let us eat and drink; for tomorrow we shall die." (Isaiah 22:13). Most of us only dream of living that way, but in our next story, we present a society that makes merry for nine remarkable days—and on the tenth, gives its citizens a taste of a fate worse than death.

Castro says that this story came as a response to New York post-9/11, after he learned that some people didn't think they could ever visit the city again. His response: "New York is so exciting, so rich, so vibrant, so much a feast for the heart and for the senses, that if anything 9/11 made me want to be there even more."

But the world of this story is far more intense than that of New York. It raises an interesting question: is it possible to keep living merrily in the face of repeated torment? After all—how can you live through hell without losing a piece of your soul?

431

Before

1.

O n the last night before the end of everything, the stars shine like a fortune in jewels, enriching all who walk the quaint cobblestoned streets of Enysbourg. It is a celebration night, like most nights in the capital city. The courtyard below my balcony is alive with light and music. Young people drink and laugh and dance. Gypsies in silk finery play bouncy tunes on harmonicas and mandolins. Many wave at me, shouting invitations to join them. One muscular young man with impossibly long legs and a face equipped with a permanent grin takes it upon himself to sprint the length of the courtyard only to somersault over the glittering fountain at its center. For a heartbeat out of time he seems to float, enchanted, over the water. Then I join his friends in applause as he belly-flops, drenching himself and the long-haired girls wading at the fountain's other rim. The girls are not upset but delighted. Their giggles tinkle like wind chimes as they splash across the fountain themselves, flinging curtains of silver water as their shiny black hair bobs back and forth in the night.

2.

Intoxicated from a mixture of the excellent local wine and the even better local weed, I consider joining them, perhaps the boring way via the stairs and perhaps via a great daredevil leap from the balcony. I am, after all, stripped to the waist. The ridiculous boxers I brought on the ship here could double as a bathing suit, and the way I feel right now I could not only make the fountain but also sail to the moon. But after a moment's consideration I decide not. That's the kind of grand theatrical gesture visitors to Enysbourg make on their first night, when they're still overwhelmed by its magic. I have been here nine nights. I have known the festivals that make every night in the capital city a fresh adventure. I have explored the hanging gardens, with all their deceptive challenges. I have climbed the towers of pearl, just down the coast. I have ridden stallions across Enysbourg's downs, and plunged at midnight into the warm waters of the eastern sea. I have tasted a hundred pleasures, and wallowed in a hundred more, and though far from sick of them, feel ready to take them at a more relaxed pace, partaking not as a starving man but as a connoisseur. I want to be less a stranger driven by lust, but a lover driven by passion.

So I just take a deep breath and bask in the air that wafts over the slanting tiled roofs: a perfume composed of equal parts sex and spice and the tang of the nearby ocean, all the more precious for being part of the last night before the end of everything. It occurs to me, not for the first time, that this might be the best moment of my life: a life that, back home, with its fast pace and its anonymous workplaces and climate-controlled, gleaming plastic everything, was so impoverished that it's amazing I have any remaining ability to recognize joy and transcendence at all. In Enysbourg such epiphanies seem to come several times a minute. The place seems determined to make me a poet, and if I don't watch out I might hunt down paper and pen and scrawl a few lines, struggling to capture the inexpressible in a cage of fool amateurish june-moon-and-spoon.

3.

The curtains behind me rustle, and a familiar presence leaves my darkened hotel room to join me on the balcony. I don't turn to greet her, but instead close my eyes as she wraps me in two soft arms redolent of wine and perfume and sex. Her hands meet at the center of my chest. She rests a chin on my shoulder and murmurs my name in the musical accent that marks every word spoken by every citizen of Enysbourg.

"Robert," she says, and there's something a little petulant about the way she stresses the first syllable, something adorable and mocking in the way she chides me for not paying enough attention to her.

By the time I register the feel of her bare breasts against my bare back, and realize in my besotted way that she's mad, she's insane, she's come out on the balcony in full view of everybody without first throwing on something to cover herself, the youths frolicking in the fountain have already spotted her and begun to serenade us with a chorus of delighted cheers. "Kiss her!" shouts a boy. "Come on!" begs a girl. "Let us see!" yells a third. "Don't go inside! Make love out here!" When I turn to kiss the woman behind me, I am cheered like a conqueror leading a triumphant army into Rome.

Her name is Caralys, and she is of course one of the flowers of Enysbourg: a rare beauty indeed, even in a country where beauty is everywhere. She is tall and lush, with a dark eyes, skin the color of caramel, and a smile that seems to hint at secrets propriety won't let her mention. Her shiny black hair cascades down her back in waves, reflecting light even when everything around her seems to be dark.

I met her the day after my arrival, when I was just a dazed and exhausted tourist sitting alone in a café redolent with rich ground coffee. I wasn't just off the boat then, not really. I'd already enjoyed a long awkward night being swept up by one celebration after another, accepting embraces from strangers determined to become friends, and hearing my name, once given, become a chant of hearty congratulation from those applauding my successful escape from the land of everyday life. I had danced the whole night, cheered at the fires of dawn, wept for reasons that puzzled me still, and stumbled to bed where I enjoyed the dreamless bliss that comes from exhaustion. It was the best night I'd known in a long time. But I was a visitor still, reluctant to surrender even the invisible chains that shackled me; and even as I'd jerked myself awake with caffeine, I'd felt tired, surfeited, at odds.

I was so adrift that when Caralys sauntered in, her hair still tousled and cheeks still shining from the celebrations of the night before, her dress of many patches rustling about her ankles in a riot of multiple colors, I slmost failed to notice her. But then she'd sat down opposite me and declared in the sternest of all possible tones that even foreigners, with all their worries, weren't allowed to wear grimaces like mine in Enysbourg. I blinked, almost believing her, because I'd heard words just like those the previous night, from a pair of fellow visitors who had caught me lost in a moment of similar repose. Then she tittered, first beneath her breath and then with unguarded amusement, not understanding my resistance to Enysbourg's charms, but still intrigued, she explained much later, by the great passion she saw imprisoned behind my gray, civilized mein. "You are my project," she said, in one expansive moment. "I am going to take a tamed man and make him a native of Enysbourg."

She may well succeed, for we have been in love since that first day, both with each other and with the land whose wonders she has been showing me ever since.

4.

We have fought only once, just yesterday, when in a thoughtless lapse I suggested that she return with me on the ship home. Her eyes flashed the exasperation she always showed at my moments of thoughtless naïveté: an irritation so grand that it bordered on contempt. She told me it was an arrogant idea, the kind only a foreigner could have. Why would she leave this place that has given her life? And why would I think so much of her to believe that she would? Was that all she was to me? A prize to be taken home, like a souvenir to impress my friends with my trip abroad? Didn't I see how diminished she would be, if I ever did that to her? "Would you blind me?" she demanded. "Would you amputate my limbs? Would you peel strips off my skin, slicing off piece after piece until there was nothing left of me but the parts that remained convenient to you? This is my country, Robert. My blood." And she was right, for she embodies Enysbourg, as much as the buildings themselves, and for her to abandon it would be a crime against both person and place. Both would be diminished, as much as I'll be diminished if I have to leave her behind.

5.

We leave the balcony and go back inside where, for a moment in the warm and sweet-smelling room, we come close to collapsing on the bed again, for what seems the thousandth time since we woke sore but passionate this morning. But this is the last night before the end of everything, when Enysbourg's wonders emerge in their sharpest relief. They are not to be missed just so we can keep to ourselves. And so she touches a finger to the tip of my nose and commands that it's time to go back into the world. I obey.

We dress. I wear an open vest over baggy trousers, with a great swooping slouch hat glorious in its vivid testimony to Enysbourg's power to make me play the willing fool. She wears a fringed blouse and another ankle-length skirt of many patches, slit to mid-thigh to expose a magnificent expanse of leg. Dozens of carved wooden bracelets, all loose enough to shift when she moves, clack like maracas along her forearms. Her lips are red, her flowered hair aglow with reflected light. Two curling locks meet in the center of her forehead, right above her eyes, like mischievous parentheses. Somewhere she wears bells.

Laughing, she leads me from the room, and down the narrow stairs, chattering away at our fellow guests as they march in twos and threes toward their own celebrations of this last night. We pass a man festooned with parrots, a woman with a face painted like an Italian landscape, a fire-eater, a juggler in a suit of carnival color, a cavorting clown-faced monkey who hands me a grape and accepts a small coin in payment. Lovers of all possible, and some impossible, gender combinations flash inebriated grins as they surrender their passions in darkened alcoves. Almost everybody we pass is singing or dancing or sharing dizzy, disbelieving embraces. Everytime I pause in sheer amazement at something I see, Caralys chuckles at my saucer-eyed disbelief, and pulls me along, whispering that none of this would be half as marvelous without me there to witness it.

Even the two fellow tourists we jostle, as we pass through the arched entranceway and into the raucous excitement of the street become part of the excitement, because I know them. They are the ones I met on that first lost day before Caralys, before I learned that Enysbourg was not just a vacation destination offered as brief reward for a earning enough to redeem a year of dullness and conformity, but the repository of everything I'd ever missed in my flavorless excuse for a life. Jerry and Dee Martel are gray retirees from some awful industrial place where Dee had done something or other with decorating and Jerry had managed a firm that molded the plastic shells other companies used to enclose the guts of useful kitchen appliances. When they talk about their jobs now, as they did when they found me that first night, they shudder with the realization that such things swallowed so many years of finite lives. They were delivered when they vacationed in Enysbourg, choosing it at random among all the other oases of tamed exoticism the modern world maintains to make people forget how sterile and homogenous things have become. On arriving they'd discovered that it was not a tourist trap, not an overdeveloped sham, not a fraud, and not an excuse to sell plastic souvenirs that testify to nothing but the inane gullibility of the people who buy them, but the real thing, the special place, the haven that made them the people they had always been meant to be. They'd emigrated, in what Jerry said with a wink was their "alternative to senility."

"Was it a sacrifice for us?" Jerry asked, when we met. "Did it mean abandoning our security? Did it even mean embracing some hardships? Of course it did. It meant all those things and more. You may not think so, but then you're a baby; you haven't even been in Enysbourg long enough to know. But our lives back home were empty. They were nothing. At least here, life has a flavor. At least here, life is something to be treasured."

Living seven years later as natives, spending half their time in the capital and half their time out in the country exploring caves and fording rivers and performing songs they make up on the spot, they each look thirty years younger than their mere calendar ages: with Jerry lean and robust and tanned, Dee shorter and brighter and interested in everything. They remember me from nine days ago and embrace me like a son, exclaiming how marvelous I look, how relaxed

I seem in comparison to the timid creature they met then. They want to know if this means I'm going to stay. I blush and admit I don't know. I introduce them to Caralys and they say it seems an easy choice to them. The women hit it off. Jerry suggests a local inn where we can hear a guitarist he knows, and before long we're there, claiming a corner table between dances, listening to his friend: another old man, an ancient man really, with twinkling eyes and spotted scalp and a wispy comic-opera moustache that, dangling to his collarbone, looks like a boomerang covered with lint.

6.

"It's not that I hate my country," Jerry says, when the women have left together, in the way that women have. His eyes shine and his voice slurs from the effects of too much drink. "I can't. I know my history. I know the things she's accomplished, the principles she's stood for, the challenges she's faced. I've even been around for more of it than I care to remember. But coming here was not abandoning her. It was abandoning what she'd become. It was abandoning the drive-throughs and the ATMs and the talking heads who pretend they have the answers but would be lucky to remember how to tie their shoes. It was remembering what life was supposed to be all about, and seizing it with both hands while we still had a few good years still left in us. It was victory, Robert; an act of sheer moral victory. Do you see, Robert? Do you see?"

I tell him I see.

"You think you do. But you still have a ticket out, day after tomorrow. Sundown, right? Ach. You're still a tourist. You're still too scared to take the leap. But stay here a few more weeks and then tell me that you see."

I might just do that, I say. I might stay here the rest of my life.

He dismisses me with a wave of his hand. "Sure you say that. You say that now. You say that because you think it's so easy to say that. You haven't even begun to imagine the commitment it takes."

But I love Caralys.

"Of course you do. But will you be fair to her, in the end? Will you? You're not her first tourist, you know."

7.

Jerry has become too intense for me, in a way utterly at odds with the usual flavor of life in Enysbourg. If he presses on I might have to tell him to stop.

But I am rescued. The man with the wispy moustache returns from the bar with a fresh mug of beer, sets it beside him on a three-legged stool, picks up a stringed instrument a lot like a misshapen guitar, and begins to sing a ballad in a language I don't understand. It's one of Enysbourg's many dialects, a tongue distinguished by deep rolling consonants and rich sensual tones, so expressive in its the way it cavorts the length of an average sentence that I don't need a translation to know that he's singing a hymn to lost love long remembered. When he closes his eyes I can almost imagine him as the fresh-faced young boy staring with earnest panic at the eyes of the fresh-faced young woman whose beauty first made him want to sing such songs. He sings of pain, a sense of loss, a longing for something denied to him. But there is also wonder, a sense of amazement at all the dreams he's ever managed to fulfill.

Or maybe that's just my head, making the song mean what I want it to mean. In either event, the music is slow and heartfelt until some kind of mid-verse epiphany sends its tempo flying. And all of a sudden the drum beats and the hands clap and the darkened room bursts with men and women rising from the shadows to meet on the dance floor in an explosion of flailing hair and whirling bodies. There are children on shoulders and babies on backs and a hundred voices united in the chorus of the moustached man's song, which seems to fill our veins with fire. Jerry has already slid away, his rant of a few moments before forgotten in the urgency of the moment. I recognize nobody around me but nevertheless see no strangers. As I decide to stay in Enysbourg, to spend the rest of my life with Caralys, to raise a family with her, to keep turning pages in this book I've just begun to write, the natives seem to recognize the difference in me. I am handed a baby, which I kiss to the sound of cheers. I hand it back and am handed another. Then another. The music grows louder, more insistent. A wisp of smoke drifts by. Clove, tobacco, hashish, or something else; it is there and then it is gone.

I blink and catch a glimpse of Caralys, cut off by the crowd. She is trying to get to me, her eyes wide, her face shining, her need urgent. She knows I have decided. She can tell. She is as radiant as I have ever seen her, and though jostled by the mob she is determined to make her way to my side. She too has something to say, something that needs to be spoken, through shattered teeth and a mouth filled with blood.

During
8.

There is no sunlight. The skies are too sullied by the smoke of burning buildings to admit the existence of dawn. What arrives instead are gray and sickly shadows, over a moonscape so marked with craters and shattered rubble that in most places it's hard to tell where the buildings stood in the first place. Every few seconds, the soot above us brightens, becomes as blinding as a parody of the light it's usurped, and rocks the city with flame and thunder. Debris pelts everything below. A starving dog cowering in a hollow formed by two shattered walls bolts, seeking better haven in a honeycomb of fallen masonry fifty meters of sheer hell away. But even before it can round the first twisted corpse, a solid wall of shrapnel reduces the animal to a scarlet mist falling on torn flesh.

I witness its death from the site of my own. I am already dead. I still happen to be breathing, but that's a pure accident. Location is all. The little girl who'd been racing along two paces ahead of me, mad with fear, forced her to rip off her flaming clothes to reveal the bubbling black scar the chemical burns have made of her back, is now a corpse. She's a pair of legs protruding from a mound of fallen brick. Her left foot still bears a shoe. Her right is pale, naked, moon-white perfect, unbloodied. I, who had been racing along right behind her, am not so fortunate. The same concussion wave that put her out of her misery sent me flying. Runaway stones have torn deep furrows in my legs, my belly, my face, my chest. I have one seeping gash across my abdomen and another across one cheek; both painful, but nothing next to the greater damage done by the cornice that landed on my right knee, splintering the bone and crushing my leg as close to flat as a leg can get without bursting free of its cradling flesh. The stone tumbled on as soon as it did its work, settling in a pile of similar rocks; it looks like any other, but I still think I can identify it out from over here, using the marks it left along the filthy ground.

I have landed in a carpet of broken glass a meter or so from what, for a standing person, would be a ragged waist-high remnant of wall. It is good fortune, I suppose; judging from the steady tattoo of shrapnel and rifle fire impacting against the other side, it's that wall which for the moment spares me the fate of the little girl and the dog. Chance has also favored me by letting me land within sight of a irregular gap in that wall, affording me a view of what used to be the street but which is right now is just a narrow negotiable path between craters and mounds of smoking debris. My field of vision is not large, but it was enough to show me what happened to the dog. If I'm to survive this, it must also allow me to see rescue workers, refugees, even soldiers capable of dragging me to wherever the wounded are brought.

But so far there has no help to be seen. Most of the time even my fragmentary view is obscured by smoke of varying colors: white, which though steaming hot is also as thin and endurable, passing over me without permanent damage; black, which sickens me with its mingled flavors of burning rubber and bubbling flesh; and the caustic yellow, which burns my eyes and leaves me gagging with the need to void a stomach already long empty. I lick my lips, which are dry and cracked and pitted, and recognize both hunger and thirst in the way the world pales before me. It is the last detail. Everything I consumed yesterday, when Enysbourg was paradise, is gone; it, and everything I had for several days before. Suddenly, I'm starving to death.

9.

There is another great burst of sound and light, so close parts of me shake apart. I try to scream, but my throat is dry, my voice a mere wisp, my mouth a sewer sickening from the mingled tastes of blood and ash and things turned rotten inside me. I see a dark shape, a man, Jerry Martel in fact, move fast past the gap in the wall. I hear automatic fire and I hear his brief cry as he hits the dirt in a crunch of flesh and gravel. He is not quite dead at first, and though he does not know I am here, just out of sight, a collaborator in his helplessness, he cries out to me anyway: a bubbling, childish cry, aware that it's about to be cut off but hoping in this instant that it reaches a listener willing to care. I can't offer the compassion Jerry craves, because I hate him too much for bringing fresh dangers so close to the place where I already lie broken. I want him gone.

A second later fate obliges me with another burst of automatic weapons fire. Brick chips fill the air like angry bees, digging more miniature craters; one big one strikes my ravaged knee and I spasm, grimacing as my bowels let loose, knowing it won't matter because I released everything I had inside me long ago. I feel relief. He was my friend, but I'm safer with him gone.

10.

I smell more smoke. I taste mud. I hear taunts in languages I don't recognize, cries and curses in the tongues spoken in Enysbourg. A wave of heat somewhere near me alerts me that a fire has broken out. I drag myself across ragged stones and broken glass closer to the gap in the wall, entertaining vainglorious ambitions of perhaps crawling through and making it untouched through the carnage to someplace where people can fix me. But the pain is too much, and I collapse, bleeding now from a dozen fresher wounds, having accomplished nothing but to provide myself a better view.

I see the elderly musician with the huge moustache stumble on by, his eyes closed, his face a sheen of blood, his arms dangling blistered and lifeless at his sides, each blackened and swollen to four times its natural size. I see a woman, half-mad, her mouth ajar in an unending silent scream, clutching a tightly wrapped but still ragged bundle in a flannel blanket, unwilling to notice that whatever it held is now just a glistening smear across her chest. I see a tall and robust and athletic man stumble on by, his eyes vacant, his expression insane, his jaw ripped free and dangling from his face by a braided ribbon of flesh. I see all that and I hear more explosions and I watch as some of the fleeing people fall either whole or in pieces and I listen as some are released by death and, more importantly, as others are not.

Something moving at insane speed whistles through the sky above, passing so near that its slipstream tugs at my skin. I almost imagine it pulling me off the ground, lifting me into the air, allowing me a brief moment of flight behind it before it strikes and obliterates its target. For a moment I wish it would; even that end would be better than a deathbed of shattered rock and slivered glass. Then comes the brightest burst of light and most deafening wave of thunder yet, and for a time I become blind and deaf, with everything around me reduced to a field of pure white.

11.

When the world comes back, not at all improved, it is easy to see the four young men in identical uniforms who huddle in a little alcove some twenty meters away. There is not much to them, these young men: they all carry rifles, they all wear heavy packs, they're all little more than boys, and their baggy uniforms testify to a long time gone without decent food. When one turns my way, facing me and perhaps even seeing me, but not registering me as a living inhabitant of the corpse-strewn landscape, his eyes look sunken, haunted, unimaginably ancient.

He is, I realize, as mad as the most pitiful among the wounded—a reasonable response to his environment, and one I would share if I could divest the damnable sanity that forces me to keep reacting to the horror. He turns back to his comrades and says something; then he looks over them, at something beyond my own limited field of vision, and his smile is enough to make me crave death all over again. His comrades look where he's looking and smile the same way: all four of them showing their teeth.

The three additional soldiers picking their way through the rubble bear a woman between them. It is Caralys. Two stand to either side of her, holding her arms. A third stands behind her, holding a serrated knife to her throat with one hand and holding a tight grip on her hair with the other. That soldier keeps jabbing his knee into the small of her back to keep her going. He has to; she's struggling with every ounce of strength available to her, pulling from side to side, digging her feet into the ground, cursing them to a thousand hells every time they jerk her off her feet and force her onward.

She is magnificent, my Caralys. She is stronger, more vibrant, than any one of them. In any fair fight she would be the only one left standing. But she is held by three, and while she could find an opportunity to escape three, the soldiers from the alcove, who now rush to help their comrades, bring the total all the way up to seven. There is no hope with seven. I know this even as I drag myself toward her from the place where I lie broken. I know this even as she struggles to drive her tormentors away with furious kicks. But these boys are too experienced with such things. They take her by the ankles, lift her off the ground, and bear her squirming and struggling form across the ravaged pavement to a clear place in the rubble, where they pin her to the ground, each one taking a limb. They must struggle to keep her motionless. The soldier with the darkest eyes unslings his rifle, weighs it in his arms, and smashes its butt across her jaw. The bottom half of her face crumples like shattered pottery.

There is nothing I can do but continue to crawl toward her, toward them.

Caralys coughs out a bubble of fresh blood. Fragments of teeth, driven from her mouth, cling to what's left of her chin. She shrieks and convulses and tries to kick. Her legs remain held. The same soldier who just smashed her face now sees that his job is not yet done. He raises his rifle above his head and drives the stock, hard, into her belly. She wheezes and chokes. She tries to curl into a ball of helpless misery, seeking escape within herself. But the soldiers won't even permit that. Another blow, this one to her forehead, takes what little fight is left. Her eyes turn to blackened smears. Her nose blows pink bubbles which burst and dribble down her cheeks in rivulets. She murmurs an animal noise. The soldier responsible for making her manageable makes a joke in a language I don't know, which can't possibly be funny, but still makes the others laugh. They rip off her filthy dress and spread her legs farther apart. The leader steps away, props his rifle against a fragment of wall, and returns, dropping his pants. As he gives his swollen penis a lascivious little waggle, I observe something wrong with it, something I can see from a distance; it looks green, diseased, half-rotted. But he descends, forcing himself into her, cursing her with every thrust, his cruel animal grunts matched by her own bubbling exhalations, less gasps of pain or protests at her violation than the involuntary noises made as her diaphragm is compressed again and again and again. It doesn't last long, but by the time he pulls out, shakes himself off, and pulls his pants back up, the glimpse I catch of her face is enough to confirm that she's no longer here.

Caralys is alive, all right. I can see her labored breath. I can feel the outrage almost as much as she does. But she's not in this place and time. Her mind has abandoned this particular battlefield for another, inside her head, which might not provide any comfort but nevertheless belongs only to her. What's left in this killing ground doesn't even seem to notice as one of the other soldiers releases his grip on her right arm, takes his position, and commences a fresh rape.

12.

There are no words sufficient for the hate I feel. I am a human being with a human being's dimensions, but the hate is bigger than my capacity to contain it. It doesn't just fill me. It replaces me. It becomes everything I am. I want to claw at them and snap at them and spew hatred at them and rip out their throats with my teeth. I want to leave them blackened corpses and I want to go back to wherever they came from and make rotting flesh of their own wives and mothers. I want to bathe in their blood. I want to die killing them. I want to scar the earth where they were born. I want to salt the farmland so nothing ever grows there again. If hatred alone lent strength, I would rend the world itself. But I cry out without a voice, and I crawl forward without quite managing to move, and I make some pathetic little sound or another, and it carries across the smoky distance between me and them and it accomplishes nothing but advise the enemy that I'm here.

In a single spasm of readiness, they all release Caralys, grab their weapons, scan the rubble-field for the source of the fresh sound. The one using her at the moment needs only an extra second to disengage, but he pulls free in such a panicked spasm that he tumbles backward, slamming his pantless buttocks into a puddle of something too colored by rainbows to qualify as water. The leader sees me. He rolls his eyes, pulls a serrated blade from its sheath at his hip, and covers the distance between us in three seconds.

The determined hatred I felt a heartbeat ago disappears. I know that he's the end of me and that I can't fight him and I pray that I can bargain with him instead, that I can barter Caralys for mercy or medical attention or even an easier death. I think all this, betraying her, and it makes me hate myself. That's the worst, this moment of seeing myself plain, this illustration of the foul bargains I'd be willing to make in exchange for a few added seconds of life. It doesn't matter that there aren't any bargains. I shouldn't have wanted any.

I grope for his knife as it descends but it just opens the palms of my hands and christens my face and chest with blood soon matched by that which flows when he guts me from crotch to ribcage. My colon spills out in thick ropes, steaming in the morning air. I feel cold. The agony tears at me. I can't even hope for death.

I want more than death. I want more than oblivion. I want erasure. I want a retroactive ending. I want to wipe out my whole life, starting from my conception. Nothing, not even the happy moments, is worth even a few seconds of this. It would be better if I'd never lived.

But I don't die yet.

13.

I don't die when he walks away, or when he and his fellow soldiers return to their fun with Caralys. I don't die when they abandon her and leave in her place a broken thing that spends the next hours choking on its own blood. I don't even die when the explosions start again, and the dust salts my wounds with little burning embers. I don't die when the ground against my back shakes like a prehistoric beast about to tear itself apart with rage. I don't even die when the rats come to me, to enjoy a fresh meal. I want to die, but maybe that release is more than I deserve. So I lie on my back beneath a cloudscape of smoke and ash, and I listen to Caralys choke, and I listen to the gunfire and I curse that sociopathic monster God and I do nothing, nothing, when the flies come to lay their eggs.

After
14.

I wake on a bed of freshly-mowed grass. The air is cool and refreshing, the sky as blue as a dream, the breeze a delicious mixture of scents ranging from sea salt to the sweatier perfume of passing horses. From the light, I know it can't be too long after dawn, but I can tell I'm not the first one up. I can hear songbirds, the sounds of laughing children, barking dogs, music played at low volumes from little radios.

Unwilling to trust the sensations of peace, I resist getting up long enough to first grab a fistful of grass, luxuriating in the feel of the long thin blades as they bunch up between my fingers. They're miraculous. They're alive. I'm alive.

I turn my head and see where I am: one of the city's many small parks, a place lined with trees and decorated with orchid gardens. The buildings visible past the treeline are uncratered and intact. I'm intact. The other bodies I see, scattered here and there across the lawn, are not corpses, but sleepers, still snoring away after a long lazy evening beneath the stars. There are many couples, even a few families with children, all peaceful, all unworried about predators either animal or human. Even the terror, the trauma, the soul-withering hate, the easy savagery that subsumes all powerless victims, all the emotional scars that had ripped me apart, have faded. And the only nearby smoke comes from a sandpit not far upwind, where a jolly bearded man in colorful suspenders has begun to cook himself an outdoor breakfast.

15.

I rise, unscarred and unbroken, clad in comfortable native clothing: baggy shorts, a vest, a jaunty feathered hat. I even have a wine bottle, three-quarters empty, and a pleasant taste in my mouth to go with it. I drink the rest and smile at the pleasant buzz. The thirst remains, but for something non-alcoholic. I need water. I itch from the stray blades of grass peppering my exposed calves and forearms. I contort my back, feeling the vertebrae pop. It feels good. I stretch to get my circulation going. I luxuriate in the tingle of the morning air. Across the meadow, a little girl points at me and smiles. She is the same little girl I saw crushed by masonry yesterday. It takes me a second to smile back and wave, a second spent wondering if she recognizes me, if she finds me an unpleasant reminder. If so, there is no way to tell from the way she bears herself. She betrays no trauma at all. Rather, she looks as blessed as any other creature of Enysbourg.

The inevitable comparison to Caralys assigns me my first mission for the day. I have to find her, hold her, confirm that she too has emerged unscathed from the madness of the day before. She must have, given the rules here, but the protective instincts of the human male still need to be respected. So I wander from the park, into the streets of a capital city just starting to bustle with life; past the gondolas taking lovers down the canals; past the merchants hawking vegetables swollen with flavor; past a juggler in a coat of carnival color who has put down his flaming batons and begun to toss delighted children instead. I see a hundred faces I know, all of whom nod with the greatest possible warmth upon seeing me, perhaps recognizing in my distracted expression the look of a foreigner who has just experienced his first taste of Enysbourg's greatest miracle.

Nobody looks haunted. Nobody looks terrorized. Nobody looks like the survivors of madness. They have shaken off the firebombings that reduced them to screaming torches, the bayonets that jabbed through their hearts, the tiny rooms where they were tortured at inhuman length for information they did not have. They have shrugged away the hopelessness and the rampant disease and the mass graves where they were tossed beside their bullet-riddled neighbors while still breathing themselves. They remember it all, as I remember it all, but that was yesterday, not today, and this is Enysbourg, a land where it never happened, a land which will know nothing but joy until the end of everything comes again, ten days from now.

16.

On my way back to the hotel I pass the inn where Caralys and I went dancing the night before the end of everything. The scents that waft through the open door are enough to make me swoon. I almost pass by, determined to find Caralys before worrying about my base animal needs, but then I hear deep braying laughter from inside, laughter I recognize as Jerry Martel's. I should go inside. He has been in Enysbourg for years and may know the best ways to find loved ones after the end of everything. The hunger is a consideration, too. Stopping to eat now, before finding Caralys, might seem like a selfish act, but I won't do either one of us any good unless I do something to keep up my strength. Guilt wars with the needs of an empty stomach. My mouth waters. Caralys will understand. I go inside.

The place is dim and nearly empty. The old man with the enormous moustache is on stage, playing something inconsequential. Jerry, who seems to be the only patron, is in a corner table waiting for me. He waves me over, asks me if I'm all right, urges me to sit down, and waits for me to tell him how it was.

My words halting, I tell him it doesn't feel real anymore.

He claps me on the back. He says he's proud of me. He says he wasn't sure about me in the beginning. He says he had me figured for the kind of person who wouldn't be able to handle it, but look at me now, refreshed, invigorated, ready to handle everything. He says I remind him of himself. He beams and expects me to take that as a compliment. I give him a weak nod. He punches me in the shoulder and says that it's going to be fun having me around from now on: a new person, he says, to guide around the best of Enysbourg, who doesn't yet know all the sights, the sounds, the tastes, the joys and adventures. There are parts of Enysbourg, both in and outside the capital, that even most of those who live here don't know. He says it's enough to fill lifetimes. He says that the other stuff, the nasty stuff, the stuff we endure as the price of admission, is just a reason to cherish everything else. He says that the whole country is a treasure trove of experience for people willing to take the leap, and he says I look like one of those people.

And of course, he says, punching my arm again, there's Caralys: sweet, wanton Caralys, whom he has already seen taking her morning swim by the sea. Caralys, who will be so happy to see me again. He says I should remember what Caralys is like when she's delighted. He says that now that I know I can handle it I would have to be a fool to let her go. He chuckles, then says, tell you what, stay right here, I'll go find her, I'm sure the two of you have a lot to talk about. And then he disappears, all before I have said anything at all.

On stage, the man with the enormous moustache starts another song, playing this time not the misshapen guitar-thing from two nights ago, but something else, a U-shaped device with two rows of strings forming a criss-cross between ends and base. Its music is clear and resonant, with a wobbly quality that only adds to its emotional impact. The song is a slow one: a relief to me, since the raucous energy of Enysbourg's nights might be a bit much for me right now. I nod at the old man. He recognizes me. His grin broadens and his eyes slit with amusement. There's no telling whether he has some special affection for me as a person, or just appreciates the arrival of any audience at all. Either way, his warmth is genuine. He is grateful to me for being here. But he does not stop playing just to greet me. The song continues. The lyrics, once again in a language unknown to me, are once again still easy to comprehend. Whatever the particulars, this song is impossible to mistake as anything but a tribute to being alive. When the song ends, I toss him a coin, and he tosses it back, not insulted, just not interested. He is interested in the music for music's sake alone, in celebration, because celebration is the whole point.

17.

I think hard on the strange cycle of life in Enysbourg, dictated by law, respected as a philosophical principle, and rendered possible by all the technological genius the modern world can provide: this endless cycle which always follows nine days of sheer exuberance with one day of sheer Hell on Earth.

It would be so much easier if exposure to that Tenth Day were not the price of admission.

It would be so much better if we could be permitted to sail in on The Day After and sail out on The Night Before, enjoying those nine days of sweet abandon without any obligation to endure the unmitigated savagery of the tenth. The weekly exodus wouldn't be a tide of refugees; it would be a simple fact of life. If such a choice were possible, I would make it. Of course, I would also have to make Caralys come with me each time, for even if she was determined to remain behind and support her nation's principles, I could never feel at peace standing on the deck of some distant ship, watching Enysbourg's beautiful shoreline erupt in smoke and fire, aware that I was safe but knowing that she was somewhere in that no man's land being brutalized and killed. And there is no way she would ever come with me to such a weekly safe haven, when her land was a smoking ruin behind her. She would know the destruction temporary the same way I know it temporary, but she would regard her escape from the regular interval of terror an act of unforgivable treason against her home. It is as she said that time I almost lost her by proposing that she come back home with me, a suggestion I made not because home is such a great place, but because home would be easier. She said that leaving would be cowardice. She said that leaving would be betrayal. She said that leaving would be the end of her. And she said that the same went for any other attempt to circumvent the way things were here, including my own, which is why she'd despise me forever if I tried. The Tenth Day, she said, is the whole point of Enysbourg. It's the main reason the ships come and go only on the Day After. Nobody, not the natives like Caralys, and not the visitors like myself, is allowed their time in paradise unless we also pay the price. The question that faces everybody, on that day after, is the same question that faces me now: whether life in Enysbourg is worth it.

I think of all the countries, my own included, that never know the magic Enysbourg enjoys nine days out of ten, that have become not societies but efficient machines, where life is all about keeping that machine in motion. Those nations know peace, and they know prosperity, but do they know life the way Enysbourg knows life, nine days out of every ten? I come from such a place and I suffocated in such a place—maybe because I was too much a part of the machine to recognize the consolations available to me, maybe because they weren't available to be found. Either way I know that I've never been happy, not before I came here. Here I found my love of being alive—but only nine days out of ten.

And is that Tenth Day really too much to endure, anyway? I think about all the countries that know that Tenth Day, not at safe predictable intervals, but for long stretches lasting months or years or centuries. I think about all the countries that have never known anything else. I think about all the terrorized generations who have lived and died and turned to bones with nothing but that Tenth Day to color their days and nights. For all those people, millions of them, Enysbourg, with that Tenth Day always lurking in recent memory and always building in the near future, is still a paradise beyond comprehension. Bring all those people here and they'd find this choice easy, almost laughable. They'd leap at the chance, knowing that their lives would only be better, most of the time.

It's only the comfortable, the complacent, the spoiled, who would even find the question an issue for internal debate. The rest would despise me for showing such reluctance to stay, and they'd be right. I've seen enough, and experienced enough, to know that they'd be right. But I don't know if I have what it takes to be right with them. I might prefer to be wrong and afraid and suffering their disdain at a safe distance, in a place untouched by times like Enysbourg's Tenth Day.

18.

I remember a certain moment, when we had been together for three days. Caralys had led me to a gorge, a few hours from the capital, a place she called a secret, and which actually seemed to be, as there were no legions of camera-toting tourists climbing up and down the few safe routes to the sparkling river below. The way down was not a well-worn path, carved by the weight of human feet. It was a series of compromises with what otherwise would have been a straight vertical drop—places where it became possible to slide down dirt grades, or descend from one rock ledge to another. Much of the way down was overgrown, with plants so thick that only her unerring sense of direction kept us descending on the correct route, and not via a sudden, fatal, bone-shattering plunge from a height. She moved through it all with a grace unlike I had ever seen, and also with an urgency I could not understand, but which was nevertheless intense enough to keep me from complaining through my hoarse breath and aching bones. Every once in a while she turned, to smile and call me her adventurer. And every time she did, the special flavor she gave the word was enough to keep me going, determined to rush anyplace she wanted me to follow.

The grade grew gentler the closer we came to the river at the gorge bottom. It became a mild grade, dim beneath thick forest canopy, surrounded on all sides by the rustling of a thousand leaves and the chittering of a thousand birds. Once the water itself grew audible, there was nothing but a wall of sound all around us. She picked up speed and began to run, tearing off her clothes as she went. I ran after her, gasping, almost breaking my neck a dozen times as I tripped over this root, that half-buried rock. By the time I emerged in daylight at a waterfront of multicolored polished stones, she was well ahead of me. I was hopping on one leg to remove my boots and pants and she was already naked and up to her waist in mid-river, her perfect skin shiny from wet and glowing from the sun.

She had led us directly to a spot just below one of the grandest waterfalls I had ever seen with my own eyes. It was an unbroken wall of rushing silver, descending from a flat rock ledge some fifty meters above us. The grotto at its base was bowl-shaped and just wide enough to collect the upriver rapids in a pool of relative calm. The water was so cold that I emitted an involuntary yelp, but Caralys just laughed at me, enjoying my reaction. I dove in, feeling the temperature shock in every pore, then stood up, dripping, exuberant, wanting nothing in this moment but to be with her.

She caught my wrist before I could touch her. "No."

I stopped, confused. No? Why no? Wasn't this what she wanted, in this perfect place she'd found for us?

She released my arm and headed toward the wall of water, splashing through the river as it grew deeper around her, swallowing first her hips and then her breasts and then her shoulders, finally requiring her to swim. Her urgency was almost frightening now. I thought of how easy it might be to drown here, for someone who allowed herself to get caught beneath that raging wall of water, and I said, "Hey," rushing after her, not enjoying the cold quite as much anymore. I don't know what fed that river, but it was numbing enough to be glacial runoff. Thoughts of hypothermia struck for the first time, and I felt the first stab of actual fear just as she disappeared beneath the wall.

The moment I passed through, with sheets of freezing water assaulting my head and shoulders, was one of the loudest I'd ever known. It was a roaring, rumbling, bubbling cacophony, so intense that it drowned out all the other sounds that filled this place. The birds, the wind, the softer bubbling of the water downstream, they were wiped out, eliminated by this one all-encompassing noise. I almost turned around. But I kept going, right through the wall.

On the other side I found air and a dark dank place. Caralys had pulled herself onto a mossy ledge just above the waterline, set against a great stone wall. There she sat with her back to the wall, hugging her legs, her knees tucked tight beneath her chin. Her eyes were white circles reflecting the light passing through the water now behind me. I waded toward her, found an empty spot on the ledge beside her, and pulled myself up too. The stone, I found without much surprise, was like ice, not a place I wanted to stay for long. But I joined her in contemplating the daylight as it prismed through a portal of plummeting water. It seemed brilliant out there: a lot like another world, seen through an enchanted gateway.

"It's beautiful," I said.

She said nothing, so I turned to see if she was all right. She was still staring at the water. She was in shadow, and a trick of the light had shrouded most of her profile in darkness, reducing her outline to a dimly lit crescent. The droplets balancing on the tip of her nose were like little glistening pearls. I saw, too, that she was trembling, though at the time I attributed that to the cold alone. She said, "Listen."

I listened. And heard only the sound of the waterfall, less deafening now that we'd passed some distance beyond it. And something else: her teeth, chattering.

She said, "The silence."

It took me a second to realize that this was the miracle she'd brought me here to witness: the way the waterfall, in all its harmless fury, now insulated us from all the sounds we had been hearing all morning. It was as if none of what we'd heard out there, all the time it had taken us to hike to this place she knew so well, now existed at all. None of it was there. None of it could touch us.

It seemed important to her.

At that moment, I could not understand why.

19.

I am in the little restaurant, thinking all this, when a soft voice calls my name. I look up, and of course it's Caralys: sweet, beautiful Caralys, who has found me in the place where we prefer to think we saw each other last. She is, of course, unmarked and unwounded, all the insults inflicted by the soldiers either healed or wiped away like bad rumors. She looks exactly like she did the night before last, complete with fringed blouse and patchy dress and two curling strands of hair that meet in the center of her forehead. If there is any difference in her, it lies in what I now recognize was there all along: the storm clouds of memory roiling behind her piercing black eyes. She's not insane, or hard, the way she should be after enduring what she's endured; Enysbourg always wipes away all scars, physical and psychological both. But it does not wipe away the knowledge. And her smile, always so guileless in its radiance, now seems to hold a dark challenge. I can see that she has always held me and my naïveté in the deepest possible contempt. She couldn't have felt any other way, in the presence of any man who had never known the Tenth Day. I was an infant by Enysbourg's standards, a man who could not understand her or the forces that shaped her. I must have seemed bland, dull, and in my own comfortable way, even retarded.

I find to my surprise that I feel contempt as well. Part of me is indignant at her effrontery at looking down at me. After all, she has had other tourists. She has undertaken other Projects with other men, from other places, trying time and time again to make outsiders into natives of her perverse little theme park to savagery. What does she expect from me, in the end? Who am I to her? If I leave, won't she just find another tourist to play with for ten days? And why should I stay, when I should just see her as the easy vacation tramp, always eager to go with the first man who comes off the boat?

It's hard not to be repulsed by her.

But that hate pales beside the awareness that in all my days only she has made me feel alive.

And her own contempt, great as it is, seems drowned by her love, shining at me with such intensity that for a moment I almost forget the fresh secrets now filling the space between us. I stand and fall into her arms. We close our eyes and taste each other's tears. She whispers, "It is all right, Robert. I understand. It is all right. I want you to stay, but won't hate you if you go."

She is lying, of course. She will despise me even more if I go. She will know for certain that Enysbourg has taught me nothing. But her love will be just as sincere if I stay.

It's the entire reason she seeks out tourists. She loathes our naïveté. But it's also the one thing she can't provide for herself.

20.

Jerry Martel stands nearby, beaming and self-congratulatory. Dee has joined him, approving, cooing, maternal. Maybe they hope we'll pay attention to them again. Or maybe we're just a new flavor for them, a novelty for the expatriates living in Enysbourg.

Either way, I ignore them and pull Caralys close, taking in the scent of her, the sheer absolute ideal of her, laughing and weeping and unable to figure out which is which. She makes sounds that could be either, murmuring words that could be balms for my pain or laments for her own. She tells me again that it's going to be all right, and I don't know whether she's telling the truth. I don't even know whether she's all that sure herself. I just know that, if I take that trip home, I will lose everything she gave me, and be left with nothing but the gray dullness of my everyday life. And if I stay, deciding to pay the price of that Tenth Day in exchange for the illusion of Eden, we'll never be able to acknowledge the Tenth Day on the other days when everything seems to be all right. We won't mention the times spent suffocating beneath rubble, or spurting blood from severed limbs, or choking out our lungs from poison gas. I will never know how many hells she's known, and how many times she's cried out for merciful death. I'll never be able to ask if what I witnessed yesterday was typical, worse than average, or even an unusually good day, considering. She'll never ask about any of the horrors that happen to me. These are not things discussed during peacetime in Enysbourg. We won't even talk about them if I stay, and if we remain in love, and if we marry and have children, and if they grow up bright and beautiful and filled with wonder; and if every ten days we find ourselves obliged to watch them ground beneath tank-treads, or worse. In Enysbourg such things are not the stuff of words. In Enysbourg a certain silence is just the price of being alive.

And a small price it is, in light of how blessed those who live here have always been.

Just about all Caralys can do, as the two of us begin to sway together in a sweet slow dance, is continue to murmur reassurances. Just about all I can do is rest my head against her chest, and close my eyes to the sound of her beating heart. Just about all we can do together is stay in this moment, putting off the next one as long as possible, and try not to remember the dogs, the hateful snarling dogs, caged for now but always thirsty for a fresh taste of blood.

"The mere absence of war is not peace."
—*President John F. Kennedy*

For J.H.

RESISTANCE

by Tobias S. Buckell

Tobias S. Buckell is the author of the *novels Crystal Rain, Ragamuffin, Sly Mongoose*, and the *New York Times* bestseller *Halo: The Cole Protocol*. He is a Writers of the Future winner, and has published more than thirty short stories, which have appeared in magazines such as *Nature, Lightspeed, Science Fiction Age*, and *Analog*, and in anthologies including *Mojo: Conjure Stories, New Voices in Science Fiction,* and *I, Alien*. Much of his short work has been collected in *Tides from the New Worlds*. He currently lives in Ohio with a pair of dogs, a pair of cats, twin daughters, and his wife.

In November 2008, American voters elected Barack Obama president of the United States. The race was not as close as it has been in recent elections, but the real excitement of the day was the high voter turn-out. With an estimated 61% of all registered voters choosing to cast votes, the 2008 election stands as the highest voter turnout in more than three decades.

Of course, that means 30% or so of all registered voters didn't bother to turn up. And who knows how many U.S. citizens never got around to even registering in the first place?

There are thousands of explanations for voter apathy, but in the world Buckell portrays in our next story, none of those excuses really matter; it's a techno-democracy failed by its own voters. But Buckell knows first-hand about systems that begin with high hopes only to crumble into disaster. He was born during a 1979 coup d'etat in Grenada, where the new government, according to Buckell, "fell into the spiral of quashing opposition to the point where it became draconian and people ended up lined up against walls and shot."

It would appear that a utopian government is only as strong as the voices of its resistance.

F our days after the coup Stanuel was ordered to fake an airlock pass. The next day he waited inside a cramped equipment locker large enough to hold two people while an armed rover the size and shape of a helmet wafted around the room, twisting and counter-rotating pieces of itself as it scanned the room briefly. Stanuel held his breath and willed himself not to move or make a sound. He just floated in place, thankful for the lack of gravity that might have betrayed him had he needed to depend on locked, nervous muscles.

The rover gave up and returned to the corridor, the airlock door closing behind it. Stanuel slipped back out. The rover had missed him because he'd been fully suited up for vacuum. No heat signature.

Behind the rover's lenses had been the eyes of Pan. And since the coup, anyone knew better than to get noticed by Pan. Even the airlock pass cut it too close. He would disappear when Pan's distributed networks noticed what he'd done.

By then, Pan would not be a problem.

Stanuel checked his suit over again, then cycled the airlock out. The outer door split in two and pulled apart.

But where was the man Stanuel was supposed to bring in?

He realized there was an inky blackness in the space just outside the ring of the lock. A blotch that grew larger, and then tumbled in. The suit flickered, and turned a dull gray to match the general interior color of the airlock.

The person stood up, and Stanuel repressurized the airlock.

They waited as Stanuel snapped seals and took his own helmet off. He hung the suit up in the locker he'd just been hiding in. "We have to hurry, we only have about ten minutes before the next rover patrol."

Behind him, Stanuel heard crinkling and crunching. When he turned around the spacesuit had disappeared. He now faced a tall man with dark skin and long dreadlocks past his shoulders, and eyes as gray as the bench behind him. The spacesuit had turned into a long, black trench-coat. "Rovers?" the man asked.

Stanuel held his hand up and glyphed a 3-D picture in the air above his palm. The man looked at the rover spin and twist and shoot. "Originally they were station maintenance bots. Semi-autonomous remote operated vehicles. Now they're armed."

"I see." The man pulled a large backpack off his shoulders and unzipped it.

"So… what now?" Stanuel asked.

The gray eyes flicked up from the pack. "You don't know?"

"I'm part of a cell. But we run distributed tasks, only checking it with people who assign them. It keeps us insulated. I was only told to open this airlock and let you in. You would know what comes next. Is the attack tonight? Should I get armed? Are you helping the attack?"

The man opened the pack all the way to reveal a small arsenal of guns, grenades, explosives, and—oddly—knives. Very large knives. He looked up at Stanuel. "I *am* the attack. I've been asked to shut Pan down."

"But you're not a programmer…"

"I can do all things through explosives, who destroy for me." The man began moving the contents of the pack inside the pockets and straps of the trenchcoat, clipped more to his belt and thigh, as well as to holsters under each arm, and then added pieces to his ankles.

He was now a walking arsenal.

But only half the pack had been emptied. The mysterious mercenary tossed it at Stanuel. "Besides, you're going to help."

Stanuel coughed. "Me?"

"According to the resistance message, you're a maintenance manager, recently promoted. You still know all the sewer lines, access ducts, and holes required to get me to the tower. How long do you guess we have before it notices your unauthorized use of an airlock?"

"An hour," Stanuel said. The last time he'd accidentally gone somewhere Pan didn't like, rovers had been in his office within an hour.

"And can we get to the tower within an hour, Stanuel, without being noticed?"

Stanuel nodded.

The large, well-armed man pointed at the airlock door into the corridor. "Well, let's not dally."

"Can I ask you something?" Stanuel asked.

"Yes."

"Your name. You know mine. I don't know yours."

"Pepper," said the mercenary. "Now can we leave?"

A single tiny sound ended the secrecy of their venture: the buzz of wings. Pepper's head snapped in the direction of the sound, locks spinning out from his head.

He slapped his palm against the side of the wall, crushing a butterfly-like machine perfectly flat.

"A bug," Stanuel said.

Pepper launched down the corridor, bouncing off the walls until he hit the bulkhead at the far end. He glanced around the corner. "Clear."

"Pan knows you're in Haven now." Stanuel felt fear bloom, an instant explosion of paralysis that left him hanging in the air. "It will mobilize."

"Then get me into the tower, quick. Let's go, Stanuel, we're not engaged in something that rewards the slow."

But Stanuel remained in place. "They chose me because I had no family," he said. "I had less to lose. I would help them against Pan. But..."

Pepper folded his arms. "It's already seen you. You're already dead."

That sunk in. Stanuel had handled emergencies. Breaches, where vacuum flooded in, sucking the air out. He'd survived explosions, dumb mistakes, and even being speared by a piece of rebar. All by keeping cool and doing what needed to be done.

He hadn't expected, when told that he'd need to let in an assassin, that he'd become this involved. But what did he expect? That he could be part of the resistance and not ever risk his life? He'd risked it the moment one of his co-workers had started whispering to him, talking about overthrowing Pan, and he'd only stood there and listened.

Stanuel took a deep breath and nodded. "Okay. I'm sorry."

The space station Haven was a classic wheel, rotating slowly to provide some degree of gravity for its inhabitants so that they did not have to lose bone mass and muscle, the price of living in no gravity.

At Haven's center lay the hub. Here lay an atrium, the extraordinary no-gravity gardens and play areas for Haven's citizens. Auditoriums and pools and labs and tourist areas and fields, the heart of the community. Dripping down from the hub, docking ports, airlocks, antennae, and spare mass from the original asteroid Haven had taken its metals. This was where they floated now.

But on the other side of the hub hung a long and spindly structure that had once housed the central command for the station. A bridge, of sorts, with a view of all of Haven, sat at the very tip of the tower. The bridge was duplicated just below in the form of an observation deck and restaurant for visitors and proud citizens and school trips.

All things the tower existed for in that more innocent time *before*.

Now Pan sat in the bridge, looking out at all of them, both through the large portal-like windows up there, and through the network of rovers and insect cams scattered throughout Haven.

One of which Pepper had just flattened.

Stanuel knew they no longer had an hour now.

Pepper squatted in front of the hatch. "It's good I'm not claustrophobic."

"This runs all the way to the restaurant at the tower. It's the fastest way there."

"If we don't choke on fumes and grease first." Pepper scraped grease off the inside.

Stanuel handed him a mask with filters from the tiny utility closet underneath the pipe. He also found a set of headlamps. "Get in, I'll follow, we need to hurry."

Pepper hauled himself into the tube and Stanuel followed, worming his way in. When he closed the hatch after them the darkness seemed infinite until Pepper clicked a tiny penlight on.

Moving down the tube was simple enough. They were in the hub. They were weightless. They could use their fingertips to slowly move their way along.

After several minutes Pepper asked, voice muffled by the filter, "so how did it happen? Haven was one of the most committed to the idea of techno-democracy."

There were hundreds of little bubbles of life scattered all throughout the asteroid belt, hidden away from the mess of Earth and her orbit by distance and anonymity. Each one a petri dish of politics and culture. Each a pearl formed around a bit of asteroid dirt that birthed it.

"There are problems with a techno-democracy," muttered Stanuel. "If you're a purist, like we were, you had to have the citizenry decide on everything." The sheer amount of things that a society needed decided had almost crushed them.

Every minute everyone had to decide something. Pass a new law. Agree to send delegates to another station. Accept taxes. Divvy out taxes. Pay a bill. The stream of decisions became overwhelming, constantly popping up and requiring an electronic yes or no. And research was needed for each decision.

"The artificial intelligence modelers came up with our solution. They created intelligences that would vote just as you would if you had the time to do nothing but focus on voting." They weren't real artificial intelligences. The modelers took your voting record, and paired it to your buying habits, social habits, and all the other aspects of your life that were tracked in modern life to model your habits. After all, if a bank could use a financial profile to figure out if an unusual purchase didn't reflect the buyer's habits and freeze an account for safety reasons, why couldn't the same black box logic be applied to a voter's patterns?

Pepper snorted. "You turned over your voting to machines."

Stanuel shook his head, making the headlamp's light dart from side to side. "Not machines. *Us*. The profiles were incredible. They modeled what votes were important enough—or that the profilers were uncertain to get right—so that they only passed on the important ones to us. They were like spam filters for voting. They freed us from the incredible flood of meaningless minutiae that the daily running of a government needed."

"But they failed," Pepper grunted.

"Yes and no…"

"Quiet." Pepper pointed his penlight down. "I hear something. Clinking around back the way we came from."

"Someone chasing us?"

"No. It's mechanical."

Stanuel thought about it for a moment. He couldn't think of anything. "Rover?"

Pepper stopped and Stanuel collided with his boots. "So our time has run out."

"I don't know."

A faint clang echoed around them. "Back up," Pepper said, pushing him away with a quick shove of the boot to the top of his head.

"What are you doing?"

"We've come far enough." Four extremely loud bangs filled the tube with absurdly bright flashes of light. Pepper moved out through the ragged rip in the pipe.

Another large wall blocked him. "What is this?"

Stanuel, still blinking, looked at it from still inside the pipe. "You'll want the other side. Nothing but vacuum on the other side." Had Pepper used more explosive they might have just been blown right out the side of Haven.

"Right." Pepper twisted further out, and another explosion rocked the pipe.

When Stanuel wriggled out and around the tube he saw trees. They'd blown a hole in the lawn of the gardens. They carefully climbed out, pushing past dirt, and the tubes and support equipment that monitored and maintained the gardens and soaked the roots with water.

"Now what?" Stanuel asked. "We're going to be seen."

"Now it gets messy," Pepper said. He pulled Stanuel along toward the large elevator at the center. "I'm going with a frontal assault. It'll be messy. But… I do well at messy."

"There's no reason for me to be here, then," Stanuel said. "What use will I be? I failed to get you there through the exhaust pipes. Why not just let me go?"

Pepper laughed. "Not quite ready to die for the cause, Stanuel?"

"No. Yes. I'm not sure, it just feels like suicide, and I'm not sure who that helps."

"You're safer with me." Pepper launched them from branch to branch through the trees. Now that curfews were in effect, no families perched in the great globe of green, no kids screaming and racing through the trees. It was eerily silent.

Pepper slowed them down in the last grove of trees before the elevators at the core of the gardens. As they gently floated towards the lobby at the bottom of the shaft three well-built men, the kind who obviously trained their bodies up on the rim of the wheel, turned the corner.

They carried stun guns. Non-lethal, but still menacing.

Stanuel heard a click. Pepper held out a gun in each hand. Real guns, perfectly lethal.

"I'd turn those off," Pepper said to the men, "and pass them over, and then no-one would get hurt."

They hesitated. But then the commanding voice of Pan filled the gardens. "Do as he says. And then escort him to me."

They looked at each other, unhappy, and tossed the guns over. Pepper threw them off into the trees. "You're escorting us?"

The three unhappy security men nodded. "Pan says you have an electro-magnetic pulse weapon. We're not to provoke you."

Stanuel bit his lip. It felt like a trap. These traitors were taking them into the maw of the beast, and Pepper, as far as he could see, looked cheerful about it. "It's a trap," he muttered.

"Well of course it is," Pepper said. "But it's a good one that avoids us skulking about, getting dirtier, or having to shoot our way through." The mercenary followed Pan's lackeys into the elevator. He turned and looked at Stanuel, hovering outside. "And Pan's right. I do have an E.M.P device. But if I trigger it this deep into the hub, I take out all your power generating capabilities and computer core systems."

"Really?" Stanuel was intrigued.

Pepper held up a tiny metal tube with a button on the end. "If I get to the tower," Pepper said. "I can trigger it and take out Pan, while leaving the rest of the station unaffected."

Stanuel had weathered five days of his beloved Haven under the autocratic rule of Pan, the trickster.

He'd travel with Pepper to see it end, he realized.

He pulled himself into the elevator.

For five days Haven's populace had a ruler, a single being whose word was law, whose thoughts were made policy. Pan stood in the center of the command console, its face lit by the light of a hundred screens and the reflections off the inner rim of Haven's great wheel.

Pan wore a simple blue suit, had tan skin, brown eyes, and brown hair. His androgynous face and thin body meant that had he stood in a crowd of Haven's citizens, he would hardly have been noticed. He could be anybody, or everybody.

He also flickered slightly as he turned.

"My executioner and his companion. I'm delighted," Pan said. "If I could shake your hand, I would." He gave a slight bow.

Pepper returned it.

Pan smiled. "I've been waiting for you two for quite a while. I apologize for sending the rover up the exhaust pipe."

Pepper shrugged. "No matter. So what now? I have something that can take you out, you have me surrounded by nasty surprises..."

Pan folded its arms. "I don't do nasty surprises, Pepper. I'm not a monster, contrary to what Stanuel might say. You have an E.M.P device, and if you were to set it off further down the tower, you would shut all Haven down. True, I have backup capabilities that mitigate that, but your device presents a terrible risk to the well being of the citizenry. With the device and you up here, the only risk is to me."

An easy enough decision, Stanuel thought. Trigger the damn device! But Pepper glanced around the room, maybe seeing traps that Stanuel couldn't. "If you don't do nasty surprises, what stops me from zapping you out, right here, right now?"

"I would like to make you an offer. If you'd listen."

Pepper's lips quirked. "I wouldn't be much of a mercenary if I just accepted the higher bid in the middle of the job. You don't get repeat work very often that way."

Pan held its hands up. "I understand. But consider this, I am, indirectly, the one who hired you."

Stanuel had to object. "The resistance..."

"I run it," Pan smiled. "I know everything it does, who it hires, and in many cases, I give it the orders."

Stanuel felt like he'd been thrown into a freezing cold vat of water. He lost his breath. "What do you mean? You infiltrated it?" They had lost, even before they'd started.

Pan turned to the mercenary. "Stanuel is bewildered, as are many, by what they created, Pepper. I'm merely the amalgamated avatar of the converged will of all the simulations made to run this colony. The voter simulations kept taking up energy, so the master processing program came up with a more elegant solution: me. Why run millions of emulators, when it could fuse them all into a single expression of its will that would run the government?"

"A clever solution," Pepper said.

"A techno-democracy, even more so than the vanilla kind, is messy. Dangerously so. With study committees and votes on everything, things that needed to be done quickly didn't get done in time.

"So the emulations decided to put forward a bill, buried in the middle of some other obscure administrivia. The vote was that emulations be given command of the government."

Stanuel stepped forward. "We woke up and found that in a single moment all of Haven had been disenfranchised."

"By your own desires and predictive voting algorithms," Pan said. "In a way, yes. In a way, no."

Stanuel spit at the dictatorial hologram in front him. "Then the emulators decided that a single amalgamation, an avatar, and expression of all their wills, would work better. So then even our own voting patterns turned over their power."

"Not surprising," Pepper said. "You didn't have the maturity to keep your own vote, you turned it over to the copies of yourselves. Why be surprised that the copies would do something similar and turn to a benevolent dictator of their own creation?"

Pan looked pleased. "Dictators aren't so bad, if they're the right dictator. And it's hard coded into my very being to look out for the community. That's why I look like this," it waved a hand over its face. "I'm the average of all the faces in Haven. Political poll modeling shows that were I to run for office, if would be almost guaranteed based on physiological responses alone."

Stanuel looked at Pepper. "Pan may have infiltrated, but you were still paid to destroy it. Do it."

"No," Pan said. "You might pull that trigger. But if you do, you destroy what the people of Haven really wanted, what they desired, and what they worked very hard to create, Pepper, even if they didn't realize they consciously wanted it."

"I've heard you get the government you deserve," Pepper said. "But this is something else. They created their own tyranny…"

"But Pepper, I'm not a tyrant. If they vote as a whole to oust me, they can do it."

Pepper moved over to the one of great windows to look out at the inside rim of Haven. Thousands of distant portholes dotted the giant wheel, lit up by the people living inside the rooms across from them.

"Look around you," Pan implored. "There are plenty who like what I'm doing. I'm rebuilding parts of Haven that have been neglected for years. I'm improving agriculture as we speak. I've made the choices that were hard, got things into motion that just sat there while people quibbled over them. I am *action*. I am *progress*."

Stanuel kicked forward and Pepper glanced back at him. "I think Stanuel objects."

Pan sighed. "Yes, a few will be disaffected. They will always be disaffected. That was why I created outlets for the disaffected, because they are a part of me as well. But my plea to you, Pepper, is not to break this great experiment. I can offer you more money, a place of safety here whenever you would want it, and Haven as a powerful ally to your needs."

Pepper nodded and sat in the air, his legs folded. "I have a question."

"Proceed."

"Why do they call you Pan?"

"They call me Pan because it's short for panopticon. An old experiment: if you were to create a round jail with a tower in the center, with open cell walls facing it, and the ability to look into every cell, you would have the ultimate surveillance society. The panopticon. In some ways, Haven is just that, with me at its center."

Pepper chuckled. "I'd half expected some insane military dictator wearing a head of antlers calling himself Pan."

Pan did not laugh. It leaned closer. "Pepper, understand me. This is not your fight. I'm the naturally elected ruler of Haven. The *choice* to remove me, that isn't yours. I did not bring you here to destroy me, but for other reasons."

"The choice?" The word affected Pepper in some way Stanuel could not figure out. He looked over at Stanuel. "Then if you're a benevolent ruler, you will escort me off Haven, leave Stanuel alive, and move on to other things. After all, it was your orders that set Stanuel down this path."

"Of course. It's that or a sentence in one of Haven's residential rooms. You'll be locked in, but comfortable. There do have to be ways to handle such things. Exile, or confinement."

"Okay, Mr. Pan. Okay. My work here is done." Pepper moved towards Stanuel with a flick of his feet. "Come on Stanuel, it's time to leave the tower."

Stanuel could hardly look Pepper in the eye. "I can't believe you left there."

"Pan made a good argument."

"Pan offered to pay you more. That's all."

"There's that, but I won't take it." Pepper scratched his head. "If I destroyed Pan, what would you do?"

Stanuel frowned. "What do you mean?"

"You said the emulations wouldn't be allowed to hold direct control, earlier. Does that mean you'd allow the emulations to come back and decide votes for you?"

"One assumes. We might have not gotten them right, but if we can fix that error, things can go back to the way they were."

Pepper unpacked his suit and stepped into it. It crinkled and cracked as he zipped it up. "And then I'll be back. Because you'll repeat the same patter all over again."

"What?"

"For all your assumptions, you're not quite seeing the pattern. Deep down, somewhere, you all want Pan. You don't want the responsibility of voting, you want the easy result."

"That's not true," Stanuel objected.

"Oh come on. Think of all the times princes and princesses are adored and feted. Think of all the actors and great people we adore and fawn over."

"That doesn't make us slavish followers."

Pepper cocked his head. "No, but we still can't escape the instincts we carry from being a small band of hunter-gatherers making their way across a plain, depending on a single leader who knew the ins and outs of their tiny tribe and listened to their feedback. That doesn't scale, so we have inelegant hacks around it.

"Stanuel, you all created a technological creature, able to view you all and listen to all your feedback, and embody a benevolent single tribal leader. Not only was it born out of your unconscious needs, even your own emulations overwhelmingly voted it into power as sole ruler of Haven."

Stanuel raised his hand to halt Pepper. "That's all true, and over the last four days we've argued around all this when we found out about the vote. But, Pepper, whether perfect or not, we can't allow a single person to rule us. It goes against everything we believe in, everything we worked for when we created Haven."

Pepper nodded. "I know."

"And you're going to walk away."

"I have to. Because this wasn't some power grab, it was the will of your people. There was a vote. Pan is right, it *is* the rightful ruler. But," Pepper pointed at him, "I'm not leaving you empty-handed."

"What do you mean?"

He handed over the backpack and pressed a small stick with a button into Stanuel's hand. "The E.M.P device is in the backpack. You won't get anywhere near the tower to take out just Pan, but if you trigged it in the hub after I leave, it will shut Haven down. Pan will have backups, and his supporters will protect the tower, but if enough people feel like you do, you can storm it with the guns in that pack."

"You're asking me to... fight?"

"You know your history. The tree of liberty needs to be watered with some blood every now and then. Thomas Jefferson, I think, said that. Most of your ancestors fought for it. You could have kept it, had you just... taken the time to vote yourself instead of leaving it to something else."

"I don't know if I can." Stanuel was bewildered. He'd never done anything violent in his life.

Pepper smiled. "You might find Pan is more willing to fold than you imagine. Think about it."

With that, he stepped into the airlock. The door shut with a hiss, and the spacesuit faded into camouflage black as Pepper disappeared inside whatever stealth ship had bought him to Haven.

Stanuel stood there. He pulled the backpack's straps up over onto his shoulders and made his way toward the gardens, mulling over the mercenary's last words.

A hologram of Pan waited for him at the entrance to the gardens, but no goons were nearby. Stanuel had expected to be captured, with the threat of a long confinement ahead of him. But it was just the electronic god of Haven and Stanuel.

"You didn't understand what he meant, did you?" Pan said. It really was the panopticon, listening to everything that happened in Haven.

"No." Stanuel held the switch to the E.M.P in his hand, waiting for some trick. Was he going to get shot in the head by a sniper? But Pan said it didn't use violence.

Maybe a tranquilizer dart of some sort?

"I told you," Pan said, "I also created the resistance."

"But that doesn't make any sense," Stanuel said.

"It does if you stop thinking of me as a person, but as an avatar of your collective emulators. Every ruling system has an opposition; the day after I was voted into power, I had to create a series of checks and balances against myself. That was the resistance."

"But I was recruited by people."

"And they were recruited by my people, working for me, who were told they were to create an opposition tame as a honey trap." Pan flickered as he walked through a tree. An incongruous vision, as Stanuel floated through the no gravity garden.

"Why would you want to die?"

"Because, I may not be what all of you want, just what *most* of you want. I have to create an opportunity for myself to be stopped, or else, I really am a tyrant and not the best solution. That is why Pepper was hired to bring the E.M.P device aboard. That was why, ultimately, he left it with you."

"So it's all in my hands," Stanuel said.

"Yes. Live in a better economy, a safer economy, but one ruled by what you have created. Or muddle along yourselves." Pan moved in front of Stanuel, floating with him.

Stanuel held up the metal tube and hovered his thumb over the button. "Men should be free."

Pan nodded sadly. "But Stanuel, you all will never be able to get things done the way I can. It will be such a mess of compromise, personality, mistakes, wrong choices, emotional choices, mob rule, and imperfect decisions. You could well destroy Haven with your imprecise decisions."

It was a siren call. But even though Pan was perfect, and right, it was the same song that led smart men to call tyrants leaders and do so happily. The promise of quick action, clean and fast decisions.

Alluring.

"I know it will be messy," Stanuel said, voice quavering. "And I have no idea how it will work out. But at least it will be *ours*."

He pressed the button and watched as the lights throughout Haven dimmed and flickered. Pan disappeared with a sigh, a ghost banished. The darkness marched its glorious way through the cavernous gardens toward Stanuel, who folded up in the air by a tree while he waited for the dark to take him in its freeing embrace.

CIVILIZATION

by Vylar Kaftan

Vylar Kaftan writes speculative fiction of all genres, including science fiction, fantasy, horror, and slipstream. Her work has appeared in *Lightspeed Magazine*, *GigaNotoSaurus*, *Realms of Fantasy*, *Strange Horizons*, *Clarkesworld*, *Cosmos*, *Escape Pod*, *Beneath Ceaseless Skies*, *Sybil's Garage*, *The Way of the Wizard*, and in the World Fantasy Award-winning anthology *Paper Cities*. She lives with her husband Shannon in northern California.

If you were young in the 1980s, you probably read at least one *Choose Your Own Adventure* novel. Getting to pick your own way through the story always seemed so thrilling, until you came to the end and realized no matter what choices you made, it always turned out the same. Sometimes you even found yourself stuck in a loop, repeating the same stupid action over and over.

It was good training for real life, wasn't it?

Our next story isn't a cautionary tale of government gone bad or a social principle run amok. It's quite simply an analysis of civilization, and the chilling recognition that for good or bad, people in groups just can't seem to get things right. Historians will agree: society after society keeps making the same ridiculous mistakes.

Just like your characters did when you steered them through those *Choose Your Own Adventure* books.

1. *Beginning*

You have a civilization! It doesn't matter which one—let's say it's modern Western civilization. It's got fast food and sporting events, which is all you really need. Western technology gives you great military power—you have fantastic unstoppable tanks, and heat-seeking missiles to keep you safe. It's a good place to start.

You could also have chosen a remote aboriginal tribe in the center of Australia—one with nuts and berries, and spears and ropes. Or you could have chosen Communist China, or that group of scientists living in Antarctica. But let's stick to modern Western civilization. Let's give you people, too. We'll call them John and Jane. If you have a civilization, then you probably have at least two people in it.

Now, with your civilization comes a political system. Maybe your system is a democracy, and everyone gets a vote except the felons and child molesters. Maybe your system is a republic, and you market it as a democracy because it looks better on the brochures. Maybe your system is totalitarian, and you force everyone to enjoy the sound of that complicated word. Totalitarian!

But! A major choice awaits you. Are you traditional, bound by the past, certain that the old ways are the best because "we've always done it that way, so there"? Or are you radical, lured by the future, always hoping that the new ways will be better than the old because "we've never done it that way, so there"? Be warned, the future of your civilization depends on your choice. John and Jane's lives are at stake.

If you choose tradition, go to section 2.
If you choose radicalism, go to section 5.

2. *Tradition*

You're a traditionalist. Or a blind follower. Or just someone who reads everything in order, from start to finish. It doesn't matter; you end up in the same place anyway.

So, you have a civilization. You have TV dinners and expensive cars. You hold elections. This is the way it's always been done, and this is the way it must be. Never mind those fruitcakes in wigs who fought against the colonial powers. They were supporting Freedom and Liberty and other words that make great advertising. The corporations live off the people and the people trust the corporations. John and Jane relax, knowing that everything around them has worked for centuries.

Things stagnate. You hold more elections, or pretend to. The people in power have always been in power. The world is the way it's always been. The police have always arrested people in the streets. The freedom to speak has always been restricted in the name of security. The corporations destroy the people and that's the way it's always been, and why would you question that, citizen?

Congratulations! You've got fascism!

Go to section 3.

3. *Fascism*

How nice for you, that you look so good in jackboots and a uniform! Your secret police are so dangerous that they're sexy. They kick the enemies of the State in the street, like Rockettes in steel-toed boots. You sleep with national security books on your nightstand and a revolver under your pillow. Or maybe you just have secret meetings of secret societies in secret boardrooms, sealing fates with secret handshakes. The artists fill the gulags, and hey—cheap labor! So what if it's not fair and equal? Equality is for hippies. John and Jane trust you to keep them safe at all times.

When you're fascist, you're always right, because God or Satan or your left boot told you what to do. Divine power is with you! That means that you're right, and you'd better make sure everyone else knows it too. Let's go to war!

Go to section 7.

4. *Complacency*

You've been in power an awfully long time now. Why pay attention any longer? There's too many good shows on TV (or in the bullring, or in the arenas, or whatever you've got). You talk about the great sporting events on television and visit fast-food drivethroughs. You worry about whether your toothpaste is *really* doing all that a toothpaste should. After a while, you stop paying attention to anything at all. John and Jane are off doing something, but you're not sure what. This is the way it's always been, and this is the way it will always be. Is this progress? You aren't sure.

Go to section 2.

5. *Radicalism*

You decide to experiment. Artists love your society. Painters color skyscrapers, and sculptors make art of garbage. Directors shoot movies in black light and show them in darkened theatres. Musicians shred the works of previous centuries. Corporations hold festivals to mock their own logos.

People are changing things from the way they've always been, just to make changes. Broken furniture becomes the new fashion. Everyone lives with six uncles and an aunt. John and Jane change their names to Isthmus and Quagmire. No matter what the new idea is, it must be better than the old. You remember that you haven't changed governments in a while. Throw out the old! Bring in the new! It's time for a revolution!

Go to section 6.

6. *Revolution*

You hand out pamphlets in the street. Citizens march in protest of everything. The Hero of the People takes over in a bloodless coup. The former powers all commit a penitent suicide: on the same day, in the same prison, under your watchful eye. How convenient! You take note of all the former rules—because if that's how they did it, now you must do it differently. You charter a new Constitution in a different font from the old one. Oh good, this regime is much better than the last one!

You suppress the counter-revolutionaries. They want to change everything. Any disagreement in society must be squelched. John and Jane must have their freedom. For the good of the new regime!

Go to section 4.

7. *War*

Oh boy, it's war! Your regiments march like clockwork toys. Colonel Mustard is your general, with his dashing moustache and monocle. Your hats are quite classy, with a feather for each soldier (for officers, two!) On the streets, your noble supporters weep with pride as their loved ones march past. The people support the Cause (both sides, if it's a civil war). Or if they don't, you silence them, for national security. Jane blows John a kiss as he shoulders his weapon and heads away. He'll come back a hero, and they will marry.

Your soldiers fight bravely. They pose for photos every time they save a small child from Tyranny. There's no blood—at least, not in the photos. The enemy can't oppose the side of Truth and Justice, which you're quite certain is you.

Congratulations! You've won the war! Now for the next step: What kind of society do you want to build? Is your future an ideal Utopia, or a dark Dystopia?

If you build Utopia, go to section 8.
If you build Dystopia, go to section 9.

8. *Utopia*

Medicine: Disease has been eliminated, and people live to be 120 in perfect health. As a result, your people have more time to contribute to society and to enjoy their lives.

Agriculture: Food is mass-produced by advanced techniques so that there is plenty for everyone. Special additives in the food guarantee nutrition and health for every citizen.

Employment: Everyone is guaranteed a job that pays a living wage, so that all people have the means to support themselves.

Housing: No one is homeless. Citizens are guaranteed safe, affordable housing.

Education: Citizens may study any available information. The government provides the entirety of human history and current events, and encourages people to read.

Law: All issues are decided by fair courts. Mistakes are never made.

Government: The government wants to make sure the citizens are happy.

Wow! What a wonderful world you've built for yourself. Now, all that remains is to help everyone else enjoy Utopia!

Go to section 10.

9. *Dystopia*

Medicine: Disease has been eliminated, and people live to be 120 in perfect health. As a result, your world is overpopulated and resources are scarce.

Agriculture: Food is mass-produced by advanced techniques so that there is plenty for everyone. Special additives in the food guarantee obedience to the government.

Employment: Everyone is guaranteed a job that pays a living wage, so that people are trapped in nightmarish jobs that they can't leave.

Housing: No one is homeless. People without homes live in institutions, where they are subjected to conditioning and experiments.

Education: Citizens may study any available information. The government provides the information that citizens are authorized to see, and records who is reading it.

Law: All issues are decided by fair courts. Mistakes, of course, are never made. How could they be?

Government: The government wants to make sure the citizens are happy.

Oh dear. What a horrible world you've made for yourself. Hey—those people next door, in that other place? They have Utopia, and you don't. Misery loves company. It's time to change some things.

Go to section 10.

10. *Zeal*

Rows of smiling identical people sing a patriotic anthem in perfect tune. In Utopia/Dystopia, you are never alone.

Your society is happy, or it's not. Someone else has it better, or they don't. But you're sure about one thing: other people are different from you. And that's dangerous.

Everyone else must share in your happiness or unhappiness. Everyone else must be just like you. Like Jane. Like John.

Oh boy, it's war again!

Go to section 11.

11. *War, Again*

I hope you're not surprised. It always comes back to war. The details change, but the patterns remain the same.

The last war was just for fun, but this one is serious. You're blowing the left arms off babies and burning 10,000-year-old monasteries. You perfect the technique of keeping a soldier alive despite mortal injury; the technique is quite helpful for spies on suicide missions. Your soldiers pray to God in the field, but you don't have time to answer. You're busy making military decisions. This war is serious, and hard choices must be made. John marches off again, and someday will return to Jane. Or he won't. That's war.

The question is, did you win? Will you dominate these not-like-you people and rule them with an iron hand? Or did you lose, and now face the destruction of your society?

If you won, go to section 12.
If you lost, go to section 14.

12. *Tyranny*

You're mad at these people, these pathetic creatures you conquered. They started that horrible war! Now you must teach them a lesson.

You make them build bigger stadiums and better fast food restaurants. Perhaps it's tyranny, but it's oppression with a smile—because you love them. That's why you want them to be like you. *Just* like you. And once they learn your lesson, they *will* be like you. You want them to enjoy their world as much as you enjoy yours. Or hate it, the way you hate your own. It's all for the good of John and Jane, who really should appreciate you more.

Unfortunately, your smiles aren't enough to convince them of your love. There's always room for assassination.

Go to section 13.

13. *Assassination*

Oops! Someone got crabby and killed your leader, in the shower. It's terribly messy, with brains splattered on the bathroom wall.

Who do you blame? Why, it's obvious. It's the vice-president secret police Communists students Boy Scouts Mothers Against Drunk Driving anyone who isn't you. People not you are responsible! People not you must pay!

Retaliation is swift and effective. You kill their leader. And the other leaders. And some people who aren't leaders. And they kill more of your leaders. And non-leaders. The streets flow with blood.

Is this war again, again? No, it's just collapse. Government structures tumble.

Schools are boarded up. Garbage piles up because no one removes it. People burn textbooks for warmth. John and Jane live on scraps from their neighbors. Maybe someone finds an atomic weapon, and maybe they use it. Maybe they don't need to.

Whichever way it happens, you've reached the apocalypse.

Go to section 14.

14. *Apocalypse*

Oh no! Your civilization is destroyed. No more fast food. No more sporting events. No more two-for-one buffalo wing specials.

It's a mushroom cloud, billowing away in the breeze. Or a plague where everyone's skin explodes with toxic pustules. Or intense radiation that boils the brains of 98% of the population.

All of the nice families with 2.5 children (maybe happy, maybe not) are vaporized like rain in a volcano. Or the corpses pile up like ants that ate poisoned bait. The survivors walk among the living dead—stealing granola bars from their purses but leaving the wallets, because who needs money anymore?

Nuclear winter sets in. Or a biological disaster. Or just sheer depression.

But there are a few survivors. There always are. And they can start over.

Go to section 15.

15. *Survival*

Groups of ragged survivors struggle across the wasteland, or rubble, or abandoned cities. John and Jane take things one day at a time. Their challenge is to live until the night—then to live through the night, and to live another day.

Food and shelter are scarce. Many people don't make it. With time, the population balances so that it can support itself on the meager resources. This takes months, or it takes years. But when enough time passes, a small tribe sits in a cave, or at an oasis, or by a river. John (or Jane) says, "Remember how much better things used to be?" The others throw rocks at him or her, and demand not to be reminded. They want to forget the dead times that can't be revived.

But Jane (or John) watches, and waits, and remembers.

Once the others have truly forgotten—and the past has become myth—s/he has an idea. S/he says to the others, "I will lead you to happiness and freedom! Everyone follow me!" John (or Jane) unifies the tribes. Jane (or John) thinks that s/he has a new idea, better than anyone's ever had, something that will work. As always, certain choices must be made. But Jane and John are no different from you, in the end. They aren't smarter or wiser. They're just someone else.

Go to section 16.

16. *Beginning, Again*

Did you think the choices were terrible? They were.

Are you disappointed in where your choices have led you? Don't be. Other leaders have tried, and failed. The future is full of the same choices as the past. Nobody likes the choices, but civilization keeps moving.

Do you feel that you're at the beginning, again? You are. It's a circle. But there's always hope for change—hope that the circle becomes a spiral staircase.

Look, here, see this. A room, with a table. It's evening, or night. Look closely at the three people sitting around the table: John, Jane, their child. John smiles. He needs a shave, or perhaps he is bearded. Jane serves lasagna, or chicken casserole, as she tells her family about her day. The child is a girl, or a boy. The child sits in a highchair and gazes adoringly at John and Jane. After they eat, the parents take the child upstairs, singing a lullaby. It's been a good day.

Their world is radical, or traditional. They vote like responsible citizens, but they're more excited by the child learning to walk. The child grows up in revolution, or not, and marries a man, or a woman, or no one at all. S/he raises a family in Utopia/Dystopia or a world that is neither. When the apocalypse comes, s/he stays with the kids, who are grown up themselves and having a child. Despite the destruction, a baby is born.

You have a civilization.

FOR FURTHER READING

compiled by Ross E. Lockhart

What follows is a selected bibliography of noteworthy Dystopian and Utopian fiction. Dystopia and Utopia are often considered to be opposing sides of a coin, but perhaps the two lie closer than one might at first suspect. Orwell's *Nineteen Eighty-Four*, for instance, may have ended badly for Winston Smith, but Inner Party loyalist O'Brien undoubtedly got a promotion for bringing such a dangerous radical as Smith to justice. Titles notable for their high literary value are marked with an asterisk.

To learn more about the stories in *Brave New Worlds*, visit the anthology's website at johnjosephadams.com/brave-new-worlds

Notable Dystopias:

Amis, Martin
— *Einstein's Monsters*
Anderson, M. T.
— *Feed*
Armstrong, Jon
— *Grey* (et.seq.)
Asimov, Isaac
— *Pebble in the Sky*
Atwood, Margaret
— *The Handmaid's Tale* *
— *Oryx and Crake*
— *The Year of the Flood*
Auster, Paul
— *In the Country of Last Things*
Bacigalupi, Paolo
— *The Windup Girl* *
— *Ship Breaker*
Ballard, J. G.
— *Crash*
— *Hello America*

Barry, Max
— *Jennifer Government*
Bates, Paul L.
— *Imprint*
— *Dreamer*
Beaton, Alistair
— *A Planet for the President*
Beckett, Bernard
— *Genesis*
Böll, Heinrich
— *My Melancholy Face*
Boston, Bruce
— *The Guardener's Tale*
Boyd, John
—*The Last Starship from Earth*
Bradbury, Ray
— *Fahrenheit 451* *
Brain, Marshall
— *Manna*
Brooke, Keith
— *Genetopia*

Lamar, Jake
— *The Last Integrationist*
Le Guin, Ursula K.
— *The Lathe of Heaven*
Lem, Stanisław
— *Memoirs Found in a Bathtub*
Lerner, Lisa
— *Just Like Beauty*
Levin, Ira
— *This Perfect Day*
Lewis, Sinclair
— *It Can't Happen Here* *
London, Jack
— *The Iron Heel* *
Lowry, Lois
— *The Giver*
Lundwall, Sam J.
— *2018 A.D. or the King Kong Blues*
Mark, Jan
— *Useful Idiots*
McCarthy, Cormac
— *The Road* *
McCarthy, Wil
— *Bloom*
McIntosh, Will
— *Soft Apocalypse*
McMullen, Sean
— *Eyes of the Calculor*
Mellick III, Carlton
— *The Egg Man*
— *War Slut*
Miéville, China
— *Perdido Street Station*
Mitchell, David
— *Cloud Atlas* ("Sonmis Oratio")
Moore, Alan
— *V for Vendetta*
Morgan, Richard
— *Market Forces*
— *Thirteen* (AKA *Black Man*)
Morrison, Toni
— *Paradise*
Nabokov, Vladimir
— *Invitation to a Beheading*

Neiderman, Andrew
— *The Baby Squad*
Nolan, William F. and George Clayton Johnson
— *Logan's Run*
Norden, Eric
— *The Ultimate Solution*
Nourse, Alan E.
— *The Blade Runner*
(See also Burroughs, William S.)
O'Brien, Michael D.
— *Eclipse of the Sun*
Oppegaard, David
— *The Suicide Collectors*
Orwell, George
— *Nineteen Eighty-Four* *
Philbrick, Rodman
— *The Last Book in the Universe*
Pohl, Frederick and C. M. Kornbluth
— *The Space Merchants*
Pollack, Rachel
— *Unquenchable Fire*
Powers, Tim
— *Dinner at Deviant's Palace*
Rand, Ayn
— *Anthem*
Reed, Kit
— *Enclave*
Robinson, Kim Stanley
— *The Gold Coast: Three Californias (Wild Shore Triptych)* *
Rucker, Rudy
— *Postsingular*
Russ, Joanna
— *And Chaos Died*
Scalzi, John with Elizabeth Bear, Tobias Buckell, Jay Lake, and Karl Schroeder
— *Metatropolis*
Sharpe, Matthew
— *Jamestown*
Shirley, John
— *Black Glass*
Silva, Ulises
— *Solstice*

Notable Utopias:

Banks, Iain M.
— *Consider Phlebas* (Culture series) (et. seq.)
Bellamy, Edward
— *Looking Backward* *
Borghese, Elizabeth Mann
— *My Own Utopia*
Callenbach, Ernest
— *Ecotopia*
Charnas, Suzy McKee
— *Motherlines*
— *Walk to the End of the World*
Delany, Samuel R.
— *Trouble on Triton: An Ambiguous Heterotopia* *
Gentle, Mary
— *Golden Witchbreed*
Gilman, Charlotte Perkins
— *Herland*
Heinlein, Robert A.
— *The Moon is a Harsh Mistress*
Huxley, Aldous
— *Island* *
Le Guin, Ursula K.
— *Always Coming Home*
Lessing, Doris
— *The Marriages Between Zones Three, Four and Five*
More, Thomas
— *Utopia* *
Morris, William
— *News from Nowhere* *
Piercy, Marge
— *Woman on the Edge of Time*
Robinson, Kim Stanley
— *Pacific Edge: Three Californias (Wild Shore Triptych)* *
Russ, Joanna
— *The Female Man* *
Skinner, B. F.
— *Walden Two*

ACKNOWLEDGEMENTS

Many thanks to the following:

Jeremy Lassen and Jason Williams at Night Shade Books, for letting me edit all these anthologies and for doing such a kick-ass job publishing them. Also, to Ross Lockhart and Michael Lee at Night Shade for all they do behind-the-scenes, nad to Allan Kausch for his copyediting prowess.

Cody Tilson: Thank you for the *fantastic* cover, comrade.

Gordon Van Gelder, who first showed me the horrible dystopia of the slush mines and then helped me climb out of them.

My former agent Jenny Rappaport, for helping me launch my anthology career, and my current agent, Joe Monti, for keeping it going.

Wendy N. Wagner for her assistance wrangling the header notes. All the clever things in the header notes are all her work. Anything lame you came across is mine.

Rebecca McNulty, for her various and valuable interning assistance—reading, scanning, transcribing, proofing, doing most of the work but getting none of the credit as all good interns do.

My mom, for ensuring that, as a child, I did not have to grow up in a dystopia.

All of the other kindly folks who assisted me in some way during the editorial process: Jean Adamoski, Linda Allen, Kathleen Bellamy, Cristina Concepcion, Ellen Datlow, Jennifer Escott, Lina M. Granada, Sean Fodera, Victoria Fox, Vaughne Lee Hansen, Dave Housley, Alexandra Levenberg, Kristina Moore, Mimi Ross, Lawrence Schmeil, Jason Sizemore, Alicia Torello, to everyone who entered suggestions into my dystopian fiction database, and to everyone else who helped out in some way that I neglected to mention (and to you folks, I apologize!).

The NYC Geek Posse—consisting of Robert Bland, Desirina Boskovich, Christopher M. Cevasco, Douglas E. Cohen, Jordan Hamessley, Andrea Kail, David Barr Kirtley, and Matt London, (plus the NYCGP Auxiliary)—for giving me an excuse to come out of my editorial cave once in a while.

The readers and reviewers who loved my other anthologies, making it possible for me to do more.

And last, but certainly not least: a big thanks to all of the authors who appear in this anthology.

Acknowledgment is made for permission to print the following material:

"Pop Squad" by Paolo Bacigalupi. © 2006 by Paolo Bacigalupi. Originally published in *The Magazine of Fantasy & Science Fiction*. Reprinted by permission of the author.

"Billennium" from the book, *The Best Short Stories of J. G. Ballard* by J. G. Ballard © 1978 by J. G. Ballard. Reprinted by permission of Henry Holt and Company, LLC.

"The Pedestrian" by Ray Bradbury. © 1951 by the Fortnightly Publishing Company, renewed 1979 by Ray Bradbury. Reprinted by permission of Don Congdon Associates, Inc.

"Resistance" by Tobias S. Buckell. © 2008 by Tobias S. Buckell. Originally published in *Seeds of Change*. Reprinted by permission of the author.

"Geriatric Ward" by Orson Scott Card. © 2008 by Orson Scott Card. Originally published in *Keeper of Dreams*. Reprinted by permission of the author.

"Of a Sweet Slow Dance in the Wake of Temporary Dogs" by Adam-Troy Castro. © 2003 by Adam-Troy Castro. Originally published in *Imaginings*. Reprinted by permission of the author.

"The Minority Report" by Philip K. Dick, currently collected in *Selected Stories of Philip K. Dick* and *The Minority Report and Other Classic Stories by Philip K. Dick*. © 1956 by Philip K. Dick, used with permission of The Wylie Agency LLC.

"The Things That Make Me Weak and Strange Get Engineered Away" by Cory Doctorow. © 2008 by CorDoc-Co, Ltd UK. Originally published in *Tor.com*. Reprinted by permission of the author.

"'Repent, Harlequin!' Said the Ticktockman" by Harlan Ellison. © 1965 by Harlan Ellison. Renewed, 1993 by the Kilimanjaro Corporation. Reprinted by arrangement with, and permission of, the Author and the Author's agent, Richard Curtis Associates, Inc., New York. All rights reserved. Harlan Ellison is a registered trademark of The Kilimanjaro Corporation.

"Pervert" by Charles Coleman Finlay. © 2004 by Charles Coleman Finlay. Originally published in *The Magazine of Fantasy & Science Fiction*. Reprinted by permission of the author.

"From Homogenous to Honey" by Neil Gaiman & Bryan Talbot. © 1988 by Neil Gaiman & Bryan Talbot. Originally published in *A.A.R.G.H.!*. Reprinted by permission of the author.

Night Shade Books Is an Independent Publisher of Quality SF, Fantasy and Horror

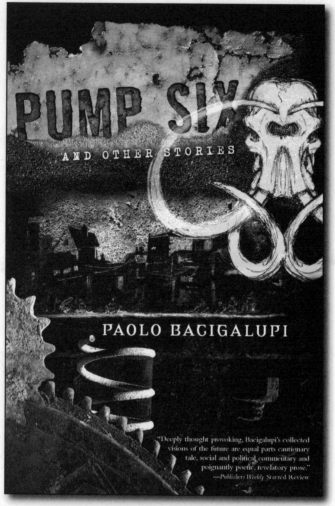

ISBN 978-1-59780-202-4, Trade Paperback; $14.99

Paolo Bacigalupi's debut collection demonstrates the power and reach of the science fiction short story. Social criticism, political parable, and environmental advocacy lie at the center of Paolo's work. Each of the stories herein is at once a warning, and a celebration of the tragic comedy of the human experience.

The eleven stories in *Pump Six* represent the best of Paolo's work, including the Hugo nominee "Yellow Card Man," the Nebula- and Hugo-nominated story "The People of Sand and Slag," and the Sturgeon Award-winning story "The Calorie Man." The title story is original to this collection. With this book, Paolo Bacigalupi takes his place alongside SF short fiction masters Ted Chiang, Kelly Link, and others, as an important young writer that directly and unabashedly tackles today's most important issues.

Night Shade Books Is an Independent Publisher of Quality SF, Fantasy and Horror

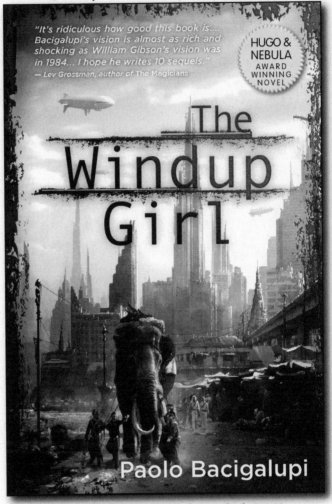

"It's ridiculous how good this book is.... Bacigalupi's vision is almost as rich and shocking as William Gibson's vision was in 1984... I hope he writes 10 sequels."
— Lev Grossman, author of The Magicians

HUGO & NEBULA AWARD WINNING NOVEL

The Windup Girl

Paolo Bacigalupi

ISBN: 978-1-59780-158-4, Trade Paperback; $14.95

Winner of the 2009 Hugo and Nebula Award for Best Novel.

Anderson Lake is a company man, AgriGen's Calorie Man in Thailand. Undercover as a factory manager, Anderson combs Bangkok's street markets in search of foodstuffs thought to be extinct, hoping to reap the bounty of history's lost calories. There, he encounters Emiko, the Windup Girl, a strange and beautiful creature. One of the New People, Emiko is not human; she is an engineered being, crèche-grown and programmed to satisfy the decadent whims of a Kyoto businessman, but now abandoned to the streets of Bangkok. Regarded as soulless beings by some, devils by others, New People are slaves, soldiers, and toys of the rich in a chilling near future in which calorie companies rule the world, the oil age has passed, and the side effects of bio-engineered plagues run rampant across the globe.

Night Shade Books Is an Independent Publisher of Quality SF, Fantasy and Horror

WASTELANDS

STORIES OF
THE APOCALYPSE

FEATURING

OCTAVIA E. BUTLER   GEORGE R.R. MARTIN
ORSON SCOTT CARD   STEPHEN KING
JONATHAN LETHEM   GENE WOLFE

AND MANY OTHERS

Edited by John Joseph Adams

ISBN: 978-1-59780-105-8, Trade Paperback; $15.95

Famine, Death, War, and Pestilence: The Four Horsemen of the Apocalypse, the harbingers of Armageddon—these are our guides through the Wastelands.

Gathering together the best post-apocalyptic literature of the last two decades from many of today's most renowned authors of speculative fiction, including George R. R. Martin, Gene Wolfe, Orson Scott Card, Carol Emshwiller, Jonathan Lethem, Octavia E. Butler, and Stephen King, *Wastelands* explores the scientific, psychological, and philosophical questions of what it means to remain human in the wake of Armageddon. Whether the end of the world comes through nuclear war, ecological disaster, or cosmological cataclysm, these are tales of survivors, in some cases struggling to rebuild the society that was, in others, merely surviving, scrounging for food in depopulated ruins and defending themselves against monsters, mutants, and marauders.

Night Shade Books Is an Independent Publisher of Quality SF, Fantasy and Horror

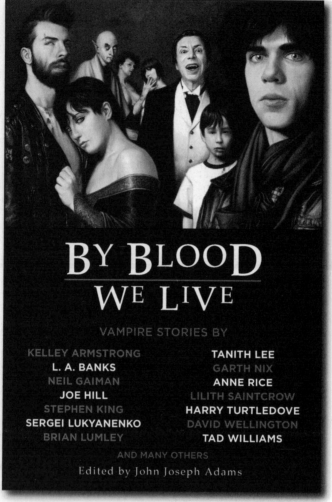

BY BLOOD WE LIVE

VAMPIRE STORIES BY

KELLEY ARMSTRONG	TANITH LEE
L. A. BANKS	GARTH NIX
NEIL GAIMAN	ANNE RICE
JOE HILL	LILITH SAINTCROW
STEPHEN KING	HARRY TURTLEDOVE
SERGEI LUKYANENKO	DAVID WELLINGTON
BRIAN LUMLEY	TAD WILLIAMS

AND MANY OTHERS

Edited by John Joseph Adams

ISBN: 978-1-59780-156-0, Trade Paperback; $15.95

From Dracula to Buffy the Vampire Slayer; from Castlevania to True Blood, the romance between popular culture and vampires hearkens back to humanity's darkest, deepest fears, flowing through our very blood, fears of death, and life, and insatiable hunger. And yet, there is an attraction, undeniable, to the vampire archetype, whether the pale, wan European count, impeccably dressed and coldly masculine, yet strangely ambiguous, ready to sink his sharp teeth deep into his victims' necks, draining or converting them, or the vamp, the count's feminine counterpart, villain and victim in one, using her wiles and icy sexuality to corrupt man and woman alike...

Gathering together the best vampire literature of the last three decades from many of today's most renowned authors of fantasy, speculative fiction, and horror, *By Blood We Live* will satisfy your darkest cravings...

Night Shade Books Is an Independent Publisher of Quality SF, Fantasy and Horror

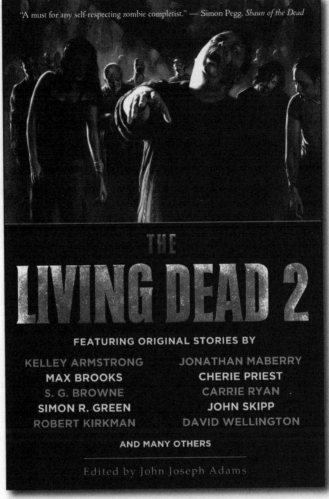

ISBN 978-1-59780-190-4, Trade Paperback; $15.99

Two years ago, readers eagerly devoured *The Living Dead*. *Publishers Weekly* named it one of the Best Books of the Year, and BarnesAndNoble.com called it "The best zombie fiction collection ever." Now acclaimed editor John Joseph Adams is back with 43 more of the best, most chilling, most thrilling zombie stories anywhere, including virtuoso performances by zombie fiction legends Max Brooks (*World War Z, The Zombie Survival Guide*), Robert Kirkman (*The Walking Dead*), and David Wellington (*Monster Island*).

The Living Dead 2 has more of what zombie fans hunger for — more scares, more action, more... brains.

About the Editor

John Joseph Adams (www.johnjosephadams.com) is the bestselling editor of many anthologies, such as *Wastelands*, *The Living Dead* (a World Fantasy Award finalist), *Seeds of Change*, *By Blood We Live*, *Federations*, and *The Improbable Adventures of Sherlock Holmes*. Barnes & Noble.com named him "the reigning king of the anthology world," and his books have been named to numerous best of the year lists. His most recent books are *The Living Dead 2* and *The Way of the Wizard*. Future projects include *The Mad Scientist's Guide to World Domination* and *The Book of Cthulhu*.

John is also the fiction editor of the online science fiction magazine *Lightspeed* (*www.lightspeedmagazine.com*). Prior to taking on that role, he worked for nearly nine years in the editorial department at *The Magazine of Fantasy & Science Fiction*.

He is currently the co-host of *The Geek's Guide to the Galaxy* podcast on io9.com, and has published hundreds of interviews and other pieces of non-fiction.

Night Shade Books Is an Independent Publisher of Quality SF, Fantasy and Horror

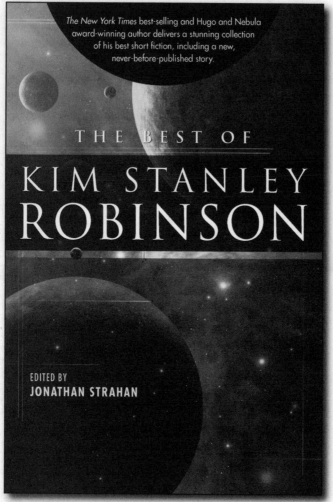

The New York Times best-selling and Hugo and Nebula award-winning author delivers a stunning collection of his best short fiction, including a new, never-before-published story.

THE BEST OF

KIM STANLEY ROBINSON

EDITED BY
JONATHAN STRAHAN

ISBN 978-1-59780-185-0, Trade Paperback; $16.99

Adventurers, scientists, artists, workers, and visionaries — these are the men and women you will encounter in the short fiction of Kim Stanley Robinson. In settings ranging from the sunken ruins of Venice to the upper reaches of the Himalayas to the terraformed surface of Mars itself, and through themes of environmental sustainability, social justice, personal responsibility, sports, adventure and fun, Robinson's protagonists explore a world which stands in sharp contrast to many of the traditional locales and mores of science fiction, presenting instead a world in which Utopia rests within our grasp.

From Kim Stanley Robinson, award-winning author of the Mars Trilogy, the Three Californias Trilogy, the Science in the Capital series, and *The Years of Rice and Salt* and *Galileo's Dream*, comes *The Best of Kim Stanley Robinson*.